Praise for *The Book of Cthulhu*:

"Gathering Cthulhu-inspired stories from both 20th and 21st century authors, this collection provides such a huge scope of styles and takes on the mythology that there are sure to be a handful that surprise and inspire horror in even the most jaded reader."

—Josh Vogt, *Examiner.com*

"There are no weak stories here—every single one of the 27 entries is a potential standout reading experience. *The Book of Cthulhu* is nothing short of pure Lovecraftian gold. If fans of H. P. Lovecraft's Cthulhu mythos don't seek out and read this anthology, they're not really fans—it's that simple."

—Paul Goat Allen, *Explorations: The BN SciFi and Fantasy Blog*

"…thanks to the wide variety of contributing authors, as well as Lockhart's keen understanding of horror fiction and Lovecraft in particular, [*The Book of Cthulhu*] is the best of such anthologies out there."

—Alan Cranis, *Bookgasm.com*

"*The Book of Cthulhu* is one hell of a tome."

—Brian Sammons, *HorrorWorld.org*

"…an impressive tribute to the enduring fascination writers have with Lovecraft's creation. […] Editor Ross E. Lockhart has done an excellent job of ferreting out estimable stories from a variety of professional, semi-professional, and fan venues […] to establish a sense of continuity and tradition."

—Stefan Dziemianowicz, *Lo

Praise for *The Book of Cthulhu*:
(*continued*)

"For anyone who has been a life-long fan of Cthulhu, or anyone looking to start into this universe, *The Book of Cthulhu* is a wonderful collection."

—Andrew Keyser, *Portland Book Review*

"The enduring allure of H. P. Lovecraft's Cthulhu Mythos, now nearly a century old, is evident in this representative anthology of modern tales, most of which were written in the last decade. [...] To the book's credit, none of the twenty-seven stories read like slavish Lovecraft pastiche, which makes this volume all the more enjoyable."

—*Publishers Weekly*, starred review

"This smorgasbord of Lovecraftian horror should gratify the author's many fans."

—*Library Journal*

the **BOOK** of CTHULHU **II**

Other books edited by Ross E. Lockhart

The Book of Cthulhu

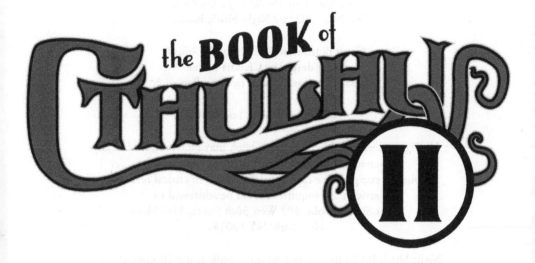

the **BOOK** of **CTHULHU** **II**

More Tales Inspired by H. P. Lovecraft

edited by
Ross E. Lockhart

Night Shade Books
New York

For Madeline…
…Chasing the Cats of Ulthar

And for Mike Roth
Friend, Brother, Sounding-board, Fellow Dreamer on the Nightside

Table of Contents

Introduction

I can't help but wonder what H. P. Lovecraft would have made of his continuing literary legacy and current pop culture prominence. On the one hand, I'm sure he would have been pleasantly surprised, once he got past the shock of seeing works he considered disposable pulp entertainments, or worse, stories and fragments he never intended to see the light of day, in print, thriving, and continuing to inspire readers and writers some seventy-five years after his death. After all, tales by the Gent from Providence are widely available in packages ranging from lurid-covered paperbacks and e-books to more scholarly tomes curated and introduced by well-respected author/editors like Joyce Carol Oates and Peter Straub. HPL possibly would have affected embarrassment over the scholarly attention afforded his fiction by the likes of Houellebecq, Joshi, and Price, but I'm sure he would also have felt a swell of pride over the recognition by these writers, and of his place in American letters, and his recognition as, as Fritz Leiber described him, "the Copernicus of the horror story."

On the other hand, there is also the matter of Lovecraft's place in popular culture. What would HPL have remarked upon discovering that his Jeffrey Coombs-voiced cartoon avatar—H. P. Hatecraft—has solved mysteries alongside the Scooby-Doo gang (and a cartoon avatar of Harlan Ellison®)? Would he have been offended or amused upon seeing *South Park's* Cartman team-up with Cthulhu against Justin Beiber to a *My Neighbor Tortoro*-inspired soundtrack? Would he have tried for a high score in *Cthulhu Saves the World*? Likewise, what might HPL have made of his recent cinematic legacy, from the titillating gore-fests of Stuart Gordon to the retro reconstructions of the H. P. Lovecraft Historical Society to the recently-aborted multi-million-dollar Guillermo del Toro adaptation of *At the Mountains of Madness*?

Regardless of what Lovecraft himself would have taken away from the various offshoots his fiction has inspired over the decades, a handful of simple facts remain. Today, H. P. Lovecraft is more popular than ever, and generations of new readers have discovered—and continue to discover—the fictional universe he created, and the philosophy of cosmicism he pioneered. Authors continue to draw inspiration from Lovecraft's life and works, setting their own tales of cosmic horror, pitting scholars, dreamers, and occult investigators against terrifying cosmic indifference and the machinations of the Great Old Ones in Lovecraftian venues such as Arkham, Dunwich, and Innsmouth.

Part of the continuing appeal of Lovecraft's universe of cosmic terror is that HPL, unlike fantasists such as J. R. R. Tolkien and C. S. Lewis, actively encouraged writers he admired or mentored to play in his creation. By doing this, HPL inadvertently created an open source fantastic universe unlike any other, ultimately grounded in the modern world, but enriched by secret histories and weird cults, and populated by ghouls, night-gaunts, and Elder Things. And while some focus only on the outlying horrors of the Cthulhu Mythos, it is Lovecraft's overarching sense of connectedness, bridging Randolph Carter's Dunsanian oneiric journey to Kadath and beyond with the still-shocking schlock of "Herbert West—Reanimator." It all integrates.

But it takes more than a few unpronounceable names, moldy tomes, and tentacles to successfully write a story in the Lovecraftian mode. To succeed, an author must not only internalize Lovecraft's materialistic meme, but must innovate, rather than imitate, recasting Grandpa Theobald's broad creation, unmooring it from the social mores of Lovecraft's time and truly making it their own. The tales collected in this volume—and the previous—do just that.

But now, the stars grow right, and the sleeper stirs. Welcome, readers to *The Book of Cthulhu II. Iä! Iä! Cthulhu Fhtagn!*

Shoggoth's Old Peculiar

Neil Gaiman

BENJAMIN LASSITER was coming to the unavoidable conclusion that the woman who had written *A Walking Tour of the British Coastline*, the book he was carrying in his backpack, had never been on a walking tour of any kind, and would probably not recognise the British coastline if it were to dance through her bedroom at the head of a marching band, singing "I'm the British Coastline" in a loud and cheerful voice while accompanying itself on the kazoo.

He had been following her advice for five days now and had little to show for it, except blisters and a backache. *All British seaside resorts contain a number of bed-and-breakfast establishments, who will be only too delighted to put you up in the "off-season"* was one such piece of advice. Ben had crossed it out and written in the margin beside it: *All British seaside resorts contain a handful of bed-and-breakfast establishments, the owners of which take off to Spain or Provence or somewhere on the last day of September, locking the doors behind them as they go.*

He had added a number of other marginal notes, too. Such as *Do not repeat not under any circumstances order fried eggs again in any roadside cafe* and *What is it with the fish-and-chips thing?* and *No they are not.* That last was written beside a paragraph which claimed that, if there was one thing that the inhabitants of scenic villages on the British coastline were pleased to see, it was a young American tourist on a walking tour.

For five hellish days, Ben had walked from village to village, had drunk sweet tea and instant coffee in cafeterias and cafes and stared out at grey rocky vistas and at the slate-coloured sea, shivered under his two thick sweaters, got wet, and failed to see any of the sights that were promised.

Sitting in the bus shelter in which he had unrolled his sleeping bag one night, he had begun to translate key descriptive words: *charming* he decided, meant *nondescript*; *scenic* meant *ugly but with a nice view if the rain ever lets up*; *delightful* probably meant *We've never been here and don't know anyone who has*. He had also come to the conclusion that the more exotic the name of the village, the duller the village.

Thus it was that Ben Lassiter came, on the fifth day, somewhere north of Bootle, to the village of Innsmouth, which was rated neither *charming*, *scenic* nor *delightful* in his guidebook. There were no descriptions of the rusting pier, nor the mounds of rotting lobster pots upon the pebbly beach.

On the seafront were three bed-and-breakfasts next to each other: Sea View, Mon Repose and Shub Niggurath, each with a neon VACANCIES sign turned off in the window of the front parlour, each with a CLOSED FOR THE SEASON notice thumbtacked to the front door.

There were no cafes open on the seafront. The lone fish-and-chip shop had a CLOSED sign up. Ben waited outside for it to open as the grey afternoon light faded into dusk. Finally a small, slightly frog-faced woman came down the road, and she unlocked the door of the shop. Ben asked her when they would be open for business, and she looked at him, puzzled, and said, "It's Monday, dear. We're never open on Monday." Then she went into the fish-and-chip shop and locked the door behind her, leaving Ben cold and hungry on her doorstep.

Ben had been raised in a dry town in northern Texas: the only water was in backyard swimming pools, and the only way to travel was in an air-conditioned pickup truck. So the idea of walking, by the sea, in a country where they spoke English of a sort, had appealed to him. Ben's hometown was double dry: it prided itself on having banned alcohol thirty years before the rest of America leapt onto the Prohibition bandwagon, and on never having got off again; thus all Ben knew of pubs was that they were sinful places, like bars, only with cuter names. The author of *A Walking Tour of the British Coastline* had, however, suggested that pubs were good places to go to find local colour and local information, that one should always "stand one's round", and that some of them sold food.

The Innsmouth pub was called *The Book of Dead Names* and the sign over the door informed Ben that the proprietor was one A. Al-Hazred, licensed to sell wines and spirits. Ben wondered if this meant that they would serve Indian food, which he had eaten on his arrival in Bootle and rather enjoyed. He paused at the signs directing him to the *Public Bar* or the *Saloon Bar*, wondering if British Public Bars were private like their Public Schools, and eventually, because it sounded more like something you would find in a Western, going into the Saloon Bar.

The Saloon Bar was almost empty. It smelled like last week's spilled beer and the day-before-yesterday's cigarette smoke. Behind the bar was a plump woman with bottle-blonde hair. Sitting in one corner were a couple of gentlemen wearing long grey raincoats and scarves. They were playing dominoes and sipping dark brown foam-topped beerish drinks from dimpled glass tankards.

Ben walked over to the bar. "Do you sell food here?"

The barmaid scratched the side of her nose for a moment, then admitted, grudgingly, that she could probably do him a ploughman's.

Ben had no idea what this meant and found himself, for the hundredth time, wishing that *A Walking Tour of the British Coastline* had an American-English phrase book in the back. "Is that food?" he asked.

She nodded.

"Okay. I'll have one of those."

"And to drink?"

"Coke, please."

"We haven't got any Coke."

"Pepsi, then."

"No Pepsi."

"Well, what do you have? Sprite? 7UP? Gatorade?"

She looked blanker than previously. Then she said, "I think there's a bottle or two of cherryade in the back."

"That'll be fine."

"It'll be five pounds and twenty pence, and I'll bring you over your ploughman's when it's ready."

Ben decided as he sat at a small and slightly sticky wooden table, drinking something *fizzy* that both looked and tasted a bright chemical red, that a ploughman's was probably a steak of some kind. He reached this conclusion, coloured, he knew, by wishful thinking, from imagining rustic, possibly even bucolic, ploughmen leading their plump oxen through fresh-ploughed fields at sunset and because he could, by then, with equanimity and only a little help from others, have eaten an entire ox.

"Here you go. Ploughman's," said the barmaid, putting a plate down in front of him.

That a ploughman's turned out to be a rectangular slab of sharp-tasting cheese, a lettuce leaf, an undersized tomato with a thumb-print in it, a mound of something wet and brown that tasted like sour jam, and a small, hard, stale roll, came as a sad disappointment to Ben, who had already decided that the British treated food as some kind of punishment. He chewed the cheese and the lettuce leaf, and cursed every ploughman in England for choosing to dine upon such swill.

The gentlemen in grey raincoats, who had been sitting in the corner, finished their game of dominoes, picked up their drinks, and came and sat beside Ben. "What you drinking?" one of them asked, curiously.

"It's called cherryade," he told them. "It tastes like something from a chemical factory."

"Interesting you should say that," said the shorter of the two. "Interesting you should say that. Because I had a friend worked in a chemical factory and he *never drank cherryade*." He paused dramatically and then took a sip of his brown drink. Ben waited for him to go on, but that appeared to be that; the conversation had stopped.

In an effort to appear polite, Ben asked, in his turn, "So, what are *you* guys drinking?"

The taller of the two strangers, who had been looking lugubrious, brightened up. "Why, that's exceedingly kind of you. Pint of Shoggoth's Old Peculiar for me, please."

"And for me, too," said his friend. "I could murder a Shoggoth's. 'Ere, I bet that would make a good advertising slogan. 'I could murder a Shoggoth's.' I should write to them and suggest it. I bet they'd be very glad of me suggestin' it."

Ben went over to the barmaid, planning to ask her for two pints of Shoggoth's Old Peculiar and a glass of water for himself, only to find she had already poured three pints of the dark beer. *Well,* he thought, *might as well be hung for a sheep as a lamb,* and he was certain it couldn't be worse than the cherryade. He took a sip. The beer had the kind of flavour which, he suspected, advertisers would describe as *full-bodied,* although if pressed they would have to admit that the body in question had been that of a goat.

He paid the barmaid and manoeuvered his way back to his new friends.

"So. What you doin' in Innsmouth?" asked the taller of the two. "I suppose you're one of our American cousins, come to see the most famous of English villages."

"They named the one in America after this one, you know," said the smaller one.

"Is there an Innsmouth in the States?" asked Ben.

"I should say so," said the smaller man. "He wrote about it all the time. Him whose name we don't mention."

"I'm sorry?" said Ben.

The little man looked over his shoulder, then he hissed, very loudly, "H. P. Lovecraft!"

"I told you not to mention that name," said his friend, and he took a sip of the dark brown beer. "H. P. Lovecraft. H. P. bloody Lovecraft. H. bloody P. bloody Love bloody craft." He stopped to take a breath. "What did he know. Eh? I mean, what did he bloody know?"

Ben sipped his beer. The name was vaguely familiar; he remembered it from rummaging through the pile of old-style vinyl LPs in the back of his father's garage. "Weren't they a rock group?"

"Wasn't talkin' about any rock group. I mean the writer."

Ben shrugged. "I've never heard of him," he admitted. "I really mostly only read Westerns. And technical manuals."

The little man nudged his neighbour. "Here. Wilf. You hear that? He's never heard of him."

"Well. There's no harm in that. *I* used to read that Zane Grey," said the taller.

"Yes. Well. That's nothing to be proud of. This bloke—what did you say your name was?"

"Ben. Ben Lassiter. And you are...?"

The little man smiled; he looked awfully like a frog, thought Ben. "I'm Seth," he said. "And my friend here is called Wilf."

"Charmed," said Wilf.

"Hi," said Ben.

"Frankly," said the little man, "I agree with you."

"You do?" said Ben, perplexed.

The little man nodded. "Yer. H. P. Lovecraft. I don't know what the fuss is about. He couldn't bloody write." He slurped his stout, then licked the foam from his lips with a long and flexible tongue. "I mean, for starters, you look at them words he used. *Eldritch*. You know what *eldritch* means?"

Ben shook his head. He seemed to be discussing literature with two strangers in an English pub while drinking beer. He wondered for a moment if he had become someone else, while he wasn't looking. The beer tasted less bad, the farther down the glass he went, and was beginning to erase the lingering aftertaste of the cherryade.

"*Eldritch*. Means weird. Peculiar. Bloody odd. That's what it means. I looked it up. In a dictionary. And *gibbous*?"

Ben shook his head again.

"*Gibbous* means the moon was nearly full. And what about that one he was always calling us, eh? Thing. Wossname. Starts with a b. Tip of me tongue..."

"Bastards?" suggested Wilf.

"Nah. Thing. You know. *Batrachian*. That's it. Means looked like frogs."

"Hang on," said Wilf. "I thought they was, like, a kind of camel."

Seth shook his head vigorously. "S'definitely frogs. Not camels. Frogs."

Wilf slurped his Shoggoth's. Ben sipped his, carefully, without pleasure.

"So?" said Ben.

"They've got two humps," interjected Wilf, the tall one.

"Frogs?" asked Ben.

"Nah. Batrachians. Whereas your average dromederary camel, he's only got one. It's for the long journey through the desert. That's what they eat."

"Frogs?" asked Ben.

"Camel humps." Wilf fixed Ben with one bulging yellow eye. "You listen to me, matey-me-lad. After you've been out in some trackless desert for three or four weeks, a plate of roasted camel hump starts looking particularly tasty."

Seth looked scornful. "You've never eaten a camel hump."

"I might have done," said Wilf.

"Yes, but you haven't. You've never even been in a desert."

"Well, let's say, just supposing I'd been on a pilgrimage to the Tomb of Nyarlathotep…"

"The black king of the ancients who shall come in the night from the east and you shall not know him, you mean?"

"Of course that's who I mean."

"Just checking."

"Stupid question, if you ask me."

"You could of meant someone else with the same name."

"Well, it's not exactly a common name, is it? Nyarlathotep. There's not exactly going to be two of them, are there? 'Hello, my name's Nyarlathotep, what a coincidence meeting you here, funny them bein' two of us,' I don't exactly think so. Anyway, so I'm trudging through them trackless wastes, thinking to myself, I could murder a camel hump…"

"But you haven't, have you? You've never been out of Innsmouth harbour."

"Well…No."

"There." Seth looked at Ben triumphantly. Then he leaned over and whispered into Ben's ear, "He gets like this when he gets a few drinks into him, I'm afraid."

"I heard that," said Wilf.

"Good," said Seth. "Anyway. H. P. Lovecraft. He'd write one of his bloody sentences. Ahem. 'The gibbous moon hung low over the eldritch and batrachian inhabitants of squamous Dulwich.' What does he mean, eh? *What does he mean?* I'll tell you what he bloody means. What he bloody means is that the moon was nearly full, and everybody what lived in Dulwich was bloody peculiar frogs. That's what he means."

"What about the other thing you said?" asked Wilf.

"What?"

"*Squamous*. Wossat mean, then?"

Seth shrugged. "Haven't a clue," he admitted. "But he used it an awful lot." There was another pause.

"I'm a student," said Ben. "Gonna be a metallurgist." Somehow he had managed to finish the whole of his first pint of Shoggoth's Old Peculiar, which was, he realised, pleasantly shocked, his first alcoholic beverage. "What do you guys do?"

"We," said Wilf, "are acolytes."

"Of Great Cthulhu," said Seth proudly.

"Yeah?" said Ben. "And what exactly does that involve?"

"My shout," said Wilf. "Hang on." Wilf went over to the barmaid and came back with three more pints. "Well," he said, "what it involves is, technically speaking, not a lot right now. The acolytin' is not really what you might call laborious employment in the middle of its busy season. That is, of course, because of his bein' asleep. Well, not exactly *asleep*. More like, if you want to put a finer point on it, *dead*."

" 'In his house at Sunken R'lyeh dead Cthulhu lies dreaming,' " interjected Seth. "Or, as the poet has it, 'That is not dead what can eternal lie—' "

" 'But in Strange Aeons—' " chanted Wilf.

"—and by *Strange* he means *bloody peculiar*—"

"Exactly. We are not talking your normal Aeons here at all."

" 'But in Strange Aeons even Death can die.' "

Ben was mildly surprised to find that he seemed to be drinking another full-bodied pint of Shoggoth's Old Peculiar. Somehow the taste of rank goat was less offensive on the second pint. He was also delighted to notice that he was no longer hungry, that his blistered feet had stopped hurting, and that his companions were charming, intelligent men whose names he was having difficulty in keeping apart. He did not have enough experience with alcohol to know that this was one of the symptoms of being on your second pint of Shoggoth's Old Peculiar.

"So right now," said Seth, or possibly Wilf, "the business is a bit light. Mostly consisting of waiting."

"And praying," said Wilf, if he wasn't Seth.

"And praying. But pretty soon now, that's all going to change."

"Yeah?" asked Ben. "How's that?"

"Well," confided the taller one. "Any day now, Great Cthulhu (currently impermanently deceased), who is our boss, will wake up in his undersea living-sort-of quarters."

"And then," said the shorter one, "he will stretch and yawn and get dressed—"

"Probably go to the toilet, I wouldn't be at all surprised."

"Maybe read the papers."

"—And having done all that, he will come out of the ocean depths and consume the world utterly."

Ben found this unspeakably funny. "Like a ploughman's," he said.

"Exactly. Exactly. Well put, the young American gentleman. Great Cthulhu will gobble the world up like a ploughman's lunch, leaving but only the lump of Branston pickle on the side of the plate."

"That's the brown stuff?" asked Ben. They assured him that it was, and he went up to the bar and brought them back another three pints of Shoggoth's Old Peculiar.

He could not remember much of the conversation that followed. He remembered finishing his pint, and his new friends inviting him on a walking tour of the village, pointing out the various sights to him "that's where we rent our videos, and that big building next door is the Nameless Temple of Unspeakable Gods and on Saturday mornings there's jumble sale in the crypt..."

He explained to them his theory of the walking tour book and told them, emotionally, that Innsmouth was both *scenic* and *charming*. He told them that they were the best friends he had ever had and that Innsmouth was *delightful.*

The moon was nearly full, and in the pale moonlight both of his new friends did look remarkably like huge frogs. Or possibly camels.

The three of them walked to the end of the rusted pier, and Seth and/or Wilf pointed out to Ben the ruins of Sunken R'lyeh in the bay, visible in the moonlight, beneath the sea, and Ben was overcome by what he kept explaining was a sudden and unforeseen attack of seasickness and was violently and unendingly sick over the metal railings into the black sea below...After that it all got a bit odd.

Ben Lassiter awoke on the cold hillside with his head pounding and a bad taste in his mouth. His head was resting on his backpack. There was rocky moorland on each side of him, and no sign of a road, and no sign of any village, scenic, charming, delightful, or even picturesque.

He stumbled and limped almost a mile to the nearest road and walked along it until he reached a petrol station.

They told him that there was no village anywhere locally named Innsmouth. No village with a pub called *The Book of Dead Names*. He told them about two men, named Wilf and Seth, and a friend of theirs, called Strange Ian, who was fast asleep somewhere, if he wasn't dead, under the sea. They told him that they didn't think much of American hippies who wandered about the countryside taking drugs, and that he'd probably feel better after a nice cup of tea and a tuna and cucumber sandwich, but that if he was dead set on wandering the country taking drugs, young Ernie who worked the afternoon shift would be all too happy to sell him a nice little bag of homegrown cannabis, if he could come back after lunch.

Ben pulled out his *A Walking Tour of the British Coastline* book and tried to find Innsmouth in it to prove to them that he had not dreamed it, but he was unable to locate the page it had been on—if ever it had been there at all. Most of one page, however, had been ripped out, roughly, about halfway through the book.

And then Ben telephoned a taxi, which took him to Bootle railway station, where he caught a train, which took him to Manchester, where he got on an aeroplane, which took him to Chicago, where he changed planes and flew to Dallas, where he got another plane going north, and he rented a car and went home.

He found the knowledge that he was over 600 miles away from the ocean very comforting; although, later in life, he moved to Nebraska to increase the distance from the sea: there were things he had seen, or thought he had seen, beneath the old pier that night that he would never be able to get out of his head. There were things that lurked beneath grey raincoats that man was not meant to know. *Squamous.* He did not need to look it up. He knew. They were *squamous.*

A couple of weeks after his return home Ben posted his annotated copy of *A Walking Tour of the British Coastline* to the author, care of her publisher, with an extensive letter containing a number of helpful suggestions for future editions. He also asked the author if she would send him a copy of the page that had been ripped from his guidebook, to set his mind at rest; but he was secretly relieved, as the days turned into months, and the months turned into years and then into decades, that she never replied.

Nor the Demons Down Under the Sea (1957)

Caitlín R. Kiernan

The late summer morning like a shattering blue-white gem, crashing liquid seams of fluorite and topaz thrown against the jagged shale and sandstone shingle, roiling calcite foam beneath the cloudless sky specked with gulls and ravens. And Julia behind the wheel of the big green Bel Air, chasing the coast road north, the top down so the Pacific wind roars wild through her hair. Salt smell to fill her head, intoxicating and delicious scent to drown her city-dulled senses and Anna's alone in the backseat, ignoring her again, silent, reading one of her textbooks or monographs on malacology. Hardly a word from her since they left the motel in Anchor Bay more than an hour ago, hardly a word at breakfast, for that matter, and her silence is starting to annoy Julia.

"It was a bad dream, that's all," Anna said, the two of them alone in the diner next door to the motel, sitting across from one another in a Naugahyde booth with a view of the bay, Haven's Anchorage dotted with the bobbing hulls of fishing boats. "You know that I don't like to talk about my dreams," and then she pushed her uneaten grapefruit aside and lit a cigarette. "God knows I've told you enough times."

"We don't have to go on to the house," Julia said hopefully. "We could always see it another time, and we could go back to the city today, instead."

Anna only shrugged her shoulders and stared through the glass at the water, took another drag off her cigarette and exhaled smoke the color of the horizon.

"If you're afraid to go to the house, you should just say so."

Julia steals a glance at her in the rearview mirror, wind-rumpled girl with shiny sunburned cheeks, cheeks like ripening plums and her short, blonde hair twisted into a bun and tied up in a scarf. And Julia's own reflection stares back at her from the glass, reproachful, desperate, almost fifteen years older than Anna, so close to thirty-five now that it frightens her; her drab hazel eyes hidden safely behind dark sunglasses that also conceal nascent crow's feet, and the wind whips unhindered through her own hair, hair that would be mouse brown if she didn't use peroxide. The first tentative wrinkles beginning to show at the corners of her mouth, and then she notices that her lipstick is smudged and licks the tip of one index finger and wipes at the candy-pink stain.

"You really should come up for air," Julia shouts, shouting just to be heard above the wind, and Anna looks slowly up from her book. She squints and blinks at the back of Julia's head, an irritated, uncomprehending sort of expression and a frown that draws creases across her forehead.

"You're missing all the scenery, dear."

Anna sits up, sighs loudly and stares out at a narrow, deserted stretch of beach rushing past, the ocean beyond. "Scenery's for the tourists," she says. "I'm not a tourist." And she slumps down into the seat again, turns a page and goes back to reading.

"You could at least tell me what I've done," Julia says, trying hard not to sound angry or impatient, sounding only a little bit confused, instead, but this time Anna doesn't reply, pretending not to hear or maybe just choosing to ignore her altogether.

"Well, then, whenever you're ready to talk about it," Julia says, but that isn't what she *wants* to say; she wants to tell Anna she's getting sick of her pouting about like a high-school girl, sick of these long, brooding silences, and more than sick of always feeling guilty because she doesn't ever know what to say that will make things better. Always feeling like it's her fault, somehow, and if she weren't a coward she would never have become involved with a girl like Anna Foley in the first place.

But you are a coward, Julia reminds herself. *Don't ever forget that, not even for a second*, and she almost misses her exit, the turnoff that would carry them east to Boonville if she stayed on the main road. Julia takes the exit, following the crude map Anna drew for her on a paper napkin; the road dips and curves sharply away from the shoreline, and the ocean is suddenly lost behind a dense wall of redwoods and blooming rhododendrons, the morning sun traded for the rapid flicker of forest shadows. Only a few hundred yards from the highway there's another, unpaved road, unnamed road leading deeper into the trees, and she slows down, and the Chevrolet bounces off the blacktop onto the rutted, pockmarked logging trail.

ভৈ

The drive up the coast from San Francisco to Anchor Bay was Anna's idea, even though they both knew it was a poor choice for summertime shelling. But still a chance to get out of the laboratory, she said, to get away from the city, from the heat and all the people, and Julia knew what she really meant. A chance to be alone, away from suspicious, disapproving eyes, and besides, there had been an interesting limpet collected very near there a decade or so ago, a single, unusually large shell cataloged and tucked away in the vast Berkeley collections and then all but forgotten. The new species, *Diodora thespesius*, was described by one of Julia Winter's male predecessors in the department, and a second specimen would surely be a small feather in her cap.

So, the last two days spent picking their way meticulously over the boulders, kelp- and algae-slick rocks and shallow tide pools consistently buried and unburied by the shifting sand flats; hardly an ideal place for limpets, or much of anything else, to take hold. Thick-soled rubber boots and aluminum pails, sun hats and gloves, knives to pry mollusks from the rocks, and little reward for their troubles but scallops and mussels. A few nice sea urchins and sand dollars, *Strongylocentrotus purpuratus* and *Dendraster excentricus*, and the second afternoon Anna had spotted a baby octopus, but it had gotten away from them.

"If we only had more time," Anna said. "I'm sure we would have found it if we had more time." She was sitting on a boulder, smoking, her dungarees soaked through to the thighs, staring north and west towards the headland and the dark silhouette of Fish Rocks jutting up from the sea like the scabby backs of twin leviathans.

"Well, it hasn't been a total loss, has it?" Julia asked and smiled, remembering the long night before, Anna in her arms, Anna whispering things that had kept Julia awake almost until dawn. "It wasn't a *complete* waste."

And Anna Foley turned and watched her from her seat on the boulder, sloe-eyed girl, slate-gray irises to hide more than they would ever give away; *She's taunting me,* Julia thought, feeling ashamed of herself for thinking such a thing, but thinking it anyway. *It's all some kind of a game to her, playing naughty games with Dr. Winter. She's sitting there watching me squirm.*

"You want to see a haunted house?" Anna asked, finally, and whatever Julia had expected her to say, it certainly wasn't that.

"Excuse me?"

"A haunted house. A *real* haunted house," and Anna raised an arm and pointed northeast, inland, past the shoreline. "It isn't very far from here. We could drive up tomorrow morning."

This is a challenge, Julia thought. *She's trying to challenge me, some new convolution in the game meant to throw me off balance.*

"I'm sorry, Anna. That doesn't really sound like my cup of tea," she said, tired and just wanting to climb back up the bluff to the motel for a hot shower and an early dinner.

"No, really. I'm serious. I read about this place last month in *Argosy*. It was built in 1890 by a man named Machen Dandridge who supposedly worshipped Poseidon and—"

"Since when do you read *Argosy*?"

"I read everything, Julia," Anna said. "It's what I do," and she turned her head to watch a ragged, commingled flock of Mew and Herring gulls flying by, ash and charcoal wings skimming just above the surface of the water.

"And an article in *Argosy* magazine said that this house was *really* haunted?" Julia asked skeptically, watching Anna watch the gulls as they rose and wheeled high over the Anchorage.

"Yes, it did. It was written by Dr. John Montague, an anthropologist, I think. He studies haunted houses."

"Anthropologists aren't generally in the business of ghost-hunting, dear," Julia said, smiling, and Anna glared at her from her rock, her stormy eyes narrowing the slightest bit.

"Well, this one seems to be, *dear*."

And then neither of them said anything for a few minutes, so there were no sounds but the wind and the surf and the raucous gulls, all the soothing, lonely ocean noises. Finally the incongruent, mechanical rumble of a truck up on the highway broke the spell, the taut, wordless space between them.

"I think we should be heading back now," Julia said finally. "The tide will be coming in soon."

"You go on ahead," Anna whispered and chewed at her lower lip. "I'll catch up."

Julia hesitated, glancing down at the cold saltwater lapping against the boulders, each breaking and withdrawing wave tumbling the cobbles imperceptibly smoother. Waves to wash the green-brown mats of seaweed one inch forward and one inch back; *Like the hair of drowned women*, she thought and then pushed the thought away.

"I'll wait for you at the top, then," she said. "In case you need help."

"Sure, Dr. Winter. You do that," and Anna turned away again and flicked the butt of her cigarette at the sea.

ဆဲ

Almost an hour of hairpin curves and this road getting narrower and narrower still, strangling dirt road with no place to turn around, before Julia finally comes to the edge of the forest, and the fern thickets and giant redwoods release her to rolling, open fields. Tall yellow-brown pampas grass that sways gently in the breeze, air that smells like sun and salt again, and she takes a deep breath. A relief to breathe air like this after the stifling closeness of the forest, all those old trees with their shaggy, shrouding limbs, and this clear blue sky is better, she thinks.

"There," Anna says, and Julia gazes past the gleaming green hood of the Chevy, across the restless grass, and there's something dark, outlined against the western horizon.

"That's it," Anna says. "Yeah, that *must* be it," and now she's sounding like a kid on Christmas morning, little girl at an amusement park excitement; she climbs over the seat and sits down close to Julia.

I could always turn back now, Julia thinks, her hands so tight around the steering wheel that her knuckles have gone a waxy white. *I could turn this car right around and go back to the highway. We could be in the city in a few hours. We could be home before dark.*

"What are you *waiting* for?" Anna asks anxiously, and she points at the squat rectangular smudge in the distance. "That's it. We've found it."

"I'm beginning to think this is what you wanted all along," Julia says, speaking low, and she can hardly hear herself over the Bel Air's idling engine. "Anchor Bay, spending time together, that was all just a trick to get me to bring you out here, wasn't it?"

Anna looks reluctantly away from the house. "No," she says. "That's not true. I only remembered the house later, when we were on the beach."

Julia looks towards the faraway house again, if it *is* a house. It might be almost anything, sitting out there in the tall grass, waiting. It might be almost anything at all.

"You're the one that's always telling me to get my nose out of books," snaps Anna, starting to sound angry, cultivated indignation gathering itself protectively about her like a caul, and she slides away from Julia, slides across the vinyl car seat until she's pressed against the passenger door.

"I don't think this was what I had in mind."

Anna begins kicking lightly at the floorboard, then, the toe of a sneaker tapping out the rhythm of her impatience like a Morse code signal.

"Jesus," she says, "It's only an old house. What the hell are you so afraid of, anyway?"

"I never said I was afraid, Anna. I never said anything of the sort."

"You're *acting* like it, though. You're acting like you're scared to death."

"Well, I'm not going to sit here and argue with you," Julia says and tells herself that just this once it doesn't matter if she sounds more like Anna's mother than her lover. "It's my car, and we never should have driven all the way out here alone. I would have turned around half an hour ago, if there'd been enough room on that road." And then she puts the Bel Air into reverse and backs off the dirt road, raising an alarmed and fluttering cloud of grasshoppers, frantic insect wings beating all about them as she shifts into drive and cuts the wheel sharply in the direction of the trees.

"I thought you'd understand," Anna says. "I thought you were different," and she's out of the car before Julia can try to stop her, slams her door shut and walks quickly away, following the path that leads between the high and whispering grass towards the house.

Julia sits in the Chevy and watches her go, watches helplessly as Anna seems to grow smaller with every step, the grass and the brilliant day swallowing her alive, wrapping her up tightly in golden stalks and sunbeam teeth. And Julia imagines driving away alone, simply taking her foot off the brake pedal and retracing that twisting, tree-shadowed path to the safety of paved roads. How *easy* that would be, how perfectly *satisfying*, and then she watches Anna for a few minutes more before she turns the car to face the house and tries to pretend that she never had any choice in the matter at all.

ॐ

The house stands like a grim and untimely joke, like something better off in a Charles Addams cartoon than perched on the high, sheer cliff, the pampas grass and a bumpy ride ends. This ramshackle grotesquerie of boards gone the silver-gray of old oyster shells, the splinterskin walls with their broken windows and crooked shutters, steep gables and turrets missing half their slate shingles, and there are places where the roof beams and struts show straight through the house's weathered hide. One black lightning rod still standing guard against the weather, a rusting garland of wrought iron filigree along the eaves, and the uppermost part of the chimney has collapsed in a red-green scatter of bricks gnawed back to soft clay by moss and the corrosive sea air. Thick weeds where there might once have been a lawn and flower beds, and the way the entire structure has begun to list perceptibly leaves Julia with the disconcerting impression that the house is cringing, or that it has actually begun to pull itself free of the earth and is preparing to crawl, inch by crumbling inch, away from the ocean.

"Anna, wait," but the girl's already halfway up the steps to the wide front porch, and Julia's still sitting behind the wheel of the Chevy. She closes her eyes for a moment, better to sit listening to the wind and the waves crashing against the cliffs and the smaller, hollow sound of Anna's feet on the porch, than to let the house think that she *can't* look away. Some dim instinct to tell her that's how this works, the mere sight of it enough to leave you dumbstruck and vulnerable.

My god, she thinks. *It's only an ugly old house. An ugly old house that no one wants anymore,* and then she laughs out loud, like it can hear.

As if it's listening.

After she caught up with Anna and made her get back into the car, and after Julia agreed to drive her the rest of the way out to the house, Anna Foley started talking about Dr. Montague's article in *Argosy* again, talking as though there'd never been an argument. The tension between them forgotten or discarded in a flood of words, words that came faster and faster as they neared the house, almost piling atop each other towards the end of her monologue.

"There were stories that Dandridge murdered his daughter as a sacrifice, sometime after his wife died in 1914. But no one ever actually found her body. No, she just vanished one day, and no one ever saw her again. The daughter, I mean. The daughter vanished, not the wife. His wife is buried behind the house, though I'm not sure..."

Only an ugly, old house sitting forgotten beside the sea.

"...to Poseidon, or maybe even Dagon, who was a sort of Mesopotamian corn king, half man and half fish. Dandridge traveled all over the Middle East and India before he came back and settled in California. He had a fascination with Indo-Iranian antiquities and mythologies."

Then open your eyes and get this over with, and she does open her eyes, then, staring back at the house, and Julia relaxes her grip on the steering wheel. Anna's standing on the porch now, standing on tip-toes and peering in through a small shattered window near the door.

"Anna, wait on me. I'm coming," and Anna turns and smiles, waving to her, then goes back to staring into the house through the broken window.

Julia leaves the keys dangling in the ignition and picks her way towards the house, past lupine and wild white roses and a patch of poppies the color of tangerines, three or four orange-and-black monarch butterflies flitting from blossom to blossom, and there's a line of flagstones almost lost in the weeds.

The stones lead straight to the house, though the weedy patch seems much wider than it did from the car.

I should be there by now, she thinks, looking over her shoulder at the convertible and then ahead, at Anna standing on the porch, standing at the door of the Dandridge house, wrestling with the knob. *No. I'm so anxious, it only seems that way*, but five, seven, ten more steps, and the porch seems almost as far away as it did when she got out of the car.

"Wait on me," she shouts at Anna, who doesn't seem to have heard. Julia stops and wipes the sweat from her forehead before it runs down into her eyes. She glances up at the sun, directly overhead and hot against her face and bare arms, and she realizes that the wind has died. The blustery day has grown suddenly so still, and she can't hear the breakers anymore, either. Only the faint and oddly muted symphony of the gulls and grasshoppers.

She turns to face the sea, and there's a brittle noise from the sky that makes her think of eggshells cracking against the edge of a china mixing bowl, and on the porch Anna's opening the door. And the shimmering darkness, somehow wet and sticky, that flows out and over and *through* Anna Foley makes a different sound, and Julia shuts her eyes so she won't have to watch whatever comes next.

ଔଔ

The angle of the light falling velvet soft across the dusty floor, the angle and the honey color of the sun, so Julia knows that it's late afternoon, and somehow she's lost everything in between. That last moment in the yard before entering this place without even unconsciousness to bridge the gap, *then* and *now*, and she understands it's as simple as that. Her head aches and her stomach rolls when she tries to sit up to get a better look at the room, and Julia decides that maybe it's best to lie still a little while longer. Just lie here and stare out that window at the blue sky framed in glass-jagged mouths. There might have been someone there a moment ago, a scarecrow face looking in at her through the broken window, watching, waiting, and there might have been nothing but the partitioned swatches of the fading day.

She can hear the breakers again, now only slightly muffled by the walls and the wind around the corners of the house; these sounds through air filled with the oily stench of rotting fish and the neglected smell of any very old and empty house. A barren, fishstinking room and a wall with one tall arched window just a few feet away from her, sunbleached and peeling wallpaper strips, and she knows that it must be a western wall, the sunlight through the broken window panes proof enough of that.

Unless it's morning light, she thinks. *Unless it's morning light, and this is an-other day entirely. Unless the sun is rising now instead of setting.* Julia wonders why she ever assumed it was afternoon, how she can ever again assume any-thing. And there's a sound, then, from somewhere behind her, inside the room with her or very close to it; the crisp sound of a ripe melon splitting open, scarlet flesh and black teardrop seeds, sweet red juice, and now the air smells even worse. Fish *putrefying* under a baking summer sun, beaches strewn with bloated fish-silver bodies as far as the eye can see, beaches littered with every-thing in the sea heaved up onto the shore, an inexplicable, abyssal vomit, and she closes her eyes again.

"Are you here, Anna?" she whispers. "Can you hear me?"

And something quivers at the edge of her vision, a fluttering darkness deep-er than the long shadows in the room, and she ignores the pain and the nau-sea and rolls over onto her back to see it more clearly. But the thing on the ceiling sees her, too, and it moves quickly towards the sanctuary of a corner; all feathery, trembling gills and swimmerets, and its jointed lobster carapace almost as pale as toadstools, chitin soft and pale, and it scuttles backwards on raw and bleeding human hands. It drips and leaves a spattered trail of itself on the floor as it goes.

She can see the door now, the absolute blackness waiting in the hall through the doorway, and there's laughter from that direction, a woman's high, hysteri-cal laugh, but so faint that it can't possibly be coming from anywhere inside the house.

"Anna," she calls out again, louder than before, and the laughter abruptly stops, and the thing on the ceiling clicks its needle teeth together.

"She's gone down, *that* one," it mutters. "She's gone all the way down to Mother Hydra and won't hear you in a hundred, hundred million years."

And the laughing begins again, seeping slyly up through the floorboards, through every crack in these moldering plaster walls.

"I saw a something in the sky," the ceiling crawler whispers from its corner, "No bigger than my fist."

And the room writhes and spins around her like a kaleidoscope, that tum-bling gyre of colored shards, remaking the world, and it wouldn't matter if there were anything for her to hold onto. She would still fall; no way not to fall with this void devouring even the morning, or the afternoon, whichever, even the colors of the day sliding down that slick gullet.

"I can't *see* you," Anna says, definitely Anna's voice, though Julia's never heard her sound this way before: so afraid, so insignificant.

"I can't see *you* anywhere," Julia replies and reaches out (or down or up) into the furious storm that was the house, the maelstrom edges of a collapsing universe, and her arm sinks in up to the elbow. Sinks through into dead-star cold, the cold ooze of the deepest seafloor trench. "Open your eyes," Anna says, and she's crying now. "Please, god, open your *eyes*, Julia."

But her eyes *are* open, and she's standing somewhere far below the house, standing before the woman on the rock, the thing that was a woman once, and part of it can still recall that lost humanity. The part that watches Julia with one eye, the desperate, hate-filled, pale-green eye that hasn't been lost to the seething ivory crust of barnacles and sea lice that covers half its face. The woman on the great rock in the center of the phosphorescent pool, and then the sea rushes madly into the cavern, surges up and foams around the rusted chains and scales and all the squirming pink-white anemones sprouting from her thighs.

Alone, alone, all all alone,

The woman on the rock raises an arm, her ruined and shell-studded arm, and reaches across the pool towards Julia.

Alone on the wide wide sea

Her long fingers and the webbing grown between them, and Julia leans out across the frothing pool, ice water wrapping itself around her ankles, filling her shoes, as she strains to take the woman's hand. Straining to reach while the jealous sea rises and falls, rises and falls, threatening her with the bottomless voices of cachalots and typhoons. But the distance between their fingertips doubles, triples, origami space unfolding itself, and the woman's lips move silently, yellow teeth and pleading, gill-slit lips as mute as the cavern walls.

—murdered his daughter, sacrificed her—

Nothing from those lips but the small and startled creatures nesting in her mouth, not *words* but a sudden flow of surprised and scuttling legs, the claws and twitching antennae, and a scream that rises from somewhere deeper than the chained woman's throat, deeper than simple flesh, soulscream spilling out and swelling to fill the cave from wall to wall. This howl that is every moment that she's spent down here, every damned and salt-raw hour made aural, and Julia feels it in her bones, in the silver amalgam fillings of her teeth.

Will you, won't you, will you, won't you, will you join the dance?

And the little girl sits by the fire in a rocking chair, alone in the front parlor of her father's big house by the sea, and she reads fairy tales to herself while her father rages somewhere overhead, in the sky or only upstairs, but it makes no difference, in the end. Father of black rags and sour, scowling faces, and she tries not to hear the chanting or the sounds her brother is making again from his attic prison, tries to think of nothing but the Mock Turtle and Alice, the Lobster Quadrille by unsteady lantern light. *Don't look at the windows,* she thinks, or Julia tries to warn her. Don't look at the windows ever again.

Well, there was mystery. Mystery, ancient and modern, with Seaography: then Drawling—the Drawling-Master was an old conger-eel…

An old *conjure* eel—

Don't ever look at the windows even when the scarecrow fingers, the dry-grass bundled fingers, are tap-tap-tapping their song upon the glass. And she has seen the women dancing naked by the autumn moon, dancing in the tall moonwashed sheaves, bare feet where her father's scythe has fallen again and again, every reaping stroke to kill and call the ones that live at the bottom of the pool deep below the house. Calling them up and taunting them and then sending them hungrily back to down to Hell again. Hell or the deep, fire or ice-dark water, and which makes no difference whatsoever in the end.

Would not, could not, would not, could not, would not join the dance.

Julia's still standing at the wave-smoothed edge of the absinthe pool, or she's only a whispering, insubstantial ghost afraid of parlor windows, smoke-gray ghost muttering from nowhen, from hasn't-been or never-will-be, and the child turns slowly towards her voice as the hurting thing chained to the rock begins to tear and stretches itself across the widening gulf.

"Julia, *please.*"

"You will be their queen, in the cities beneath the sea," the old man says. "When I am not even a *memory*, child, you will hold them to the depths."

And they all dead did lie, And a million million slimy things Liv'd on—and so did I…

"Open your eyes," Anna says, and this time Julia does. All these sights and sounds flicker past like the last frames of a movie, and she's lying in Anna's arms, lying on her back in the weedy patch between the car and the brooding, spiteful house.

"I thought you were dead," Anna says, holding onto her so tightly she can hardly breathe. Anna sounds relieved and frightened and angry all at once, the tears rolling down her sunburned face and dripping off her chin onto Julia's cheeks.

"You were so goddamn cold. I thought you were dead. I thought I was alone."

Alone, alone, all all alone…

"I smell flowers," Julia says, "I smell roses," because she does, and she can think of nothing else to say, no mere words to ever make her forget, and she stares up past Anna, past the endless, sea-hued sky, at the summer sun staring back down at her like the blind and blazing eye of Heaven.

This Is How the World Ends

John R. Fultz

They always said the world would end in fire.

Mushroom clouds, atomic holocaust, the pits of Hell opening up and vomiting flame across a world of sin, corruption, and greed. The world would be a cinder, and Christ would come down from the clouds to lift the faithful skyward.

I used to believe those things. My daddy taught me the Bible, and Revelations was his favorite chapter. He believed in the wrath of God, and he feared the fires of Hell.

But the world wasn't burned away by righteous fires. There was no great conflagration.

The world didn't burn.

It drowned.

One thing the Bible did get right: the sea did turn to blood.

The coastal cities were the first to go. Two years ago the first of the Big Waves hit. The newscasters called them "mega-tsunamis." Los Angeles, San Diego, Seattle, San Francisco...so many sandcastles flattened and drowned. Watery graves for millions. New York, Miami, even Chicago when the Great Lakes leapt out of their holes like mad giants. A single day and all the major cities...gone.

After the tsunamis came the *real* terror. The waves washed terrible things onto the land...things that had never seen the light of day. Fanged, biting, *hungry* things. They fed on the bodies of the drowned, laid their eggs in the gnawed bodies. Billions of them...the seas ran red along the new coastlines. Survivors from Frisco fled inland, carrying tales of something even *worse* than the vicious Biters. Something colossal...some called it the Devil himself. It took the fallen skyscrapers as its nesting ground, ruling a kingdom of red waters.

I heard similar tales from western and eastern refugees. They fled inland, away from the stench of brine and blood, and the drifting islands of bloated bodies.

The military tried fighting back, but there were too many of those things claiming the coast. That's when the plague started. It floated across the land in great, black clouds, like dust storms during the Depression. Those who breathed the stuff didn't die...they *changed*. They grew gills, and fangs, and writhed like snakes, spitting venom. Feeding on each other. Soon there weren't any more soldiers.

I heard they tried nuking Manhattan, where something big as the moon crawled out of the ocean. The missiles didn't fire. Something shorted out all the technology, every computer on the continent...probably the planet...every piece of electronic equipment...all dead. Air Force jets fell out of the sky like dead birds. Somebody called it an electromagnetic pulse. As if the rules of the universe had shifted. In a flash, the modern world was done.

There was nothing to do but run. Hide.

Hordes of the Biters took to roaming the plains, the hills, the valleys and mountains. Those poor souls that didn't get taken by the rolling clouds eventually got rooted out by the Biters, or the worm-things that followed them around. Big, saw-toothed bastards, like leeches the size of semi-truck trailers. I saw one of the Biter hordes hit Bakersfield, saw a school bus full of refugees swallowed whole by one of those worms. Still see that in my nightmares sometimes...the faces of those kids...sound of their screams.

Whiskey helps, when I can get it.

About fifty of us from farms in the San Joaquin Valley had banded together, loaded up with guns, ammo, and canned food from Lloyd Talbert's bomb shelter, and headed east in a convoy of old pick-ups and decommissioned Army jeeps. We figured out that the black clouds usually preceded the Biters, so we stayed one step ahead of them. We tried to pick up some relatives in Bakersfield, or we would have avoided it altogether. Barely made it out of there, and we lost twelve good men in the process. Nobody got rescued.

It had rained for two months straight in California, nonstop ever since the Big Waves. Farther inland we went, the less rain we got. We figured out that the Biters liked the wet…they hated the dry lands, so we went on into Nevada. Thought we'd find kindred souls in Vegas.

That was a mistake.

Sin City had been smashed flat by something terrible that came out of Yucca Mountain, where they buried all that nuclear waste. We couldn't tell what it was, but we saw it slithering through hills of rubble, rooting up corpses like a hog sniffing for truffles. We watched it for awhile from a high ridge, until it raised itself up and howled at the moon. Its head was larger than a stadium, and it split open like a purple orchid lined with bloody fangs. What grew along the bulk of its shapeless body I can only call…tentacles. Looked like something from a B-movie filmed in Hell. It was the Beast That Ate Vegas.

Then it belched out one of those black clouds, and slammed itself back into a sea of debris that used to be a sparkling dream of a city. This cloud wasn't like the others. There were things inside it…flying things…maybe they were miniature versions of the Vegas-eater. We thought our vehicles could outrun the cloud, so we headed back west, until the Flyers came down on us.

I was riding in a jeep driven by Adam Ortega, a man I'd known since Iraq. We were two lone wolves who had gone through a lot of shit together and somehow came out alive. One of those Flyers swooped out of the dark and landed on his face. It smelled like fish guts. He screamed, and the beast pointed its orchid-face at me. A cluster of pinkish tongues quivered between the rows of fangs, and I raised my shotgun just in time to blow that thing to Hell. My shot also took Ortega's head off. God knows I didn't mean to do that. I was scared.

The jeep veered off the road, hit an embankment, and sent me flying. I blacked out, and when I woke up the entire convoy was in flames, every man lost beneath a mess of black-winged monsters. But they had forgotten me, at least for a few minutes.

They were good men, all of them, but there was no helping them now. Some had brought families with them. I heard women screaming. And children. Me, I'd always been alone, ever since my divorce. Farm life was lonely life, but it was good. My daddy passed away three years previous. Now that I think about it, I'm glad he went before all this happened. And that I never had kids of my own to see all this evil shit coming down. But some of my friends had loved ones they weren't about to leave behind, so there they were…deep in the middle of the shitstorm with the rest of us. I hid in a ditch and watched a few stragglers try to escape, but the Flyers tore away from carcasses like flocks of ravens and flapped after them.

I still had my .45 Desert Eagle and knew I was probably dead anyway. I could run, maybe live awhile longer. But one of the women trying to outrun those things was pregnant. So I started picking off the Flyers chasing her, one by one. A man ran behind her, and the things took him down. He screamed her name and I knew who she was.

"Evelyn!"

That was Johnny Colton and his wife. They hadn't been married more than a year.

Johnny's blood spouted as the damned things tore his heart out, then set to work on his face.

I ran toward Evelyn, shooting two more Flyers out of the air. I'm a pretty good shot. Got a lot of practice in the Mideast. Kept up my skills at the shooting range over the years.

One of them landed on her back and she fell, not twenty feet from me. I was afraid of shooting her, so I came at it with the hunting knife from my boot. Sliced it clean in half, but its blood was some kind of acid, splashed across my left cheek...burned like the Devil's piss. Still have one helluva scar from that.

I helped Evelyn to her feet, and we ran together. She cried out for Johnny, but I wouldn't let her look back. The black cloud was bearing down on us, blotting out the stars and moon. I smelled the stink of the ocean rolling over the desert...the smell of dead and rotted marine life.

I grabbed a satchel of gear from the overturned jeep, and we took off into the desert. The Flyers must have forgot us after awhile. They had a big enough feast back on the highway.

As the sun came up, red and bloated in the purple sky...it had never looked right since the Big Waves...we came into Pahrump. The tiny town was deserted, and corpses littered the streets. We saw they had been gnawed up pretty good, probably by the Flyers...or something just as bad. There wasn't a single living soul there. But we did find a good supply of canned food, bottled water, a gun shop full of ammo and a few rifles, and some other odds-and-ends.

It was Evelyn who told me about the old silver mine on the edge of town. She was a Nevada girl before she married Johnny.

"Maybe we can hide there...in the mine tunnels," she said. "Maybe they won't go underground. Those mines are pretty deep. We'll be safe down there, Joe."

I didn't believe we would, but I looked into her big, blue eyes, crystalline with tears shed for her dead husband, for her dead relatives in San Joaquin... for the whole damn world gone to Hell.

"Yeah." I lied to her. "We'll be safe down there. Good idea."

We loaded wheelbarrows with provisions, water, guns, blankets, and I picked up an old ham radio from the gun store. I didn't expect it to work, but it was something. Something to pin our hopes on. When the world is ending, you'll take anything you can get.

Evelyn was five months along when we moved into the mine. We weren't exactly *comfortable* down there in the belly of the cool earth, but it was as close as we were going to get. Even a blanket laid over hard stones feels good when you're half dead from exhaustion and worry. She tended the wound on my face, and I told her hopeful lies to settle her nerves. I said this would all blow over and things would be back to normal in a few months. I didn't believe a word of it. Maybe she did, or at least she wanted to.

I started playing with the radio, hooking it up to a portable battery and listening to the static. I scanned every frequency, every day for weeks, but there was nothing out there. Nothing at all. I imagined all those ham radio geeks lying dead in their basements, or their bones in the bellies of nameless beasts, their radios crushed to splinters or lying in forgotten barns covered with dust.

Slowly, the months crept by. It turned out Evelyn was right. We were safe underground. Her belly grew bigger, and she stopped moving around so much. I started mentally preparing myself to deliver the baby, something I had never done before. But I'd seen so much blood and suffering, first in the war, now at the end of the world, that I knew it wouldn't matter. How hard could it be to pull this little bugger out of his momma's belly? *She* would do most of the work.

"I'm gonna name him Johnny," she said. "Like his father."

I smiled as if it mattered. The kid had no future in a world like this. I cleaned my .45 and contemplated putting us both out of our misery. Why go on living? What was the point? We'd both be better off dead. I loaded a clip into the chamber and tucked the gun behind my belt buckle. I went over to sit by her on the makeshift bed we'd been sharing. I had never touched her sexually, but we'd hold hands in the dead of night. It brought some measure of comfort…more for her than for me, I told myself.

The baby was kicking today, and she was excited. I lowered the flame in our lantern and told her to get some sleep. I might sneak out later and hunt a hare for dinner, I told her. I always said that, but I'd never found any living game outside in the three months we'd been there. Still, sometimes I'd sneak out between the rolling black clouds and scavenge, or look for signs of life. I knew I was kidding myself, and I was tired of it.

She would nod off soon and I would end her life painlessly, one clean shot through her skull and another to finish off the unborn child.

Then one last round through the roof of my mouth and right into my brain pan.

All this suffering would be over for us. The baby would never know a world of crawling Biters and hungry Flyers. It was the right thing to do, I told myself, my mind made up.

But Evelyn…she stopped me without ever knowing my plan.

She looked up at me with those big, blue eyes, her dark lids heavy, and she raised her head a bit.

She kissed me, damn her.

She kissed me like she loved me, and I took her into my arms. We lay there for awhile, then fell to sleep. After that I knew I could never kill her. Not even to spare her the pain of living in this dying world.

Two weeks later she went into labor. I had the towels and the boiling water, and even some painkillers I'd looted from a burned-out drug store in Pahrump. She started screaming, and I could see the baby pressing outward from inside her belly.

She screamed, and I coached her to breathe, breathe, breathe. She pushed, and she screamed. A gout of blood and placenta flowed out of her, and I knew something was wrong. Her screams reached a higher pitch, and she called out for Jesus, for her mommy and daddy, for poor old Johnny.

I fell back when her stomach burst like a ripe melon, a gnarled claw protruding like a dead tree branch. She writhed like a snake, and her wailing was a white noise in my ears as the thing inside her *ripped* its way out. It slithered across her splayed abdomen, and she fainted. I couldn't move…I stared at Johnny Colton's baby, my mouth hanging open, my heart a hunk of lead in my chest. The stench of the deep ocean filled the cavern, overpowering the human odors of blood and afterbirth.

Its head was a bulbous thing…emerald and coated with bloody slime. Two lidless eyes bulged like black stones, but it had no other face to speak of. A mass of quivering tendrils writhed below the eyes, headless snake-things dripping with gore and mucous. It crawled out of Evelyn's body, and I knew she was dead. Nobody could lose that much blood and still be alive. She was a hollow shell. Her vacant eyes stared at the tunnel's rough ceiling. I remember thinking it was a good thing she didn't live to see this thing that had grown inside her.

It hopped from her corpse in a splash of dark fluids, walking on its clawed arms and feet. Two more appendages grew from its hunched little back, and as they spread I heard a crackling sound like stretching leather. They looked like the wings of a big bat, though far too small to carry this thing with its melon-like head and bloated stomach. It had to weigh at least twenty-five, thirty pounds, I was sure.

It looked at me for a timeless moment, then turned to explore its dead mother's body with those twitching facial tentacles. I heard a horrible sucking sound as it lapped up Evelyn's blood like mother's milk, and then the cracking of bones as its tendrils encircled and *squeezed* her body into pulp. Already it looked somehow larger.

The sound of her bones snapping broke my trance, and I leapt for a sawed-off shotgun I kept near the blankets. It turned to face me again, as if it knew I was about to put an end to it. The big, black eyes narrowed in their sockets, and the remnants of its own afterbirth sluiced from its hidden squid-mouth. It stared down the twin barrels of my gun, and I swear it *spoke*.

Even though it was only minutes old, it hissed at me, a single word I had never heard before, but somehow sounded familiar. Maybe I'd heard it in a nightmare.

Cthulhu, it whispered before I blew its head off.

I've heard that word for months now. Every time I close my eyes.

Sometimes I dream of New York, or Los Angeles, or even London. I see the great landmarks of the world that was...the towers that once conquered the sky...I see them tilted and crumbling and fallen into the sea, and a mass of cold-blooded amphibian things swirling about them like maggots on a decaying corpse.

I see Evelyn Colton's baby, too, or something like it. It stands above those ruined cities, wings spread like thunderheads, singing a wild song of triumph and murder. It squats like a colossal ape on the skeleton of the Empire State Building as if it were no more than a fallen log in some world-sized swamp.

I see its *children*, spreading across the globe, filling the low places with brackish seawater, turning the high places into wastelands. A billion-billion monsters spew from the angry seas, screaming its name beneath the bloody moon.

Cthulhu.

Flocks of Colton-babies fly down from the cold stars, soaring around their god like masses of buzzing flies.

That's what it is, I come to understand...it's their god.

It's the god of this new world.

It's been a year now since I buried Evelyn. Her grave sits in one of the mine's westernmost tunnels, marked with a cross I took from the husk of an old church.

I listen to the endless static on the ham radio every day. Found a little generator in the ruined town, and I've been siphoning gasoline from an abandoned filling station to power it. The static fills my ears, and sometimes it even drowns out the echoes of Evelyn's wailing as that thing tore itself out of her. Sometimes I broadcast, not giving away my location, but hoping someone—anyone—will answer. I feel like those SETI scientists who used to beam radio messages out into space, into the darkness of infinity, on the off chance that someone out there is listening.

But there's only static.

It rains all the time now, up there. I can't even go topside anymore because strange things move through the rain clouds, and the puddles breed miniature terrors.

The world is still drowning.

The stink of oceanic brine rolls down into the tunnels of the mine.

I tune the dials of the ham radio, call out a few more S.O.S. messages.

The .45 sits on the blanket before me. I stare at it, gleaming with silver promise.

Evelyn isn't here to stop me this time. One quick, clean shot, and I won't smell the ocean stench any more, won't have the dreams anymore, won't hear the static. The unbroken, white static.

My bottled water is running out. I can't drink the rain, but I know sooner or later I'll have to. I don't want to think what it will do to me. But thirst is a demon no man can outrun for long. I sit staring at the gun, listening to the radio static, making my decision.

I pick up the .45 and slide the barrel into my mouth. It tastes cold and bitter. Static fills my ears. I fix my thumb so that it's resting on the trigger. I say a silent prayer, and think of my daddy's face.

Something breaks the static.

A momentary glitch in the wall of white noise. I blink, my lips wrapped around the gun. I pull it from my mouth and fiddle with the nobs. There it is again! A one-second break in the static...a voice!

I turn the volume up, wait a few moments, then pick up the mic, dropping the pistol.

"Hello!" I say, my voice hoarse like sand on stone. "Hello! Is anybody there?"

White noise static...then a pause, followed by a single word, ringing clear as day from the dusty speaker, thick as mud.

Cthulhu.

I drop the mic. Something twists in my gut, and I step back from the radio like it's another monstrosity burst from Evelyn Colton's belly.

Again it speaks to me, a voice oozing out of the cold ocean depths.

Cthulhu.

The word sinks into me like a knife, a smooth incision...a length of cold metal between the eyes would be no less effective. The pain is a spike of understanding. I bend over, my hand hovering between the silver-plated pistol and the radio mic. I grab the mic, not the gun, and raise it to my lips.

I stare into the darkness at the back of the cavern and sigh out my reply.

"Cthulhu..."

I drop it to the floor and kick over the little table where the radio sits. It crashes against the stone, spilling the lantern. Flaming oil ignites the blankets, and the cavern fills with noxious smoke. I turn my back on it and walk toward the smell of briny rain, my throat dry as bone.

As I come up out of the silver mine for the last time, the storm rages, winged things soar between the clouds, and I hear a chorus of howling and screeching punctuated by moaning thunder. Thirst consumes me.

I open my mouth to the black skies and drink the oily rain. It flows down my throat like nectar, quenching my terrible thirst in the most satisfying way. It sits cool and comforting in my belly, and I drink down more of it.

I'll never again be thirsty, I realize.

This isn't the end of the world.

It's the beginning.

My body trembles with hidden promise. I know I've got a place in this new world.

Towering things with shadow-bright wings descend to squat about me, staring with clusters of glazed eyes as I crumple…shiver…evolve.

I raise my blossoming face to the storm and screech my joy across the face of the world.

His world.

Cthuuuuulhuuuuu…

Spreading black wings, I take to the sky.

The Drowning At Lake Henpin

Paul Tobin

I have never before filed a shooting report and I appreciate your patience in this matter. It has taken me some time to steady myself, to steel my nerves and commit this queer incident to paper. Writing has been difficult, and not only from a standpoint of my mental state. For these past several days my fingers have been… wet. They made the paper slippery. Smeared the ink. I have been sweating. It's only sweat. Nothing else. I'm sure of it. There's no reason to be alarmed. To be honest I'm still somewhat shaken, and while it's customary for police officers to deny any need for psychiatric help, I think it's best that I do speak with someone in some official capacity. Someone who will understand me. If such a thing is anymore possible.

Perhaps I shouldn't have so clearly stated my above thoughts here in this file. I do not personally believe that asking for help is a sign of weakness, but there are those that do and it may come back to haunt me. I hope that I will not be denied advancement in the force. To be candid, I hope to be transferred to another district, to act as a constable somewhere away from the village of Leighton, certainly away from Lake Henpin and any members of the Cabershaw family. It's only that these visions won't leave my head. I can see Marken in that damnable pool of blood. Or what should have been blood. I cannot be mistaken on this. It most definitely should have been blood. Correct? It should have been blood. Of course.

Despite my earlier statements, such as those when I was being removed from the scene, I now realize it's not possible that I saw my bullet leaving the barrel of my Webley. A bullet moves too quickly to be seen. That's rather the point of a bullet. But I saw it. I witnessed it coming from the barrel. There was an explosion of light. Not the bright kind of light. It was the dull variety. Until that singular moment I hadn't known of this blacker light, that there is a light that steals brightness as it travels along its path. It was a light that did not share. It... it was a greedy light. That's all I can say about it. And the bullet came from my barrel and it paused and then something spoke. Not the bullet. I don't mean that. I've been misquoted. What I meant to say it that there was something else at the scene. I mean *someone* else, of course. Not *something* else. Someone said something that I could not understand, that I dared not understand, and I was only screaming in the hopes of driving out the damnable noise but nothing was working because the words were dripping inside my head and I could see the air moving aside from the bullet as if it were plunging through water. The air was rippling. My bullets were curving in arcs.

I am told that Christopher Marken, there with Cecil Cabershaw at the lake house shooting, was long dead. Dead for two days, I've heard. Drowned and dead before I fired the shots that killed him. I'm told that my shots (there were three bullets missing from my Webley, but I stand by my earlier testimony that I fired four rounds) were not the cause of Christopher Marken's death. The reports say he drowned. I cannot account for whatever results Marken's autopsy have brought forth. I can only say that they are a mistake. Some vials must have been mistakenly tagged. Perhaps tampered with. The samples must have been compromised. I tell you that Marken screamed when I shot him, and I can tell you that he lunged for me, that he had me by my collar, that he whispered words to me as he died, that his hands began dripping a foul wetness down the front of my uniform and that his eyes were screaming. He was screaming. I tell you he was screaming.

You must believe me.

଼ଌ

I feel better now.

My visits with Mr. Ulton have helped. He agrees with me that there is no reason to feel weak merely because I'm seeing a psychiatrist like him. We have decided, after some discussion, that my shooting report should involve the whole of the incident. That it should not be a simple statement of, "*Marken had an axe and I shot him.*" It is best that I begin with the first disappearance, that I speak of the first bodies, of the shooting itself and, of course, of the lake where I was found. Lake Henpin.

Cecil Cabershaw was the first to go missing and I, of course, was assigned to the case. Cecil has lived for some time, alone, more or less, in the abbey. It is not much of an abbey, I'd say. Arrogant to call it as such, but it has been known by the name for some three or four centuries, now. The villagers wouldn't know what else to call it. They're simple, as a rule. I do not mean to fault them for that.

Cecil lives in the main house. That sprawling ancient mess. Not as old as the tower building, of course, but it still reaches back some few hundreds of years. It's been anyone's guess why the tower and the house, being part of the same estate, were built so far apart. Half a mile at the least. The tower is near the lake. My father always wondered why a defense tower would be so far removed from the main house and the main road. He wondered why it was so close to the lake. I could tell him, now. I've solved the mystery. I am pleased that my father is no longer with us. He would not want this knowledge.

Cecil spent the greater part of his life caring for his elder sister, Maple, doing so since the days of her near-drowning at Lake Henpin. This was some fifteen years ago. She'd been a bright child, but she'd slipped beneath the waves one afternoon, foundered by a cramp is the general belief, though she hasn't spoken a word since that day. By chance my father and mother were on the lake as part of a boating party, like the ones you see in Impressionist paintings, my father said. He was fond of art. He was fond of calling the Cabershaw house an abbey. The cancer took him on my twenty-sixth birthday, but that's nothing to this story. Nothing at all.

My father saved her. He was the very one who pulled Maple from the waters. She was limp. Like a rag, he was fond of saying. She'd been down for some time before my father found her. He hauled her up into his boat and he tried to get air back in her lungs, blowing at her mouth and massaging her lungs, pushing at her ribs, literally rocking the boat, as it were, so that the other boats (there were three in the party) came close in order to steady my father's boat, so that it would not be spilled.

Maple gasped back to life. Heaving air. Father said she wasn't the only one who gasped. It was like watching the dead come back to life. They'd all given up hope. They'd all thought the water had taken her life and spat back her body. It wasn't far from the truth, I suppose, because she's been silent ever since and holds a strange fascination with water. When her parents committed suicide (Albert and Dorline drank cyanide some few months after the lake incident, and then slid into the warm waters of their bathtub, to be found by their maid) Cecil was all that Maple had left. She is beautiful, in a wasted way. Haunting, I'd say. Almost as if her beauty was frozen away in time, caught in some trap with her words. She needs constant care. Cecil gave his life to her. For nearly fifteen years. Then, he went missing. There were signs of a struggle. The bathroom, the same room where Cecil had lost his parents, was smashed up a bit, as if men had been wrestling, tossing each other about. Maple was found sitting quietly in her own room. There was a bowl of oats on her lap. Half eaten. She would not give it up. She still kept the bowl, even when she was moved to the psychiatric ward of the hospital in Wath-upon-Dearne. She said nothing, of course, about any attacks or her missing brother.

The villagers widely regarded Cecil's disappearance as a simple case of a young man (he was thirty, but that's young enough) deciding that his life must be lived, and his sister must therefore be abandoned. There were few who blamed him. Few who wondered at the signs of the scuffle in the bathroom. Perhaps he had been in a rage, mad at himself over his upcoming flight? It was a plausible theory, but it is not the work of a policeman to devise interesting theories and move on. We must have our proof.

There were several tracks outside the bathroom. A toothbrush. A razor and a strop. These footprints, though, were largely upon a bed of Copper Beech tree leaves, making it impossible to determine their outlines or origins. My theory was that there was more than one set. I still hold this to be true.

The footprints led to the woods. I lost them several times. I had the dog with me. The one Captain Levetts had trained. Steggs was his name. An Irish Setter. Named after an army friend of the captain's, I believe. The dog was eager for the run, at the first, but as the woods closed in the hound was less in love with the game. He was shivering, and there was a wetness to him, as if he'd been romping through the morning dew. The woods were humid. The dog was unnerved. Oh, he was still barking and such, but he was looking to me in question. I urged him on. Several times. He kept on past the clearing where the festivals are held. He circled. He whined. We carried on past the tower and its recent renovations, but Steggs did not find it to be of any interest. We moved through the woods. There were more tracks, now. I wish someone else would have seen them. I am sure of them. The late September heat had been about, but the footprints were wet. I can remember thinking that perhaps young Cecil had been in his bath. That his kidnappers had taken him straight from his daily preparations.

The dog and I emerged from the woods at the edge of Lake Henpin on the opposite side from the old docks, across from the boarded up lake house that had been built when the lake was considered a tourist attraction, in the days before the stuffy bastards from Basil College ran their experiments but could not tell us why all the fish in the lake have perished.

Steggs was no longer barking. He was, in fact, hiding behind me, and he was glad of it when I eventually determined that there was nothing to be seen. Had Cecil's kidnappers taken a boat across the waters? If so, I could find no hint of a mooring or any place where a boat had been slid into the waters. I could find nothing at all, and the dog's unease was wearing on my mood. When Steggs ran off, I followed after him willingly enough. I wanted nothing of the lake.

The Miller girl went missing only three days after.

ജ

Christopher Marken had been raised in these parts, if you'll remember. I was actually with him in school. Up to Third Year, I mean. We learned our numbers together, but little else, for we did not mingle. He was standoffish, and to be honest I was a bit of a bully in those days. Marken (we called him Markie) was picked up after school by his father, having been deposited by his governess in the morning. He was good at his books, which none of the rest of us cared for. He left almost before we were out of our short pants. He was little remembered, his absence less mourned.

When he returned last year he purchased Cabershaw Tower. You'll remember the outcry, at first, when the villagers did not believe an outsider should be in charge of any part of the abbey. The tower has been vacant for some hundred years, and we were content for it to remain as such. Cecil Cabershaw had argued for the sale, argued that he needed the money for Maple's medicines, and that he didn't give a tick about heritage or the past, not when his sister needed help in the present. Still...still... it didn't seem right. It wasn't settled until the town meeting where Marken reminded us of the boy he had been. That he was indeed a child of Leighton. That he was little Markie. Returned.

Extensive renovations began on the abbey's tower. Marken had the audacity to hire outside workers. A scandal, there, owing to how there are good men in Leighton who need a hammer to swing and fresh bread on their plates.

As like any village policeman, it is my duty to make sure each and everything is proper, not just the laws but the morals. I surprised Marken and his men one day by touring the restorations. They were superficial in the upper tower, where Marken was making his rooms, but the renovations were more extensive in the lower basements. And the wet of the lake was coming through the walls, so much so that I wished I'd brought my rubber boots. I was past my ankles at some points, sploshing about. The waters were chilly. The abbey tower is well above the lake and I would not have thought the basements could be so damp, but I suppose earth draws water like a napkin on a table. Water goes where it wishes, if you give it a path.

Marken was not on the premises. Not for the first hour.

The workers were an ill sort. Dark men. Not dark skinned, I mean, but dark eyed. And they kept their gaze away from me and did not speak. You'll remember they never came into the village. Not for the dances or the taverns. Not to flirt with our women or play darts with our champions. Marken bought all the supplies himself. There were meats and cheeses, but no liquors, which we all thought a bit odd. A man needs his drink, of course. When I began my surprise inspection, one of Marken's men tried his best to bar me from the door but I had my badge and I've never been a man too easily put off my course. I took my tour.

The interior walls, down below, were strange. Perhaps it was just the water playing havoc with all the angles. I thought as much, any way, at the time, though it did not explain how the walls and the ceiling met at such sharp angles that I could not poke my fingers along the edges. It was ancient architecture, of course. Likely settled poorly over the centuries. The abbey is one of those places that is built upon one thing that is built upon an earlier dwelling that is built upon an earlier structure and so on. It likely goes all the way back to some distant bonfire, my father was fond of saying.

I was well beneath the old abbey and there were carvings on the wall. Intricate scratchings. Marken later told me the abbey had often held prisoners (political prisoners, I assumed) and they'd scratched their words on the walls, using spoons and such. Much of it was vulgar. And there were also crude drawings clearly spat out from diseased minds. Drawings of men with no heads. Men with no legs, pulling themselves along the ground in the manner of a caterpillar. Women being bothered by fantastical creatures. The water was so blasted cold, around me. I had to throw away my shoes, in the end. Damn good shoes, too.

I'd never been in the tower, before. Not below, I mean. As children, I suppose it was a Leighton tradition to shiver ourselves through the gaps in the blocked outer doors, explore the upper tower, imagine ourselves as adventurers with princesses to be won and dragons to be gutted, but none of us ever thought to tear away the boards that kept the basement sealed. I can remember, myself, being dared to do it, to venture below. I remember willing my hands to tear away the first of the boards, but the wood was cold and quite moist and I lost my nerve. We all did. This too, was a Leighton tradition. We all knew the tower, but none of us knew the basements. It was strange to be down in them. Like sealing away part of my childhood... gaining a man's knowledge of somewhere else that had been only lurking, waiting below.

I discovered a small room with what appeared to be a stone altar. I suppose it could have been a bed. I've seen enough books to know ancient people made .

their beds of stone. They'd have been piled high with cushions, of course. The stone altar (I still couldn't help but think of it as such, and of course now I know so much of the truth) was carved of all one piece. Rough on its surface, like pumice. Small bits of it broke off when I touched the damn thing. I watched the bits settle in the water. The ripples disappearing. Then I turned, hearing a sloshing behind me, and it seemed every one of the damned workers was in the doorway, staring at me. I asked them about the room but they said nothing. The room's ceiling had a vault design, but curved and twisted, as if had at one point been a proper dome but some divine hand had reached down and twisted it into the shape of carnival ice cream on a cone. It was unsettling. Water was dripping down from above. I could hear it up above, trickling and rippling along the odd curves before it fell to the waters around me.

There were many more carvings on the walls of this room. Better ones, I might add. Whatever prisoner had been kept in this room, he or she was a more talented artist. Likely as insane, I might add. The carved figures were just as fantastical. Men with multiple arms. Fish with legs. There were several images of what I assume was the sun, with radiant energy spread out all around it. Words were carved into the walls of this room as well. Not a word of it in English, though, this time. Latin, I presumed. Or a barbaric tongue. I speak and read nothing but the King's own, if you take my meaning. Captain Levetts fancies himself a scholar, though, and I took a rubbing of some of the words so that he could make of it what he would. I used the back of a summons and a stub of pencil and put it on the wall right above the strange stone altar. I still have the rubbing. *"Ph'nglui mglw'nafh Cthulhu R'lyeh wgah'nagl fhtagn - Lw'nafh ch'Henpin."* Seems to be utter nonsense, though it ends with *Henpin*, an obvious reference to our lake, so I thought the captain might like it for local lore.

Right as I was taking the rubbing, Marken returned. I'd known he'd gone off to the Leighton general store, seeing about pickaxes and wheelbarrows, and I'd timed my visit while he was out. It's always best to poke around a bit oneself.

"Why are you here?" he demanded. He was holding a pickaxe. I didn't like it. My feet were wet and the workmen's constant presence had given me a tension in my neck.

"Poking around," I told him. "Seeing about the tower." Marken's hands were twisting on the handle of his pickaxe. He was a good seven or eight feet distant, and of course the water meant he wouldn't be dashing closer any too quickly, but I've seen a man hit with a pickaxe before, in the days before the mines flooded, and the thought of it put my hand on the handle of my Webley. Only in a casual manner, mind you. Still... a message.

Marken saw where my hand had gone and, I think, for the first time truly noted the pickaxe in his hands. He immediately handed it over to one of the workmen, but the fellow's hands were wet and he dropped it into the water, then fished around for a bit, trying to find it, not having much luck. It was comical enough to break the mood, and Marken and I were soon up on dry land having tea on the lawn in front of the abbey, as my shoes and pants were no longer fit for any indoor conversations.

I found Markie to be pleasant enough. A great wit, truth be told. He remembered me a good deal more than I remembered him, though when he talked of my earlier bullying I felt a few flashes of the old memories returning. I'd been an awful bastard, but Markie thought it was funny, now. Days gone by and all that. I caught him up to speed on the village (he seemed to know everything already, as if it were only another of the tests he always studied for) and I caught him up on the story of my life, which wasn't much. A few women. My wife, now. The futility of fishing the lake. The best places to sit in each of Leighton's three pubs.

Marken's life had gone in more interesting directions. He'd taken in with an antiquarian up in Bradford. Playing the part of an apprentice. Learning to tell if a scarab was four thousand years old, or only four weeks. He'd also gone crazy for languages, learning them by the basket. I asked about the writing in the rooms below the abbey and the rubbing I had taken, but he said he couldn't read a word of it. Looking back, he was lying, of course. Looking back, I know I missed his reluctance to return the paper to my grasp.

I asked why he wanted to restore the old tower. Nobody had lived within its premises for some hundred years, and there were further centuries of accumulated dust even so, and a man of his means (trading in antiquities seemed to be remarkably profitable, though I might add that Marken comes from money, and a rich man slides along the path to money, while a poor man stumbles) might well have had any house in Leighton, or perhaps even renovated the lake house, a far more modern and hospitable structure. He'd shuddered when I mentioned the lake house. I need no hindsight, here. I noticed it even then.

We talked of women, of course... of our own wives and other women, and also of women we wished had been our wives. Much laughter, of course. Women may weep over spoiled romance, but men such as Marken and I see the comic side. We also spoke of the local football clubs and how strikers seem to be born and goalkeepers seem to be idiots. Women see the comic side in such things as that, but men such as Marken and I are nearly driven to tears.

What I mean to say is that the mood had been good until I spoke of the renovations, the strange quality of the basements. Marken did not speak for some moments and I had the feeling that I should remain quiet as well. He looked off in the distance, mostly, but his eyes kept returning to mine. I could see that he was calculating. Gauging. Weighing facts and emotions. That sort of thing. All nonsense. We know in an instant whether we trust a man. All the rest is mere twaddle.

Marken did a very extraordinary thing.

Before finally speaking, he nabbed up the teapot, still half filled with water. Cooled by then, of course, as we'd been talking for nearly an hour.

He poured it on the lawn. Not in any casual manner, but in that precise and sadly focused way a man will line up a good shot on a dog that's gone bad.

I took a long look at Marken, then. The cut of his suit was beyond adequate. Much better than mine, and I do take some care with my general grooming. He had the sideburns of a learned Bradford man. His hair was perhaps longer than we prefer in Leighton, but there's no law against a man's hair catching the wind. His hands were strong, and his general form was that of a fellow who could ride a horse or swing a golf club without huffing or heaving. His eyes were dark and there was a certain moistness to his skin that I assumed was sweat, as the day was balmy and we'd taken chairs in the sun to hasten the drying process of our shoes and trouser legs, soaked as they were by the excursion into the renovations.

His skin was somewhat leathery, and dark and spotted by the sun, but that's as a man should be.

Marken placed the teapot upended on the table and emptied both our cups into the grass. I did not protest. Too curious to form words, I admit.

Then, he said, "Have you heard of the Book of Eibon? Or the Cthäat Aquadingen?"

It is that moment that I consider my first step into madness.

&

Joslie Miller was a peach of a girl. A peach. She had been visiting her friend, thirteen-year-old Constance Grane, a visit during which the two of them had crafted several paper dolls, clever cutouts from newspapers Joslie's father had brought back from a recent excursion to Stoke-on-Trent for medical reasons. Joslie's mother had taken ill. Some sort of wasting sickness. A cancer, I hear, but I hear other things and give them more credit, now.

The paper dolls had been connected to each other, cut away from the papers so that each of the duplicate figures was holding hands. I heard people talking, later, of how the search parties were similar, with all of us holding hands, moving across the meadows and through the woods as best we could, staying within reach of each other because Joslie was such a small girl and could be missed so easily.

She'd never come home from the Granes' house. Joslie's mother had waited a fretful time and then come to me, and I take things seriously at all times and the disappearance of Cecil Cabershaw was still biting at my mind. I rounded up as many of the villagers as I could, and we took such lanterns and torches as were available, and we set out.

As it happens, I was the one to find her. Joslie's little body was crumpled no more than a hundred feet from her mother's house. Caught in the weeds, she was, at the edge of the fallow field, half hidden by the tall grass and the wheat. She was cracked and she was broken as if some monster had crumpled her there, or she'd fallen from a cloud. She was soaking wet and… just before I found her, I could have sworn I heard a running stream, but the nearest river was a half mile distant. These phantom sounds were drowned away by the swish of running men as they came plunging through the wheat when I cried out, and of course soon there was nothing but her mother's wails.

෨

By the time the dogs began to disappear, over the course of the next several days, Marken and I had become friends. We were something, anyway. I take to friends slow, I admit, but Marken was on his way. It would have gone quicker without the disappearances, and without his madness, and certainly without the way his madness began to make sense. I think that was what disturbed me most of all.

He had theories about Leighton. About the town and the lake. He explained these theories to me when we were drinking, and once I had his words in my head I didn't want to stop drinking. Not ever. I didn't want to be sober in my bed, my wife going about her duties in the kitchen, me listening to my thoughts and to the raindrops coming off my roof, or the hissing complaints of a teapot set to boil.

"The tower is old," Marken told me. He had several papers spread out on his table. Drawings of the tower within which we were sitting. I say they were papers but they were not. They were on parchment. Papyrus. Or leather. And there was one drawing of the tower in a book that Marken called the Cthäat Aquadingen, as old a book as I've ever seen. I've never been a book man, and now I never will be, because that book is in my head. It got in my head. Dripped inside. It has me.

Marken said, "Versions of this book first appeared in the 5th century. Nobody knows who wrote it. God give him a good grave, though. God grant him that. This one is in English, and there was a Latin version mentioned in damnation by the first of the Knights Templar, and they called it a new book, then, which I suppose would date it to the 11th or 12th century."

"I suppose," I said. I was looking at the book. It was stained. Stained with what I hoped were coffees or wines or waters. And the book seemed to be creaking. A thick and ugly thing, it was. Several hundred pages long. A folio. Bound in a leather of which I wanted no knowledge. Bulging. That book was bulging. Solid and resting motionless on Marken's table, but it felt like it was creaking open nonetheless. I was sweating. The circulation in the abbey tower is not good. Marken had opened the book to an image of the very tower we were in. The image was hundreds of year old, but the base structure of the tower was unmistakable, as was its proximity to the lake. Unsettling, then, to see how the tower was only the beginning of the image, with the earth cut away beneath, basements and cellars and caverns reaching down an unimaginable depth. Strange creatures roamed below, and channels were connected to the lake. And then, far beneath, a being of inconceivable size. A protoplasmic blob that could have stretched itself from Leighton to London.

"This is Ubbo-Sathla, the Unbegotten Source," Marken told me. He was hesitant to even touch the image. I could hear a rustling from below, in the basements beneath us, and while I knew it would only be Marken's workmen going about their tasks, I still shuddered. We were drinking wine. I drank more. More than I should have. Or less.

"It looks like some viscous fluid," I told Marken. "An oil stain. A jam spilt upon the floor." I was making light of it. I could see outside the window and down to the lake, where it was black. A dog was howling, somewhere. The days had been playing hell with their kind. The villagers were pressing hard at me on the disappearances. The hounds. Cecil Cabershaw. Especially little Joslie's murder. But I had nothing. No gypsies to roust or travelers to condemn. No donkey where I could pin the murderous tail. Now, ten dogs dead or missing in the last week. The dog that Marken and I could hear howling was undoubtedly being kept at home, mournful that it was not allowed to roam free at night.

"Ubbo-Sathla is the creator of all life on Earth," Marken told me, and he began to spin a fantastical tale of the vastness of space, of visitors marooned on our planet, stranded long before life here began. It was a story of Ubbo-Sathla huddled beneath ice, spitting forth creatures into a glacier melt... drop after drop of life, small organisms that soon sprang into the strange and foul creatures Ubbo-Sathla created at whim, life as no more than a toy, these beings stumbling away to cover the Earth, passing the centuries, the millennia, hundreds of millions of years, becoming grotesque fish, or dogs that howl in the night, or the villagers in every English town.

"But not every creature changed," Marken told me. We were on our third bottle of wine. I excused myself to the bathroom, standing over the toilet and listening to Marken's words as he called out, as I relieved myself, as I watched the faucet of Marken's sink dripping out, drop after drop. I was thinking of my wife, alone, at home. She would be mending. Reading. Having tea. I thought of her running the faucets. I thought of her hair. Her smile. I thought of going home but in my madness I needed to hear what Marken had to say.

He called out, "Some of the foulest creatures kept their form, kept their hatred for their new home and for all their brothers. Unchanged, they watched as eternity cantered by, with endless steps. Or perhaps they do have an end."

I returned to my chair. To my cups of wine. I asked, "What do you mean?"

"The Cabershaw family," he spoke. There was great import in his words, but I had no idea of his meaning. There was little left to the Cabershaw family. They were dying out. Was this what he meant?

"Cecil has gone missing," I said. "Maple is in Wath-upon-Dearne. A hospital. For her mind."

"You don't understand. Time has no meaning. None at all. To the ones who came before, to Cthulhu, to Kassogtha, to the Black *Goat* of the Woods with his *thousand* young, time is only a tool. We are neither here nor there. Not in the past or the future. Every Cabershaw who has ever lived, they are still here. Still among us. Still going about their tasks."

"Their... tasks?" I asked. I felt as a man who cannot help himself from entering a cavern's depths. The dogs of Leighton were all howling, now, calling from off in the distance, for the most part, though some were coming closer. The night had gone so dark that I could no longer see the lake from my seat next to the window. The curtains were rustling. A wind was visiting.

"They are caretakers since time immemorial," Marken said. "Since before they were human. Since before there *were* humans." He was turning pages of the Cthäat Aquadingen. The book was hundreds of years old, but the pages were not brittle. I wondered of their origin. Inside, there were texts in several languages. Most of them alien to my eyes. There were chunks of pages filled with nothing but dots in intricate patterns. And pictograms with figures that made my eyes itch and burn. I wondered of the illustrations I was seeing as Marken heaved page after page of the giant tome aside, all the images of fantastical creatures that I would never have believed existed, except Marken believed, and he did not seem as if any madness had taken him, or the wine had misguided him. My father had often told me that sometimes it is only a madman that see or speaks the truth.

"Here," Marken said. "The Cabershaw family." He made as if to speak more, but then stopped, said nothing. I wondered, with all that he had been speaking, what madness he had decided was best left unsaid. He tapped on the pages and at first I did not look. I only reached for more wine. We'd opened another bottle. Outside, there were the sounds of dogs moving closer, racing through the woods and towards, I somehow felt, the lake.

There was an image of the Cabershaw family in the book. Of Cecil Cabershaw. An exact likeness. Even, God help me, the clothes that he had been wearing the last time he'd been seen, when he was at the general store retrieving an order of two hundred canning jars suitable for vegetables or meats. The clerk remembered him well, wondering of such an order from a man not known to garden or to prepare much for the future.

But there he was, just as the clerk had described, just in the clothes that Cecil normally wore... the same vest and the pocket watch and the hat and everything in place, even the cut of his hair, and all of it in a book whose pages had been created while the Vandals were still sacking Rome. My forehead was moist. My hand was on my Webley, for reassurance. The metal felt cold and real. It began raining outside. Soft rain. Dribbles and drops. One after the other. I could hear a pack of hounds racing past. An awful racket. I could hear the blood in my ears. A small thump in my temple. I'd have a headache, soon, I believed. I wanted to be home in bed with a cloth on my head, with my wife's loving hands holding it in place.

Instead of this, I said, "What role do you have? Why are you here, Marken? Why have you come back to Leighton?"

He pondered my question. No immediate answer. I could see another of those rounds of calculation in his eyes. This time, I sensed, he was deciding not if he would answer, but only how he would answer.

Finally, he said, "You've heard the dogs?"

I nodded. The dogs were gathering by Lake Henpin. I could hear their baying, their growls, their whimpers and such. The wine and Marken and the strange leather book had put me in a mood where the dogs seemed unreal, foreign, as far away as the stars. At any other time I would have sprang to my feet and raced outside in wonder at their actions. Dogs are wise, you know. My father said to trust a dog more than a man, because a dog has never learned to lie.

"Dogs are not the only ones that hunt," Marken told me.

The dogs had been disappearing at night. For a week. One a night. Sometimes two. At first it was assumed they'd simply run off. Dogs need freedom. They'd soon come home. There were one or two jokes gamboled about... talk of how something was in the air. Cecil had started a trend by running away on his sister. The dogs were following suit. I didn't laugh at these jokes. It is not my job to do so. And Joslie had been put to rest in her grave. A policeman can't be seen to be smiling when a girl's grave is still so fresh.

As the disappearances continued, there were no more jokes. Leashes were found chewed apart. Or broken. And then the dogs began to wash up on the lake. Drowned, they were. And some animal had been at them. Dogs are not talented swimmers, and nobody could hazard a guess why they'd been going into the waters. Nobody but me, that is, standing at the shore, watching the small waves lapping for a foothold on land, and remembering the tales I'd been hearing from Marken.

∾

We followed the dogs to the lake, did Marken and I. There wasn't any part of me that wanted to be near Lake Henpin at night, not since seeing the drawings in that damned book, not since hearing tales of the *Sathlattae*, rituals and chants and spells related to Ubbo-Sathla. Incantations with which water spirits could be raised. Summoned. Created. And, thankfully destroyed. It was the last knowledge that Marken had been seeking. Not just since he'd come back to Leighton. From earlier. Much earlier.

"My family is charged with destroying the Old Ones," he said as we moved through the woods. I had my Webley and he an old axe that looked brittle, carved with pictograms and strange words. More a work of art than a weapon, though he clenched it as tight as his teeth.

Marken said, "The tower wasn't erected to stop any Saxons. Not for any Vikings or Normans, either. It's a defense against invaders from the lake. It wasn't part of the original abbey. Has nothing to do with it, unless you count fighting for the other side." The dogs were still howling at the lake, but it was too dark, too many trees in the way. I could see nothing. My heart was a hammer, beating against my chest in waves.

"I've travelled the globe. Fighting. Well... not much fighting. Acquiring artefacts, mostly. Stopping others from fighting. And I've been learning about the Cabershaw family. Learning about the lake house. Learning about... God help me and keep my soul in His hands... Lake Henpin."

It was then that I saw the glow from the lake. And as sure as a man knows light from dark, I knew that light was wrong. It was unsettled. Not shimmering, but... moving. Creeping out from the lake. Like a mist. The dogs were growling. Whining. I think they would have fled if they weren't all together in a pack, with a thousand teeth and a mob's nerves.

I realized at that moment that I had a hundred questions for Marken. That

I'd finally begun to understand. That the wet coming down from the sky in infinite raindrops was different than the wet that was gathered together in the lake. And that Marken was, I suppose, an officer of a greater law than I'd ever served, with answers as far above my own eyes as if a child had been asking me about mine.

I began to understand that he had much to tell me. That he had been keeping many things hidden. That I wasn't ready. That I had only a drop of knowledge. Just the taste of an ocean.

We were still, I swear and believe, a hundred feet from the edges of the lake. But that makes no matter. None at all.

We still fell in.

There was a rush of earth, of water, as if the lake had nabbed us from below in the manner of a mole stealing vegetables from a garden. The dogs were in chaos, paddling as best they could, but the water was churning and alive and I lost sight of the surface, of Marken, of everything. I tumbled and flailed. There was nothing but the water. For long moments, there was nothing but the water. And me, of course, being drawn down below. Then… old Steggs, the police dog, came sinking past me, struggling as he was for air. I dove for him, needing to save something, to act for a cause, to believe in something. I dove for that dog. Down and down. Down and down. Always down. My lungs should have been bursting. My lungs should have been furious. But I felt nothing. Only dove for the dog. He was just out of reach. Looking to me. Scared. Trusting. But I couldn't reach him.

I pulled up short when I saw the city.

Nothing could induce me to put onto paper what I saw of that city. Of its people. Police psychiatry be damned… I will not bid my mind to speak of what I will never forget. Those temples of stone. Those streets made of nothing but water, curling through and around and over the buildings, and men walking about them as if these streets were a true surface, as if water could hold them, as if the wet were solid. And the men were not men, of course. I only call them men to save my mind. They were as much slugs as men. Creatures of jelly. Blobs of flesh that changed shape with every facsimile of a step. Tendrils always and ever reaching out, but tendrils changing to arms, to wings, to faces, to legs, then all of these at the same time, and then they were nothing, nothing at all, only whisked away by the water that whirled around the spires and the rooftops, each surface of each building worn by untold millennia of footsteps, grooves worn into the stone of the rooftops and the walls and everywhere, all of the motion a mad whirl around me, and down past it all at the bottom, down at the bed of the lake, past Steggs, past the sinking dogs, there was the source of the light. A glacier, I thought, at first. A strange white glacier that was beneath the water, that covered the bottom of the lake, that stretched into caverns that went even farther below, that sank deep into the heart of this world.

A glacier.

But of course it was not. I will not write anything more of it in this report. Nothing of how, without eyes, it looked up to me. Nothing of how, without a mouth, it spoke my name.

I swam madly for the surface. I swam away from the buildings, from the city that stretched beneath me. I abandoned the dogs that were floating past me, their dead eyes bulging in fear, then closing in death, then opening once more, staring at me, though I had no thought that they had come back to life. None of that.

I could see the surface. It was like a roll of clouds above me. A hundred feet, it seemed. I swam as a madman. Closing the distance. Planning how I would run when I was on land. No destination. No stopping. Just running. I would run.

A hand went on my shoulder.

Marken, I hoped. I hoped for Christopher Marken.

But when I turned it was Maple Cabershaw.

At first I thought she was drowning. At first I wondered how she had traveled from Wath-upon-Dearne, where I knew she was being kept, to find herself in the waters of Lake Henpin. But then I saw the look of blackness in her eyes. The depths of space within her. The smile that was somehow both uncaring and malignant at the same time. I heard her laugh, even underwater, casting aside Earth's rules and speaking to me even as water filled her lungs, even as her skin flashed into impossible colors and her limbs flickered into tendrils, or thick seaweeds, and then back to human again.

But she was not human. She had never been human. The Cabershaw family were guardians and I had come too close to their secrets and their domain. Maple slid her fingers into my hair and began to pull me back down, back down, laughing at my struggles and whispering through the water and into my ears. She spoke of citadels. Of rulers. Of servants. Of sustenance. Of life. But nothing of her words was of Earth. It was all madness. Grand madness. And all true. Her madness was true.

I fought. I fought and I clubbed her with the Webley that I still held clutched in my hands. I brought it down on her face, shattering nothing. Her features merely moved aside. Slid around the impact. My lungs were heaving and I clutched at her throat; I clenched at her throat while trying to choke the life out of the beautifully strange creature, but her smile never changed. I was nothing. Only a minnow swimming against a whale. Still, a minnow may fight, and fought I did. I fought until I saw how we were near the surface of the lake, how I was nearly to freedom, separated momentarily from the creature I once believed was human, who I once believed was Maple Cabershaw, a woman who had sat for long years in silence, and who had once nearly drowned in this lake.

She swam for me, and I saw no humanity in her eyes. Only death.

But then, before she could reach me, hands came down from above. A man's hands. Maple gave a start of surprise, and then a grin of realization, and then she smiled at me as she was plucked up and out of the waters. She went limp as she surfaced.

Air. Sweet air. I heaved to the surface and into... sunlight. My face was barely above the waves. My face was only inches from a boat. My eyes, looking up, saw my father, my father who has been dead so many years. He was gasping and he was holding the still frame of Maple Cabershaw, desperately trying to breathe life into her limp form, as all around him the boating party came to the aid of the young girl who had nearly drowned in the lake.

❧

Time is nothing to them. What of it to me, then? Why should I care how I found myself in the lake house? Why should I care that the floors were new? The curtains clean? The smells of fresh bread in the kitchen so delicious? I remembered little of finding my way. Of slipping beneath the waves, away from the past, away from my father, swimming unseen and away from the newest madness, rising from the lake, sodden, dripping, always dripping, hearing nothing but the echoes of barking dogs but being drawn by something, some thread that was dancing me on its string, and then I was in the great hall of the lake house, where I found Christopher Marken holding Cecil Cabershaw by his hair, raising his brittle-looking axe and bringing it down, beheading the man. There was a hiss of smoke without flame, cold without a source, and Cabershaw's body shivered, but the head, God save us, still lived. The head still lived. It grew tentacles, tendrils like seaweed, and it began to run, to escape, to flee the promised kiss of that brittle axe.

"Shoot it!" Marken said, seeing me. "We can't let it escape! Bring it down!"

And I rose my gun, and I fired four shots. Four. Only three bullets missing from my Webley, but I know what I have done. I fired four shots. Four bullets. But they curved. The trajectory of my bullets curved. They slammed into Marken. Brought him down. He was an innocent. He was a good man.

I have been misquoted, you understand. I never said he killed the dogs. I never said he killed young Joslie. I only said he was responsible. He said as much to me, cursing his failure, as he died.

It was not blood that came from his veins. It was water. Water from the lake. Despite this, I believe that Markie was a good man.

When I awoke, I was sprawled outside the decrepit and long-unused lake house, with the waters of Lake Henpin slapping at my feet.

☙❧

Captain Levetts, I fear I am no longer writing a shooting report. This is now a note to you. And to my wife, if you think that is best. I have learned many things in the days since Marken's death. I have recovered some of what he left behind in the tower, ferreting them away before the mysterious fire that claimed the lives of his workmen and collapsed the entire tower into the basements and caverns below. I have read of the Cabershaw family in such books as the Cthäat Aquadingen and Unaussprechlichen Kulten. I now have more knowledge that I can possibly hold. My brain wants to scream it away. I will allow my brain to do this in the only way possible. I am writing this in your office bathroom, now, where I have excused myself for some moments from Mr. Ulton, the psychiatrist, and where I am watching the sink in your bathroom dripping and dripping and dripping, and I could stand here and speak to it. But I won't. I won't do that.

I know that you have my gun in your desk. My Webley is there. Taken from me. For the best, it was said. It will be a simple matter to force open your locked desk. I will find my gun.

First, before that, I will save you from the embarrassment of having a suicide on your force. I hereby resign.

It has been a great honor to serve the people of Leighton. Tell my wife I love her, and to never let the water run for too long. It's a waste, you know. An awful waste.

Oh.

A thought.

I have just now solved the mystery of my Webley.

Three bullets or four?

I understand, now.

Time means nothing to them.

The fourth shot has yet to be fired.

The Ocean and All Its Devices

William Browning Spencer

*Left to its own enormous devices the sea
in timeless reverie conceives of life,
being itself the world in pantomime.*

—Lloyd Frankenberg, *The Sea*

The hotel's owner and manager, George Hume, sat on the edge of his bed and smoked a cigarette. "The Franklins arrived today," he said.

"Regular as clockwork," his wife said.

George nodded. "Eight years now. And why? Why ever do they come?"

George Hume's wife, an ample woman with soft, motherly features, sighed. "They seem to get no pleasure from it, that's for certain. Might as well be a funeral they come for."

The Franklins always arrived in late fall, when the beaches were cold and empty and the ocean, under dark skies, reclaimed its terrible majesty. The hotel was almost deserted at this time of year, and George had suggested closing early for the winter. Mrs. Hume had said, "The Franklins will be coming, dear."

So what? George might have said. Let them find other accommodations this year. But he didn't say that. They were sort of a tradition, the Franklins, and in a world so fraught with change, one just naturally protected the rare, enduring pattern.

They were a reserved family who came to this quiet hotel in North Carolina like refugees seeking safe harbor. George couldn't close early and send the Franklins off to some inferior establishment. Lord, they might wind up at The Cove with its garish lagoon pool and gaudy tropical lounge. That wouldn't suit them at all.

The Franklins (husband, younger wife, and pale, delicate-featured daughter) would dress rather formally and sit in the small opened section of the dining room—the rest of the room shrouded in dust covers while Jack, the hotel's aging waiter and handyman, would stand off to one side with a bleak, stoic expression.

Over the years George had come to know many of his regular guests well. But the Franklins had always remained aloof and enigmatic. Mr. Greg Franklin was a man in his mid or late forties, a handsome man, tall—over six feet—with precise, slow gestures and an oddly uninflected voice, as though he were reading from some internal script that failed to interest him. His much younger wife was stunning, her hair massed in brown ringlets, her eyes large and luminous and containing something like fear in their depths. She spoke rarely, and then in a whisper, preferring to let her husband talk.

Their child, Melissa, was a dark-haired girl—twelve or thirteen now, George guessed—a girl as pale as the moon's reflection in a rain barrel. Always dressed impeccably, she was as quiet as her mother, and George had the distinct impression, although he could not remember being told this by anyone, that she was sickly, that some traumatic infant's illness had almost killed her and so accounted for her methodical, wounded economy of motion.

George ushered the Franklins from his mind. It was late. He extinguished his cigarette and walked over to the window. Rain blew against the glass, and lightning would occasionally illuminate the white-capped waves.

"Is Nancy still coming?" Nancy, their daughter and only child, was a senior at Duke University. She had called the week before saying she might come and hang out for a week or two.

"As far as I know," Mrs. Hume said. "You know how she is. Everything on a whim. That's your side of the family, George."

George turned away from the window and grinned. "Well, I can't accuse your family of ever acting impulsively—although it would do them a world of good. Your family packs a suitcase to go to the grocery store."

"And your side steals a car and goes to California without a toothbrush or a prayer."

This was an old, well-worked routine, and they indulged it as they readied for bed. Then George turned off the light and the darkness brought silence.

ఴ

It was still raining in the morning when George Hume woke. The violence of last night's thunderstorm had been replaced by a slow, business-like drizzle. Looking out the window, George saw the Franklins walking on the beach under black umbrellas. They were a cheerless sight. All three of them wore dark raincoats, and they might have been fugitives from some old Bergman film, inevitably tragic, moving slowly across a stark landscape.

When most families went to the beach, it was a more lively affair.

George turned away from the window and went into the bathroom to shave. As he lathered his face, he heard the boom of a radio, rock music blaring from the adjoining room, and he assumed, correctly, that his twenty-one-year-old daughter Nancy had arrived as planned.

Nancy had not come alone. "This is Steve," she said when her father sat down at the breakfast table.

Steve was a very young man—the young were getting younger—with a wide-eyed, waxy expression and a blond mustache that looked like it could be wiped off with a damp cloth.

Steve stood up and said how glad he was to meet Nancy's father. He shook George's hand enthusiastically, as though they had just struck a lucrative deal.

"Steve's in law school," Mrs. Hume said, with a proprietary delight that her husband found grating.

Nancy was complaining. She had, her father thought, always been a querulous girl, at odds with the way the world was.

"I can't believe it," she was saying. "The whole mall is closed. The only—and I mean only—thing around here that is open is that cheesy little drugstore, and nobody actually buys anything in there. I know that, because I recognize stuff from when I was six. Is this some holiday I don't know about or what?"

"Honey, it's the off season. You know everything closes when the tourists leave."

"Not the for-Christ-sakes mall!" Nancy said. "I can't believe it." Nancy frowned. "This must be what Russia is like," she said, closing one eye as smoke from her cigarette slid up her cheek.

George Hume watched his daughter gulp coffee. She was not a person who needed stimulants. She wore an ancient gray sweater and sweatpants. Her blonde hair was chopped short and ragged and kept in a state of disarray by the constant furrowing of nervous fingers. She was, her father thought, a pretty girl in disguise.

ଔଧ

That night, George discovered that he could remember nothing of the spy novel he was reading, had forgotten, in fact, the hero's name. It was as though he had stumbled into a cocktail party in the wrong neighborhood, all strangers to him, the gossip meaningless.

He put the book on the nightstand, leaned back on the pillow, and said, "This is her senior year. Doesn't she have classes to attend?"

His wife said nothing.

He sighed. "I suppose they are staying in the same room."

"Dear, I don't know," Mrs. Hume said. "I expect it is none of our business."

"If it is not our business who stays in our hotel, then who in the name of hell's business is it?"

Mrs. Hume rubbed her husband's neck. "Don't excite yourself, dear. You know what I mean. Nancy is a grown-up, you know."

George did not respond to this and Mrs. Hume, changing the subject, said, "I saw Mrs. Franklin and her daughter out walking on the beach again today. I don't know where Mr. Franklin was. It was pouring, and there they were, mother and daughter. You know..." Mrs. Hume paused. "It's like they were waiting for something to come out of the sea. Like a vigil they were keeping. I've thought it before, but the notion was particularly strong today. I looked out past them, and there seemed no separation between the sea and the sky, just a black wall of water." Mrs. Hume looked at herself in the dresser's mirror, as though her reflection might clarify matters. "I've lived by the ocean all my life, and I've just taken it for granted, George. Suddenly it gave me the shivers. Just for a moment. I thought, Lord, how big it is, lying there cold and black, like some creature that has slept at your feet so long you never expect it to wake, have forgotten that it might be brutal, even vicious."

"It's all this rain," her husband said, hugging her and drawing her to him. "It can make a person think some black thoughts."

George left off worrying about his daughter and her young man's living arrangements, and in the morning, when Nancy and Steve appeared for breakfast, George didn't broach the subject—not even to himself.

Later that morning, he watched them drive off in Steve's shiny sports car—rich parents, lawyers themselves?—bound for Wilmington and shopping malls that were open.

The rain had stopped, but dark, massed clouds over the ocean suggested that this was a momentary respite. As George studied the beach, the Franklins came into view. They marched directly toward him, up and over the dunes, moving in a soldierly, clipped fashion. Mrs. Franklin was holding her daughter's hand and moving at a brisk pace, almost a run, while her husband faltered behind, his gait hesitant, as though uncertain of the wisdom of catching up.

Mrs. Franklin reached the steps and marched up them, her child tottering in tow, her boot heels sounding hollowly on the wood planks. George nodded, and she passed without speaking, seemed not to see him. In any event, George Hume would have been unable to speak. He was accustomed to the passive, demure countenance of this self-possessed woman, and the expression on her face, a wild distorting emotion, shocked and confounded him. It was an unreadable emotion, but its intensity was extraordinary and unsettling.

George had not recovered from the almost physical assault of Mrs. Franklin's emotional state, when her husband came up the stairs, nodded curtly, muttered something, and hastened after his wife.

George Hume looked after the retreating figures. Mr. Greg Franklin's face had been a mask of cold civility, none of his wife's passion written there, but the man's appearance was disturbing in its own way. Mr. Franklin had been soaking wet, his hair plastered to his skull, his overcoat dripping, the reek of salt water enfolding him like a shroud.

George walked on down the steps and out to the beach. The ocean was always some consolation, a quieting influence, but today it seemed hostile.

The sand was still wet from the recent rains and the footprints of the Franklins were all that marred the smooth expanse. George saw that the Franklins had walked down the beach along the edge of the tide and returned at a greater distance from the water. He set out in the wake of their footprints, soon lost to his own thoughts. He thought about his daughter, his wild Nancy, who had always been boy-crazy. At least this one didn't have a safety-pin through his ear or play in a rock band. *So lighten up*, George advised himself.

He stopped. The tracks had stopped. Here is where the Franklins turned and headed back to the hotel, walking higher up the beach, closer to the weedy debris-laden dunes.

But it was not the ending of the trail that stopped George's own progress down the beach. In fact, he had forgotten that he was absently following the Franklins' spoor.

It was the litter of dead fish that stopped him. They were scattered at his feet in the tide. Small ghost crabs had already found the corpses and were laying their claims.

There might have been a hundred bodies. It was difficult to say, for not one of the bodies was whole. They had been hacked into many pieces, diced by some impossibly sharp blade that severed a head cleanly, flicked off a tail or dorsal fin. Here a scaled torso still danced in the sand, there a pale eye regarded the sky.

Crouching in the sand, George examined the bodies. He stood up, finally, as the first large drops of rain plunged from the sky. No doubt some fishermen had called it a day, tossed their scissored bait and gone home.

That this explanation did not satisfy George Hume was the result of a general sense of unease. *Too much rain.*

ಜ

It rained sullenly and steadily for two days during which time George saw little of his daughter and her boyfriend. Nancy apparently had the young man on a strict regime of shopping, tourist attractions, and movies, and she was undaunted by the weather.

The Franklins kept inside, appearing briefly in the dining room for bodily sustenance and then retreating again to their rooms. And whatever did they do there? Did they play solitaire? Did they watch old reruns on TV?

On the third day, the sun came out, brazen, acting as though it had never been gone, but the air was colder. The Franklins, silhouetted like black crows on a barren field, resumed their shoreline treks.

Nancy and Steve rose early and were gone from the house before George arrived at the breakfast table. George spent the day endeavoring to satisfy the IRS's notion of a small businessman's obligations, and he was in a foul mood by dinner time.

After dinner, he tried to read, this time choosing a much-touted novel that proved to be about troubled youth. He was asleep within fifteen minutes of opening the book and awoke in an overstuffed armchair. The room was chilly, and his wife had tucked a quilt around his legs before abandoning him for bed. In the morning she would, he was certain, assure him that she had tried to rouse him before retiring, but he had no recollection of such an attempt.

"Half a bottle of wine might have something to do with that," she would say. He would deny the charge.

The advantage of being married a long time was that one could argue without the necessity of the other's actual, physical presence.

He smiled at this thought and pushed himself out of the chair, feeling groggy, head full of prickly flannel. He looked out the window. It was raining again—to the accompaniment of thunder and explosive, strobe-like lightening. The sports car was gone. The kids weren't home yet. Fine. Fine. None of my business.

Climbing the stairs, George paused. Something dark lay on the carpeted step, and as he bent over it, leaning forward, his mind sorted and discarded the possibilities: cat, wig, bird's nest, giant dust bunny. Touch and a strong olfactory cue identified the stuff: seaweed. Raising his head, he saw that two more clumps of the wet, rubbery plant lay on ascending steps, and gathering them—with no sense of revulsion for he was used to the ocean's disordered presence—he carried the weed up to his room and dumped it in the bathroom's wastebasket.

He scrubbed his hands in the sink, washing away the salty, stagnant reek, left the bathroom and crawled into bed beside his sleeping wife. He fell asleep immediately and was awakened later in the night with a suffocating sense of dread, a sure knowledge that an intruder had entered the room.

The intruder proved to be an odor, a powerful stench of decomposing fish, rotting vegetation and salt water. He climbed out of bed, coughing.

The source of this odor was instantly apparent and he swept up the wastebasket, preparing to gather the seaweed and flush it down the toilet.

The seaweed had melted into a black liquid, bubbles forming on its surface, a dark, gelatinous muck, simmering like heated tar. As George stared at the mess, a bubble burst, and the noxious gas it unleashed dazed him, sent him reeling backward with an inexplicable vision of some monstrous, shadowy form, silhouetted against green, mottled water.

George pitched himself forward, gathered the wastebasket in his arms, and fled the room. In the hall he wrenched open a window and hurled the wastebasket and its contents into the rain.

He stood then, gasping, the rain savage and cold on his face, his undershirt soaked, and he stood that way, clutching the window sill, until he was sure he would not faint.

Returning to bed, he found his wife still sleeping soundly and he knew, immediately, that he would say nothing in the morning, that the sense of suffocation, of fear, would seem unreal, its source irrational. Already the moment of panic was losing its reality, fading into the realm of nightmare.

The next day the rain stopped again and this time the sun was not routed. The police arrived on the third day of clear weather.

Mrs. Hume had opened the door, and she shouted up to her husband, who stood on the landing. "It's about Mr. Franklin."

Mrs. Franklin came out of her room then, and George Hume thought he saw the child behind her, through the open door. The girl, Melissa, was lying on the bed behind her mother and just for a moment it seemed that there was a spreading shadow under her, as though the bedclothes were soaked with dark water. Then the door closed as Mrs. Franklin came into the hall and George identified the expression he had last seen in her eyes for it was there again: fear, a racing engine of fear, gears stripped, the accelerator flat to the floor.

And Mrs. Franklin screamed, screamed and came falling to her knees and screamed again, prescient in her grief, and collapsed as George rushed toward her and two police officers and a paramedic, a woman, came bounding up the stairs.

Mr. Franklin had drowned. A fisherman had discovered the body. Mr. Franklin had been fully dressed, lying on his back with his eyes open. His wallet—and seven hundred dollars in cash and a host of credit cards—was still in his back pocket, and a business card identified him as vice president of marketing for a software firm in Fairfax, Virginia. The police had telephoned Franklin's firm in Virginia and so learned that he was on vacation. The secretary had the hotel's number.

After the ambulance left with Mrs. Franklin, they sat in silence until the police officer cleared his throat and said, "She seemed to be expecting something like this."

The words dropped into a silence.

Nancy and Steve and Mrs. Hume were seated on one of the lobby's sofas. George Hume came out of the office in the wake of the other policeman who paused at the door and spoke. "We'd appreciate it if you could come down and identify the body. Just a formality, but it's not a job for his wife, not in the state she's in." He coughed, shook his head. "Or the state he's in, for that matter. Body got tore up some in the water, and, well, I still find it hard to believe that he was alive just yesterday. I would have guessed he'd been in the water two weeks minimum—the deterioration, you know."

George Hume shook his head as though he did know and agreed to accompany the officer back into town.

∞

George took a long look, longer than he wanted to, but the body wouldn't let him go, made mute, undeniable demands.

Yes, this was Mr. Greg Franklin. Yes, this would make eight years that he and his wife and his child had come to the hotel. No, no nothing out of the ordinary.

George interrupted himself. "The tattoos…" he said.

"Didn't know about the tattoos, I take it?" the officer said.

George shook his head. "No." The etched blue lines that laced the dead man's arms and chest were somehow more frightening than the damage the sea had done. Frightening because… because the reserved Mr. Franklin, business-man and stolid husband, did not look like someone who would illuminate his flesh with arcane symbols, pentagrams and ornate fish, their scales numbered according to some runic logic, and spidery, incomprehensible glyphs.

"Guess Franklin wasn't inclined to wear a bathing suit."

"No."

"Well, we are interested in those tattoos. I guess his wife knew about them. Hell, maybe she has some of her own."

"Have you spoken to her?"

"Not yet. Called the hospital. They say she's sleeping. It can wait till morning."

An officer drove George back to the hotel, and his wife greeted him at the door.

"She's sleeping," Mrs. Hume said.

"Who?"

"Melissa."

For a moment, George drew a blank, and then he nodded. "What are we going to do with her?"

"Why, keep her," his wife said. "Until her mother is out of the hospital."

"Maybe there are relatives," George said, but he knew, saying it, that the Franklins were self-contained, a single unit, a closed universe.

His wife confirmed this. No one could be located, in any event.

"Melissa may not be aware that her father is dead," Mrs. Hume said. "The child is, I believe, a stranger girl than we ever realized. Here we were thinking she was just a quiet thing, well behaved. I think there is something wrong with her mind. I can't seem to talk to her, and what she says makes no sense. I've called Dr. Gowers, and he has agreed to see her. You remember Dr. Gowers, don't you? We sent Nancy to him when she was going through that bad time at thirteen."

George remembered child psychiatrist Gowers as a bearded man with a swollen nose and thousands of small wrinkles around his eyes. He had seemed a very kind but somehow sad man, a little like Santa Claus if Santa Claus had suffered some disillusioning experience, an unpleasant divorce or other personal setback, perhaps.

Nancy came into the room as her mother finished speaking. "Steve and I can take Melissa," Nancy said.

"Well, that's very good of you, dear," her mother said. "I've already made an appointment for tomorrow morning at ten. I'm sure Dr. Gowers will be delighted to see you again."

"I'll go too," George said. He couldn't explain it but he was suddenly afraid.

≫

The next morning when George came down to breakfast, Melissa was already seated at the table and Nancy was combing the child's hair.

"She isn't going to church," George said, surprised at the growl in his voice.

"This is what she wanted to wear," Nancy said. "And it looks very nice, I think."

Melissa was dressed in the sort of outfit a young girl might wear on Easter Sunday: a navy blue dress with white trim, white knee socks, black, shiny shoes. She had even donned pale blue gloves. Her black hair had been brushed to a satin sheen and her pale face seemed just-scrubbed, with the scent of soap lingering over her. A shiny black purse sat next to her plate of eggs and toast.

"You look very pretty," George Hume said.

Melissa nodded, a sharp snap of the head, and said, "I am an angel."

Nancy laughed and hugged the child. George raised his eyebrows. "No false modesty here," he said. At least she could talk.

On the drive into town, Steve sat in the passenger seat while George drove. Nancy and Melissa sat in the back seat. Nancy spoke to the child in a slow, reassuring murmur.

Steve said nothing, sitting with his hands in his lap, looking out the window. *Might not be much in a crisis*, George thought. *A rich man's child.*

≫

Steve stayed in the waiting room while the receptionist ushered Melissa and Nancy and George into Dr. Gowers' office. The psychiatrist seemed much as George remembered him, a silver-maned, benign old gent, exuding an air of competence. He asked them to sit on the sofa.

The child perched primly on the sofa, her little black purse cradled in her lap. She was flanked by George and Nancy.

Dr. Gowers knelt down in front of her. "Well, Melissa. Is it all right if I call you Melissa?"

"Yes sir. That's what everyone calls me."

"Well, Melissa, I'm glad you could come and see me today. I'm Dr. Gowers."

"Yes sir."

"I'm sorry about what happened to your father," he said, looking in her eyes.

"Yes sir," Melissa said. She leaned forward and touched her shoe.

"Do you know what happened to your father?" Dr. Gowers asked.

Melissa nodded her head and continued to study her shoes.

"What happened to your father?" Dr. Gowers asked.

"The machines got him," Melissa said. She looked up at the doctor. "The real machines," she added. "The ocean ones."

"Your father drowned," Dr. Gowers said.

Melissa nodded. "Yes sir." Slowly the little girl got up and began wandering around the room. She walked past a large saltwater aquarium next to a teak bookcase.

George thought the child must have bumped against the aquarium stand—although she hardly seemed close enough—because water spilled from the tank as she passed. She was humming. It was a bright, musical little tune, and he had heard it before, a children's song, perhaps? The words? Something like *by the sea, by the sea.*

The girl walked and gestured with a liquid motion that was oddly sophisticated, suggesting the calculated body language of an older and sexually self-assured woman.

"Melissa, would you come and sit down again so we can talk? I want to ask you some questions, and that is hard to do if you are walking around the room."

"Yes sir," Melissa said, returning to the sofa and resettling between George and his daughter. Melissa retrieved her purse and placed it on her lap again.

She looked down at the purse and up again. She smiled with a child's cunning. Then, very slowly, she opened the purse and showed it to Dr. Gowers.

"Yes?" he said, raising an eyebrow.

"There's nothing in it," Melissa said. "It's empty." She giggled.

"Well yes, it is empty," Dr. Gowers said, returning the child's smile. "Why is that?"

Melissa snapped the purse closed. "Because my real purse isn't here. It's in the real place, where I keep my things."

"And where is that, Melissa?"

Melissa smiled and said, "You know, silly."

৪৫

When the session ended, George phoned his wife.

"I don't know," he said. "I guess it went fine. I don't know. I've had no experience of this sort of thing. What about Mrs. Franklin?"

Mrs. Franklin was still in the hospital. She wanted to leave, but the hospital was reluctant to let her. She was still in shock, very disoriented. She seemed, indeed, to think that it was her daughter who had drowned.

"Did you talk to her?" George asked.

"Well yes, just briefly, but as I say, she made very little sense, got very excited when it became clear I wasn't going to fetch her if her doctor wanted her to remain there."

"Can you remember anything she said?"

"Well, it was very jumbled, really. Something about a bad bargain. Something about, that Greek word, you know 'hubris.'"

"Hewbris?"

"Oh, back in school, you know, George. Hubris. A willful sort of pride that angers the gods. I'm sure you learned it in school yourself."

"You are not making any sense," he said, suddenly exasperated—and frightened.

"Well," his wife said, "you don't have to shout. Of course I don't make any sense. I am trying to repeat what Mrs. Franklin said, and that poor woman made no sense at all. I tried to reassure her that Melissa was fine and she screamed. She said Melissa was not fine at all and that I was a fool. Now you are shouting at me, too."

George apologized, said he had to be going, and hung up.

On the drive back from Dr. Gowers' office, Nancy sat in the back seat with Melissa. The child seemed unusually excited: her pale forehead was beaded with sweat, and she watched the ocean with great intensity.

"Did you like Dr. Gowers?" Nancy asked. "He liked you. He wants to see you again, you know."

Melissa nodded. "He is a nice one." She frowned. "But he doesn't understand the real words either. No one here does."

George glanced over his shoulder at the girl. *You are an odd ducky*, he thought.

A large, midday sun brightened the air and made the ocean glitter as though scaled. They were in a stretch of sand dunes and sea oats and high, wind-driven waves and, except for an occasional lumbering trailer truck, they seemed alone in this world of sleek, eternal forms.

Then Melissa began to cough. The coughing increased in volume, developed a quick, hysterical note.

"Pull over!" Nancy shouted, clutching the child.

George swung the car off the highway and hit the brakes. Gravel pinged against metal, the car fishtailed and lurched to a stop. George was out of the car instantly, in time to catch his daughter and the child in her arms as they came hurtling from the back seat. Melissa's face was red and her small chest heaved. Nancy had her arms around the girl's chest. "Melissa!" Nancy was shouting. "Melissa!"

Nancy jerked the child upwards and back. Melissa's body convulsed. Her breathing was labored, a broken whistle fluttering in her throat.

She shuddered and began to vomit. A hot, green odor, the smell of stagnant tidal pools, assaulted George. Nancy knelt beside Melissa, wiping the child's wet hair from her forehead. "It's gonna be okay, honey," she said. "You got something stuck in your throat. It's all right now. You're all right."

The child jumped up and ran down the beach.

"Melissa!" Nancy screamed, scrambling to her feet and pursuing the girl. George ran after them, fear hissing in him like some power line down in a storm, writhing and spewing sparks.

In her blue dress and knee socks—shoes left behind on the beach now—Melissa splashed into the ocean, arms pumping.

Out of the corner of his eye, George saw Steve come into view. He raced past George, past Nancy, moving with a frenzied pinwheeling of arms. "I got her, I got her, I got her," he chanted.

Don't, George thought. *Please don't.*

The beach was littered with debris, old ocean-polished bottles, driftwood, seaweed, shattered conch shells. It was a rough ocean, still reverberating to the recent storm.

Steve had almost reached Melissa. George could see him reach out to clutch her shoulder.

Then something rose up in the water. It towered over man and child, and as the ocean fell away from it, it revealed smooth surfaces that glittered and writhed. The world was bathed with light, and George saw it plain. And yet, he could not later recall much detail. It was as though his mind refused entry to this monstrous thing, substituting other images—maggots winking from the eye sockets of some dead animal, flesh growing on a ruined structure of rusted metal—and while, in memory, those images were horrible enough and would not let him sleep, another part of his mind shrank from the knowledge that he had confronted something more hideous and ancient than his reason could acknowledge.

What happened next, happened in an instant. Steve staggered backwards and Melissa turned and ran sideways to the waves.

A greater wave, detached from the logic of the rolling ocean, sped over Steve, engulfing him, and he was gone, while Melissa continued to splash through the tide, now turning and running shoreward. The beast-thing was gone, and the old pattern of waves reasserted itself. Then Steve resurfaced, and with a lurch of understanding, as though the unnatural wave had struck at George's mind and left him dazed, he watched the head bob in the water, roll sickeningly, bounce on the crest of a second wave, and disappear.

Melissa lay face down on the wet sand, and Nancy raced to her, grabbed her up in her arms, and turned to her father.

"Where's Steve?" she shouted over the crash of the surf.

You didn't see then, George thought. *Thank God.*

"Where's Steve," she shouted again.

George came up to his daughter and embraced her. His touch triggered racking sobs, and he held her tighter, the child Melissa between them.

And what if the boy's head rolls to our feet on the crest of the next wave? George thought, and the thought moved him to action. "Let's get Melissa back to the car," he said, taking the child from his daughter's arms.

It was a painful march back to the car, and George was convinced that at any moment either or both of his charges would bolt. He reached the car and helped his daughter into the back seat. She was shaking violently.

"Hold Melissa," he said, passing the child to her. "Don't let her go, Nancy."

George pulled away from them and closed the car door. He turned then, refusing to look at the ocean as he did so. He looked down, stared for a moment at what was undoubtedly a wet clump of matted seaweed, and knew, with irrational certainty, that Melissa had choked on this same seaweed, had knelt here on the ground and painfully coughed it up.

He told the police that Melissa had run into the waves and that Steve had pursued her and drowned. This was all he could tell them—someday he hoped he would truly believe that it was all there was to tell. Thank god his daughter had not seen. And he realized then, with shame, that it was not even his daughter's feelings that were foremost in his mind but rather the relief, the immense relief, of knowing that what he had seen was not going to be corroborated and that with time and effort, he might really believe it was an illusion, the moment's horror, the tricks light plays with water.

He took the police back to where it had happened. But he would not go down to the tide. He waited in the police car while they walked along the beach.

If they returned with Steve's head, what would he say? *Oh yes, a big wave decapitated Steve. Didn't I mention that? Well, I meant to.*

But they found nothing.

ॐ

Back at the hotel, George sat at the kitchen table and drank a beer. He was not a drinker, but it seemed to help. "Where's Nancy?" he asked.

"Upstairs," Mrs. Hume said. "She's sleeping with the child. She wouldn't let me take Melissa. I tried to take the child and I thought... I thought my own daughter was going to attack me, hit me. Did she think I would hurt Melissa? What did she think?"

George studied his beer, shook his head sadly to indicate the absence of all conjecture.

Mrs. Hume dried her hands on the dish towel and, ducking her head, removed her apron. "Romner Psychiatric called. A doctor Melrose."

George looked up. "Is he releasing Mrs. Franklin?" *Please come and get your daughter*, George thought. *I have a daughter of my own.* Oh how he wanted to see the last of them.

"Not just yet. No. But he wanted to know about the family's visits every year. Dr. Melrose thought there might have been something different about that first year. He feels there is some sort of trauma associated with it."

George Hume shrugged. "Nothing out of the ordinary as I recall."

Mrs. Hume put a hand to her cheek. "Oh, but it was different. Don't you remember, George? They came earlier, with all the crowds, and they left abruptly. They had paid for two weeks, but they were gone on the third day. I remember being surprised when they returned the next year—and I thought then that it must have been the crowds they hated and that's why they came so late from then on."

"Well…" Her husband closed his eyes. "I can't say that I actually remember the first time."

His wife shook her head. "What can I expect from a man who can't remember his own wedding anniversary? That Melissa was just a tot back then, a little mite in a red bathing suit. Now that I think of it, she hasn't worn a bathing suit since."

Before going to bed, George stopped at the door to his daughter's room. He pushed the door open carefully and peered in. She slept as she always slept, sprawled on her back, mouth open. She had always fallen asleep abruptly, in disarray, gunned down by the sandman. Tonight she was aided by the doctor's sedatives. The child Melissa snuggled next to her, and for one brief moment the small form seemed sinister and parasitic, as though attached to his daughter, drawing sustenance there.

"Come to bed," his wife said, and George joined her under the covers.

"It's just that she wants to protect the girl," George said. "All she has, you know. She's just seen her boyfriend drown, and this… I think it gives her purpose."

Mrs. Hume understood that this was in answer to the earlier question and she nodded her head. "Yes, I know dear. But is it healthy? I've a bad feeling about it."

"I know," George said.

∞

The shrill ringing of the phone woke him. "Who is it?" his wife was asking as he fumbled in the dark for the receiver.

The night ward clerk was calling from Romner Psychiatric. She apologized for calling at such a late hour, but there might be cause for concern. Better safe than I sorry, etc. Mrs. Franklin had apparently—well, had definitely—left the hospital. Should she return to the hotel, the hospital should be notified immediately.

George Hume thanked her, hung up the phone, and got out of bed. He pulled on his trousers, tugged a sweatshirt over his head.

"Where are you going?" his wife called after him.

"I won't be but a minute," he said, closing the door behind him.

The floor was cold, the boards groaning under his bare feet. Slowly, with a certainty born of dread, expecting the empty bed, expecting the worst, he pushed open the door.

Nancy lay sleeping soundly.

The child was gone. Nancy lay as though still sheltering that small, mysterious form.

George pulled his head back and closed the door. He turned and hurried down the hall. He stopped on the stairs, willed his heart to silence, slowed his breathing. "Melissa," he whispered. No answer.

He ran down the stairs. The front doors were wide open. He ran out into the moonlight and down to the beach.

The beach itself was empty and chill; an unrelenting wind blew in from the ocean. The moon shone overhead as though carved from milky ice.

He saw them then, standing far out on the pier, mother and daughter, black shadows against the moon-gray clouds that bloomed on the horizon.

Dear God, George thought. *What does she intend to do?*

"Melissa!" George shouted, and began to run.

He was out of breath when he reached them. Mother and daughter regarded him coolly, having turned to watch his progress down the pier.

"Melissa," George gasped. "Are you all right?"

Melissa was wearing a pink nightgown and holding her mother's hand. It was her mother who spoke: "We are beyond your concern. Mr. Hume. My husband is dead, and without him the contract cannot be renewed."

Mrs. Franklin's eyes were lit with some extraordinary emotion and the wind, rougher and threatening to unbalance them all, made her hair quiver like a dark flame.

"You have your own daughter, Mr. Hume. That is a fine and wonderful thing. You have never watched your daughter die, watched her fade to utter stillness, dying on her back in the sand, sand on her lips, her eyelids; children are so untidy, even dying. It is an unholy and terrible thing to witness."

The pier groaned and a loud crack heralded a sudden tilting of the world. George fell to his knees. A long sliver of wood entered the palm of his hand, and he tried to keep from pitching forward.

Mrs. Franklin, still standing, shouted over the wind. "We came here every year to renew the bargain. Oh, it is not a good bargain. Our daughter is never with us entirely. But you would know, any parent would know, that love will take whatever it can scavenge, any small compromise. Anything less utter and awful than the grave."

There were tears running down Mrs. Franklin's face now, silver tracks. "This year I was greedy. I wanted Melissa back, all of her. And I thought, I am her mother. I have the first claim to her. So I demanded—demanded—that my husband set it all to rights. 'Tell them we have come here for the last year,' I said. And my husband allowed his love for me to override his reason. He did as I asked."

Melissa, who seemed oblivious to her mother's voice, turned away and spoke into the darkness of the waters. Her words were in no language George Hume had ever heard, and they were greeted with a loud, rasping bellow that thrummed in the wood planks of the pier.

Then came the sound of wood splintering, and the pier abruptly tilted. George's hands gathered more spiky wooden needles as he slid forward. He heard himself scream, but the sound was torn away by the renewed force of the wind and a hideous roaring that accompanied the gale.

Looking up, George saw Melissa kneeling at the edge of the pier. Her mother was gone.

"Melissa!" George screamed, stumbling forward. "Don't move,"

But the child was standing up, wobbling, her nightgown flapping behind her.

George leapt forward, caught the child, felt a momentary flare of hope, and then they both were hurtling forward and the pier was gone.

They plummeted toward the ocean, through a blackness defined by an inhuman sound, a sound that must have been the first sound God heard when He woke at the dawn of eternity.

And even as he fell, George felt the child wiggle in his arms. His arms encircled Melissa's waist, felt bare flesh. Had he looked skyward, he would have seen the nightgown, a pink ghost shape, sailing toward the moon.

But George Hume's eyes saw, instead, the waiting ocean and under it, a shape, a moving network of cold, uncanny machinery, and whether it was a living thing of immense size, or a city, or a machine, was irrelevant. He knew only that it was ancient beyond any land-born thing.

Still clutching the child he collided with the hard, cold back of the sea.

George Hume had been raised in close proximity to the ocean. He had learned to swim almost as soon as he had learned to walk. The cold might kill him, would almost certainly kill him if he did not reach shore quickly—but that he did. During the swim toward shore he lost Melissa and in that moment he understood not to turn back, not to seek the child.

He could not tell anyone how he knew a change had been irretrievably wrought and that there was no returning the girl to land. It was not something you could communicate—any more than you could communicate the dreadful ancient quality of the machinery under the sea.

Nonetheless, George knew the moment Melissa was lost to him. It was a precise and memorable moment. It was the moment the child had wriggled, with strange new, sinewy strength, flicked her tail and slid effortlessly from his grasp.

Take Your Daughters to Work

Livia Llewellyn

Sadie smoothes down her long brown hair, then fastens a choker around her neck. She stares at herself in the mirror. Today her father is taking her to work, and she must be perfect. There will be other girls there, other daughters brought to work by their fathers. But her father runs the company, and so she sets the example. All who look on her must see perfection—otherwise, her father will be shamed.

From the darkened master bedroom, weeping rises. Sadie adjusts the heavy gold at her throat—her mother gave it to her this morning. It's been in the family at least a thousand years. She leans close to the mirror, and smiles.

"Don't worry," she tells her quicksilver self. "You'll do just fine."

The train station swells with the chatter of a thousand excited girls. Sadie walks slowly, her head held high. Her father's fingers trace patterns in the air as they climb the metal steps to his private car, fathers and first-born daughters crowding into the rest. Beneath her feet, engines throb. A lurch and a thrust: now the city parts as the train flows inside.

Sadie perches on the stiff horsehair seat, watching rooftops sail past the elevated tracks. Young men in brown livery pour tea into porcelain cups, and Sadie remembers to hold her little finger out, like a lady. The tea is the color of the sky—sulphur tinged with whorls of cloudy grey. It is the color of the webbing between the young mens' fingers, the color of milky pupils in their lidless eyes.

"Will we see the ocean behind the factories? You promised."

Sadie's father smiles.

"I did indeed. You'll see all the waters of the world."

Sadie sips her tea, touches her throat with nervous hands. Outside, the horizon rushes toward them, a forest of massive smokestacks pumping out fire and haze under a burnt orange sun. The liveried men bow and sway, strange words bursting in wet pops from their lips. Fire makes them nervous. Sadie understands. She's nervous, too.

Her father leads her to the observation car as they pass the first edges of the factory. Sadie stares in wonder at blackened brick rising all around her, at steel pipes tangled around cauldrons larger than her house. Red sparks float in the air like weightless rubies. The factory is the only ocean she's ever seen, and it crashes against the city like a storm. Every year, another row of crumbling homes are eaten away. This is the way of the world, *His* way, her father has explained. If they cannot raise the old city with the old ways, they will bring it up from the deep, piece by piece, and the factory will rebuild it. Sadie cranes her neck, staring at thick columns blotting out the sky—she can see their fixed surfaces, but feels the walls bleeding through other dimensions, dragging a bit of her soul with them. Nauseous, she swallows hard.

"Remember what I told you, Sadie?" Her father touches her lightly, and she turns away.

"Never look directly at the edges," she recites, and he gives her shoulder a quick squeeze.

"That's my girl." He fingers the choker, moving the interlocking hydras into place. Two small rings hang down from either side, like gaping mouths. His fingers hook them, gently. "You're the reason I work so hard. You're our future. I know you'll make me proud."

Alien emotion swims up from Sadie's heart, and catches in her throat. The skin beneath the metal swells and chafes.

"I know," she replies. "I know."

Deep within the heart of the factory, Sadie shakes the scaled hands of many important men. Secretaries slither before her, leaving trails of damp that evaporate quickly in the factory heat. They give her gifts of seashells, and lovely historicals of the factory's beginnings, bound in gilt-edged skin. Sadie eats lunch on a courtyard crowned by pyramids of slag, at a coral table set just for the daughters. Metal fines cling to their skin, settle in their food. Sometimes, Sadie lays down her fork and gasps for a bit of air. Just nerves, she tells herself, and wills herself to breathe.

Afternoon fades, as small trams whisk them down mile-long shafts to a room of pale rib and abalone, where dry air gives way to plump humidity, ocean-sweet. Sadie licks her lips, and tugs at the heavy gold around her neck. Her father holds her hand as they cross the floor, and when they reach the double doors at the far wall, it's as if she's traveled to the end of Time. Behind them, vice-presidents and company managers hover, their daughters clinging anxiously to their coats.

"Open the door, Sadie."

Sadie wipes the sweat from her hands, and pushes. Brisk wind and the roar of surf rush in as Sadie leads them onto the balcony. Below, black sands speckled with skulls descend in jagged dunes down to the endless sea. It is everything her father promised, and more.

"Can we go down?" Her lungs expand, and baleen inside her corset snaps.

"Lead the way." He points to wide steps plunging into the coarse sands. Sadie skips down the steps and into the dunes, all the girls following behind like a veil of trailing flowers. Overhead, pipes larger than the train thrust from the factory walls, plunging straight into iron-grey waves. As she reaches the beach's edge, factory horns sound one by one, great spine-shuddering cries that send the waters rushing back. Sadie stops and turns. All along the curving coast, green light explodes from pockets of the factory—signal fires lighting the way.

The men spread out across the beach, directing their daughters to the edge of the tide line. Before them, dark shapes rise from receding waves—cobblestone roads slick with foam, low houses clustered like rotting mushrooms, and beyond... The sandy ridge breaks off and free-falls into the rift. Sadie spies chimney stacks peeking up from the depths, bioluminescent smoke coiling in the air, freed of the weight of water. Soft movements appear, as flippers and webbed feet emerge from gaping doors. More employees of her father, ready to greet them all. Sadie spies the liveried young man from the train car, and her heart skips a beat.

Some of the girls cry as their fathers pull chains up from the sands, hooking them at the loops in their golden hydra chokers. The chains stretch out along the ancient roads and over the edges of the rift, ending in the city below. Sadie trembles slightly as her father stretches out his hand, links of black metal dripping off his palm. Beneath her choker, skin stretches wide, half-developed gills sucking at the moisture in the air as they vaguely remember what to do.

"I'll always love you. Remember that, in the last moments." Her father looks down at her, the tentacles of his beard coiling into a hundred tender smiles.

"Of course." Sadie covers his hand with her own. In the dying light, the silver of her bones shine through the flesh, luminous and pure. "When my bones are added to the city, you'll see me. We'll never be apart. It is my honor to join the work."

"You are my greatest gift, my greatest sacrifice." As he kisses her forehead, his tears fall onto her skin. Sadie feels the chain slide through the hoops as he carefully hooks it. Somewhere, beneath the rift, strong tentacles hold the other end. Sadie prays to the Mother that whoever accepts her, he is vast and terrible. After all, her father runs the factory, and she is her father's daughter. She sets the example till the day her chained bones, heavy with spawn, are pulled back from her bridal grave.

"Our work renews our world," her father says. "Our daughters renew our lives. In His name we bring them together. In His name, we take our daughters to work."

Sadie steps onto the slick cobblestones, and the employees of New Y'ha-nthlei Steelworks follow, each of them walking their daughters into the rising waves.

The Big Fish

Kim Newman

The Bay City cops were rousting enemy aliens. As I drove through the nasty coast town, uniforms hauled an old couple out of a grocery store. The Taraki family's neighbors huddled in thin rain howling asthmatically for bloody revenge. Pearl Harbor had struck a lot of people that way. With the Tarakis on the bus for Manzanar, neighbors descended on the store like bedraggled vultures. Produce vanished instantly, then destruction started. Caught at a sleepy stop light, I got a good look. The Tarakis had lived over the store; now, their furniture was thrown out of the second-story window. Fine china shattered on the sidewalk, spilling white chips like teeth into the gutter. It was inspirational, the forces of democracy rallying round to protect the United States from vicious oriental grocers, fiendishly intent on selling eggplant to a hapless civilian population.

Meanwhile my appointment was with a gent who kept three pictures on his mantelpiece, grouped in a triangle around a statue of the Virgin Mary. At the apex was his white-haired mama, to the left Charles Luciano, and to the right, Benito Mussolini. The Tarakis, American-born and registered Democrats, were headed to a dustbowl concentration camp for the duration, while Gianni Pastore, Sicilian-born and highly unregistered *capo* of the Family Business, would spend his war in a marble-fronted mansion paid for by nickels and dimes dropped on the numbers game, into slot machines, or exchanged for the favors of nice girls from the old country. I'd seen his mansion before and so far been able to resist the temptation to bean one of his twelve muse statues with a bourbon bottle.

Money can buy you love but can't even put down a deposit on good taste.

The palace was up in the hills, a little way down the boulevard from Tyrone Power. But now, Pastore was hanging his mink-banded fedora in a Bay City beachfront motel complex, which was a real estate agent's term for a bunch of horrible shacks shoved together for the convenience of people who like sand on their carpets.

I always take a lungful of fresh air before entering a confined space with someone in Pastore's business, so I parked the Chrysler a few blocks from the Seaview Inn and walked the rest of the way, sucking on a Camel to keep warm in the wet. They say it doesn't rain in Southern California, but they also say the U.S. Navy could never be taken by surprise. This February, three months into a war the rest of the world had been fighting since 1936 or 1939 depending on whether you were Chinese or Polish, it was raining almost constantly, varying between a light fall of misty drizzle in the dreary daytimes to spectacular storms, complete with DeMille lighting effects, in our fear-filled nights. Those trusty Boy Scouts scanning the horizons for Jap subs and Nazi U-Boats were filling up influenza wards and manufacturers of raincoats and umbrellas who'd not yet converted their plants to defense production were making a killing. I didn't mind the rain. At least rainwater is clean, unlike most other things in Bay City.

A small boy with a wooden gun leaped out of a bush and sprayed me with sound effects, interrupting his onomatopoeic chirruping with a shout of "die you slant-eyed Jap!" I clutched my heart, staggered back, and he finished me off with a quick burst. I died for the Emperor and tipped the kid a dime to go away. If this went on long enough, maybe little Johnny would get a chance to march off and do real killing, then maybe come home in a box or with the shakes or a taste for blood. Meanwhile, especially since someone spotted a Jap submarine off Santa Barbara, California was gearing up for the War Effort. Aside from interning grocers, our best brains were writing songs like "To Be Specific, It's Our Pacific", "So Long Momma, I'm Off to Yokahama", "We're Gonna Slap the Jap Right Off the Map" and "When Those Little Yellow Bellies Meet the Cohens and the Kellys". Zanuck had donated his string of Argentine polo ponies to West Point and got himself measured for a comic opera Colonel's uniform so he could join the Signal Corps and defeat the Axis by posing for publicity photographs.

I'd tried to join up two days after Pearl Harbor but they kicked me back onto the streets. Too many concussions. Apparently, I get hit on the head too often and have a tendency to black out. When they came to mention it, they were right.

The Seaview Inn was shuttered, one of the first casualties of war. It had its own jetty, and by it were a few canvas-covered motor launches shifting with the waves. In late afternoon gloom, I saw the silhouette of the *Montecito*, anchored strategically outside the three-mile limit. That was one good thing about the Japanese; on the downside, they might have sunk most of the U.S. fleet, but on the up, they'd put Laird Brunette's gambling ship out of business. Nobody was enthusiastic about losing their shirt-buttons on a rigged roulette wheel if they imagined they were going to be torpedoed any moment. I'd have thought that would add an extra thrill to the whole gay, delirious business of giving Brunette money, but I'm just a poor, twenty-five-dollars-a-day detective.

The Seaview Inn was supposed to be a stopping-off point on the way to the *Monty* and now its trade was stopped off. The main building was sculpted out of dusty ice cream and looked like a three-story radiogram with wave-scallop friezes. I pushed through double-doors and entered the lobby. The floor was decorated with a mosaic in which Neptune, looking like an angry Santa Claus in a swimsuit, was sticking it to a sea-nymph who shared a hairdresser with Hedy Lamarr. The nymph was naked except for some strategic shells. It was very artistic.

There was nobody at the desk and thumping the bell didn't improve matters. Water ran down the outside of the green-tinted windows. There were a few steady drips somewhere. I lit up another Camel and went exploring. The office was locked and the desk register didn't have any entries after December 7, 1941. My raincoat dripped and began to dry out, sticking my jacket and shirt to my shoulders. I shrugged, trying to get some air into my clothes. I noticed Neptune's face quivering. A thin layer of water had pooled over the mosaic and various anenome-like fronds attached to the sea god were apparently getting excited. Looking at the nymph, I could understand that. Actually, I realised, only the hair was from Hedy. The face and the body were strictly Janey Wilde.

I go to the movies a lot but I'd missed most of Janey's credits: *She-Strangler of Shanghai*, *Tarzan and the Tiger Girl*, *Perils of Jungle Jillian*. I'd seen her in the newspapers though, often in unnervingly close proximity with Pastore or Brunette. She'd started as an Olympic swimmer, picking up medals in Berlin, then followed Weissmuller and Crabbe to Hollywood. She would never get an Academy Award but her legs were in a lot of cheesecake stills publicising no particular movie. Air-brushed and made-up like a good-looking corpse, she was a fine commercial for sex. In person she was as bubbly as domestic champagne, though now running to flat. Things were slow in the detecting business, since people were more worried about imminent invasion than missing daughters or misplaced love letters. So when Janey Wilde called on me in my office in the Cahuenga Building and asked me to look up one of her ill-chosen men friends, I checked the pile of old envelopes I use as a desk diary and informed her that I was available to make inquiries into the current whereabouts of a certain big fish.

Wherever Laird Brunette was, he wasn't here. I was beginning to figure Gianni Pastore, the gambler's partner, wasn't here either. Which meant I'd wasted an afternoon. Outside it rained harder, driving against the walls with a drumlike tattoo. Either there were hailstones mixed in with the water or the Jap air force was hurling fistfuls of pebbles at Bay City to demoralise the population. I don't know why they bothered. All Hirohito had to do was slip a thick envelope to the Bay City cops and the city's finest would hand over the whole community to the Japanese Empire with a ribbon around it and a bow on top.

There were more puddles in the lobby, little streams running from one to the other. I was reminded of the episode of *The Perils of Jungle Jillian* I had seen while tailing a child molester to a Saturday matinee. At the end, Janey Wilde had been caught by the Panther Princess and trapped in a room which slowly filled with water. That room had been a lot smaller than the lobby of the Seaview Inn and the water had come in a lot faster.

Behind the desk were framed photographs of pretty people in pretty clothes having a pretty time. Pastore was there, and Brunette, grinning like tiger cats, mingling with showfolk: Xavier Cugat, Janey Wilde, Charles Coburn. Janice Marsh, the pop-eyed beauty rumored to have replaced Jungle Jillian in Brunette's affections, was well represented in artistic poses.

On the phone, Pastore had promised faithfully to be here. He hadn't wanted to bother with a small-timer like me but Janey Wilde's name opened a door. I had a feeling Papa Pastore was relieved to be shaken down about Brunette, as if he wanted to talk about something. He must be busy because there were several wars on. The big one overseas and a few little ones at home. Maxie Rothko, bar owner and junior partner in the *Monty*, had been found drifting in the seaweed around the Santa Monica pier without much of a head to speak of. And Phil Isinglass, man-about-town lawyer and Brunette frontman, had turned up in the storm drains, lungs full of sandy mud. Disappearing was the latest craze in Brunette's organisation. That didn't sound good for Janey Wilde, though Pastore had talked about the Laird as if he knew Brunette was alive. But now Papa wasn't around. I was getting annoyed with someone it wasn't sensible to be annoyed with.

Pastore wouldn't be in any of the beach shacks but there should be an apartment for his convenience in the main building. I decided to explore further. Jungle Jillian would expect no less. She'd hired me for five days in advance, a good thing since I'm unduly reliant on eating and drinking and other expensive diversions of the monied and idle.

The corridor that led past the office ended in a walk-up staircase. As soon as I put my size nines on the first step, it squelched. I realised something was more than usually wrong. The steps were a quiet little waterfall, seeping rather than cascading. It wasn't just water, there was unpleasant, slimy stuff mixed in. Someone had left the bath running. My first thought was that Pastore had been distracted by a bullet. I was wrong. In the long run, he might have been happier if I'd been right.

I climbed the soggy stairs and found the the apartment door unlocked but shut. Bracing myself, I pushed the door in. It encountered resistance but then sliced open, allowing a gush of water to shoot around my ankles, soaking my dark blue socks. Along with water was a three-weeks-dead-in-the-water-with-rotten-fish smell that wrapped around me like a blanket. Holding my breath, I stepped into the room. The waterfall flowed faster now. I heard a faucet running. A radio played, with funny little gurgles mixed in. A crooner was doing his best with "Life is Just a Bowl of Cherries", but he sounded as if he were drowned full fathom five. I followed the music and found the bathroom.

Pastore was face down in the overflowing tub, the song coming from under him. He wore a silk lounging robe that had been pulled away from his back, his wrists tied behind him with the robe's cord. In the end he'd been drowned. But before that hands had been laid on him, either in anger or with cold, professional skill. I'm not a coroner, so I couldn't tell how long the Family Man had been in the water. The radio still playing and the water still running suggested Gianni had met his end recently but the stench felt older than sin.

I have a bad habit of finding bodies in Bay City and the most profit-minded police force in the country have a bad habit of trying to make connections between me and a wide variety of deceased persons. The obvious solution in this case was to make a friendly phone call, absent-mindedly forgetting to mention my name while giving the flatfeet directions to the late Mr. Pastore. Who knows, I might accidentally talk to someone honest.

That is exactly what I would have done if, just then, the man with the gun hadn't come through the door…

I had Janey Wilde to blame. She'd arrived without an appointment, having picked me on a recommendation. Oddly, Laird Brunette had once said something not entirely uncomplimentary about me. We'd met. We hadn't seriously tried to kill each other in a while. That was as good a basis for a relationship as any.

Out of her sarong, Jungle Jillian favored sharp shoulders and a veiled pill-box. The kiddies at the matinee had liked her fine, especially when she was wrestling stuffed snakes, and dutiful Daddies took no exception to her either, especially when she was tied down and her sarong rode up a few inches. Her lips were four red grapes plumped together. When she crossed her legs you saw swimmer's smooth muscle under her hose.

"He's very sweet, really," she explained, meaning Mr. Brunette never killed anyone within ten miles of her without apologising afterwards, "not at all like they say in those dreadful scandal sheets."

The gambler had been strange recently, especially since the war shut him down. Actually the *Montecito* had been out of commission for nearly a year, supposedly for a refit although as far as Janey Wilde knew no workmen had been sent out to the ship. At about the time Brunette suspended his crooked wheels, he came down with a common California complaint, a dose of crack-pot religion. He'd been tangentally mixed up a few years ago with a psychic racket run by a bird named Amthor, but had apparently shifted from the mostly harmless bunco cults onto the hard stuff. Spiritualism, orgiastic rites, chanting, incense, the whole deal.

Janey blamed this sudden interest in matters occult on Janice Marsh, who had coincidentally made her name as the Panther Princess in *The Perils of Jungle Jillian*, a role which required her to torture Janey Wilde at least once every chapter. My employer didn't mention that her own career had hardly soared between *Jungle Jillian* and *She-Strangler of Shanghai*, while the erstwhile Panther Princess had gone from Republic to Metro and was being built up as an exotic in the Dietrich-Garbo vein. Say what you like about Janice Marsh's *Nefertiti*, she still looked like Peter Lorre to me. And according to Janey, the star had more peculiar tastes than a seafood buffet.

Brunette had apparently joined a series of fringe organisations and become quite involved, to the extent of neglecting his business and thereby irking his long-time partner, Gianni Pastore. Perhaps that was why person or persons unknown had decided the Laird wouldn't mind if his associates died one by one. I couldn't figure it out. The cults I'd come across mostly stayed in business by selling sex, drugs, power or reassurance to rich, stupid people. The Laird hardly fell into the category. He was too big a fish for that particular bowl.

The man with the gun was English, with a Ronald Colman accent and a white aviator's scarf. He was not alone. The quiet, truck-sized bruiser I made as a fed went through my wallet while the dapper foreigner kept his automatic pointed casually at my middle.

"Peeper," the fed snarled, showing the photostat of my license and my supposedly impressive deputy's badge.

"Interesting," said the Britisher, slipping his gun into the pocket of his camel coat. Immaculate, he must have been umbrella-protected between car and building because there wasn't a spot of rain on him. "I'm Winthrop. Edwin Winthrop."

We shook hands. His other companion, the interesting one, was going through the deceased's papers. She looked up, smiled with sharp white teeth, and got back to work.

"This is Mademoiselle Dieudonné."

"Geneviève," she said. She pronounced it "Zhe-ne-vyev", suggesting Paris, France. She was wearing something white with silver in it and had quantities of pale blonde hair.

"And the gentleman from your Federal Bureau of Investigation is Finlay."

The fed grunted. He looked as if he'd been brought to life by Willis H. O'Brien.

"You are interested in a Mr. Brunette," Winthrop said. It was not a question, so there was no point in answering him. "So are we."

"Call in a Russian and we could be the Allies," I said.

Winthrop laughed. He was sharp. "True. I am here at the request of my government and working with the full co-operation of yours."

One of the small detective-type details I noticed was that no one even suggested informing the police about Gianni Pastore was a good idea.

"Have you ever heard of a place called Innsmouth, Massachusetts?"

It didn't mean anything to me and I said so.

"Count yourself lucky. Special Agent Finlay's associates were called upon to dynamite certain unsafe structures in the sea off Innsmouth back in the twenties. It was a bad business."

Geneviève said something sharp in French that sounded like swearing. She held up a photograph of Brunette dancing cheek to cheek with Janice Marsh.

"Do you know the lady?" Winthrop asked.

"Only in the movies. Some go for her in a big way but I think she looks like Mr. Moto."

"Very true. Does the Esoteric Order of Dagon mean anything to you?"

"Sounds like a Church-of-the-Month alternate. Otherwise, no."

"Captain Obed Marsh?"

"Uh-uh."

"The Deep Ones?"

"Are they those colored singers?"

"What about Cthulhu, Y'ha-nthlei, R'lyeh?"

"*Gesundheit.*"

Winthrop grinned, sharp moustache pointing. "No, not easy to say at all. Hard to fit into human mouths, you know."

"He's just a bedroom creeper," Finlay said, "he don't know nothing."

"His grammar could be better. Doesn't J. Edgar pay for elocution lessons?"

Finlay's big hands opened and closed as if he would rather there were a throat in them.

"Gené?" Winthrop said.

The woman looked up, red tongue absently flicking across her red lips, and thought a moment. She said something in a foreign language that I did understand.

"There's no need to kill him," she said in French. Thank you very much, I thought.

Winthrop shrugged and said "fine by me." Finlay looked disappointed.

"You're free to go," the Britisher told me. "We shall take care of everything. I see no point in your continuing your current line of inquiry. Send in a chit to this address," he handed me a card, "and you'll be reimbursed for your expenses so far. Don't worry. We'll carry on until this is seen through. By the way, you might care not to discuss with anyone what you've seen here or anything I may have said. There's a War on, you know. Loose lips sink ships."

I had a few clever answers but I swallowed them and left. Anyone who thought there was no need to kill me was all right in my book and I wasn't using my razored tongue on them. As I walked to the Chrysler, several ostentatiously unofficial cars cruised past me, headed for the Seaview Inn.

It was getting dark and lightning was striking down out at sea. A flash lit up the *Montecito* and I counted five seconds before the thunder boomed. I had the feeling there was something out there beyond the three-mile limit besides the floating former casino, and that it was angry.

I slipped into the Chrysler and drove away from Bay City, feeling better the further inland I got.

I take *Black Mask*. It's a long time since Hammett and the fellow who wrote the Ted Carmady stories were in it, but you occasionally get a good Cornell Woolrich or Erle Stanley Gardner. Back at my office, I saw the newsboy had been by and dropped off the *Times* and next month's pulp. But there'd been a mix-up. Instead of the *Mask*, there was something inside the folded newspaper called *Weird Tales*. On the cover, a man was being attacked by two green demons and a stereotype vampire with a widow's peak. "'Hell on Earth', a

Novelette of Satan in a Tuxedo by Robert Bloch" was blazed above the title. Also promised were "A new Lovecraft series, 'Herbert West—Reanimator'" and "'The Rat Master' by Greye la Spina". All for fifteen cents, kids. If I were a different type of detective, the brand who said *nom de* something and waxed a moustache whenever he found a mutilated corpse, I might have thought the substitution an omen.

In my office, I've always had five filing cabinets, three empty. I also had two bottles, only one empty. In a few hours, the situation would have changed by one bottle.

I found a glass without too much dust and wiped it with my clean handkerchief. I poured myself a generous slug and hit the back of my throat with it.

The radio didn't work but I could hear Glenn Miller from somewhere. I found my glass empty and dealt with that. Sitting behind my desk, I looked at the patterns in rain on the window. If I craned I could see traffic on Hollywood Boulevard. People who didn't spend their working days finding bodies in bathtubs were going home not to spend their evenings emptying a bottle.

After a day, I'd had some excitement but I hadn't done much for Janey Wilde. I was no nearer being able to explain the absence of Mr. Brunette from his usual haunts than I had been when she left my office, leaving behind a tantalising whiff of *essence de chine*.

She'd given me some literature pertaining to Brunette's cult involvement. Now, the third slug warming me up inside, I looked over it, waiting for inspiration to strike. Interesting echoes came up in relation to Winthrop's shopping list of subjects of peculiar interest. I had no luck with the alphabet soup syllables he'd spat at me, mainly because "Cthulhu" sounds more like a cough than a word. But the Esoteric Order of Dagon was a group Brunette had joined, and Innsmouth, Massachusetts, was the East Coast town where the organisation was registered. The Esoteric Order had a temple on the beach front in Venice, and its mumbo-jumbo hand-outs promised "ancient and intriguing rites to probe the mysteries of the Deep." Slipped in with the recruitment bills was a studio biography of Janice Marsh, which helpfully revealed the movie star's place of birth as Innsmouth, Massachusetts, and that she could trace her family back to Captain Obed Marsh, the famous early 19th Century explorer of whom I'd never heard. Obviously Winthrop, Geneviève and the FBI were well ahead of me in making connections. And I didn't really know who the Englishman and the French girl were.

I wondered if I wouldn't have been better off reading *Weird Tales*. I liked the sound of Satan in a Tuxedo. It wasn't Ted Carmady with an automatic and a dame, but it would do. There was a lot more thunder and lightning and I finished the bottle. I suppose I could have gone home to sleep but the chair was no more uncomfortable than my Murphy bed.

The empty bottle rolled and I settled down, tie loose, to forget the cares of the day.

Thanks to the War, Pastore only made Page 3 of the *Times*. Apparently the noted gambler-entrepreneur had been shot to death. If that was true, it had happened after I'd left. Then, he'd only been tortured and drowned. Police Chief John Wax dished out his usual "over by Christmas" quote about the investigation. There was no mention of the FBI, or of our allies, John Bull in a tux and Mademoiselle la Guillotine. In prison, you get papers with neat oblongs cut out to remove articles the censor feels provocative. They don't make any difference: all newspapers have invisible oblongs. Pastore's sterling work with underprivileged kids was mentioned but someone forgot to write about the junk he sold them when they grew into underprivileged adults. The obit photograph found him with Janey Wilde and Janice Marsh at the premiere of a George Raft movie. The phantom Jap sub off Santa Barbara got more column inches. General John L. DeWitt, head of the Western Defense Command, called for more troops to guard the coastline, prophesying "death and destruction are likely to come at any moment". Everyone in California was looking out to sea.

After my regular morning conference with Mr. Huggins and Mr. Young, I placed a call to Janey Wilde's Malibu residence. Most screen idols are either at the studio or asleep if you telephone before ten o'clock in the morning, but Janey, with weeks to go before shooting started on *Bowery to Bataan*, was at home and awake, having done her thirty lengths. Unlike almost everyone else in the industry, she thought a swimming pool was for swimming in rather than lounging beside.

She remembered instantly who I was and asked for news. I gave her a *precis*.

"I've been politely asked to refrain from further investigations," I explained. "By some heavy hitters."

"So you're quitting?"

I should have said yes, but "Miss Wilde, only you can require me to quit. I thought you should know how the federal government feels."

There was a pause.

"There's something I didn't tell you," she told me. It was an expression common among my clients. "Something important."

I let dead air hang on the line.

"It's not so much Laird that I'm concerned about. It's that he has Franklin."

"Franklin?"

"The baby," she said. "Our baby. My baby."

"Laird Brunette has disappeared, taking a baby with him?"

"Yes."

"Kidnapping is a crime. You might consider calling the cops."

"A lot of things are crimes. Laird has done many of them and never spent a day in prison."

That was true, which was why this development was strange. Kidnapping, whether personal or for profit, is the riskiest of crimes. As a rule, it's the province only of the stupidest criminals. Laird Brunette was not a stupid criminal.

"I can't afford bad publicity. Not when I'm so near to the roles I need."

Bowery to Bataan was going to put her among the screen immortals.

"Franklin is supposed to be Esther's boy. In a few years, I'll adopt him legally. Esther is my house-keeper. It'll work out. But I must have him back."

"Laird is the father. He will have some rights."

"He said he wasn't interested. He ... um, moved on ... to Janice Marsh while I was ... before Franklin was born."

"He's had a sudden attack of fatherhood and you're not convinced?"

"I'm worried to distraction. It's not Laird, it's her. Janice Marsh wants my baby for something vile. I want you to get Franklin back."

"As I mentioned, kidnapping is a crime."

"If there's a danger to the child, surely..."

"Do you have any proof that there is danger?"

"Well, no."

"Have Laird Brunette or Janice Marsh ever given you reason to believe they have ill-will for the baby?"

"Not exactly."

I considered things.

"I'll continue with the job you hired me for, but you understand that's all I can do. If I find Brunette, I'll pass your worries on. Then it's between the two of you."

She thanked me in a flood and I got off the phone feeling I'd taken a couple of strides further into the LaBrea tar pits and could feel sucking stickiness well above my knees.

I should have stayed out of the rain and concentrated on chess problems but I had another four days' worth of Jungle Jillian's retainer in my pocket and an address for the Esoteric Order of Dagon in a clipping from a lunatic scientific journal. So I drove out to Venice, reminding myself all the way that my wipers needed fixing.

Venice, California, is a fascinating idea that didn't work. Someone named Abbot Kinney had the notion of artificially creating a city like Venice, Italy, with canals and architecture. The canals mostly ran dry and the architecture never really caught on in a town where, in the twenties, Gloria Swanson's bathroom was considered an aesthetic triumph. All that was left was the beach and piles of rotting fish. Venice, Italy, is the Plague Capital of Europe, so Venice, California, got one thing right.

The Esoteric Order was up the coast from Muscle Beach, housed in a discreet yacht club building with its own small marina. From the exterior, I guessed the cult business had seen better days. Seaweed had tracked up the beach, swarmed around the jetty, and was licking the lower edges of the front wall. Everything had gone green: wood, plaster, copper ornaments. And it smelled like Pastore's bathroom, only worse. This kind of place made you wonder why the Japs were so keen on invading.

I looked at myself in the mirror and rolled my eyes. I tried to get that slap-happy, let-me-give-you-all-my-worldly-goods, gimme-some-mysteries-of-the-orient look I imagined typical of a communicant at one of these bughouse congregations. After I'd stopped laughing, I remembered the marks on Pastore and tried to take detecting seriously. Taking in my unshaven, slept-upright-in-his-clothes, two-bottles-a-day lost soul look, I congratulated myself on my foresight in spending fifteen years developing the ideal cover for a job like this.

To get in the building, I had to go down to the marina and come at it from the beach-side. There were green pillars of what looked like fungus-eaten cardboard either side of the impressive front door, which held a stained glass picture in shades of green and blue of a man with the head of a squid in a natty monk's number, waving his eyes for the artist. Dagon, I happened to know, was half-man, half-fish, and God of the Philistines. In this town, I guess a Philistine God blended in well. It's a great country: if you're half-fish, pay most of your taxes, eat babies and aren't Japanese, you have a wonderful future.

I rapped on the squid's head but nothing happened. I looked the squid in several of his eyes and felt squirmy inside. Somehow, up close, cephalopod-face didn't look that silly.

I pushed the door and found myself in a temple's waiting room. It was what I'd expected: subdued lighting, old but bad paintings, a few semi-pornographic statuettes, a strong smell of last night's incense to cover up the fish stink. It had as much religious atmosphere as a two-dollar bordello.

"Yoo-hoo," I said, "Dagon calling…"

My voice sounded less funny echoed back at me.

I prowled, sniffing for clues. I tried saying *nom de* something and twiddling a non-existant moustache but nothing came to me. Perhaps I ought to switch to a meerschaum of cocaine and a deerstalker, or maybe a monocle and an interest in incunabula.

Where you'd expect a portrait of George Washington or Jean Harlow's Mother, the Order had hung up an impressively ugly picture of "Our Founder". Capt. Obed Marsh, dressed up like Admiral Butler, stood on the shore of a Polynesian paradise, his good ship painted with no sense of perspective on the horizon as if it were about three feet tall. The Capt., surrounded by adoring if funny-faced native tomatoes, looked about as unhappy as Errol Flynn at a Girl Scout meeting. The painter had taken a lot of trouble with the native nudes. One of the dusky lovelies had hips that would make Lombard green and a face that put me in mind of Janice Marsh. She was probably the Panther Princess's great-great-great grandmother. In the background, just in front of the ship, was something like a squid emerging from the sea. Fumble-fingers with a brush had tripped up again. It looked as if the tentacle-waving creature were about twice the size of Obed's clipper. The most upsetting detail was a robed and masked figure standing on the deck with a baby's ankle in each fist. He had apparently just wrenched the child apart like a wishbone and was emptying blood into the squid's eyes.

"Excuse me," gargled a voice, "can I help you?"

I turned around and got a noseful of the stooped and ancient Guardian of the Cult. His robe matched the ones worn by squid-features on the door and baby-ripper in the portrait. He kept his face shadowed, his voice sounded about as good as the radio in Pastore's bath and his breath smelled worse than Pastore after a week and a half of putrefaction.

"Good morning," I said, letting a bird flutter in the higher ranges of my voice, "my name is, er…"

I put together the first things that came to mind.

"My name is Herbert West Lovecraft. Uh, H.W. Lovecraft the Third. I'm simply fascinated by matters Ancient and Esoteric, don't ch'know."

"Don't ch'know" I picked up from the fellow with the monocle and the old books.

"You wouldn't happen to have an entry blank, would you? Or any incunabula?"

"Incunabula?" he wheezed.

"Books. Old books. Print books, published before 1500 *anno domini*, old sport." See, I have a dictionary too.

"Books…"

The man was a monotonous conversationalist. He also moved like Laughton in *The Hunchback of Notre Dame* and the front of his robe, where the squidhead was embroidered, was wet with what I was disgusted to deduce was drool.

"Old books. Arcane mysteries, don't ch'know. Anything cyclopaean and doom-haunted is just up my old alley."

"The *Necronomicon*?" He pronounced it with great respect, and great difficulty.

"Sounds just the ticket."

Quasimodo shook his head under his hood and it lolled. I glimpsed green-ish skin and large, moist eyes.

"I was recommended to come here by an old pal," I said. "Spiffing fellow. Laird Brunette. Ever hear of him?"

I'd pushed the wrong button. Quasi straightened out and grew about two feet. Those moist eyes flashed like razors.

"You'll have to see the Cap'n's Daughter."

I didn't like the sound of that and stepped backwards, towards the door. Quasi laid a hand on my shoulder and held it fast. He was wearing mittens and I felt he had too many fingers inside them. His grip was like a gila mon-ster's jaw.

"That will be fine," I said, dropping the flutter.

As if arranged, curtains parted, and I was shoved through a door. Crack-ing my head on the low lintel, I could see why Quasi spent most of his time hunched over. I had to bend at the neck and knees to go down the corridor. The exterior might be rotten old wood but the heart of the place was solid stone. The walls were damp, bare and covered in suggestive carvings that gave primitive art a bad name. You'd have thought I'd be getting used to the smell by now, but nothing doing. I nearly gagged.

Quasi pushed me through another door. I was in a meeting room no larger than Union Station, with a stage, rows of comfortable armchairs and lots more squid-person statues. The centrepiece was very like the mosaic at the Seaview Inn, only the nymph had less shells and Neptune more tentacles.

Quasi vanished, slamming the door behind him. I strolled over to the stage and looked at a huge book perched on a straining lectern. The fellow with the monocle would have salivated, because this looked a lot older than 1500. It wasn't a Bible and didn't smell healthy. It was open to an illustration of some-thing with tentacles and slime, facing a page written in several deservedly dead languages.

"The *Necronomicon*," said a throaty female voice, "of the mad Arab, Abdul Al-Hazred."

"Mad, huh?" I turned to the speaker. "Is he not getting his royalties?"

I recognised Janice Marsh straight away. The Panther Princess wore a turban and green silk lounging pajamas, with a floorlength housecoat that cost more than I make in a year. She had on jade earrings, a pearl cluster pendant and a ruby-eyed silver squid brooch. The lighting made her face look green and her round eyes shone. She still looked like Peter Lorre, but maybe if Lorre put his face on a body like Janice Marsh's, he'd be up for sex goddess roles too. Her silk thighs purred against each other as she walked down the temple aisle.

"Mr. Lovecraft, isn't it?"

"Call me H.W. Everyone does."

"Have I heard of you?"

"I doubt it."

She was close now. A tall girl, she could look me in the eye. I had the feeling the eye-jewel in her turban was looking me in the brain. She let her fingers fall on the tentacle picture for a moment, allowed them to play around like a fun-loving spider, then removed them to my upper arm, delicately tugging me away from the book. I wasn't unhappy about that. Maybe I'm allergic to incunabula or perhaps an undiscovered prejudice against tentacled creatures, but I didn't like being near the *Necronomicon* one bit. Certainly the experience didn't compare with being near Janice Marsh.

"You're the Cap'n's Daughter?" I said.

"It's a honorific title. Obed Marsh was my ancestor. In the Esoteric Order, there is always a Cap'n's Daughter. Right now, I am she."

"What exactly is this Dagon business about?"

She smiled, showing a row of little pearls. "It's an alternative form of worship. It's not a racket, honestly."

"I never said it was."

She shrugged.

"Many people get the wrong idea."

Outside, the wind was rising, driving rain against the Temple. The sound effects were weird, like sickening whales calling out in the Bay.

"You were asking about Laird? Did Miss Wilde send you?"

It was my turn to shrug.

"Janey is what they call a sore loser, Mr. Lovecraft. It comes from taking all those bronze medals. Never the gold."

"I don't think she wants him back," I said, "just to know where he is. He seems to have disappeared."

"He's often out of town on business. He likes to be mysterious. I'm sure you understand."

My eyes kept going to the squid-face brooch. As Janice Marsh breathed, it rose and fell and rubies winked at me.

"It's Polynesian," she said, tapping the brooch. "The Cap'n brought it back with him to Innsmouth."

"Ah yes, your home town."

"It's just a place by the sea. Like Los Angeles."

I decided to go fishing, and hooked up some of the bait Winthrop had given me. "Were you there when J. Edgar Hoover staged his fireworks display in the twenties?"

"Yes, I was a child. Something to do with rum-runners, I think. That was during Prohibition."

"Good years for the Laird."

"I suppose so. He's legitimate these days."

"Yes. Although if he were as Scotch as he likes to pretend he is, you can be sure he'd have been deported by now."

Janice Marsh's eyes were sea-green. Round or not, they were fascinating. "Let me put your mind at rest, Mr. Lovecraft or whatever your name is," she said, "the Esoteric Order of Dagon was never a front for boot-legging. In fact it has never been a front for anything. It is not a racket for duping rich widows out of inheritances. It is not an excuse for motion picture executives to gain carnal knowledge of teenage drug addicts. It is exactly what it claims to be, a church."

"Father, Son and Holy Squid, eh?"

"I did not say we were a Christian church."

Janice Marsh had been creeping up on me and was close enough to bite. Her active hands went to the back of my neck and angled my head down like an adjustable lamp. She put her lips on mine and squashed her face into me. I tasted lipstick, salt and caviar. Her fingers writhed up into my hair and pushed my hat off. She shut her eyes. After an hour or two of suffering in the line of duty, I put my hands on her hips and detached her body from mine. I had a fish taste in my mouth.

"That was interesting," I said.

"An experiment," she replied. "Your name has such a ring to it. Love ... craft. It suggests expertise in a certain direction."

"Disappointed?"

She smiled. I wondered if she had several rows of teeth, like a shark.

"Anything but."

"So do I get an invite to the back-row during your next Dagon hoe-down?"

She was businesslike again. "I think you'd better report back to Janey. Tell her I'll have Laird call her when he's in town and put her mind at rest. She should pay you off. What with the War, it's a waste of manpower to have you spend your time looking for someone who isn't missing when you could be defending Lockheed from Fifth Columnists."

"What about Franklin?"

"Franklin the President?"

"Franklin the baby."

Her round eyes tried to widen. She was playing this scene innocent. The Panther Princess had been the same when telling the white hunter that Jungle Jillian had left the Tomb of the Jaguar hours ago.

"Miss Wilde seems to think Laird has borrowed a child of hers that she care-lessly left in his care. She'd like Franklin back."

"Janey hasn't got a baby. She can't have babies. It's why she's such a psy-cho-neurotic case. Her analyst is getting rich on her bewildering fantasies. She can't tell reality from the movies. She once accused me of human sacrifice."

"Sounds like a square rap."

"That was in a film, Mr. Lovecraft. Cardboard knives and catsup blood."

Usually at this stage in an investigation, I call my friend Bernie at the District Attorney's office and put out a few fishing lines. This time, he phoned me. When I got into my office, I had the feeling my telephone had been ringing for a long time.

"Don't make waves," Bernie said.

"Pardon," I snapped back, with my usual lightning-fast wit.

"Just don't. It's too cold to go for a swim this time of year."

"Even in a bathtub."

"Especially in a bathtub."

"Does Mr. District Attorney send his regards?"

Bernie laughed. I had been an investigator with the DA's office a few years back, but we'd been forced to part company.

"Forget him. I have some more impressive names on my list."

"Let me guess. Howard Hughes?"

"Close."

"General Stillwell?"

"Getting warmer. Try Mayor Fletcher Bowron, Governor Culbert Olson, and State Attorney General Earl Warren. Oh, and Wax, of course."

I whistled. "All interested in little me. Who'd 'a thunk it?"

"Look, I don't know much about this myself. They just gave me a message to pass on. In the building, they apparently think of me as your keeper."

"Do a British gentleman, a French lady and a fed the size of Mount Rush-more have anything to do with this?"

"I'll take the money I've won so far and you can pass that question on to the next sucker."

"Fine, Bernie. Tell me, just how popular am I?"

"Tojo rates worse than you, and maybe Judas Iscariot."

"Feels comfy. Any idea where Laird Brunette is these days?"

I heard a pause and some rumbling. Bernie was making sure his office was empty of all ears. I imagined him bringing the receiver up close and dropping his voice to a whisper.

"No one's seen him in three months. Confidentially, I don't miss him at all.

But there are others…" Bernie coughed, a door opened, and he started talking normally or louder. "…of course, honey, I'll be home in time for Jack Benny."

"See you later, sweetheart," I said, "your dinner is in the sink and I'm off to Tijuana with a professional pool player."

"Love you," he said, and hung up.

I'd picked up a coating of green slime on the soles of my shoes. I tried scraping them off on the edge of the desk and then used yesterday's *Times* to get the stuff off the desk. The gloop looked damned esoteric to me.

I poured myself a shot from the bottle I had picked up across the street and washed the taste of Janice Marsh off my teeth.

I thought of Polynesia in the early 19th Century and of those fish-eyed native girls clustering around Capt. Marsh. Somehow, tentacles kept getting in the way of my thoughts. In theory, the Capt. should have been an ideal subject for a Dorothy Lamour movie, perhaps with Janice Marsh in the role of her great-great-great and Jon Hall or Ray Milland as girl-chasing Obed. But I was picking up Bela Lugosi vibrations from the set-up. I couldn't help but think of bisected babies.

So far none of this running around had got me any closer to the Laird and his heir. In my mind, I drew up a list of Brunette's known associates. Then, I mentally crossed off all the ones who were dead. That brought me up short. When people in Brunette's business die, nobody really takes much notice except maybe to join in a few drunken choruses of "Ding-Dong, the Wicked Witch is Dead" before remembering there are plenty of other Wicked Witches in the sea. I'm just like everybody else: I don't keep a score of dead gambler-entrepreneurs. But, thinking of it, there'd been an awful lot recently, up to and including Gianni Pastore. Apart from Rothko and Isinglass, there'd been at least three other closed casket funerals in the profession. Obviously you couldn't blame that on the Japs. I wondered how many of the casualties had met their ends in bathtubs. The whole thing kept coming back to water. I decided I hated the stuff and swore not to let my bourbon get polluted with it.

Back out in the rain, I started hitting the bars. Brunette had a lot of friends. Maybe someone would know something.

By early evening, I'd propped up a succession of bars and leaned on a succession of losers. The only thing I'd come up with was the blatantly obvious information that everyone in town was scared. Most were wet, but all were scared.

Everyone was scared of two or three things at once. The Japs were high on everyone's list. You'd be surprised to discover the number of shaky citizens who'd turned overnight from chisellers who'd barely recognise the flag into true red, white and blue patriots prepared to shed their last drop of alcoholic blood for their country. Everywhere you went, someone sounded off against Hirohito, Tojo, the Mikado, *kabuki* and *origami*. The current rash of accidental deaths in the Pastore-Brunette circle were a much less popular subject for discussion and tended to turn loudmouths into closemouths at the drop of a question.

"Something fishy," everyone said, before changing the subject.

I was beginning to wonder whether Janey Wilde wouldn't have done better spending her money on a radio commercial asking the Laird to give her a call. Then I found Curtis the Croupier in Maxie's. He usually wore the full soup and fish, as if borrowed from Astaire. Now he'd exchanged his carnation, starched shirtfront and pop-up top hat for an outfit in olive drab with bars on the shoulder and a cap under one epaulette.

"Heard the bugle call, Curtis?" I asked, pushing through a crowd of patriotic admirers who had been buying the soldier boy drinks.

Curtis grinned before he recognised me, then produced a supercilious sneer. We'd met before, on the *Montecito*. There was a rumour going around that during Prohibition he'd once got involved in an honest card game, but if pressed he'd energetically refute it.

"Hey cheapie," he said.

I bought myself a drink but didn't offer him one. He had three or four lined up.

"This racket must pay," I said. "How much did the uniform cost? You rent it from Paramount?"

The croupier was offended. "It's real," he said. "I've enlisted. I hope to be sent overseas."

"Yeah, we ought to parachute you into Tokyo to introduce loaded dice and rickety roulette wheels."

"You're cynical, cheapie." He tossed back a drink.

"No, just a realist. How come you quit the *Monty*?"

"Poking around in the Laird's business?"

I raised my shoulders and dropped them again.

"Gambling has fallen off recently, along with leading figures in the industry. The original owner of this place, for instance. I bet paying for wreaths has thinned your bankroll."

Curtis took two more drinks, quickly, and called for more. When I'd come in, there'd been a couple of chippies climbing into his hip pockets. Now he was on his own with me. He didn't appreciate the change of scenery and I can't say I blamed him.

"Look, cheapie," he said, his voice suddenly low, "for your own good, just drop it. There are more important things now."

"Like democracy?"

"You can call it that."

"How far overseas do you want to be sent, Curtis?"

He looked at the door as if expecting five guys with tommy guns to come out of the rain for him. Then he gripped the bar to stop his hands shaking.

"As far as I can get, cheapie. The Philippines, Europe, Australia. I don't care."

"Going to war is a hell of a way to escape."

"Isn't it just? But wouldn't Papa Gianni have been safer on Wake Island than in the tub?"

"You heard the bathtime story, then?"

Curtis nodded and took another gulp. The juke box played "Doodly-Acky-Sacky, Want Some Seafood, Mama" and it was scary. Nonsense, but scary.

"They all die in water. That's what I've heard. Sometimes, on the *Monty*, Laird would go up on deck and just look at the sea for hours. He was crazy, since he took up with that Marsh popsicle."

"The Panther Princess?"

"You saw that one? Yeah, Janice Marsh. Pretty girl if you like clams. Laird claimed there was a sunken town in the bay. He used a lot of weird words, dar-kie bop or something. Jitterbug stuff. Cthul-whatever, Yog-Gimme-a-Break. He said things were going to come out of the water and sweep over the land, and he didn't mean U-Boats."

Curtis was uncomfortable in his uniform. There were dark patches where the rain had soaked. He'd been drinking like W.C. Fields on a bender but he wasn't getting tight. Whatever was troubling him was too much even for Jack Daniel's.

I thought of the Laird of the *Monty*. And I thought of the painting of Capt. Marsh's clipper, with that out-of-proportion squid surfacing near it.

"He's on the boat, isn't he?"

Curtis didn't say anything.

"Alone," I thought aloud. "He's out there alone."

I pushed my hat to the back of my head and tried to shake booze out of my mind. It was crazy. Nobody bobs up and down in the water with a sign round their neck saying "Hey Tojo, Torpedo Me!" The *Monty* was a floating target.

"No," Curtis said, grabbing my arm, jarring drink out of my glass.

"He's not out there?"

He shook his head.

"No, cheapie. He's not out there alone."

All the water taxis were in dock, securely moored and covered until the storms settled. I'd never find a boatman to take me out to the *Montecito* tonight.

Why, everyone knew the waters were infested with Japanese subs. But I knew someone who wouldn't care any more whether or not his boats were being treated properly. He was even past bothering if they were borrowed without his permission.

The Seaview Inn was still deserted, although there were police notices warning people away from the scene of the crime. It was dark, cold and wet, and nobody bothered me as I broke into the boathouse to find a ring of keys.

I took my pick of the taxis moored to the Seaview's jetty and gassed her up for a short voyage. I also got my .38 Colt Super Match out from the glove compartment of the Chrysler and slung it under my armpit. During all this, I got a thorough soaking and picked up the beginnings of influenza. I hoped Jungle Jillian would appreciate the effort.

The sea was swelling under the launch and making a lot of noise. I was grateful for the noise when it came to shooting the padlock off the mooring chain but the swell soon had my stomach sloshing about in my lower abdomen. I am not an especially competent seaman.

The *Monty* was out there on the horizon, still visible whenever the lightning lanced. It was hardly difficult to keep the small boat aimed at the bigger one.

Getting out on the water makes you feel small. Especially when the lights of Bay City are just a scatter in the dark behind you. I got the impression of large things moving just beyond my field of perception. The chill soaked through my clothes. My hat was a felt sponge, dripping down my neck. As the launch cut towards the *Monty*, rain and spray needled my face. I saw my hands white and bath-wrinkled on the wheel and wished I'd brought a bottle. Come to that, I wished I was at home in bed with a mug of cocoa and Claudette Colbert. Some things in life don't turn out the way you plan.

Three miles out, I felt the law change in my stomach. Gambling was legal and I emptied my belly over the side into the water. I stared at the remains of my toasted cheese sandwich as they floated off. I thought I saw the moon reflected greenly in the depths, but there was no moon that night.

I killed the engine and let waves wash the taxi against the side of the *Monty*. The small boat scraped along the hull of the gambling ship and I caught hold of a weed-furred rope ladder as it passed. I tethered the taxi and took a deep breath.

The ship sat low in the water, as if its lower cabins were flooded. Too much seaweed climbed up towards the decks. It'd never reopen for business, even if the War were over tomorrow.

I climbed the ladder, fighting the water-weight in my clothes, and heaved myself up on deck. It was good to have something more solid than a tiny boat under me but the deck pitched like an airplane wing. I grabbed a rail and hoped my internal organs would arrange themselves back into their familiar grouping.

"Brunette," I shouted, my voice lost in the wind.

There was nothing. I'd have to go belowdecks.

A sheet flying flags of all nations had come loose, and was whipped around with the storm. Japan, Italy and Germany were still tactlessly represented, along with several European states that weren't really nations any more. The deck was covered in familiar slime.

I made my way around towards the ballroom doors. They'd blown in and rain splattered against the polished wood floors. I got inside and pulled the .38. It felt better in my hand than digging into my ribs.

Lightning struck nearby and I got a flash image of the abandoned ballroom, orchestra stands at one end painted with the name of a disbanded combo.

The casino was one deck down. It should be dark but I saw a glow under a walkway door. I pushed through and cautiously descended. It wasn't wet here but it was cold. The fish smell was strong.

"Brunette," I shouted again.

I imagined something heavy shuffling nearby and slipped a few steps, banging my hip and arm against a bolted-down table. I kept hold of my gun, but only through superhuman strength.

The ship wasn't deserted. That much was obvious.

I could hear music. It wasn't Cab Calloway or Benny Goodman. There was a Hawaiian guitar in there but mainly it was a crazy choir of keening voices. I wasn't convinced the performers were human and wondered whether Brunette was working up some kind of act with singing seals. I couldn't make out the words but the familiar hawk-and-spit syllables of "Cthulhu" cropped up a couple of times.

I wanted to get out and go back to nasty Bay City and forget all about this. But Jungle Jillian was counting on me.

I made my way along the passage, working towards the music. A hand fell on my shoulder and my heart banged against the backsides of my eyeballs.

A twisted face stared at me out of the gloom, thickly-bearded, crater-cheeked. Laird Brunette was made up as Ben Gunn, skin shrunk onto his skull, eyes large as hen's eggs.

His hand went over my mouth.

"Do Not Disturb," he said, voice high and cracked.

This wasn't the suave criminal I knew, the man with tartan cummerbunds and patent leather hair. This was some other Brunette, in the grips of a tough bout with dope or madness.

"The Deep Ones," he said.

He let me go and I backed away.

"It is the time of the Surfacing."

My case was over. I knew where the Laird was. All I had to do was tell Janey Wilde and give her her refund.

"There's very little time."

The music was louder. I heard a great number of bodies shuffling around in the casino. They couldn't have been very agile, because they kept clumping into things and each other.

"They must be stopped. Dynamite, depth charges, torpedoes..."

"Who?" I asked. "The Japs?"

"The Deep Ones. The Dwellers in the Sister City."

He had lost me.

A nasty thought occurred to me. As a detective, I can't avoid making deductions. There were obviously a lot of people aboard the *Monty*, but mine was the only small boat in evidence. How had everyone else got out here? Surely they couldn't have swam?

"It's a war," Brunette ranted, "us and them. It's always been a war."

I made a decision. I'd get the Laird off his boat and turn him over to Jungle Jillian. She could sort things out with the Panther Princess and her Esoteric Order. In his current state, Brunette would hand over any baby if you gave him a blanket.

I took Brunette's thin wrist and tugged him towards the staircase. But a hatch clanged down and I knew we were stuck.

A door opened and perfume drifted through the fish stink.

"Mr. Lovecraft, wasn't it?" a silk-scaled voice said.

Janice Marsh was wearing pendant squid earrings and a lady-sized gun. And nothing else.

That wasn't quite as nice as it sounds. The Panther Princess had no nipples, no navel and no pubic hair. She was lightly scaled between the legs and her wet skin shone like a shark's. I imagined that if you stroked her, your palm would come away bloody. She was wearing neither the turban she'd affected earlier nor the dark wig of her pictures. Her head was completely bald, skull swelling unnaturally. She didn't even have her eyebrows pencilled in.

"You evidently can't take good advice."

As mermaids go, she was scarier than cute. In the crook of her left arm, she held a bundle from which a white baby face peered with unblinking eyes. Franklin looked more like Janice Marsh than his parents.

"A pity, really," said a tiny ventriloquist voice through Franklin's mouth, "but there are always complications."

Brunette gibbered with fear, chewing his beard and huddling against me.

Janice Marsh set Franklin down and he sat up, an adult struggling with a baby's body.

"The Cap'n has come back," she explained.

"Every generation must have a Cap'n," said the thing in Franklin's mind. Dribble got in the way and he wiped his angel-mouth with a fold of swaddle.

Janice Marsh clucked and pulled Laird away from me, stroking his face.

"Poor dear," she said, flicking his chin with a long tongue. "He got out of his depth."

She put her hands either side of Brunette's head, pressing the butt of her gun into his cheek.

"He was talking about a Sister City," I prompted.

She twisted the gambler's head around and dropped him on the floor. His tongue poked out and his eyes showed only white.

"Of course," the baby said. "The Cap'n founded two settlements. One beyond Devil Reef, off Massachusetts. And one here, under the sands of the Bay."

We both had guns. I'd let her kill Brunette without trying to shoot her. It was the detective's fatal flaw, curiosity. Besides, the Laird was dead inside his head long before Janice snapped his neck.

"You can still join us," she said, hips working like a snake in time to the chanting. "There are raptures in the deeps."

"Sister," I said, "you're not my type."

Her nostrils flared in anger and slits opened in her neck, flashing liverish red lines in her white skin.

Her gun was pointed at me, safety off. Her long nails were lacquered green.

I thought I could shoot her before she shot me. But I didn't. Something about a naked woman, no matter how strange, prevents you from killing them. Her whole body was moving with the music. I'd been wrong. Despite everything, she was beautiful.

I put my gun down and waited for her to murder me. It never happened.

I don't really know the order things worked out. But first there was lightning, then, an instant later, thunder.

Light filled the passageway, hurting my eyes. Then, a rumble of noise which grew in a crescendo. The chanting was drowned.

Through the thunder cut a screech. It was a baby's cry. Franklin's eyes were screwed up and he was shrieking. I had a sense of the Cap'n drowning in the baby's mind, his purchase on the purloined body relaxing as the child cried out.

The floor beneath me shook and buckled and I heard a great straining of abused metal. A belch of hot wind surrounded me. A hole appeared. Janice Marsh moved fast and I think she fired her gun, but whether at me on purpose or at random in reflex I couldn't say. Her body sliced towards me and I ducked.

There was another explosion, not of thunder, and thick smoke billowed through a rupture in the floor. I was on the floor, hugging the tilting deck. Franklin slid towards me and bumped, screaming, into my head. A half-ton of water fell on us and I knew the ship was breached. My guess was that the Japs had just saved my life with a torpedo. I was waist deep in saltwater. Janice Marsh darted away in a sinuous fish motion.

Then there were heavy bodies around me, pushing me against a bulkhead. In the darkness, I was scraped by something heavy, cold-skinned and foul-smelling. There were barks and cries, some of which might have come from human throats.

Fires went out and hissed as the water rose. I had Franklin in my hands and tried to hold him above water. I remembered the peril of Jungle Jillian again and found my head floating against the hard ceiling.

The Cap'n cursed in vivid 18th Century language, Franklin's little body squirming in my grasp. A toothless mouth tried to get a biter's grip on my chin but slipped off. My feet slid and I was off-balance, pulling the baby briefly underwater. I saw his startled eyes through a wobbling film. When I pulled him out again, the Cap'n was gone and Franklin was screaming on his own. Taking a double gulp of air, I plunged under the water and struggled towards the nearest door, a hand closed over the baby's face to keep water out of his mouth and nose.

The *Montecito* was going down fast enough to suggest there were plenty of holes in it. I had to make it a priority to find one. I jammed my knee at a door and it flew open. I was poured, along with several hundred gallons of water, into a large room full of stored gambling equipment. Red and white chips floated like confetti.

I got my footing and waded towards a ladder. Something large reared out of the water and shambled at me, screeching like a seabird. I didn't get a good look at it. Which was a mercy. Heavy arms lashed me, flopping boneless against my face. With my free hand, I pushed back at the thing, fingers slipping against cold slime. Whatever it was was in a panic and squashed through the door.

There was another explosion and everything shook. Water splashed upwards and I fell over. I got upright and managed to get a one-handed grip on the ladder. Franklin was still struggling and bawling, which I took to be a good sign. Somewhere near, there was a lot of shouting.

I dragged us up rung by rung and slammed my head against a hatch. If it had been battened, I'd have smashed my skull and spilled my brains. It flipped upwards and a push of water from below shoved us through the hole like a ping-pong ball in a fountain.

The *Monty* was on fire and there were things in the water around it. I heard the drone of airplane engines and glimpsed nearby launches. Gunfire fought with the wind. It was a full-scale attack. I made it to the deck-rail and saw a boat fifty feet away. Men in yellow slickers angled tommy guns down and sprayed the water with bullets.

The gunfire whipped up the sea into a foam. Kicking things died in the water. Someone brought up his gun and fired at me. I pushed myself aside, arching my body over Franklin and bullets spanged against the deck.

My borrowed taxi must have been dragged under by the bulk of the ship.

There were definitely lights in the sea. And the sky. Over the city, in the distance, I saw firecracker bursts. Something exploded a hundred yards away and a tower of water rose, bursting like a puffball. A depth charge.

The deck was angled down and water was creeping up at us. I held on to a rope webbing, wondering whether the gambling ship still had any lifeboats. Franklin spluttered and bawled.

A white body slid by, heading for the water. I instinctively grabbed at it. Hands took hold of me and I was looking into Janice Marsh's face. Her eyes blinked, membranes coming round from the sides, and she kissed me again. Her long tongue probed my mouth like an eel, then withdrew. She stood up, one leg bent so she was still vertical on the sloping deck. She drew air into her lungs—if she had lungs—and expelled it through her gills with a musical cry. She was slim and white in the darkness, water running off her body. Someone fired in her direction and she dived into the waves, knifing through the surface and disappearing towards the submarine lights. Bullets rippled the spot where she'd gone under.

I let go of the ropes and kicked at the deck, pushing myself away from the sinking ship. I held Franklin above the water and splashed with my legs and elbows. The *Monty* was dragging a lot of things under with it, and I fought against the pull so I wouldn't be one of them. My shoulders ached and my clothes got in the way, but I kicked against the current.

The ship went down screaming, a chorus of bending steel and dying creatures. I had to make for a launch and hope not to be shot. I was lucky. Someone got a polehook into my jacket and landed us like fish. I lay on the deck, water running out of my clothes, swallowing as much air as I could breathe.

I heard Franklin yelling. His lungs were still in working order.

Someone big in a voluminous slicker, a sou'wester tied to his head, knelt by me, and slapped me in the face.

"Peeper," he said.

"They're calling it the Great Los Angeles Air Raid," Winthrop told me as he poured a mug of British tea. "Some time last night a panic started, and everyone in Bay City shot at the sky for hours."

"The Japs?" I said, taking a mouthful of welcome hot liquid.

"In theory. Actually, I doubt it. It'll be recorded as a fiasco, a lot of jumpy characters with guns. While it was all going on, we engaged the enemy and emerged victorious."

He was still dressed up for an embassy ball and didn't look as if he'd been on deck all evening. Geneviève Dieudonné wore a fisherman's sweater and fatigue pants, her hair up in a scarf. She was looking at a lot of sounding equipment and noting down readings.

"You're not fighting the Japs, are you?"

Winthrop pursed his lips. "An older war, my friend. We can't be distracted. After last night's action, our Deep Ones won't poke their scaly noses out for a while. Now I can do something to lick Hitler."

"What really happened?"

"There was something dangerous in the sea, under Mr. Brunette's boat. We have destroyed it and routed the ... uh, the hostile forces. They wanted the boat as a surface station. That's why Mr. Brunette's associates were eliminated."

Geneviève gave a report in French, so fast that I couldn't follow.

"Total destruction," Winthrop explained, "a dreadful set-back for them. It'll put them in their place for years. Forever would be too much to hope for, but a few years will help."

I lay back on the bunk, feeling my wounds. Already choking on phlegm, I would be lucky to escape pneumonia.

"And the little fellow is a decided dividend."

Finlay glumly poked around, suggesting another dose of depth charges. He was cradling a mercifully sleep-struck Franklin, but didn't look terribly maternal.

"He seems quite unaffected by it all."

"His name is Franklin," I told Winthrop. "On the boat, he was..."

"Not himself? I'm familiar with the condition. It's a filthy business, you understand."

"He'll be all right," Geneviève put in.

I wasn't sure whether the rest of the slicker crew were feds or servicemen and I wasn't sure whether I wanted to know. I could tell a Clandestine Operation when I landed in the middle of one.

"Who knows about this?" I asked. "Hoover? Roosevelt?"

Winthrop didn't answer.

"Someone must know," I said.

"Yes," the Englishman said, "someone must. But this is a war the public would never believe exists. In the Bureau, Finlay's outfit are known as 'the Unnameables', never mentioned by the press, never honoured or censured by the government, victories and defeats never recorded in the official history."

The launch shifted with the waves, and I hugged myself, hoping for some warmth to creep over me. Finlay had promised to break out a bottle later but that made me resolve to stick to tea as a point of honour. I hated to fulfil his expectations.

"And America is a young country," Winthrop explained. "In Europe, we've known things a lot longer."

On shore, I'd have to tell Janey Wilde about Brunette and hand over Franklin. Some flack at Metro would be thinking of an excuse for the Panther Princess's disappearance. Everything else—the depth charges, the sea battle, the sinking ship—would be swallowed up by the War.

All that would be left would be tales. Weird tales.

Rapture of the Deep

Cody Goodfellow

The old man tried to walk on his own as they lifted him off the chopper. They let him fall on his face, then lifted him off the helipad deck by his handcuffed wrists and drove him up the catwalk.

His mangled nose spewed blood over his mustachioed mouth, glazed eyes rolled back in his bald, heavily sedated head, but the image he sent her almost blinded her with its intensity. She shivered as the brilliant sunny day and the endless ocean vanished behind a wave of frigid white mind-noise.

Cold.

White cold. Snow flurries. Cold white and hot red splashing from his frostbitten hand, as he tries to get his black severed fingers from the wolves that haunt the perimeter of the gulag. The laughing guards, the long red wolf-tongues panting behind clouds of breath-mist…

And then… blackness. Total and crushing darkness. Buried alive under five miles of bone-chilling cold, sunless ocean.

She gagged on the flood of phantom sensation and clung to the railing as they carried him out of sight.

The message was clear. Their cruelty was amateurish, next to that of his old masters. An unaccustomed treat they would gorge themselves on until it made them sick.

He told her even more by assaulting her so, even as they led him down below the waterline, to the interrogation cells. He was more powerful than even his old Soviet handlers had known… but maybe he could only do it when they hurt him.

Beside her, Roger Mankiw shook the crushed ice in his mojito and turned to look at her through green lenses. "You're afraid of him, Ingrid?"

Not half as afraid of him as you should be of me, she thought back, and he might have tasted the sting of it, even he, her skeptical boss. His reedy neck straightened. The sweat rings on his linen shirt deepened. "He's capable, but he's a coward," she told him. "He's afraid of something he saw down there."

"He led us a merry chase, you know. Two contractors topped, untold collateral damage over there. Thailand's off-limits, now. Our legal eagles are triple-billing us for—"

"Three."

"Pardon?"

"A contractor jumped out of the chopper, a half hour out. Pulled his grenade pins and jumped. Sergei touched him, they say. Just once."

He didn't ask her how she knew. "Christ!" He tossed his drink over the side. The glass shattered on the lower railings of the research ship and dimpled the heaving sea. Some lucky fish got the bits of mint and ice. Some luckier fish in the indigo deeps far below would get the ones who ate the glass.

"I never signed on for any of this *One Step Beyond* shit," Mankiw growled. "The data shows a steady warming trend with trace radioactivity that's sweeping the whole South Pacific starting right here, but I'd just as soon keep tossing five million-dollar drone submersibles into the breach, until the head office wises up and drops this entire idiotic venture."

Easy for him to say. He was vested, and would fail up the ladder to a corner office in Hong Kong. She would sink like a stone. "Roger, pressing with that kind of urgency sends the wrong message. Sergei will read it as weakness—"

"Then show none. If you don't get anything out of him now, I for one will go to the mat for you. But if he doesn't produce immediately, no more games. No more threats. One way or the other, he's going to the bottom of the Marianas Trench. Today."

❧

She waited until he was lucid and beginning to show visible discomfort before she entered his cell. "Perhaps now, Sergei Vasilievich, you will take us a bit more seriously."

"This is why you did this? So I would respect you? I know a thing or two about torture. You could have asked me for advice…"

"We don't do torture, Sergei. We do negotiation. Nobody forced you to take our money. We only want what we paid for."

A fat girl, gobbling sweets and cake under a table at a wedding reception.

Sergei Lyubyenko reclined as much as his shackles and the bolted-down steel chair allowed, and slid his mangled, three-fingered hand out of its cuff. He flashed his sly, sorry grin, as if they'd both tried to flee, as if they'd been caught together, and would both be punished.

A gray-faced mastiff rolls in a laboratory cage, licking his prodigious cock and balls.

"I need your goodwill like my asshole needs a tongue," he finally replied. "I told you where to find the *Rybinsk* in less than an hour. I assumed our business was concluded. Was I wrong?"

The dog again, now busily devouring its own hind legs.

Ingrid pinched the bridge of her nose. She could smell the dog with the clarity of memory. "You described something else you saw while under hypnosis..."

"Remote viewing is not hypnosis, but no matter. You got what you paid for. The *Rybinsk* is unrecoverable, yes? But you know exactly where she is. Now, I believe when I came in, I had a hat..."

"We paid you to remote view the wreck, but also the source of the unusual radiation signatures, and to find out what happened to the *Nereid* and *Triton 3* submersibles."

Sergei produced a pouch from his breast pocket and, using only one hand and his agile lips, rolled a scrawny cigarette. "You rose to this job not just for your good looks, yes? You are a sensitive, but your talents are unformed. They have never been *pushed*..." He waggled the cigarette at her. She lit it, hand shaky, flinching when he almost touched her.

"Sergei, my superiors are very disappointed in you and, to put it frankly, they're also highly dubious of your alleged abilities."

He smiled and shrugged. *President Nixon hunches over on the toilet aboard Air Force One, masturbating grimly into a Sears catalog.*

"Maybe you think that because you survived the KGB treatment, you're invincible and answerable to no one. But we are not a government. This is not a country. This is a private ship in international waters, over the deepest hole in the earth. And my superiors in Hong Kong, Moscow and San Francisco may deal in shit most of them don't believe in, but they expect results. Whatever you think you've endured before, I can guarantee you it's nothing compared to what'll happen to you, if you don't show us what we want to know."

Sergei yawned, exposing yellow but sturdy, straight teeth. "Do you know where I was going? I stopped in Bangkok, who would not, but I was going back to Russia. If you truly know anything about me, think about that."

She nodded. When Sergei slipped the KGB and defected, they arrested his wife and two sons. Somewhere in that dizzying succession of Premiers in the late 80's, all of them were executed. They did this to make him come out to the South Pacific to view something they called Opaque Zone 38a, so they could drop a tactical nuclear weapon on it.

"Moscow is worse than ever, but is five time zones from nearest water." He sighed and rolled another smoke. "You were a very fat girl, when young, yes, Ingrid? Nobody liked you or understood, but is clear to me."

"This is not getting us any closer to our objective, Sergei."

"You were not just piggy little girl, no. You thought if you ate faster, if you ate everything, you would grow up faster, not so? But you only grew fat."

Ingrid declined to play his game.

"It must eat at you, no?" he pressed. "To be unable to do this, yourself. Such a fool, you actually want to do it, don't you?"

Her doctorate was in psychology, but her training as a remote observer required intense concentration on a host vector—the pair of eyes through which she would see whatever her handlers set as her objective. Her success rate was near perfect, with targets she'd slept with.

Sergei was more properly classified as a projector. He could leave his body and roam freely on what mediums used to call the astral plane or the aether. He needed no prior contact with the target, nothing but a cigarette and his preposterous fee. His hit rate was legendary, before Opaque Zone 38a drove him insane.

He killed the cigarette and gestured for another. In the past, he would go into his trance after taking his first drag, and rest his hand on the table before him with the lit cigarette gnawing away at the stained paper. In about seven minutes, the cigarette burned his fingers, and jolted him awake. Back into his body.

She reached out with her Bic disposable lighter and lit the shaking cigarette. He took one hit off it and held the smoke in until the burst capillaries on his nose and cheeks flared deep violet. His frosty blue eyes sparkled at her, then went vague and rolled back under drooping lids.

Ingrid reached out and took the cigarette from his unfeeling fingers, stubbed it out on the table.

Now, they would get to the bottom of this. He would not come back without answers.

His three-fingered hand shot out and seized her arm, pulling her across the table towards his empty face. His other arm snaked around her neck to cradle her head, and somehow, she was powerless to push back or strike him.

When her body fell across the table and settled against Sergei, Ingrid was not inside it.

‌‌‍❧

Everything goes blue.

A blue so pure and bright, she thinks, *he's taken my sight, I'm blind.*

Blue deepened to indigo as she began to understand that she was seeing all there was to see. When confronted by a featureless color field, the human eye tends to fill the void with visual hallucinations—the *ganzfeld* effect—but no optical illusions rose up out of the darkening blue, leaving her to conclude that she was not viewing this with her eyes.

Let us go and see, Sergei whispered, *let us go together.* She did not hear him or feel him—or anything else—but he was there. The only sensation she felt was a tugging that echoed his gnarled, nicotine-stained grip on her wrist, dragging her inexorably down into the void.

One time on assignment in Thailand, Ingrid got so stoned on opium that she felt like she tumbled up out of her body. She saw her empty vessel on the silk pallet, drooling as the boy loaded another bolus of tarry resin into her bowl, and then the jumbled rooftops and skeins of wires and cables connecting every synapse of the city, and she was terrified beyond anything she ever experienced before. She fought a raging riptide that tried to pull her up into the smoggy sky, battled back to her body to find herself shivering in a pool of cold urine as the boy and his family went through her pockets.

Sergei chuckled at her panic, and offered her a body.

Through a pair of dead black eyes that perceived the ocean as layers of heat and gradients of food trails, she watched the light fail and felt the pressure build as their perfect cruise missile dove beyond the reach of the sun.

The rude nub of brain that housed them both was little more than a binary box flashing *eat/don't eat* as it scented trails of organic waste streaming away from the research ship.

You could learn to love life as a shark, I think, he thought at her. *I could leave you here—*

Sergei trampled the mako shark's hardwired instincts and drove it to descend ever deeper. The indigo zone gave way to a blue-black twilight, broken by the murky horizon of the ocean floor at the edge of the Marianas Trench. The sheer cliffs of slimy basalt tumbled away into perfect blackness.

The flow of water over their gills grew frigid and forced them back. Expelling the contents of its bowels and compressing its tissues with the agonizing relentlessness of a wringer, the shark struggled downward for another mile until the pressure crushed its cartilaginous skeleton.

Expelled out through the shark's collapsed eyes, she spilled helplessly down into almost total darkness that soon became a starry night sky filled with swooping, stalking, luminescent life.

An anglerfish drifted past, bloated black head bisected by a grin of needles painted eerie thallium green by the glow of its bobbing barbel lures. Other creatures she saw only by the fitful glow of their beguiling witch-lights, fluttering or skulking through the drifting sleet of organic debris from the surface.

Tiny jewels of glistering ectoplasm and endless garlands of stinging tendrils and greedy gullets seemed to pulsate with arousal at the passage of their bodiless ghosts, but the predators' attentions were diverted by the rich feast of the imploded shark's carcass that came tumbling after them.

It abruptly dawned upon her that, as a mote of pure intelligence, her senses were limited solely by her will. Whatever caught her mind's eye seemed to magnify itself until it loomed over her bodiless mind or engulfed her whole. And yet she was drawn inexorably downward, into zones of pure darkness and paralyzing cold, by the invisible grip of the mad Russian psychic.

Falling, flowing through the inky void, she still felt some inkling of the mounting pressure above them. Water is a thousand times denser than air, yet seawater is only one tenth as dense as lead. The pressure at their destination would exceed six tons per square inch. Exposed to this environment, her physical body would implode long before it could drown.

Ingrid was not claustrophobic, and as her instinctual fears for her body receded, she began to feel a kind of creeping exhilaration, the euphoria that submariners called the rapture of the deep. No human had ever been where they were going. No one had ever seen what they were going to see. Not like this.

The last fleeting traces of glowing marine life faded away far above, and the blackness again became absolute. Only by painful degrees did her mind begin to discern the deeper contours of tortured stone, little more solid than the water laying heavy upon them.

They touched down before a cathedral of bones—the skeleton of a whale, trailing tattered banners of putrefied blubber to feed swarms of gulper eels and dragonfish. Swarms of giant brittle stars squirmed and spawned in the calcareous ooze that coated the ocean floor.

How deep? she asked.

This is the bottom of your bottomless pit. We are nearly five miles beneath the surface. You are only a breath away from your body, but the mind plays tricks, yes? To return so quickly would kill us both.

Floating over a plain of basalt slabs fragmented into disturbingly tessellated geometrical patterns, they approached a towering column like a skyscraper volcano, easily twelve stories high.

Festooned with giant tubeworms and anemones that twisted in the gelid gloom to bask in the torrent of superheated water and clouds of molten minerals that gushed from its peak.

Swarms of enormous shrimp sported on the corona of the boiling outflow, only to be ensnared and devoured by monstrous arachnids, which farmed globules of cooling heavy metals, and bore them off across the plain, like leaf cutter ants harvesting fungi from carrion.

And beyond the chimney lay more chimneys, and larger ones. Hundreds of them, in a uniform field. A farm.

This was what they had really been sent to find, though Ingrid knew the company would lie to her as blithely as they'd deceived Sergei. The energy wasted here could power a city, if only they could harness it.

Beyond the last chimney, the plain was broken by dozens of octagonal pits, each hundreds of yards across, and seemingly bottomless. But as she reluctantly floated over them, Ingrid perceived honeycombs of wormholes in the walls. Their hypnotic complexity suggested that they were inhabited by something utterly alien, yet older—and perhaps wiser—than humankind.

They live, Ingrid railed, *and they're still active, the ones you supposedly exterminated at Opaque Zone 38a?*

Men try to steal the power from their enemies by numbering them. Call it what it was, and what it will be again—R'lyeh.

Something gleamed in the nearest pit, and she warily reached down to focus on it. Massive metal hulks hung suspended over the void—the missing company submersibles, and the sunken Soviet sub. All were badly crushed, but also dismantled. *Rybinsk's* empty nuclear missile silos gaped like the holes in a toothless jaw.

The Russians said they destroyed them all, Ingrid railed.

Destroyed them! Girl, even if you could believe a Russian, never suppose that they can be destroyed. This is their world. We live in it only so long as they sleep.

Beyond the wells lay a vast plain of fluted lava spires and craters that might have covered a mile. They sped over it to stop suddenly at a gaping, glowing rift in the abyssal plain, which seemed to hold the sun in it.

No, my dear. All we did was wake them up...

Tornadoes of heavy black smoke roared up out of the spreading rift in the floor of the trench, which seemed far too hot for even the best-adapted inhabitants of the ocean floor. Slurping waves of fresh magma oozed up over the lips of the rift, melting the crust of Archaean basalt and remaking the earth's crust at the rate of a flood engulfing a levee.

This isn't natural, is it?

Everything is natural, you fool. Watch...

Something splashed in the white lava flow, lurched up out of the molten stone and thrust a net of barbed tentacles after her. She almost felt their razored heat, until she was chilled by Sergei's intangible laughter.

It was at least as large as the biggest submersible in the company fleet, and resembled a fusion of trilobite and salamander with snarls of segmented tentacles for a head, but only the merest portion of it emerged from the rock-river before it sank again.

This is retaliation for what you did, twenty years ago.

What we did, all those years ago, was done with your country's secret blessing. It was perhaps Soviet Russia's first and last true selfless act for the good of the world. To end the nightmares, yes? Or perhaps it was not so pure... Moscow could not imagine a world without itself at the helm. Perhaps they meant to rid the world of its nightmares by awakening the sleeper who sent them.

But it mattered not. The bomb hit its target, and the mission was a success, yes? And yet the one they sought to slay, they did not even disturb his sleep. His children... they are awake again, but they would not trifle in revenge upon insects.

Away across the plain they flew, to the red mouth of the lava river. A glowing seam of fresh faultline sprouted from it and arrowed away across the plain. The cracked earth subsided like a misfit jigsaw puzzle, and eager gouts of magma bubbled up between the jagged edges.

At last, they came upon a mountain that crawled across the murky plain, gouging open the earth's brittle crust with thousands of armored claws like steamshovels. Pitted with age and clotted with colorless, glowing coral reefs, infested by clouds of submarine parasites, its colossal, chitinous shell hid all but the countless antennae and eyestalks that emerged from seams, fissures and faults in the cyclopean exoskeleton.

The size of a city, the creature yet bore some kinship with the lava-borne larvae. In its wake, the mountainous isopod left glowing opals which bored into the splintered earth like depth charges, like the treasures carelessly spilled by a god, or the eggs sown by a devil.

There are no gods, as you mean it, Sergei interrupted. *There are those who dwell outside, and who neither live nor die, as we know of life and death. They answer prayers, but only when offered in blood and geometry, and their miracles...*

But if they're not gods, then they can be stopped.

Stopped! This is their world. It always was, and will be again. They do not seek our extinction, but only to hasten the day when the world will be ripe for their dominion, and His awakening. They redraw the faultlines of the ocean floor to drive the continents back beneath the waves, and raise the Pacific seamounts to the sky, as it was when they came down from the stars.

But it's not their world, it's ours! We'll destroy them, or send them back where they came from—

If you could but see them, you would know how insane that is. And why should you care? In two thousand years, their plans will bear fruit. In two hundred years, the ice caps will melt, the ocean will rise and drown all human cities, anyway. But this is not their concern—

Ingrid ripped free of Sergei and fled away across the shattered abyssal plain, back to the bottomless pits. Diving into an octagonal well, she made her focus into a sword that slashed at the darkness. Before she could find anything upon which to practice her attack, something found her, and seized her in talons of icy, paralyzing pain.

A gargantuan humanoid form reached up out of the pit with mammoth forelimbs cloaked in crawling, viscous flesh, and unfurled vast black wings or outsized dorsal fins that effortlessly beat back the lead-dense water.

Trapped and suddenly feeling as corporeal as she was helpless, she cried out.

Sergei answered, instantly beside her as always, yet even he trembled in fear before her captor. *See!* he raved. *Behold what we hoped to destroy, and what you hope to plunder, and what will bury us all!*

It stretched out to nearly fill the vast pit, yet only the roughest outline of its titanic form could be picked out of the darkness, for its body was festooned with crinoids, clams and tubeworm colonies. So glacially slow and deliberate were its movements, that life thrived on it undisturbed; and yet now, it flew faster than she could perceive to draw her bodiless ghost up to its inscrutable, luminous eyes.

A rugose, boneless sac bearded with restless coiling tentacles, the creature's head was an octopoid of obscenely magnified proportions. There was no escaping those clutching, prescient tentacles, or the piercing gaze of its hideously lambent eyes, which seemed to turn her mind inside out.

For all its awesome size and unfathomable intelligence, the godlike monster seemed to retreat into a fugue for an age of endless moments, until some decision was made.

What does it want? she demanded.

Suddenly, the colossal prodigy bombarded her with convoluted psychic hymns. It sang to her of One older and more terrible than all its kind beneath the sea, the One who slept until the world was perfect, and of the rapture of His imminent return.

I am most disturbed to report, Sergei numbly sent, *that it wishes to… what is your word…? Negotiate.*

What could such a creature want from her, that it could not simply take? Ingrid retreated into the innermost bolthole of herself and pulled the cerebral dirt in after her, but the psychic onslaught only redoubled as it sought to crush her with understanding.

What do they want?

They want to share their knowledge with the human race. For your benefit and theirs.

Why would they do this?

The power to harness the fire of the earth's core… they want you to have it. They have come to understand only dimly how quick, how fragile, is the human mind, but how devastating the effects of its tiny genius. In human hands, that power will hasten their ends a hundredfold.

But why? Who would have given them such an idea?

I believe you *did, my dear…*

Ingrid feigned shock and let herself seem dead, until the tentacles and talons relaxed their grip. She pulled away and forced herself to visualize her body, miles above her, lying prone on the table in the holding cell on the research ship.

She willed herself across that distance instantly, as she would will herself out of a nightmare. For in the end, that was all this was. Sergei was a master manipulator. Somehow, he got inside the minds of his mercenary captors and drove three of them to suicide. Surely, he was trying to do the same to her, but she was not so powerless.

She opened her eyes, and the cell, dingy and too brightly lit, surrounded her. Her body hung heavy from her exhausted mind, an exquisite assembly of dead weight that trembled when she sought to draw in a breath of fresh air.

Her hands lay on the table, trapped in the scarred, stained hands of Sergei Lyubyenko. His eyes floated up behind drooping lids, regarding her with empty, bloodshot orbs.

Her arms dangled from her shoulders like concrete counterweights with the cables cut. She struggled to make her body move, to sever the contact from her that seemed to hold her still, that yet trapped a part of her beneath the sea.

Abruptly, Sergei's eyes opened impossibly wide and stared at her. An eerie, yellow-green light kindled within them and ate through the cornea and iris, spreading until his slack, waxen face gleamed like a torch blazed within it.

"*I will negotiate with your masters now,*" he said, with no trace of an accent, no scintilla of humanity.

Ingrid fought to free herself. She raked his hands with her nails and hurled herself back in her chair to sprawl across the uncarpeted steel floor. Sergei made no move to pursue her, but repeated his demand in the same flat, untenanted tone, as he shuffled towards the door.

Ingrid had to stop him. She had to get to Mankiw first, and try to make him understand what they would be dealing with.

Her head boiled with the opening salvo of a five-alarm migraine. Her body resisted her best efforts to climb to her feet. The door swayed and rocked before her, but she was resolute, even if her body was not.

Blood dripped from both her nostrils, and her muscles began to ache, then to tear themselves apart. Her bowels and bladder explosively evacuated and swelling bubbles of pure agony erupted in her belly and chest and every muscle, in the marrow of her bones, and the pressurized cage of her skull.

She screamed, but she could hear only the teapot whistle of compressed gases pouring out of her burst eardrums, her tear ducts and sinuses, forcing its way out of her pores.

It made no difference that she had been sitting at the table with Sergei the entire time, or even if the entire jaunt was only a dream or a telepathic fantasy. *The mind plays tricks*, Sergei had said, and he was not lying.

The agony of explosive decompression swept aside all doubts and points of debate and devoured her whole. And still, she tried to stop them. Still, she tried to beat Sergei to the door.

She almost made it.

Her outstretched hands were blue-black with burst capillaries and liquefied muscle tissue. The steel mirror on the back of the sealed hatch showed her only a shapeless red collage, doubly filtered through the blood flooding her eyeballs. Her tongue swelled to fill her mouth and block her throat, but her brain exploded out her eye sockets before she could drown on the briny tide of her own fluids.

Ingrid flew away, taking the only escape left to her—out of her body and down into the dark to claim a sleek new body. And this time, she felt no fear, for she was going home.

"Once More, from the Top..."

A. Scott Glancy

"**T**his is the fourth time," the old man grumbled, shifting his gaze out the window to the sparsely planted grounds of the VA hospital. "How many more times do we have to go through this?"

"Just a couple more, Sergeant Hennessey," said Levine, stooping to plug the power cord into the cracked and yellowed wall socket. "Your memory being what it is, we need to go through this as many times as possible. You added some details the second and third times through. Maybe you'll remember something more this time." As Levine busied himself with the camera, his partner, Henry Parker, unpacked the files and laid them out on the card table in front of Sergeant Hennessey, like he was dealing out a game of solitaire.

Hennessey angrily gripped the arms of his wheelchair with trembling hands. "It's been seventy years! That's more years than the both of you and 'Sambo' stacked together. You can't know what it's like trying to remember that far back."

"You're right about that," Levine said as he laid his jacket over the back of a folding chair and loosened his tie. The staff kept the veterans' hospital uncomfortably warm. But, that's why people retire to Florida, Levine thought. To warm their bones. "Of course, some things are harder to forget than others."

"Seventy years," Hennessey sighed as he ran a gnarled hand over his snow-white hair. "Why the hell is the Navy interested again after seventy years?"

"They didn't tell us," Levine lied as he sighted the video camera on Hennessey and hit the record button. "'Need-to-know' means they don't need us to know." Levine checked to see that the camera was running and then took his seat across the table from Hennessey. "After a lifetime in the Marine Corps, you must've learned that if you're not cleared for the answer, don't ask the question."

"I suppose," Hennessey said, eyeing the pair of men as they settled into their seats and continued unpacking their files. Levine, the younger of the two, was thin, with glasses like an accountant and fingers like a pianist. As part of his cover, Levine had cut his hair to military regulation for this op, but he figured Hennessey could tell he wasn't really Navy. Levine was a civilian from his scuffed shoes to his J.C. Penney suit. Parker, on the other hand, was military to the bone, thick-featured and barrel-chested, his ebony scalp cleanly shaven, but nonetheless a "landlubber." If he was getting steamed about Hennessey calling him "Sambo," he wasn't showing it.

As he pulled out his notepad and pen, Levine could feel Hennessey dissecting them with his eyes, trying to figure out what they were really up to and who'd really sent them. Being kept in the dark was grating to Hennessey. Levine supposed it was almost ironic. Seventy years ago Hennessey and the rest of the 3rd Battalion walked into a small town in Massachusetts without a clue as to what they were facing. Somewhere up the chain of command somebody, probably someone who hadn't joined Hennessey and his fellow Marines on their little excursion, made the decision that the guys on the ground just weren't cleared to know what was going on. And here they were, seventy years later, debriefing Hennessey about a mission he never learned the particulars about and lying to him about who was asking the questions. The more things change, the more they remain the same.

Of course, thought Levine, if those men had told the truth, told Hennessey and the other Marines what was waiting in those rotting piles of moldy stone, he never would have believed them. But if he had…if he had believed the unbelievable, he would have deserted before ever setting foot in Innsmouth. Levine wondered what Hennessey would do if he knew the truth about why he and Parker were there.

"So? Ready to begin?" Levine asked without much enthusiasm.

"Ready?" Hennessey spit back. "Ready to dredge up the worst fucking night of my entire life? Ready to get the shakes and not be able to keep down the swill they serve here or even close my eyes all night 'cuz if I do I'll be right back there in the middle of it all killing those things in the snow?" Hennessey tried his best to rivet the two of them with a withering stare. It may have worked on Marine recruits forty years ago, but it had lost much of its power since then.

Embarrassed and resigned, Levine quickly glanced to Parker. Parker remained as inscrutable as one of those Easter Island statues. With no apparent support from Parker, Levine answered weakly, "Uh, yeah."

Hennessey rolled his eyes. He bowed his head to pinch the bridge of his nose, as *if warding off an impending migraine.* "Sure," *he mumbled.* "Of course. Let's get to it then."

"When did you first get wind that your battalion was being tasked for something special?" *asked Levine.*

Hennessey shifted uncomfortably in his wheelchair. "We knew something was up when the entire battalion was assembled in Punta Gorda. Companies and platoons that were dispersed all over the country chasing Sandino were suddenly called back to the coast and immediately herded onto a Navy transport. Everyone knew the big brass had something in mind. Rumor was, even the Colonel didn't know."

Levine scribbled a few notes. "Do you remember the ship's name?"

"No. I told you that the last time. I thought Jews were supposed to be smart."

"I'm not Jewish," *Levine said without looking up from his notes. Levine figured it was the only way the old bastard could get back at the two of them for making him go through the story over and over again. Since he couldn't intimidate them, he would suffice with insults.*

"Yeah. Next you're going to tell me he ain't a nigger either." *Hennessey laughed mirthlessly. One again, Parker didn't even blink. Something in Parker's poker face told Levine the big man was thinking, 'I bet you're going to die soon, old man.'*

"Where were you first briefed on the details of the Innsmouth operation?"

"The Boston Naval Annex; the same day our ship docked."

"And that day was?" *Levine volleyed.*

"It was February 23rd, 1928. They marched the entire battalion into a warehouse in the Annex and sat us down on these wooden benches. There were already about a hundred guys in suits in there, T-men we were told, and nearly a dozen Navy officers in their faggoty dress whites. They had this big map of the town and all the approaches. Plus a screen set up for the movie and slides they showed later."

"Do you remember the name of the operation? What was it code-named?" *Levine interrupted.*

"Just what I told you before," *Hennessey said irritably.* "It was something biblical, like Project Moses, or Pharisees, or something. Y'know, Old Testament."

"And who gave the briefing?" *Levine prodded.*

"There was a Captain from Naval Intelligence and a T-man. I got the impression he was Secret Service. I don't remember their names 'cuz I never saw 'em again. There was one fella, though, I seen plenty of since."

"We know," *interrupted Levine.* "You already mentioned Hoover."

Hennessey glared at Levine and leaned forward onto the table. "Are you going to let me tell the damn story or not?"

"Sorry," *said Levine, leaning back to keep the distance between them.* "Please continue." *Levine felt a flush of embarrassment at the clumsiness of his questions.*

He was an Elint Specialist, not an interrogator. Listen in while the Kremlin orders out for pizza? No problem. But interrogation? And Parker? As far as Levine could figure, he was some DOD mechanic currently on loan to the Company. If this was the best debriefing team Alphonse could put together, it meant that either this was a low priority op, or things at Delta Green were well and truly fucked.

"'Military support for civilian law enforcement' he called us," Hennessey hissed. "But the operation the brass laid out was more like the kind of thing we'd been doing for United Fruit in Nicaragua."

"What exactly had you been doing for United Fruit?" asked Parker.

"Whatever we were told to do," Hennessey snapped, glaring angrily at Parker's interruption. But Hennessy's watery eyes couldn't hold Parker's cold stare and he quickly looked down to his own trembling, knotted hands. After a second, Hennessey cleared his throat and looked up. "'Bout the same thing our boys did in Vietnam. 'Cept we didn't have TV cameras breathing down our necks. We'd move into a pueblo that our officers said was supporting Sandino, round all the spics up, shoot those that gave us any trouble, burn the corn and rice in the field, torch the huts, and march everyone out to a 'controlled area' where they couldn't support Sandino. 'Course, often as not those same corn fields would be turned into banana plantations by the next time we marched through, but what the hell did we care. It ain't changed much since '27 as far as I can see."

"The film," said Levine.

"Huh?"

"Could you tell us again about the film they showed you." Levine had not only undone his tie, but also rolled up his sleeves. He could feel the sweat in his armpits and around his collar. Parker, however, didn't spill a drop—lotsa jungle work.

"Did I leave that out? Well, there was some film shot from an airplane. It showed the town and the surrounding countryside. The captain described the main features of the town, pointing out this road and that. The last part of the film showed a small, black, rocky island, or maybe it was the top of a reef poking out of the sea. But they stopped the film before that got too far along. The captain acted like it was something we weren't supposed to see.

"Then there were the slides. Someone, probably one of Hoover's boys, had wandered through town with a hidden camera in a suitcase. The shots weren't very well aimed and most were out of focus. The camera must've been hid real good and run real quiet because some of the locals were awful close when he snapped the shutter. One just about looked right in the camera lens. When that blotchy, goggle-eyed face flashed onto the screen, I guess I must've gasped along with everybody else. Everybody except Paskow, of course. Fucker's heart pumped ice water.

"But that face...it was like something out of Lon Chaney's makeup kit. The head was all wrong. During Korea I saw a kid in Seoul with the same kind of head.

'Water Heads' they're called. The skull was somehow soft and bloated-looking. The guy's eyes were bulging and watery, and even though it was just a still shot, those eyes seemed not to have any lids. That's when I knew this was going to be worse than anything I could imagine."

ॐ

"You Marines better get used to that face; you're going to be seeing a lot of that the next couple of days," roared the Captain from Naval Intelligence. "The federal agents who've been conducting surveillance of the town have reported a high incidence of …inbreeding." The Captain said the word "inbreeding" like he could taste it. "This town has been isolated from the rest of Massachusetts for nearly eighty years. The people up there have been marrying their second and first cousins for three or four generations. During the Civil War federal draft agents determined that over half the males of combat age in Innsmouth were unfit for military service." The Captain paused to let that sink in. "Do not be surprised by anything you see. Appearances to the contrary, they're not congenital idiots. They've used their appearance as part of their propaganda campaign to keep the uninvolved locals quiet and outsiders away."

Private First Class Robert Hennessey sat there in that drafty warehouse, on those polished benches and listened aghast to that Navy prick spin a yarn about rum-running, drug smuggling, white slavery, murder, piracy and an elaborate scare-story crafted to frighten away the curious. The captain pointed out the objectives with a collapsible metal pointer. As he ticked off the objectives, he struck the map like he was disciplining it for getting caught in the liquor cabinet.

"First Company will deploy along the docks on both sides of the Manuxet. Your mission will be to prevent anyone from fleeing the city by sea. First Company's Second Platoon will move with a detachment of Treasury agents and secure the Marsh Refinery and the company offices. Second Company will be assigned to hold a perimeter along Southwick Street in the north while its Third Platoon will move to the Marsh estate and secure the Mansion and assist the Treasury agents in serving the arrest and search warrants. Second Company, Second Platoon will move to secure the former Masonic Hall on Federal Street, which now serves as the headquarters of a quasi-spiritualist group calling itself The Esoteric Order of Dagon. There are three churches—here!—" cracking the map again—"along Church Street. Current intelligence indicates that all three have lost their original congregations and are now used by the Esoteric Order of Dagon."

Hennessey hung on every unbelievable word. He'd done sweeps of hostile pueblos down in Bananaland, but this was Massachusetts, for Christ's sake. Hennessey turned to Lance Corporal Charlie Paskow, who was sitting with his elbows on his knees. A Camel hung limply from his mouth, slowly dripping ash. "Hey, Charlie?" Charlie turned and pushed a lazy cloud of smoke out of the corner of his mouth. He raised an eyebrow to invite the question. "Are they serious? Are we really going to attack a town here in America?"

"I certainly hope so," Charlie hissed. His thin mouth was wrinkled into something akin to wry amusement. Once, outside Bluefields on the Mosquito Coast, Hennessey had seen Charlie shoot a ten-year-old kid out of the saddle from two hundred and fifty yards. Charlie's only comment, as he ejected the spent round from his Springfield, was, "Spics oughtn't give rifles to kids." Charlie was as cold-blooded a fish as Hennessey had seen in the Corps. It should have come as no surprise that Paskow was getting a chuckle out of doing to an American town what they'd been doing to Nicaraguan pueblos.

The Captain had already run through the information on the "Esoteric Order of Dagon." Some kind of creepy South-Seas religion as far as Hennessey could follow the Captain's lecture. Like something out of a Fu Manchu pulp. Idolatry. Secret initiations. Murder and human sacrifice. It was all too much. Maybe this kinda thing could happen in Borneo or the Amazon, but this was America, less than thirty miles from Boston Common.

Hennessey's head was spinning by the time the lecture was done. His company, the Third, was to cross the Manuxet to the north side of town, then cut west along Martin Street to Phillips Place. There they would break into four platoons and begin "internment operations." They were to round up everyone in a four-block area and march them to the old railway station, where battalion HQ would have a processing center set up with the Bureau of Investigation to sort out the "criminal aliens" from the rest of the townsfolk. When their blocks were cleared, the company would work its way eastward, clearing the next four blocks and so on until they reached the harbor. To the north, Second Company would be doing the same, while on the south side of town, Fourth Company would be spread out along Garrison Street clearing blocks and moving north. The noose would be drawn tighter and tighter until everyone in town was accounted for and "sorted out." A couple platoons of Marine sappers were standing by to begin "excavating certain structures" once the population was clear. Hennessey figured that when the Captain said "excavate," he probably meant "blow up."

After the briefing, the battalion was marched out by platoons to a staging area. Cold-weather gear, helmets, and winter camouflage was passed out. Then came the weapons. It looked like jungle warfare all over again. Most Marines were issued a pump-action Winchester trench gun or a Thompson subma-chine gun, with only a few bolt-action Springfields and Browning Automatic Rifles thrown in. After all, if they were going to be operating in a town, there wasn't going to be much call to shoot anyone two or three hundred yards away. Everyone was also issued four grenades, and a Colt .45 sidearm, too. Clearing blocks of teetering old tenements room by room would be claustro-phobic work, often without the luxury of enough space to maneuver a rifle or shotgun. It looked to Hennessey like the Brass had put some thought into the weapons mix.

Which is why the flamethrowers really scared him. Hennessey counted at least six flamethrower teams. Plus the quartermaster was handing out white-phosphorous grenades and satchel charges like it was the Battle of Beallue Wood all over again. "They wouldn't be handing those out unless they were expecting us to have to burn the locals out their houses."

Hearing Hennessey's comment, Charlie Paskow looked over at the Marine sappers strapping the tanks of jellied gasoline onto their backs. Paskow's bay-onet-thin figure was practically swallowed by the heavy winter greatcoat and steel helmet. He shrugged noncommittally as he shouldered his trench gun. "I s'pect so." Paskow turned away to join the rest of Third Company, Third Platoon by the four military trucks that would soon be bearing them north up the Ippswich road to the doomed town of Innsmouth.

The drive north was bitterly cold. Snow was fresh on the ground and shone pale in the moonlight. The sea winds blowing in along the shore cut right through the canvas-covered truck. It froze the Marines' helmets to the tops of their ears. The draft tugged at their clothes and swept their steaming breath away like the exhaust from the rattling tailpipe. A few silently cursed the T-men, who were making the trip in a long train of big, black Packards. The oth-ers gripped their weapons upright between their knees, curled up inside their fear and adrenaline, and tried to focus. Focus on not getting killed.

As their truck crested the top of yet another hill, Lieutenant Cobb shouted a warning from the cab to the men bundled in the rear. "We just topped the last hill. We'll hit town in three minutes! Nobody does nothing until we deploy." The driver ground the gears as he down-shifted for the descent into town. That's when the stench hit them.

At first Hennessey thought they'd passed some road kill, some dog or farm animal on the side of the road. But the smell was more like rotten fish than any other smell he could think of.

"Jeezus," choked Deerborn. "What the hell is that?"

"Smells like the crack on a two-pesos whore!" Lyman gasped, holding his nose.

"Shut the hell up, Marine," barked Sergeant Miles. The Sergeant preferred to dispense discipline with the butt of his Thompson. No one said a word after that, even though the eye-watering stink just kept getting worse.

Hennessey's first glimpse of the town was lost in the glare of the headlights of the trucks behind his. Now and again he could see windows staring back, like the empty sockets of a skull. It just seemed incredible that any of the buildings could possibly be inhabited. They were crumbling heaps. Regardless, they were going to have to clear those heaps room by room. Clearing an intact building is hard enough, but when the walls look like Swiss cheese and you can see the attic while standing in the basement, there's just no way to know where that next shot is coming from. No way to know if that wall to your back is going to give way to a sniper's killing zone. It made Hennessey's guts twist just thinking about it.

Suddenly they were crossing a large square. The Gilman Hotel leaned drunkenly to the right, on the left the First National Grocery. In the blink of an eye, the trucks were rattling across the Federal Street Bridge and into the north side of town. Just across Dock Street they sped past the columned facade of a Romanesque building. Its granite pillars and steps were fleetingly illuminated as one of the trucks from the convoy peeled off and began disgorging troops. Hennessey could just make out the building's graven title above the door: "The Esoteric Order of Dagon." The building was out of Hennessey's sight even before the Marines began vaulting up the front steps, their bayonets flashing in the passing headlights.

As their trucks drove deeper into Innsmouth, the buildings along Federal Street grew even more dilapidated; some were little more than four hollow walls cradling collapsed roofs and floors. Crossing Church and Martin Streets, more trucks veered off to their targets. Hennessey's truck and three others made a hard left onto Martin and gunned their engines. "First squad!" barked Lieutenant Cobb from the front cab. "You will move south and secure the southwest block. Round everyone up and get them ready to move to the train station. Have you got that?"

"Yes, Sir!" came the chorus. Hennessey looked across the truck to Charlie Paskow. Hennessey knew that faraway look meant that Paskow was winding his clock springs. Hennessey loved having Charlie with him in a firefight: the guy moved like a wind-up soldier. No hesitation, no frenzy, just one fluid action after another.

The truck turned right again, shot forward maybe thirty yards, and jammed on the brake, skidding slightly as snow chains bit into the icy cobblestones. "Go! Go! Go!" barked Sergeant Miles as he jumped down from the truck, hoisting his Thompson in one hand while waving the men forward with the other. Hennessey jumped down, holding the barrel of the Thompson skyward, slipping slightly in the ice. "Corporal Paskow! Take Hennessey, Lyman, and Boyle and clear that house there!" Miles indicated a sagging heap that had once been a quaint, gambrel-roofed Georgian home. In any small town in America, it might have passed as a haunted house. Here in Innsmouth, a city of haunted houses, its intact windowpanes made it look upscale.

Paskow got to the door first and began pounding with his gloved fist. "Open the door! This is the U.S. Marine Corps! Open up!" Hennessey hung back with Lyman and Boyle at the foot of the steps, keeping an eye on the windows. Boyle, a steady Tennessee farmboy, had been in Hennessey's company for six months in Nicaragua. Hennessey had no worries about him. Lyman, on the other hand, had just gotten off the boat from Camp LeJune when the battalion was turned around and sent back to the States. He was nervous as a cat and kept dancing around, shifting his weight from one foot to the other like he had to pee.

The owner was fairly slow to come to the door, but that was to be expected. It was 2:00 A.M., after all, and his reactions were dulled from having to wrench himself out of a warm winter slumber. For a half awake fella, dressed only in his nightshirt and facing four Marines armed with bayonet-tipped shotguns and Thompson machine-guns, the man took it fairly well.

"What th'sweet Jay-sus is gowin' ahn!" he shouted. Hennessey sincerely hoped the ol' fella didn't give Paskow too much trouble. Last fella who did, Paskow put out most of his teeth with the butt of his Springfield.

"Town's being evacuated. You and anyone else you've got in there are going to have to go with us. Right now," Paskow said flatly. It wasn't much of an explanation. For a second Hennessey thought the old man was going to give Paskow an opportunity to do a little more dental work. Instead he smiled. It wasn't much of a smile, what with more than a few teeth missing or gone gray with rot, but his face lit up like they'd just reported the end of Prohibition.

"Y'all are Marines? Yav come t'clear the town?" he beamed.

"Yes we are and yes we have," Paskow answered.

"Thank th' Lawd! Ah just need t'get dressed!" Without closing the door the man turned and ran back into his bedroom leaving the four slightly puzzled Marines on his doorstep.

"Maybe we won't need to burn 'em out after all," Hennessey said hopefully.

In less than four minutes the old man had himself, his wife, and his two sons dressed and out the door. Then it was on to the next house. This time when Paskow pounded on the door, the only answer he got was a curt "Go ahway!"

"We are authorized to use whatever force is necessary to evacuate the inhabitants of this town, sir!" Paskow bellowed back through the door. "If you don't open up right now, we're kicking the door in!"

"Dammit t'Hell, Jawsef!" the old man cried from the street behind the Marines. "They'ah from th'government! They'ah here t'help!"

Paskow was just about to tell the old man to keep quiet when the front door unbolted. "Ah can't believe it," said the weathered face that peered out. "Afta all this time. Yav come t'put it right then?"

Paskow gripped his trench gun a little tighter in frustration. "I don't know nuthin' 'bout that. My orders are to move everyone to the train station for evacuation."

"Ever'one? Even th' others?" the man asked tentatively.

"I don't know anything about any others, but if you don't open the door this second, my men will smash it in."

The man looked resigned and cast his eyes to the floor. "What'll Ah need t'bring?"

"Warm clothes is all," Paskow urged. "And make it fast." Once the weathered face disappeared back into the house, Paskow turned to Hennessey. "It'll be a damn shame if we don't get to use the flamethrowers." Hennessey was fairly sure this wasn't meant in jest.

As the weathered man bundled his wife and daughter down to the sidewalk, he turned to Hennessey and hissed, "Be careful of th' Sahgents. Ah ain't seen his waaf for better-on four months. Ah think she's beginnin' t'turn." Hennessey hadn't the slightest clue what the fella was talking about, but he could still see the genuine fear in the man's watery gray eyes.

"Thanks, sir. We'll watch out for that."

By 2:30 A.M., Third Company had cleared all the blocks north of Pierce Street and west of Phillips and was ready to move south towards the river and east towards the bay. Now the situation was beginning to rapidly change. Lights were on in many of the windows on Hancock Street. It made it a lot easier for the Marines to pick out which doors to knock on, only now the inhabitants were beginning to resist. Up and down Hancock Street Marines were kicking in doors and smashing open windows with their buttstocks. Despite the quality and state of repair of the houses on this street, the attitude of the locals was one of defiance and loathing. At one house, Hennessey saw a woman standing at her front door brandishing a frying pan and screaming, "Ah won't stand far it!"

"Get off mah yaad," was the reply from the first house they came to.

"Open this door or we'll smash it in!" Paskow said loudly, but without a hint of anger.

"Yav got no right t'be turnin' us outta our homes in th'dead o'night!"

"I've all the rights I need right here." Paskow worked the action on his trench gun with a resounding "cha-chak!" The door opened without much more to-do about "rights." The man who greeted them was stooped and bow-legged. His age was hard to determine, being somewhere between thirty and fifty. He had big bulging eyes and a wide, thick-lipped mouth that probably turned down at the corners even when he wasn't being rounded up in the middle of the night. His fat eyes were filled to the brim with fear and loathing for the men outside. Hennessey could not help but think that the hate wasn't because he and his fellow Marines represented the unbridled power of the government. Instead this parody of a man hated them for being straight-backed and clear-skinned. He hated them for being normal. His wife and children showed many of the same signs as their father: over-large eyes, rough, scaly skin, too-wide mouths. Even his fat wife was showing signs of encroaching baldness. As she called the children together, the woman's voice sounded badly scarred. Maybe it had something to do with the thick wrinkles on her neck? The family had to be prodded and pushed down to the street where a crowd of equally repugnant locals was being gathered together.

The name on the mailbox of the next house read "Sergeant." A rickety-look-ing motor coach, dirty gray in color, was parked at the curb. The half-illegible sign in the windshield read "Arkham-Innsmouth-Newb'port." Whoever was inside the house was awake with a light on. He croaked at the four Marines before they even got to the first step. "Ah can't leave th'house! Mah wife's very sick. She can't be moved."

"We'll have a doctor look her over," Paskow called back.

"She can't walk. She's an invalid."

"We'll get a couple of medics to carry her on a stretcher."

"No, she's too sick. Go away, d'ya hear? Ah've got a shotgun and ah'll use it!"

Paskow stepped to the right side of the door and motioned Hennessey and Lyman to take the left and Boyle to join him on the right. "You shoot at us and we'll damn well toss a grenade in there with you. You want to be blown to Kingdom Come?" Paskow took the silence to mean that Mr. Sergeant was thinking about it. "Now open the door and toss the shotgun out!" The four held their breaths as they listened to the bolts turn in the door. The hand that held the shotgun barrel and placed it on the doormat was as dry and scaly-looking as any from the last house full of inbreds, only this one was webbed up to the second knuckle.

As Sergeant released the shotgun, Hennessey, with a nod from Paskow, threw himself against the door. At age twenty, Hennessey was a horse of a man: six-foot-two and two hundred and twenty pounds of combat-honed muscle. Under that kind of force, the door swung open like a spring-loaded trap and struck Sergeant in the chin. He stumbled backwards and landed hard on his rump. Hennessey put a boot in his chest and shoved him back down on the floor. "Stay down! Don't get up!"

True to what his hand had suggested, Sergeant presented another fine example of Innsmouth's poor breeding habits. He was thin, with stooped shoulders. Like his neighbors, he had the same flaky, peeling skin, almost like he'd been sunburnt. His eyes, mouth, and lips were disproportionately large, and his sloping forehead and chin seemed to simply fall into his strangely creased neck. "Where's your wife?"

The question filled Sergeant's bulging blue eyes with terror. "Ya can't take her. She's too sick ah tell ya."

"We'll be the judge of that," Paskow said as he coolly surveyed the interior of the house. The furnishings seemed oddly antiquated, as if Sergeant lived in a house full of his grandfather's furnishings. The room was lit by a single oil lamp. "Boyle, check the rooms on this floor. Lyman, check upstairs." Boyle quickly set off, but Lyman hesitated a moment. Paskow's bark of "Get a move on!" sent him scurrying up the stairs.

"Don't go up thar!" Sergeant croaked from the floor. As he began to pull himself off the floor, Hennessey put him back down again with the boot.

"Stay there!"

"Ya don't understand!" Sergeant looked absolutely panicked now. "Ma wife, she needs me!"

"If he tries to get up again, shoot him," Paskow said with finality. On that note Hennessey pulled back the action lever on the Thompson's bolt and aimed the muzzle right at Sergeant's face. His complexion, already quite gray, grew considerably less healthy.

From upstairs Lyman called down, "I think I found it, Corporal. There's a padlocked door."

Paskow looked down at Sergeant. "Where's the key?" Sergeant just looked away at the floor. "Fine. We'll break it open. Boyle! Get back here and watch the prisoner." As Boyle came back in through the dining room from the kitchen Paskow turned and trudged up the stairs.

"Just sit still," Hennessey warned. "We'll have your wife down in a jiffy." Despite the reassurance, Sergeant looked like a coiled spring. Hennessey could hear the crunching thuds of a shotgun butt smashing at the padlock upstairs. Once. Twice. The third crack was followed by a sharp crash, and then a scream.

No, not a scream. More like a roar.

What followed was a scream, like nothing Hennessey had heard since the time his uncle gelded one of the horses on his Oklahoma ranch: high-pitched and piercing, almost like a whistle. Both Hennessey and Boyle reflexively looked up to the source of the sound. That was when Sergeant made his move. He swung his leg with speed and strength so shocking that Hennessey had no time to comprehend before he landed flat on his back. Sergeant gained his feet in a flash, and just as fast jumped across the room to grab Boyle's trench gun and try to wrench it away. Boyle was a strong man, strong as an ox, and he swung Sergeant around and sent the two of them crashing into the dining room table.

Hennessey rolled to his feet just in time to jump clear of two figures tumbling down the stairs together. One was a Marine; the other, something out of a sideshow. Sparse strands of hair were plastered to a head the size and shape of a pumpkin. A sheen of moisture extended from its scalp down its back. The thing had rubbery, bloated skin, mottled gray in color, gone green in patches, and peeling like someone was halfway through skinning it when it tumbled down the stairs. Its feet were huge with widely splayed toes that showed more of the curious webbing between them. The same was true of the hands, except these were tipped by hideously curved nails over two inches long. The Marine it had locked itself around screamed hysterically and beat at its back and sides with his fists. Hennessey couldn't open up with the Thompson for fear of shooting the man to pieces. Instead, he swung the machine gun's buttstock down onto the thing's skull. The noise was like Joe Jackson hitting a home run, but it didn't let go. He brought the weapon down again and again. Still nothing. Then the Marine's screaming cut off with a wet tearing sound.

"Get th'hell outta the way." Paskow's voice was strangely calm. He stood at the top of the landing, taking careful aim with his trench gun, blood running from a pair of long scratch marks from just under his left eye down to his jaw line. Hennessey jumped back and Paskow blew off the back of the thing's upturned rump. The thing sat bolt upright, its huge, lidless eyes and its mouth locked open in an almost comical look of surprise. Rows of pointed teeth hung clotted with bits of Lyman's throat. Hennessey could plainly see the blood-red gills on the sides of its greasy neck open and close spasmodically. Then most of the head above the eyes exploded in a fine mist as Paskow put it down.

Over in the corner of the dining room, Boyle still grappled with Sergeant for the trench gun. Paskow calmly walked down the stairs, stepped over the two corpses, and bellowed, "Boyle! Hit the deck!" Boyle got the message and let go of the shotgun, dropping to the floor. Sergeant looked up just in time to see the muzzle flash before the contents of his chest splashed the dining room's brown, peeling wallpaper.

Hennessey looked away and became transfixed by the thing sprawled atop Lyman. Now that he could see the front of it, he noticed details of even more terrible proportion. It wasn't that it was inhuman. No, the problem was that it was so very human. Pendulous breasts would seem to signify a mammal, but the other features suggested a mix of fish and frog, as did the rotting, nearly choking stench.

Suddenly Hennessey remembered to see if Lyman were still alive. Most of the kid's throat had been torn out. His esophagus was laid wide open and the gleaming bones of his vertebrae were clearly visible. No blood pumped from the severed veins.

Someone appeared at the door.

"What the hell's—" Sergeant Miles' demand was cut short when he saw the bloated woman-thing. "Jesus! I...I'd better go get the Lieutenant."

Pulling up a chair at the overturned dinner table, Paskow plopped himself down. "Yeah. I'm sure Cobb'll know just what to do," he muttered sardonically.

"Christ Almighty," Boyle whispered after retrieving his shotgun. "What is that thing?"

"That guy on the other street knew," Hennessey muttered. "He said to watch out for Mrs. Sergeant. He said she was beginning to change."

"Change into what?" Boyle sounded shaky.

"Nothing good," Paskow added as he lit a cigarette with his lighter.

Just then, Lieutenant Cobb strode in and boggled at the sight of the thing that had torn the throat out of one of his Marines. It took him a second to compose himself enough to ask Paskow what had happened.

Without bothering to put out his smoke, Paskow stood and faced Lieutenant Cobb. "This fella on the floor barred our entry, so we had t'force our way in. Then this thing over here, which the first fella had padlocked in a room upstairs, busted out. It opened up my face and tore out Private Lyman's throat with its teeth. I had to kill it and the other fella since he was trying to take Private Boyle's weapon away from him."

"I think it's his wife," Hennessey added weakly.

"What?" snapped Lieutenant Cobb.

Feeling all the eyes in the room on him, Hennessey felt himself shrink. "One of the other folks on the last street said something about Mrs. Sergeant changing and that we ought to watch out for her."

"And you think this...this aberration is his wife?" Lieutenant Cobb shot back.

"He did say his wife was in the house, sir," Paskow said, tapping his ash. "And there's nobody else here but him and her...or it, if you prefer."

"She must have slipped out of the house while you were fighting with this... thing."

"I don't think this is the only one of these things we're going to find, sir," Paskow continued painfully. "I think we're going to find one of these in every attic."

"Don't be ridiculous," Cobb said, without much conviction. The Lieutenant's rejoinder was cut off by the sound of gunfire out in the street. Facing something as mundane as bullets was infinitely preferable to puzzling over the dead heap on the floor. "C'mon, men! Let's go!" Lieutenant Cobb turned and bolted out the door. The other Marines followed him into the yard and were greeted by the sight of three Marines spraying the front of a brick house with their Thompsons. Sergeant Fields was stumbling around holding a glove to a bullet-hole in his upper left arm. The gunfire quickly subsided and the three Marines charged up the front steps and kicked in what was left of the bullet-ridden door.

"Got 'er," one called down after a quick look inside.

"Sergeant! What's the situation?"

"The woman shot me, sir!" the Sergeant roared. "She pulled out an honest t'god revolver and started shootin'!"

"Did you provoke her?"

Sergeant Fields looked sincerely insulted. "No sir. We told her we were comin' in and she started shootin' is all."

Just then they heard a hoarse caterwaul from the basement window to the left of the front steps. As the Marines peered into the darkness, they were startled by the sound of breaking glass. A long, rubbery-looking arm groped through the window's clinging shards and rattled the bars beyond. "Mah-ree!" it croaked. "Mah-ree! Whar's mah waaf? Whaat ave yoo dun t' mah waaf?"

Again, those nearest the window hit a choking, fishy odor. Lieutenant Cobb's face wrinkled in an expression of confusion and disgust. He turned to Sergeant Miles and gagged out the order, "Get the Captain."

Captain Kardashian didn't exactly look like the guy on the recruiting poster. He was short but straight-backed, with olive skin and a bad complexion. His black eyes and mustache could have been found on a Hollywood villain. Rumor was, he'd come up from the ranks with a battlefield commission during the Great War. He was accompanied by one of the T-men bundled in a dark topcoat and fedora.

As soon as he approached, Cobb said, "There's one in that basement, sir. My men killed another one across the street in that house there."

"Let's have a look at this one here, Lieutenant."

The creature bellowed and cried for its wife, Mary, and shook the bars with its webbed hands. After a few moments of staring noncommittally, Kardashian announced, "I'll see the dead one now."

Hennessey and some other Marines had begun to follow the entourage across the street when Sergeant Miles turned and roared, "What th' hell d'ya think yer doin'! Don't stand around like a bunch'a ducks in a shootin' gallery! Spread out and form a perimeter to secure this block!" The Marines scrambled into position instantly.

Although they were supposed to be watching the streets and windows, many of the Marines were asking each other what was going on and trying to get Boyle, Hennessey, or Paskow to tell them what they'd seen in the Sergeant house and what had happened to Lyman. Paskow kept his views to himself, but Boyle and Hennessey ended up repeating the story about a dozen times.

Then, from the east, towards the docks, the sounds of a full-scale battle shattered the calm. The avenue echoed with the clattering of Thompsons and the booming of shotguns. All the Marines looked east like dogs catching a scent. It wasn't like the earlier gunfire. Once or twice before they'd heard the odd angry shot, but this was something else. Those who'd seen the fields of Flanders in the Great War had heard the sound before: a "Big Push," hundreds of men charging across No Man's Land into the blazing muzzles of enemy machine guns and barbed wire. But it wasn't quite the same. Instead of the roaring hurrah of the advancing troops, there was another sound. Something like a swamp filled with frogs, only deeper and fuller. Then they saw the flare pop high to the east. Under its parachute, the white magnesium glare threw stark, crazily jumping shadows down alleys and through hollow windows. Hennessey stood transfixed, watching it drift behind the building and into the midst of the still-raging battle.

"Marines! Listen up!" It was Captain Kardashian standing atop the hood of the dilapidated motor coach in front of the Sergeant house. "These are your new orders concerning evacuation. Any local who looks abnormal is to be treated as a hostile. Take no chances. If they resist for even a second, shoot 'em. If you come across any locked or padlocked doors, don't open 'em. We'll just keep the things in there bottled up until we're ready for 'em. Mark every house where you find one of those things with an 'X.' Carve it in the front door and move on to the next house. Do you understand?"

The cry of "yessir" went up all down the line. Just then a young Marine came charging up Martin Street and onto Phillips at a dead run.

"Captain! Captain Kardashian!"

"What is it, soldier?"

"Captain Frost sent me, sir," he gasped. "First Company is under attack on the docks. We need reinforcements immediately!" A spatter of blood marked his white winter camouflage.

Kardashian spun around on Lieutenant Cobb. "That'll be you, Bill. Get your platoon down there right now! Double-time!"

"Yessir! Third Platoon to me!" Cobb shouted. Hennessey and the rest of the men quickly converged and set off at a jog down Martin Street to the sea. As they ran, the pounding of thirty pairs of boots thumped in counterpoint to the rattling bullets in the Thompsons' drum-magazines. Even above that din, Hennessey could hear the battle raging in front of them. Another parachute flare arched skyward. Even eight hundred yards away, down the sloping hill to the harbor, the Marines could see flashes of gunfire.

As they crossed Lafayette Street, the brooding shape of the Marsh Mansion loomed above them to their left. The grounds stretched all the way along Martin between Lafayette and Washington, while the mansion itself, with its wide-terraced parterres, towered three stories. Its top was crowned by an iron-railed widow's walk. Big black Packard sedans and military trucks filled the driveway and yard. Flanking the front gate and door, pairs of dark-coated T-men in fedoras cradled their Thompsons. Marines were lifting some kind of stone statue into the back of one of the trucks while a nervous T-man kept saying, "Easy! Go easy with that!" More Marines prodded a handcuffed figure down the front walk with their bayonets. Whatever it was, it wore a bloodied nightshirt and stumbled along with a curious hopping limp. Four Marines had been laid out on the front lawn, side by side, their helmets placed over their faces, their white camouflage torn and crusted with blood.

The docks were five more blocks ahead, nearly four football fields away, down a corridor of crumbling warehouses and office buildings, obviously long-abandoned. Hennessey's lungs burned as he ran. He could now hear screams, shouted orders, and cries of agony. And behind that din, the chorus of croaking and braying rumbled. Suddenly out of the blackness a baby-faced Marine emerged running straight for them. His face was as white as his camouflage. He didn't slow down for a second, just swerved to the right and flew right past Hennessey's platoon, tears of mindless panic streaming down his face.

On Water Street, right in front of the wharf, Thompsons and Browning machine-guns fired such long bursts they should have melted the barrels into slag. Marines ran this way and that. It appeared at first as if every Marine in First Company was trying to spend every last round as quickly as possible by firing into the blackness under the docks. A wild-eyed corporal ran past Lieutenant Cobb, a can of belted machine-gun ammo in each hand, screaming, "They're under the docks! Get 'em! Get 'em!"

The air burned with cordite. Every breath scalded the lungs. But even above the scent of war, a more ponderous stench asserted itself, the old rotting smell of dead fish, now grown monumental. It displaced the air and seemed to steal the last usable oxygen. Hennessey almost believed that his stomach would surrender its contents to the stink, when he noticed the croaking, bellowing chorus rising from the wharves of Innsmouth blending with the splashing of hundreds of flailing limbs. The men of Third Company, Third Platoon stumbled forward to the edge of the sea wall, peering down among the jumble of ships' masts and pilings. Hennessey followed, straining into the dark tangle. And at that moment, everyone wished they were back in the jungle with Sandino.

Below the docks, outlined by the strobing muzzle flashes of nearly a hundred weapons, clinging to wharf pilings, hanging from the masts and rigging, and crouched on the listing decks of Innsmouth's worm-eaten fishing fleet, squirmed an army out of drowned nightmares. Two arms, two legs, and a bloated, lolling head—each stood like a man with a cork-screwed spine. But the similarity to terrestrial life ended at that, for these were creatures of the deep. The white gleam of the flare reflected in hundreds of pairs of fat, oily eyes mounted on the sides of scaly heads, the eyes of creatures crafted by evolution to strain every last particle of light from their environment. Wet, lazy gills opened and closed on the sides of their stout necks. Their taloned, webbed hands and feet, like baseball gloves, were splayed wide. Their bottom jaws dropped open like the cavernous mouths of sea bass and again those barking croaks issued forth. "Iä! Iä!" came the war cry from the deep. "Iä!"

Nobody had to give the order to open fire. It erupted in a spasmodic fusillade that sent dozens more of the barking horde tumbling into the black waters. Hennessey brought his Thompson to his shoulder and began firing bursts into the thickest knot of them, chopping through rubbery hide, sending gouts of scarlet and other colors over the rotten timbers. They fell, only to be immediately replaced by a dozen more. The Marines, Hennessey included, were all screaming now, nearly drowning out the croaking of the fish-men. But they could not slow the charge. Pump-action shotguns worked with blinding speed, Thompsons raked over the braying throng, but it was not enough. Within seconds the things gained the sea wall and began to climb.

As the clouds of burnt powder obscured the leaping, flopping carnage, Hennessey saw some of the creatures haul themselves atop the docks and begin running toward the wall. He sighted the Thompson and fired a burst. Two of the things dropped like stringless marionettes, but eight more leapt forward. To his right, Charlie Paskow was calmly racking round after round through his trench gun, ejecting spent casings that sizzled in the snow. Hennessey could see he'd never get a bead before the things crashed into the Marines. "They're on top of the docks!" he screamed. Paskow jerked his head up and put his next 12-gauge round into the closest thing's chest, blowing it off its feet and into the bay. PFC Grodin, a tough kid from Pittsburgh, snapped off a load of buckshot that caught the next beast in the leg, nearly severing it at the knee. And then they were among the Marines, webbed, talon-tipped fingers raking into winter coats.

The mayhem was total. Private Franklin, a Marine from Second Squad, went down under two of them, his Thompson crushed to his chest. Razor-sharp talons sliced divots out of his jawbone and tore open his equipment harness. One clawed at his face and neck as he struggled to kick away and bring his weapon to bear. The other thing threw itself onto his legs and sank its fangs into his groin. Franklin's keening scream was broken as the first tore out his throat. A private by the name of McVeigh, his bayonet driven up to its hilt in the belly of an onrushing fish-man, danced in circles as the beast tried to claw its way up the Springfield rifle to get him. After desperately chambering a fresh round, McVeigh blew it off the end with a resoundingly wet report. Grodin put a load of buckshot into the head of the beast shredding Franklin's throat and, with a scream, drove his bayonet through the neck of the beast locked to Franklin's crotch. He twisted the trench gun, wrenching its jaws open as it gargled madly, spraying angry red blood from its twitching gill slits. "Die! Fucking die!" He stepped over the thing, straddling its back, jerked out the weapon and thrust it into the thing's spine, quelling the spastic twitch of its limbs. Meanwhile, Paskow held his empty trench gun in his left hand and serenely dropped one charging nightmare after another with careful slugs from his .45 automatic.

Hennessey brought his Thompson to bear in time to catch the second wave, which was running—no, hopping—across the docks. He held the trigger and hosed them down with a twenty-round burst, barrel low, the barrage knocking seven off the dock as they croaked in shock and anger. Hennessey's mind was running on little more than adrenaline and boot-camp training. The fifty-round drum was empty and there was no time to change magazines. He dove to his left, rolled the slippery monstrosity off the corpse of Private Franklin, scooped up the fallen Marine's Thompson, and spun on the icy cobblestones to loose another stream of fire.

Privates Bromley and Helms thrust their bayonets at the creatures scrabbling up the stone sea wall, bursting the soft, fat eyes like egg yolks. One screamed an almost human wail, clutched its oozing eye with both claws and pitched backwards onto its fellows. A creature straddling Private Dean's back sunk its teeth into his shoulder, and tore loose a bloody chunk of meat and wool just a second before Paskow blew off the top of its skull with the .45. Meanwhile, McVeigh and Boyle were finishing off two wounded creatures. The flopping abominations croaked and brayed pathetically, gagging on their blood as the Marines thrust and twisted their bayonets. Boyle jerked his bayonet out of the creature at his feet just in time to turn, reverse grip, and swing the butt like a golf club into the face of one struggling to hoist itself over the sea wall. Grodin loosed another's grip on the wall by pulping its head with a load of buckshot.

Hennessey had exhausted a second drum when the things gave up rushing along the tops of the tattered docks. But they were still scrambling up the sea wall. Most of the trench guns had quickly emptied their five rounds and were slow to reload. With the onslaught coming so fast, there was little time to shove the shells into the tube one at a time. The battle at the sea wall was rapidly coming down to buttstocks and bayonets against raking claws and dripping fangs.

A rushing sound and rising light caught Hennessey's attention as a ball of flame rose up from one of the fishing boats, splashing gasoline over the rotten timbers. At the northernmost end of the docks, a Marine from First Company was pouring a can of gasoline over the sea wall onto the scaly, flopping horde while another lit them with a flare pistol. Burning, keening beasts tossed themselves back into the bay, extinguishing the flames, and then scrambled right back over the mounting dead at the wall's base. Another Marine tossed a gas can onto the deck of a fishing boat and was followed by a shot from Lieutenant Cobb's flare pistol, sending it up with a cheerful whump.

Hoskins, a private from Second Squad, held tight to his trench gun as one of the creatures below grabbed the barrel. He went over the side like a Vaudeville comedian getting the hook, shrieking loudly. But not for long. Within seconds something at the foot of the sea wall tossed his head back up onto Water Street, still seated in its helmet and trailing a few links of spine. Hoskins looked more surprised than upset. The demonstration had its effect. All along the sea wall the Marines backed away from the edge, just long enough for the things to haul themselves up. It was one thing to kill the monsters from atop the wall while they tried to climb, but another to face them on equal ground. All along the edge, the sea wall was topped by another wall, this one made of slippery green flesh and glittering talons, rearing up as if in triumph. Or, at least, until the Browning opened up.

The first tracer Hennessey saw looked like it passed about a half-foot in front of his nose. He slipped and scrabbled on the icy cobbles, trying to backpedal in time to avoid getting mowed down. To Hennessey's right, in front of the Marsh fish-packing plant, First Company's water-cooled Browning gobbled belt after belt of ammunition, turning Water Street into a shooting gallery. The things hopped forward into the crossfire like a wave, dozens and dozens of them. Bullets and tracers ripped down Water Street, a wall of invisible razors shot through with lightning. The beasts charging through it simply came apart. Everywhere, monsters burst from a thousand miraculous stigmata. Most squawked and croaked as they crashed to the ground, but even stitched with dozens of bullet wounds, a few crawled forward, sliding over the bodies of their brethren, dragging themselves on hemorrhaging stumps and trailing ropy intestines. From behind their invisible fortress of screaming metal, the Marines desperately reloaded their weapons and blasted any lucky enough to cross the barrier of flying lead and magnesium.

"Grenade!" bellowed Sergeant Miles, holding one of the metal pineapples over his head. "Grenade!" With that, he lobbed it over the sea wall. The grenade exploded with a dull, wet thump, punctuated by inhuman shrieks of agony. Mud and other less wholesome semi-solids flew into the night air. Marines began tearing grenades from their harnesses, ripping the pins out, and hurling them after the first. Hennessey ripped a grenade off his harness and tossed it clear into Innsmouth Bay. Then the air was torn apart by a staccato barrage of ear-splitting explosions. It looked to Hennessey as if a dozen photographers beyond the wall were snapping flashbulbs at some Broadway celebrity. The Marines kept throwing their grenades over the side, some laughing hysterically. Within thirty seconds, the only thing answering the explosions was the sound of debris pattering to the earth or splashing into the harbor.

Nothing climbed up the sea wall now. No tracers screamed down Water Street. There was no movement except the slow, painful wriggling of the dying. Slowly the Marines began picking their way through the tangle of carnage. Hennessey felt drunk, lightheaded. As he inched through the dead, he jumped at the crack of gunfire as here and there a Marine delivered a perfunctory coup de grace.

In the light from the fires, Hennessey could now see that the area beneath the dock was awash with broken bodies. Fins, scales, and gills glistened in the orange flames. They'd killed far more of the creatures than Hennessey had suspected. The scene was almost like that of a beach after a red-tide fish-kill. And at the base of the sea wall, the bodies piled one atop the other in a bloody pyramid. The pile of gutted and boned fish-men had brought the shoal at least six feet higher. Hennessey had never seen such a slaughter, not even in picture books about the Great War.

A few of the fishing boats moored beneath the drunkenly listing docks still had fuel in their tanks. As they cooked off one by one, they sent fireballs roaring skyward. It wouldn't take too long for the docks to turn into a twisted maze of blazing timbers and planks. Hennessey strained for any movement in the thick gray haze. There was nothing. The fish-men had had enough. For the moment.

"Sound off by squads, you fucking apes!" bellowed Sergeant Miles. "First Squad!" Only five out of eight men barked out their names. As the rest of the platoon sounded off, Hennessey took a quick mental inventory of the remaining men in his squad. Lyman...he was still lying at the foot of the stairs at the

Sergeants' house. Paskow was dropping the magazine from his .45 and slapping another in place. He didn't even look out of breath. Boyle's pants were torn open at the left knee and his boot was wet with his blood. McVeigh and Grodin were panting like dogs but unmarked. The other two, Baldwin and Rhodes, had ended up on the north end of the defense line and had come through unscathed.

The rest of Third Platoon was mauled. Four Marines were dead, including Franklin with his throat torn out and balls bitten off. Eleven men were wounded, two so badly they'd soon be joining the dead. Out of the thirty-two men who comprised Third Platoon, only twenty-one were still able to fire a weapon. By some miracle, seven of them were in Hennessey's squad. There was a platoon from Second Company stumbling about with just seventeen men still standing, and the two platoons from First Company who'd begun the defense of the sea wall couldn't even form a full platoon between them. The wounded screamed and moaned; the others prayed and even wept. The only sounds of sanity came from Sergeant Miles bellowing orders to the survivors, policing up weapons and the dead.

At that moment, Lieutenant Cobb was standing next to First Company's Captain Frost. The Captain was screaming and gesturing wildly with his .45. "They came out of the sea, goddammit! Right out of the sea! They were all over us before we knew what was happening. It's a goddamn miracle it was only a dozen or so to start with. If they'd hit us with that second wave first..." Frost's quavering voice trailed off and then rose hysterically again. "We gotta get the Navy! We gotta get depth charges!"

"Sir! Sir!" Cobb hissed, shaking the man. "Calm down, sir. I need to know what you want us to do?"

"Do?" Frost shrieked. "What can we do? We've got to get out of here is what!"

"Dammit, sir, if we pull out, those things will overrun the town." Cobb gripped the Captain's shoulders in a vise-grip. "The battalion will be overrun. We're all spread out policing up the locals. If we're overrun, it'll unravel. It'll be a slaughter!"

"Fuck them!" Frost giggled hysterically. "We've gotta get out of here!"

Suddenly, the loudest noise on the docks was the sound of Lieutenant Cobb slapping Captain Frost's face. Frost trembled with anger, his red-rimmed eyes jumping in their sockets. "I'll see you broken for that."

Cobb drew in a measured breath and set his jaw. "Yes, sir. And if you run, or do anything to incite others to run, they'll be trying me for murder as well." Then he turned to Sergeant Miles. "Put the Captain someplace where he'll be out of the way, Sergeant."

For the next ten minutes, Lieutenant Cobb turned into Blackjack Pershing, barking commands in rapid succession, imposing order through his own force of personality. He sent the severely wounded off in a truck to the Battalion HQ with a situation report and request for reinforcements. He got the rest of the men to police up the extra ammo off the dead, tip the slain creatures back into the bay, and set the Browning machine gun up in the second-floor window of an abandoned warehouse at the end of Pierce Street.

Across the river, along the docks on the south side, Hennessey could see a couple of Brownings raking back and forth across the docks and shore. Then a tongue of liquid fire leapt out and showered the docks with jellied gasoline. As soon as Hennessey saw that, he knew that the fish-men would quickly figure to give the north docks another try.

"There they are!" A stout Montana Sergeant named Dollins stabbed a trembling finger towards the bay. Bobbing on the surface about a hundred yards out, scores of squat heads listed atop powerful shoulders. Their fat eyes reflected the orange light from the fires on the docks.

"Let 'em have it!" roared Cobb. With that, the Browning cut loose. The fusillade peppered the water, tore open misshapen skulls and sent the rest of the creatures diving under the waves. "Cease fire!" Cobb called up to the machine-gun nest. "Hold your fire!"

Hennessey waited silently. None of the Marines spoke. No one breathed. The sounds of the little battles behind them in Innsmouth faded from their perception as they focused on the black waters of Innsmouth Bay. Every fiber of their beings reached out to try to pick out a sound, a movement, anything that would tell them where the attack would come. But nothing came, nothing moved but the waves lapping against the shore and the horrible bodies stacked along its edge. Hennessey waited in the snow with the rest of the Marines and listened to the waves breaking.

Charlie Paskow broke the silence. "Tide's comin' in," he whispered. Hennessey, lost in concentration, didn't bother to answer him. "Tide's not due till dawn," he continued gravely. Hennessey was about to shush him when he caught Paskow's eye. He was looking at the waves cresting against the shore. They were strong and insistent. And they didn't wash back out. They just kept pushing one atop the other against the shore. The tide was coming in all right. In one single surge of water. Then Hennessey saw it. One of the fishing boats, nearly burned down to the waterline, rose as if a whale, pushing thousands of gallons of water before it, had just passed beneath. Before he could even register what he'd seen, Hennessey saw one of the dock's still-standing pilings plow under, like a road sign struck by an out-of-control truck.

"Under the water!" Lieutenant Cobb bellowed. "They're under the water!" Marines surged forward to the edge of the sea wall to fire down into the submerged beasts. But it wasn't a horde of sea devils.

It was just one.

Hennessey would later describe it to his Naval Intelligence de-briefers as being like an avalanche. An avalanche of tar that jumped up out of the sea.

A fair description. Except it was far more than that. An avalanche may be animate, but it is lifeless. The thing that erupted from the sea was anything but lifeless. It veritably boiled with life, like a steaming, maggot-filled turd. There were the eyes, and the mouths, the teeth, the tongues, the tentacles, the pincers, the claws, the talons. It was the whole Bronx Zoo boiled down to a thick, viscous paste and then filled with lightning. Even the parts that looked like little more than fibrous snot moved and coiled with a terrible strength. Within a second, it rolled straight up the sea wall. Private Rhodes was standing right on the edge when it reared up like a wave cresting in reverse and then slapped its weight down on him. His helmet slammed down onto his bootlaces and most everything in between shot liquidly out the sides.

Mere feet away, Sergeant Dollins screamed, along with almost everyone else who could find their voice, and opened up with his Thompson. A slimy rope jerked him into a gaping mouth and for a second the Marines nearby could see his muzzle flash through the semi-transparent slime. Then the bulk coiled up and Sergeant Dollins was squeezed back out an aperture roughly the size of an egg, like the suppurating contents of a lanced boil. About half the guys in Dollins' squad were now either running blindly or trying to get their Sergeant out of their eyes.

All the while, every Marine blasted away with everything he had. Bullets splashed into it and vanished with no more effect than firing into a lake. Hennessey was trying to seat a second drum magazine when he was jerked backwards off his feet. "Waddaminit! Waddaminit!" he screamed. Charlie Paskow didn't wait a minute. Swinging Hennessey around by his equipment harness, Paskow dragged him stumbling down Water Street towards the boarded-up customs house at the corner of Elliot. Hennessey couldn't believe what the hell he was doing. *Why am I running?* he wondered as he fled along the loading docks.

Behind Paskow and Hennessey the other Marines were scattering in every direction. Most weren't fast enough. As the thing sucked Sergeant Miles into its obscene bulk, he pulled the pins on the two grenades on his belt. He died quicker than Lieutenant Cobb, who was being used by a tentacle to smash a military truck's cab into junk.

Hennessey lost track of where he was for a second. For some reason, he thought he saw McVeigh put his .45 under his chin as he was being sucked into the monster. Then Paskow shoved him through the front window of the customs house. Inside was blackness, the floor a maze of broken furniture and coated with shards of glass. Paskow kept pushing Hennessey forward until they emerged out the back, onto the corner of Church Street. Hennessey looked over his shoulder back towards the docks. Paskow was right behind him, his eyes burning like magnesium. "Don't look! Keep running!"

They were passing something like a churchyard when a shot from one of the second- or third-story windows kicked a piece of the cobblestones loose just a foot or two to their left. With no time to slow down, no time to determine where the shot came from, they ran straight for one of the abandoned office buildings on their left. Not even slowing to try the doorknob, Hennessey threw his shoulder into the darkly stained wood, which burst apart like a rotten log, spilling him inside onto the floor. He got up, took a step, and fell screaming into open air. He pictured twisted, rusty machinery rising out of the blackness, a dozen lethal points.

He was wrong, of course. Nothing waited but a stone floor. Hennessey landed extremely well, keeping his feet together and rolling forward. Even so, he could feel something stab his left ankle and he cried out as he rolled on his side.

From above Paskow yelled down, "Bob! Bob!"

"I'm okay, I think," Hennessey added weakly, suddenly realizing that he couldn't see his Thompson anywhere.

"Stay put. I'll find the stairs." Hennessey could hear Paskow picking his way over the creaking timbers above. Alone in the dark, he began groping for the submachine gun. His gloved hands ranged back and forth over the cold stone for what seemed like forever. Then, with trembling relief, he lit on the still-warm barrel and pulled it to him, hugging it like a lost child. For a moment, Hennessey almost sobbed his relief. Then he heard the movement.

Something was with him in the dark.

He backed up until he hit the wall, bringing the Thompson up to his hip, but there was nothing to see. Nothing but blackness. Even so, he caught that fishy smell again, pricking at his nose. "Charlie! Don't come down here!"

"What?"

"There's some of those things down here! Stay upstairs!" Hennessey tested the weight of the weapon and figured he had better than forty rounds left in the drum. Plenty for what he was going to try. Holding tight on the fore grip to keep the barrel low, Hennessey squeezed the trigger and swung the barrel in a long arc from left to right. Suddenly the cluttered basement was illuminated by the strobing muzzle-flash. Then the things started jumping and moving, scrambling from between the rotten crates and collapsed shelves. Hennessey swung the Thompson and hosed them down. First one, then another, then two more went down howling. Then nothing. Silence.

"Bob? Bob, are you okay?"

Hennessey felt dizzy with relief. "Sure. I'm fine. C'mon down." To his right Hennessey could hear the stairs creaking under Paskow's weight. After peeling off the exhausted drum, Hennessey replaced it with a thirty-round stick and began to pick his way through the rubble to the stairs. A moment later the room was bathed in white light by another parachute flare, gleaming through the Swiss cheese holes of the roof. Gaping craters in the floors above were plainly visible for the second it passed overhead. And so were the four bodies of the family Hennessey had slaughtered.

The mother and father had the signs. The bulging eyes, the fish-like mouths, the skin that seemed too dry. But the two kids—the girl maybe six, the boy just a toddler—they looked just fine. It was hard to tell, of course. Firing from the hip, Hennessey had caught each in the head with a whopping .45 round. "Ah Jesus!"

Paskow looked down at the scene just before the flare drifted away and took their light with it. "C'mon, we gotta go."

"Jesus, Charlie, I fuckin' killed 'em."

"Nice shootin'." Paskow grabbed Hennessey's equipment harness and pulled him up the stairs. "Now move it!"

"But—"

"They ain't people," Paskow hissed. "They're deviates. Sub-humans. Understand this, Bob, we ain't Marines tonight. We're exterminators. This town, and everyone in it…We're gonna hafta burn it all." Paskow looked positively gleeful at the prospect. "But first we gotta get out of here." With that, Paskow pulled Hennessey up the steps and out a door onto Fall Street. To their left was the Manuxet River and the Federal Street bridge back into the south side of town.

All around them the operation was coming apart. Men ran every direction, screaming, firing their weapons at who knows what. At the intersection of Fall and Dock Streets, Paskow and Hennessey were nearly run down by a careening truck full of Marines. It took the turn onto the Federal Street Bridge rather poorly and slammed into the railing at about forty miles an hour. The driver shot out through the front window like a human cannonball, arching through the air, his arms pinwheeling until he slammed into the frozen Manuxet river with a crack that was part ice, part bone. The Marines on the truck fell over themselves pouring out the back.

Then there was a crash like thunder behind them. Six feet tall and spread across Dock Street like an enormous black mound of dough, the horror from Water Street rolled into the fish-packing plant five blocks away and splintered the loading docks like dry kindling. It was a freight train. An avalanche. A tidal wave. Hennessey was distantly aware he'd shat himself.

"Don't look! Run!" Paskow screamed. On the bridge, Paskow stopped. "Waddaminit!" His iron grip brought Hennessey to a sliding halt. Then Hennessey saw it too. Downstream, past the ruins of the Fish Street Bridge was a second bridge, one linking both sides of the wharf across the Manuxet. The mountain of slime wasn't crossing that bridge; in fact it was moving away. Someone down there had a pair of flamethrowers going. The long geysers of fire shot out and bathed the creature, driving it back against the fish-packing plant, collapsing the outer wall like something built out of a child's blocks. The plant disintegrated as the thing rolled through its interior, smashing walls and support beams. It was coming their way now. Right towards their bridge.

"Fire," Paskow hissed. "It don't like fire! We gotta seal off this bridge with flamethrowers!" Whirling around, Paskow stopped and stared at two Marines stumbling out of the crashed truck. They were shrugging their flamethrowers off their backs and turning to run.

"You!" shouted Paskow. He let go of Hennessey's equipment harness, sending him sprawling into the snow. "Get over here with those torches!"

"Fuck you!" screamed the ashen-faced kid, his acne scarlet against his snow-white skin. Paskow shot the kid right in the face. Paskow turned the .45 on the second Marine.

"Are your tanks full?"

He nodded furiously. Paskow shot him through the heart for good measure. Jamming the .45 in his belt, Paskow jerked Hennessey to his feet and hurled him towards the first flamethrower. "Strap that torch on!" Hennessey was weeping with exhaustion, but did as he was told. Meanwhile dozens of Marines raced past them, heading for the Arkham road and out of town. Out of Massachusetts if they could manage it. Fuck Innsmouth. Fuck Massachusetts. Fuck New England. No fucking way were they slowing down before they hit Tierra del Fuego.

Paskow snapped the chest buckle from the flamethrower's harness into place and ran to the truck. He flipped up the canvas flap and began rummaging in the back. Hennessey was just shrugging the tanks full of liquid fire onto his shoulders when Paskow said, "Bob! Heads up!" Hennessey turned in time to catch a pineapple-sized white phosphorous grenade. Paskow tossed him two more. Then, shouldering a satchel charge, he craned his neck and looked back behind them; his pupils widened. "Move your ass, Bob!" Hennessey saw the rolling obscenity coming down Dock Street right towards them. It wasn't alone. Right behind it, hopping and leaping around the fat, greasy bag of slime were more of the sea devils, barking and croaking. One carried a human arm as a club. And alongside them were men, men like Mr. Sergeant, carrying shot-guns and rifles and cleavers and scooping up the weapons of the fallen Marines.

Paskow pulled the fuse pin from a second satchel charge and tossed it into the back of the truck. It landed right between the three cases of white phos-phorous grenades and the six cases filled with bricks of TNT. "Runrunrun-run!" Paskow and Hennessey tore across the bridge with fifty pounds of jellied fuel sloshing on their backs. *Just one hot fragment! Just one!* was the only coher-ent thought in Hennessey's head. As they reached the south end of the bridge, they peeled off to the right around the grimy Waite and Sons' Restaurant, with its swinging placard showing a fish-head impaled on an enormous barbed hook. A moment later, Hennessey saw the searing flash of light and earth-shaking concussion send the placard airborne, flying over New Town Square.

The blast wave surged outward like an invisible wall of cement traveling at the speed of sound, trailing a cloud of debris that included head-sized cobble-stones. Laying flat on their faces, their hands over their ears, Hennessey and Paskow would have been torn to rags if not for the thick walls of the Waite and Sons' Restaurant. As it was, over a hundred yards away, they still felt the concussion suck the air out of their mouths and noses. When the wind sub-sided, Hennessey heard the townsfolk screaming, heard the fish-men braying and then a horrible unearthly keening, louder than the rest. They dragged themselves off the cobbles and emerged in Federal Street to find that most of the abandoned mill, which had been just yards from the truck, had disinte-grated and its water wheel blown out of the ice. The Esoteric Order of Dagon was gone. The side of the building facing the explosion had smashed through the opposite wall, squeezing the shattered interior onto Federal Street. Flam-ing shards of its timbers lay all about amid far more magnificent fires: the three cases of white phosphorous grenades, with the assistance of the TNT and satchel charges, had spread their contents over most of the area in front of the north end of the Federal Street Bridge. Those made of bone and meat who hadn't been disintegrated by the concussion had been showered with a downpour of burning metal; everywhere figures flopped amid the rubble, skin and clothing ignited by white-hot fragments like a thousand little suns.

The source of the keening revealed itself then, as the polymorphous horror emerged from the wreck of a nearby warehouse, a hundred mouths boiling out of its flesh amid blazing chunks of phosphorous. It rolled towards the riv-er, crushing the faint life out of a dozen or so maimed and burning townsfolk. The faster it sped, the more the air whipped its coat of stars to new brilliance. The thing somehow knew it had to get back to the sea; it crashed into the ice and poured like lightning through the hole.

Unfortunately, phosphorus burns just as well with the oxygen in water as it does with the oxygen in air. The water under the ice began to boil.

Hennessey began laughing like a fool. It was so fucking beautiful. The whole north end of the bridge was an inferno. All along Dock Street blazing scarecrows that used to be men, and less wholesome things, ran back and forth trying to extinguish themselves. Some rolled down the embankment to dive into the river, its uniform sheet of ice now a broken tangle of bergs. "Burn! Burn, you sonzabitches! Burn!" Hennessey sang as he danced in a circle waving his arms, the nozzle of his flamethrower clattering against the cobblestones at his feet.

But then the groan of the rending ice brought him back.

"Light your torch!" shouted Paskow. Charlie's eyes were still black and hot, and Hennessey dared not disobey. Cranking the ignition nozzle to full, he lit the blow-torch-like stream of gas off a burning fragment of the mill's water wheel. Over the thick granite railing on the bayward side of the bridge, about forty yards from where they were, Hennessey could see a two-foot-thick sheet of ice being levered out of the river by a muscular pseudopod. The thing began flowing out onto the ice like a rope uncoiling in reverse. Glittering black eyes winked open across its steaming surface. Alone but for Charlie, not a single Marine in sight, Hennessey wasn't even remotely scared. *They burn*, he thought gleefully. *They burn and they scream!* The fifty pounds of jellied gasoline on his back didn't scare him anymore, either. He loved it.

Paskow ran to the railing's edge. The shiny black thing was done shitting itself out of the hole it had punched. "I'll get its attention," he grunted. First, he pulled his .45 out of his belt and emptied the magazine at it. The bullets dimpled its plastic flesh with no effect other than to send it rolling towards them. They each uncorked a phosphorus grenade, Paskow barely breathing, Hennessey giggling like a girl.

"Wait," murmured Paskow. The thing was at the river's edge and rolling up the bank. Sweat stung Hennessey's eyes.

"Closer," Paskow hissed. At ten yards, Hennessey could see mouths and eyes rolling over the surface of its twenty-five-foot-wide amoeba-like surface.

The black tide hit the bridge supports and flowed upwards, grasping and reaching hungrily. "Now!"

Hennessey hurled his grenade after Paskow's down into the flabby bulk and then ducked behind the bridge's stone wall. The sizzling splash of phosphorous was followed by the hideous wail of a pipe organ made from burning men. Rising up to bring his flamethrower to bear, Hennessey could see tongues waving like snakes in dozens of mouths. Despite the phosphorous, the thing rolled forward. Some of those mouths were no longer screaming; instead, their teeth were bared in what could only be a grimace of hate. Hennessey cackled like a maniac as he hosed it down with blinding flame.

Like burning water, the jellied gasoline filled every open orifice. At first, the thing kept coming, stupid with hate and pain and wanting to kill the tiny thing that was hurting it. But suddenly it must have realized that it was not just hurting, it was dying. It hesitated in Hennessey's shower for a second, before retreating under the bridge.

"Keep it under there!" Paskow yelled as he ran to the opposite side of the bridge. Paskow let loose a blast of fire a moment later. "It's coming back your way!" The thing's wailing peaked, hit an octave that was too human. Hennessey greeted it with flame the instant it poked out.

Then the shooting started. A stuttering fusillade of bullets peppered the bridge, knocking razor-sharp chips of masonry loose with their impact. Somewhere across the river, the freakish townsfolk were rallying to the defense of their aquatic angel. One slug missed the fuel hose on Hennessey's flamethrower by about half an inch. Both Marines dropped to their knees.

"Did you see where it—oh fuck!" Paskow cut himself short. The white phosphorous grenade clipped to his belt was missing its spoon. It had been shot away in the hail of bullets. The fuse was lit on Charlie Paskow. With two grenades, a satchel charge of TNT, and at least forty pounds of gasoline on his back, it pretty much meant Hennessey was fucked, too.

Charlie stood up and, without even meeting Hennessey's horrified gaze or uttering a word, vaulted over the side of the bridge. Neither the creature nor Charlie Paskow had time to scream.

Hennessey was thrown face down on the stones by the concussion. Twin fireballs rolled out from either side of the bridge, flashing the snow and ice into steam and blackening Hennessey's white winter greatcoat. Forcing himself up onto his knees, his bones still ringing with the blast, Hennessey immediately thought, *I hope Charlie's okay.* With shame and horror, he realized then that he was alone. No, not alone. Those fuckers who'd killed Charlie were out there somewhere.

Hennessey shrugged the tanks of fuel off his back and cast around for a discarded weapon. There were plenty to be had. Spotting a Lewis Gun that still had a magazine loaded, he pulled it to him by its barrel sheath. He checked the drum-pan magazine. Not jammed. Never even fired. He poked his head over the bridge's upstream wall for a second. The shots came fast, from somewhere downstream. The Marsh Refinery. Hennessey scrambled to the opposite side of the bridge and hugged the wall. He poked his head up again and this time at least three rifles opened up on him. Still, the shots did little more than reveal their positions. The snipers were on the roof, no doubt huddled together for safety. Good, Hennessey thought warmly. Grouped nice and tight.

Hennessey crawled forward about ten yards and then came up again, this time with the Lewis Gun. He balanced the bi-pod the bridge's stone railing as a bullet bit the masonry right in front of him. He had his sight picture and then he opened up. Hennessey's first burst got him his range to the refinery's roof, the second found the snipers' roost. Then he poured it on. All three flopped like rag-dolls. One lost his weapon over the side.

More weapons opened up on his position from the black shuttered windows and doorways across the Manuxet. Hennessey had forgotten all about dying. He was too angry. Angry that these things had wiped out his platoon. Angry that he'd shit his pants with fear. Angry that Charlie was dead. Angry that he'd felt bad for killing the basement family of abominations. Hennessey wound his clock springs and went to work.

First, the one on the crumbling roof at the corner of Fall Street. Then the two down by the shore to the right. Then the one in the doorway nearly a hundred yards along Federal Street. A hunched thing broke for cover on the left and got about two hopping steps. Then back to Federal Street, where four of them tried to advance around the burning debris from the Esoteric Order of Dagon. Then another at the window a block over on Church Street.

Now they were running, turning tail and running. Just like Hennessey had minutes before. Running like women. But not from a monster. Not from a living mountain of shit that gobbled men and shrugged off bullets. *No. They're running from me!* Hennessey thought. *They're afraid of me!*

"Run!" he screamed, laughing. "Run!" He held the trigger down and chewed the rest of the magazine up in seconds. "Run, you fuckers!"

Somewhere he could hear a Browning machine gun chattering away. Turning back around, he felt a little disappointed to see the bridge filled with Marines, all of them firing past him and advancing by squads. All around him Marines were firing and charging forward. Suddenly two grabbed him by his numb arms and began to pull him back to the south bank.

Are we winning? he thought, and then blearily asked the question aloud to a Marine on his right.

"Jay'sus, lad!" the guy sounded like they'd just whisked him out of County Kildair. "If'n we aren't, it'll be no fault'a yore own. Who'dya think yar? Sah'gent Yark?"

"What're you talkin' about?"

"'Bout half the battalion saw you two on the bridge," said a mustached Marine sergeant, grinning foolishly. "I heard the old man himself say you fellas looked like Horatius times two out there. He'll want to see you after you're fixed up." Some kind of triage station had been set up behind the First National Grocery. Hennessey was gently lowered to the ground.

"Congressional Medal of Honor, f'sure," the grinning sergeant said. "You just sit tight and a corpsman'll be 'long t'check you out, okay?" Hennessey could do little more than dumbly nod his assent. The night was passing like a blur. Someone came and looked him over, but Hennessey had no idea whether the guy was checking him for wounds or rummaging through his pockets. Sometime later he noticed that his face and neck were burned, and his greatcoat was actually smoldering. He leapt to his feet to shrug off the flamethrower before he exploded like a Roman candle, but suddenly remembered he'd ditched it back on the bridge.

Swaying on his feet, Hennessey could see that he was not alone in the square. It had become a sort of rally point for the battalion. Trucks were rolling in and out. Wounded and dead were being sorted in front of the Gilman Hotel. And there on the southernmost side, two Marines with trench guns were standing guard over twenty or so battered-looking townsfolk.

It only took a few seconds for Hennessey to cross the square to the prisoners. As Hennessey walked along the knot of men and women, he carefully studied each of the bloated, inhuman faces. The only thing he saw in their fat, bulging eyes was hatred. From the mother clutching a wailing brat to her fat breasts, to the men, tattered, bloodied, and bruised from the beatings the Marines had given them, all Hennessey saw was red-rimmed hatred. They didn't hate the Marines for burning their temples and smashing their idols. They hated them for what they were: normal, clean, and human.

Hennessey didn't want their hate. He wanted their fear.

He returned a few minutes later with a Thompson he got off a dead Marine at the triage station and killed them all. The two Marines who had been guarding the civilians were so shocked they almost let him load a second drum into the Thompson before they tackled him and wrestled the empty weapon away. Hennessey was cuffed and placed under arrest.

Major Walsh, the battalion's commanding officer, was a bit disappointed that his nominee for the Congressional Medal of Honor was now a "baby-killing sonuvabitch." But, as Hennessey heard one of the T-men explain to the Major, "How're you going to court-martial the man when none of this ever happened and we were never here?"

Later Hennessey was taken under guard to the Battalion HQ outside Innsmouth. He sat and watched a mortar battery dump hundreds of shells onto the north side of town where things were still flopping and twisting in the rubble. Next a convoy of motor coaches arrived. Hennessey watched as Navy doctors carefully examined the captured townsfolk and directed them onto the waiting buses. Some people got to go on the buses on the right; others were sent to the left. To Hennessey the folks going to the left seemed a good deal more squamous.

Hennessey soon found himself joined by three other handcuffed Marines: a captain by the name of Houseman, a sergeant named Dylan, and a private who claimed his name was "Death." The feeling of kinship was immediate and mutual. After the debriefing back at the Boston Naval Annex's brig, Hennessey was reassigned to units of the 6th Marine Regiment based in San Diego. He never again saw the men he'd spent the night handcuffed to in that truck. Except for one, decades later, at the Chosin Reservoir. That had been even colder than Innsmouth. Maybe the coldest place this side of Hell. Hennessey saw Private "Death," this time sporting a gold oak leaf and quartering a Chinese soldier with an entrenching tool. For a second, recognition passed between them, but nothing was ever said. By the end of that day, the Chinese, like the monsters of Innsmouth, had learned to fear them.

And their fear was all he'd ever wanted.

∞

"Sergeant Hennessey?" Levine thought the old man was dead. The way he started stuttering and then slumped over with that outrush of breath, Levine was sure he'd just had a coronary. He reached forward and grasped Hennessey's stick-thin wrist to search for a pulse. As soon as he felt the bird-like bones, Hennessey jumped to life again and snatched his hand away as if the young Delta Green agent were made of red-hot coals. "I'm sorry!" Levine stammered. "Are you all right?"

The question tugged an involuntary and terrible giggle out of Hennessey. "Awl'right? Shit no! I'm not all awlright at all! How many more times I gotta go through that fucking nightmare with you?"

Nearly as soaked with perspiration as Hennessey, Levine glanced to Parker and noted the big Army Major's nearly imperceptible nod. "I think this will be the last time, Sergeant," Levine said. "We've got all we need, I think. You've been extremely helpful, and your government appreciates the service you've done us today."

"And did for us back then as well," Parker added flatly. That was about as many words as Levine had heard Parker speak at one time.

"That was it?" Hennessey looked more surprised than relieved. "You won't be coming back?"

"No, sir," Levine said as he moved to turn off the video camera.

"Are you sure, son? 'Cuz you know, I might remember more next time." The voice went thin with desperate entreaty.

Levine turned and looked at the old gnarled root of a man coiled in the wheelchair in front of him and instantly recognized that he wasn't the same man he'd spent the last four days with. That man was filled with hate and jealousy for the men who were still young enough to walk to the bathroom and have a regular bowel movement. This new man was filled with fear, fear that he would die alone in this VA hospital with no one to even notice.

"I'm...I'm afraid we have other duties waiting for us back in Washington."

"That's not the only time I saw them fish men, y'know," Hennessey blurted out.

That stopped them cold. "I thought you said you never saw where they took the prisoners?"

"Not the prisoners," Hennessey chattered. "Others. And others sorta like them. During the war in the Pacific I got picked up by a section of the OSS. I went on a dozen missions in the Marshalls, the Philippines, Manchuria, and even French Indochina. I saw stuff. I could tell ya all about it."

"Really?" Parker's voice sounded like the earth moving.

Hennessey took a deep breath and let it out slow. "Maybe you can answer me one question first? Why is the Navy coming to me for answers? Why ask me when you guys have a whole filing cabinet full of debriefings on this? I ain't telling you anything I didn't tell Naval Intelligence right afterwards. So why ask me all over again seventy years later?"

"Sergeant Hennessey," Levine said evenly, "please believe me when I tell you that I truly wish I could tell you what this is all about. But it's national security. You understand, don't you?"

Hennessey apparently tried to look angry, but instead he just looked tired, old and tired. His head dangled at the end of his stumpy neck and he rubbed his eyes with his swollen-jointed fingers. "Maybe you can't tell me who sentcha, but I can sure as hell tell you who you smell like to me. You smell like those OSS guys. Answered every question with 'Sorry, that's Delta Green clearance only.' I know you ain't gonna tell me whether I'm right or not, but before I tell you one more thing, there's something I gotta know. And dammit, you owe me.

"I've done a lot of hard shit for my country. Forty-two years in the Marine Corps: Guadalcanal, Saipan, Tinian, Iwo Jima, Chosin. And those are just the ones I can talk about, if there was even anyone around to listen. After forty-two years in a business where doing anything, including doing nothing, can get you killed, somebody or something should have punched my ticket. Instead I'm propped up in this fuckin' chair, my legs next to useless, my back and fingers twisted with arthritis. Everything's failing except my memories. From breakfast to bedtime, all I do all day is wait for my heart to stop. So I've paid my dues and done my duty thirty times over and you assholes owe me this answer before I say another word.

"You can't make me talk. I'm too old to threaten. The only reason I'm still alive is that I'm still a good Catholic and suicide's a one-way ticket to Hell, so killin' me would be doing me a big fuckin' favor. I'm too old to bribe, either. There's nothing you can promise me that I've got the capacity to even enjoy anymore. So don't even try.

"So if you want to know more, you'll have to answer one question first."

"What is it?" Levine asked.

The old bastard looked up. He looked terribly small and frail just then.

"Are we winning?" he asked.

Levine knew the answer to that question. Everyone in Delta Green knew the answer. Some more than others. Some wouldn't admit it, but they knew. What the hell could Levine tell him? The truth? That rather than face what Innsmouth meant the government had chosen to ignore it? That when others formed a force to fight the war anew, they were disbanded, not once but twice? That all those precious files were either misplaced or destroyed? Could he really look the old man in the eye and tell him that the Delta Green Hennessey knew was now a pack of renegades having to beg, borrow, and steal to fight a war for the very survival of the human species, all because nobody wanted to believe in the things Hennessey fought seventy years ago?

Levine knew that he sure enough owed the old bastard. He'd fought the first battle in a war that raged behind the shadows even today. A war with no end in sight. Hennessey won the first battle and made the first advances. He'd beaten the ugliness back. And then some other assholes had pissed it all away.

Levine owed the old bastard a few restful nights, a few nights of sleep where he could lay his head down and know that he had not sacrificed in vain. That the world was safe. That Jerusalem was delivered from the infidel.

"We're winning, Sergeant. Of course we are."

The Hour of the Tortoise

Molly Tanzer

4 April 1887, early morning. Traveling.

I sat alone in my train-carriage watching the beech-copses and white sheep and mist-wreathed fields flashing by. I am sure this countryside could be anywhere in England, but these were the trees and fields of Devon, my home county! And I had not seen them from the time I was sent away to learn what I could at Miss Coote's Academy for Young Women of Breeding and Promise.

More than a decade has passed, but the native beauty of this place remains ever-first in my heart. How could it not be but so? My happiest days were spent in Devonshire, when I was but a lass running hither and yon, and always by the side of my cousin Laurent. Two years my junior, he had been my constant childhood companion—but what of now? What sort of man has he grown into?

'Twas a kiss that separated us, a kiss seen by his mother, Lady Fanchone. That woman, whom some would call great, mistook our embrace for the blossoming of love rather than the affection shared by near-siblings, and would brook no explanations. Laurent became but a memory, and Devon, too—until now! For I am coming home…

ꙮ

Yes, that should do nicely, I think, for the introduction. A heroine at the end of her pupal stage, all grown up and ready to break through childhood's chrysalis.

Christ above, save me from choking upon my own vomit.

I must find a way to add some spice directly lest I bore myself into an early grave, to say nothing of losing us the whole of our readership. Perhaps she (need name, floral in nature: Violet? Camilla? Camilla is nice) shall lose her maidenhead on the train. But to whom: the conductor? A handsome fellow-traveler? I must think on it.

No, I should delay the jimmying open of Love's crimson gate slightly longer. She could be introduced to the art of prick-sucking by a gallant stranger...but then he leaves her unsatisfied?

Better, better, and yet while it's true my editrix has never once given me poor counsel regarding my pornographies, I find Gothic fiction so very tiresome. I really cannot account for its popularity, but I am sure that is the reason Susan is so beside herself with excitement over this project. "Dearest Chelone, you shall write me *Jane Eyre*—but with lots and lots of fucking! It shall be our new serial and make us ever so much money!" Not exactly the response I anticipated when I told her I must take an extended leave of absence from *Milady's Ruby Vase* so I might journey into the dreariest parish in Devon to sit by the side of my former guardian while he lies gasping out his last upon his deathbed.

To stay once again under the gabled roof of Calipash Manor, after being so unceremoniously chucked out a decade ago...I have mixed feelings about this journey, to say the least. I am certain Susan believes I am going to encounter a country house full of secret passages, drafty towers, mysterious mysteries, and handsome cousins. Well, that will happen in the pornography, of course, and to be fair, Calipash Manor *does* have a tower. And, I suppose, its share of silly rumors about the family. But the reality is far more boring: An old man in his tidy house, wasting away with few to comfort him, having alienated himself during his life from those who might have loved him unto death.

I suppose there is something rather *Wuthering Heights* about that, but not like any of the better parts, like when So-and-So threatens to cut off the boy's ears or whatever it is that happens.

Later—Funny, how I had thought to include a handsome stranger-*cum*-deflowerer in my story; I just met a rather natty fellow that will do nicely as a model! I should liked to have had some sport with him myself, except, it was so queer. He apologized for approaching me without a proper introduction, but asked if I was by chance related to the Calipash family. I told him I wasn't—which isn't strictly true, of course, but we illegitimate children of the noblesse are trained to be discreet—but he would not let the matter go. He shook his head and apologized, with the excuse that he was a native of Ivybridge, so knew "the Calipash look," and said I had a serious case of it.

"The Calipash look!" I exclaimed, delighted. "Surely you must be referring to the Calipash Curse?"

"I suppose I am," said he. I was surprised by how alarmed he seemed by my amusement. "You know of the curse, miss?"

"Of course I do, but I have not heard anybody mention it for nigh ten years!"

"You may smile," he said, furrowing his brow at me as if his very life depended on it, "but we Ivybridge folk know nothing connected with that family is a laughing matter. Bad blood, they have—diabolists, deviants, and necromancers all!"

"I am acquainted with the Lord Calipash, and a better man I have rarely met." Well, it was true enough statement. I let this cove take it as he would.

"He's a good sort, true enough, but they go bad easy. I'd be on the lookout, miss. You surely look like a Calipash, perhaps you were...well, I won't curse you by suggesting you have a twin lurking somewhere—but best to stay out of the ponds, just the same!"

I told him I had every intention of staying out of ponds, lakes, rivers, streams, sloughs, and for that matter, lagoons. He seemed relieved, but the way such a dapper young man took notice of piffling country legends, well, it gave me pause.

Of course when I used to go into the village as a girl I heard tell of the Calipash family curse—when twins are born, the devil is their father, and something about taking to the sea, or to ponds, and something about frog people maybe, of all the outlandish claims! I may not be remembering it all correctly; as a girl once I came home enquiring about it, but Lizzie, the housekeeper, reprimanded me for repeating such twaddle and I never again mentioned it. I am glad I was taught at a young age to be skeptical of supernatural nonsense.

Really, what family that lives in a manor-house rather than a cottage doesn't have some sort of rumor or another hanging over them like the sword of Damocles?

Rum analogy to use when going to see a dying man, perhaps.

Ooh—but we are slowing, and there is the whistle! I must ready myself.

Evening. In my old room—The dolls I left behind are still here, and the white bedstead still has its rose-sprigged coverlet and pink frilly canopy. It is only how yellowed and worn everything appears that keeps me from thinking I have stepped back into another time. I feel fourteen years old in this room.

Ah well, why bother changing the décor? I was always made to maintain the illusion of juvenescence to please my guardian, so why not keep my chambers in a state of static girlishness, too?

But I should not speak ill of Lord Calipash, or rather, he who was Lord Calipash until his death—his death that I fear I may have caused not an hour ago! And already there is a new lord under the manor-roof tonight...

Things are far stranger here at Calipash Manor than I anticipated. Perhaps there is something to the idea of a family curse—no! Stop that, Chelone. You are simply tired from your journey, and overwrought.

Here is what happened, the facts, I mean: I arrived at the Ivybridge station on time, but no one was waiting for me, to my distress. The skies promised rain, and it was miles to walk to Calipash Manor.

After waiting at the station for some time, I begged the use of a little wheeled cart for my trunk and went into Ivybridge proper, thinking I would visit the post office. It was from thence I had received the letter from my guardian summoning me hither. I thought perhaps I could, rather than sending a message by courier, ride with said courier (if the horse would bear us both) and come back later for my luggage.

The town looked the same, snug stone houses and muddy streets, the occasional chicken scurrying across the main thoroughfare. The post office was in the same dilapidated cottage, I was happy to discover, with what could have been the same geraniums as when I was a girl blooming in the window-box. I went inside and explained my situation.

"Quite a lot of traffic to and from the manor-house of late," remarked the woman at the window, not answering my query of how I might get myself to Calipash Manor. "Telegraph yesterday, and was barely a week ago the prodigal son come in to send a letter. Queer fellow."

"Mr. Vincent has come home, then?"

"Aye, for his father is soon for the grave, they say."

"How is he queer?" I was madly curious about Orlando Vincent, the cousin I had never seen. I should remember later to ask him about Rotterdam, where he was educated. Might be able to write something for the *Vase* about Dutch schoolboys or something...

"Didn't say nothing when he came in." The woman's frown would have shamed the devil himself. "Grunted his yeses and noes as if he had no human power of speech in him. Gave me a turn, he did. At first I thought he was the Ghast o'the Hills, come to take my soul. Mr. Vincent is very like the apparition, though of course his clothing is different."

Her words made me laugh, which I could tell displeased her. As a child I heard tell of the 'Ghast o'the Hills,' some sort of spirit in a frock-coat that is said to haunt the parish of Ivybridge. Once I even thought I saw it...a childish fancy, of course. I am lucky that education—and, of course, living in London—has disabused me of such country superstitions.

"So you've seen the Ghast?" I asked, amused.

"You may laugh, miss, but around here, there's precious few who haven't seen the Ghast! He's as real as you or I, and wanders at night moanin and groanin. It's said he seeks a wife to keep him company."

"And Mr. Vincent looks like him?"

"Well, he's thin, tall, with that Calipash face. All thems what come from the Manor have a look, don't they? In fact, you have it too, my girl. Are you related?"

I didn't want to get into that. "I didn't realize the Ghast was part of the Calipash Curse?"

"Well, that family's queer, of course, so if this town had some sort of malign spirit, it'd come from thems what—"

"You hush your foolish old mouth, Hazel Smith! Telling ghost stories like a heathen. You ought to be ashamed!"

I turned 'round, surprised, and was pleased to see Old Bill, the groundskeeper and jack-of-all for Calipash Manor, standing behind me.

"Bill!" I cried, and embraced him. "How are you? Oh, just look at you!"

"Let us be gone, Miss Burchell," he said gruffly. "Waited for you at the station, but they said you'd traipsed hither for your own purposes. Hold your tongue, we can talk on the drive. Lord Calipash is not long for this world and I have no wish to follow him into the grave if this weather turns wet."

At first I attributed his poor spirits to his age, for he must be closer to seventy than sixty these days, white-haired and gaunt as a skeleton. But he got my trunk onto his skinny back and into the cart quickly enough; indeed, by the time he had scrambled onto the seat, ready to leave, I had hardly finished saying hello and asking after my guardian.

"Things are quite dire," was his reply. "'Tis good you've come now, though you might've sent more notice of your arriving. Lizzie is beside herself getting your old room ready, not to mention the cooking for an extra person."

"I telegraphed yesterday," I replied, rather taken aback by this admonition. "And really, Lord Calipash himself invited me—bid me come with all possible haste!"

"As you say," said Bill, looking at me askance as he chucked the reins.

"What do you mean by that?"

"Master's not been able to lift a quill in some time," he said with a shrug. "Before his son come home, I was writing all his letters for him."

"You, Bill!"

"Aye. I went to the village school as a youth and learned to read, write, and cipher—no need to look so surprised, Miss! I do tolerable justice to my lord's handwriting, he himself asked me to learn the trick of it when he was struck with arthritis. But now him that's to be the next Lord Calipash has taken over the duty, so he says, but unless he posts the letters himself, nothing's gone out in some time. Hasn't asked me to go into the village since his arrival anyways."

"But that woman said Mr. Vincent delivered the letter himself!"

"Did she now?"

"Yes...perhaps Mr. Vincent was the one who wrote to me. But, then, why disguise his writing? I should have come if he had extended the invitation to me, of course."

"Couldn't say, Miss. He's a strange creature, full of notions and temper. Perhaps he thinks you are like him. I had to write to him in the Lord Calipash's own hand, begging for his return, to get him to come! Ignored all the letters I wrote as myself."

"Rotterdam is a very far distance to travel on short notice ..."

"Aye, and the road to hell is a short and easy path! Honor thy father says the Bible."

"Oh, Bill. I've missed you," said I, shocked to find it was the truth, as I had always remembered him as the bane of my childhood. Somehow he knew when I was up to mischief and would foil my plans if he could, with a Bible verse ready to shame me for my willfulness.

I opened my mouth to ask him another question, one about Mr. Vincent, but my power of speech left me entirely at that moment. We'd crested a hill, and Calipash Manor had come into view.

I looked upon the ivy-wreathed front doors and the ancient moldering stone of the house, pale in the weird light of the coming storm, and felt a strange flutter inside my chest. I could not help thinking that the manor looked as if it had weathered a good deal more than ten years during my decade-long absence. The tower, where I had once held tea-parties with my dolls, or played at being Rapunzel, now looked so rickety it would not support a dove's nest; the plentiful windows, upon which I had painted frost-pictures in the winter and opened to feel the breeze during the mild country summers, looked smaller, and dark with the kind of soot and filth one sees in London but few other places.

"I have been away a very long time," I whispered hoarsely. "Drive 'round, Bill, so I may get inside and see the place."

"Go through the front doors, Miss Burchell," urged Bill.

This drew a laugh to my lips, and I wiped my eyes. "I am no lady, and certainly not the lady of the house. Drive 'round, the servants' door was always good enough for me."

"No, Miss. You're here as our guest now, after all."

I knew that tone, and it meant no arguing, so I thanked Bill and hopped down from the haywain. I was seized with a girlish fancy to take the steps two at a time as I had always used to do, but I only managed a few such leaps before my corset prevented further exertion. Thus I was sweaty-faced and breathing hard when I threw open the door—and saw the foyer for the first time in ten years.

The floorboards groaned under my shoes as I entered, and the high ceilings amplified the echoes of both footfall and wood-creak. The first thing I noticed was the watery light spilling in from the door was hazy with little swirling motes of dust. My hasty entrance had stirred the air more than it had been in some time. Indeed, filth and grime lay thick on every surface, and I was overwhelmed by the smell of mold. When I looked up, I saw the chandelier was missing more than one pendalogue, and the candle-cups did not look like they had held tapers in recent memory.

I could not move for astonishment. I remembered this room as a bright and welcoming space; recalled the sound of my guardian's laughter as he would chase me, shrieking, through the hallways, much to the displeasure of the housekeeper, Lizzie, who said I should grow up wild.

Shouting and stomping startled me out of my reverie. It was a man's voice I heard coming from the interior of the house—and all of a sudden there was a tall, thin fellow with messy black hair and bulging eyes at the top of the front staircase, then galloping down it! He was too busy howling at the top of his lungs to notice me.

"Bill! Lizzie! Anyone! The old bastard is in need of something, but I cannot understand his infernal mumblings!"

It was such an excellent entrance that upon recollection, I cannot help but now contemplate how I will translate it into my narrative of Camilla's coming-of-age:

I have no words to express my surprise when I saw that Laurent was all grown up! Pale of skin and darkly handsome, his face held a haughty, cruel expression that checked my first impulse to rush into his arms and demand a longed-for kiss from my oldest, dearest friend in the world. How serious he looked! His black coat and trousers would have been better suited for a funeral in London than his ancestral country home. Still, I blushed to see him—and felt a blush where not three hours ago I had been brought to the golden threshold of love by the gamahuching of Mr. Reeves. I never thought I would see my cousin in such a light—and yet...

But of course, my Camilla has her memories of Laurent to *contrast* with the man she meets upon arriving at The Beeches, as I think I shall call her former home. ("A Camilla Among The Beeches" sounds like an excellent title to me— we shall see what Susan thinks.) I, however, had never before laid eyes upon Orlando Vincent. My first impression was of a flustered wretch of about my own age, clad in a wrinkled suit, and waving his arms about and carrying on in a dreadful manner. I could see how someone might mistake him for the Ghast o'the Hills—if one were inclined to see ghosts and spirits everywhere, that is.

"Why Mr. Vincent, I declare!" cried Lizzie, stepping into the dusty foyer, drying her hands with a dingy rag. How old must she be now, I wondered? Always slender and tall, she was now made all of angles, and her impressive mane of dark hair was now a lustrous gray—handsome, to be sure, but no longer youthful. "And here's our Chelone! Why, just look at you, grown! I'm surprised at you, Mr. Vincent. Let the young lady come in and rest herself before alarming her with your profuse ejaculations!"

I am aware those not in my profession use that word without heed for its alternative definition, but I confess I giggled—which caused Mr. Vincent to blush very pink indeed, and sneer at me down his long narrow nose.

"It is good to meet you at last," said I, to cover the awkwardness I had caused. "I used to read your letters to the Lord Calipash. How was your journey from Rotterdam?"

"Spare me this nonsense," he snapped. "You must come, Lizzie—now—he gurgles and sweats out his very life, I think. You can understand him better than I, come and discover what it is he wants!"

Lizzie looked appalled. "Mr. Vincent, you must not—"

"I shall make love to the chit later if it please you—only come now and see to my father! Are you so silly that the health of your lord does not take precedence over your sense of decorum?"

"Excuse me, Chelone," said Lizzie. "I shall get you settled directly, but if you like, please go now to your old room. I know you know the way."

"Let me come with you," I suggested. I had no wish to be left alone in this dreary, unremembered house! "Perhaps I can be of some help."

"You'll be the most help if you shut your mouth and stop distracting us all! Why you have come now, at the eleventh hour, is a mystery to me!" Mr. Vincent turned on his heel and fairly ran away from us, taking the steps two at a time.

I was, of course, concerned that he who had posted, and I had supposed, written the letter to me also had no notion of my coming, but I had no time to muse on this—Lizzie had followed after him, saying over her shoulder:

"Come along, then. You always had a certain rapport with the Lord Calipash, perhaps the unexpected sight of you will restore him."

"I cannot account for this," I said, as I followed her. "Why did he not tell anyone of his invitation to me, I wonder? And how did he get the letter into the post?" I laughed. "Perhaps it really was the Ghast!"

"I beg your pardon?"

"Oh, nothing—just, the woman at the post office said Mr. Vincent was very like the Ghast o'the Hills, you know, the ghost that—"

"There's no such thing as ghosts," interrupted Lizzie. "Let us see what the Lord Calipash requires, yes?"

During our trip upstairs to my guardian's chambers I had noticed the same disrepair and neglect throughout Calipash Manor as had been evident in the foyer. The banisters were unpolished and slick with moisture; the carpet felt damp beneath my feet. Even the portrait-frames looked strangely aged. The gold leaf had flaked away and, curiously, the people in the pictures appeared older than I remembered them. The Calipash family has always been an attractive one, though just as the gentleman on the train mentioned, bizarrely alike in aspect, and with frequent incidences of twins. Long did I study their thin, aristocratic faces as a girl, making up silly stories about their lives—but today, instead of looking like an ancient and noble line, all seemed to carry in their eyes a hateful and sinister expression I had never before noticed. It made me shiver.

Yet the dilapidation of the house was most evident when Lizzie turned the brass knob of the door into my lord's chambers and pushed through the decaying portal into the interior. The horrible smell of warm putrefaction hit me first, and then, through the gloom—for the thick window-dressings blocked most of the already-dim light—I could see more of the awful dust that coated every surface. Soiled garments were piled upon the floor, and his desk was messy with papers and spilled candle-wax.

This place had always been so fastidiously-kept when I was a child! Nauseated, shocked, I looked to my left and saw my guardian in his bed, the curtains of which were stained and the linens unclean. And then there was my lord himself...I remembered him as a vigorous older man, with thick white hair swept back from his temples and a ruddy, narrow, pleasant face, but the person I saw gave me no hint as to his former appearance. He was swollen, bloated even; his hair was thinner, and his face drooped horribly on the left side from the palsy that struck him some weeks back. His skin was as brown as a walnut, and had a patchy, unwholesome appearance.

I was glad Bill had prepared me for the sight, I do not know if I could have kept from crying out had I gone to see him unaware.

Lizzie bustled into the room saying, "Well, well, my lord, what may I fetch you?"

The series of sounds that came from my guardian's mouth could not be called speech, yet Lizzie seemed to understand them well enough.

"Such a fuss and for what? Only the want of a cup of Darjeeling!" she exclaimed.

"My God, is that all?" cried Mr. Vincent, giving me quite a fright—I had not noticed him lurking like a spider on the other side of my lord's bed.

"I'll have it for you before you can say Jack Robinson," said Lizzie, "but while you wait, here's something for you, my lord—your guest is here!"

More wet grunting and smacking. Lizzie's face fell.

"Well, surely you will be pleased when you see who it is—come closer, my dear, don't hang in the doorway like some sort of apparition!"

With not a little trepidation I took a few faltering steps toward the bed. He really looked as miserable as the house itself; indeed, the only thing bright or beautiful about him was a curious jade pendant he wore on a chain upon his breast, just visible where his nightshirt was unbuttoned. Carved in the shape of a winged tortoise, it had a face more lupine than reptilian, and great clawed monkey-paw hands that gave the impression that the ornament was clinging to his skin. The craftsmanship looked almost Egyptian, and it glowed faintly in the gloaming. I thought I recognized the image…but I know not where, for surely he never wore it while I lived in this house.

Something about it captivated me, made me long to look upon it further, to hold it in my hand and run my fingertips over the smoothness of the stone.

"What a lovely necklace," I blurted, unable to help myself.

A grunt that sounded like agreement came from him—and then his bleary eyes focused on my face.

"Whooo?" he said, like a tubercular owl.

"Your letter bid me come," said I, remembering myself at last. I took his hand in mine, but almost dropped it in surprise. It felt leathery and chitinous at once; I could not feel the bones beneath the skin. "It is I, Chelone Burchell, your ward. I had not expected to see you again. I am so glad—"

There was more I was going to say, but, unexpectedly, my greeting induced a sort of apoplexy in the Lord Calipash. He began to cry out and wheeze and make such a ruckus I let go his hand immediately.

"Never!" I managed to understand through it all, and also, "Begone!"

This cut me to the quick. It was not as though I had forgotten what was supposed to be my permanent banishment when I received his missive! How could I fail to recall the day I was turned out of the house and sent alone in a coach to attend Miss Redcombe's School for Girls of Quality? I was not even allowed to pack, my things were sent after me. All I had were the clothes on my back, a few shillings in my pocket, and a letter of explanation in my hand that stated, among other things, that payment would soon arrive to cover my education until I came of age; that I should stay at the school for all holidays unless invited to a friend's house, and that every effort must be taken to keep me away from young men!

And yet I had always hoped we would be reconciled, despite his returning every letter I ever sent him, unopened; that he would come to regret punishing me so severely for such a trifling youthful indiscretion ...

"I'm—sorry, the letter, it must have, I don't know," I stammered, backing away from the bed. The old man had begun to twitch and froth at the mouth, looking wildly back and forth between myself and Mr. Vincent.

"Begone!" he cried again, and then he fell back on the pillows—stone dead!

Lizzie, Mr. Vincent, and I stood still for some minutes, all shocked by what had transpired.

I was the first to speak.

"I brought the letter," I heard myself saying, protesting this awful scene and my part in it. "You can see it for yourselves!"

Mr. Vincent—or rather, Lord Calipash, as I should start to call him, checked for the old man's pulse.

"Well," he sighed. "That's that. There is nothing to be done but prepare ourselves for the funeral and legal expenses. A damned nuisance, I'll warrant, but it shall be soon done with."

"My lord," said Lizzie, in her *how shameful* voice that I knew too well. "How can you say such things? And at a time like this?"

"I barely knew the man," said the new Lord Calipash with a dismissive wave of his pale hand. "He sent me away to live with strangers as soon as I could walk, and called me home only so he could instruct me as to the management of this estate. He cared nothing for me, nor I for him. Now get thee to the kitchen to make my supper, and have Bill dress the body and put it in the crypt to keep it cool until the official burial. Oh—and have him go into the village to send a telegram to our lawyer in London, too."

And he left the room, slamming the door behind him.

I jumped—and then jumped again. The skies had made good on the storm promised since I arrived at the station; thunder crashed, a sudden spatter of thick raindrops hit the glass window. The room lit up with lightning, then fell dark again.

"For goodness' sake, it's only rain," said Lizzie, reprimanding me for my jumpiness. I detected a note of bitterness in her voice. "You'd better go settle in. You will not want to try to return to London tonight."

"Of course," I heard myself say. "I—I am sorry…"

"And what good does that do anybody?" she said, not looking at me. She looked wracked, grief-stricken, bereft even. "You've ruined so much this day, girl."

Then she said what I had been feeling since my arrival:

"You should never have come back to this house, Chelone Burchell. Not for love or money."

Night. In my room—I thought I should not to go down to supper, but hunger drove me from my chambers. Out of respect I dressed in my most somber gown—but I found the new Lord Calipash tipsy as a lord in his father's chair at the head of the table, cravat untied, his meal unfinished before him. A cold collation awaited me on the dirty sideboard; apparently Lizzie was too occupied to cook something hot. At least the platters looked clean.

"My lord," I said, entering the shabby dining room. "You must allow me to apologize—I had no notion my presence would so upset your late father. If I had known—"

"If *I* had known, I should have invited you myself, and weeks ago," he slurred, looking at me half-lidded. "Have some wine, cousin? And some salad, and meat? The cold boiled is particularly good."

I was surprised to hear him address me as *cousin*, for while that is certainly true, I was taught from a young age that my illegitimate origins prevented me from claiming such a connection with the Calipash family.

I could not bring myself to be so informal with him.

"Thank you, my lord. I am thirsty," I said, and he poured me a large glass out of the crystal decanter by his elbow. The claret was blood-red, and sparkled as it flowed. I knew just by looking at it that it was of a better vintage than I had ever before tasted.

"Allow me to apologize for the rude hello I gave you earlier," he said. "I was flustered and not myself."

"It has already been forgotten," I said, accepting the glass he handed me. I took nothing else, I found I did not wish to eat just then, during our first real encounter. "I understand. Meeting each other—now! It is a queer thing."

"What, that a strumpet's whelp should have lived here, in this house, while the son of the lord was exiled? Yes, that is a queer thing," he said. His eyes finally focused on me. "A queer thing indeed."

I knew not what to make of his mood, so I said nothing. I do not enjoy verbal fencing with mercurial gentlemen, that is for sharp-tongued spinsters with many cats and well-thumbed copies of *Emma*.

"Well, let bygones be bygones," he said at last. "'Twas not your fault, my situation, and it would make me unreasonable to blame you. Tell me about yourself, Miss Burchell. What do you do?"

"I am—a writer," I said. "I live in London, where I work for a ladies' periodical."

"Which?"

"You would not have heard of it," I said demurely. Experience has taught me not to reveal my status as pornographer too readily, I have found it is better to let people form an opinion of me before revealing how disreputable I am.

"You might be surprised," he said. "I read all sorts of things."

"Indeed?"

"Things that would make you blush, I'll warrant."

I thought this a sorry attempt at rakishness. "My lord?"

"I should show you my collection sometime...even though you are but a distant, and to be truthful, unwanted relation, you have Calipash blood in you, and thus should appreciate certain genres considered *outré* by the masses. It is really too bad the Private Library was burned to ashes—"

A clap of thunder from outside, where the storm still raged, silenced him, but I did not mind. I needed a moment to recover myself: He had mentioned the Private Library! That was what had been written on each bookplate: *This Book Belongs to the Private Library of the Calipash Family.*

"Perhaps you are referring to the collection of infamous volumes that used to be housed on the leftmost bookcase of the library? The one that required spinning about to find what it *really* housed?"

It was my turn to surprise him! He sat up in his chair and looked at me keenly. I began to doubt he had drunk as much wine as I had first thought.

"Yes—yes I do! Ach, how can it be that such a lowly urchin has sampled the legendary delights of the Calipash Private Library, and yet I have never done so?"

"I could not say, my lord."

"Perhaps—do you then know why it was burned? I could not understand what my father said regarding the matter. His speech was too far gone when I asked."

I was happy to have something to hold over him, so instead of answering him directly, I stood and began to fill a plate from the contents of the sideboard—salmon salad, cold chicken, succulent orange-slices, tongue in aspic. I avoided the cold boiled.

As I selected the last elements of my repast, over my shoulder I said, "Your father did not share your opinions, my lord."

"Oh? How so?"

"He burned the collection after finding me perusing an illustrated copy of *Fanny Hill*—or, at least, what I know now was a...let us say *variant* edition of that classic pornography, rewritten to emphasize deviant black magicks than matters carnal. He was so very horrified that he whipped me out the door and into his coach, to be taken directly to school, never permitted to return."

I did not add that he had discovered me with my hand under my own skirts, frigging myself furiously whilst looking at the naughty pictures, strange though some surely were.

It had been a humid summer day, and I had just that year discovered the delights of that revolving bookcase. Actually, I do not believe my guardian knew of the Private Library before that day, as when the old Lord Calipash walked in on me, he snatched the book away, and, eyes wide, had demanded to know where I found such a thing; after seeing what else the collection held he had shouted that he would burn the lot of it, that such titles could do nothing but induce evil in women and men alike.

Though I have never had any reason to doubt my lord's having followed through on the threat, it made me sad to hear he had really done so. It was, after all, an impressive collection of very rare, decadent, and often shockingly corrupt tomes. Those on the subject of fornication were my favorite, of course, but those were fewer and farther between than I liked. Far more of the collection was made up of rather mouldy books on performing dark sorceries and profane rituals to honor a pack of heathen gods who sounded rather rum compared to Zeus or Thor. There was one I recall that had loads of filthy pictures—a translation of some sort of foreign sex and murder manual, it seemed to me. I can't recall the title but I know an Englishman named Dee saw fit to have the book available in our tongue, but I question his decision there. It was a far cry from Burton's *Kama Sutra*; I can't imagine anyone would find those positions or actions pleasurable, but there's no accounting for taste, I suppose. But that wasn't all: there were books on horrid-sounding cannibal cults of the ancient world—*Nameless Cults*, I think the title was—and I recall there was even a treatise on the delights of necromancy by a young woman of the family, Rosemary Vincent, whose portrait still hangs in the gallery! Though a stilted homage—or, funny, it must have been a precursor, for she lived during the eighteenth century—to Shelley's *Frankenstein*, my ancestor's manual, *Resurrecting the Dead for Work and Pleasure* was entertaining reading at the very least, as it detailed how one might create some sort of composite creature from dead bodies using common household items and magic spells, many drawn from some of the other books in the Private

Library. I had even cross-referenced a few, bored creature that I was...I wonder if Shelley had a copy of her work? It seems the sort of thing Byron would have had lying about.

It occurs to me as I write this that it was in that strange sex-manual where I had once before seen the chimerical tortoise-image my guardian had been wearing. There had been two creatures hand-drawn upon the page, one very like my guardian's pendant, and another in the same style, of a winged, hound-faced sphinx. I saw the same image in a few books, come to think of it, though those had Latin titles and were indecipherable to me.

"Well well well, *Fanny Hill*," said Orlando Vincent, interrupting my thoughts as he poured himself another tipple from the decanter. "Variant or not, it seems the adage *is* true—what is bred in the bone will come out in the flesh. The slut's pup is a slut herself!"

"Then you must be as illegitimate as I, for you are no gentleman!" I said hotly.

"Mind that temper, cousin," he said, and slurped his wine at me lewdly.

"And you mind your manners!" said I. "I shall not be calumniated by a messy-haired stripling, drunk on his father's wine. Good night, sir!" Thus I rose, and took my leave of him.

I wasn't really that offended, I just wanted to make it clear to him that he could not speak to me like that. But upon reaching my rooms I regretted my decision; I was not yet tired. The strange day had enlivened me rather than the reverse.

Remembering that when I was a girl and wakeful in the night I used to sit at my window and brush my hair until I was sleepy, I changed into my night-clothes and blew out the candle. Yet while I thought the ritual would settle my mind, when I saw how ill-tended the storm-lit grounds of Calipash Manor were, instead of relaxing me, looking upon them brought back my earlier feelings of gloom, horror, and ruination.

Especially when I saw that the woods were not so overgrown as to prevent me from seeing the Calipash family crypt through the pine-boughs!

I felt a shock when I saw the crumbling Doric structure, quite as if I had been struck by a bolt of the lightning still occasionally illuminating the night sky—how had I forgotten the nightmarish sepulcher until that very moment? Not that there was anything actually frightening about the place, of course. I had merely scared myself nearly out of my wits in there as a child.

What it is about graveyards that so captivate children I know not, but I would venture there often as a girl. It was far from the house proper, which made it exciting, and overgrown, which put me in mind of fairy-circles or some such nonsense. The day I found enough bravery in myself to push open the door—and found it unlocked—I made my one and only exploration of its interior. There I had fancied I saw a ghost, or perhaps it was the Ghast, a puerile notion I know…though I confess, looking out upon that temple in miniature again, the little hairs on the back of my neck rose quivering.

A sudden movement tore my eyes away from the loathsome mausoleum. A lone figure ran across the grounds. It was, of all people, Orlando Vincent! Pell-mell he pelted over the grass and through the dregs of the rainstorm, and he was headed toward the graveyard, curiously enough. I wondered on what errand he went; it must be something so urgent it could not wait until morning, so I watched him dash to the crypt and duck inside its carven doorway.

It could not have been five minutes later that he emerged, though with quite a different air about him. Instead of seeming like a man possessed of a desperate mission, he had the lackadaisical aspect of a gentleman very much at his leisure. He stood casually under the overhang of the crypt-entrance for a moment, hands in his pockets—and then he looked up at me!

How he knew I was at my casement I could not say, but I am sure he knew, and I felt another strange shock when his shadowed eyes met mine. I raised my hand in greeting, not knowing if he could see the gesture, but he mirrored it. When a final flash of lightning illuminated the grounds I saw he was smiling at me.

I felt a flush of passion worthy of my heroine Camilla and rose from my seat, alarmed at myself. It was then that I re-lit the candle and sat down here—to write—to try to settle my mind. I am not sure if it has worked…

I was too disturbed by my newfound carnal thoughts about my cousin to sleep, so I crept from my room to the tower stairs, thinking I should like to see how altered was the place we had used to play together as children. Up and up I climbed, my candle casting strange shadows on walls of the staircase, until I reached the door. Upon pushing it open, I found the room unchanged by time. There was even still a sheet strung from wall to wall, the roof of our play-castle in which we had pretended to be lords and ladies. I took a faltering step and my foot hit something—looking down, I saw it was the play-sword that Laurent once used to carve dragons and monsters to pieces. That sword was the only thing that had gotten me to come up to the tower, for the first time we braved the stairs, I had believed it haunted!

A sudden movement made me scream—perhaps there really was a ghost that haunted this room! But then my cousin emerged from the shadows, grinning at me.

"Why Camilla! Venturing up here—and in the dark!"

"Oh, Laurent! You gave me such a fright!" I cried. My legs were trembling beneath my night-dress; perceiving this, he offered me his arm and led me to a dusty sofa.

"Will you allow me to make it up to you?" said he. "I know a treatment that is said to cure nervousness in women, it is called *fucking*."

"Oh, I know all about fucking," I laughed weakly. "I have never done it, but nearly everything but. The girls at school said I could lick a quim better than anybody, and a gentleman on the train said my cock-sucking was first rate!"

"Let us see about that," he said, putting my hand on his stiffening prick. It was quite a large affair, larger than anything I had yet encountered. "If you are as good as you say, then I shall introduce you to the very best pleasure of all!"

5 April 1887, Morning. In my room—Oh, what a good night's sleep can do to improve one's spirits! Or at the very least, a good night's *something*. Susan was right, my visit home has yielded quite a lot of inspiration for my serial!

Not a quarter of an hour after I blew out my candle for the second time I heard a soft knock at my door. Somehow I knew who was outside—the new Lord Calipash—but unsure if I wanted to see him, I did not answer. He had been unpleasant, yes, but he was also rather attractive, at least in a squirrely sort of way, and I have enjoyed my share of casual romps with far more irksome men. Many and manifest are the advantages of having no inclination to marry and an excellent understanding of abortifacients.

A second knock, then the handle turned. Without lifting my head from my pillow I saw in the doorway the outline of Orlando, whom I think I may now safely call by his Christian name!

He stole into my chamber, closing the door softly behind him, and then shed his coat, throwing it upon the chair in which I had earlier sat scribbling on my latest story, which, if I do say so myself, is coming along nicely. After kicking off his shoes, to my surprise, he slid wordlessly into bed beside me.

"My God," I whispered, for he stank of death from his trip into the family crypt. "What is it you want so badly that you could not bathe before coming to me, I wonder?"

He said nothing—merely groaned in the most fetching, desperate manner, and put his hand on where my right breast swelled beneath my nightgown. I turned over, and his lips found mine.

I drew back, appalled by his stench. It emanated from every pore in his body; his mouth was foul with the reek of the grave.

"Go and wash," I said. I love an unexpected frolick, but the unclean human body is disgusting to me.

He groaned again, urgently, but due to his odor I was no longer inclined to engage in any amorous endeavors. I pushed him away, but he grabbed my wrist, and held up something in his other hand. It swung to and fro in the moonlight, for the fading storm had parted her clouds to reveal the last sliver of that waning sphere, and I could just see what he held out to me.

It was the jade tortoise I had earlier seen hanging 'round my guardian's neck!

"For me?" I asked him, surprised. He grunted his assent, and then fastened the clasp around my neck.

When I felt the weight of the cold stone on my skin (I am ashamed to write this, for I cannot account for it—not even to myself, here in my private diary) I was possessed of a passion stronger than any I have ever felt before. I was ever so desperate to be fucked, more than when I finally managed to sneak Lord Crim-Con away from his wife for a quick one in a servant's bed at their tenth anniversary party, more even than the time on the occasion of my twenty-third birthday when Susan surprised me by taking me on holiday to Winsor, and snuck me into her brother's dormitory so I could have some sport with five handsome youths of that year's senior class.

"Why, Lord Calipash," said I, snaking my hand down his chest and under the lip of his trousers. "You have inflamed—bewitched me! I simply must have you! Do let us make love!"

He kissed his answer upon my neck, and then lower, lower. I know I am in the habit of describing my encounters in detail here, for my personal enjoyment when I am in my dotage, but we sported for so long, and in so many ways, I fear I shall miss breakfast if I record everything. Suffice it to say, a more tender, compassionate lover I could never want, and he made full use of every place of pleasure I possess. It is sadly rare to find a man as able with bottom-hole as with cunt, but Orlando knew the unique needs, challenges, and delights to be had behind as well as in front. He also had no reservations allowing me to do what I would with him, even going so far as to allow me to work my favorite dildoe (I always take it with me) up into his fundament to induce the truly copious spending which is nigh impossible for men to produce any other way.

Good Lord, but I am hungry! It's only natural after taking so much exercise in the night, I suppose.

Later—Orlando was not at breakfast. Lizzie says he will not come out of his room.

Later still—Feeling rather lonely, for neither Lizzie nor Bill seem to want much to do with me (they are holed up in the kitchen, apparently "doing what must be done" regarding the Lord Calipash's death, though I swear I saw Bill sweep away a trick of bezique when I came into the room...but I must have imagined it, for the sanctimonious old ferret never trucks with any games at all, and certainly not cards!) I went for a walk after my meal.

The grounds are still very lovely here, I think their being so overgrown actually adds to their savage charm. And yet...one would think such a wilderness
would attract more wild creatures, but I saw no life within the twilit deeps except for a tiny, but bright red bird of a type I had never seen before. It landed
on a tree and peered at me silently. I know it will sound strange, but I swear
that once it was sure it held my attention, it fluttered to a close-by tree and
did not move until I stepped toward it. Then it did the same thing again, and
again, until it led me—by chance, surely—to the Calipash family crypt. There
it landed on the pediment—and after a moment, flew inside the crypt itself.
The door was ajar from Orlando's midnight sojourn.

The charnel smell that had clung to Orlando's flesh last night whilst we frol-
icked emanated from the black interior; I found it nauseating but strangely
compelling, and reached out my hand to push open the door and further
investigate what lay inside the sepulcher. In I went, and once again braved the
stone steps down into the crypt proper.

It is a horrid place, the crypt, a burial-place worthy of the strange legends
concocted by the locals. Grinning carven demons watch over the bodies of
former Calipash lords, and from their mouths emanate awful orange and purple light, very like sunlight through filtered glass, but they shine even at night!
My steps echoed on the granite floor as I peered about, revisiting that dead
place where the dead dwell, thinking of the strange ghost I had thought I had
seen as a child—but then I am ashamed to say my courage failed me. I fancied
I heard the ghost groaning at me; looking up, I saw a shadow of a man, tall
and thin—and screamed!

"It is surely the Ghast!" I cried, and fled, nearly falling back down the mois-
ture-slick stairs several times in my haste, but by the time the handle of the
garden-door of Calipash Manor was in my hand I was laughing at myself for
being such a noodle. The wind often moans when it passes over stone, does it
not, and I had left the door ajar—and why, I wondered, had it not occurred
to me that Orlando could have walked in front of the crypt-door? That would
have cast a shadow very like the "ghost" I saw.

If there is any *real* danger here at Calipash Manor, it is too much sunshine. I
must be more careful of my skin—my complexion will be ruined if I continue
taking morning walks. My skin is browner already, I am sure of it.

Afternoon—Orlando did not come down to dinner. I fear I must have done
him a mischief. Perhaps attempting to induce a fourth occasion took more out
of him than I anticipated?

I had a solitary, silent meal in the dining room; again, Lizzie and Bill would not allow me to dine with them. They were really rather stern with me about it.

"We would have notions of rank preserved in this house, Chelone," said Lizzie. "Anarchy results elseways."

"Yes indeed, a woman of your breeding mustn't break bread with those such as us," said Bill—which in anyone else I would think to be a crack about my lack of proper parentage, but not from Bill!

Ah well. I have eaten lonelier meals.

I wonder, though, if I didn't work myself into rather an agitated state, too— I could stomach only the vegetable courses.

Late Afternoon—Something strange is going on, I am sure of it. Orlando *must* be ill. Before going down to tea I knocked on the door of his room, and heard nothing. I raised my voice and told him it was tea-time, and I heard a faint moan from within. Who declines tea? Even invalids must have their refreshing cuppa and hot buttered toast, surely.

After Tea—I went to consult with Lizzie about Orlando, though I hated to disturb her again after her earlier sternness with me. It is funny, as I approached the kitchen-door, I am sure I misheard her, but before I knocked, I heard her conversing with Bill. He said, "that he will not stir is a good sign," and I thought I overheard her say, "Soon will come the hour of the tortoise," which made Bill laugh, a harsh sound. Then I knocked; they fell silent as I entered.

"I fear the Lord Calipash may be ill," said I.

"As I said, he was up late last night," said Lizzie. "When I retired he had called Bill to bring him another bottle of wine. Have you never had a hangover?"

"Even if he was up late—"

"Likely he's a cold upon him," said Bill. He had obviously been doing something that required his high boots (come to think of it, he could have been the source of the shadow, as he is tall and thin, too). Mud plastered his feet and calves nearly to the knee, but he had not shed his footwear before coming to sit at the table. Lizzie, I was surprised to note, did not chide him for this; indeed, she seemed hardly to notice his mess. This was quite a change from the attitude she used to take when I came in from outside without a care!

"A cold!" I exclaimed.

"He went outside last night, in the storm," said Bill, and shrugged at me as he put his boots up on one of the kitchen chairs, fouling it horribly. "I tried to speak reason to him, but he would not listen. Said he wished to keep vigil by the side of his dead father. Heathen notion—perhaps it is as you say, and the Lord has punished him with an ailment."

"Then he must be in need of at least a cup of tea," I said, exasperated. "Let me bring it to him, you needn't trouble yourselves."

"Oh, go on then," said Lizzie, pouring some liquid the color of wash-water into a chipped cup. "Take him this, if you must be meddlesome."

It was in low spirits indeed that I went up to Orlando's room, tea in hand. I have rarely felt so depressed. This slapdash housekeeping and surly language would be understandable, of course, if Bill and Lizzie seemed distraught over my guardian's death, but neither seem to care tuppence about it—they have not even mentioned it to me! And come to think of it, the house was topsy-turvy when I arrived. From what I saw, taking care of the former Lord Calipash would not have occupied the whole of their waking hours, so how can they account for how decrepit Calipash Manor has become? It pains me to write this, but I feel as though the two of them have no emotion whatsoever as regards their former master; I get the strange feeling if no one would notice the irregularity of it, they would not even attend to the funereal arrangements. When I was a girl neither one of them seemed the sort of servant who would take a "when the cat's away" attitude toward their duties, but perhaps I was not a perceptive child?

Well, regardless, I went up to Orlando's room and entered without knocking, only to find him prostrate on the bed, sheets wound around him like a shroud. The curtains were drawn and I could barely see my way over to him.

"Lord Calipash?" I whispered. "It is I—Chelone, your cousin, come to see if you need anything?"

He groaned and stirred, and I took this as a good sign. Setting the cup of tea down beside him, I took the liberty of seating myself on his bed and patting his shoulder.

"It is after tea-time, please—won't you take a bite or sip of anything?"

"My head," he groaned. "Oh, Chelone—I was beastly to you last night, was I not?"

"Never mind that," I said. "I believe you have already apologized enough."

"Did I?" He flopped over onto his side and looked at me. "I must have had more wine than I thought."

"Not all apologies must be spoken," I said, and touched where my new lovely necklace hung below my blouse. Stroking the pendant, even through the fabric, gave me the most visceral shock! Plenty of times I have received trinkets from lovers, but this—it comforted me to have it about my neck, as if it were a warm extension of my very flesh.

"True enough, I suppose! Draw back the curtains, cousin, and hand me that tea—ahh," he said, sipping it. "Better. I should not have lingered in bed so long, but ach—my head! How it aches!"

"Well, you had a long night," I said over my shoulder.

"Indeed I did. Ventured out to that tomb—well, you must know that already. Dreadfully wet, and I fell—or hit my head—or something. Must have slipped." He took another long slurp of tea and fell back upon the pillows of his bed. "Well, no lasting harm done. Still feel miserable, though."

"Is there anything I can do?"

"I wonder ..." He looked at me. "You seem in a maternal sort of mood, eh? Would you be so kind—no."

"Ask anything and it shall be yours, if it is within my power to give it."

"Just sit with me, talk to me. Keep me company. I never had a relative to look after me before."

Poor dear! "Let me read to you, then—and perhaps you will doze until supper-time."

"Smashing idea, Chelone. What would you like to read?"

"You claimed to have a collection that would make me blush," I suggested, having retained no small curiosity regarding his literary tastes. "Even if you no longer think me so easily shocked, I should like to see what you have."

Even in the dim light—for though I had drawn back the drapes, the hour was late, and the sunlight waning—I saw him blush pinker than a rose! I had no expectation of his showing any shyness after the events of last night, and felt such a rush of tenderness for the dear boy that I kissed him on the forehead.

"N—no," he stammered. "I was, ah, drinking last night, you see, and loose-tongued; I was not myself, and should not have mentioned such things about—about my family, myself, and ..."

Such an endearing display! Charmed, I put my finger to his lips and shook my head. I was not to be dissuaded.

"Let me read something—I shall pick it. Just nod where you have stowed them. Coyness will only make me all the more eager!"

He looked miserable as a wet cat, but pointed with a trembling finger towards a valise not yet unpacked. Opening the top, I discovered to my delight that it was entirely full of pornography! He had a lovely old edition of *Juliette*, several volumes of *The Pearl* and *The Oyster* (I cannot fault him; though Lazenby has always been a competitor, his work is very fine), a chapbook of Swinburne's "Reginald's Flogging," *The Sins of the Cities of the Plain*, which perhaps would explain his ability with arses—and, I was happy to see, quite a few editions of *Milady's Ruby Vase*!

"I see you are quite an avid reader," said I, which caused him to choke on the dregs of his tea. "Here, I have selected something. Let me read to you—ah, yes! Here is a good-sounding yarn, 'What My Brother Learned in India' by a

Rosa Birchbottom."

"Not that one," he said with such trepidation I felt rather wounded.

"Why ever not?"

"I…please, Chelone. She is my very favorite author, and I fear I should—embarrass myself."

"Rosa Birchbottom is your favorite author?" How could I not laugh! "Let me read this story, then. I trust your taste, cousin."

"I—"

"My brother studied a great many things whilst in India, and upon his return he was good enough to teach me some of what he learned about the voluptuous peculiarities of the human body," I read, or rather, recited half from memory. *"Given that I am soon to die of a wasting sickness that has claimed my beauty, rendering me unfit to engage in any amorous sport, I have decided to spend my remaining days writing down some of the most exotic techniques he taught me, techniques to induce to sensual erotic pleasure in man or woman…Orlando!"*

He had begun to weep, and I set aside the volume, feeling rather rotten indeed.

"Whatever is the matter?" I asked him.

"I am a disgusting creature," said he, "to own such wicked books—and to ask a young lady to read them! Here I have you debasing yourself before me, and—"

"None of that," I said sternly. "It is no debasement to read these words, pornography is not a wicked art! Oh, Orlando, I apologize. I was only so very amused. You see, *I* am Rosa Birchbottom. It tickled me last night when you implied I should read pornography—I write it for my living!"

"You?" he sat up straight and looked at me with fresh, adoring eyes. "You wouldn't tease me, cousin?"

"Never, I assure you. I told you I worked for a periodical, did I not? I authored 'What My Brother Learned in India,' 'The Personal Papers of Lady Strokinpoke,' 'A Penny Spent,' and 'A Sporting Attitude Indeed.' I had to take a *nom de plume* or risk all sort of unpleasantness if our publication is ever shut down on obscenity charges. It is a bad pun, I know, but my very first story was a Mrs. Lechworthy tale, you see."

"I have it in my collection," said he, placing his hand upon my knee in an endearingly familiar manner. "I really think 'Le Vice Anglese' is one of the very best stories ever written."

"Flatterer," I said.

"Not at all—but …" He blushed again.

"What?"

"I am sorry, I was about to trouble you with an impertinence …"

"What could be impertinent between us, cousin?".

"Do you...ever...do you write from experience? Or is it all...imagination?"

The dear young man! "I know why you ask, Orlando, but fear not. Though I have in the past used my experiences to inform my writings, I never do so directly. And I never name names."

"I see...so you are not, oh, how did you put it so delightfully in 'A Penny Spent'? *Burdened by an exasperating virginity?*"

I laughed. "Is that a question you needed to ask me? Could you not tell?"

Orlando's lip twitched and then his face lit up in the most handsome smile I had ever seen on a man's face. "Oh, Chelone, I am feeling ever so much better now, you have raised my spirits to the point I think I could manage a bit of supper! Would you like to dress and come down with me?"

"Very much so, my dear Orlando," said I.

"I am ever so glad you came to Calipash Manor," he said. "Why—I feel as though I've known you my whole life. It is funny, before you arrived my father was speaking of twins, twins born into this family—do you not think we could be siblings? Look in the mirror, there—are not our faces quite alike?"

"I hope we are not twins," said I, though it gave me quite a start to see how alike we were. "Are not Calipash twins always supposed to be cursed? Evil?"

"That was what my father told me, at least. Well, well, it seems an unlikely coincidence, does it not? But we shall talk more about it over dinner, eh, cousin?"

And thus I must hurry—he will be awaiting me! Oh, I am ever so glad I came home again. It is rare, when one writes under a false name, to meet one's public in person! Very enjoyable, as is Orlando himself. I do think I shall have another go with him after our meal, if he is willing and able...

The dress I wore that night was not expensive, and though it had been turned once, I thought it looked well enough when I gazed at my reflection in the glass. My only regret was how high the neckline, for though I wore his gift none could see it. Still, its warm weight was a secret comfort to me, for he had given this present to me as a token of affection, and feeling it 'round my neck reminded me that I needed not fear disgracing myself in front of my nobler relation with my ignorant manners and common conversation.

When I heard the knock at my door I very nearly turned my ankle in my dash to answer the summons. It was Laurent, looking very dashing indeed, and he even took my hand and kissed it when he saw me!

"Dearest Camilla, how beautiful you look," he said, lasciviously licking his lips with his red tongue. "Why, my cock is half-standing just looking at you, remembering the rapturous sensation of Mr. John Thomas battering his way up inside of you, taking for my own your troublesome maidenhead! Careful, or I might make a mistake—and eat *you* instead of my supper."

"I am glad you have not had your fill of me. I have heard it said in town that you are indeed a rake and libertine."

"It is all in the past," he assured me. "I have never thought to marry, but you, my cousin, have won my heart, body, and soul."

Alas, for I was a fool to believe such words! I assure you, as I write this, locked up for crimes I did not commit, that no woman has ever suffered more than I on account of love!

We lingered over supper, which consisted of every food known to inspire amorous devotion: caviar, asparagus, oysters, champagne, artichokes in white wine, and finally, a tiny cup of potent chocolate. By the end of it I was swooning with passion and anxious to retire, but it was not to be. As a final course, Laurent's housekeeper surprised us by coming in with two chilled glasses of a French anisette liqueur as a digestif—but when I reached to take mine off the silver tray, the silver-filigreed cameo Laurent had given me spilled out from the neckline of my gown.

"Thief!" cried his housekeeper. "Why, it is Lady Fanchone's favorite ornament, long thought to be missing! How did it come to be concealed on your person, I wonder?"

"Laurent gave it to me last night," said I, shocked by her implication.

"How could he, when it has been gone these ten years? As I recall it, Lady Fanchone wished to bequeath it to her only son and heir—and could not, for it had vanished!"

I thought Laurent would come to my defense, but when I raised my tear-filled eyes to meet his, I saw only cruelty there.

"Indeed, it had long been my desire to have that ornament turned into a cravat-pin—and here you are, possessed of it! My, my…Camilla! I never thought you would be the sort of girl around whom I should have to count the silver! To discover the woman I thought to make my bride is actually a low thief—and a thief so bold as to wear her ill-gotten possessions around those who might miss them!"

I know it does not speak to my honesty to confess here that I bolted from the table then, thinking to leave The Beeches on foot. But I ask you, dearest reader, what hope I had of protesting my innocence when Laurent—he whom I had thought devoted to me—was speaking such dreadful falsehoods? You, my friend, know that I am innocent, that I would never steal, but I was apprehended by the handyman before I had taken ten steps out the front door. I screamed and beat his breast with my fists, demanding he release me, but he was far stronger than I, and restrained me easily. Then a policeman was called, and the matter seemed more and more hopeless. My character is no longer known in these parts, after all, and so it was the easiest thing to conclude I was a thief!

To keep me from fleeing before my trial, I was locked into the tower with only a meager supply of candles to keep me from the grim darkness at night.

It seems a century past, but it was less than a fortnight ago that I was found guilty of the crime of stealing the cameo necklace, and tomorrow I shall be hanged for it. The town being so small I was locked back into the tower at The Beeches for safekeeping; they bring me my meals fairly regularly, but already my dress hangs off my body, so hungry, cold, and lonely am I. Woe is me! I asked my jailers for paper and pencil so I could write my story; this, as it is my last request, they have given me. Thus I have recorded all that transpired during my fateful journey to my home county, where, instead of love, I have found only death. My only conclusion is that Laurent always intended to cast me aside, and gave me the necklace to have a good reason to do so.

I have no regrets but one as to my actions in life, the things I have enjoyed and done—but trusting such a knave as Laurent and his hateful staff was a greater mistake than any of my amorous encounters. Would that I had taken Mr. Milliner up on his offer to elope with him! I am sure I should be happier than here, alone, in the darkness, awaiting my death.

That should do; I shall copy it out now.

Date unknown, time of day uncertain, languishing in the crypt—My plan has not worked, all hope has left me. I must conclude that either my dear editrix Susan did not perceive the cipher I painstakingly included in the handwritten conclusion I composed for "A Camilla Among the Beeches," or it has not been sent to her was promised. I suspect the latter; given the extent of the treachery I have experienced, I cannot believe in human kindness any longer.

Here I shall record what actually befell me more than a fortnight ago, if my sense of time has not been too much disturbed by living as I have been, in the Calipash family crypt. (I have counted meals, but they have been thrown down to me at strange intervals with no difference between breakfast and dinner, as I can no longer stomach much.) It pains me to write about my misfortunes, for this honors a hideous request, but at the very least I know this document will live on in the Private Library—which I have found out was never burnt, and exists today, and now one book richer. I suppose it is every writer's wish to compose something that others might enjoy, and though future Calipash heirs may take pleasure in the real account which inspired 'A Camilla Among the Beeches' more for my suffering than any greatness of prose, such is life.

I went down to dinner in my most modest gown, for when I was dressing for dinner I saw how brown and mottled my skin had become. I thought then it was from too much sun during my earlier walk; I know better now. Regardless, Orlando, sweet boy, remarked upon my dress favorably, and we enjoyed our meal.

But when Lizzie came in with our dessert, I reached for the decanter of wine upon the table—and the jade tortoise pendant fell from my décolletage. Then all was confusion!

"My God, it is my father's necklace!" cried Orlando, pointing at the glowing object dangling before my bosom. "How has it come into your possession, Chelone?"

"It is the potent thing itself!" cried Lizzie, dropping the tray of blancmange. "Bill!" she screeched at the top of her lungs. "Brother! Come! I have discovered it! It is *not* lost!"

"What?" said I, backing away quickly from the table. "Orlando! Tell them you gave it to me late last night!"

"I did not give it to you, nor did I see you after you left this room!" he exclaimed. "I drank and drank, then went down into the crypt after Bill came to me and told me he had forgotten to strip the pendant from my father's body. I went to get it—and there was my father's corpse, cold on the marble slab where Bill had put him, but the necklace was gone! And then there was a strange sound...and I startled away from the body—and hit my head—and woke up in my own bed!"

"Indeed," said Bill, coming into the room, "I think I have an explanation for that, dearest Lizzie. I've just had a visit with Rosemary's golem."

"The golem!" exclaimed Lizzie. "Well, I never!"

"Explain yourselves," demanded Orlando. He was standing between myself and Lizzie and Bill. "Tell me what is happening here!"

At this, Bill backhanded Orlando across the mouth, and the young Lord fell to the carpet, howling and clutching his mouth.

"Silence, churl," said Bill, and spat on his master. "You speak unto your rightful lord! I am William Fitzroy, Lord Calipash, and you are nothing but a lesser man's son, thou shameful usurper!"

It was such a strange scene—and my confusion so great—that I made to run away from the room; indeed, I wished to quit the house entirely, but Lizzie stuck out her foot and tripped me. After I fell to the ground with a cry, I tried to claw my way to the door with my hands, but she lifted up her skirts and sat upon my chest to hold me hostage. When I cried out she punched me in the side so hard I wept for the pain.

"Dearest William," said she, "why is it you suspect the golem?"

"He told me—or rather, I had him write it all down for me," said Bill. "When I saw how fit and healthy Orlando looked when he came down to dinner, I knew his earlier indisposition must be from some other source than the necklace's transformative properties. Looking upon Chelone, how dreadful her skin appears now, I suspected some trickery, and went to the crypt for insight. And look at this!"

He held up a scrap of paper before Lizzie's eyes, and I caught a glimpse of it—the note was in my guardian's own handwriting!

"It wrote to her," said Bill. "It apparently saw her as a girl and took a fancy to her, and in the confusion over our brother's decline it thought it could safely invite her back and have some sport with her. It's smarter than I ever realized, and it *does* look rather like Orlando—if one doesn't peer too closely. Thus it was able to sneak down to the village and send her the note that called her hither! It wants a *bride*, dear sister. Just like the legends about it! Imagine that—the peasants knew something we didn't!"

"It seems from this note that they had quite a wedding night," said Lizzie, looking up from the parchment to leer at me.

I could barely breathe for her sitting on me, and choked on my tears. What, I wondered, was a golem, to live in a crypt, and send false letters?

"Careful, sister, or you'll give her fits," said Bill. "We can't have another one die on us, after the failure with our brother."

"I shan't let her suffocate. If we keep her and allow her to pupate into the Guardian, then all we'll have to worry about is *that*," here she pointed to where Orlando whimpered on the ground, "We can't have him destroying the illusion that we are a happy family…"

"Indeed," said Bill. "We can use him for all sorts of things, actually. I believe he's a virgin, which could prove…useful."

"What is happening," I wept. "Oh, do get up, do let me go, please!"

"It's too late for you, stupid girl," said Lizzie, and kicked me in the side with her boot-heel. "Though it may please you to know you alone have been the agent of your undoing. Rather amusing! If you hadn't surprised the former Lord into death, then he would have completed his transmutation, and you should have gotten away from here safely."

"Sister, do think—if she had not been discovered perusing the Private Library, inducing the anger that made our loathsome brother wish to destroy it, then we never would have thought to create a Guardian to protect our family legacy from future well-meaning fools! Ha! It is very funny, how a young girl's curiosity can result in such tragedy." He smiled thinly. "Rather Gothic, really. Isn't the bitch some sort of petty writer? Too bad she'll never put it all into a story."

"Perhaps we should have her chronicle her transformation!" sniggered Lizzie. "It might be of great scientific interest one day."

"So it is *you* who are the twins of whom my father spoke," mumbled Orlando, his hand raised to where his cheek still bled. "I thought he had become completely insensible when he began to rant about how he had siblings— twins, yes, but not terrible he thought, though he said to be on the lookout for you, lest you show some sign of treachery! Alas—I have realized it too late!"

I know it sounds incredible, that in this modern time such things as curses are real, but as I languish in the crypt, surrounded by my mummified ancestors and these strange stone gargoyles that emit the weird light by which I can see to write this, gradually changing into the creature whose jade likeness I so unwittingly wore upon my breast, I have been forced to admit I should have heeded the warning given to me during my train-ride home to Ivybridge. Lizzie and Bill, two people whom I should never have suspected of evil, have been proven to be nothing but. Long did they plot their revenge on my former guardian for his decision to destroy the Private Library; long have they cursed fortune for having made he who I knew as the Lord Calipash the legitimate heir, and them the servitors of an estate they could claim no right to manage.

The worst part is, Bill was not being hyperbolic when he accused me of authoring my own undoing—indeed, it is the case, in so very many ways. When the former Lord Calipash found me so entranced by that strange, deviant copy of *Fanny Hill*, he resolved to burn the collection. Bill told me that, horrified by the idea of his family's Private Library destroyed, *he* offered to do it for his master and half-brother—but instead he stoked the bonfire with other books, all the while secreting the foul tomes of the Private Library in the family crypt, where I will now dwell until the end of my life, which I think will not be for decades, if not centuries, if what I have been told is true.

It seems the very day I was sent away to school, Lizzie and Bill resolved to create for the Calipash family's possessions a Guardian, immortal and terrible, who would protect the satanic heirlooms of this degenerate family if again they were threatened. Such will be my fate. The golem—he with whom I am miserably and all-too-closely acquainted—would not do for the office, being constructed by his mistress, as I understand it, out of dead Calipash males for pleasure-purposes, and thus is more lover than fighter.

But the twins, like me, had gazed upon the fell contents of that strange, leather-bound book wherein I first saw the image of the winged tortoise, only they knew how to decipher its malignant text. Discovering that the pendant would transform its owner into rabid protectors of mortal treasure, long did they search for the idol that has changed me, and when they at last found it, they gave it unto my guardian—but I surprised him into death before he could fully transmute! Thus I was many times over my own executioner, and I use that word for I sense I shall be Miss Chelone Burchell for not too much more of my life. I can tell by the thickening of my skin and the swelling of my belly; the seizing of my hands into clawed monkey's paws, the growing of two strange protuberances upon my already insensate back.

The twins had wanted the old Lord Calipash for a guardian, to punish him for his attempt to destroy the Private Library; my heinous half-aunt and half-uncle, evil though they surely are, held no ill-will towards me, and to their credit have expressed some regret over the unfortunate circumstances that have led me to this very particular doom. Their next victim was to have been Orlando; indeed, Bill himself had sent my cousin out to the crypt that night, to suffer the transformation himself. Now they are holding him for purposes of their own, I know not what—and likely never shall. They have told me only that Bill, shaven, is very like the old Lord Calipash, and so plans on impersonating his old master until the end of his days, claiming to have had a miraculous recovery from the illness that, unexpectedly, claimed his own groundskeeper!

At least I shall not be lonely. There is the voiceless golem who tries in his way to comfort me, poor creature, and the massive Private Library to read, and demoniac treasures I have found, and spend many hours contemplating. Oh, but none of it is any comfort to me; how I wish I had never come home! Calipash Manor is a blasphemous, unthinkable place, and to visit here is to face not death, but the vast terror of selfish, unfathomable evil. So ends my tale—my hands stiffen, my eyes dull—and the world shall never know what became of me. Beware those who would seek to rob my family: Soon it shall come the hour of the tortoise!

I Only Am Escaped Alone to Tell Thee

Christopher Reynaga

Whatever you do, don't call me Ishmael.

Don't call me anything at all. Give me my pint of piss-poor ale and leave me be in this yellowed corner where men relieve themselves when they are too lazy to make three extra stumbling steps to the streets of Nantucket. I am done. Finished. Come to this hole to die—and if you insist on speaking to me, I'll find a deeper hole than this dying excuse of a whaling town can offer.

No, I do not want another round, nor your sick curiosity. Why can't New Englanders, most stoic of men, keep to their business when a dead man walks among them. Yes dead, though life still beats in this heart. It does not matter that I am the only survivor of what happened to the Pequod out there in the deep. I am marked by it—

I see now. It's not me you want at all, it's him. Captain Ahab. Old Thunder. The god and monster among men. Ahab the cracked, the insane. The captain who would cut the throat of his own wife and son and lap up the blood, if it would give him revenge on the white beast he hunted. I heard the rumors of his madness on these very docks before we shipped out. And now you want to know all.

How wrong you are of him. He does not deserve your eager eyes and poison tongues. He was nothing of the monster you imagine. For his sake alone, I will set his tale to right.

The captain was no saint, I'll have you that. My first sight of him was his savage backhand to Pip, the cabin boy, for touching the scar on the captain's face as he made his way up to the quarter deck to address us. Ahab was the iron hand on the ship's tiller, as all good captains are. A good captain would have you in irons if he smelled mutiny in your blood. I saw in Ahab's eyes that he'd heave you over the side.

"There's no man on this boat fool enough to have signed on without having heard the tales. I have seen to that. Ye are not the finest whalers to board this ship. Ye are the boldest, the most dangerous, the most desperate. *I have seen to that*. I want no common harpooneers here. I hunt greater game."

"Ye have heard of the white leviathan that took my leg and left me with this." The captain lifted the shroud of his pant, revealing the greasy white bone, carved in queer, twisted angles that made Pip gasp and me squint my eyes till he dropped the cuff again. "Ye know the wealth in gold I offer. This much is true. The rest has been lies. Ones you have told yourselves. It is not a whale we hunt... but a god. A tentacled and winged god greater than the greatest whale that ever lived.

"Ye must think me mad! And I am. But mad with knowing what is in store for this earth. For when that beast took my leg as I dangled in the green moss that grows from its fishbelly white tentacles, I saw into its mind, and it left a splinter of itself in mine. It means to kill us all, and not because it is the Lord's instrument hailing the end of days. This beast is the end of all gods and men.

"If there is any of ye that wants no part of this hunt, I will leave ye in a whaling skiff with a day's food and water to row the thousand miles back to shore. I do this not to doom ye, but because it would make no difference to your fate. This thing does not care that ye exist. We are krill to its massive jaws and it will eat ye here or in the deepest landlocked desert ye can hide."

You laugh. You drag me from my corner to hear his tale and now you laugh just as we sailors did. You there, hold your tongue—and you, shut up and hear me well. You would not laugh had you seen the worms that clawed their way from QueeQueg's belly, or the ungodly glow that led the ship into the beast's waters, or the madness that took Pip as the boy began convulsing and speaking in tongues.

You could not have laughed the night Ahab pulled me aside on deck and tapped the hollow-sounding horror of his leg. "Ye looked upon this," he told me.

"Yes sir," I said, "and beg your pardon, have no desire to again."

"You looked," croaked the mad cabin boy, Pip, hanging from the rigging above, "I looked, it looked, it looked, *It looked...*"

"Ye were the only one, besides the boy, to not close your eyes to it," said Ahab, pulling me closer. "Do ye know what it is?"

"A peg leg carved from a whale's bone, sir."

"No, Ishmael," he said drawing up his trouser again. "It is my leg. All of it." Those twisting angles were in my eye again, an impossible shape of horrifying white melded to the flesh of his knee like wet, diseased wood. It stung my eyes to look upon it, and in the moon's glare it seemed to writhe in impossible directions as if the twisting point of it met not the deck, but plunged through to some other realm. Pip began screaming above and did not stop until the captain cloaked his leg once more. "It's growing up my thigh, making more of me itself each day. Do ye think me mad now? Do ye know why I hunt a beast I know I'll never kill?"

"Why, Sir?"

"I have a wife, Ishmael, and a son. A boy who loves singing and counting the stones he lines up on the porch steps. A boy with my voice and his mother's sweet blue eyes. I will not tell ye their names for I will not let *it* hear me say them aloud. My life is over. I do this for them. I do not think we will ever succeed in killing the beast, but if I can slow it down for one moment, I will gladly throw my life into its jaws *for them*."

None of you are laughing now are you? I see I have your rapt attention, eyes to mine, mugs not quite meeting your lips.

You could never find it in you to laugh again had you seen *it* the morning it rose from the waters to greet us. God almighty.

The watch on the mast-head that cried, "There she breaches!" tore the eyes from his sockets even before he tumbled to the deck.

"Aye, breach your last to the sun!" cried Ahab. "Thy hour and thy harpoon are at hand!" He turned to the whalers and shouted, "Down, down all of ye but one man at the fore! Look not upon the beast! The boats—stand by!"

Ahab gripped my arm, "Ishmael, ye are my bowsman, for I know ye can cast your eyes at its horizon without going mad. Do not be tempted to look directly upon it!"

It amazes me still that I had the fortitude to step into that whaleboat. The oarsmen pulled for their lives, knowing they had no life left, but they were blessedly turned away from the rising horror that only I, and the captain at his steering, could see with averted eyes. I cannot describe the wrinkles and scars that covered the monster's forehead like hieroglyphics, tangled with the stumps of rusted harpoons. I focused on the green moss that grew across its dead-white flesh, pretending that I was racing toward moss-wet cliffs that did not have great claws rising from the depths. It must have been one of these claws that reached over us and tore the ship down into the sea with a terrible chorus of screams and breaking timber. I could not look. Ahab was already at my side, harpoon in hand, screaming to the men, "My God, stand by me now!"

Stand by I could not, for the crashing wave of the monster rushing to meet us swamped me and my oarsmen overboard and into the milky churn. Ahab rode through it like a titan going forth to meet a god, buoyed up by the strength of his unnatural leg, his blessed spear gripped in his hands.

"From hell's heart I stab at thee!" Ahab cried and flung the harpoon from the sinking whaleboat. It flew true into the great god's bottomless right eye, the only moment I glanced into those eyes. Those eyes knew me, and in that moment I knew I was forever marked.

The beast flew forward with igniting velocity, wanting to swallow us with those eyes. The great tentacles reached to grasp us like a lover. Ahab gripped the harpoon line and heaved against it, twisting the spear in the great socket with a spray of black ichor. Something gave in the beast, some impossible nerve and the creature lashed backwards into the sea, dragging the harpoon line down with it. The loop of it caught Ahab around the neck and voicelessly he shot out of the boat before he even knew he was gone. Next instant, the heavy eyesplice in the rope's final end flew out of the stark empty tub, and smiting the sea, disappeared into its depths.

I do not know why that great man sacrificed himself for you, but no man here deserves his providence. You believe Ahab is mad. He is the Christ come to try and deliver us all, and there's not enough blood in him to save us.

None laugh now. None of you can laugh. My words have hooked into you like fishing lines, like the rope that dragged poor Ahab down into the depths. I see that when I tug that portion of my mind, I can make the cup roll lifelessly from your hands, make you twitch where you stand, the spit running from your chins. I too have something twisted and white that the great god gave to me but it is growing someplace deep in my skull.

I hear it now. I know what it wants. I know I am no safer than you, but even as I hear the distant screams of Nantucket begin to roll in like the tide, and watch the flood of seawater fan beneath the door, that twisted white part of me knows that I will be the last to die in this world. It is my fate to tell the world *its* story and hold you fast with the harpoon of my voice. 'Twas rehearsed by thee and me a billion years before this ocean roiled.

Fool, I am your eulogist as it slouches toward us like some rough beast waiting to be born.

Objects from the Gilman-Waite Collection

Ann K. Schwader

t was the strange appearance of the gold and coral sculptures—their ethereal moon-white luster—that first drew Wayland's eyes to the museum poster. *Objects From the Gilman-Waite Collection*, its formal script announced. *Unique cultural art-forms of Pohnpei.*

The poster copy continued with a Scientific and Cultural Facilities District note, plus heartier thanks to the Manuxet Seafood Corporation for additional funds, but he was distracted by the sculptures themselves. Arranged on sea-green velvet with a tasteful scattering of shells, they still exuded a feeling he could only describe as otherworldly.

Yet, at the same time, their design seemed oddly familiar. He felt certain he had never been to this museum before—nor to any other displaying Objects from this particular Collection. *Gilman* and *Waite* were equally mysterious. But *Manuxet*? Was that where his déjà vu came in?

Wayland stepped closer to the poster, trying to decide. The museum lobby was almost deserted this afternoon. The desk attendant, a plain-faced older woman, sat silently at her terminal.

Just as well. He had no other hope of amusement, stranded by business obligations in this glorified cow town he had never visited before and was not eager to see again. Purchasing admission, he headed for the elevator and was soon navigating a maze of display rooms on one of the upper floors, searching for the Objects that had so intrigued him.

He finally located a small placard by one entryway: *Gilman-Waite*, with an even smaller notation forbidding photography. Wayland peered inside.

Aside from low-wattage spotlights illuminating various cases and signage, the narrow room was almost dark. And, apparently, deserted. A faint labored hissing came from one corner. Approaching cautiously, he was relieved—and slightly ashamed—to discover a dehumidifier, the first he had noticed in this building.

It too had a placard. This one warned how important it was not to turn the machine off, as excess humidity could endanger the Objects.

Wayland snorted. This high desert climate had kept his throat miserably dry all day. Still, the air here did seem moister than it had elsewhere in the museum. The thick shadowy carpet clung to his feet as he turned to read the nearest Object's label.

RITUAL(?) ARMLET. *Circa 18?? C.E., gold with coral embellishment.* Embellishment wasn't the word he'd have chosen. This coral mimicked the exact shade of pallid flesh—down to delicate blue vein-shadows, running through it by some trick of the light. Partially encased by the strange whitish gold, it twisted and writhed through the armlet's design. Rather than accenting the precious metal, the coral appeared enslaved—even tormented—by it.

Wayland's breath caught as he examined the goldwork more closely. What he had taken at first for arabesques now appeared as lithe, androgynous figures. The cast of their features disturbed him, though it took a few moments to see why. They echoed the armlet's aquatic flora and fauna: bulging eyes and piscine faces, gill-slitted throats and shimmering suggestions of scales on shoulder and thigh. Spread fingers and toes revealed membranes as they wound through their strange environment, occupied in ways he did not care to consider.

He began examining the armlet's shape instead. It seemed intended for a woman, but its wearer would have to be oddly muscled indeed to carry it comfortably on her bicep.

The strain and twist of muscles under slick cold skin, almost slipping from his grasp as she struggled...

"May I help you, sir?"

Wayland started. The young woman standing only a few feet from his elbow wore a docent's badge. Its white plastic and her pale face bobbed in the dimness.

"I was wondering about the provenance of this piece," he said. "Even if the artist is unknown, shouldn't there be a tribal group or something?"

The wide dark eyes in that face stared at him, unblinking.

"Assigning such a label would add little to your experience of these Objects. This exhibit's intent is to help viewers appreciate them purely as art."

Eyes wider than human and darker than night ocean, boring into his soul...

Something in the back of Wayland's mind shuddered. "Purely as art," he echoed, feeling another unwelcome twinge of déjà vu.

Even if he let himself remember clearly what had happened that night, this couldn't be her. It had been over fifteen years since that drunken, disastrous party back East. The townie girl one of his buddies had set him up with wouldn't *be* a girl any more. She'd be nearly his age, and look older.

The docent gave him a sympathetic glance. "Perhaps you missed the first placard by the door."

As she indicated it, he had an urge to bolt for the corridor, with its bright lights and desiccated air. If anything, the atmosphere here felt even moister than it had a few minutes ago. A faint whiff of decay rose from the carpet as he returned to read the sign he'd overlooked.

Aside from another nice fat thank you to the Manuxet Seafood Corporation, it didn't say much. There was even some question about these Objects being from Pohnpei, as they represented "a design tradition divergent from all documented native cultures of that region." The ritual aspect of many of the Objects was speculative, though Wayland had no doubts. There was too much reverence in the postures of some of the armlet's aquatic figures.

The placard didn't explain what was being reverenced.

Reading on more carefully, Wayland learned that most of the Objects had been brought to America early in the nineteenth century by one O. Marsh, a New England trading captain. How they wound up in the Gilman-Waite Collection was not noted. Instead, the placard quoted several local art critics, some of them specialists in native art of the Pacific region. To a man—or woman—they praised the exhibit's "vibrant energy" and "mythic overtones," without specifying which myths.

Wayland doubted they had a clue either. Turning away, he headed for one of the largest cases, gleaming under a spotlight in the center of the room. It held a single tall Object cushioned on green velvet.

To his relief, this one had no coral. It appeared to be a highly baroque sculpture—or at least, it did until he read its label.

RITUAL(?) TIARA OR HEADPIECE. *Circa 18?? C.E., gold.*

Which is clearly impossible. The "gold" looked even paler and more lustrous than it had in the armlet, suggesting (at best) some odd precious-metal alloy.

Odder still was the tiara's shape. Though it did seem intended to be worn around something, that something could not be a human skull. The base was all wrong: more elliptical than round, with accommodations for odd bumps and hollows. It was also much too narrow even for a woman's head—though the design suggested femininity.

He looked closer, trying to figure out why.

Cigarette smoke and liquor and beer, far too much beer, mingled with the tang of female sweat. With that shining, baby-silk curtain of hair, obscuring half her face as he pulled her down onto his lap. Even then, he'd felt her muscles resisting...

Wayland swallowed hard. Where had *that* come from? Surely not from these intricately entwined aquatic motifs—though there was something suggestive in all that twining. Suggestive and malignant, as though the lightless, sightless couplings of deep ocean denizens had been frozen in gold forever, survivals of another eon.

And where exactly had that eon passed? Like the Objects on the poster downstairs, this tiara reflected no familiar artistic tradition. Its craftsmanship was exquisite, but by whose standards? Another sensibility—another aesthetic entirely—had formed this piece.

As if reading his thoughts, the docent reappeared at his elbow.

"The ceremonial feeling of this Object is particularly strong, isn't it?" Her voice was muted and liquid, tinged with some accent he hadn't noticed before. "Let the design draw your eye upwards...engage with the flow of the piece. It makes all the difference."

Suppressing a cynical comment, Wayland tried it. At first, he didn't notice much difference: the design did "flow" towards its delicate apex above the center of the wearer's forehead, but...

He gasped at a stab of nausea.

What he had taken for several motifs intertwining at irregular intervals was actually *one* motif, or rather one entity. One grotesque entity. Its face was mercifully obscured by other design elements, but he could still trace the body as it twisted through what had first seemed a stylized undersea forest.

He didn't need the docent's encouragement to know what he was really looking at.

Taste of the ocean on her lips...deep night ocean...primal salts and darkness and undying secrets. All the beer and smoke in the world couldn't wash it away. And when he'd brushed back that curtain of hair and looked into her eyes for the first and only time, he'd seen that she wasn't young at all, no matter what her body said against his.

Not a drunken, ignorant little townie he'd managed to steer into a convenient bedroom. Not an easy score. What stared back at him was ancient and cunning, inhuman...

Wayland turned away. Cold sweat trickled down the back of his neck as he moved on to another Object, hoping the docent didn't follow. The room was dank with shadows, but he could still see (*imagine, only imagine*) those faint lines on the skin of her throat, just above her collar.

Like gills.

Maybe I ought to leave right now, he thought as his feet propelled him through the clinging strands of carpet. *The humidity or the lighting or something is getting to me.*

Then he stopped and drew a deep breath. *Get a grip.* These Objects gleaming faintly in their cases (*had there been so many, earlier?*) were on display as art. Not as triggers for unpleasant recollections, and certainly not as prods for a neglected conscience. He had come here to pass an afternoon admiring some bizarre bits of goldwork, period.

Still, he avoided reading any more labels. The docent was right: if these were true art-forms, he shouldn't need to. Their craftsmanship and design should speak for themselves.

Faint gleam of gold around one skinny wrist as he pushed her backwards…as he grabbed both those wrists with one hand and pulled them over her head…

He started bypassing Objects with coral in them. The material was too disturbing, triggering fragmentary memories as his eyes slid away. Wayland made himself pause before each of the other cases, though, trying to limit his observations to pure aesthetics.

It wasn't easy. The style of these pieces—mostly jewelry or small figurines—had a cumulative effect on the imagination. Engaging with the design flow of a single Object sent ice prickles down his spine. Watching that same flow twist and twine *between* Objects did something else entirely. He became aware how relentlessly aquatic it was, ebbing and pulsing in an ageless rhythm which was subtly wrong. Offbeat from any human rhythm, even that of his heart.

"You're beginning to feel it now, aren't you?"

Wayland flinched. The docent's face, isolated by the general murkiness, floated near his left shoulder. She resembled a swimmer emerging from night water, her eyes bulging with exertion. Lips parted to breathe, revealing…

…white white teeth, tinier and sharper and way too many more than any girl's…laughing silently at him even as he did what he'd done in anger. What he would deny doing at all later, and later still make himself forget…

"Yes."

The word emerged without volition. It too floated in the dark between them, confirming something hidden beyond language.

Wayland stared past her at the next case. Staggered glass shelves held half a dozen small white-gold figurines. Any pattern here—of those shelves or of the Objects themselves—would have to be human, the work of some museum employee. Safe.

That security lasted all of two seconds as he took in the details of the top-most statuette.

Then he glanced away, dry-mouthed, for the exit.

"Is there a problem, sir?"

Damn. The docent was still there, goggling at him in the murk. She had remarkably ugly eyes: puglike or maybe froglike, with a flat, cold curiosity.

"Just wondering what time it was getting to be," he lied. "Seems like I've been here a while, and it's a pretty intense experience."

She nodded. "There's one larger piece you ought to see, though. Its design flow is...extraordinary. A multi-figure grouping with complex mythic structure, and the finest coral work in this exhibit."

Sweat broke on his forehead as she mentioned the coral. Still, there was no turning away from those eyes—or their unspoken challenge. Wayland disliked women who challenged him. Fists clenched at his sides, he asked where this marvelous piece was and why it didn't appear on the exhibit posters.

The docent shrugged and gestured left toward a deep alcove.

Wayland scowled, annoyed at having overlooked it himself. Without thanking her, he headed for that oblong of darker shadow, trying to ignore his shoes squishing in the carpet.

Wet carpet *and* damp air, despite the prominent warning on that dehumidifier. Worse, the carpet exuded an unpleasant vegetative smell, like something long dead on a beach. Was the curator an idiot? After he saw this "complex mythic structure," he was heading downstairs to complain.

The alcove was longer than it had looked from outside—and darker. He squinted around for any sign of another large display case.

When his foot hit the tiny switch concealed by the carpet, it took him a few seconds to connect that click with the rising light up ahead. Not a spotlight, exactly, but a series of tiny recessed spots, each illuminating the target briefly before winking out again. The flickering effect resembled candles seen through water.

Long twining shadows swayed to that same rhythm on all the walls. They urged his attention forward, to the very end of what now seemed more tunnel than alcove.

Wayland gasped.

He'd been wrong about the display case. No glass glinted between him and this last, largest Object. Despite the unmistakable value of the strange whitish gold—and the coral's fleshy masses—it stood unprotected on a block of dark stone. Raw and unpolished, that base drew the viewer's full attention upward.

As promised, the sculpture was a multi-figure grouping. And certainly mythic, since it depicted a ritual sacrifice about to begin.

The entity Wayland had first recognized as a design element—*the* design element—in the misshapen tiara seemed to be the object of that sacrifice. Surging up from the rough stone, it curved its shining, sleek-muscled, and utterly inhuman body over the ritual's participants. Arms twisted and supple as seaweed spread wide, ending in long-fingered hands with delicate webbing between the digits. Polished black coral nails scythed out from each of those digits. And its face...

Her face...

"You're allowed to touch this one." The docent's voice behind him was muted but insistent, her odd accent stronger in the alcove's hush. "In fact, you're encouraged to. It will enhance your appreciation of the design flow."

Even as some desperate bit of Wayland's consciousness recoiled, he felt his feet propelling him forward. Strands of carpet clung to his ankles as he reached the base of the massive sculpture.

"If you can reach that high," her soft voice continued, "the textural quality of the hair is quite extraordinary."

Wayland didn't want to reach that high. Even from here, gazing straight ahead, he could see thick ropy strands coiling down from the entity's shoulders. Shifting light from the ceiling spots added an illusion of motion, making individual strands "flow" around the bodies of the ritualists—all female, he noted automatically. Female and either naked or getting there.

But not human. Not even remotely, despite the yammering of his hormones.

"And the sensual flow of precious metal, those flawless additions of coral..."

Wayland's hands trembled. He remembered these feelings: desire and rage and disgust all at once, the strong hot undertow of temptation. He didn't want to touch this sculpture. He didn't even want to stand close to it, yet he was already here—already reaching out for the nearest gleaming gold-white form.

The taste of cheap beer and cigarette smoke filled his mouth. The docent's voice beside him was *her* voice now, as his nightmares remembered it.

"*I'll see you again,*" she'd whispered as he left her. At the time, half drunk himself and hoping she was worse off, he'd forced a smile. Even muttered something back, though he had no intention of revisiting that decrepit Massachusetts college town.

"That's right. You have to touch the design flow to experience it."

The docent's smile flashed white in the alcove's wavering illumination. White and sharp. As Wayland recoiled from her, turning for the exit (*but where?*), his left ankle twisted in the sodden carpet. He felt himself tumbling backwards, though he didn't have far to fall. He'd already been close enough to brush one golden thigh with his fingertips.

"Iä, Hydra Mother!"

Wayland's last coherent thought was that there had been no placard, so how the hell did she know what this sculpture depicted? Then he was falling, *flowing*, inexorably toward its center, where a moment ago there had been only an empty carved slab. The rest of the figures swayed outward to envelop him, then closed again into their circle which turned as the stars must…forever and forever…towards the rightness of Her dead and dreaming lord's return.

Wayland's scream froze deep in his lungs. His flesh writhed as the sea-change took it, turning meat to blue-veined coral—living, feeling coral—of a uniquely disturbing hue. Spread-eagled upon the sacrificial platform, bound ankle and wrist with fetters of pale oceanic gold, that material awaited only the descent of Her priestess's gutting hook, forged in the image of the Mother's own smallest claw.

The wait was not long.

Of Melei, of Ulthar

Gord Sellar

Haunted went Melei that evening into the streets of Ulthar, haunted by what she had seen in the dream-voyage of the night before; desert fires burning distant across the dark and dusty plain, and an immense black silhouette of some enormous outcropping of rock rising up, upward into the sky to blot out the tiny flickering stars across half of the heavens. In a dream, too, had she heard voices echoing against the stone walls of buildings crammed together along narrow streets, voices laden with care and worry, crying her name out into the blackness of deepening night.

Her name—but *not* Melei, not that name she used in waking—had crouched in wait beneath her tongue; perhaps it was only natural, in the dreaming, in this other world, to be called something else. *That* name, strange in her mouth, cold and quivering when she nearly whispered it to herself, was *hers*. And why not? She was alone, she lived alone, and with nobody shared the secrets of her nocturnal voyages, for who would call her anything but mad…?

So that awake, by the lengthening hours of that slow, still-warm autumn endlessness, Melei stalked the cozy, jumbled streets of Ulthar. Listlessly; suffering through a sunny afternoon as faraway gleam of dreamt flames in darkness, and the tempo of faint faraway cries and chanting, haunted her waking mind.

Cats—for in Ulthar, where there was one, there were ten—traipsed past in little dainty-footed troupes, eyeing her with the wary look of beings that glimpsed her dark secret as no human could. She yielded the road to them just as everyone in Ulthar did, occasionally stooping to rub one behind the ear. Briefly, just until its tail batted back against her elbow and it turned its head slightly before going on along its carefree, shiftless way. Always one with black and white patches, always with white paws, she knelt to touch *those* chiaroscuro beasts with the slightest hesitation only, with a trepidation she prayed nobody noticed, most of all the beasts themselves. And yet she was sure in her heart's blood that they knew. They *knew*.

And then, round some corner would she follow the troupe of cats, and find a pack of soldiers standing together. Staring at her from behind grilled black faceplates. She would stop, as other citizens did not, and stare into those night-dark eyes, glimpse the dark folds of eyelids surrounding those bold orbs, and sigh gently and slowly to herself, for these people looked to her like the folk of her dreams, almost. Swarthy, yes, and smelling of exotic, perplexing spices. Beside them, in the street, as clouds drifted in overhead, over the tops of gods-haunted mountains, she took comfort in that strange aroma, the hint of myrrh and tehenna and cinnamon, the broad brown lips pursed stern. The foreign soldiers looked at this bold young woman with wonder, for none of Ulthar had done as she, pausing to gaze into their eyes with something like recognition, perhaps, or fascination, in their own.

Only Melei.

She gazed thus, for a few brief moments, upon these strange and ever-surly foreigners, as a wanderer sometimes, but only sometimes, looks upon the walls of the city where her people have dwelt since forgotten ages. In dreaming, she often had seen folk like these, sat at fires and eaten with them, sung songs she only half-understood, songs shared with that hopeful, dire world which filled her waking days with longing.

But no songs now. Instead, she whispered a word to them, a single word in her own language. One of them, in his fluted blue steel armor, shrugged slightly. They looked at one another, and then at her again, the expectation being that she would move on.

"Atal," she asked them, a name, a single word so pathopoeic that the warriors could do nothing but ache from it, and she nodded her fair head past them, to a distant gate behind, up to the high temple carved from hillstone there, where ancient Atal was, in those days, thought still to linger. His image had been painted last as a priest in repose, feeble and centuries-worn Atal in white robes, shaven head resting upon a stone pillow; his eyes full of longing, staring up from the canvas. Melei had seen the picture in a public hall, gazed reverently on it for an hour while closing her eyes and opening them again, over and over until the image was stamped upon her mind perfectly, indelibly.

The soldiers only pursed their dark, broad lips harder and shook their heads. They nodded down the road. Not towards wherever Atal now was, if indeed the old priest lived still; these footmen of the new conqueror were directing her nowhere except away. Melei gazed upon them a moment more. What songs had they sung as boys? What games had they played amidst fires burning among the darkling foothills surrounding the great peaks of the south? Slowly, she turned and followed a quiet old striped tomcat away, along a gutter. But she heard them speak of her, then, to one another.

And then, suddenly, Ulthar was no longer tinged by her dreams, no longer dressed in that enchantment she had smuggled back from the world of her slumbering voyages. As the soldiers spoke with muted words at once utterly gibberish and completely familiar, she gave up on her earlier half-fancies that she might even have understood them, at least the sense in them, if only she could have heard their voices a little more clearly. It was a lie. They were not mystical creatures. They were quotidian men of muscle and sinew, and Ulthar was simply a holding in their masters' empire.

And Melei longed for more.

She felt their eyes upon her as she wandered down the road, and round a corner, her eyes searching the sky for the first stars, that she might turn homeward and settle herself down to the repose and reverie that only sleep could bring her.

ಬಿ

The black night-ocean roared beneath, broad and noisy with the lapping of waves that she could hear clear as children's voices, so silently did she glide through the deep, familiar sepia that always preceded sunrise on these flights.

The ocean was new: often, she had soared above grasslands, occasionally among the buildings of a smog-choked city, but tonight, this dream-morning, she found herself above some expansive southern ocean. Below, from time to time, a lumbering darkness could be seen, spilling light from tiny windows, luminance far different from any reflection of the whole and simple face of the single crescent moon above her. These were windows in the hulls of lumbering ships that crawled across the ruined sea.

As sepia slowly burnt into orange with the coming of the morning sun, Melei spied the coast ahead. It was an immense and hideous metal graveyard, the hulls and decks of broken ships protruding from the sand, their bare bones laid out as if upon an examiner's table. Among them gathered labouring men, already at work hauling enormous rusty chains and ruined slabs of metal ashore. The ships looked as if they had been hewn in half by some enormous, awful blade and left to bleed into the ocean. For the waters, too, were sullied here, stained black and putrid. The rancid stink of the waters wafted up into the air, and Melei gasped in stunned disbelief.

This was not the same site as she had visited in previous dream-flights, though the people shared the same dark hue of skin, wore the same resignation on their faces. A man beneath her dropped his load, a gargantuan link of chain slamming down onto his leg, and he collapsed upon the poisoned sand with a cry so loud she could hear it as she soared past.

It was exquisite, wrenching but enchanting. It was a place where mistakes mattered, and this was why Melei kept returning. Because this world was one of consequences and dire meanings, godless and hard and amazing. But this beach was not the precise place she sought. In Ulthar, Melei was a mere seamstress, a needle-girl who day in and day out walked the streets careful not to step in cat shit. But in this strange world, she found herself possessed of powers beyond anything a real person in Ulthar could have boasted in millennia. She could soar in the sky, and she could go anywhere.

And there was a place that she was seeking, these nights.

Below her, a fence surrounded an enormous tent village. Men shouted, and there was a violent clattering sound, and screams. She saw people running, people clothed in white that shone against their dark flesh. To Melei they were unspeakably beautiful in their terror. Running for their lives, panicked. She felt her tears welling up. Such awful lives; and yet they held onto them so desperately. What humbling beauty, what endless rapture, that beings could live that way, in a world so starved of magic and gods. It enchanted her, as she swooped down low enough to brush her fingertips against the tattered hems of a few of the dingy white shirts that ran long enough to reach down past the knees of the scrambling men and women.

Melei concentrated, and suddenly spun in the air, soaring now into the northwest. There was a city there that she had read of in secret books hidden in the drab tearooms of Ulthar, books only secret because nobody read them—for the denizens of Ulthar spoke only of the failed expeditions to unearth Kadath, old dead Kadath, and of gossip in the wracked court of Ulthar that was now under Southern rule. But Melei had read on fragile, forgotten pages of the wild tangled passage-roads that ran between the great grey monoliths of that old city on the coast, the city with the unbroken towers and the bridges and the streets laden with music and voices and wavering lights. Across an ocean, it lay: unutterably far by the standards of these folk; but for a dream-traveler, its bright roads and bustling noise lay within reach, if the will was strong.

If only she could find that strange and mystic polis... nobody had done so in aeons of dreaming, not in the lifetimes even of gods. The sky swallowed her, and she soared into it not lightly, but as an arrow soars toward its victim's death: unstoppable, unabashed, and filled with the most resolute certainty imaginable.

სე

Excrescences thick and strange rose from the drowned streets, wafting steam-ily up from broad, jagged-barred holes in the ground, and Melei swept down into the fog of the broken city. This was the place, but no longer the city of the pages, not the city about the magnificences of which had been whispered and scribbled out by dream-wanderers in ancient tomes long-lost. This polis had changed, its million secret details discarded like the flimsy skin of an ancient serpent drifting through the slow eternity of its being.

The city had, by some horrid magic or doom, been drowned, and slain. Ru-ined, its towering spirit smashed apart, the smithereens tossed into cold water and frozen away into bitter ice.

Here, a great library stood encrusted in ice that gleamed chill as diamonds in darkness; and before it, barges poled by men in thick woolen coats, shiver-ing and calling out in their strange tongues, baleful cries. Old men and wom-en gathered upon the library steps and huddled at its high windows as flakes of snow fell enormous and faintly grey with the ash of fires half a world away.

And there, further along, the great old temples of the last true religion in that world, the fanatic cult-houses of the worshippers of the magical curve, the endless blessed marketeers and insatiable blood-hungry pirates of water and light and time. There, these rectangular temples of lost merchandises stood with windows smashed, empty from lootings, empty except for the poor useless souls who took refuge in their icy halls remaining since the cult had loosed its foul and terrible powers upon the world, and toppled everything that humankind had once built up.

Thence flew Melei, deeper into the city, over crumbled steel bridges and the steeples of abandoned, burnt-down churches. She heard singing, not of human voices, not of ghosts—for this world, haunted though its inhabitants' faces were, was a place bereft of stalking ghūls and spirits hungrily wandering. No, not like the frightening lands that lay distant from Ulthar; nothing like the shadowy passes near high Old Kadath or the caverns of B'thaniss. Only the wretched faces of the living gazed out through the smashed-glass windows. The voice she heard was none other than her own, crying out her exultant terror.

An open square between the broken buildings spread out below her, and she wondered whether this had been a park, or the base of some enormous destroyed temple, or perhaps that square where, in ancient frigid nights, the folk of the city had gathered to witness the death-knell of the ending year and cry out jubilant with the beginning of the new. No hint suggested which guess might be correct.

She thought again of living here, in this strange world of cold consequences, as often she had before. Shivering—not from cold, for her dreaming self was swaddled in thick, warm wool, and something of the power of her dream-voyaging shielded her from the worst of the awful, ruined clime—but rather from a titillation derived less from horror at the ruined city, or that such ruination was possible, than out of the purer terror that shook her upon witnessing the magnificent finality of the fact of the ruination itself.

Broken buildings slumbered all around her as she flew past, and she marveled that this world was thus; a place where ruinations could be visited upon mighty civilizations in a generation, yet where the people here would endure on, shivering and hungry, fighting to continue. Whisperings of the fate of Sarnath bubbled up from the silence of her forgotten childhood, but there peered no specters from the windows of this city, at least none that had died. Only the pale and sallow faces of the hungry stared out at her, living scavengers looking out, lit by fires and shame.

Terror. The terror of finding oneself before a mountain to be scaled, a mountain the height of a dozen nations piled upon one another, end to end, boasting whole civilizations and waste lands between them, upon a slope rising unceasingly upward into the sky. The terror of looking upon the ocean stirred into a raging turmoil of violence. Terror at confronting the great secret of this world: that all things had endings, all things could be destroyed just as they had once, long ago, been built up. That terror swept through Melei, thrilled her.

That was when her name in this world, that *other* name, pierced up into her tongue, begging again to be spoken and seal itself upon her.

She bit her tongue, bit down into it so hard that it ached and bled a little. To *say* the name… to consign herself among the living shades… such a temptation…

The name fought relentlessly. It *would* be said, she realized, someday. She would come to live here, in this drowned city of humbling, awful beauty. It would be her home, someday, taking her into its brutal black arms like a lover would do, grinding its iciness against her shivering flesh.

Still she fought, clenching her teeth and grinding them together so violently that she felt they might break off in her mouth. She pushed herself upward, into the sky, letting go of the city even as she stared into the watery canal grid-work of its forgotten, worthless streets. She let herself ascend, into the foul clouds that were heavy with strange poisons, up into the cold nebulousness that lay beyond them, falling away from this awful and lovely world that was her constant obsession, this place of strange meanings and consequences and cruel finalities.

The city and all of its broken, awful grandeur blurred into a mere patch of indistinct darkness dotted with scattered open fires, blending into the sur-rounding darkness and becoming nothingness as she fell upward, outward; away from the world once again.

సౌ

Melei's eyes opened slowly as the sunrise just finished and serene Ulthar grad-ually stirred from its long nocturnal slumber. She slid her prodigious bedding aside, and took up her scribbling-notebook in one hand, searching for the words that would draw the magnificently drab colors across from that other world into hers.

A troupe of cats passed by her window, miaowing gleefully at one another, and she rose to peer out at them, as if to divine some portent from the colors of their coats; but they were a motley pack, impossible to read even for a girl as bright as Melei.

Waking, dreaming. She felt as if a woman torn between two lovers—one of them calm, and sweet, and still and good, and the other magnificent, stone-muscled and taciturn and bold enough to seize her and pull her close to him in the darkness of night.

She set the notebook down, ruminating. There was a choice coming. She would have to choose a name. Said she, in that world, "Melei," then her dark lover would listen, and hear, and understand what her heart said. The deli-cious torture would end, and he would send her home… never to return. Yet said she that other name, that strange name that even now squirmed beneath her tongue, prickling her mouth and fighting to be pronounced in the sunny morning calm of Ulthar, then her dark lover would seize her, all at once, and carry her off into the delightful terror of the world of her dreams, leaving the streets of Ulthar forever empty of her.

She could feel the city's ache, at the very thought of her leaving. The city's ache, or perhaps it was her own.

No harm could come of writing the name, she decided. She had written it upon her own palm, in different scripts, one by one, and not a thing had hap-pened save that she had dreamt of the other world sooner, and more fiercely, each time. She could write it upon a page, she was sure. It was not the same as saying it. She could still decide. Melei, or...

She took a quill, unlidded a jar of sepia ink, and touched the quill's tip into the inky darkness. Without speaking—with her jaw locked firmly, to guard against accidental pronouncement—she touched the tip of the quill against the gently yellowed page. The dawn sunlight cast a shadow from the feather quill, throwing a line of gentle shading across the page and into her lap. She shut her eyes, and opened them, and shut them again, and once more opened them, so as to let the shadow find a place in her heart's memory.

She realized, then, she was building up a storehouse of memories already. The faces of the swarthy guards. The troupes of cats mewing happily all around her. She had stopped hating Ulthar, wincing at the summery stink of the cat turds and grumbling at the foreign power that ruled the place. She had found the kind of love that wells up one when she abandons her lover for another, her world for another's; that sort of love that is rooted in impossibility that cannot be prevented even by sorrow, even by fear, even by the movement of the shadow across a page as the sun slips up into the sky.

She did not write the name, but instead rose, scribbling-book still in hand, and went back to her window. The sweetest cottages of Ulthar lay just there, empty of terror but touching in their way, stirring memories of the games she had played in these dusty streets during what felt like another life. Laughter and the voices of children who had somehow become half-forgotten friends, folk whose faces that she had seen not once in ages and ages.

And Melei knew, then, that she *would* say the name. Perhaps not that night. Not so soon as that, she told herself. But she *would* say it, and go, and old Ulthar would continue on without her, as it had done before her birth, with its cats and gentle sunny days and whispering old women and men.

She filled a basin with warm water, and carried it to a high table in her room, her feet padding upon the wooden planks of the floor. Outside, a bird sang a snatch of birdsong she had heard dozens of times before, though she could not name what type of bird it was. She splashed the water on her face, delighting in its gentle warmth, steeling herself.

For there would be precious little warmth like this in the other world, in the arms of her dark dream lover.

And then she donned a bright and comfortable silk, light in shade to suit the warm day, and crossed the threshold of her home, going out into a street that smelled of blooming cherry flowers and apple orchards that had been planted by the Southerners. There, in the street, a trio of cats gazed up at her, curiously eyeing her approach with heads tilted one way or another. They seemed, like all cats in Ulthar, almost as if they wished to ask her something, or to dispense some holy secret to her, but if indeed this was so, they said nothing, their own jaws as firmly locked as hers had been minutes before.

An old man made his way down the street, comfortable and calm though his back was a little bent. He smiled at her, and a cock crowed in the distance, and Melei closed her eyes. And opened them again.

And closed them.

And opened them again, committing every breath of it, every shade and tiny noise and scent, to the strongest urn in the storehouse of her memory. The voices of children long gone echoed, now, within that storehouse, and the image of her mother baking sour bread, and the laughter of cats—for in Ulthar, by nights, cats do laugh, though only the most blessed ever hear it more than once—and the sunrises, the sunrises that had saddened her so often.

Perplexed, she went through the streets, dazed, eyes and heart drinking Ulthar in deeply and constantly until she was drunk with the place. It was her farewell kiss to the world of her birth, a kiss of the eyes upon the forehead. It was her last embrace of the little city, day-long as she wandered and rambled from shop to temple to the current doorsteps of present friends and the abandoned doorways of friends long-lost. She met those she had once loved, and said nothing of leave-taking, though she wondered if they could see it in her eyes. Yet she asked not a soul as she spoke to them of nothings, of needle work and gossip and of the latest news from other cities and lands. As she walked those quiet, calm streets, her footsteps tapping gently the beat of her last ballad to Ulthar, she realized she loved this city, loved it unceasingly and would do so evermore though she would not live here any longer.

For as the sun began slowly to draw itself down unto the horizon, and the shadows lengthened across the streets as another shadow had done upon her page that morning, the name beneath Melei's tongue stirred once more, this final time irresistibly...

A Gentleman from Mexico

Mark Samuels

"Barlow, I imagine, can tell you even more about the Old Ones."
—Clark Ashton Smith to August Derleth, April 13th 1937.

Víctor Armstrong was running late for his appointment and so had hailed a taxi rather than trusting to the metro. Bathed in cruel noon sunlight, the green-liveried Volkswagen beetle taxi cruised down Avenida Reforma. In the back of the vehicle, Armstrong rummaged around in his jacket pocket for the pack of Faros cigarettes he'd bought before setting off on his rendezvous.

"Es OK para mí a fumar en tu taxi?" Armstrong said, managing to cobble together the request in his iffy Spanish.

He saw the eyes of the driver reflected in the rear-view mirror, and they displayed total indifference. It was as if he'd made a request to fold his arms.

"Seguro," the driver replied, turning the wheel sharply, weaving his way across four lines of traffic. Armstrong was jolted over to the left and clutched at the leather handle hanging from the front passenger door. The right hand seat at the front had been removed, as was the case with all the green taxis, giving plenty of leg-room and an easy entrance and exit. Like most of the taxi drivers in Mexico City, this one handled his vehicle with savage intent,

determined to get from A to B in the minimum possible time. In this almost permanently gridlocked megalopolis, the survival of the fastest was the rule.

Armstrong lit up one of his untipped cigarettes and gazed out the window. Brilliant sunshine illuminated in excruciating detail the chaos and decay of the urban rubbish dump that is the Ciudad de México, Distrito Federal, or "D.F." for short. A great melting pot of the criminal, the insane, the beautiful and the macho, twenty-five million people constantly living in a mire of institutionalised corruption, poverty and crime. But despite all this, Mexico City's soul seems untouched, defiant, and no other great city of the world is so vividly alive, dwelling as it does always in the shadow of death. Another earthquake might be just around the corner, the Popocatéptl volcano might blow at any hour, and the brown haze of man-made pollution might finally suffocate the populace. Who knows? What is certain is that the D.F. would rise again, as filthy, crazed and glorious as before.

They were approaching La Condesa, a fashionable area to the north of the centre that had attracted impoverished artists and writers ten years ago, but which had recently been overrun with pricey restaurants and cafés. Armstrong had arranged to meet with an English-speaking acquaintance at the bookshop café La Torre on the corner of Avenida Nuevo León. This acquaintance, Juan San Isidro, was a so-called underground poet specialising in sinister verse written in the Náhuatl language and who, it was rumoured, had links with the *narcosatánicos*. A notorious drunk, San Isidro had enjoyed a modicum of celebrity in his youth but had burnt out by his mid-twenties. Now in his mid-thirties, he was scarcely ever sober and looked twice his actual age. His bitterness and tendency to enter into the kind of vicious quarrels that seem endemic in Latin American literary circles had alienated him from most of his contemporaries. Armstrong suspected that San Isidro had requested a meeting for one of two reasons; either to tap him for money or else to seek his assistance in recommending a translator for a re-issue of his poetical work in an English language edition in the United States. It was highly unlikely that San Isidro was going to offer him a work of fiction for one of his upcoming anthologies of short stories.

The taxi pulled up alongside the bookshop.

"*¿Cuánto es?*" Armstrong asked.

"*Veintiún pesos,*" the driver responded. Armstrong handed over some coins and exited the vehicle.

Standing on the corner outside the bookshop was a stall selling tortas, tacos and other fast-food. The smell of the sizzling meat and chicken, frying smokily on the hob, made Armstrong's mouth water. Despite the call of *¡Pásele, señor!* Armstrong passed by, knowing that, as a foreigner, his stomach wouldn't have lasted ten minutes against the native bacteria. Having experienced what they called "Montezuma's Revenge" on his first trip to D.F. a year ago, there was no question of him taking a chance like that again. Across the street an argument was taking place between two drivers, who'd got out of their battered and dirty cars to trade insults. Since their abandoned vehicles were holding up the traffic, the rather half-hearted battle (consisting entirely of feints and shouting) was accompanied by a cacophony of angry car-horns.

La Torre was something of a landmark in the area, its exterior covered with tiles, and windows with external ornate grilles. A three-storey building with a peaked roof, and erected in the colonial era, it had been a haunt for literati of all stripes, novelists, poets and assorted hangers-on, since the 1950s. During the period in which La Condesa had been gentrified some of La Torre's former seedy charm had diminished and, as well as selling books, it had diversified into stocking DVDs and compact discs upstairs. Part of the ground floor had been converted into an expensive eatery, whilst the first floor now half occupied a café-bar from where drinkers could peer over the centre of the storey down into the level below, watching diners pick at their food and browsers lingering over the books on shelves and on the display tables. As a consequence of these improvements, the space for poetry readings upstairs had been entirely done away with, and Juan San Isidro haunted its former confines as if in eternal protest at the loss of his own personal stage.

As Armstrong entered he glanced up at the floor above and saw the poet already waiting for him, slumped over a table and tracing a circle on its surface with an empty bottle of Sol beer. His lank black hair hung down to his shoulders, obscuring his face, but even so his immense bulk made him unmistakable.

Armstrong's gaze roved around and sought out the stairway entrance. He caught sight of the only other customer in La Torre, besides himself and San Isidro. This other person was dressed in a dark grey linen suit, quite crumpled, with threadbare patches at the elbows and frayed cuffs. The necktie he wore was a plain navy blue and quite unremarkable. His shoes were badly scuffed and he must have repeatedly refused the services of the D.F.'s innumerable *boleros*. They keenly polished shoes on their portable foot-stands for anyone who had a mere dozen pesos to spare. The man had an olive complexion, was perfectly clean-shaven, and about forty years old. His short black hair was parted neatly on the left-hand side. He had the features of a *mestizo*, a typical Mexican of mingled European and Native Indian blood. There was something in the way that he carried himself that told of a gentleman down on his luck, perhaps even an impoverished scholar given his slight stoop, an attribute often acquired by those who pore over books or manuscripts year after year.

He was browsing through the books on display that were published by the likes of *Ediciones Valdemar* and *Ediciones Siruela* that had been specially imported from Spain. These were mostly supernatural fiction titles, for which many Mexican readers had a discerning fondness. Armstrong was glad, for his own anthologies invariably were comprised of tales depicting the weird and uncanny, a market that, at least in the Anglophone countries, seemed to have self-destructed after a glut of trashy horror paperbacks in the 1980s. But these were not junk, they were works by the recognised masters and a quick glance over the classics available for sale here in mass-market form would have drawn the admiration of any English or American devotee. Here were books by Arthur Machen, Algernon Blackwood, M.R. James and Ambrose Bierce, amongst dozens of others. Most striking however, was the vast range of collections available written by H. P. Lovecraft. The browsing man in the dark suit picked up one after the other, almost reluctant to return each to its proper place, although if his down-at-heel appearance were an indication, their price was surely beyond his limited means. New books in Mexico are scarcely ever cheap.

Armstrong looked away. He could not understand why this rather ordinary gentleman had stirred his imagination. He was, after all, merely typical of the sort of book-addict found anywhere and at any time. Meanwhile Juan San Isidro had noticed Víctor's arrival and called down to him.

"¡Ay, Víctor, quiero más chela! Lo siento, pero no tengo dinero."

Armstrong sighed, and made his way up the stairs.

When they were eventually sat opposite one another, Armstrong with a bottle of Indio and San Isidro with a fresh bottle of Sol, the Mexican switched from Spanish to English. He was always keen to take whatever opportunity he could to converse in the language. A huge bear of a man, he'd recently grown a shaggy goatee beard and the T-shirt he wore bore the logo of some outlandish band called "Control Machete", whose music Armstrong did not know and did not want to know. Years ago Armstrong had foolishly mentioned San Isidro's literary efforts to the publisher of a small press imprint in California who was looking for cosmic or outré verse. The result had been a chapbook with a selection of San Isidro's Aztec-influenced work translated into English, and thereafter Armstrong had never been able to entirely shake off his "discovery".

"So," he said, "how are things with you? Still editing those *antologías?*"

"There's scarcely any money in them, Juan," Armstrong replied, "unless I've managed to wrangle something original out of Steve King, the publishers want to nail my balls to the wall."

"You know him? King? Do you think he'd give me a loan? He's very rich, no? Help out a struggling brother artist?"

Armstrong tried not to smile inappropriately. He could only imagine how quickly San Isidro would piss away any handouts he'd receive on booze. No one other than their agents, accountants, lawyers or publishers milks cash-cow authors.

"He's a busy man. I don't think he'd appreciate my..."

"You mean he's a *pinche cabrón*. Keeps his money up his *culo* where no one else can get at it. That's why *todos los gringos* walk around with their legs apart, like cowboys, no? All those dollar bills stuffed in there."

Armstrong was relieved to be British. Even liberal Americans who came south, seeking to atone for the recent sins of NAFTA and a long history of land grabbing, were objects of ridicule here. They might get away with such conscience posturing in the north, in cities like Monterrey that were closer to the border and which looked to rich U.S. states like Texas for inspiration, but in Mexico D.F. *gringos* are only ever *pinches gringos* and no amount of self-loathing or atonement on their part could ever erase the fact. The British, on the other hand, despite their Imperial past, were redeemed by virtue of having given the Beatles and association football to the world.

"Why did you want to see me, Juan?" Armstrong asked, taking out his packet of *Faros* and putting them on the table. His companion looked at the cheap brand with amused contempt. Nevertheless, this attitude did not stop him from smoking them.

"I want you to take a look at some *cuentos*," San Isidro replied, puffing away on the cigarette he'd taken. "Read them and make me an offer. They're in your line of work."

He delved into a shoulder bag lying underneath the table and took out a pile of papers, individuated into sections by rubber bands, and handed them over.

"I thought you didn't write short stories," Armstrong said.

"I didn't write them. I'm acting as the exclusive agent. They're in English, as you see, and they're the type of horror stories you like. I handle all his stuff."

"Who's this author," Armstrong said, looking at the top sheet, "Felipe López? I can't say I've heard of him."

"*El señor López* has only been writing for a couple of years. He's my personal discovery, like you discovered me, no? *Es un autor auténtico*, not some hack. *Mira al cabellero* down there, the one who's looking through the books? That's *el señor López*. He doesn't want to meet you until you've read his stuff. I told him I knew you, and that you weren't the same as all those other *culeros* who'd rejected him."

So that man in the crumpled grey suit was San Isidro's first client, Armstrong thought. He hesitated for a moment but then relented. At least this man López had the appearance of being literate.

"Alright," Armstrong said, "I'll take them away with me and call you once I've read them. I can't promise anything though."

"Why not sit here and read them now, *compañero*? I tell you, these things are a goldmine. We can have a few more *chelas* while I wait for you to finish. He also does his own proofreading, so you won't need to *trabajar mucho* yourself."

"Short stories," Armstrong riposted, "are fool's gold, Juan. I told you, there's no real money in them anymore. Have another on me if you like, but I've got to go. I'll be in touch."

With that closing remark Armstrong stood up, left a hundred pesos note on the table, and made his exit. He didn't notice whether or not *el Señor López* saw him leave.

৩১

Over the next few days Armstrong almost forgot about the stories by Felipe López. He hated being asked to read fiction by an unknown author that had been praised by one of his friends. All too often he had to prick their enthusiasm, usually fired by beer and comradeship rather than from an objective assessment of literary merit. And San Isidro had never acted as an agent for anybody before; he was far too consumed by his own literary ambitions. So it appeared obvious to Armstrong that San Isidro was paying back a favour of some sort. Though it seemed unlikely given the down-at-heel appearance of López, but perhaps it was a case of San Isidro owing him money.

Armstrong was staying close to Cuauhtémoc metro station in an apartment owned by Mexican friends of his, a couple, Enrique and María, who were in London for a few weeks, staying in his flat there in an exchange holiday. It was something they did every other year to save on hotel bills. There were only three days left before they were due to cross each other high over the Atlantic in flights going in the opposite direction. Enrique and María were both involved in publishing themselves, and he'd struck up a friendship with them in 1995 whilst attending a fantasy and horror convention held in San Francisco.

Since he was staying in an apartment belonging to friends, Armstrong paid little attention to the telephone, as he knew he'd just be taking messages for his absent hosts. Anything desperately important that needed to be passed on to them would be left on the answerphone machine. When he got around to checking it, there were three messages, two for Enrique and María, and one for him. It was left by Juan San Isidro:

"*Oye, ¿qué onda?* Man, don't fuck me over. Have you read *los cuentos?* I think not. Otherwise you'd be chasing my ass like a *puto*. You don't leave Mexico until I hear from you, *¿te queda claro?*"

Despite his reluctance, Armstrong didn't see any alternative but to look the stories over. He took them out onto the little balcony overlooking the *privada* in which the apartment was situated. It was pleasantly warm outside in the evening, being October, and since the only traffic passing below consisted of pedestrians it was easy to concentrate. He sat down on the chair he'd moved out there, put the papers that he'd retrieved from his suitcase on his lap, and looked them over.

San Isidro had given him four stories, the longest of which was the third at around forty thousand words.

Armstrong had seen this type of story on dozens of occasions in the past, usually sent for his consideration by "fan authors" who were obsessed with the life and works of H. P. Lovecraft. Most of these pastiches contained long lists of clichéd forbidden books and names of unpronounceable entities to be incorporated into the so-called "Cthulhu Mythos". As he turned the pages of the first of López's tales though, he was surprised to discover that they did not also contain the other feature associated with Lovecraft fan pastiches: there were no obvious grammatical, spelling or common textual errors. The work had already been gone over by an author with a keen eye for copyediting. Additionally, it had to be the case that Felipe López was fluent in English to the degree of being able to pass completely for a native. The text contained no trace of any Spanish language idioms indicating his Mexican nationality. Indeed, López even favoured the British spelling of certain words, rather than that used in the United States, in exactly the same fashion as Lovecraft had done himself.

Despite his disdain for pastiche, Armstrong kept reading. Eventually, to his surprise, he found that López's mimetic skills were so expert that he could almost believe that he was reading a previously undiscovered work written by Lovecraft himself. The story had the exact same sense of nightmarish authenticity as the best of the Providence author's tales. By the time he'd finished reading the first story, Armstrong was in a state of dazed wonder. Of course he realised, on a professional level, that the thing had no commercial potential. It smacked far too much of an in-joke, or a hoax, but it was nevertheless profoundly impressive in its own right. He began to wonder what this López person might be able to achieve were he to wean himself from the Lovecraft influence and produce fiction utilising a distinct authorial voice. It might result in another modern-day writer of the order of Thomas Ligotti.

Armstrong was dimly aware of the telephone ringing in the background. He ignored the sound, allowing the answer-machine to deal with whoever it was. He supposed that it could be San Isidro again and that it might have been better to pick up, but he was too eager to discover whether the story he'd just read was a fluke or not. Since the mosquitoes were now busy in the night air, he took the manuscripts inside and carried on reading.

ʬ

Whoever had left the weird message on Enrique and María's answer-machine was obviously some crank, thought Armstrong. He played it back again the morning after it was recorded.

There was click on the line and the sound of unintelligible voices conferring amongst themselves and then a jarring, discordant muttering in English. The voice had a Mexican accent but was unknown to Armstrong. It said:

"*He belongs to us. His products belong to us. No-one will take him from us.*"

That was all.

After listening to the message one more time, Armstrong wondered if it were not simply San Isidro playing a joke on him, pretending to be another rival party involved with the works of Felipe López. Perhaps he thought the idea of some competition might spur Armstrong to a quick decision. If so, it was an unnecessary ploy.

After having read the second of López's tales he was convinced that the author had unmatched imagination and ability, despite being almost ruinously handicapped by his slavish mimicry of Lovecraft's style and themes. However, there was more than enough pure genius in there to convince Armstrong to take the matter further. If he could meet with López in person, he was determined to press upon him the necessity of a last revision of the texts: one that removed entirely the Cthulhu Mythos elements and replaced the florid, adjective-ridden prose with a minimalist approach.

When he telephoned Juan San Isidro it was no surprise that the poet-turned-agent was deeply suspicious about Armstrong's insistence that he must meet López alone.

"You want to cut me out of the deal, *¡estás loco!* Forget it, man. Now you know *que es un maestro, lo quieres todo para ti.*"

"I only want to suggest a few changes to the texts, Juan. Nothing sinister in that, really. You'll get your commission, I'll not cheat you, believe me."

Their conversation went round in circles for ten minutes before Armstrong eventually convinced San Isidro that he had no underhand motive with regards to López's work. Even so, Armstrong realised that there was something more going on between the two of them than the usual protective relationship between an agent and his client. Nevertheless he successfully elicited a promise from San Isidro that he would ensure López met with him alone in the Café la Habana on La Calle de Bucareli at 2:00 pm that same afternoon.

ಐಐ

The Café la Habana was a haunt for distinguished old men who came to play chess, smoke their pipes or cigars and spend the better part of the afternoon dreaming over coffee or beer. It had a high ceiling and was decorated with framed photographs of Havana from the time before Castro's revolution. Many communist exiles from Batista Cuba came here, having fled persecution, and its fame dated from that period. The number of exiles had dwindled as the years passed, but it still had a reputation amongst all those who championed leftist defiance. The place had a long pedigree, having been a favourite meeting place, in even earlier decades, of those Spanish Republican refugees who'd settled in D.F. after escaping the wrath of General Franco's regime.

Armstrong sat in a corner, lingering over a glass of tequila with lime, when López walked in. He was half-an-hour late. His lean form was framed in the doorway by the brilliant sunshine outside. López cast his glance around the place before spotting Armstrong and making for the table at which he sat.

López had changed his dark grey suit for a cream-coloured one, and this time he was wearing a matching panama hat. He gave a nod of recognition towards Armstrong as he approached.

Before he sat down he shook Armstrong's hand and apologised in English:

"I hope that you will excuse my tardiness, Mr. Armstrong, but the truth is that I was distracted by a particularly fascinating example of 18th Century colonial architecture whilst making my way over here."

Armstrong did not reply at once. He was taken aback by López's accent. Unless he was mistaken, it was pure, authentic New England Yankee. There was not a trace of Mexican in it.

"No need to apologise," Armstrong finally said, "can I get you a drink; some beer or tequila perhaps?"

"Thank you but no. I never partake of alcoholic beverages, even for the purposes of refreshment. However, a cup of coffee, perhaps a double espresso, would be most welcome."

Armstrong ordered López's coffee and asked for another tequila with lime to be brought to their table.

"I liked your tales very much, it was quite an experience reading through them I can tell you. Of course they're overly derivative, but I imagine that you easily could tone down all the Lovecraft elements…"

"I'm afraid, Mr. Armstrong," López said, with a chill tone entering his voice, "that alterations of any sort are completely out of the question. The stories must be printed as written, down to the last detail, otherwise this conversation is simply a waste of my time and your own."

The drinks arrived. López calmly began to shovel spoonful after spoonful of sugar into his cup, turning the coffee into treacly, caffeine-rich syrup. Armstrong looked at him incredulously. Now he understood what was going on. San Isidro was definitely having a joke at his expense. He must have coached this López character, telling him all about H. P. Lovecraft's mannerisms and …to what end?

"Why are you persisting with this absurd Lovecraft impersonation?" Armstrong blurted out. "It's ridiculous. San Isidro put you up to it, I suppose. But what I can't figure out is why, so let me in on the joke."

López looked up from his coffee and his eyes were deadly serious. And here it comes, boy and girls, thought Armstrong; here comes the line we've all been waiting for:

This is no joke, Mr. Armstrong, far from it, for I am in reality Howard Phillips Lovecraft of Providence, Rhode Island.

"Surely the only rational answer has already suggested itself," López replied, very calmly and without any melodrama, "you are in fact sitting across the table from a certifiable lunatic."

Armstrong leaned back in his seat and very carefully considered the man opposite. His manner betrayed no sign of humour and he spoke as if what he'd suggested was an established truism.

"Then despite your behaviour, you know that you're not really Lovecraft?" Armstrong said.

"Howard Phillips Lovecraft died in agony on the morning of Monday the 15th of March 1937 in Providence's Jane Brown Memorial Hospital. I cannot be him. However, since Tuesday the 15th of March 2003, I have been subject to a delusion whereby the identity of Lovecraft completely supplanted my own. I currently have no memories whatsoever of having once been Felipe López of Mexico City. His family and friends are complete strangers to me. Meanwhile everyone Lovecraft knew is dead. I have become an outsider in this country and in this time. Unless one accepts the existence of the supernatural, which I emphatically do not, then only the explanation I have advanced has any credence."

Armstrong was taken aback by these remarks. This was like no madman he'd heard of: one who was not only able to recognise his derangement, but who also was totally a slave to it. It was more like some bizarre variant of a multiple personality disorder.

"What did the doctors here have to say?" Armstrong asked.

"They did their best, but with no appreciable effect, let alone any amelioration, upon my malady. They tended to agree with my analysis of the situation," López said, after taking a sip of his coffee.

"What about López before this happened? Did he have any interest in Lovecraft prior to your—umm—alteration? I can't believe something like that would come out of nowhere."

It was annoying, but Armstrong found himself questioning López as if he were actually addressing Lovecraft inhabiting another body.

"Quite so. I have discovered that López was a fanatical devotee of Love-craft's life and work. Moreover, he was one of that rather contemptible breed of freaks who adhere to the outlandish belief that, rather than writing fiction, Lovecraft had unconscious access to ultra-mundane dimensions. The group to which he belonged, who styled themselves 'The Sodality of the Black Sun', advocated the piteous theory that Lovecraft was an occult prophet instead of a mere scribbler. This indicates to me a brain already on the brink of a potential collapse into total chaos. You see before you the inevitable consequence."

There are a lot of sad crazies out there, thought Armstrong, who believe in nothing except the power of their own imaginations to create whatever they want to create from a supposedly malleable reality. A whole bunch of them had doubtless fastened upon Lovecraft's mythos for inspiration, but he doubted that any others had wound up like Felipe López.

"Well," Armstrong said, "I don't know what to make of all this. But surely one consideration has occurred to you already? If you really were Lovecraft, you'd know certain things that only he could possibly have known."

"An ingenious point," said López, "but with all his contemporaries in the grave, how then to verify that information? Mr. Armstrong, I must remind you that the idea of Lovecraft's consciousness not only surviving the death of his physical form, but also transferring itself to another body, is patently ridiculous. I make no such claim."

López stared at him wordlessly and then, having finished the dregs of his coffee, got up and left.

When Armstrong arrived back at Enrique and María's apartment, he found the door already ajar. Someone had broken in, forcing their entrance with a crowbar or similar tool judging by the splintered wound in the side of the door's frame. He was relieved to find that the intruders had not torn the place apart and seemed to have scarcely disturbed anything. When he examined his own room however, he noted at once that the López manuscripts were missing. He unmistakably remembered having left them on his bedside table. However, in their place, was a note left behind by whoever had stolen them. It read:

Do not meddle in our affairs again, lest the darkness seek you out.

Obviously, this was a targeted burglary by the people who'd left that answerphone message warning him off having dealings with López. They must have wanted to get hold of the López stories extremely badly, and, whoever they were, must have also known that San Isidro had passed them to him, as well as knowing that Armstrong had an appointment with López, thus giving them the perfect moment to strike while he was out.

It was difficult to figure out what to do next. Everyone in Mexico City realises that to call the police regarding a burglary has two possible outcomes. The first is that they will turn up, treat it as a waste of their time and do nothing. The second is that things will turn surreal very quickly, because they will casually mention how poorly paid police officers are, and, in return for a "donation", they are able to arrange for the swift return of your goods with no questions asked. Given that the burglary was not the work of organised crime but some nutty underground cult, Armstrong thought better of involving the police.

Great, thought Armstrong, now I'm in trouble not only with the local branch of occult loonies, but with San Isidro and López for having lost the manuscripts. The first thing to do was give San Isidro the bad news. Since a matter of this delicate nature was best dealt with face-to-face Armstrong decided to make his way over to the poet's apartment, after he'd arranged for someone to come over and fix the door.

∾

A cardinal, though unspoken, rule of travelling by metro in Mexico City is not to carry anything of value. If you're a tourist, look like a tourist with little money. The security guards that hover around the ticket barriers are not there just for show. They carry guns for a reason. D.F. is the kidnapping capital of the world. Armstrong had always followed the dress-down rule and, although he stood out anyway because he was a pale-skinned *güerito*, he'd encountered no problems on his travels. The stations themselves were grimy, functionalist and depressing. Architecturally they resembled prison camps, but located underground. Nevertheless Armstrong enjoyed travelling by metro; it was unbelievably cheap, the gap between trains was less than a minute, and it was like being on a mobile market place. Passengers selling homemade CDs would wander up and down the carriages, with samples of music playing on ghetto blasters slung over their shoulders. Others sold tonics for afflictions from back pain to impotence. Whether these worked or not there was certainly a market for them, as the sellers did a brisk trade.

One of the carriages on the train that Armstrong took must have been defective. All its lights were out and, curiously, he noticed that when anyone thought to board it anyway changed their minds at once and preferred to either remain on the platform or else rush over into one of the adjacent carriages instead.

Armstrong alighted at Chapultepec station, found his way through the convoluted tunnels up to the surface and turned left alongside the eight-lane road outside. The noise of the traffic blocked out most other sounds, and the vehicle fumes were like a low-level grey nebula held down by the force of the brilliant afternoon sunshine. People scurried to and fro along the pavement, their gazes fixed straight ahead, particularly those of any lone women for whom eye-contact with a *chilango* carried the risk of inviting a lewd suggestion.

A long footbridge flanked the motorway, and was the only means of crossing for pedestrians for a couple of miles or so. At night it was a notorious crime spot and only the foolhardy would cross it unaccompanied. However, at this time of the day everyone safely used it and a constant stream of people went back and forth.

Juan San Isidro's apartment was only five minutes walk from the bridge, and was housed in a decaying brownstone building just on the fringes of La Condesa. Sometimes Armstrong wondered whether the poet was the structure's only occupant, for the windows of all the other apartments were either blackened by soot or else broken and hanging open day and night to the elements.

He pushed the intercom button for San Isidro, and, after a minute, heard a half-awake voice say:

"*¿Quién es?*"

"It's me, Victor, come down and let me in, will you?" Armstrong replied, holding his mouth close to the intercom.

"Stand in front where I can see you," he said, "and I'll give you *mis llaves.*"

Armstrong left the porch, went onto the pavement and looked up. San Isidro leaned out of one of the third floor windows, his lank black hair making a cowl over his face. He tossed a plastic bag containing the keys over the ledge, and Armstrong retrieved it after it hit the ground.

The building had grown even worse since the last time he'd paid a visit. If it was run-down before, now it was positively unfit for human habitation and should have been condemned. The lobby was filled with debris, half the tiles had fallen from the walls and a dripping waterpipe was poking out from a huge hole in the ceiling. Vermin scurried around back in the shadows. The building's staircase was practically a deathtrap, for if a step had not already collapsed, those that remained seemed likely to do so in the near future. As Armstrong climbed he clutched at the shaky banister with both hands, his knuckles white with the fierce grip, advancing up sideways like a crab.

San Isidro was standing in the doorway to his apartment, smoking a fat joint with one hand and swigging from a half-bottle of Cuervo with the other. The smell of marijuana greeted Armstrong as he finally made it to the fourth floor. Being continually stoned, he thought, was about the only way to make the surroundings bearable.

"*Hola, compañero,* good to see you, come on inside."

His half-glazed eyes, wide fixed smile and unsteady gait indicated that he'd been going at the weed and tequila already for most of the day.

"This is a celebration, no? You've come to bring me *mucho dinero,* I hope. I'm honoured that you come here to see me. *Siéntate, por favor.*"

San Isidro cleared a space on the sofa that was littered with porno magazines and empty packets of Delicados cigarettes. Armstrong then sat down while San Isidro picked up an empty glass from the floor, poured some tequila in it and put it in his hand.

"*Salud,*" he said "to our friend and saviour Felipe López, *el mejor escritor de cuentos macabros del mundo, ahora y siempre.*"

"I want you to tell me, Juan, as a friend and in confidence, what happened to López and how he came to think and act exactly like H. P. Lovecraft. And I want to know about the people that are after him. Were they people he knew before his—um—breakdown?" Armstrong said, looking at the glass and trying to find a clean part of the rim from which to drink. At this stage he was reluctant to reveal that the López manuscripts had been stolen. San Isidro was volatile, and Armstrong wasn't sure how he might react to the news.

San Isidro appeared to start momentarily at the mention of "H. P. Lovecraft" but whether it was the effect of the name or the cumulative effect of the booze and weed, it was difficult to tell.

"So he told you, eh? Well, not all of it. *No recuerda nada de antes,* when he was just Felipe López. *No importa qué pasó antes,* sure, there was some heavy shit back then. *Si quieres los cuentos, primero quiero mucho dinero.* Then maybe I'll tell you about it, eh?"

"I'll pay you Juan, and pay you well. But I need to understand the truth," Armstrong replied.

What San Isidro told Armstrong over the next half-hour consisted of a meandering monologue, mostly in Spanish, of a brilliant young *gringo* who had come to Mexico in the 1940s to study Mesoamerican anthropology. This man, Robert Hayward Barlow, had been Lovecraft's literary executor. Armstrong had heard the name before but what little he knew did not prepare him for San Isidro's increasingly bizarre account of events.

He began plausibly enough. Barlow, he said, had taken possession of Lovecraft's papers after his death in 1937. He had gone through them thereafter and donated the bulk to the John Hay Library in Providence, in order to establish a permanent archival resource. However he was ostracised by the Lovecraft circle, a campaign driven by Donald Wandrei and August Derleth, on the basis that he had supposedly stolen the materials in the first place from under the nose of the Providence author's surviving aunt.

However, what was not known then, San Isidro claimed, was that Barlow had kept some items back, the most important of which was the *Dream Diary of the Arkham Cycle*, a notebook in longhand of approximately thirty or so pages and akin to Lovecraft's commonplace book. It contained, so San Isidro claimed, dozens of entries from 1923 to 1936 that appeared to contradict the assertion that Lovecraft's mythos was solely a fictional construct. These entries are not suggestive by and of themselves *at the time they were supposedly written*, for the content was confined to the description of dreams in which elements from his myth-cycle had manifested themselves. These could be accepted as having no basis in reality had it not been for their supposedly *prophetic* nature. One such entry San Isidro quoted from memory. By this stage his voice was thick and the marijuana he'd been smoking made him giggle in a disquieting, paranoid fashion:

A dream of the bony fingers of Azathoth reaching down to touch two cities in Imperial Japan, and laying them waste. Mushroom clouds portending the arrival of the Fungi from Yuggoth.

To Armstrong, this drivel seemed only a poor attempt to turn Lovecraft into some latter-day Nostradamus, but San Isidro clearly thought otherwise. Armstrong wondered what López had to do with all of this, and whether he would repudiate the so-called "prophecies" by sharing Lovecraft's trust in indefatigable rationalism. That would be ironic.

"How does all this tie in with López?" Armstrong said.

"In 1948," San Isidro slurred, "there were *unos brujos, se llamaban La Sociedad del Sol Oscuro*, cheap *gringo* paperbacks of Lovecraft were their inspiration. They were interested in revival of worship for the old Aztec gods before they incorporated Cthulhu mythology. The gods of the two are much alike, no? *Sangre, muerte y la onda cósmica.* They tormented Barlow, suspected that's why he came to Mexico, because of the connection. Barlow was a *puto*, he loved to give it to boys, and soon they found out about the dream-diary. That was the end. Blackmail. He killed himself in 1951, took a whole bottle of seconal."

"But what about López?"

"They had to wait *cincuenta años para que se alinearan las estrellas.* Blood sacrifices, so much blood, the police paid off over decades. But it was prophesised in his own dream-diary: *El espléndido regreso.* Even the exact date was written in there. López was the chosen vessel. "

"How do you know all this, Juan?"

"I chose him from amongst us, but I betrayed them, the secret was passed down to me, and now I need to get out of this *pinche* country *rápido*, before *mis hermanos* come for me. López, he wants to go back to Providence, one last time," San Isidro giggled again at this point, "though I reckon it's changed a lot, since he last saw it, eh? But, me, I don't care."

He's as insane as López, Armstrong thought. This is just an elaborate scheme cooked up by the two of them to get money out of someone they think of as simply another stupid, rich foreigner. After all, what evidence was there that any of this nonsense had a grain of truth in it? Like most occultists, they'd cobbled together a mass of pseudo-facts and assertions and dressed it up as secret knowledge known only to the "initiated". Christ, he wouldn't have been surprised if, at this point, San Isidro produced a "Dream Diary of the Arkham Cycle", some artificially-aged notebook written in the 1960s by a drugged-up kook who'd forged Lovecraft's handwriting and stuffed it full of allusions to events after his death in 1937. They'd managed to pull off a pretty fair imitation of his stories between themselves and whoever else was involved in the scam. The results were certainly no worse than August Derleth's galling attempts at "posthumous collaboration" with Lovecraft.

At last, as if San Isidro had reached a stage where he had drunk and smoked himself back to relative sobriety, he lurched up from the easy chair in which he'd been sitting. He ran his fingers through his beard, stared hard at Armstrong and said:

"We need to talk business, how much are you going to give me?"

"I'll give you enough to get out of Mexico, for the sake of our friendship, but I can't pay for the stories, Juan, anyway someone has stolen them," Armstrong replied.

Probably you or López, he thought cynically.

The only reaction from San Isidro was that he raised his eyebrows a fraction. Without saying a word he went into the kitchen next door and Armstrong could hear him rattling around in some drawers.

"If you're going to try to fleece me," Armstrong said, raising his voice so that he could be heard in the adjacent room, "then you and López will have to do better than all this Barlow and the 'Sodality of the Black Sun' crap."

When San Isidro came back into the room, his teeth were bared like those of a hungry wolf. In his right hand he was clutching a small calibre pistol, which he raised and aimed directly at Armstrong's head.

"*Cabrón, hijo de puta, di tus últimas oraciones, porque te voy a matar.*"

Sweat broke out on Armstrong's forehead. His thoughts raced. Was the gun loaded or was this only bravado? Another means of extorting money from him? Could he take the chance?

Just as Armstrong was about to cry out, everything went black. Despite the fact that it was the middle of the afternoon, with brilliant sunshine outside, the room was immediately swallowed up by total darkness. Armstrong could not believe what was happening. He thought, at first, that he had gone blind. Only when he stumbled around in the inky void and came right up against the window did he see the sunlight still outside, but not penetrating at all beyond the glass and into the room. Outside, the world went on as normal. Armstrong turned back away from the window and was aware of a presence moving within the dark. The thing emitted a high-pitched and unearthly whistle that seemed to bore directly into his brain. God, he thought, his train of reasoning in a fit of hysterical chaos, something from Lovecraft's imagination had clawed its way into reality, fully seventy years after the man's death. Something that might drive a man absolutely insane, if it was seen in the light. Armstrong thought of the hundreds of hackneyed Cthulhu Mythos stories that he'd been forced to read down the years and over which he'd chortled. He recalled the endless ranks of clichéd yet supposedly infinitely horrible monstrosities, all with unpronounceable names. But he couldn't laugh now, because the joke wasn't so funny anymore.

So he screamed instead—

"Juan! Juan!"

Armstrong bumped into the sofa in a panic, before he finally located the exit. From behind him came the sound of six shots, fired one after the other, deafeningly loud, and then nothing but dead, gaunt silence. He staggered into the hallway and reached the light outside, turned back once to look at the impenetrable darkness behind him, before then hurtling down the stairs. He now gave no thought, as he had done when coming up, as to how precarious they were. He did, however, even in the grip of terror, recall that the building was deserted and that no one could swear to his having been there.

৩

After what had happened to him, Armstrong expected to feel a sense of catastrophic psychological disorientation. Whatever had attacked San Isidro, he thought, carrying darkness along with it so as to hide its deeds, was proof of something, even if it did not prove that everything San Isidro had claimed was in fact true. At the very least it meant that the "Sodality of the Black Sun" had somehow called a psychic force into existence through their half-century of meddling with rituals and sacrifices. Armstrong had no choice but to discount the alternative rational explanation. At the time when day had become night in San Isidro's apartment he had been afraid, but nothing more, otherwise he was clear-headed and not prone to any type of hysterical interlude or hallucinatory fugue. Rather than feeling that his worldview had been turned upside-down however, he instead felt a sense of profound loneliness. What had happened had really happened but he knew that if he tried to tell anyone about it, they would scoff or worse, pity him, as he himself would have done, were he in their position.

Enrique and María returned to their apartment on schedule and Armstrong told them of his intention to remain in Mexico City a while longer. They noticed the curious melancholy in him, but did not question him about it in any detail. Nor would he have told them, even if prompted. Armstrong moved out the next day, transferring his meagre belongings to a room in a seedy hotel overlooking La Calle de Bucareli. From there he was able to gaze out of a fifth-floor window in his *cuartito* and keep watch on the Café la Habana opposite. His remaining connection to the affair was with Felipe López, the man who had the mind of Lovecraft, and he could not leave without seeing him one last time. He had no idea whether San Isidro were alive or dead. What was certain was that it was inconceivable that he attempted to make contact with him. Were San Isidro dead, it would arouse suspicion that Armstrong had been connected with his demise, and were he alive, then Armstrong had little doubt that he'd want to exact revenge.

Days passed, and Armstrong's vigil yielded no results. There was no sign of López and he had no way of contacting him directly, no phone number, and no address. He was fearful that the Mexican police might call upon him at any instant, and scanned the newspapers daily in order to see if there were any reports mentioning San Isidro. He found nothing at all relating to him and recalled what he'd been told about the authorities having been paid off with blood money over decades. When Armstrong left his room it was only to visit the local Oxxo convenience store in order to stock up on *tortas de jamón y queso, Faros, y tequila barato*. The last of these items was most important to him. He spent most of the time pouring the tequila into a tumbler and knocking it back, while sitting at his pigeon-shit stained window, hoping to see López finally enter the Café la Habana in search of him. All he saw was the endless mass of frenzied traffic, drivers going from nowhere to anywhere and back in a hurry, oblivious to the revelation that separated him from such commonplace concerns, and which had taken him out of the predictable track of everyday existence.

And then, twelve days after he'd rented the room in the hotel, he finally saw a slightly stooped figure in a grey suit making his way towards the Café la Habana. It was López; there could be no doubt about it.

ଓ

López was seated in a table in the corner of the Café, reading a paperback book and sipping at a cup of coffee. As Armstrong approached he saw that the book was a grubby second-hand copy of *Los Mitos de Cthulhu por H. P. Lovecraft y Otros.* The edition had a strange green photographic cover, depicting, it appeared, a close-up of a fossil. López immediately put down the volume once he caught sight of Armstrong.

"San Isidro seems to have disappeared off the face of the earth," he said. "I've been endeavouring to contact him for the last two weeks, but all to no avail. I admit to feeling not a little concern in the matter. Have you crossed paths with him of late?"

Armstrong could not take his eyes off the man. Could "The Sodality of the Black Sun" have succeeded? Was the creature that conversed with him now actually the mind of Lovecraft housed in the body of some Mexican occultist called López? God, what a disappointment it must have been for them, he thought. What irony! To go to all that trouble to reincarnate the consciousness of the great H. P. Lovecraft, only to find that after his return he denied his own posthumous existence! But why keep such a survival alive, why allow the existence of the last word on the subject if it contradicted their aims? It made no sense.

"I'm afraid," said Armstrong, "that San Isidro has vanished."

"I don't see..." said López.

"Not all of Lovecraft came back, did it? I don't think they salvaged the essence, only a fragment. A thing with his memories, but not the actual man himself. Some sort of failed experiment. You're the one who's been leaving me those warning notes, aren't you?" Armstrong said, interrupting.

"You presume too much, Mr. Armstrong, and forget," replied López, "that I have not, at any stage, asserted that I believe myself to be anything other than the misguided individual called Felipe López."

"That's just part of the deception!" Armstrong said, getting to his feet and jabbing his finger at López, "that's what you *know* Lovecraft would have said himself!"

"How on earth could I be of benefit to the designs of an occult organisation such as 'The Sodality of the Black Sun' if I deny the very existence of supernatural phenomena? You make no sense, Sir."

López's lips had narrowed to a thin cruel line upon his face and he was pale with indignation. His voice had dropped to a threatening whisper.

Everyone in the Café la Habana had turned around to stare, stopped dreaming over their pipes, newspapers and games of chess, and paused, their attention drawn by the confrontation being played out in English before them.

"The Old Ones are only now being born, emerging from your fiction into our world," Armstrong said, "the black magicians of 'The Sodality of the Black Sun' want to literally become them. Once they do, the Old Ones will finally exist, independent of their creator, with the power to turn back time, recreating history to their own design as they go along."

"You, Sir," said López, "are clearly more deranged than am I."

"Tell me about the notebook, Lovecraft, tell me about your 'Dream-Diary of the Arkham Cycle'," Armstrong shouted.

"There is no record of such a thing," López replied, "there are no indications that such an item ever existed amongst Lovecraft's papers, no mention of anything like it in his letters or other writings, no evidence for…"

"Tell me whether history is already beginning to change, whether the first of the Old Ones has begun manipulating the events of the past?"

As Armstrong finished asking his question he saw a shocking change come over López's features. Two forces seemed to war within the Mexican's body and a flash of pain distorted his face. At that moment the whites of his eyes vanished, as if the darkness of night looked out through them. But then he blinked heavily, shook his head from side to side, and finally regained his composure. As he did so, his usual aspect returned. The change and its reversal had been so sudden that, despite how vivid it had been, Armstrong could have just imagined it. After all, his nerves were already shredded, and he jumped at shadows.

"I can tell you nothing. What you are suggesting is madness," López said, getting to his feet and picking up the copy of the book he'd left on the table. He left without looking back.

Armstrong did not return to London. He acquired a certain notoriety over the years as the irredeemably drunk English bum who could be found hanging around in the Café la Habana, talking to anyone who would listen to his broken Spanish. However, he was never to be found there after nightfall or during an overcast and dark afternoon. At chess, he insisted on playing white, and could not bear to handle the black pieces, asking his opponent to remove them from the board on his behalf.

The Hands That Reek and Smoke

W. H. Pugmire

I.

Lisa came to me on that fateful night of revelation, her purple hair as wild as her intoxicated eyes. Her pixy face had lost is usual mirth. She was dead serious. "You must see Nyarlathotep," she panted, refusing the chair that I had offered her, preferring to pace the wooden floor instead. One hand clutched a canvas that was covered with a sheet of cloth.

"It amazes me," I answered, "that hair as short as yours can look so disarrayed."

"Screw the hair," she shot back, at the same time running a gloved hand through the unruly mess. "You've been moaning for months about your inability to write. I tell you, go see Nyarlathotep, and he will *drench* your dreams with wondrous vision."

I blew air. "I doubt that the parlor tricks of some cult figure will inspire new work from my dead pen. No new Lord of Disillusion can save me. Stephen was here, too, yakking about this bloke of yours. Seems he's arrived three months ago to set up in some building downtown. No, I have no need of tricks."

"You know, it's really stupid the way you allow your cynicism to keep you cooped up in this depressing little apartment. Things are happening, can't you feel it?"

"I feel only this intolerable heat wave. Such appalling weather for mid-October. Autumn is my favorite time of year; it heralds absolutely the death of torturous summer, that wretched period when ugly human apes strip off their gaudy attire and shriek to cancerous sun. How you can wear such thick gloves when it's so hot quite bewilders me."

How oddly she smiled as she placed one hand before her face and gazed at it as if in rapture. As she did so I noticed two curious things. First, the gloves that encased her hands were not composed of cloth but rather of some fine mesh of metal. Second, with the movement of her hand there came a wave of smell, a scent not unlike the festering of dead lilies. I watched as she silently stared at her gloved hand, and something in her expression unnerved me. I jabbered on. "I've not been able to sleep because of this diabolic heat. When I am able to catch a few winks I have monstrous dreams, horrid visions that soak my sheets and shake me out of slumber."

She looked at me with her serious face. "*He* will make you dream," she sang. "You would find your muse again if you knelt before him."

"Oh, please. You speak of this freak as if he were a god."

"By god, he could be! He looks supernal, with his golden eyes and scarlet robes. I worship him."

"Great Jesu, you're worse than little Stephen. But, no. I fear I'm far too old and faded for such radical wonder as you hint of."

She looked like she would spit at me. "You see, you do that all the time. Using your age as an excuse to be a boring little shut-in. You could be the poet you once were! *He* will show you the way!"

"Enough!" I shouted. "You've gone on long enough about bold new vision and great creative guts. Stop your mouth and *show* me this new thing that you've done, if that's what you think will induce me to rush in fevered pitch to kiss this Narlywhosit's hand. *Show me*," I told her, indicating her canvas.

Lisa set the canvas onto the floor and let it lean against a chair. Deeply inhaling, she placed her hands together in a semblance of prayer. With the movement of her hands there came again the peculiar odor, one that did not inspire my lips to smile. Expecting her to remove the gloves, I frowned in perplexity when she did not. Pulling my desk chair out, she placed the covered canvas on it so that the sheeted work sat upright. Irritated with her theatrical manner, I yawned in feigned *ennui*. She took no notice of me, choosing rather to place her face into her gloved hands and rock to and fro as her mouth hummed an odd melody.

"First," she whispered, "tell me what you know of Nyarlathotep."

I spat air, annoyed. "Very well. What did little Stephen tell me? Let me rack my brain." Delicately, I touched hand to brow. I, too, can be dramatic. "This

Messiah with the preposterous name came to our city in middle or late June. He has rented the old lecture hall where the J. Duds used to hold meetings. It is claimed that this Nyarlathotep has crawled through the blackness of several centuries to our modern age, and thus we see proven that the more outlandish a cult leader's claims the more anxious are fools to follow him. I'm told they do follow—in droves."

I watched as Lisa stopped her swaying as she listened to my reply. She continued to clasp her face with those gloved hands, and I looked at their strange material, which queerly caught the light of my little room. "I'm told," I continued, "that he won't allow his image to be photographed or his voice to be recorded. Early on some friend of Stephen's smuggled a recording device into a lecture, but when the tape was played back all they could hear was a weird variety of buzzing sounds. You remember Stephen's pal, the boy who recently disappeared?"

"I remember," her low voice answered.

Really, her odd attitude was too much. I spoke with more frivolity, in a voice that mocked. "It seems this darkie is a splendid showman and works a multiplicity of mechanical geegaws with which he spellbinds the rabble. Funny, how little Stevie shuddered when he mentioned these devices. Like you, he urged me to go and witness this fantastic creature. I declined then, as I do now. The only beast I choose to worship is myself."

Lisa's hands fell from her face. "What a lonely veneration yours must be. You're so full of empty talk. But I remember a dim and distant time when you spoke beautifully, when you penned exquisite verse."

I sighed sadly. "Dim and distant indeed."

"Look, Hyrum, I know what it's like to lose energy and vision—it sucks. But you can regain yours. As I have recovered and cultivated mine. Look at how Nyarlathotep has inspired me!"

Summarily, she pulled the sheet from the canvas. I shouted in shock and outrage. Lisa's wonderful work had always been delightfully inventive and filled with color, in the tradition of Gorky. I was thus expecting a work of multi-hued genius. Instead, I was confronted with a vile composition of filthy soot and fuzzy ink and wash, with here and there a bruise of blue and purple. The scene was a gargantuan ruins set deep within a riotous growth of jungle. Standing among the debris of antiquity was a shrouded figure that wore no face, yet by its stance seemed haughty and implacable. The entire scene unnerved me. I knew not the origin of the ruins, for they were nothing I had known in history or art. Oh, yes, it was original, this vision, but not one that I could embrace or applaud. I hated it absolutely, and yet I could not turn my eyes away. The image beguiled as much as it appalled. My senses were stunned by the aspect of *age* that Lisa had been able to evoke. But what a horrid medium for she who had once been so clever with color! Quavering with emotion, I turned to the witch.

"*This* is your new achievement?" Oh, how I wailed. "This *sorry* depiction of a dead and haunted past?"

How oddly she smiled. "My dear Hyrum, this is a vision of the dead and haunted *future*."

I gagged with choked fury. My emotions seethed. "Really, this is too utterly nauseating. Please, *do* cover the wretched thing. I'm sorry to be so blunt, but you have shocked me." She made no movement, and although I turned my face away, my eyes slid inexorably to the painted surface. "And what in the blessed name of all the gods is *that* supposed to be? You've not given the silly creature a face!"

"The faceless god wears no visage."

I could not refrain from shuddering. Muttering profanely, I reached for the sheet of cloth and tossed it over the canvas; yet even as I did so my eyes ached to look again upon the painted surface. My companion smiled in eerie triumph. I rose and paced the wooded floor. "I simply do not understand why you should surrender your wonderful sense of vibrant color and sensuous line to replace them with ink and wash and whatever the hell else this new medium is. The thing lacks life. It is naught but a concoction of blur and blotch. What did you use, an old bath sponge?"

Ye gods, her peculiar smile! "I used my fingers." She grabbed hold of me and stopped my movement. One gloved hand stroked my cheek. Great Saturn, what was that monstrous stench? It was a stink of decay, yet tainted with some fragrance the likes of which I had never inhaled. It revolted and enthralled, like her painting. "I used these fingers that he has kissed." One metallic finger smoothed my eye. I watched as she slowly removed the glove that touched my face. Horrified at the nefarious sight, I cried and fell into the nearest chair. I cowered from her hand. But, oh, I longed to feel its touch upon my brow. The pale mists of smoke that spilled from the tiny wounds and bruises were the origin of the unholy stench. She bent to me, and I pretended to cover my eyes. What could have caused such mutation in hands that had once been so lovely? How could fingers become so disfigured? What could cause them to become so flattened, their tips so *erased*?

She removed the other glove. "These hands that he has sanctified."

"No...no..." Yet even as I whimpered I reached for one of her smoky hands and brought it to my lips. It tasted of nightmare. The nauseating smoke plunged into my nostrils and found my brain, which it teased ruthlessly with esoteric shape and shadow. I curled my nails into her transformed flesh. Lisa hissed with pain and drew her hands away. With cloudy sight I saw her indistinctly. I beheld the fuming appendages that bled from where I had clutched them, saw them slide into their outré gloves. I watched as they reached for the sheeted painting.

"New vision requires radical treatment. This is the sacrosanct gift with which I have been blessed. Perhaps you lack backbone and prefer to sit here and quiver in your impotent existence. So be it. But, oh, I remember a time when your world was filled with magnificent language and stunning vision. You could find that world anew." Her words were like needles in my brain. Weakly, I tried to rise from the chair, only to slip from it to the floor. Blinking streaming liquid from my eyes, I crawled to where she stood. My fingers found her shoes. I reached for but could not find her hands, the palsied flesh of which I ached to kiss.

Cool breath bathed my ear. "You must see Nyarlathotep. He is wonderful, and dreadful. He will show you prophecies of the cold bleak abysses between the stars, where dead gods fumble in dream-infested slumber. The great ones were. They are. They shall be."

A hot tongue licked my lobe. I listened as she sucked in breath, then jolted as she uttered unearthly howling. Instantly afterward, I was alone.

II.

Thus it was in that hot October that I ventured forth one night in pursuit of Nyarlathotep. As I crept along the silent sidewalks, I passed certain individuals who looked at me queerly and askance. I sensed that they had been to see this foreigner from an alien land. How anxious they seemed to speak to me, and yet how timid and hesitant they looked, peering at me in silence as I passed them by. I came at last to the lecture hall and gaped at the throngs of lingering rabble. They leaned against the building and sat on the curbing; they congregated near the threshold that led to a narrow stairway. One man was especially fidgety. I watched as he snatched at his hair and muttered lowly. I watched as he rushed into an alley and disappeared from view, and I shivered at the sound of anguished howling that issued from that alley. The noise sent a quiver of emotion through the crowd.

Pushing through the horde at the threshold I climbed the silent stairway. From somewhere above I could hear low fluted music. I walked down a dimly lit hallway that led to the double doors of a lecture room wherein I would confront the alien. The piping of discordant music came from behind the closed doors, and my old flesh prickled at its sound. Shutting my eyes, I leaned my forehead against one of the doors, pushing it open. With eyes still shut, I stumbled into the room. I could smell the candlelight. My eyelids opened.

He stood on a slightly raised platform, the shrouded one. Swarthy, slender, sinister, he was robed in scarlet silk. On a table beside him was a device similar to a child's magic lantern. Its diseased illumination cast obscene shapes that moved along the walls. My attention was caught by the nebulous form that squatted at the feet of Nyarlathotep, the thing that held in clumsy paw an apparatus of tinted ivory or pale gold. It was from this instrument that the fluted music emerged. Yet the more I tried to scrutinize the gadget, the more it seemed to subtly fluctuate in form, reshaping with a sensual movement that ached my skull. I listened to what sounded like whipping wings, as the music melted into silence. My heavy eyes demanded closure, and shutting them I saw upon their lids a multitude of spinning shapes that caused a vertigo that weakened my knees. I crashed onto the floor.

Weakly, I raised my agonizing head. He stood before me—grim, austere, merciless. My hungry mouth kissed his chilly feet. The room was still and silent, and I looked about but could not see the thing that had played the music of the spheres. Boldly, I clung to Nyarlathotep's garment and pulled myself to my feet. Swirling light and blackness played upon his regal visage. Fantastically, he smiled; and as he did so his face slipped, as though he wore some tight-fitting mask that had momentarily lost its hold. He lifted a hand, and I saw upon his palm a living symbol. Tilting to it, I licked the pulsing insignia. It was sharp and ripped the tongue that touched it. As I swallowed blood, the daemon moved his hand away, then thrashed that hand against my forehead. Splinters of bubbling ice pierced my brain.

I was inside Lisa's painting. The awful heat that had so plagued our autumn season weighed heavily in dead air. To breathe was to burn. He stood before me still, the black alien, in shapes that did and undid his being. I looked beyond him at the mammoth buildings, the ruins of distant time. It was a time over which Nyarlathotep was Lord Supreme. But how could he exist in future epoch? How had he escaped the nip of Death?

"That cannot die which stands outside time."

Behind him I detected throngs of writhing black gargoyles that mindlessly pranced beneath a dying sun. Why did I ache to join in their frolic? Oh, how his liquid mark burned upon my brow. Scorching wind arose and pushed into my eyes, burning wind that blinded.

A large rough hand poked at my face. Rubbing torment from my eyes, I beheld the young man who gaped at me in desperation. I watched his mouth twitch in an effort to talk, but which was unable to function. I saw him pound with fists at his head, as if to knock some profane vision from his brain. I saw the blackness that crept into his eyes as he raised his head and wailed in lunacy.

I escaped, fleeing the place and running until I came to the street where Lisa lived with her epileptic mother. My brain buzzed with semi-vision, with a prophecy of disaster that I ached to share with she who understood. And I overflowed with lust to see again her painting. Not pausing to knock, I boldly entered the quiet house. A lamp burned with pallid light next to a sofa on which I saw the twitching form. The elderly woman did not look at me as she spoke.

"She's quiet now, perhaps we don't want to disturb her. Yes, quiet, quiet. No more howling now. What a funny sound. But she's quiet now. You don't need to stay."

I left the creature to her confusion and walked the cluttered hallway to Lisa's studio. I could smell incense, could smell that other fragrance of my friend's altered state. Stopping before the studio door, I leaned my head upon it, pushing it open. Her lifeless form lay on the floor, its arms sprawled over a canvas. An overwhelming stench emanated from the stubs that had once been hands, those nubs that stank and smoked. I knelt beside her and saw that her terrible eyes wore a wild expression. I looked at the image on canvas, that image composed of a filament of transfigured flesh. I saw the hooded thing composed of soot. From deep within the folds of its hood I could discern the shifting features of his many forms. Yet even as I watched his image faded and was gone.

I raised my shivering face. I closed my liquid eyes. I stretched my mouth with noise.

Akropolis

Matt Wallace

Danny's eight and the world is coming to an end. Chicken Little was right; the sky is falling. It begins as a big black ball high above the Earth, the blotted-out stars defining its shape. It burns yellow, then red before it descends over the farmlands of Danny's home. It seems to draw the night, gathering the sky beneath it like miles of black silk sucked into a jet. The furls become a wave, fluid, chaotic, raging. Danny stands at the edge of the cornfield and waits to be crushed by it, his tiny mouth hanging open and the apocalypse reflected in the dark droplets of his pupils.

When the wave finally breaks against the Earth they feel the tremors five miles away. It's the dry season, and the heat blast causes the cornhusks to burst, creating a pestilence of shredded seed membranes that fall like snowflakes siphoned of their essence. The autumn wind carries them away, and Danny realizes it wasn't the end of the world. His house is still there, the three lighted windows that make up its jack-o-lantern face shining out at him across their back field. The stars return. It was just something that fell from the sky, like Dorothy's house, only bigger. Much, much bigger. A falling star.

Danny follows his father, the musky old man lighting the way with an ancient Coleman lantern. Along the way they collect the Smiths from the next farm over. Their boy, Eric, is a few years younger than him, little more than a toddler trundling at his own father's heels. The group follows the sky-streaked path above their heads for miles, to a crater the size of a lake, and the soil inside of it has been caramelized. It breaks like hardened wax beneath Danny's tiny feet. His father grips him by the wrists and pulls his ankles free.

It's not a star. It's a city. An entire stone city, an alien Atlantis, and steps above it leading to a high place of battlements and thick walls. Danny's eyes are drawn to it immediately. A castle in the sky...

∾

Danneth is thirty-six and he still dreams of it. Five of them entered the Akropolis that night; the first ones. It should've been hot, but the stone was cold when they touched it. They wandered the empty city for hours before finally making the trek up the long, steep steps. They made their way to the highest room in the Akropolis. It was empty too, a room with veined walls, lines thick and twisting like petrified kudzu. The strange runes that they would come to know as runati surrounding the throne-like chair with its stone skull cap, the dome designed to open heads and burn the runati into brains.

Somehow it spoke to Danneth's father. What it later took the scientists months to begin to decipher, the old man knew that first night. But he let them fumble with it, allowed them to study it, to begin to expose it to the world. He let them believe he was a simple farmer just happy to have made first contact with such a discovery. And when the time came that their inept ministrations were of no more use, he, the simple farmer, ejected the government from the Akropolis.

Danneth is awakened from the dream by a Summoning in the back of his brain. Arric's there, his words that aren't really words, but an intangible form of understanding, conveying a message:

"Two of our akropophytes are trapped in EV-Z-5. They were sweeping for rats and wandered right into an ambush. They're panicking. It's rendered them unable to cast. I would've interceded myself, but your orders are to be informed."

Arric is his second. He is ambitious, powerful, and devoid of all human mercy. Danneth keeps him close. Yes, because he is useful, but also because he has to.

"I'll meet you a hundred yards out," is the message he transmits back.

∾

Danny's twelve and he knows that his father is no longer his father. Maybe he hasn't been since that night. He comes to think of it as trial software. His father was the first human being to enter the Akropolis, that's all. He was the connector to the human interface, the port that downloaded the Akropolis' directions. But it's more than a sterile program, it's an entity, and when the old man finally dies, that consciousness dies with him. It is not passed on. It has served its purpose. It has done its job.

∞

Danneth dresses quietly, watching Brya slumber in their bed as he does, listening to her breath, to the blood pumping warm and strong beneath her perfect breast.

The akropolia uniform is his second skin. The cassock with its sleek black lines, the non-conductive pauldron fitted over his left shoulder, guarding his heart, the half-cape draped from its edges that conceals his arm, the arm that is the reason for his single glove. It's become a cephalopod appendage, suckered and shiny and pronged like a spade. The left side of his face has abscessed to match it, a new lobe forming with each spell cast, swelling as his power swells. His children do not know. His wife does not know. They see only the glamour he casts over that part of himself: Five perfect, strong digits, and a chiseled profile.

It begins in the second year of akropolia training, the runati changing dormant parts of their brains. Danneth has seen the resonance scans. Some think the new tissue looks like faces, like small alien cameos carved in gray matter. Danneth knows better. The physical manifestations are just a sacrifice, a side effect of power never meant for humans.

He leaves their bedchamber and walks along the Akropolis parapets with their jeweled eyes shut tight against the crater below. The crater's soil is fertile again, but scorched patches of earth as tall as men are lined up like memorials atop it. A month after they established rule, the United States armed forces launched a coordinated assault on the Akropolis. The stone lids covering the eyes of the parapets scraped back and the soldiers were reduced to shadows of ash cast forever against the ground.

The akropolia, their families, and the first citizens of the city were never even roused from their beds.

Danneth arrives at the needleport chamber. It has a name in the Akropolis language, but they've come to call it that because it's a literal translation of passing yourself through the eye of a needle. Microscopic beams of light transport them across the globe in minutes.

There is no navigational system. The akropolia controls his own destination.

∞

Danny's fourteen and he's having trouble gripping a fork with his left hand. His fingers have begun to merge and his thumb grows suckers. But he can split tree trunks with invisible blades created by his mind, and more. He's to be the first of the akropolia, an extension of the Akropolis itself, a force with the power to bring order to the world. His father laid the foundation for him before the stroke claimed him, and now the Akropolis will care for Danny until he comes of age, while he prepares.

Himself, and the others. More coming every day.

∞

Danneth and Arric walk over the ruins of 57th Street. Danneth was here when the city still stood. New York was the last major American metropolis to submit to their leadership.

The rioters fall over each other like lobsters in a tank. They're massed around one of the freestanding fall-out bunkers that are the only remaining structures intact throughout the city. The stragglers who infest these evacuation zones think they've formed some sort of resistance movement.

"Let me bring what's left of these buildings down on their greasy heads," Arric imports.

"I'm going to talk to them."

Danneth can feel Arric's eyes on him. The fact that he doesn't voice the thoughts they're conveying reassures Danneth, but only a little.

He murmurs at first, the verbal commands accessing those parts of his brain changed by the runati. The akropolia have come to call these commands "spells" and think of their effects in the same terms. The spell Danneth casts will enhance his vocal range and affect the waves that carry it.

"Disperse," his voice booms across the ruins like an angry god. "Disperse, or be dealt with. The choice is yours."

The strength of a mob is the strength of the sea, and they surge toward Danneth and Arric in the same way. Their obsolete guns crackle and pop, producing all the affectation of children's fireworks. With a wave of his distorted left hand, Arric magnetizes a dented blue-flecked mailbox. The tide of bullets part from their chosen course and riddle the aging receptacle, followed by the weapons that fired them, flying from the hands of their owners. There's a mashed chorus of screams as fillings are ripped from teeth.

This time when Danneth opens his mouth his voice turns into a nuclear-amplified shriek. The sonic wave brushes them back, peeling layers of bodies like a razor on skin. Limbs break and necks snap under its force. The ones left standing belong to Arric. He focuses on the emergency floodlights hung along the street. Their gas and luminescence are converted into laser beams that descend as Zeusian thunderbolts, striking down the rest.

They step over the wracked corpses, smoke pouring from their mouths, from the gaping holes in their chests. A few are still alive. One, a middle-aged man in a Navy surplus flight jacket, grabs the harness of Danneth's boot.

"I know what you are," he croaks.

Danneth crouches down low, sweeping back the half-cape. "Do you think us inhuman?" he asks the man, making no move to disengage the hand on his boot. "In a literal sense, I mean."

"I know what you are," the man repeats. These are his last words.

Arric removes the door of the bunker without laying a finger on it and the akropophytes stagger out into the morning sun. Before they can speak, Arric has cast a binding spell around them. The electromagnetic field engulfs the akropophytes. By Arric's hand they rise through the air.

"You two are pathetic. We give you the power of the akropolia and you hide like children while monkeys shake you in a can."

Defiant beasts live in the dark caves of Arric's eyes. Danneth knows he has overridden his second-in-command enough for the day. The next action is his to take alone.

Electricity crackles up through the stream tethering Arric to the field and infects the spherical force surrounding the young men. They begin screaming as it courses through their muscles.

Danneth turns away, leaving the akropophytes to be disciplined.

I know what you are.

"So do I," Danneth says to no one.

ᛒᛟ

Danneth is eighteen and he has the power to eat worlds. The government has no choice but to deal with him. At first the akropolia supplement the old forces; they did in the Middle East in two weeks what the president was still stumbling over after twenty years. Traditional police are obsolete. Two akropolia can maintain order in each city. Armies follow. Soldiers, weapons, technology, they all become meaningless. Danneth can render a nuclear reactor inert from halfway around the world. He can boil submarines at the farthest depths of the ocean. He can bring down planes or cast a spell that causes the sky to swallow them.

Their power is as absolute as the protests are inevitable. Congress passes a bill to restrict the akropolia's authority. The bill is ignored. Danneth learns the United States government is conspiring with three rival nations to develop a technology that will retard the runati's effect on human brain chemistry.

The akropolia make their first true alliance with the Chinese. Danneth will oversee the construction of a Manchurian Akropolis. The American government considers this an act of war.

The war lasts approximately 18 hours.

ဆ

When Danneth and Arric return to the Akropolis, a page is waiting with an official communiqué from the LSoN. Danneth has been invited to a summit in Geneva, hosted by what's being called The Last Stand of Nations, to negotiate a treaty between the akropolia and the final holdouts of human civilization.

"It was a mistake to let them regroup there," Arric says. "And I don't understand this need of yours to negotiate. Imbuing them with power they don't have. I could pacify the entire continent myself, tonight."

" 'Pacify.' You mean subjugate."

"Semantical horse shit. The akropolia rule this planet, Danneth. We don't govern. We don't serve. We rule. You can dance around the word, but its meaning dictates our actions. It baffles me how you've brought us this far with your attitude."

A crowd has gathered, akropophytes and akropolia alike, black cassocks and gleaming pauldrons. Arric has sympathizers, admirers, followers. Soon he'll challenge Danneth for leadership of the akropolia.

"I'll take the evening to consider it," he says.

ဆ

Danneth is twenty-four and the last vestige of the American government has been swept away. Fort Braddock fell at 6:13 this morning, Akropolis time. Danneth pulled the general's skeleton through his skin. He orders it to be cast in bronze above the fort's welcome banner as a memorial. And a warning.

The akropolia now rule unopposed.

ဆ

The next morning at breakfast in the main hall, Brya, forever Danneth's most loyal supporter, publicly accuses Arric of committing a very ugly assault against her. Arric is surprised, but only for a moment. Then he looks to Danneth. Arric is smart. That's the problem.

Danneth makes the challenge that Brya's accusation has allowed him to make. The duel is epic. Arric thinks it's because he and Danneth are so evenly matched. Danneth knows it's because that's what they expect, the other akropolia and their citizens. They've bought into the myth they've become, the myth Danneth helped architect.

In the end he superheats Arric's blood to a temperature of roughly one thousand degrees. His body does not melt, it explodes. A grand deathblow. It's a feat beyond Arric's ability to defend, beyond any of the akropolia's ability to cast. But that will change. In time, their power will grow. Danneth, however, will always be one level beyond their reach, and that is how he will lead.

That night he dispatches the akropolia to lay waste to Western Europe. The Last Stand of Nations is barely that. The remaining populace surrender unconditionally.

∞

Danneth is sixty and he is no longer recognizable as human.

∞

Danneth is one hundred and seventy-four years old and he awaits their arrival.

Many seconds have served under him, but he still remembers Arric well. Arric was right about Geneva. Danneth realized that then. But he was wrong about the akropolia. They were never meant to rule.

They are meant to serve.

Soon there'll come a night like the one when he was a boy. A night when the sky falls again, and their masters, the true masters of the Akropolis, will come home.

Boojum

Elizabeth Bear & Sarah Monette

The ship had no name of her own, so her human crew called her the *Lavinia Whateley*. As far as anyone could tell, she didn't mind. At least, her long grasping vanes curled—affectionately?—when the chief engineers patted her bulkheads and called her "Vinnie," and she ceremoniously tracked the footsteps of each crew member with her internal bioluminescence, giving them light to walk and work and live by.

The *Lavinia Whateley* was a Boojum, a deep-space swimmer, but her kind had evolved in the high tempestuous envelopes of gas giants, and their offspring still spent their infancies there, in cloud-nurseries over eternal storms. And so she was streamlined, something like a vast spiny lionfish to the earth-adapted eye. Her sides were lined with gasbags filled with hydrogen; her vanes and wings furled tight. Her color was a blue-green so dark it seemed a glossy black unless the light struck it; her hide was impregnated with symbiotic algae.

Where there was light, she could make oxygen. Where there was oxygen, she could make water.

She was an ecosystem unto herself, as the captain was a law unto herself. And down in the bowels of the engineering section, Black Alice Bradley, who was only human and no kind of law at all, loved her.

Black Alice had taken the oath back in '32, after the Venusian Riots. She hadn't hidden her reasons, and the captain had looked at her with cold, dark, amused eyes and said, "So long as you carry your weight, cherie, I don't care. Betray me, though, and you will be going back to Venus the cold way." But it was probably that—and the fact that Black Alice couldn't hit the broad side of a space freighter with a ray gun—that had gotten her assigned to Engineering, where ethics were less of a problem. It wasn't, after all, as if she was going anywhere.

Black Alice was on duty when the *Lavinia Whateley* spotted prey; she felt the shiver of anticipation that ran through the decks of the ship. It was an odd sensation, a tic Vinnie only exhibited in pursuit. And then they were underway, zooming down the slope of the gravity well toward Sol, and the screens all around Engineering—which Captain Song kept dark, most of the time, on the theory that swabs and deckhands and coal-shovelers didn't need to know where they were, or what they were doing—flickered bright and live.

Everybody looked up, and Demijack shouted, "There! There!" He was right: the blot that might only have been a smudge of oil on the screen moved as Vinnie banked, revealing itself to be a freighter, big and ungainly and hopelessly outclassed. Easy prey. Easy pickings.

We could use some of them, thought Black Alice. Contrary to the e-ballads and comm stories, a pirate's life was not all imported delicacies and fawning slaves. Especially not when three-quarters of any and all profits went directly back to the *Lavinia Whateley*, to keep her healthy and happy. Nobody ever argued. There were stories about the *Marie Curie*, too.

The captain's voice over fiber optic cable—strung beside the *Lavinia Whateley*'s nerve bundles—was as clear and free of static as if she stood at Black Alice's elbow. "Battle stations," Captain Song said, and the crew leapt to obey. It had been two Solar since Captain Song keelhauled James Brady, but nobody who'd been with the ship then was ever likely to forget his ruptured eyes and frozen scream.

Black Alice manned her station, and stared at the screen. She saw the freighter's name—the *Josephine Baker*—gold on black across the stern, the Venusian flag for its port of registry wired stiff from a mast on its hull. It was a steelship, not a Boojum, and they had every advantage. For a moment she thought the freighter would run.

And then it turned, and brought its guns to bear.

No sense of movement, of acceleration, of disorientation. No pop, no whump of displaced air. The view on the screens just flickered to a different one, as Vinnie skipped—apported—to a new position just aft and above the *Josephine Baker*, crushing the flag mast with her hull.

Black Alice felt that, a grinding shiver. And had just time to grab her console before the *Lavinia Whateley* grappled the freighter, long vanes not curling in affection now.

Out of the corner of her eye, she saw Dogcollar, the closest thing the *Lavinia Whateley* had to a chaplain, cross himself, and she heard him mutter, like he always did, *Ave, Grandaevissimi, morituri vos salutant.* It was the best he'd be able to do until it was all over, and even then he wouldn't have the chance to do much. Captain Song didn't mind other people worrying about souls, so long as they didn't do it on her time.

The captain's voice was calling orders, assigning people to boarding parties port and starboard. Down in Engineering, all they had to do was monitor the *Lavinia Whateley's* hull and prepare to repel boarders, assuming the freighter's crew had the gumption to send any. Vinnie would take care of the rest—until the time came to persuade her not to eat her prey before they'd gotten all the valuables off it. That was a ticklish job, only entrusted to the chief engineers, but Black Alice watched and listened, and although she didn't expect she'd ever get the chance, she thought she could do it herself.

It was a small ambition, and one she never talked about. But it would be a hell of a thing, wouldn't it? To be somebody a Boojum would listen to?

She gave her attention to the dull screens in her sectors, and tried not to crane her neck to catch a glimpse of the ones with the actual fighting on them. Dogcollar was making the rounds with sidearms from the weapons locker, just in case. Once the *Josephine Baker* was subdued, it was the junior engineers and others who would board her to take inventory.

Sometimes there were crew members left in hiding on captured ships. Sometimes, unwary pirates got shot.

There was no way to judge the progress of the battle from Engineering. Wasabi put a stopwatch up on one of the secondary screens, as usual, and everybody glanced at it periodically. Fifteen minutes ongoing meant the boarding parties hadn't hit any nasty surprises. Black Alice had met a man once who'd been on the *Margaret Mead* when she grappled a freighter that turned out to be carrying a division's-worth of Marines out to the Jovian moons. Thirty minutes ongoing was normal. Forty-five minutes. Upward of an hour ongoing, and people started double-checking their weapons. The longest battle Black Alice had ever personally been part of was six hours, forty-three minutes, and fifty-two seconds. That had been the last time the *Lavinia Whateley* worked with a partner, and the double-cross by the *Henry Ford* was the only reason any of Vinnie's crew needed. Captain Song still had Captain Edwards' head in a jar on the bridge, and Vinnie had an ugly ring of scars where the *Henry Ford* had bitten her.

This time, the clock stopped at fifty minutes, thirteen seconds. The *Josephine Baker* surrendered.

෪ඏ

Dogcollar slapped Black Alice's arm. "With me," he said, and she didn't argue. He had only six weeks seniority over her, but he was as tough as he was devout, and not stupid either. She checked the Velcro on her holster and followed him up the ladder, reaching through the rungs once to scratch Vinnie's bulkhead as she passed. The ship paid her no notice. She wasn't the captain, and she wasn't one of the four chief engineers.

Quartermaster mostly respected crew's own partner choices, and as Black Alice and Dogcollar suited up—it wouldn't be the first time, if the *Josephine Baker*'s crew decided to blow her open to space rather than be taken captive—he came by and issued them both tag guns and x-ray pads, taking a retina scan in return. All sorts of valuable things got hidden inside of bulkheads, and once Vinnie was done with the steelship there wouldn't be much chance of coming back to look for what they'd missed.

Wet pirates used to scuttle their captures. The Boojums were more efficient.

Black Alice clipped everything to her belt and checked Dogcollar's seals.

And then they were swinging down lines from the *Lavinia Whateley*'s belly to the chewed-open airlock. A lot of crew didn't like to look at the ship's face, but Black Alice loved it. All those teeth, the diamond edges worn to a glitter, and a few of the ship's dozens of bright sapphire eyes blinking back at her.

She waved, unselfconsciously, and flattered herself that the ripple of closing eyes was Vinnie winking in return.

She followed Dogcollar inside the prize.

They unsealed when they had checked atmosphere—no sense in wasting your own air when you might need it later—and the first thing she noticed was the smell.

The *Lavinia Whateley* had her own smell, ozone and nutmeg, and other ships never smelled as good, but this was... this was...

"What did they kill and why didn't they space it?" Dogcollar wheezed, and Black Alice swallowed hard against her gag reflex and said, "One will get you twenty we're the lucky bastards that find it."

"No takers," Dogcollar said.

They worked together to crank open the hatches they came to. Twice they found crew members, messily dead. Once they found crew members alive.

"Gillies," said Black Alice.

"Still don't explain the smell," said Dogcollar and, to the gillies: "Look, you can join our crew, or our ship can eat you. Makes no never mind to us."

The gillies blinked their big wet eyes and made fingersigns at each other, and then nodded. Hard.

Dogcollar slapped a tag on the bulkhead. "Someone will come get you. You go wandering, we'll assume you changed your mind."

The gillies shook their heads, hard, and folded down onto the deck to wait.

Dogcollar tagged searched holds—green for clean, purple for goods, red for anything Vinnie might like to eat that couldn't be fenced for a profit—and Black Alice mapped. The corridors in the steelship were winding, twisty, hard to track. She was glad she chalked the walls, because she didn't think her map was quite right, somehow, but she couldn't figure out where she'd gone wrong. Still, they had a beacon, and Vinnie could always chew them out if she had to.

Black Alice loved her ship.

She was thinking about that, how, okay, it wasn't so bad, the pirate game, and it sure beat working in the sunstone mines on Venus, when she found a locked cargo hold. "Hey, Dogcollar," she said to her comm, and while he was turning to cover her, she pulled her sidearm and blastered the lock.

The door peeled back, and Black Alice found herself staring at rank upon rank of silver cylinders, each less than a meter tall and perhaps half a meter wide, smooth and featureless except for what looked like an assortment of sockets and plugs on the surface of each. The smell was strongest here.

"Shit," she said.

Dogcollar, more practical, slapped the first safety orange tag of the expedition beside the door and said only, "Captain'll want to see this."

"Yeah," said Black Alice, cold chills chasing themselves up and down her spine. "C'mon, let's move."

But of course it turned out that she and Dogcollar were on the retrieval detail, too, and the captain wasn't leaving the canisters for Vinnie.

Which, okay, fair. Black Alice didn't want the *Lavinia Whateley* eating those things, either, but why did they have to bring them *back?*

She said as much to Dogcollar, under her breath, and had a horrifying thought: "She knows what they are, right?"

"She's the captain," said Dogcollar.

"Yeah, but—I ain't arguing, man, but if she doesn't know…" She lowered her voice even farther, so she could barely hear herself: "What if somebody *opens* one?"

Dogcollar gave her a pained look. "Nobody's going to go opening anything. But if you're really worried, go talk to the captain about it."

He was calling her bluff. Black Alice called his right back. "Come with me?"

He was stuck. He stared at her, and then he grunted and pulled his gloves off, the left and then the right. "Fuck," he said. "I guess we oughta."

∽∽

For the crew members who had been in the boarding action, the party had already started. Dogcollar and Black Alice finally tracked the captain down in the rec room, where her marines were slurping stolen wine from broken-necked bottles. As much of it splashed on the gravity plates epoxied to the *Lavinia Whateley*'s flattest interior surface as went into the marines, but Black Alice imagined there was plenty more where that came from. And the faster the crew went through it, the less long they'd be drunk.

The captain herself was naked in a great extruded tub, up to her collarbones in steaming water dyed pink and heavily scented by the bath bombs sizzling here and there. Black Alice stared; she hadn't seen a tub bath in seven years. She still dreamed of them sometimes.

"Captain," she said, because Dogcollar wasn't going to say anything. "We think you should know we found some dangerous cargo on the prize."

Captain Song raised one eyebrow. "And you imagine I don't know already, cherie?"

Oh shit. But Black Alice stood her ground. "We thought we should be *sure*."

The captain raised one long leg out of the water to shove a pair of necking pirates off the rim of her tub. They rolled onto the floor, grappling and claw-ing, both fighting to be on top. But they didn't break the kiss. "You wish to be sure," said the captain. Her dark eyes had never left Black Alice's sweating face. "Very well. Tell me. And then you will know that I know, and you can be *sure*."

Dogcollar made a grumbling noise deep in his throat, easily interpreted: *I told you so.*

Just as she had when she took Captain Song's oath and slit her thumb with a razorblade and dripped her blood on the *Lavinia Whateley*'s decking so the ship might know her, Black Alice—metaphorically speaking—took a breath and jumped. "They're brains," she said. "Human brains. Stolen. Black-market. The Fungi—"

"Mi-Go," Dogcollar hissed, and the captain grinned at him, showing ex-traordinarily white strong teeth. He ducked, submissively, but didn't step back, for which Black Alice felt a completely ridiculous gratitude.

"Mi-Go," Black Alice said. Mi-Go, Fungi, what did it matter? They came from the outer rim of the Solar System, the black cold hurtling rocks of the Öpik-Oort Cloud. Like the Boojums, they could swim between the stars. "They collect them. There's a black market. Nobody knows what they use them for. It's illegal, of course. But they're... alive in there. They go mad, supposedly."

And that was it. That was all Black Alice could manage. She stopped, and had to remind herself to shut her mouth.

"So I've heard," the captain said, dabbling at the steaming water. She stretched luxuriously in her tub. Someone thrust a glass of white wine at her, condensation dewing the outside. The captain did not drink from shattered plastic bottles. "The Mi-Go will pay for this cargo, won't they? They mine rare minerals all over the system. They're said to be very wealthy."

"Yes, Captain," Dogcollar said, when it became obvious that Black Alice couldn't.

"Good," the captain said. Under Black Alice's feet, the decking shuddered, a grinding sound as Vinnie began to dine. Her rows of teeth would make short work of the *Josephine Baker*'s steel hide. Black Alice could see two of the gillies—the same two? she never could tell them apart unless they had scars—flinch and tug at their chains. "Then they might as well pay us as someone else, wouldn't you say?"

❧

Black Alice knew she should stop thinking about the canisters. Captain's word was law. But she couldn't help it, like scratching at a scab. They were down there, in the third subhold, the one even sniffers couldn't find, cold and sweating and with that stench that was like a living thing.

And she kept wondering. Were they empty? Or were there brains in there, people's brains, going mad?

The idea was driving her crazy, and finally, her fourth off-shift after the capture of the *Josephine Baker*, she had to go look.

"This is stupid, Black Alice," she muttered to herself as she climbed down the companion way, the beads in her hair clicking against her earrings. "Stupid, stupid, stupid." Vinnie bioluminesced, a traveling spotlight, placidly unconcerned whether Black Alice was being an idiot or not.

Half-Hand Sally had pulled duty in the main hold. She nodded at Black Alice and Black Alice nodded back. Black Alice ran errands a lot, for Engineering and sometimes for other departments, because she didn't smoke hash and she didn't cheat at cards. She was reliable.

Down through the subholds, and she really didn't want to be doing this, but she was here and the smell of the third subhold was already making her sick, and maybe if she just knew one way or the other, she'd be able to quit thinking about it.

She opened the third subhold, and the stench rushed out.

The canisters were just metal, sealed, seemingly airtight. There shouldn't be any way for the aroma of the contents to escape. But it permeated the air nonetheless, bad enough that Black Alice wished she had brought a rebreather.

No, that would have been suspicious. So it was really best for everyone concerned that she hadn't, but oh, gods and little fishes, the stench. Even breathing through her mouth was no help; she could taste it, like oil from a fryer, saturating the air, oozing up her sinuses, coating the interior spaces of her body.

As silently as possible, she stepped across the threshold and into the space beyond. The *Lavinia Whateley* obligingly lit the space as she entered, dazzling her at first as the overhead lights—not just bioluminescent, here, but LEDs chosen to approximate natural daylight, for when they shipped plants and animals—reflected off rank upon rank of canisters. When Black Alice went among them, they did not reach her waist.

She was just going to walk through, she told herself. Hesitantly, she touched the closest cylinder. The air in this hold was so dry there was no condensation—the whole ship ran to lip-cracking, nosebleed dryness in the long weeks between prizes—but the cylinder was cold. It felt somehow grimy to the touch, gritty and oily like machine grease. She pulled her hand back.

It wouldn't do to open the closest one to the door—and she realized with that thought that she was planning on opening one. There must be a way to do it, a concealed catch or a code pad. She was an engineer, after all.

She stopped three ranks in, lightheaded with the smell, to examine the problem.

It was remarkably simple, once you looked for it. There were three depressions on either side of the rim, a little smaller than human fingertips but spaced appropriately. She laid the pads of her fingers over them and pressed hard, making the flesh deform into the catches.

The lid sprang up with a pressurized hiss. Black Alice was grateful that even open, it couldn't smell much worse. She leaned forward to peer within. There was a clear membrane over the surface, and gelatin or thick fluid underneath. Vinnie's lights illuminated it well.

It was not empty. And as the light struck the grayish surface of the lump of tissue floating within, Black Alice would have sworn she saw the pathetic unbodied thing flinch.

She scrambled to close the canister again, nearly pinching her fingertips when it clanked shut. "Sorry," she whispered, although dear sweet Jesus, surely the thing couldn't hear her. "Sorry, sorry." And then she turned and ran, catching her hip a bruising blow against the doorway, slapping the controls to make it fucking *close* already. And then she staggered sideways, lurching to her knees, and vomited until blackness was spinning in front of her eyes and she couldn't smell or taste anything but bile.

Vinnie would absorb the former contents of Black Alice's stomach, just as she absorbed, filtered, recycled, and excreted all her crew's wastes. Shaking,

Black Alice braced herself back upright and began the long climb out of the holds.

In the first subhold, she had to stop, her shoulder against the smooth, velvet slickness of Vinnie's skin, her mouth hanging open while her lungs worked. And she knew Vinnie wasn't going to hear her, because she wasn't the captain or a chief engineer or anyone important, but she had to try anyway, croaking, "Vinnie, water, please."

And no one could have been more surprised than Black Alice Bradley when Vinnie extruded a basin and a thin cool trickle of water began to flow into it.

❦

Well, now she knew. And there was still nothing she could do about it. She wasn't the captain, and if she said anything more than she already had, people were going to start looking at her funny. Mutiny kind of funny. And what Black Alice did *not* need was any more of Captain Song's attention and especially not for rumors like that. She kept her head down and did her job and didn't discuss her nightmares with anyone.

And she had nightmares, all right. Hot and cold running, enough, she fancied, that she could have filled up the captain's huge tub with them.

She could live with that. But over the next double dozen of shifts, she became aware of something else wrong, and this was worse, because it was something wrong with the *Lavinia Whateley*.

The first sign was the chief engineers frowning and going into huddles at odd moments. And then Black Alice began to feel it herself, the way Vinnie was... she didn't have a word for it because she'd never felt anything like it before. She would have said *balky*, but that couldn't be right. It couldn't. But she was more and more sure that Vinnie was less responsive somehow, that when she obeyed the captain's orders, it was with a delay. If she were human, Vinnie would have been dragging her feet.

You couldn't keelhaul a ship for not obeying fast enough.

And then, because she was paying attention so hard she was making her own head hurt, Black Alice noticed something else. Captain Song had them cruising the gas giants' orbits—Jupiter, Saturn, Neptune—not going in as far as the asteroid belt, not going out as far as Uranus. Nobody Black Alice talked to knew why, exactly, but she and Dogcollar figured it was because the captain wanted to talk to the Mi-Go without actually getting near the nasty cold rock of their planet. And what Black Alice noticed was that Vinnie was less balky, less *unhappy*, when she was headed out, and more and more resistant the closer they got to the asteroid belt.

Vinnie, she remembered, had been born over Uranus.

"Do you want to go home, Vinnie?" Black Alice asked her one late-night shift when there was nobody around to care that she was talking to the ship. "Is that what's wrong?"

She put her hand flat on the wall, and although she was probably imagining it, she thought she felt a shiver ripple across Vinnie's vast side.

Black Alice knew how little she knew, and didn't even contemplate sharing her theory with the chief engineers. They probably knew exactly what was wrong and exactly what to do to keep the *Lavinia Whateley* from going core meltdown like the *Marie Curie* had. That was a whispered story, not the sort of thing anybody talked about except in their hammocks after lights out.

The *Marie Curie* had eaten her own crew.

So when Wasabi said, four shifts later, "Black Alice, I've got a job for you," Black Alice said, "Yessir," and hoped it would be something that would help the *Lavinia Whateley* be happy again.

It was a suit job, he said, replace and repair. Black Alice was going because she was reliable and smart and stayed quiet, and it was time she took on more responsibilities. The way he said it made her first fret because that meant the captain might be reminded of her existence, and then fret because she realized the captain already had been.

But she took the equipment he issued, and she listened to the instructions and read schematics and committed them both to memory and her implants. It was a ticklish job, a neural override repair. She'd done some fiber optic bundle splicing, but this was going to be a doozy. And she was going to have to do it in stiff, pressurized gloves.

Her heart hammered as she sealed her helmet, and not because she was worried about the EVA. This was a chance. An opportunity. A step closer to chief engineer.

Maybe she had impressed the captain with her discretion, after all.

She cycled the airlock, snapped her safety harness, and stepped out onto the *Lavinia Whateley*'s hide.

That deep blue-green, like azurite, like the teeming seas of Venus under their swampy eternal clouds, was invisible. They were too far from Sol—it was a yellow stylus-dot, and you had to know where to look for it. Vinnie's hide was just black under Black Alice's suit floods. As the airlock cycled shut, though, the Boojum's own bioluminescence shimmered up her vanes and along the ridges of her sides—crimson and electric green and acid blue. Vinnie must have noticed Black Alice picking her way carefully up her spine with barbed boots. They wouldn't *hurt* Vinnie—nothing short of a space rock could manage that—but they certainly stuck in there good.

The thing Black Alice was supposed to repair was at the principal nexus of Vinnie's central nervous system. The ship didn't have anything like what a human or a gilly would consider a brain; there were nodules spread all through her vast body. Too slow, otherwise. And Black Alice had heard Boojums weren't supposed to be all that smart—trainable, sure, maybe like an Earth monkey.

Which is what made it creepy as hell that, as she picked her way up Vinnie's flank—though *up* was a courtesy, under these circumstances—talking to her all the way, she would have sworn Vinnie was talking back. Not just tracking her with the lights, as she would always do, but bending some of her barbels and vanes around as if craning her neck to get a look at Black Alice.

Black Alice carefully circumnavigated an eye—she didn't think her boots would hurt it, but it seemed discourteous to stomp across somebody's field of vision—and wondered, only half-idly, if she had been sent out on this task not because she was being considered for promotion, but because she was expendable.

She was just rolling her eyes and dismissing that as borrowing trouble when she came over a bump on Vinnie's back, spotted her goal—and all the ship's lights went out.

She tongued on the comm. "Wasabi?"

"I got you, Blackie. You just keep doing what you're doing."

"Yessir."

But it seemed like her feet stayed stuck in Vinnie's hide a little longer than was good. At least fifteen seconds before she managed a couple of deep breaths—too deep for her limited oxygen supply, so she went briefly dizzy—and continued up Vinnie's side.

Black Alice had no idea what inflammation looked like in a Boojum, but she would guess this was it. All around the interface she was meant to repair, Vinnie's flesh looked scraped and puffy. Black Alice walked tenderly, wincing, muttering apologies under her breath. And with every step, the tendrils coiled a little closer.

Black Alice crouched beside the box, and began examining connections. The console was about three meters by four, half a meter tall, and fixed firmly to Vinnie's hide. It looked like the thing was still functional, but something—a bit of space debris, maybe—had dented it pretty good.

Cautiously, Black Alice dropped a hand on it. She found the access panel, and flipped it open: more red lights than green. A tongue-click, and she began withdrawing her tethered tools from their holding pouches and arranging them so that they would float conveniently around.

She didn't hear a thing, of course, but the hide under her boots vibrated suddenly, sharply. She jerked her head around, just in time to see one of Vinnie's feelers slap her own side, five or ten meters away. And then the whole Boojum shuddered, contracting, curved into a hard crescent of pain the same way she had when the *Henry Ford* had taken that chunk out of her hide. And the lights in the access panel lit up all at once—red, red, yellow, red.

Black Alice tongued off the *send* function on her headset microphone, so Wasabi wouldn't hear her. She touched the bruised hull, and she touched the dented edge of the console. "Vinnie," she said, "does this *hurt?*"

Not that Vinnie could answer her. But it was obvious. She was in pain. And maybe that dent didn't have anything to do with space debris. Maybe—Black Alice straightened, looked around, and couldn't convince herself that it was an accident that this box was planted right where Vinnie couldn't... quite... reach it.

"So what does it *do?*" she muttered. "Why am I out here repairing something that fucking hurts?" She crouched down again and took another long look at the interface.

As an engineer, Black Alice was mostly self-taught; her implants were second-hand, black market, scavenged, the wet work done by a gilly on Providence Station. She'd learned the technical vocabulary from Gogglehead Kim before he bought it in a stupid little fight with a ship named the *V. I. Ulyanov*, but what she relied on were her instincts, the things she knew without being able to say. So she *looked* at that box wired into Vinnie's spine and all its red and yellow lights, and then she tongued the comm back on and said, "Wasabi, this thing don't look so good."

"Whaddya mean, don't look so good?" Wasabi sounded distracted, and that was just fine.

Black Alice made a noise, the auditory equivalent of a shrug. "I think the node's inflamed. Can we pull it and lock it in somewhere else?"

"No!" said Wasabi.

"It's looking pretty ugly out here."

"Look, Blackie, unless you want us to all go sailing out into the Big Empty, we are *not* pulling that governor. Just fix the fucking thing, would you?"

"Yessir," said Black Alice, thinking hard. The first thing was that Wasabi knew what was going on—knew what the box did and knew that the *Lavinia Whateley* didn't like it. That wasn't comforting. The second thing was that whatever was going on, it involved the Big Empty, the cold vastness between the stars. So it wasn't that Vinnie wanted to go home. She wanted to go *out*.

It made sense, from what Black Alice knew about Boojums. Their infants lived in the tumult of the gas giants' atmosphere, but as they aged, they pushed higher and higher, until they reached the edge of the envelope. And then—following instinct or maybe the calls of their fellows, nobody knew for sure—they learned to skip, throwing themselves out into the vacuum like Earth birds leaving the nest. And what if, for a Boojum, the solar system was just another nest?

Black Alice knew the *Lavinia Whateley* was old, for a Boojum. Captain Song was not her first captain, although you never mentioned Captain Smith if you knew what was good for you. So if there *was* another stage to her life cycle, she might be ready for it. And her crew wasn't letting her go.

Jesus and the cold fishy gods, Black Alice thought. Is this why the *Marie Curie* ate her crew? Because they wouldn't let her go?

She fumbled for her tools, tugging the cords to float them closer, and wound up walloping herself in the bicep with a splicer. And as she was wrestling with it, her headset spoke again. "Blackie, can you hurry it up out there? Captain says we're going to have company."

Company? She never got to say it. Because when she looked up, she saw the shapes, faintly limned in starlight, and a chill as cold as a suit leak crept up her neck.

There were dozens of them. Hundreds. They made her skin crawl and her nerves judder the way gillies and Boojums never had. They were man-sized, roughly, but they looked like the pseudoroaches of Venus, the ones Black Alice still had nightmares about, with too many legs, and horrible stiff wings. They had ovate, corrugated heads, but no faces, and where their mouths ought to be sprouted writhing tentacles.

And some of them carried silver shining cylinders, like the canisters in Vinnie's subhold.

Black Alice wasn't certain if they saw her, crouched on the Boojum's hide with only a thin laminate between her and the breathsucker, but she was certain of something else. If they did, they did not care.

They disappeared below the curve of the ship, toward the airlock Black Alice had exited before clawing her way along the ship's side. They could be a trade delegation, come to bargain for the salvaged cargo.

Black Alice didn't think even the Mi-Go came in the battalions to talk trade.

She meant to wait until the last of them had passed, but they just kept coming. Wasabi wasn't answering her hails; she was on her own and unarmed. She fumbled with her tools, stowing things in any handy pocket whether it was where the tool went or not. She couldn't see much; everything was misty. It took her several seconds to realize that her visor was fogged because she was crying.

Patch cables. Where were the fucking patch cables? She found a two-meter length of fiber optic with the right plugs on the end. One end went into the monitor panel. The other snapped into her suit comm.

"Vinnie?" she whispered, when she thought she had a connection. "Vinnie, can you hear me?"

The bioluminescence under Black Alice's boots pulsed once.

Gods and little fishes, she thought. And then she drew out her laser cutting torch, and started slicing open the case on the console that Wasabi had called the *governor.* Wasabi was probably dead by now, or dying. Wasabi, and Dogcollar, and... well, not dead. If they were lucky, they were dead.

Because the opposite of lucky was those canisters the Mi-Go were carrying. She hoped Dogcollar was lucky.

"You wanna go *out,* right?" she whispered to the *Lavinia Whateley.* "Out into the Big Empty."

She'd never been sure how much Vinnie understood of what people said, but the light pulsed again.

"And this thing won't let you." It wasn't a question. She had it open now, and she could see that was what it did. Ugly fucking thing. Vinnie shivered underneath her, and there was a sudden pulse of noise in her helmet speakers: screaming. People screaming.

"I know," Black Alice said. "They'll come get me in a minute, I guess." She swallowed hard against the sudden lurch of her stomach. "I'm gonna get this thing off you, though. And when they go, you can go, okay? And I'm sorry. I didn't know we were keeping you from..." She had to quit talking, or she really was going to puke. Grimly, she fumbled for the tools she needed to disentangle the abomination from Vinnie's nervous system.

Another pulse of sound, a voice, not a person: flat and buzzing and horrible. "We do not bargain with thieves." And the scream that time—she'd never heard Captain Song scream before. Black Alice flinched and started counting to slow her breathing. Puking in a suit was the number one badness, but hyperventilating in a suit was a really close second.

Her heads-up display was low-res, and slightly miscalibrated, so that everything had a faint shadow-double. But the thing that flashed up against her own view of her hands was unmistakable: a question mark.

<?>

"Vinnie?"

Another pulse of screaming, and the question mark again.

<?>

"Holy shit, Vinnie!... Never mind, never mind. They, um, they collect people's brains. In canisters. Like the canisters in the third subhold."

The bioluminescence pulsed once. Black Alice kept working.

Her heads-up pinged again: <ALICE> A pause. <?>

"Um, yeah. I figure that's what they'll do with me, too. It looked like they had plenty of canisters to go around."

Vinnie pulsed, and there was a longer pause while Black Alice doggedly severed connections and loosened bolts.

<WANT> said the *Lavinia Whateley*. <?>

"Want? Do I *want*...?" Her laughter sounded bad. "Um, no. No, I don't want to be a brain in a jar. But I'm not seeing a lot of choices here. Even if I went cometary, they could catch me. And it kind of sounds like they're mad enough to do it, too."

She'd cleared out all the moorings around the edge of the governor; the case lifted off with a shove and went sailing into the dark. Black Alice winced. But then the processor under the cover drifted away from Vinnie's hide, and there was just the monofilament tethers and the fat cluster of fiber optic and superconductors to go.

<HELP>

"I'm doing my best here, Vinnie," Black Alice said through her teeth.

That got her a fast double-pulse, and the *Lavinia Whateley* said, <HELP>

And then, <ALICE>

"You want to help *me?*" Black Alice squeaked.

A strong pulse, and the heads-up said, <HELP ALICE>

"That's really sweet of you, but I'm honestly not sure there's anything you can do. I mean, it doesn't look like the Mi-Go are mad at *you*, and I really want to keep it that way."

<EAT ALICE> said the *Lavinia Whateley*.

Black Alice came within a millimeter of taking her own fingers off with the cutting laser. "Um, Vinnie, that's um... well, I guess it's better than being a brain in a jar." Or suffocating to death in her suit if she went cometary and the Mi-Go *didn't* come after her.

The double-pulse again, but Black Alice didn't see what she could have missed. As communications went, *EAT ALICE* was pretty fucking unambiguous.

<HELP ALICE> the *Lavinia Whateley* insisted. Black Alice leaned in close, unsplicing the last of the governor's circuits from the Boojum's nervous system. <SAVE ALICE>

"By eating me? Look, I know what happens to things you eat, and it's not..." She bit her tongue. Because she *did* know what happened to things the *Lavinia Whateley* ate. Absorbed. Filtered. Recycled. "Vinnie... are you saying you can save me from the Mi-Go?"

A pulse of agreement.

"By eating me?" Black Alice pursued, needing to be sure she understood.

Another pulse of agreement.

Black Alice thought about the *Lavinia Whateley*'s teeth. "How much *me* are we talking about here?"

<ALICE> said the *Lavinia Whateley*, and then the last fiber optic cable parted, and Black Alice, her hands shaking, detached her patch cable and flung the whole mess of it as hard as she could straight up. Maybe it would find a planet with atmosphere and be some little alien kid's shooting star.

And now she had to decide what to do.

She figured she had two choices, really. One, walk back down the *Lavinia Whateley* and find out if the Mi-Go believed in surrender. Two, walk around the *Lavinia Whateley* and into her toothy mouth.

Black Alice didn't think the Mi-Go believed in surrender.

She tilted her head back for one last clear look at the shining black infinity of space. Really, there wasn't any choice at all. Because even if she'd misunderstood what Vinnie seemed to be trying to tell her, the worst she'd end up was dead, and that was light-years better than what the Mi-Go had on offer.

Black Alice Bradley loved her ship.

She turned to her left and started walking, and the *Lavinia Whateley*'s bioluminescence followed her courteously all the way, vanes swaying out of her path. Black Alice skirted each of Vinnie's eyes as she came to them, and each of them blinked at her. And then she reached Vinnie's mouth and that magnificent panoply of teeth.

"Make it quick, Vinnie, okay?" said Black Alice, and walked into her leviathan's maw.

ᐤᑯ

Picking her way delicately between razor-sharp teeth, Black Alice had plenty of time to consider the ridiculousness of worrying about a hole in her suit. Vinnie's mouth was more like a crystal cave, once you were inside it; there was no tongue, no palate. Just polished, macerating stones. Which did not close on Black Alice, to her surprise. If anything, she got the feeling the Vinnie was holding her... breath. Or what passed for it.

The Boojum was lit inside, as well—or was making herself lit, for Black Alice's benefit. And as Black Alice clambered inward, the teeth got smaller, and fewer, and the tunnel narrowed. Her throat, Alice thought. I'm inside her.

And the walls closed down, and she was swallowed.

Like a pill, enclosed in the tight sarcophagus of her space suit, she felt rippling pressure as peristalsis pushed her along. And then greater pressure, suffocating, savage. One sharp pain. The pop of her ribs as her lungs crushed.

Screaming inside a space suit was contraindicated, too. And with collapsed lungs, she couldn't even do it properly.

alice.

She floated. In warm darkness. A womb, a bath. She was comfortable. An itchy soreness between her shoulderblades felt like a very mild radiation burn.

alice.

A voice she thought she should know. She tried to speak; her mouth gnashed, her teeth ground.

alice. talk here.

She tried again. Not with her mouth, this time.

Talk... here?

The buoyant warmth flickered past her. She was... drifting. No, swimming. She could feel currents on her skin. Her vision was confused. She blinked and blinked, and things were shattered.

There was nothing to see anyway, but stars.

alice talk here.

Where am I?

eat alice.

Vinnie. Vinnie's voice, but not in the flatness of the heads-up display anymore. Vinnie's voice alive with emotion and nuance and the vastness of her self.

You ate me, she said, and understood abruptly that the numbness she felt was not shock. It was the boundaries of her body erased and redrawn.

!

Agreement. Relief.

I'm... in you, Vinnie?

=/=

Not a "no." More like, this thing is not the same, does not compare, to this other thing. Black Alice felt the warmth of space so near a generous star slipping by her. She felt the swift currents of its gravity, and the gravity of its satellites, and bent them, and tasted them, and surfed them faster and faster away.

I am *you.*

!

Ecstatic comprehension, which Black Alice echoed with passionate relief. Not dead. Not dead after all. Just, transformed. Accepted. Embraced by her ship, whom she embraced in return.

Vinnie. Where are we going?

out, Vinnie answered. And in her, Black Alice read the whole great naked wonder of space, approaching faster and faster as Vinnie accelerated, reaching for the first great skip that would hurl them into the interstellar darkness of the Big Empty. They were going somewhere.

Out, Black Alice agreed and told herself not to grieve. Not to go mad. This sure beat swampy Hell out of being a brain in a jar.

And it occurred to her, as Vinnie jumped, the brainless bodies of her crew already digesting inside her, that it wouldn't be long before the loss of the *Lavinia Whateley* was a tale told to frighten spacers, too.

The Nyarlathotep Event

Jonathan Wood

The Nyarlathotep Event :: Case File #1 :: *Performance*

The Oxford Playhouse. Now.

For the record, it is very difficult to pinpoint the exact moment when you went wrong if a woman with a Laura Ashley dress and blood-stained teeth is rhythmically beating your head against the floor. Just so you know.

Ten minutes before

Here's a treat: a night out at the theater courtesy of work. All expenses paid. The only catch: I might have to gun down the performer halfway through.

See, this is the problem with working for shadowy government agencies. There's always rough to go with the smooth. Yes, you get to enjoy an evening of ancient Egyptian magic, but it is being performed by an interdimensional avatar called Nyarlathotep who hales from a dimension representing humanity's collective fears. Silver lining, meet cloud.

Still, just another night out for Agent Arthur Wallace of MI37.

The niggling familiarity of the the name Nyarlathotep clears up as soon as he steps out on stage. Lovecraft. Whether the performer's the real deal or just some wacko with a penchant for non-Euclidean geometry, they're using the name of a gibbering literary horror.

Which, I feel, should inform my plan. Except the only plan I seem to remember old Lovecraft providing was running howling into the night, so I'm not sure how helpful that's going to be.

Nyarlathotep stands seven feet tall, wrapped in blood-red rags. They hang from his shoulders like a cloak. They wreathe his face. Red mist billows about his feet, spills into the theater, spreads out over feet and ankles. People in the front row let out odd barking sounds—the terrifying inbred cousin of laughter. And I'm pretty sure Nyarlathotep's not told any jokes yet.

Screw evaluating the situation. I reach for my gun.

Nyarlathotep opens his mouth.

There are no words. His mouth moves. Sounds emerge. But it is something beyond speech. Something more profound. Some kinesthetic reflex of bile and horror.

The buzzing of flies. The stench of rotting meat filling my nose, my mouth. Burning my throat. I gag. Heave up bile. A liquid scream. Pins in my arms. Needles, and nails, and shards of glass. The grind of cigarette against skin. My brain is burning, melting, is fecal matter sloshing in my skull.

And still his mouth stretches behind reams of cloth. And on and on pours out the filth. Into me.

My gun. I need—

I grab for the thing with numb fingers. Atrocities flicker at the edges of my vision. A noise like a kettle boiling. Rising. Rising. Up, and up. Like an itch I need to reach into my brain to scratch.

Somehow I get the gun loose. I half see it out of one eye, through filters of horror and peeling flesh. I try to sight Nyarlathotep, but I might as well be trying to shoot the moon.

Screw it. I pull the trigger.

The muzzle's thunderclap hits me like water to the face. Abruptly I'm just a man in a theater, waving a gun about, while around me everyone goes insane.

Men and women are on all fours. They roll in fights. Some screw. Some scream.

On stage, Nyarlathotep stands, arms wide, welcoming it all. The conductor of this pageant of madness. And, Lovecraft old buddy, running and screaming does seem like a good idea right about now.

On the other hand, that's not what I get paid to do. So I stand. I steady my gun. I draw a bead on the bastard. I think about how I should probably change careers.

Which is exactly the moment the woman in the Laura Ashley number clotheslines me around my throat and brings me down.

My gun scatters. I scrabble at her, coughing and choking, trying to pry her off me. She seizes my head. Slams it onto the floor. Crash. Crash. The room spins. Crash.

Which brings me to the point where I'm left wondering if I'm going to have the time to enumerate all the mistakes I've made before my head gives way.

Just another night out for Agent Arthur Wallace of MI37.

The Nyarlathotep Event :: Case File #2 :: *Rescue*

8:15 pm, The Oxford Playhouse, Oxford, England

There is romance to the idea of the Man Alone. Abandoned, desperate, he reaches deep inside and finds the will to go on, to do what must be done, to save the day.

But when the Man Alone is being beaten to death by a pack of insane theater-enthusiasts, the idea of back-up has a little more charm.

In those moments there is little better than a co-worker dismissing a homicidal Laura Ashley fan off your chest with a very large sword.

Kayla—co-worker, possessor of almost inhuman speed and agility, sword-wielder, dangerously psychotic person—stands over me, twirling a four-foot long katana.

It's hard to express my gratitude. I go with, "Guh-th-fuh."

"Shut up. Get up." Kayla demonstrates her social skills as a man in a three-piece suit leaps up on a chair in front of us, growls.

Kayla slams the butt of the blade into the man's forehead. The man pinwheels away over seats, head snapped back.

"Feckin' mad bastards," Kayla says. "Always the same crap with the baying at the moon and the lust for human flesh."

I have other concerns. Like putting a bullet in the interdimensional avatar of fear and chaos on the stage whose fault this all is—Nyarlathotep.

Except the stage is empty.

"Target's moving," I say. "Out back. Now."

A mass of drooling, enraged Oxonians stands between me and the stage. As one, they bay their madness.

"Lobby?" Kayla suggests.

I move. A raving student comes at me. I use both fists to club him to the floor.

The lobby is stark in its emptiness. And we're moving now. The chase is properly on. *You're mine, you interdimensional bastard.*

From nowhere, a yellow clay jar arcs through the air. I duck. It explodes against the wall behind me. Gas rushes out, a red mist. I duck, but an arm of vapor circles my head. I breathe—

A wall of flesh rises, engulfing. Jackals chase me across a desert. Water closes over my head, tentacles wrapped about my ankles, pulling, pulling—

—and crash to the lobby floor. I gasp, claw at my eyes.

Three figures in ragged yellow robes are in the doorway. They hold curved knives high. Their robes billow about them—whether it's the air-conditioning, or just the universe deciding to add cinematic flair, I'm not sure.

To be honest, I just reach for my gun.

My gun. Beaten out of my hand. By the the charming lady with a Laura Ashley dress and a mad-on for the taste of my spleen.

I do have my own sword. A recent acquisition, and one I'm rather proud of. It's a flaming sword, in fact. In fact, I'd go so far as to say it rocks so hard it makes Metallica look like a group of small girls. But it's also not the most fashionable accessory for a night out at the theater, and I left it back at the office. So no go on that front either.

The robed men charge. It's not much ground to cover. The first attacker is yards away. He stinks of decay. I catch a flash of teeth. Jaundiced skin. Black pits of eyes.

"Kayla!" My voice slides up to an octave I try to avoid hitting in public.

Her blade flies out. Yellow robes are stained with red. The leading attacker flies backwards in more parts than he entered the theater. Bits of him collide with his fellows.

I pull myself up, still blinking away the after-effects of the attacker's gas. "We need to get out of here."

"The Children of Nyarlathotep will stop you!" One of the yellow-robed men is pulling free of the tangled pile of his fellows. "We will come for you in your dreams. We will unseam your sanity."

With a speed that laughs at the conventional rules of physics, Kayla crosses the room and delivers her toecap to his forehead. The man's head slams to the ground, tongue lolling.

"Let's go." Kayla pushes through the door and out onto the street. I follow after her. Time to get finally get the bas—

I stop. I stare. The streets. The city.

Where has Oxford gone?

The road, once paved and straight, is a twisting roller coaster of asphalt and cobbles. Limestone storefronts have curled into blackened husks, glass bulging like blisters. Dreaming spires have stretched to the sky, points drawn out like knife blades. The citizenry scream, and caper, and cower.

The madness is spreading. It's not just in the citizens, it's in the city's walls, its streets, its soul.

And seriously, even an interdimensional avatar of madness is a Tim Burton fan?

"You know," I say to Kayla, "I cannot wait to find this bastard and shoot him."

The Nyarlathotep Event :: Case File #3 :: *Countdown*

8:38pm. Oxford, England.

"Derrière. To Christ Church College. Five minutes or less. Otherwise you're responsible for the end of the world." Tabitha, my handler and MI37's resident cheerleader, sets the ticking clock just in case my day wasn't going badly enough.

It had been a simple plan. Go to the theater. Make sure the performer really is an interdimensional avatar of fear and chaos. Shoot him.

All in a day's work for Agent Arthur Wallace.

Except now I'm chasing the bastard through Oxford transformed. Nyarlathotep—the aforementioned avatar—has vomited up the citizenry's collective fears and given the place a good basting. Architecture spirals out of control. Streets twist back in recursive loops. Buildings teeter and leer.

Oh, and everybody's gone mad. The insane cherry on the lunacy cake.

Ten minutes ago

Kayla—MI37's superhuman swordswoman and high-functioning psychotic—passes me a plastic earbud. "Tabitha," she says. I plug it in. Because who doesn't want a running job evaluation from a committed misanthrope?

"Screwed that up. Big time."

I close my eyes. "Where's Nyarlathotep?"

"Christ Church. Potential reality rip."

I move. Kayla follows.

Seven minutes ago

Get to Christ Church—simple enough. Run in a straight line from the playhouse.

Except every exit from this bloody traffic circle leads back to where it starts. "What the hell?"

"Reality leakage," Tabitha answers through the earbud. "Leaking into ours. Nyarlathotep's home dimension is. Distorting space. When you tear through realities and summon avatars of fear and chaos, sensible to close the door behind you. Not into common sense. People who summoning avatars of fear and chaos."

Which is all lovely to know, but, "How the hell do I get down this street?"

"Magic," Tabitha says.

Unfortunately, MI37's magician recently became a little less than corporeal so that could be a problem. But Tabitha says, "Our end. Already working on it."

There is muttering. I hear someone say, "Entropic Negotiator," and then, "No, the Phillip's version."

Tabitha comes back on the line. "Phone. Dial office. Then hold it up to the street."

I comply. Tinny nonsense syllables emerge. And then the world ripples like water, and I get to go down the street I actually want to go down for once.

When did running in a straight line get this hard?

Four minutes ago

If it's not one thing, it's bloody cultists.

The yellow-robed man comes out of nowhere. I spin just in time to catch his fist on my chin. I fall down—not very Kurt Russell of me but typical of my brand of heroism. Fortunately Kayla is close to being superwoman. Unfortunately, somewhere around eighteen cultists have surrounded her, which means I have to do something... well, not exactly heroic...

I kick my attacker in the crotch.

That buys me enough time to get up off the floor, and be taken down by a flying tackle from a second cultist.

We roll back and forth while, in my ear, Tabitha intones, "Tick tock. Tick tock."

It's more sheer frustration than anything else that lends me the strength to slam my opponent's face into the brick. Finally he stops worrying about me and just lies there, insensible.

Just enough time to put the boot in on cultist number one, watch Kayla dispatch of her final cultist with a casual backhand, and listen to Tabitha sing a line from *The Final Countdown*.

Now

Seriously. This is starting to get ridiculous.

The crowd is six rows deep, blocking the College gateway. Students mostly. And not enough sane thoughts among them to rub together and start a fire.

"Five minutes," Tabitha says.

I look around desperately. Time is not on our side.

And then I smile. Because time might be the answer after all.

"Any chance you can knock that down?" I ask Kayla. I point to the grand clock tower sitting above Christ Church College's grand entrance. It won't slow time but it'll disperse a crowd.

"Pope shit in the woods?" Kayla asks me.

Which stops me for a moment, because I didn't think he did.

A student at the edge of the crowd stops poking at his midriff with a stick and looks at us. He lets out a scream.

The attention of the crowd shifts.

Above our heads the clock's second hand ticks, once, twice.

Kayla leaps, impossibly high. She lands on the student's shoulders, sends him crumpling, but is already away, hits the college wall like a spider.

The crowd lurches towards me.

"Any chance you could do this faster?" I don't mean to be ungrateful, but there are a lot of crazy people charging me.

Kayla starts climbing. The crowd starts running. Kayla reaches the top. The second hand ticks.

Kayla hammers at stone with her blade. Her arms blur. Stonework cracks and creaks.

The crowd hesitates as one. Looks back. Looks up.

Limestone explodes away from Kayla's blade. Shards shower the crowd. The clock tower leans wildly. The second hand spins away from the clock.

Kayla breaks from her work, steps back, kicks the wobbling stone monument. She smiles. "Timber."

The Nyarlathotep Event :: Case File #4 :: *Portal*

Oxford, England. Not a good day.

Some days, I think, I really need to ask for a transfer. You get told you're going into a department called MI37, and you think, oh that sounds cloak-and-dagger exciting. They charge you with defending the realm from all things supernatural and tentacle-y, and you think, well that could be exciting.

Then you find you find yourself in the middle of Christ Church College facing a pack of yellow-robed cultists standing around a bubbling rip in reality.

"Not good," I say to Kayla, my equally up-shit-creek co-worker.

The cultists are chanting, of course. Limited options on the daily duties for a cultist, I imagine. Chant or sacrifice. And for all my bitching about my employer, at least working for MI37 isn't tedious.

Take the portal, for instance. If I don't close it in the next three minutes, all of Oxford is going to be permanently infected by another reality constructed of humanity's collective fears.

Likely a suicidal task, but not a boring one.

Unfortunately Kayla and I lack the appropriate color coordination, so cultists catch on to us pretty fast. Three break from the circle, pulling large knives.

I really wish I hadn't dropped my gun earlier. But things tend to get distracting when an entire city goes insane. Still, this is where Kayla comes in. No need for a gun when the woman next to you can make a champion sushi chef look like a sloppy amateur with a blade.

"All yours," I say.

Which is when the smoking grenade of crazy gas comes at her. It's a futile throw, of course. Kayla bats it out of the air without blinking. But the problem with a gas grenade designed to shatter is that it shatters as soon as you hit it.

Kayla disappears in a cloud of red mist. There is a scream from its depths. "No!"

I step towards it. Then leap back as Kayla emerges. She's clawing at her face with one hand. She sweeps viciously, blindly back and forth with her sword in the other. I duck a blow, another.

"Kayla!" I yell at her. "Kayla!" But she's gone, far gone. I don't think she even hears me.

And at that point, some cultists deign to leave the comfort of their fraternity and come to hand my arse to me.

The first cultist swings at me. I duck, grab a piece of shattered clocktower, use it to shatter most of his jaw.

That gives the other two a good time to sneak round behind me. One slices at me. I roll with it. My jacket takes the hit. The second cultist gets a good kick in. There's a better range of movement allowed by ragged yellow robes that you'd think. I double over, wheezing.

They come at me from opposite directions, knives held high. I do the best I can and collapse.

Knives whistle over my head. I use the rubble to crush one cultist's foot. He drops away howling. Meanwhile the other knife comes down and opens up my shoulder so I have some howling of my own to do.

I go at the guy angry then. Fighting is not exactly my forte. I resemble an off-balance ballerina pinwheeling across the Christ Church quad. Fortunately the cultist's hectic chanting schedule hasn't left him much time for self-defense classes. He swings the knife low. I stagger-step out of the way. My tie become noticeably shorter, the end fluttering away. The cultist becomes noticeably less conscious, my chunk of rubble colliding with his left ear.

And all that would be great if there were only three cultists. But three more separate from around the circle, which draws tighter.

I close fast. My shoulder connects with one before he gets his dagger free. I step into him, whirling wide with the rubble. A second cultist comes in low and hard, head slamming into my stomach, knife nicking my thigh. I bring my knee up into his nose. He drops away. The other grabs me from behind. The knife comes up. I slam my head backwards. His nose crunches. He drops me. I spin, the rubble held tight in my fist. More of his face crunches.

The guy on the floor is thinking about getting up. Me and my rubble encourage him not to.

Behind me, Kayla is on her knees, sobbing.

Three more cultists, but the circle is tight now and I'm close.

I break into a run, slam past one, spinning round but still moving. One goes to trip me, I hurdle desperately, mis-step, sprawl, roll.

I connect with the legs of a cultist in the circle. He trips, crashes forwards. Forward into the portal.

An ugly ripping sound. Then the cultists are down one member. The chanting falters. The cultists stare in a tiny moment of shocked silence.

Except... Not quite silence.

With a sound like a wet fart, the portal collapses in on itself.

Strike one for the good guys.

Now if only I hadn't just given twenty angry cultists nothing to do but use me like a piñata...

The Nyarlathotep Event :: Case File #5 :: *Nyarlathotep*

Christ Church College, Oxford, England

One thing I've always liked about Kurt Russell movies is that they end.

That sounds wrong...

I like that they conclude. Evil is defeated. The good guy wins. A sunset is ridden into.

In real life you face down a horde of angry cultists, close an interdimensional portal, get attacked, find out your incapacitated sword-wielding partner is now... capacitated?... watch her get rid of the rest of your problems, and then you find out there's a seven-foot tall avatar of fear and chaos who's all pissed about it and manifested behind you when you weren't looking.

In real life this shit never ends.

Having never faced an interdimensional avatar of fear and chaos before, I go with the nearest weapon to hand and throw a rock at him.

Apparently this avatar—Nyarlathotep is his name—is made of sterner stuff than that.

So: plan B.

It may not be overly heroic to run and hide while getting your friend to do the fighting, but Kayla virtually has superpowers and I don't, so this may not be as bad as it initially looks.

Kayla smiles. She points her sword at Nyarlathotep. They stand opposite each other, a frozen tableau for just one second, two... Kayla darts forward almost faster than the eye can see.

And then Kayla flies eight feet through the air and lands in a crumpled heap. Sort of the opposite result to the one we were going for there.

God, I wish I'd thought of a plan C.

In its absence, I stick to cowering. Nyarlathotep steps toward Kayla. He stretches out a robed arm. The impression of a hand and its end—*a claw, black leather skin, yellow nails*—and then gone, or denied. On the floor, Kayla screams.

What would Kurt Russell do? Possibly not the smartest question, but it's stood me better than you'd imagine in times of need.

Except Kurt Russell would probably charge the guy yelling. The man alone. Guns blazing.

A stupid, stupid plan.

Except I don't have any better ideas.

There's a broken chunk of wood on the floor, one end a jagged ruin of splinters. It looks sharp.

I grab it, brace myself, burst from cover. I level my weapon. I charge.

As it turns out, the key to a good battle cry is timing. Too early and, well...

Nyarlathotep turns, swings his arm from Kayla to me. Kayla finally lies still. And then—

Fear breaking over my skin like water, drenching me, drowning me. I can see it all. The inevitability. The end. He's here. Our harbinger. Our prophet. Our Nyarlathotep. He comes bearing this truth: this world collapsing under its own ragged weight, burying us in flesh and concrete; we will chew on our friends, our families—a desperate, animal need to consume, to feed, to survive. An utterly ridiculous, utterly futile urge.

I'm standing inches from him. Just standing. Weeping. Knowing how foolish this all is, how much madness it is. I stare at the wood in my hands. Better I just end my own life with it. Better I chew off the hands holding the wood. Better I claw out my eyes. Better I gut myself and feast on my own—

"Ooph!"

Breath bursts out of me. Something heavy and hard colliding with my back, sending me stumbling, staggering towards, towards...

The wood strikes Nyarlathotep's gut. It slashes through the robes. Reams of cloth without end. Still the weight drives me forward, drives the wood in. And it feels I'm crossing some terrible boundary, as if I'm wounding myself. Then: a glimpse of skin—black, yellow, green with pus. I gag, and then the wood carries on, and on, and in, and the figure, the god before me, Nyarlathotep, convulses, heaves, collapses. And the wood goes on, and in, and before my eyes, he dies.

A feeling like a whip crack inside my skull. And Jesus, did I... was I...

There's a pile of red rags on the floor next to me. I've fallen down. Kayla is on top of me. I'm holding a charred stump of blackened wood.

"Get the feck off me." Kayla stands up dusting herself off, blinking.

"What did you—?" I ask. Questioning Kayla is always tricky. I'm always concerned the answer will involve her gutting me.

"In my head." Kayla blinks a few more times. "Think I was trying to stop you from killing him." She squints at me. "Normally better at stopping people."

I am afraid I cannot sympathize with her injured professional pride. Instead I shake my head, try to clear the shrieking madness Nyarlathotep put in there. And I see the rags on the floor. Empty. Dead. Nyarlathotep... concluded.

I smile. Because that's an ending I can really enjoy.

The Nyarlathotep Event :: Case File #6 :: *Sweet Dreams*

Christ Church College, Oxford, England

Some days I really get the vastness of the universe. I'm tiny. It's big. I don't matter. I get it.

Then, some days, you save the world—you know, for example you close an interdimensional portal infecting the world with madness, kill an avatar of fear called Nyarlathotep when armed only with a bit of two-by-four—and you think the world should really pay more attention.

But no. Instead, Oxford remains a twisted fun house version of itself and the populace remains howling at the moon.

Kayla—my sword-wielding partner in government-sponsored world saving—and I exchange a look.

I put a finger to my ear. "Tabitha," I say to our handler back at MI37, "any chance you know what's going on?"

"Dimensional portal's definitely closed," Tabby says. "QED Nyarlathotep's not as dead as he looks."

Twenty or so of Nyarlathotep's cultists are scattered around us waiting for the concussion to kick in. Except one of them starts to laugh.

"You really thought just stabbing him would work?" He laughs harder.

And to be honest I rather had. But I don't want to give the bastard the satisfaction of hearing me admit it.

"Crap," says Tabitha. "Outside of his home reality. Can't kill him."

Wait… Now we realize this?

The cultist is laughing harder now. "And you closed the portal."

So we can't even get him. "Oh bugger and balls."

"Just point the damn phone," Tabitha tells me. So I dial the office, and I point it, and there are a few half-heard words. And then time and space bend. Like a bubble rising through viscous liquid.

"Ta-dah," Tabitha says.

The cultist stops laughing.

It should be a satisfying moment, except—

"Wait," I say. "We seriously have to go into a dimension representing humanity's collective fears and madness?"

"Well," Tabitha says. "Something about beaches. The travel brochure said."

It's not exactly sporting, but I relieve some of the stress by kicking the cultist in the head and sending him back to the dark sleep of unconsciousness.

"Also," Tabitha adds, "top him, get back, and close the thing in thirty minutes or less. Otherwise permanent world buggering. OK?"

Perfect. Just bloody perfect.

"Tick tock."

I brace myself and step through.

Another time. Another place.

As it turns out, humanity is afraid of pretty weird stuff. At least that's the only reason I can think of that a giant version of Snuggles the teddy bear is trying to kill me with a meat cleaver.

We're in something that looks like an airport terminal. Stepping through the portal put me six feet above the floor. With a feeling like slipping out of jello, I fell to the floor. And there was Snuggles. Six feet tall, eye buttons dangling on threadbare strings, a cleaver the size of my chest balanced in one hand.

"Passport!" he giggles and takes another swing at my head. I duck. He buries the blade into a cement pillar. He tugs it free with an adorable chuckle. A stitch bursts in his arm at the effort. Stuffing spills loose.

This is typically the point at which I cower and wait for Kayla to carry out violence that makes her seem more like a walking missile launcher than most people you meet. Except, when I look over Kayla is sitting with her hands over her eyes, screaming.

Seriously? This is Kayla's personal hell? Really?

Snuggles takes another swipe at my head. I duck, roll, come up behind him. Snuggles wrestles the cleaver out the floor. Another stitch pops while he giggles madly.

And I am not particularly good at this whole fighting thing, but at times like this you do what you have to do.

I kick at his loose arm. More stuffing spills. I kick again.

Snuggles looks back at me, his cotton line drawn up in a smile. "Playtime is over," he says as sweetly as can be. He heaves on the cleaver. I kick one last time.

Another stitch pops. Snuggles heaves. The whole joint gives way. He staggers back uttering things no beloved children's character should ever say, still laughing between the curses.

At this point, opportunity and the cleaver are same thing so I grab them both. I stagger under the massive weight. Snuggles' detached arm still clings to the cleaver. I swing madly, spin round and round.

And then the blade buries itself in Snuggles' gut, and he chuckles one last time and lies still.

I stand up sweating hard. And now would be a great time for me to snap Kayla out of it. Because I can see the Care Bears coming and they have machine guns.

The Nyarlathotep Event :: Case File #7 :: *The I in Team*

Every time I fight unspeakable horrors from alternate realities, I am reminded of the value of teamwork. Say, for example, that I am forced into a dimension of fear and madness to act as the government-sponsored assassin of its avatar, Nyarlathotep, then back-up is about my favorite thing in the world.

So now, forced into a dimension of fear and madness and acting as the government-sponsored assassin of its avatar, Nyarlathotep, it's really not an awesome time for my partner to lose her shit.

But Kayla MacDoyle, MI37 field agent, misanthrope, dangerous psychopath, and virtual superhero is lying on the ground whimpering, while I'm stuck with defending us from a reality gone awry.

Untethered nightmares come at me. Balls of blades, steely and sharp; beings of arms and bone, scratching, clawing; creeping insectile horrors; nuns with switchblades; rats the size of terriers; tentacular masses, sticky, viscous, and clutching. I scavenge weapons, improvise barriers. I duck blades, catch punches, wrestle limbs. I am beaten, blackened, bruised. I come up with something in my teeth. I am an animal. I am pissing terrified.

Space ripples and changes about us. Maybe we are traveling, some dream logic carrying us along like a current through rooms of living flesh, of bone, of chitin, rooms threatening to drown us, rooms I cannot bring myself to describe.

I can feel it slipping in behind my eyes. After-images of travesties that clamber into my brain and breed. I lose track of what is real in a place where everything is unreal. And I need to pull back. I need to get him good and grounded. But there is no ground. There is just Kayla, just me. Circling. Falling. Falling again.

I land. A plain. Some tundra. A dust cloud on the horizon. I pick myself up. And Kayla is still there, right next to me. And I know something big is coming. I just need to get to him, to get us both away. I start to run, but dream rules apply. My limbs do not obey me. Each step is a tottering nightmare of minimal increments.

And the cloud. The cloud is fast, is impossible in its speed. Closing. Closing. And in the dust I get an impression of hooves, of horns, of teeth.

"Kayla," I yell. "Kayla!" I'm begging her. She has to help. I was never built to be the man alone.

Finally I am at her side. I steel my courage, slap her, shake her. Her head lolls. Her eyes roll. "Come back," I whisper. The cloud comes closer.

She is not going to snap out of it. She is gone. I am alone.

I gather her up in my arms. I stagger. Another step of glacial slowness. The cloud's thunder shakes this world.

And it would be so easy to slip away, to give in, to let the madness take me, to be consumed by this reality.

But there is a home, a place to get back to, friends and family. And Kurt Russell movie marathons. And bacon.

And screw this. Kayla and I are getting out of here with Nyarlathotep's head on a bloody platter.

I turn. I face the cloud. It's almost on me now. Massive. Thundering.

Just a cloud, I tell myself. *Just dust and wind.* I don't know the rules of this place, but I know the rules of dreams. Of nightmares. And I pray that they apply.

The cloud breaks over me. *Just dust. Just wind.* It scours my cheeks. Hoofbeats crash around me. *Just echoes. Just the boom of the wind.*

And then peace. Then a breeze. I open my eyes. The cloud has blown away. I still hold Kayla.

Reality slips. I stand in a corridor full of doors. I can hear scampering about and above me. And I know I can hear the rats in the walls.

I am still afraid. I would still favor flight over fight. But fight I will. Because

I can face my fear. Because now, Nyarlathotep, you get bloody yours.

The Nyarlathotep Event :: Case File #8 :: *Interrogation*

I never thought I'd say it, but once you get used to a dimension of fear and chaos, it's not as bad as it sounds. Yes, it's driven my co-worker, Kayla, insane, and yes, it does keep trying to kill me with more and more depraved horrors, but, well it could be worse.

Take the field of flying knives I have to traverse. Blades whirl, shearing life from plants, small rodents, the odd offensive-looking rock. But a little concentration on my part, and I manifest a titanium steel umbrella and, with Kayla balanced on my shoulder, I cross the place in relatively safety.

Nightmare logic.

And when I reach a river of blood leeches—each creature a foot long, each with a spine-filled maw reaching for me—I just think hard and then I have wings. Kayla and I sail over them easy as blinking.

Seriously, I'm like the Green bloody Lantern in this reality. It's awesome.

Really the only serious fly in the ointment is that if I don't find its ruler, Nyarlathotep, in the next fifteen minutes or so, all of regular reality is going to be permanently buggered. And I have no idea where I'm going.

Fortunately I've always been more of a beta male, so stopping to ask for directions isn't a serious dilemma. If only I could stop people trying to kill me long enough to ask.

I finally strike gold in a castle that drips gore and is chock-full of tiny gremlin-like creatures armed with stilettos. An old-school suit of armor makes maneuvering difficult but renders their attempted stabbings utterly ineffective. After a few attempts I finally seize one around the midriff and heft it to eye height. It kicks and spits with its full eight-inch frame. Really, if it wasn't so full of bile it'd be quite adorable.

"I'm looking for Nyarlathotep," I inform it.

It lunges for my eyes, hurling its blades at the grills in my armored mask. I flinch back and fling it away. Possibly a little too hard. It hits a wall and becomes an ugly stain.

I keep the next one further from my face.

"Which way to Nyarlathotep?"

It suggests some awful things I should do to my mother.

"I'm not a violent man," I tell it, "but I can apparently crush you like an insect."

More profanities follow. Small he may be. Easily intimidated he is not.

"Please?" I venture.

Further obscenities. And then my jaw starts to tremble, because all of this abuse is delivered by a voice so high it's barely in human hearing range. And then I laugh. It doesn't feel at all appropriate as chunks of viscera rain down the castle walls, but I'm starting to become immune to the shock horror aspects of this place.

As soon as the sound is out of me, the gremlin shrieks and does its best to claw its way out of my hand. I'm so shocked I stop laughing and stare at it. It recovers slowly. I chuckle. It slams its body backwards, wrestling an arm free to cover its ears.

"Nyarlathotep now, or I bust a gut all over you," I tell it. Not the most threatening thing I've ever said, but it has the desired effect. The thing grimaces and screeches, and jabbers, and around me the walls of reality flex and then—

I stand (and Kayla whimpers) on a cliff overlooking a barren, dusty plain. Rising from the center, like red wax dripping toward the sky, is a many-spired citadel.

"Nyarlathotep," the gremlin gibbers at me. "Nyarlathotep!"

Looks like the sort of place an extradimensional avatar of fear and chaos would call home. I nod my thanks to the gremlin and then throw it over the edge of the cliff.

Seriously, the murderous bastard could have brought us a little closer.

The Nyarlathotep Event :: Case File #9 :: *Citadel*

As citadels that are the embodiment of sheer terror go, Nyarlathotep's is pretty imposing.

I mean, to be fair, he benefits from having built it in a nightmare reality based on humanity's collective fears where things like gravity and physics are apparently spongier than I'm used to, but still, he deserves points for effort. Blood-colored spires, statues that actually scream, non-Euclidean angles—he went the whole nine yards.

Still going to kill the bastard, of course.

I lower Kayla, co-worker, super-woman, and currently dribblingly insane person off my shoulders. I check my watch. If time obeys the same rules here as back home I've got about twelve minutes to get this done. Time to take some shortcuts.

Fortunately, the best thing about a nightmare reality is that nightmare rules apply. I concentrate, my dream armor disappears, I sprout wings, and I take to the air.

Hell yeah, I do.

I sweep down over spires, twist between towers, work my way deeper and deeper into the heart of the complex. A vast central tower looms before me. I aim for a window near its peak, tuck in my wings, clutch Kayla tight to my chest—

—and tentacles explode out of one wall and smash me into the tower.

And, yes, that would probably be the worst thing about a nightmare reality: nightmare rules apply.

I fall, scrabbling against the tower's sheer surface. I try to clear my mind, to focus. My fingers elongate, develop suckers. I latch on. One arm spirals away, elastic and strong, wrapping around Kayla.

I climb the wall. It ripples beneath me.

I jump as the first spike erupts from the wall's surface. I fall, but re-summon my wings. I seize Kayla. I climb. The spikes eject from the wall at speed. Jagged rain.

My body is steel before they strike me. I shelter Kayla and they clatter away.

And screw wings. I'm from the twenty-first century, dammit.

A moment is all it takes to get a jet engine strapped to my back. Going up.

The tentacles lash out as I jet upwards, but I angle away, roasting them with afterburners. They blacken, curling and falling away. Take that, you bastards.

A window looms. I blast towards it, faster, faster. And I'm outstripping the citadel's imagination. I'm outstripping its speed to respond. I'm bloody winning.

Except the window's frame twists even as I slam towards the glass, the edges stretching, stretching, until it resembles something worryingly close to a smile.

Glass shatters. A wall looms. I collide. Blackness descends.

Later

How long was I out? How long do I have left? Is it too late for reality? I look for my watch, but everything is black.

"Kayla?" I say. No reply.

"Always late," a voice says.

I recognize that voice.

"I'm very disappointed, Arthur."

It's my mother's voice.

A spotlight flicks on, a white circle of light on the floor before me. I hear footsteps. My mother comes into the circle. She's bleeding. A great gash across her neck. She collapses, reaches for me.

"Jesus!" I dash forward, grab her hand. She's trying to say something I can't hear. I read her lips. "Arthur…" There's something she's desperate to convey, but she can't …

And then it hits me. Nightmare rules apply.

And this is a cheap bloody ploy.

Lights. I summon them. Banish the darkness. My mother's body wilts in their brightness. Becomes mannequin parts falling apart beneath cheap clothes. An illusion dismissed.

The brightness illuminates a throne room, rich wall hangings, a velvet carpet, a magnificent golden chair. No Kayla. I can't see her. But there, standing before the chair, waiting for me—my target, my goal. Nyarlathotep is home.

And seeing him there, all traces of confidence drain away. No, they are violently expunged from my body. Seeing him there, finally, I am truly afraid.

The Nyarlathotep Event :: Case File #10 :: *Rematch*

Fear. It's easy enough to be ruled by it. There are a lot of things to be afraid of these days. Terrorists. Bioweapons. New Lady Gaga songs.

My personal issue with fear is a little more immediate, though. It is seven foot tall, wears red robes, and goes by the name of Nyarlathotep.

And I'm in his citadel, in his dimension, and in this moment, I realize I probably should have brought my gun. My super-powered co-worker, Kayla, is a government-paid swordswoman, but she appears to have disappeared into madness.

Crap.

Up until now it hasn't been too much of a problem. Until now, I've been able to take advantage of this being a reality other than ours, and just summoned things by concentrating hard. Apparently now I'm in Nyarlathotep's actual house, that's not an option. Not that I don't try it. I imagine swords, guns, knives, bombs, even Donkey Kong on the off chance I can catch him off guard.

No go.

Nyarlathotep steps towards me. He's got no gun either, but that's not really an issue for him.

Visions overwhelm me. Rush up at me from the floor, swallow me.

—drowning here, swallowed by surfaces suddenly turned liquid. I can feel them pressing in. Insects scuttering forward, enveloping me. In my mouth, my ears, my eyes. Peeling back my flesh. And beneath I am something other than expected. There is no flesh here, no blood and bone. Hollow glass veins. Crystalline tendons. A hammer descending, to shatter me, obliterate me. Fear building, building. My

heart beating faster in my chest until I fear even that. Until it is enough to shatter my fragile body. Overwhelming me. Drowning me—

It could go on and on. Forever. There is so much to fear. To run from. Through the vision I can see Nyarlathotep, hand outstretched, pacing slowly towards me. And I know then that all thoughts of killing him are madness. Because fear can never be killed. It will live forever, beat in my heart forever.

But there, then, I know too, that all of that doesn't mean fear can't be overcome too.

I squeeze shut my eyes as the visions press in, but I push back. I gather my breath. I open my eyes.

Nyarlathotep is a step away. His fingers an inch from my throat. I have one hope. One trick this place has taught me. I brace myself. And I laugh.

In his face, I laugh. As loud and hearty as I can make. Trying to avoid the hysteria overcoming me. I laugh, and I laugh, and I laugh.

His hand strikes me and shatters like glass. Nyarlathotep stares at it, disbelieving. He comes on, his arm grinding against me, splintering, fracturing, spilling to the floor in glistening red shards. And then his whole being smashes against me. And he is only so much dust at my feet.

And then his whole citadel trembles. Cracks run through it. The whole of this reality shatters and shakes. And then I am falling, tumbling through a tear in the world, into blackness.

Christ Church College, Oxford

I land with a crack on my back in the center of Christ Church quad.

I lie there panting. I look about me. And I realize, this is it. This is Oxford as I remember it. Regular, normal, boring Oxford. Normal, boring students staring at me, wondering where I'm from. The madness from Nyarlathotep's reality has been banished.

Kayla, my co-worker, lost to madness in that other reality, sits up next to me, paws at her eyes.

"Worst feckin' dream I've ever…" She shakes her head.

In my ear, static as my earbud reconnects with the MI37 home office. I hear Tabitha's voice. "Five, four, three… oh wait. You're back." She pauses. "Cut that bloody close. Idiots."

Yeah. Everything back to normal.

And I smile. Because, really, there's no place like home.

The Black Brat of Dunwich

Stanley C. Sargent

"In effect we have unsettled and reversed the given configuration, suggesting an alternative—culture/nature."

—Donald R. Burleson

A t the bartender's suggestion, Jeffrey and James made their way to the rear of the dimly lit Arkham bar. They saw only one person in the smokey shadows of the back room, a thin ancient man seated alone amidst the shadows and smoke; they casually approached his table.

"Pardon me, mister," Jeffrey proffered, "my friend and I are collecting data for a book we're writing about the so-called 'Dunwich horror.' The bartender said you'd actually met Wilbur Whateley and might be willing to speak with us."

The dark, seated figure offered no immediate response. After a few moments, the two intruders looked at each other, then shrugged and turned to walk away. Their retreat was halted by a gritty voice inviting them to sit. The pair eagerly retraced their steps.

Before they could seat themselves, the mysterious figure raised an empty glass and waved it in the air. Jeffrey headed back to the bar in response to the signal while James pulled a chair up to the table. During the awkward silence that followed, James noted the excellent though somewhat old-fashioned quality of the stranger's apparel. If the fellow had really been acquainted with the Whateley boy, his comments might well prove key elements for their book. He certainly looked old enough to have been Wilbur's contemporary.

Jeffrey soon returned, bearing a trio of glasses and a bottle of whiskey. He joined the silent pair, poured three drinks, and waited for the old man to speak.

As the two researchers sipped their drinks, the old man downed his shot, then poured himself another. He coughed, then gruffly blurted out, "So somebody's finally writing a book about my old friend Wilbur, are they? Well, I reckon I knew him better than anybody. I haven't spoken to anyone about him for years, but that's 'cos nobody cares to hear what I have to say on the subject. If you boys aren't prepared to hear the truth, you might as well be on your way."

Jeffrey assured the man that he and his friend wanted only the truth, which they would not hesitate to print, assuming it could in any way be verified. They explained that they hoped to write the first definitive history of the events leading up to the series of mysterious deaths in 1928, the responsibility for which had been attributed to the Whateley family of Dunwich. To date, the pair had studied police reports, newspaper articles, the famous Armitage account, and various coroner's reports.

"The circumstances surrounding the tragedy," added James, "have become so entwined with legend that it has become impossible to separate reality from fiction. We hope to clarify some of the issues and portray the Whateleys accurately. We would also like to take notes and tape record this conversation if that's acceptable to you, sir." He placed a notebook and pen on the table as Jeffrey extracted a hand-held tape recorder from his coat.

"Whatever you want to use is fine by me," responded the man seated opposite them. "Only three people ever knew the truth of what happened in Dunwich: Wilbur Whateley, that goddamned Armitage, and me, Abe Galvin," the old man proclaimed. "Since Wilbur's gone and you'd play hell finding Armitage, I'd say it's up to me to set the record straight before I die."

Despite their surprise at the aspersions cast upon a person as widely respected as Dr. Armitage, the authors encouraged Galvin to impart his recollections. If the man proved legitimate, he was undoubtedly the only person still alive to have actually known young Whateley.

৩৫

"I left Miskatonic University in the spring of 1924," Galvin began, "after spending six years in the linguistic program. Once I'd satisfied all of my commitments, I decided I'd like to wander around New England for a while, just exploring the backwater areas and maybe earning my keep by hiring myself out as a private tutor. I walked or took buses, answered newspaper ads for tutoring work, and occasionally placed an ad of my own. Between jobs, I'd sleep under the stars; the weather was warm so it was pleasurable to camp out.

"Dunwich was too small to have a newspaper of its own, but somehow Old Elezer Whateley, or 'Wizard Whateley' as most people knew him, came across my ad in the *Aylesbury Transcript* and made it his business to look me up. I'd never heard of Dunwich or the Whateleys, so I saw nothing unusual in an offer for room and board for the winter in exchange for helping Whateley's young grandson with some difficult translations of archaic Greek and Latin. I admit the old buzzard struck me as a mite strange—his eyes were about the eeriest I'd ever seen—but with winter just around the corner, I accepted his offer and accompanied him back to Dunwich in his horse-drawn wagon that very same day.

"The country was green and beautiful along the way, yet once we'd passed through an old tunnel bridge, things began looking pretty rustic and run-down. I was willing to put up with a lot rather than face winter without food or shelter, however, even if it meant spending time in a previous century."

The narrator poured himself another glass before resuming his tale. "Whateley's peak-roofed farmhouse came as one hell of a surprise. It was out in the middle of nowhere and smack up against a dirt incline, with one end extending right on into the hillside. The entire upper story had been boarded up, for reasons I didn't know at the time, and a wooden runway sloped right up from the ground to where a gable window had been replaced with a solid plank door.

"The old barn was a wreck and the cattle all looked diseased as hell. I was actually relieved to learn my quarters were to be in one of two unused tool-sheds. The inside of the shed stunk so bad I was obliged to scrub it out with disinfectant, then it still required airing out for two days before I could stand to sleep inside with the door closed."

He stopped to address James, who was furiously writing down every word. "Am I going too fast for you, son?" Galvin asked.

James put his pencil down just long enough to take a sip of whiskey and assure Galvin that, with shorthand, he could easily keep up.

"Just thought I'd check," Galvin said, before nodding and returning to his monologue. "Old Whateley occupied three ground-floor rooms of the farmhouse along with his albino daughter, Lavinia, and grandson, Wilbur. Lavinia, or 'Lavinny' as the old boy called her, struck me as a bit 'off,' though it's hard to say exactly what was wrong with her beyond her paleness and her too-long arms. She could read, though she lacked any kind of formal education. Housework wasn't exactly her forte, but she managed to keep everybody fed.

Her favorite pursuits were daydreaming and running through the hills during thunderstorms, if you can imagine. She struck me as being fidgety and afraid all the time, which tended to get on one's nerves, but I got along well enough with her. I guess you could say she spent most of her time trying to keep out of everybody's way." He paused in reflection, then added, "For some time, no one so much as hinted about who Wilbur's father might be."

The speaker suddenly burst into a fit of coughing that ended in painful wheezing and choking. Another hefty gulp of whiskey brought him temporary relief, but it was obvious his health was not good.

"Is this the kind of stuff you boys are looking for?" he asked.

The two men tripped over each other in response, agreeing that this indeed was exactly the material they were seeking. Both urged Galvin to go on with his tale, hoping to get as much information as possible before alcohol began to affect his memory.

"I couldn't believe my eyes when I saw my prospective student for the first time. Old Whateley had told me his grandson was eleven years old, then he introduces me to this fellow who looks older than me. How many eleven-year-olds you ever seen who are over six feet tall and fully bearded? I started to wonder if I'd been had, but I decided to play along and humor the old fool least I forfeit the promised winter provision. Wilbur and I took to each other right away, and that clinched the arrangement."

James leaned forward and asked hesitantly, "Could you tell us more about Wilbur's appearance?"

Galvin smiled. "I'll get to that. You two have a drink with me first." The tiny, wrinkled man winked at James. "Whiskey helps keep the throat and the mind lubricated, you know," he joked.

He waited patiently as the reluctant pair filled their half-empty glasses, then raised his own glass in a toast. "May you never know the true depths of loneliness!" Galvin called out. Although the sentiment seemed out of context, the pair obligingly clinked their glasses with his before downing the fiery liquid.

"Wilbur was a hell of a peculiar looking fellow, certainly not what one would call handsome. A goatee covered his lack of chin, but his skin had a sallowness to its hue. He had great big ears and long, black hair that framed his face and added to his goatish look.

"I guess I'd have to say his features were coarse by traditional standards, and there was something wild about his appearance, something amazingly feral that recalled the forest satyrs of the ancient Greeks. His pupils were black as coal so it was easy as hell to get lost in those eyes—he must of caught me staring a hundred times at least!"

A dreamlike tone had entered Galvin's voice as he recalled Wilbur's countenance, but he forced himself to focus on the business at hand.

"I don't think Wilbur ever got much chance to play as a child, except maybe occasionally with Lavinia. We had lots of fun, though the first time I made a joke, that booming laugh of his damn near made me jump out of my seat. He looked and sounded like an adult, but he was just a lonely kid inside. It didn't take long for me to realize he was still growing and that, plus his shuffling walk, caused me to wonder if he'd inherited some congenital deformity. He was shamed by his difference and tried to cover it by wearing two or three pairs of pants under his old fashioned cossack breeches. People said he smelled bad too, but if he did, I never noticed it."

Galvin lapsed into silence but did not reach for the bottle. When he spoke again, it was in softer, more intimate tones. "The few visitors we had, including Dr. Armitage, treated Wilbur like some kind of dangerous, deformed misanthrope, though some, like Earl Sawyer, did their best to overcome their qualms. I had mixed feelings about the boy myself, but only at first," he laughed. "He confused the hell out of me! But after a while, I developed a real respect for him and was proud to call him my friend."

An uncomfortable silence followed. Galvin's last statement had been a revelation after all the negative descriptions the authors had heard of "the black brat of Dunwich." James carefully reached over, grabbed the whiskey bottle, and refilled the others' glasses as well as his own.

Jeffrey found himself trying to picture Galvin at age twenty-five. His artistic bend made it easy to visualize a younger Galvin simply by filling in the lines and darkening the hair of the grandfatherly figure before him. He concluded that Galvin had once been the good looking, though probably not the handsome, rugged type. A man of Galvin's average height and build must have felt quite intimidated at having a student whose boyish lack of experience belied his towering visage. It suddenly occurred to Jeffrey that Galvin was reading his thoughts, and when he looked up, he saw that Galvin was looking directly at him with a knowing smile on his face. That made Jeffrey slightly uncomfortable, and he felt a certain relief when the old man resumed his account.

"Wilbur's room also came as a great surprise. It was on the eastern side of the ground floor where the house dug into the hillside. He'd hauled an old bureau into one corner and had been using it as a desk; that's where they later found the big ledger he used as a diary. Only one wall contained a window; every other wall was lined with shelves filled with hundreds of the rotting books that the family had collected through several generations. The majority of those books concerned various aspects of occultism, alchemy, black magic, and the like. I thought it strange that several of the volumes could be found outside the back rooms of university libraries. The rarer tomes must have been worth a fortune, even in their deteriorated condition. He owned copies of d'Erlette's *Cultes des Goules*, the *Liyuhh*, Borellus' forbidden text, von Junzt's *Unaussprechlichen Kulten*, and others I'd never even heard of. I held Joseph Curwen's own handwritten copy of Bryce's *Biblia Sinistre* in my hands! Hell, even Miskatonic University doesn't have a copy of that! Yet with all those treasures around him, Wilbur still craved a Latin edition of the *Necronomicon* printed in 17th century Spain. I was allowed freedom of his library, but I didn't have much interest in things about 'blasphemous outer spheres.'"

Galvin experienced a second coughing fit, this one worse than the first. In the meantime, Jeffrey managed to replace the tape in the recorder with a fresh one.

"Wilbur needed help translating certain passages from those books, only a few of which were actually written in archaic Greek and Latin. That's the reason I was there. Wilbur spoke a crude dialect he'd picked up from his mother, but his was such a brilliant mind that he could easily translate French, German, Arabic, and even enciphered passages without my aid."

James asked Galvin to wait until he got back from the restroom before proceeding.

Jeffrey stayed with Galvin. "Why weren't you afraid of Wilbur like everyone else?" he asked the shadowed figure seated across from him. "His appearance must have been intimidating."

Galvin chuckled softly and answered, "Wilbur was very special, and I guess I saw that right away. Armitage has since made Wilbur sound like a goat-faced monster, but people didn't scream and run when he came around, so even you must realize that was an exaggeration."

James returned. As he sat down, he tried to check the alcohol level in the whiskey bottle as inconspicuously as possible.

"You needn't worry, son," Galvin snidely commented, "it takes a lot more than one bottle to get me lathered."

The dim lighting hid the blush that immediately flooded James' face.

Jeffrey turned to James in an attempt to dispel the awkwardness of the situation. "Mr. Galvin," he proffered, "was just about to tell me how special Wilbur was."

Somewhat amused at his interviewers' apprehension, Galvin resumed his discourse. "That's right. For instance, we'd sneak out at night to chase across the countryside in the dark while the others slept. Wilbur would steer us safely around the deep ravines and gorges that I could barely see, past what they called the Devil's Hop Yard, to the rounded hilltops where folks said the Pocumtuck Indians had buried their dead. I'd squat among circles of ancient stone pillars while he set up an odd sort of telescope of his own design. Through that telescope we'd gaze upon a sky the rest of mankind has never seen, and he'd talk for hours about the endless universes revolving above us, just as if he'd toured them personally. What we now call nebulas, he claimed were colossal sprays of blood marking the demise of entities beyond imagination. Other entities, he said, had come to Earth eons ago and more were yet to come. He taught me about Cthulhu, Dagon, and the Winged Ones, and told me the story of Qom-maq, the blender of flesh, who'd been the scourge of ancient Crete. I'd lie next to him in the cool grass while he wove his wonderful tales. He made it easy to stare into the sky and envision other worlds as he described them."

"That's incredible!" exclaimed Jeffrey.

"Not as incredible as Wilbur himself," Galvin responded dreamily. After a few moments, he reluctantly moved on to the next phase of his account.

"Once he felt sure he could trust me, he told me about his twin brother, the 'Other' we called him, who was confined in the upper half of the house. Wilbur confessed to being only half human himself, though I didn't really believe him until later."

James nearly jumped out of his seat, exclaiming, "You mean you got a good look at him and even that didn't scare you off?"

Galvin rolled his eyes. "There's a great deal more to a person than what reveals itself to the eye, son; the ability to see beyond the physical is about the only thing that raises us above the level of monsters ourselves. All I knew was that the boy was deformed below the waist to some extent. He was always real concerned with privacy whenever he bathed, so it was obvious he was ashamed of his difference. He said the other kids had made fun of him when he'd tried to make friends; you know how cruel kids can be, and I saw the proof of pain in his eyes. He hated his difference and always fought to keep it hidden.

"I tried to get him over it, show him it didn't matter to me. I even kept talking to him on a couple occasions to keep him in the room while I took a bath, figuring he'd eventually loosen up, seeing as how I was no Adonis myself, but it didn't work. He just sat there staring at me all over, like he was studying me as an example of how folks are supposed to look. I just wanted him to accept himself for who he was and stop worrying about what anyone else thought." He stared directly at James. "You'd best get that disgusted look off your face damn quick, young man, or I'm done talking."

An embarrassed James apologized, then added, "But you didn't actually see, well, what Armitage and the others saw when Wilbur died, did you?"

Galvin responded forcefully, "No, I didn't, but Armitage had folks scared half out of their wits! I doubt any of them even know what they really saw that night! Certainly no one had the guts to refute the shiftless bastard later on, after his own written account made him out to be some kind of saviour."

His outburst was greeted with silence, so after a moment, a calmer Galvin continued. "Wilbur said Old Whateley'd done his bare best to convince Wilbur that the Other was some kind of avatar that needed nurturing until the stars came into the proper alignment for some legendary cosmic armageddon to enter our dimension through some kind of gate. As a child, Wilbur accepted his grandfather's philosophy, but as his human aspect became dominant and started thinking for itself, he began to look for a way to thwart the Other or at least keep it under control. He said all he needed were some special incantations, but only Old Whateley knew where to find those spells and he wasn't about to tell as long as he had any doubts about Wilbur's loyalty to the cause.

"Wilbur said I shouldn't worry about any cosmic disaster, though, and assured me the stars wouldn't be right yet for decades. He also said any premature attempt to open the gate would bring immediate misfortune upon the conjurer.

"He told me as much as he dared, fearing my curiosity might prove dangerous to me if I knew too much. I think he was also afraid of scaring me off and losing the only friend he knew he was ever likely to have."

During the awkward pause that followed, James and Jeffrey pretended to check their notes and recorder, respectively; obviously Galvin felt very strongly about Wilbur Whateley.

"Old Whateley spent most of his time repairing the house, whether it needed it or not," Galvin suddenly began again. "He was a nervous old codger who fussed over his pathetic livestock incessantly, often spending half the night transferring steers back and forth from the barn to holding pens he'd built on the far side of the house, adjacent to the ramp to the second story.

"Wilbur woke me up one night in August about ten o'clock. He said Old Whateley'd been taken seriously ill and he was going to Osborn's store in Dunwich to call the doctor in Aylesbury. He asked me to help Lavinia watch over the old man until he got back. I wanted to go with him since the townspeople were afraid of him, but he pointed out that no one would recognize him if he wore his grandfather's old-fashioned bang-up coat with a three-cornered hat cocked down low. He knew he could make better time alone on horseback than two of us could in the old wagon. Still, I worried about him as dogs always attacked him on sight; it got so bad at one point that he had to carry a pistol to protect himself from them.

"By the time Dr. Houghton arrived, the old man was nearly gone; Wilbur agreed, pointing out the whippoorwills that had gathered *en masse* around the house. Even the doctor noticed their cries were keeping time with Old Whateley's breathing. Houghton did his best, but Whateley's heart finally gave out long about two in the morning."

James jumped in with a question. "Were you actually in the room when Wizard Whateley passed away? Supposedly he said something very special to

Wilbur just before he died."

"You're baiting me now, son, just to see if I know what I'm talking about," Galvin answered.

The researcher admitted as much and offered an apology.

"Oh, I'd do the same if I was you," Galvin remarked. "Yes, I was in the room. I heard the same as Doc Houghton heard, but he didn't understand what was going on. The old man knew Wilbur wanted to keep the Other captive, so on his deathbed, the old man tried to bend Wilbur to his will. The first time I heard the name Yog-Sothoth was when, with his dying breath, the old wizard reminded Wilbur that his brother required constant feeding and room to expand. He also told Wilbur about a certain passage in the Spanish edition of the *Necronomicon* that would make the Other strong enough to reproduce and savage the planet.

"What Houghton didn't know was that Wilbur had absolutely no intention of carrying out that part of Old Whateley's instructions. Was he supposed to argue with a dying man? Hell, not much of it made sense to me, especially with the ruckus those damn birds were making outside.

"But the instant Old Whateley died, all the birds fell silent at exactly the same instant. Wilbur told me the locals believed whippoorwills gathered when someone was about to die; if they dispersed after the person died, like they did that night, it meant the person's soul had escaped them. I was never too clear on it all, but I guess the birds are supposed to be like psychopomps that escort the souls they catch to heaven or hell. When they miss, the soul remains earth-bound and can trouble the living. After all I've seen, I have to consider there might be some truth in that particular superstition.

"Wilbur asked me to stay on after his grandfather died. I helped him bury Old Whateley up near Sentinel Hill, then left Wilbur and his mother to say their farewells in private. Wilbur held up, but Lavinia broke down and cried some. She seemed to get progressively worse after that day, such that we worried about her sanity, and Wilbur wouldn't allow her to light fires up on Sentinel Hill anymore, like she'd always done before twice a year. He told her the neighbors didn't like it, and he didn't want her continuing the wizardry.

"The first thing he did after the burial was clear the house of all the old man's occult trappings. He single-handedly carried over a hundred jars and bottles out of Old Whateley's room and stacked them in a pyramid of glass behind and away from the house. Every one of the bottles contained some bit of alien monstrosity preserved for reasons I feared to ask. I'd wager your best biologists couldn't identify even half the things floating in those jars. After he emptied the room, he did some chanting and arm waving over the jars and such, then doused it all with kerosene and set it afire. Some of the bottles exploded right away from the heat, but some of the other specimens burned red hot for more than two days.

"Once that chore was done, Wilbur seemed to have more peace of mind. A little after that, he started boarding up the unused parts of the downstairs. I helped whenever I could, but the work took his mind off his troubles, and he said there was no rush."

Jeffrey abruptly took advantage of the lull to ask a question. "What did he tell you about Yog-Sothoth?"

A deep ridge formed upon the heavily creased brow of the old man. "I don't recall all that much of what he said about most of that hocus pocus stuff; I guess I just wasn't all that interested. But I can't forget his telling me that this Yog-Sothoth was father to both him and the Other. It belonged, he said, in some other dimension, but it wanted to infest this one too. He said it was a big formless thing that could only come into our world at all when it stretched itself out into threads or tendrils so thin that they could squeeze through the empty space between neutrons, electrons, and the like. The Other was meant to prepare the way for the time when a gate would open, giving its daddy full access to our universe, but Wilbur was dead set against letting that come about."

"Did Wilbur explain how Lavinia had a child by this non-material being?" Jeffrey asked.

Galvin chuckled. "I'd of thought you boys would be smart enough to figure that one out for yourselves! Seems self-evident to me that Wizard Whateley allowed himself to be possessed for an incestuous encounter with his daughter. You've read Armitage's account, don't you recall that Curtis Whateley described the giant face on top of the monster as bearing an unmistakable likeness to Wizard Whateley?

"Wilbur told me about it after Armitage came to the farm to check on him."

The mention of the famous doctor at that point in the story caught Galvin's listeners by surprise. "Armitage wrote that he met Wilbur at the Miskatonic library in 1926!" James objected.

Galvin smiled. "Is that so? Well, to begin with, there are a lot of things Armitage felt it prudent not to include in his 'authoritative' account. But if you read it carefully, you'll note he mentioned being sent to the Whateley farm in 1925 as a 'scholarly correspondent' for the university."

"But that makes no sense," Jeffrey piped in. "Why would the university send a head librarian somewhere as a correspondent? Let alone to the Whateley farm? The public lost all interest in the Whateleys long before 1925!"

"Curious, ain't it?" Galvin sniggered. "The truth is, Armitage had been visiting the farm for years; he and Wizard Whateley were old friends! After Old Whateley passed away, Armitage felt obliged to drop in, just to make sure

Wilbur was following the instructions his grandfather had given him. Armitage only mentioned the visit in writing because he was seen there by someone he hadn't expected to be there—me. I was introduced, then Old Whateley whisked Armitage off to talk in private."

Jeffrey couldn't believe his ears. "Mr. Galvin, are you saying Dr. Armitage knew about the twins and Old Whateley's plans for destroying mankind long before he encountered Wilbur at the library? That's diametrically opposed to everything the man has stood for!"

Galvin laughed out loud before adding, "You're slow, but I think you're finally starting to catch on!

"Armitage had what you could call a hidden agenda and the old bastard wasn't exactly pleased to hear Wilbur didn't want anything to do with him and Old Whateley's plan. By the time Armitage left the farm that day, he was madder than a hornet! He threatened Wilbur up and down, but Wilbur wouldn't budge. Wilbur wanted to find the spell that would reverse the Other's growth or even kill it if need be, but he didn't dare tell that to Armitage. But Armitage counted on Wilbur changing his mind—least he counted on it 'til Wilbur came to his library and asked to see the complete edition of the *Necronomicon* of the mad Arab. After reading the section Old Whateley had pointed out to him, Wilbur started looking for spells he could use to control or destroy the Other, unaware that Armitage was spying on him over his shoulder. When Armitage figured out what Wilbur was up to, he denied Wilbur further access to the book and ordered him out of the library.

"The bastard later admitted he'd written to the head librarians of every library that had a copy of the *Necronomicon*, advising them not to allow Wilbur or anyone named Galvin access."

James was outraged, unable to accept this new view of Armitage. "Dr. Armitage was a respected scholar!" he protested. "He held a doctorate from Princeton and a Doctor of Letters degree from Cambridge!"

Chuckling to himself, Galvin challenged, "Have you ever wondered why such a brilliant scholar ended up as a simple librarian? Truth is, the university's Board of Governors got wind of his delvings into certain unacceptable aspects of the occult, and they decided it would be best to put him where they could keep an eye on him."

Galvin openly relished the disillusioned shock now apparent on both writers' faces. After harboring Armitage's secret for so many years, it gave him immense pleasure to slaughter that sacred cow. He allowed the pair a few minutes for recovery before resuming his revelations.

"In the meantime, Wilbur managed to keep the Other fed with the cattle he got from Earl Sawyer. The house started smelling something fierce though, 'cos he couldn't always get all the chewed up carcasses out. The darn thing was getting unpredictable and didn't always recognize him anymore. Wilbur said its mind never developed beyond that of a human infant's despite its size, and it wouldn't be long before its bulk would require the whole of the house. Wilbur was still growing too, though he kept hoping to find some way to stop. By early '26, he measured over seven feet tall."

A sadness seeped into Galvin's voice as he began to impart the next chapter of his incredible tale. "Just before Halloween, or Hallowmass as they called it, that same year, we lost Lavinia. Wilbur and I were wrestling with a particularly knotty passage from Vogel's *Von denen Verdammten* one afternoon when Lavinia burst into the room in a full-blown panic. She was drenched in sweat and raving like a madwoman. Wilbur held her and stroked her hair for a while, trying to calm her, but she pushed him away, screaming: 'I cain't deny him nay longer! He needs 'es ma, an' not yew ner n'b'dy else'll keep me from a-goan' to him nay more!'

"There'd been a god-awful sloshing noise coming from the second floor all morning, but I never figured if it was a reaction to Lavinia's hysterics or vice-versa. Sounded like a herd of elephants was stomping around up there. I'd always tried to ignore the noise from up there before, but God himself must o' heard the uproar that day.

"Wilbur asked me to step outside while he reasoned with Lavinia's madness. She was twitching and a-fighting him, but Wilbur held her fast. Nobody could match Wilbur's strength by then, let alone a frail little thing like Lavinia. He finally got her to lie down in her room, and I heard him chanting or singing to her for more than an hour before she settled enough for him to leave her. He went back to his studies, thinking she was asleep, but as it turned out, she was just pretending."

James interrupted to ask, "Do you think Wilbur loved his mother?"

The question seemed to catch Galvin off guard, causing him to hesitate before answering. "I guess I never heard him say it right out, though he once recalled the fond memories he had of wandering through the hills with her when he was real young. Sometimes he spoke harshly to her, and we both ignored her ramblings, but when she was hurting, he was always real tender with her. It was kinda hard not to feel protective of her, especially when she'd get all worked up and confused."

Galvin drained the last of the bottle into his own glass. Jeffrey rushed off for another even before Galvin could set the empty bottle down. He rejoined them moments later, apparently anxious for Galvin to begin the next phase of his narration.

"Just before sunset, I heard a door slam and someone ran past my door toward the hillside. I poked my head out the door and caught sight of Lavinia's tiny, crinkly-haired form careening at top speed up the wood incline toward the boarded-up window on the east gable. The moment she reached the top, she let fly with the ax she'd brought with her, trying to hack the lock off and get inside. I was at a loss for action 'til Wilbur ran out of the house and saw what she was up to. I offered to help, but he was sure she'd gone mad and that there was no way to stop her. He told me to stay in the shed, saying he'd call me if there was anything I could do."

Galvin sighed. "A while later, I heard Lavinia screaming like all possessed. I headed for the door, but Wilbur had locked me in. I had heard him chanting or singing in his room just before the screaming started, so I knew it wasn't him that was hurting Lavinia."

"Were you frightened?" asked James.

"I was too busy trying to figure out what was going on to be too afraid. I couldn't believe the Other would hurt its own mother, but then I got scared for her when I heard whippoorwills calling. They got so loud I didn't hear the lock turn when Wilbur opened my door a while later.

"He didn't try to talk over the racket the birds were making, but I could see tears on his cheeks. He just walked over to where I was lying on the bed and picked me up. He set me on my feet, looked long and hard into my eyes, then wrapped both arms around me. I found myself returning his embrace, and we stayed there holding and comforting each other for some time. Then the tone of the birds changed, getting louder and wilder, so finally Wilbur let go of me."

James rose half way out of his seat in excitement. "Didn't he offer any sort of explanation?"

Galvin nodded. "All he said was, 'The 'wills got 'er, Abe. She'll rest easy naow. She ne'er understood all that Gran'pa got her inta; she wuz jest his pawn.'"

None of the trio spoke for several minutes. Finally, Jeffrey focused on the fresh bottle of whiskey and poured a round of drinks. All three joined in a silent toast in memory of Lavinia.

"The birds didn't fully disperse 'til dawn. Wilbur climbed the ramp with me behind him. He told me to stay back while he went through the gable to fetch Lavinia.

"My curiosity got the best of me when he didn't come right out, so I climbed up high enough to peek in. There's no way I can describe the feeling that came over me when I spotted Wilbur, standing just a little way inside, struggling in what looked like a tug o' war with Lavinia's limp and lifeless body floating like some kind of Kewpie doll about six feet in the air. Wilbur had told me the Other was invisible, but I guess I hadn't expected to see the walls right through it like there was nothing there at all. I could only really be sure there was something there by the way Lavinia's body was being pulled back and forth. The Other was grunting and whining like a frustrated child clinging onto its favorite toy.

"It let out a squeal when it saw me gaping at it in the doorway, and it let go of Lavinia. Wilbur ran by me, cradling what was left of his mother in his arms and yelling for me to shut the door on the thing, to hold it as best I could until he got back with new locks from the shed, which I did. Wilbur carried the withered body downstairs and laid Lavinia out in her room, then returned to secure the door with new locks and boards.

"Lavinia's clothes were all ripped up and her body was covered with big round welts from top to bottom. She'd been sucked dry as a leaf."

"But why did she feel compelled to go in there?" It was James this time.

Galvin poured another drink without bothering to offer the bottle to the others. He slammed it on the table before answering in a voice choked with emotion. "Wilbur just said, 'She a'ways felt it wuz her duty ta suckle us both.'

"He wouldn't accept help with her burial, and he didn't bother notifying the authorities. After performing some kind of esoteric service over her body, he never spoke her name in my presence again."

The control returned to Galvin's voice as he continued.

"Wilbur didn't need my help with translating any more, but he begged me not to leave as he couldn't bear the idea of being there alone. He had to stay to keep the Other contained. I told him I'd become too attached to just leave him there.

"During the summer of 1927, Wilbur repaired the large tool shed next to mine and moved the wood-burning stove from the house to outside so heat could be piped into both sheds. Then we started moving his books and make-shift desk from the house to Wilbur's shed as the Other was getting way too big for the upper half of the house. I boarded up the windows and doors of the house's ground floor while Wilbur gutted the remaining partitions between rooms and floors.

"That winter saw Wilbur doubling his efforts to get access to the *Necronomicon*; we didn't know then that Armitage had already contacted the libraries to warn them against him. They wouldn't even allow him to copy particular pages from the book. He was so desperate for a way to control his own growth as well as that of the Other that he travelled on horseback all the way to the library at Cambridge. Armitage had done his work well, though, so Wilbur wasn't allowed near the book."

Again Galvin paused, hesitant to relive the next series of events.

"We managed to keep things in check all that winter and on into 1928, but by late summer it became obvious that the Other was quickly outgrowing the old farmhouse. The walls bulged whenever it turned around, and its movement in general became very constrained. Something had to be done to stop its growth before all hell broke loose. That's when Wilbur realized he had to try and steal the book from the library at Miskatonic. He wouldn't allow me to come with him as someone had to keep feeding the Other while he was away or it would break out for sure and go on a killing spree."

"You blame Armitage for Wilbur's death, don't you?" James asked.

Galvin reacted adamantly. "You're damn right I blame him! He knew Wilbur couldn't control the Other any longer without the spell, yet he did everything possible to force the crisis. He wanted Wilbur to come crawling to him and agree to his hellish plan. The only other option was for Wilbur to steal the book. Armitage knew that too. Why do you think, knowing how dogs universally hated Wilbur, Armitage suddenly added watch dogs in addition to the regular security at the library? When he found Wilbur bleeding to death on the library floor, Armitage did nothing to save him. He feigned shock at seeing such an alien monster simply for the benefit of his colleagues!"

Neither interviewer knew what to say, so they waited silently for Galvin's fury to subside. His story was fascinating despite many surprising revelations.

"Wilbur felt there was a real good chance he'd be arrested while attempting to steal the book, so he made me promise to leave if he hadn't returned within a week. It never occurred to me that worse might happen, but it must have occurred to him.

"Before he left, he said he could feel the Other's claustrophobia. As often happens with twins, he and the Other shared strong emotional feelings to a certain extent. He said it felt trapped and afraid.

"I hesitated to leave, however, hoping my friend would come back safely with the means to halt or even reverse the Other's growth.

"I decided it was time to leave when I had used up all the cows to feed the Other. That was on the first of September. Earl Sawyer had been providing them regularly for that purpose, but he heard the creaking and the straining sounds coming from the house and it frightened him away. I admit I was afraid too, so on the ninth I decided to leave. I was packing a bag when I heard a real loud noise, like the logs of the farmhouse wrenching and cracking apart. I stepped out of the shed to get a better look, and the whole world exploded around me.

"It was pouring down rain so hard I could barely see. Doors, plaster, and glass filled the air; huge chunks of walls were flying in every direction. The farmhouse had been ripped into sections, parts of which were still moving. A huge chunk of roof floated in the air, the gables and chimney still intact. Mud was splashing up in waves and an ungodly stench hit me so hard, I threw up.

"The next thing I knew, something slimy grabbed one of my legs and thrust me thirty feet or so into the air. I couldn't see what had me, but it felt like a mass of wet, living rope winding and knotting all over me. I tried to get a grip on whatever held me, but it was like trying to grasp an armload of oily snakes—only these were as thick as my thigh. I could feel mouths clamping down and biting me right through my clothes, and I saw the rain turn red as it struck my body. My chest felt like it was being squeezed in a vise, so with the first air I caught, I started screaming and hollering for all I was worth.

"Everything was getting dark and blurry but I fought against passing out. All at once, a desperate clarity came over me and pushed away the fear. Without thinking, I began yelling at my invisible attacker, 'I'm Abe, Wilbur's friend! Don't you recognize me? I'm a friend! Please, put me down—you're killing me!'"

Galvin paused. "You may not believe me, but all of a sudden my feet touched the ground and the things that were binding me let go all at once."

Unable to restrain his excitement, James leaned back in his chair and shouted, "Jesus!"

Galvin, who had almost crept over the table toward his listeners, also leaned back, releasing his audience from the stifling tension he had produced as he described his ordeal.

An excited Jeffrey begged, "But why did it let go of you?"

After a moment, Galvin whispered, "I believe it remembered me from its telepathic link with Wilbur; it experienced Wilbur's trust and love for me. It was as if Wilbur reached out from beyond the grave to save me."

Galvin now sat perfectly upright in his chair. His hands were shaking to the extent that he spilled half his drink even before he could raise it to his mouth. The second bottle lay empty on the table before him.

"I never did actually see what the Other looked like, but from what I heard later about it, that was probably a blessin'.

"I guess I blacked out then, 'cos Earl Sawyer's kid stumbled across me the next morning. He fetched his daddy, who said I was more dead than alive when he found me lying half inside a footprint as big as an old hogshead barrel and over a foot deep. They took me to Dr. Houghton and so saved my life. Nearly all my ribs were crushed, my sternum was fractured, and I was bleeding all over. I swore all three to secrecy about my presence, hoping Armitage would assume the Other had killed me. He'd have come after me if he thought I was still alive."

For several minutes Galvin sat quietly in his chair, as if he had finished his tale. The whir of tape rewinding alerted Jeffrey to stop his recorder. He felt a certain relief that Galvin had reached the end of his tale before his speech got any worse. He had been slipping more and more into colloquial speech patterns for several minutes.

"Well," offered James, "I guess that's about it then. Armitage killed the Other up on Sentinel Hill for whatever motive, and the day was saved!"

Galvin leaned forward with a disgusted look on his face and sneered, "And I thought you boys was smart!"

James stumbled over a few syllables in search of some response, but Galvin wasn't finished yet.

"The whole story's in Wilbur's diary, which I read after he left for Arkham; the code wasn't all that hard to figure out. Later on, when Armitage got the diary, he read it and only let his buddies see bits and pieces so he could interpret the text to mean whatever he wanted it to mean. He burned it before anybody else got a chance to see it. Now, just how scholarly does an action like that sound to you? Yet if you read his account carefully, you'll see the wily old bastard couldn't resist tossing in a few tantalizing clues to the truth."

Galvin was obviously getting drunk, occasionally slurring a few words. "Okay, so I'll explain it to you kids. The Indians had been performing weird rites in the area in and around Dunwich for over four hundred years before Wizard Whateley came along and figured out just exactly what they were up to. And he was just crazy enough to try and do the same.

"The Indians had been breeding their women with things from other dimensions, but they were smart enough to keep the offspring imprisoned in underground caves. It was safer that way and the hybrids grew slower in the dark. Old Whateley'd thought he'd do the same, 'cept Lavinia gave birth to twins and refused to part with either of them. Living above ground, both of the twins grew a whole lot faster than their half-brothers and half-sisters below the ground."

Gasps escaped the mouths of his listeners as Galvin rambled on.

"You mean you never wondered what it was that has been rumbling and moaning under the hills? It's been consistently reported since the first white men settled on Dunwich land!

"Armitage didn't destroy the Other and make everything safe! That's all just a load of crap. Did anyone actually see what happened when the lightning struck? Nobody but Armitage and those two fools he had believing anything he told them. He said himself that the damn thing couldn't be killed! It sought out the altar stone because that stone was the door to an entrance to the pits below, where it could be safe! The Other called out for help in English, but the eyewitnesses said they heard an unearthly calling from the altar stone as well! All Armitage did was call down a bolt of lightning that lifted the altar stone up just long enough for the Other to squeeze its elastic form through and down to where the others were just waiting!

"Ain't you figured out that Sentinel Hill and all the hills in Dunwich are hollow? They're rounded 'cos the things underneath are growing and slowly pushing the earth up higher and higher. The standing stones mark the hills where the Indians 'planted' the spawn of Yog-Sothoth!"

"But Dr. Armitage..." James began.

"Dr. Armitage my arse," interrupted Galvin. "That son of a bitch high-tailed it back to Arkham and wrote his lying account before going back to live with his family..."

Jeffrey started to butt in, but fell silent after Galvin finished his sentence.

"...in Innsmouth."

"What?" James cried out in disbelief.

"Yessir, I said Innsmouth!" Galvin exclaimed. "The only thing he didn't know was that his parents were taken away by the FBI when they raided Innsmouth. And the ones they took away were the ones that weren't human, and neither was Armitage, though he covered it well. Folks think he took sick and died soon after that day on Sentinel Hill, but I defy any man to show me the record of his death."

Both Jeffrey and James were stunned.

"At least I put one over on the old bastard; I got all the Whateley gold. He wanted it bad, but Wilbur gave it to me before he left. I had it on me when Earl found me, and I've been living on it ever since. Look here if you don't believe me," he added as he tossed two shiny coins onto the table.

The two authors snatched up the coins and stared at them in disbelief. One bore the imprint of Arabic lettering that they would later learn spelled out 'Irem,' a lost city of Arabian myth; the other was impressed with the easily recognizable features of Augustus Caesar.

"Yessir, the Other and hundreds more like him are down there still, just growing and waiting for the day they're full grown and the stars all line up as their signal. When that day comes, the earth'll rise up beneath our feet and they'll emerge to smite mankind by the millions—and nothing on this Earth can stop them!"

Galvin paused, belched, then concluded with a snicker, "If you boys finish your book in a real hurry, you just might get it published afore the apocalypse!"

FOR MY RESPECTED FRIEND, WILUM HOPFROG PUGMIRE

The Terror from the Depths

Fritz Leiber

Remember thee!
Ay, thou poor ghost, while memory holds a seat
In this distracted globe.

—HAMLET

The following manuscript was found in a curiously embossed copper and German silver casket of highly individual modern workmanship which was purchased at an auction of unclaimed property that had been held in police custody for the prescribed number of years in Los Angeles County, California. In the casket with the manuscript were two slim volumes of verse: *Azathoth and Other Horrors* by Edward Pickman Derby, Onyx Sphinx Press, Arkham, Massachusetts, and *The Tunneler Below* by Georg Reuter Fischer, Ptolemy Press, Hollywood, California. The manuscript was penned by the second of these poets, except for the two letters and the telegram interleafed into it. The casket and its contents had passed into police custody on March 16, 1937, upon the discovery of Fischer's mutilated body by his collapsed brick dwelling in Vultures Roost under circumstances of considerable horror.

Today one will search street maps of the Hollywood Hills area in vain for the unincorporated community of Vultures Roost. Shortly after the events narrated in these pages its name (already long criticized) was changed upon the urging of prudent real-estate dealers to Paradise Crest, which was in turn absorbed by the City of Los Angeles—an event not without parallel in that general neighborhood, as when after certain scandals best forgotten, the name of Runnymede was changed to Tarzana after the chief literary creation of its most illustrious and blameless inhabitant.

The magneto-optical method of detection referred to herein, "which has already discovered two new elements," is neither fraud nor fancy, but a technique highly regarded in the 1930s (though since discredited), as may be confirmed by consulting any table of elements from that period or the entries "alabamine" and "virginium" in *Webster's New International Dictionary*, second edition, unabridged. (They are not, of course, in today's tables.) While the "unknown master builder Simon Rodia" with whom Fischer's father conferred is the widely revered folk architect (now deceased) who created the matchlessly beautiful Watts Towers.

It is only with considerable effort that I can restrain myself from plunging into the very midst of a description of those unequivocally monstrous hints that have determined me to take—within the next eighteen hours and no later—a desperate and initially destructive step. There is much to write and only too little time in which to write it.

I myself need no written argument to bolster my beliefs. It is all more real to me than everyday experience. I have only to close my eyes to see Albert Wilmarth's horror-whitened long-jawed face and migraine-tormented brow. There may be something of clairvoyance in this, for I imagine his expression has not changed greatly since I last saw him. And I need not make the slightest effort to hear those hideously luring voices, like the susurrus of infernal bees and glorious wasps, which impinge upon an inner ear which I now can never and would never close. Indeed, as I listen to them, I wonder if there is anything to be gained from penning this necessarily outré document. It will be found—if it is found—in a locality where serious people do not attach any importance to strange revelations and where charlatanry is only too common. Perhaps that is well and perhaps I should make doubly sure by tearing up this sheet, for there is in my mind no doubt of the results that would follow a systematic, scientific effort to investigate those forces which have ambushed and shall soon claim (and perhaps welcome?) me.

I shall write, however, if only to satisfy a peculiar personal whim. Ever since I can remember I have been drawn to literary creation, but until this very day certain elusive circumstances and crepuscular forces have prevented my satisfactorily completing anything more than a number of poems, mostly short, and tiny prose sketches. It would interest me to discover if my new knowledge has freed me to some extent from those inhibitions. Time enough when I have completed this statement to consider the advisability of its destruction (before I perpetrate the greater and crucial destruction). Truth to tell, I am not especially moved by what may or may not happen to my fellow men; there have been profound influences (yes, from the depths indeed!) exerted upon my emotional growth and upon the ultimate direction of my loyalties—as will become clear to the reader in due course.

I might begin this narrative with a bald recital of the implications of the recorded findings of Professors Atwood and Pabodie's portable magneto-optic geo-scanner, or with Albert Wilmarth's horrendous revelations of the mind-shattering, planet-wide researches made during the past decade by a secret coterie of faculty members of far-off Miskatonic University in witch-haunted, shadow-beset Arkham and a few lonely colleagues in Boston and Providence, Rhode Island, or with the shivery clues that with nefarious innocence have found their way even into the poetry I have written during the past few years. If I did that, you would be immediately convinced that I was psychotic. The *reasons* that led me, step by step, to my present awesome convictions, would appear as progressive *symptoms*, and the monstrous horror behind it all would seem a shuddersome paranoid fantasy. Indeed, that will probably be your final judgment in any case, but I will nevertheless tell you what happened just as it happened to me. Then you will have the same opportunity as I had to discern, if you can, just where reality left off and imagination took up and where imagination stopped and psychosis supervened.

Perhaps within the next seventeen hours something will happen or be revealed that will in part substantiate what I shall write. I do think so, for there is yet untold cunning in the decadent cosmic order which has entrapped me. Perhaps they will not let me finish this narrative; perhaps they will anticipate my own resolve. I am almost sure they have only held off thus far because they are sure I will do their work for them. No matter.

The sun is just now rising, red and raw, over the treacherous and crumbling hills of Griffith Park (Wilderness were a better designation). The sea fog still wraps the sprawling suburbs below, its last vestiges are sliding out of high, dry Laurel Canyon, but far off to the south I can begin to discern the black congeries of scaffold oil wells near Culver City, like stiff-legged robots massing for the attack. And if I were at the bedroom window that opens to the northwest, I would see night's shadows still lingering in the precipitous wilds of Hollywoodland above the faint, twisting, weed-encroached, serpent-haunted trails I have limped along daily for most of my natural life, tracing and retracing them ever more compulsively.

I can turn off the electric light now; my study is already pierced by shafts of low, red sunlight. I am at my table, ready to write the day through. Everything around me has the appearance of eminent normality and security. There are no signs remaining of Albert Wilmarth's frantic midnight departure with the magneto-optic apparatus he brought from the East, yet as if by clairvoyance I can see his long-jawed horror-sucked face as he clings automatically to the steering wheel of his little Austin scuttling across the desert like a frightened beetle, the geo-scanner lying on the seat beside him. This day's sun has reached him before me as he flees back toward his deeply beloved, impossibly distant New England. That sun's smoky red blaze must be in his fear-wide eyes, for I know that no power can turn him back toward the land that slips uncouth into the titan Pacific. I bear him no resentment—I have no reason to. His nerves were shattered by the terrors he bravely insisted on helping to investigate for ten long years against his steadier comrades' advice. And at the very end, I am certain, he saw horrors beyond imagining. Yet he waited to ask me to go with him and only I know how much that must have cost him. He gave me my opportunity to escape; if I had wanted to, I could have made the attempt.

But I believe my fate was decided many years ago.

My name is Georg Reuter Fischer. I was born in 1912 of Swiss parents in the city of Louisville, Kentucky, with an inwardly twisted right foot which might have been corrected by a brace, except that my father did not believe in interfering with the workings of Nature, his deity. He was a mason and stonecutter of great physical strength, vast energy, remarkable intuitive gifts (a dowser for water, oil, and metals), great natural artistry, unschooled but profoundly self-educated. A little after the Civil War, when he was a young boy, he had immigrated to this country with his father, also a mason, and upon the death of the latter, inherited a small but profitable business. Late in life he married my mother, Marie Reuter, daughter of a farmer for whom he had dowsed not only a well but a deposit of granite worth quarrying. I was the child of their age and their only child, coddled by my mother and the object of my father's more thoughtful devotion. I have few memories of our life in Louisville, but those few are eminently wholesome ones: visions of an ordered, cheerful household, of many cousins and friends, of visitings and laughter, and two great Christmas celebrations; also memories of fascinatedly watching my father at his stonecutting, bringing a profusion of flowers and leaves to life from death-pale granite.

And I will say here, because it is important to my story, that I afterward learned that our Fischer and Reuter relatives considered me exceptionally intelligent for my tender age. My father and mother always believed this, but one must allow for parental bias.

In 1917 my father profitably sold his business and brought his tiny family west, to build with his own hands a last home in this land of sunlight, crumbling sandstones, and sea-spawned hills, Southern California. This was in part because doctors had advised it as essential for the sake of my mother's failing health, slow victim of the dread tubercular scourge, but my father had always had a strong yearning for clear skies, year-round heat, and the primeval sea, a deep conviction that his destiny somehow lay west and was involved with Earth's hugest ocean: from which perhaps the moon was torn.

My father's deep-seated longing for this outwardly wholesome and bright, inwardly sinister and eaten-away landscape, where Nature herself presents the naïve face of youth masking the corruptions of age, has given me much food for thought, though it is in no way a remarkable longing. Many people migrate here, healthy as well as sick, drawn by the sun, the promise of perpetual summer, the broad if arid fields. The only unusual circumstance worthy of note is that there is a larger sprinkling than might be expected of persons of professed mystical and utopian bent. The Brothers of the Rose, the Theosophists, the Foursquare Gospelers, the Christian Scientists, Unity, the Brotherhood of the Grail, the spiritualists, the astrologers—all are here and many more besides. Believers in the need of return to primitive states and primitive wisdoms, practitioners of pseudo-disciplines dictated by pseudo-sciences—yes, even a few overly sociable hermits—one finds them everywhere; the majority awaken only my pity and distaste, so lacking in logic and avid for publicity are they. At no time—and let me emphasize this—have I been at all interested in their doings and in their ignorantly parroted principles, except possibly from the viewpoint of comparative psychology.

And they were brought here by that excessive love of sunlight which characterizes most faddists of any sort and that urge to find an unsettled, unorganized land in which utopias might take root and burgeon, untroubled by urbane ridicule and tradition-bred opposition—the same urge that led the Mormons to desert-guarded Salt Lake City, their paradise of Deseret. This seems an adequate explanation, even without bringing in the fact that Los Angeles, a city of retired farmers and small merchants, a city made hectic by the presence of the uncouth motion-picture industry, would naturally attract charlatans of all varieties. Yes, that explanation is still sufficient to me, and I am rather pleased, for even now I should hate to think that those hideously alluring voices a-mutter with secrets from beyond the rim of the cosmos *necessarily* have some dim, continent-wide *range*.

("The carven rim," they are saying now here in my study. "The proto-shoggoths, the diagramed corridor, the elder Pharos, the dreams of Cutlu...")

Settling my mother and myself at a comfortable Hollywood boardinghouse, where the activities of the infant film industry provided us with colorful distraction, my father tramped the hills in search of a suitable property, bringing to bear his formidable talent for locating underground water and desirable rock formations. During this period, it occurs to me now, he almost certainly pioneered those trails which it is my own invariable and ever more compulsive wont to walk. Within three months he had found and purchased the property he sought near a predominantly Alsatian and French settlement (a scatter of bungalows, no more) bearing the perhaps exaggeratedly picturesque name Vultures Roost, redolent of the Old West.

Clearing and excavation of the property revealed an upthrust stratum of fine-grained solid metamorphic rock, while a little boring provided an excellent well, to the incredulous astonishment of his initially hostile neighbors. My father kept his counsel and began, mostly with his own hands alone, to erect a brick structure of moderate size that by its layout and plans promised a dwelling of surpassing beauty. This occasioned more head-shaking and lectures on the unwisdom of building brick structures in a region where earthquakes were not unknown. They called it Fischer's Folly, I learned later. Little did they realize my father's skill and the tenacity of his masonry!

He bought a small truck and scoured the area as far south as Laguna Beach and as far north as Malibu, searching for the kilns that would provide him with bricks and tiles of requisite quality. In the end he sheathed the roof partly with copper, which has turned a beautiful green with the years. During these searches he became closely acquainted with the visionary and remarkably progressive Abbott Kinney, who was building the resort of Venice on the coast ten miles away, and with the swarthy, bright-eyed, unknown master builder Simon Rodia, self-educated like himself. All three men shared a rich vein of the poetry of stone, ceramics, and metals.

There must have been prodigious reserves of strength in the old man (for my father was that now, his hair whitely grizzled) to enable him to accomplish so much hard labor, for within two years my mother and I were able to move into our new home at Vultures Roost and take up our lives there.

I was delighted with my new surroundings and to be rejoined with my father, and only resentful of the time I must spend at school, to which my father drove me and from which he fetched me each day. I especially enjoyed rambling, occasionally with my father but chiefly by myself, through the wild, dry, rock-crowned hills, spry despite my twisted foot. My mother was fearful for me, especially because of the hairy brown and black tarantulas one sometimes encountered and the snakes, including venomous rattlers, but I was not to be restrained.

My father was happy, but also like a man in a dream as he worked unceasingly at the innumerable tasks, chiefly artistic, involved in finishing our home. It was a structure of rich beauty, though our neighbors continued to shake their heads and cluck dubiously at its hexagonal shape, partly rounded roof, thick walls of tightly mortared (though unreinforced) brick, and the area of brightly colored tile and floridly engraved stone. "Fischer's Folly," they'd whisper, and chuckle. But swarthy Simon Rodia nodded approvingly when he visited and once Abbott Kinney came to admire, driven in an expensive car by a black chauffeur with whom he seemed on terms of easy friendship.

My father's stone engravings were indeed quite fanciful and even a little disconcerting in their subject matter and location. One was in the basement's floor of natural rock, which he had smoothed. From time to time I'd watch him work on it. Desert plants and serpents seemed to be its subject matter, but as one studied it one became aware that there was much marine stuff too: serrated looping seaweeds, coiling eels, fishes that trailed tentacles, suckered octopus arms, and two giant squid eyes peering from a coral-crusted castle. And in its midst he boldly hewed in a flowery stone script, "The Gate of Dreams." My childish imagination was fired, but I was a little frightened too.

It was about this time—1921 or thereabouts—that my sleepwalking began, or at any rate showed signs of becoming disturbingly persistent. Several times my father found me at varying distances from the house along one of the paths I favored in my limping rambles and carried me tenderly back, chilled and shivering, for unlike Kentucky in summer, Southern California nights are surprisingly cold. And more than once I was found huddled and still asleep in our cellar alongside the grotesquely floor-set "Gate of Dreams" bas-relief-to which, incidentally, my mother had taken a dislike which she tried to conceal from my father.

At that time too my sleeping habits began to show other abnormalities, some of them contradictory. Although an active and apparently healthy boy of ten, I was still sleeping infancy's twelve hours or more a night. Yet despite this unusual length of slumber coupled with the restlessness my sleepwalking would seem to have indicated, I never dreamed or at any rate remembered dreams upon awakening. And with one notable exception this has been true for my entire life.

The exception occurred a little later on, when I was eleven or twelve—in 1923 or thereabouts. I remember those few dreams (there were no more than eight or nine of them) with matchless vividness. How else? —since they were my life's only ones and since...but I must not anticipate. At the time I was secretive about them, telling neither my father nor my mother, as if for fear my parents might worry or (children are odd!) disapprove, until one final night.

In my dream I would find myself making my way through low passages and tunnels, all crudely cut or perhaps *gnawed* from solid rock. Often I felt I was at a great distance under the earth, though why I thought this in my dream I cannot say, except that there was often a sensation of heat and an indescribable feeling of pressure from above. This last sensation was diminished almost to nothing at times, though. And sometimes I felt there were vast amounts of water far above me, though why I suspected this I cannot say, for the strange tunnels were always very dry. Yet in my dreams I came to assume that the burrows extended limitlessly under the Pacific.

There was no obvious source of illumination in the passages. My dream explanation of how I then managed to see them was fantastic, though rather ingenious. The floor of the tunnels was colored a strange purplish-green. This I explained in my dream as being the reflection of cosmic rays (which were much in the newspapers then, firing my boyish imagination) that came down through the thick rock above from distantmost outer space. The rounded ceiling of the tunnels, on the other hand, had a weird orange-blue glow. This, I seemed to know, was caused by the reflection of certain rays unknown to science that came up through the solid rock from the Earth's incandescent, constricted core.

The eerie mixed light revealed to me the strange engravings or ridgy pictures everywhere covering the tunnels' walls. They had a strong suggestion of the marine to them and also of the monstrous, yet they were strangely *generalized*, as if they were the mathematical diagrams of oceans and their denizens and of whole universes of alien life. If the *dreams* of a monster of supernatural mentality could be given visual shape, then they would be like those endless forms I saw on the tunnels' walls. Or if the *dreams* of such a monster were half materialized and able to move through such tunnels, *they would shape the walls in such fashion.*

At first in my dreams I was not conscious of having a body. I seemed to be a viewpoint floating along the tunnels at a definitely *rhythmic* rate, now faster, now slower.

And at first I never saw anything in those tormenting tunnels, though I was continually conscious of a fear that I might—a fear mixed with a desire. This was a most disturbing and exhausting feeling, which I could hardly have concealed upon awakening save that (with one exception) I never woke until my dream had played itself out, as it were, and my feelings were temporarily exhausted.

And then in my next dream I did begin to see things—creatures—in the tunnels, floating through them in the same general rhythmic fashion as I (or my viewpoint) progressed. They were worms about as long as a man and as thick as a man's thigh, cylindrical and untapering. From end to end, as many as a centipede's legs, were pairs of tiny wings, translucent like a fly's, which vibrated unceasingly, producing an unforgettably sinister low-pitched *hum*. They had no eyes—their heads were one circular mouth lined with rows of triangular teeth like a shark's. Although blind, they seemed able to sense each other at short distances and their sudden lurching swerves then to avoid colliding with each other held a particular horror for me. (It was a little like my lurching limp.)

In my very next dream I became aware of my own dream body, In brief, I was myself one of those same winged worms. The horror I felt was extreme, yet once more the dream lasted until its intensity was damped out and I could awaken with only the memory of terror, still able (I thought) to keep my dreams a secret.

The next time I had my dream it was to see three of the winged worms writhing in a wider section of tunnel where the sensation of pressure from above was minimal. I was still observer rather than participant, floating in my worm body in a narrower side passageway. How I was able to see while in one of the blind worm bodies, my dream logic did not explain.

They were worrying a rather small human victim. Their three snouts converged upon and covered his face. Their sinister buzzing had a hungry note and there were sucking sounds.

Blond hair, white pajamas, and (projecting from the right leg of those) a foot slightly shrunken and *twisted sharply inward* told me the victim was myself.

At that instant I was shaken violently, the scene swam, and through it my mother's huge terrorized face peered down at me with my father's anxious visage close behind.

I went into convulsions of terror, flailing my limbs, and I screamed and screamed. It was hours literally before I could be quieted down, and days before my father let me tell them my nightmare.

Thereafter he made a strict rule: that no one ever try to shake me awake, no matter how bad a nightmare I seemed to be having. Later I learned he'd watch me at such times with knitted brow, suppressing the impulse to rouse me and seeing to it that no one else tried to do so.

For several nights thereafter I fought sleep, but when my nightmare was never repeated and once more I could never remember having dreamed at all when I wakened, I quieted down and my life, both sleeping and waking, became very tranquil again. In fact, even my sleepwalking became less frequent, although I continued to sleep for abnormally long hours, a practice now encouraged by my father's injunction that I never be wakened unnaturally.

But I have since come to wonder whether this apparent diminishment of my unconscious night-wandering were not because I, or some fraction of me, had become more cunningly deceitful. *Habits* have in any case a way of slipping slowly from the serious notice of those around.

At times, though, I would catch my father looking at me speculatively, as though he would have dearly liked to talk with me of various deep matters, but in the end he would always restrain this impulse (if I had divined it rightly) and content himself with encouraging me in my school studies and rambling exercise despite the latter's dangers: there *were* more rattlesnakes about my favorite paths, perhaps because opossums and raccoons were being exterminated; he made me wear high laced shoes of stout leather.

And once or twice I got the impression that he and Simon Rodia were talking secretly about me when the latter visited.

On the whole my life was a lonely one and has remained so to this day. We had no neighbors who were friends, no friends who were neighbors. At first this was because of the relative isolation of our residence and the suspicion that Germanic names uniformly called forth in the years following the World War. But it continued even after we began to have more neighbors, tolerant newcomers. Perhaps things would have been different if my father had lived longer. (His health was good save for a touch of eyestrain—dancing colors he'd see briefly.)

But that was not to be. On that fatal Sunday in 1925 he had joined me on one of my customary walks and we had just reached one of my favorite spots when the ground gave way under his feet and he vanished from beside me, his startled exclamation dropped in pitch as he fell rapidly. For once his instinct for underground conditions had deserted him. There was a little scraping rumble as a few rocks and some gravel landslided, then silence. I approached the weed-fringed black hole on my belly and peered down fearfully.

From very far below (it sounded) I heard my father call faintly, "Georg! Get help!" His voice now had a strained, higher-pitched sound, as if his chest were being constricted.

"Father! I'm coming down," I cried, cupping my hands about my mouth, and I had thrust my twisted foot into the hole searching for support, when his frantic yet clearly enunciated words came up, his voice still higher-pitched and even more strained, as if he had to make a great effort to get sufficient breath for them: "Do *not* come down, Georg—you'll start an avalanche. Get help...a rope!"

After a moment's hesitation I withdrew my leg and set off for home at a hobbling gallop. My horror was heightened (or perhaps a little relieved) by a sense of the dramatic—early that year we had listened for weeks on the little crystal set I'd built to the radioed reports of the long protracted, exciting efforts (ultimately unsuccessful) to rescue Floyd Collins from where he'd got himself trapped in Sand Cave near Cave City, Kentucky. I suppose I anticipated some such drama for my father.

Most fortunately a young doctor was making a call in our neighborhood and he was foremost in the party of men I soon guided back to where my father had disappeared. No sounds at all came from the black hole, although we called and called, and I remember that a couple of men had begun to look at me dubiously, as if I'd invented the whole thing, when the courageous young doctor insisted against the advice of most on being lowered into the hole—they'd brought a strong rope *and* an electric flashlight.

He was a long time going down, descending about fifty feet in all while calls went back and forth, and almost as long being drawn up. When he emerged all smeared with sandy dirt—great orange smudges—it was to tell us (he made a point of laying his hand on my shoulder; I could see my mother hurrying up between two other women) that my father was inextricably wedged in down there with little more than his head exposed and that he was, to an absolute certainty, dead.

At that moment there was another grating rumble, and the black hole collapsed upon itself. One of the men standing on its edge was barely jerked to safety. My mother shrieked, threw herself down on the shaking brown weeds, and was drawn back too.

In the subsequent weeks it was decided that my father's body could not be recovered. Some bags of concrete and sand were dumped into what was left of the hole to seal it. My mother was forbidden to erect a monument at the spot, but in some sort of compensation—I didn't understand the logic of it—Los Angeles County presented her with a cemetery plot elsewhere. (It now holds her own body.) An unofficial funeral service conducted by a Latin American priest was eventually held at the spot, and Simon Rodia, defying the injunction, put up a small, nonsectarian ovoid monument of his own matchlessly tough white concrete bearing my father's name and beautifully inset with a vaguely aquatic or naval design in fragmented blue and green glass. It is still there.

After my father's death I became more withdrawn and brooding than ever, and my mother, a shy consumptive woman full of hysterical fears, hardly encouraged me to become sociable. In fact, almost as long as I can remember and certainly ever since Anton Fischer's tragic and abrupt demise, nothing has ever bulked large with me save my own brooding and this brick house set in the hills with its strange, queerly set stone carvings and the hills themselves, those sandy, spongy, salt-soaked, sun-baked hills. There has been altogether too much of them in my background: I have limped too long along their crumbling rims, under their cracked and treacherous overhanging sand-stones, and through the months-dry streams that thread their separating canyons. I have thought a great deal about the old days when, some Indians are said to have believed, the Strangers came down from the stars with the great meteor shower and the lizard men perished in the course of their fran-tic digging for water and the scaly sea men came tunneling in from their encampments beneath the vast Pacific which constituted a whole world to the west, extensive as that of the stars. I early developed too great a love for such savage fancies. Too much of my physical landscape has become the core of my mental landscape. And during the nights of my long, long sleepings, I hobbled through them both, I am somehow sure. While by day I had hor-rible fugitive visions of my father, underground, dead-alive, companied by the winged worms of my nightmare. Moreover, I developed the notion or fantasy that there was a network of *tunnels* underlying the paths I limped along and corresponding to them exactly, but at varying depths and coming closest to the surface at my "favorite spots."

("The legend of Yig," the voices are droning. "The violet wisps, the globu-lar nebulas, Canis Tindalos and their foul essence, the nature of the Doels, the tinted chaos, great Cutlu's minions..." I have made breakfast but I can-not eat. I thirstily gulp hot coffee.)

I would hardly keep harping on my sleepwalking and on the unnaturally long hours I spent so deeply asleep that my mother would vow that my mind was elsewhere, were it not associated with a lapse in the intellectual promise I was said to have shown in earlier years. True, I got along well enough in the semi-rural grade school I trudged to and later in the suburban high school to which a bus took me; true too that I early showed interest in many sub-jects and flashes of excellent logic and imaginative reasoning. The trouble was that I did not seem ever able to pursue any of those flashes and make a steady and persistent effort. There would be times when my teachers would worry my mother with reports of my unpreparedness and my disregard of assignments, though when examination time came I almost invariably man-aged to make a creditable showing. My interests in more personal directions, too, seemed to peter out very quickly. I was certainly peculiarly deficient in the power of attention. I remember often sitting down with a favorite book or text and then finding myself, minutes or hours later, turning over pages far ahead of anything I could remember reading. Sometimes only the memory of my father's injunctions to study, to study *deeply*, would keep me prodding on.

You may not think this matter worth mentioning. There is nothing strange in a lonely sheltered child failing to show great willpower and mental energy.

There is nothing strange in such a child becoming slothful, weak, and indecisive. Nothing strange— only much to pity and reproach. The powers that be know I reproached myself often enough, for as my father had encouraged me to, I felt a power and a capability somewhere in myself, but somehow inhibited. But there are only too many people with power they cannot loose. It is only *later* events that have made me see something significant in my lapsings.

My mother followed to the letter my father's directions for my higher education, which I only learned of now. Upon my graduation from high school I was sent to a venerable Eastern institution of learning not as well known as those of the Ivy League, but of equally high standing—Miskatonic University, which lies on the serpentine river of that name within the antique town of Arkham with its gambrel roofs and elm-shaded avenues quiet as the footsteps of a witch's familiar. My father had first heard of the school from an Eastern employer of his talents, a Harley Warren, for whom he had done some unusual dowsing in a cemetery within a swamp of cypresses, and that man's high praise of Miskatonic had imprinted itself indelibly upon his memory. My previous school record did not permit of this (I lacked certain prerequisites) but I just barely managed—much to the surprise of all my previous teachers—to pass a stiff entrance examination which required, like that of Dartmouth, some knowledge of Greek as well as Latin. Only I knew how much furious, imagination-invoking guessing that took. I could not bear to fall utterly short of my father's hopes for me.

Unfortunately, my efforts were in vain. Before the first term ended I was back in Southern California, physically and mentally depleted by a series of attacks of nervousness, homesickness, actual ailment (anemia), an increase in the hours I devoted to sleep, and an almost incredible recurrence of my sleepwalking, which more than once carried me deep into the wild hills west of Arkham. I tried for what seemed to me a long time to stick it out, but was advised by the college doctors to give it up after some particularly bad attacks. I believe that they thought I was not cut out to be even a moderately strong individual and that they pitied me more than they sympathized with me. It is not a good thing to see a youth racked by sentiments and longings proper to a fearful child.

And they appeared to be right in this (although I know now that they were wrong), for my malady turned out (*apparently*) to be simple homesickness and nothing more. It was with a feeling of immense relief that I returned to my mother and our brick home in the hills, and with each room I reentered I gained more assurance—even, or perhaps especially, the cellar with its well-swept floor of solid rock, my father's tools and chemicals (acids, etc.), and the marinely decorated, floor-set rock inscription "The Gate of

Dreams." It was as though all the time I had been at Miskatonic there had been an invisible leash dragging me back, and only now had its pressure slackened completely.

(Those voices *are* continent-wide, of course: "The essential salts, the fane of Dagon, the gray twisted brittle monstrosity, the flute-tormented pandemonium, the coral-encrusted towers of Rulay...")

And the hills helped me as much as my home. For a month I roamed them daily and walked the old familiar paths between the parched and browning undergrowth, my mind full of old tales and scraps of childhood brooding. I think it was only then, only with my returning, that I first came fully to realize how much (and a little of *what*) those hills meant to me. From Mount Waterman and steep Mount Wilson with its great observatory and hundred-inch reflector down through cavernous Tujunga Canyon with its many sinuous offshoots to the flat lands and then across the squat Verdugo Hills and the closer ones with Griffith Observatory and its lesser 'scopes, to sinister, almost inaccessible Potrero and great twisting Topanga Canyons that open with the abruptness of catastrophe upon the monstrous, primeval Pacific—all of them (the hills) with few exceptions sandy, cracked, and treacherous, the earth like rock and the rock like dried earth, rotten, crumbling, and porous: all this had such a hold on me (the limper, the fearful listener) as to be obsessive. And indeed there were more and more symptoms of obsession now: I favored certain paths over others for ill-defined reasons and there were places I could not pass without stopping for a little. My fantasy or notion became stronger than ever that there were *tunnels* under the paths, traveled by beings which attracted the venomous snakes of the outer world because they were akin to them. Could some eerie reality have underlaid my childhood nightmare? —I shied away from that thought.

All this, as I say, I realized during the month after my defeated return from the East. And at the end of that month I resolved to conquer my obsession and my revolting homesickness and all the subtle weaknesses and inner hindrances that kept me from being the man my father had dreamed of. I had found that a complete break such as my father had planned for me (Miskatonic) would not work; so I determined to work out my troubles without running away: I would take courses at nearby UCLA (the University of California at Los Angeles). I would study and exercise, build up both body and mind. I remember that my determination was intense. There is something very ironic about that, for my plan, logical as it seemed, was the one sure course to further psychological entrapment.

For quite some time, however, I seemed to be getting on successfully. With systematic exercise and better-controlled diet and rest (still my twelve hours a night), I became healthier than I ever had been before. All the troubles that had beset me in the East vanished completely away. No longer did I wake shuddering from my dreamless sleepwalking; in fact, as far as I could determine at the time, that habit had gone for good. And at college, from which I returned home nightly, I made steady progress. It was then that I first began to write those imaginative and pessimistic poems tinged with metaphysical speculation that have won me some little attention from a small circle of readers. Oddly, they were sparked by the one significant item I had brought back with me from shadow-beset Arkham, a little book of verse I'd bought at a dusty secondhand store there, *Azathoth and Other Horrors* by Edward Pickman Derby, a local poet.

Now I know that my spurt of new effort during my college years was largely deceptive. Because I had decided upon a new course of life that brought me into a few new situations (though keeping me at home), I thought I was progressing vastly. I managed to keep on believing that for all my college years. That I could never study any subject profoundly, that I could never create anything that took a protracted effort, I explained by telling myself that what I was doing was "preparation" and "intellectual orientation" for some great future effort. For several years I managed to conceal from myself the fact that I could only call a tithe of my energy my own, while the residuum was being shunted down only the powers that be know what inner channels.

(I thought I knew what books I was studying, but the voices now are telling me, "The runes of Nug-Soth, the clavicle of Nyarlathotep, the litanies of Lomar, the secular meditations of Pierre-Louis Montagny, the *Necronomicon*, the chants of CromYa, the overviews of Yiang-Li...")

(It is midday or later outside, but the house is cool. I have managed to eat a little and made more coffee. I have been down to the basement, checking my father's tools and things, his sledge, carboys of acid, et cetera, and looking at "The Gate of Dreams" and treading softly. The voices are strongest there.)

Suffice it that during my six college and "poetic" years (I couldn't carry a full load of courses) I lived not as a man, but as a fraction of a man. I had gradually given up all grand ambitions and become content to lead a life in miniature. I spent my time going to easy classes, writing fragments of prose and an occasional poem, caring for my mother (who except for her worries about me was undemanding) and for my father's house (so well built it needed hardly any care), rambling almost absentmindedly in the hills, and sleeping prodigiously. I had no friends. In fact, we had no friends. Abbott Kinney had died and Los Angeles had stolen his Venice. Simon Rodia gave up his visits, for he was now totally preoccupied with his great single-handed building project. Once on my mother's urging I went to Watts, a settlement of flower-decked humble bungalows dwarfed by his fabulous backyard towers that were rising like a blue-green Persian dream. He had trouble recalling who I was and then he watched me strangely as he worked. The money my father had left (in silver dollars) was ample for my mother and myself. In short, I had become, not unpleasantly, *resigned*.

This was all the easier for me because of my growing absorption in the doctrines of such men as Oswald Spengler who believe that culture and civilization go by cycles and that our own Faustian Western world, with all its grandiose dream of scientific progress, is headed toward a barbarism that will engulf it as surely as the Goths, Vandals, Scythians, and Huns engulfed mighty Rome and her longer-lived sister, dwindling Byzantium. As I looked from my hilltops down on bustling Los Angeles always a-building, I placidly thought of the future days when little bands of blustering, ill-kempt barbarians will walk the streets of humped and pitted asphalt and look on each of its ruined, many-purposed buildings as just another "hut"; when high-set Griffith Park Planetarium, romantically rockbuilt, high-walled, and firmly bastioned, will be the stronghold of some petty dictator; when industry and science will be gone and all their machines and instruments rusted and broken and their use forgotten...and *all* our works forgotten as completely as those of the sunken civilization of Mu in the Pacific, of the fragments of whose cities only remain Nan Matol and Rapa Nui, or Easter Island.

But *whence* did these thoughts really come? Not entirely or even principally from Spengler, I'll be bound. No, they had a *deeper* source, I greatly fear.

Yet thus I thought, thus I believed, and thus I was wooed away from the pursuits and tempting goals of our commercial world. I saw everything in terms of transciency, decadence, and decline—as if the times were as rotten and crumbling as the hills which obsessed me.

It was that I was *convinced*, not that I was morbid. No, my health was better than ever and I was neither bored nor dissatisfied. Oh, I occasionally berated myself for failure to manifest the promise my father had seen in me, but on the whole I was strangely content. I had a weird sense of power and self-satisfaction, as if I were a man in the midst of some engrossing pursuit. You know the pleasant relief and bone-deep satisfaction that comes after a day of successful hard work? Well, *that was the way I felt almost all the time, day in and day out.* And I took my happiness as a gift of the gods. It did not occur to me to ask, *"Which* gods? Are they from heaven...or from the *underworld?"*

Even my mother was happier, her disease arrested, her son devoted to her and leading a busy life (on a very small scale) and doing nothing to worry her beyond his occasional rambles in the snake-infested hills.

Fortune smiled on us. Our brick dwelling rode out the severe Long Beach earthquake of March 10, 1933, without sustaining the least damage. Those who still called it Fischer's Folly were nonplussed.

Last year (1936) I duly received from UCLA my bachelor's diploma in English literature, with a minor in history, my mother proudly attending the ceremony. And a month or so later she seemed as childishly delighted as I at the arrival of the first bound copies of my little book of verse, *The Tunneler Below*, printed at my own expense, and in my hubristic mood of auctorial conceit I not only sent out several copies for review but also donated two to the UCLA library and two more to that at Miskatonic. In my covering letter to the erudite Dr. Henry Armitage, librarian at the latter institution, I mentioned not only my brief attendance there, but also my inspiration by an Arkham poet. I also told him a little about the circumstances of my composition of the poems.

I joked deprecatingly to my mother about this last expansive gesture of mine, but she knew how deeply I had been hurt by my failure at Miskatonic and how strongly I desired to repair my reputation there, so when only a few weeks later a letter came addressed to me and bearing the Arkham postmark, she hurried out into the hills quite against her usual wont, to bring it to me, I having just gone out on one of my rambles.

From where I was, I barely heard, yet also recognized her mortal screams. I rushed back at my most desperate limping speed. At the very spot where my father had perished, I found her writhing on the hard, dry ground and screaming still—and near to her and whipping about, the large young rattle-snake that had bitten her on the calf, which was already swelling.

I killed the horrid thing with the stick I carry, then slashed the bite with my sharp pocketknife and sucked it out and injected antivenin from the kit I have always with me on my walks.

All to no avail. She died two days later in the hospital. Once more there was not only shock and depression, but also the dismal business of a funeral to get through (at least we already owned a grave lot), this time a more conventional ceremony, but this time I was wholly alone.

It was a week before I could bring myself to look at the letter she'd been bringing me. After all, it had been the cause of her death. I almost tore it up unread. But after I had got into it, I became more and more interested and then incredulously amazed .,.and frightened. Here it is, in its entirety:

118 Saltonstall St.,
Arkham, Mass.,
Aug. 12, 1936.

Georg Reuter Fischer, Esq.,
Vultures Roost,
Hollywood, Calif.

My dear Sir:—

Dr. Henry Armitage took the liberty of letting me peruse your *The Tunneler Below* before it was placed on general circulation in the university library. May one who serves only in the outer court of the muses' temple, and particularly outside Polyhymnia's and Erato's shrines, be permitted to express his deep appreciation of your creative achievement? And to tender respectfully the like admirations of Professor Wingate Peaslee of our psychology department and of Dr. Francis Morgan of medicine and comparative anatomy, who share my special interests, and of Dr. Armitage himself? "The Green Deeps" is in particular a remarkably well-sustained and deeply moving lyric poem.

I am an assistant professor of literature at Miskatonic and an enthusiastic amateur student of New England and other folklore. If memory serves, you were in my freshman English section six years ago. I was sorry then that the state of your health forced you to curtail your studies, and I am happy now to have before me conclusive evidence that you have completely surmounted all such difficulties. Congratulations!

And now will you allow me to pass on to another and very different matter, which is nonetheless peripherally related to your poetic work? Miskatonic is currently engaged in a broad interdepartmental research in the general area of folklore, language, and dreams, an investigation of the vocabulary of the collective unconscious, particularly as it expresses itself in poetry. The three scholars I have alluded to are among those active in this work, along with persons in Brown University, Providence, Rhode Island, who are carrying on the pioneering work of the late Professor George Gammell Angell, and from time to time I am honored to render them assistance. They have empowered me to ask you for your own help in this matter, which could be of signal importance. It is a matter of answering a few questions only, relating to the accidents of your writing and in no way impinging on its essence, and should not cut seriously into your time. Naturally any information you choose to supply will be treated as strictly confidential.

I call your attention to the following two lines in "The Green Deeps":

> Intelligence doth grow itself within
> The coral-palled, squat towers of Rulay.

Did you in composing this poem ever consider a more eccentric spelling of the last (and presumably invented?) word? "R'lyeh," say. And going back three lines, did you consider spelling "Nath" (invented?) with an initial "p"—i.e., "Pnath"?

Also in the same poem:

> The rampant dragon dreams in far Cathay
> While snake-limbed Cutlu sleeps in deep Rulay.

The name "Cutlu" (once more, invented?) is of considerable interest to us. Did you have phonetic difficulty in choosing the letters to represent the sound you had in mind? Did you perhaps simplify in the interests of poetic clarity? At any time did "Cthulhu" ever occur to you?

(As you can see, we are discovering that the language of the collective unconscious is almost unpleasantly guttural and sibilant! All hawking and spitting, like German.)

Also, there is this quatrain in your impressive lyric, "Sea Tombs":

> Their spires underlie our deepest graves;
> Lit are they by a light that man has seen.
> Only the wingless worm can go between
> Our daylight and their vault beneath the waves.

Were there some proofreading errors here? —or the equivalent. Specifically, in the second line should "that" be "no"? (And was the light you had in mind what you might call orange-blue or purple-green, or both?) And, in the next line, how does "winged" rather than "wingless" strike you?

Finally, in regard to "Sea Tombs" and also the title poem of your book, Professor Peaslee has a question which he calls a "long shot" about the subterranean and submarine tunnels which you evoke. Did you ever have fantasies of such tunnels really existing in the area where you composed the poem? —the Hollywood Hills and Santa Monica Mountains, presumably, the Pacific Ocean being nearby. Did you perhaps try actually to trace the paths overlying these fancied tunnels? And did you happen to notice (excuse the strangeness of this question) an unusual number of venomous serpents along such routes? —rattlers, I would presume (in our area it would be copperheads, and in the South water moccasins and coral snakes). If so, do take care!

If such tunnels should by some strange coincidence actually exist, it would be scientifically possible to confirm the fact without any digging or drilling (or by discovering an existent opening), it may interest you to know. Even vacuity—i.e., nothing—leaves its traces, it appears! Two Miskatonic science professors, who are part of the interdepartmental program I mentioned, have devised a highly portable apparatus for the purpose, which they call a magneto-optic geoscanner. (That last hybrid word must sound a most clumsy and barbarous coinage to a poet, I'm sure, but you know scientists!) It is strange, is it not, to think of an investigation of dreams having geological repercussions? The clever though infelicitously named instrument is a simplified adaptation of one which has already discovered two new elements.

I shall be making a trip west early next year, to confer with a man in San Diego who happens to be the son of the scholarly recluse whose researches led to our interdepartmental program—Henry Wentworth Akeley. (The local poet—alas, deceased—to whom you pay such generous tribute, was another such pioneer, it happens oddly.) I shall be driving my own British sports car, a diminutive Austin. I am some thing of an automobile maniac, I must confess, even a speed demon! —however inappropriate that may be for an assistant English professor. I would be very pleased to make your further acquaintance at that time, if entirely agreeable to you. I might even bring along a geoscanner and we could check out those hypothetical tunnels!

But I perhaps anticipate and presume too far. Pardon me. I will be very grateful for any attention you are able to give this letter and its necessarily impertinent questions.

Once more, congratulations on *The Tunneler!*

Yrs. very truly,
Albert N. Wilmarth.

It is quite impossible to describe all at once my state of mind when I finished reading this letter. I can only do so by stages. To begin with, I was flattered and gratified, even acutely embarrassed, by his apparently sincere praise of my verses—as what young poet wouldn't be? And that a psychologist and an old librarian (even an anatomist!) should admire them too—it was almost too much.

As soon as the man mentioned freshman English I realized that I had a vivid memory of him. Although I'd forgotten his name in the course of years, it came back to me like a shot when I glanced ahead at the end of the letter and saw it. He had been only an instructor then, a tall young man, cadaverously thin, always moving about with nervous rapidity, his shoulders hunched. He'd had a long jaw and a pale complexion, with dark-circled eyes which gave him a haunted look, as if he were constantly under some great strain to which he never alluded. He had the habit of jerking out a little notebook and making jottings without ceasing for a moment to discourse fluently, even brilliantly. He'd seemed incredibly well read and had had a lot to do with stimulating and deepening my interest in poetry. I even remembered his car—the other students used to joke about it with an undercurrent of envy. It had been a Model T Ford then, which he'd always driven at a brisk clip around the fringes of the Miskatonic campus, taking turns very sharply.

The program of interdepartmental research he described sounded very impressive, even exciting, but eminently plausible—I was just discovering Jung then and also semantics. And to be invited so graciously to take part in it—once again I was flattered. If I hadn't been alone while I read it, I might have blushed.

One notion I got then did stop me briefly and for a moment almost turned me angrily against the whole thing—the sudden suspicion that the purpose of the program might not be the avowed one, that (the presence in it of a psychologist and a medical doctor influenced me in this) it was some sort of investigation of the delusions of crankish, imaginative people—not so much the incidental insights as the psychopathology of poets.

But he was so very gracious and reasonable—no, I was being paranoid, I told myself. Besides, as soon as I got a ways into his detailed questions it was an altogether different reaction that filled me—one of utter amazement...and *fear*.

For starters, he was so incredibly accurate in his guesses (for what else could they possibly be? I asked myself uneasily) about those invented names, that he had me gasping. I *had* first thought of spelling them "R'lyeh" and "Pnath" —exactly those letters, though of course memory can be tricky about such things.

And then that *Cthulhu*—seeing it spelled that way actually made me shiver, it so precisely conveyed the deep-pitched, harsh, inhuman cry or chant I'd imagined coming up from profound black abysses, and only finally rendered as "Cutlu" rather dubiously, but fearing anything more complex would seem affectation. (And, really, you can't fit the inner rhythms of a sound like "Cthulhu" into English poetry.)

And then to find that he'd spotted those two proofreader's errors, for they'd been just that. The first I'd missed. The second ("wingless" for "winged") I'd caught, but then rather spinelessly let stand, feeling all of a sudden that I'd perpetuated something overly fantastic when I'd put a figure from my life's one nightmare (a worm with wings) into a poem.

And topping even that, how in the name of all that's wonderful could he have described unearthly colors I'd only dreamed of and never put into my poems at all? Using exactly the same color-words I'd used! I began to think that Miskatonic's interdepartmental research project must have made some epochal discoveries about dreams and dreaming and the human imagination in general, enough to turn their scholars into wizards and dumbfound Adler, Freud, and even Jung.

At that point in my reading of the letter I thought he'd hit me with everything he possibly could, but the next section managed to mine a still deeper source of horror and one most disturbingly close to everyday reality. That he should know, somehow deduce, all about my paths in the hills and my odd daydreams about them and about tunnels I'd fancied underlying them—that was truly staggering. And that he should *ask and even warn me* about venomous snakes, so that the very letter my mother was carrying unopened when she got her death sting contained a vital reference to it—really, for a moment and more then, I did wonder if I were going insane.

And finally when despite all his jaunty "fancied's" and "long shot's" and "hypothetical's" and English-professor witticisms, he began to talk as if he assumed my imaginary tunnels were real and to refer lightly to a scientific instrument that would prove it...well, by the time I'd finished his letter, I fully expected him to turn up the next minute—turn in sharply at our drive with a flourish of wheels and brakes in his Model T (no, Austin) and draw up in a cloud of dust at our door, the geo-scanner sitting on the front seat beside him like a fat black telescope directed downward!

And yet he'd been so damnably *breezy* about it all! I simply didn't know what to think.

(I've been down in the basement again, checking things out. This writing stirs me up and makes me frightfully restless. I went out front, and there was a rattlesnake crossing the path in the hot slanting sunlight from the west. More evidence, if any were needed, that what I fear is true. Or do I hope for it? At all events, I killed the brute. The voices vibrate with, "The half-born worlds, the alien orbs, the stirrings in blackness, the hooded forms, the nighted depths, the shimmering vortices, the purple haze...")

When I'd calmed down somewhat next day, I wrote Wilmarth a long letter, confirming all his hints, confessing my utter astonishment at them, and begging him to explain how he'd made them. I volunteered to assist the interdepartmental project in any way I could and invited him to be my guest when he came west. I gave him a brief history of my life and my sleep anomalies, mentioning my mother's death. I had a strange feeling of unreality as I posted the letter and waited with mixed feelings of impatience and lingering (and also regathering) incredulity for his reply.

When it came, quite a fat one, it rekindled all my first excitement, though without satisfying all my curiosity by any means. Wilmarth was still inclined to write off his and his colleagues' deductions about my word choices, dreams, and fantasies as lucky guesses, though he told me enough about the project to keep my curiosity in a fever—especially about its discoveries of obscure linkages between the life of the imagination and archaeological discoveries in far-off places. He seemed particularly interested in the fact that I generally never dreamed and that I slept for very long hours. He overflowed with thanks for my cooperation and my invitation, promising to include me on his itinerary when he drove west. And he had a lot more questions for me.

The next months were strange ones. I lived my normal life, if it can be called that, keeping up my reading and studies and library visits, even writing a little new poetry from time to time. I continued my hill-ramblings, though with a new wariness. Sometimes during them I'd stop and stare at the dry earth beneath my feet, as if expecting to trace the outlines of a trapdoor in it. And sometimes I'd be consumed by sudden, wildly passionate feelings of grief and guilt at the thought of my father locked down there and at my mother's horrible death too; I'd feel I must somehow go to them at all costs.

And yet at the same time I was living only for Wilmarth's letters and the moods of wonder, fantastic speculation, and panic—yet almost delicious terror—they evoked in me. He'd write about all sorts of things besides the project—my poetry and new readings and my ideas (he'd play the professorial mentor here from time to time), world events, the weather, astronomy, submarines, his pet cats, faculty politics at Miskatonic, town meetings at Arkham, his lectures, and the local trips he'd make. He made it all extremely interesting. Clearly he was an inveterate letter-writer and under his influence I became one too.

But most of all, of course, I was fascinated by what he'd write from time to time about the project. He told me some very interesting things about the Miskatonic Antarctic expedition of 1930–31, with its five great Dornier airplanes, and last year's somewhat abortive Australian one in which the psychologist Peaslee and his father, a one-time economist, had been involved.

I remembered having read about them both in the newspapers, though the reports there had been curiously fragmentary and unsatisfying, almost as if the press were prejudiced against Miskatonic.

I got the strong impression that Wilmarth would have liked very much to have accompanied both expeditions and was very much put out at not having been able (or allowed) to, though most of the time bravely concealing his disappointment. More than once he referred to his "unfortunate nervousness," sensitivity to cold, fierce migraine attacks, and "bouts of ill health" which would put him to bed for a few days. And sometimes he'd speak with wistful admiration of the prodigious energy and stalwart constitutions of several of his colleagues, such as Professors Atwood and Pabodie, the geo-scanner's inventors, Dr. Morgan, who was a big-game hunter, and even the octogenarian Armitage.

There were occasional delays in his replies, which always filled me with anxiety and restlessness, sometimes because of these attacks of his and sometimes because he'd been away longer than he'd expected on some visit. One of the latter was to Providence to confer with colleagues and help investigate the death under mysterious circumstances involving a lightning bolt of Robert Blake, a poet like myself, short-story writer, and painter whose work had provided much material for the project.

It was just after his visit to Providence that with a curious sort of guardedness and reluctance he mentioned visiting another colleague of sorts there (who was in poor health), a Howard Phillips Lovecraft, who had fictionalized (but quite sensationally, Wilmarth warned me) some Arkham scandals and some of Miskatonic's researches and project activities. These stories had been published (when at all) in cheap pulp magazines, especially in a lurid journal called *Weird Tales* (you'll want to tear the cover off, if ever you should dare to buy a copy, he assured me). I recalled having seen the magazine on downtown newsstands in Hollywood and Westwood. I hadn't found the covers offensive. Most of their nude female figures, by some sentimental woman artist, were decorously sleek pastels and their activities only playfully perverse. Others, by one Senf, were a rather florid folk art quite reminiscent of my father's floral chiselings.

But after that, of course, I haunted secondhand bookstores, hunting down copies of *Weird Tales* (mostly) with Lovecraft stories in them, until I'd found a few and read them—one, "The Call of Cthulhu," no less. It cost me the strangest shudders, let me tell you, to see *that* name again, spelled out in cheapest print, under such very outlandish circumstances. Truly, my sense of reality was set all askew and if the tale that Lovecraft told with a strange dignity and power was anything like the truth, then Cthulhu was real, an other-dimensional extraterrestrial monster dreaming in an insane, Pacific-sunken metropolis which sent out mental messages (and—who knows? —tunnels) to the world at large. In another tale, "The Whisperer in Darkness," *Albert N. Wilmarth* was a leading character, and that Akeley too he'd mentioned.

It was all fearfully unsettling and confounding. If I hadn't attended Miskatonic myself and lived in Arkham, I'd have thought surely they were a writer's projections.

As you can imagine, I continued to haunt the dusty bookstores and I *bombarded* Wilmarth with frantic questions. His replies were of a most pacifying and temporizing sort. Yes, he'd been afraid of my getting too excited, but hadn't been able to resist telling me about the stories. Lovecraft often laid on things *very* thickly indeed. I'd understand everything much better when we could really talk together and he could explain in person. Really, Lovecraft had an extremely powerful imagination and sometimes it got out of hand. No, Miskatonic had never tried to suppress the stories or take legal action, for fear of even less desirable publicity—and because the project members thought the stories might be a good preparation for the world if some of their more frightening hypotheses were verified. Really, Lovecraft was a very charming and well-intentioned person, but sometimes he went too far. And so on and so on.

Really, I don't think I could have contained myself except that, it now being 1937, Wilmarth sent me word that he was at last driving west. The Austin had been given a thorough overhaul and was "packed to the gills" with the geo-scanner, endless books and papers, and other instruments and materials, including a drug Morgan had just refined, "which induces dreaming and may, conceivably, he says, facilitate clairvoyance and clairaudience. It might make even you dream—should you consent to ingest an experimental dose."

While he was gone from 118 Saltonstall his rooms would be occupied and his cats, including his beloved Blackfellow, cared for by a close friend named Danforth, who'd spent the last five years in a mental hospital recovering from his ghastly Antarctic experience at the Mountains of Madness.

Wilmarth hated to leave at this time, he wrote, in particular he was worried about Lovecraft's failing health, but nevertheless he was on his way!

The next weeks (which dragged out to two months) were a time of particular tension, anxiety, and anticipatory excitement for me. Wilmarth had many more people and places to visit and investigations to make (including readings with the geo-scanner) than I'd ever imagined. Now he sent mostly postcards, some of them scenic, but they came thick and fast (except for a couple of worrisome hiatuses) and with his minuscule handwriting he got so much on them (even the scenic ones) that at times I almost felt I was with him on his trip, worrying about the innards of his Austin, which he called the Tin Hind after

Sir Francis Drake's golden one. I on my part had only a few addresses he'd listed for me where I could write him in advance—Baltimore; Winchester, Virginia; Bowling Green, Kentucky; Memphis; Carlsbad, New Mexico; Tucson; and San Diego.

First he had to stop in Hunterdon County, New Jersey, with its quaintly backward farm communities, to investigate some possibly pre-Colonial ruins and hunt for a rumored cave, using the geo-scanner. Next, after Baltimore, there were extensive limestone caverns to check out in both Virginias. He crossed the Appalachians Winchester to Clarksburg, a stretch with enough sharp turns to satisfy even him. Approaching Louisville, the Tin Hind was almost swallowed up in the Great Ohio Flood (which preoccupied the radio news for days; I hung over my superheterodyne set) and he was unable to visit a new correspondent of Lovecraft's there. Then there was more work for the geo-scanner near Mammoth Cave. In fact, caves seemed to dominate his journey, for after a side trip to New Orleans to confer with some occult scholar of French extraction, there were the Carlsbad Caverns and nearby but less well-known subterranean vacuities. I wondered more and more about my tunnels.

The Tin Hind held up very well, except she blew out a piston head crossing Texas ("I held her at high speed a little too long") and he lost three days getting her mended.

Meanwhile, I was finding and reading new Lovecraft stories. One, which turned up in a secondhand but quite recent science fiction pulp, fictionalized the Australian expedition most impressively—especially the dreams old Peaslee had that led to it. In them, he'd exchanged personalities with a cone-shaped monster and was forever wandering through long stone passageways haunted by invisible whistlers. It reminded me so much of my nightmares in which I'd done the same thing with a winged worm that buzzed, that I airmailed a rather desperate letter to Tucson, telling Wilmarth all about it. I got a reply from San Diego, full of reassurances and more temporizings, and referring to old Akeley's son and some sea caverns they were looking into, and (at last!) setting a date (it would be soon!) for his arrival.

The day before that last, I made a rare find in my favorite Hollywood hunting-ground. It was a little, strikingly illustrated book by Lovecraft called *The Shadow Over Innsmouth* and issued by Visionary Press, whoever they were. I was up half the night reading it. The narrator found some sinister, scaly human beings living in a deep submarine city off New England, realized he was himself turning into one of them, and at the end had decided (for better or worse) to dive down and join them. It made me think of crazy fantasies I'd had of somehow going down into the earth beneath the Hollywood Hills and rescuing or joining my dead father.

Meanwhile mail addressed to Wilmarth care of me had begun to arrive. He'd asked my permission to include my address on the itinerary he'd sent other correspondents. There were letters and cards from (by their postmarks) Arkham and places along his route, some from abroad (mostly England and Europe, but one from Argentina), and a small package from New Orleans. The return address on most of them was his own—118 Saltonstall, so he'd eventually get them even if he missed them along his route. (He'd asked me to do the same with my own notes.) The effect was odd, as though Wilmarth were the author of everything—it almost rearoused my first suspicions of him and the project. (One letter, though among the last to come, a thick one bearing extravagantly a six-cent airmail stamp and a ten-cent special delivery, had been addressed to George Goodenough Akeley, 176 Pleasant St., San Diego, Cal., and then forwarded care of my own address in the upper left-hand corner.)

Late the next afternoon (Sunday, April 14—the eve of my twenty-fifth birthday, as it happened) Wilmarth arrived very much as I'd imagined it occurring when I'd finished reading his first letter, except the Tin Hind was even smaller than I'd pictured—and enameled a bright blue, though now most dusty. There was an odd black case on the seat beside him, though there were a lot of other things on it too—maps, mostly.

He greeted me very warmly and began to talk a blue streak almost at once, with many a jest and frequent little laughs.

The thing that really shocked me was that although I knew he was only in his thirties, his hair was white and the haunted (or hunted) look I'd remembered was monstrously intensified. And he was extremely nervous—at first he couldn't stay still a moment. It wasn't long before I became certain of something I'd never once suspected before—that his breeziness and jauntiness, his jokes and laughs, were a mask for fear, no, for sheer terror, that otherwise might have mastered him entirely.

His actual first words were, "Mr. Fischer, I presume? So glad to meet you in the flesh! —and share your most salubrious sunlight. I look as if I need it, do I not? —a horrid sight! This landscape hath a distinctly cavish, tunnelly aspect—I'm getting to be an old hand at making such geological judgments. Danforth writes that Blackfellow has quite recovered from his indisposition. But Lovecraft is in the hospital—I do not like it. Did you observe last night's brilliant conjunction? —I *like* your clear, clear skies. No, I will carry the geo-scanner (yes, it *is* that); it's somewhat crankish. But you might take the small valise. Really, so very glad!"

He did not comment on or even seem to notice my twisted right foot (something I hadn't mentioned in my letters, though he may have recalled it from six years back) or imply its or my limp's existence in any way, as by insisting on carrying the valise also. That warmed me toward him.

And before going into the house with me, he paused to praise its unusual architecture (another thing I hadn't told him about) and seemed genuinely impressed when I admitted that my father had built it by himself. (I'd feared he'd find it overly eccentric and also question whether someone could work with his hands and be a gentleman.) He also commented favorably on my father's stone carvings wherever they turned up and insisted on pausing to study them, whipping out his notebook to make some quick jottings. Nothing would do, but I must take him on a full tour of the house before he'd consent to rest or take refreshments. I left his valise in the bedroom I'd assigned him (my parents', of course), but he kept lugging the black geo-scanner around with him. It was an odd case, taller than it was wide or long, and it had three adjustable stubby legs, so that it could be set up vertically anywhere.

Emboldened by his approval of my father's carvings, I told him about Simon Rodia and the strangely beautiful towers he was building in Watts, whereupon the notebook came out again and there were more jottings. He seemed particularly impressed by the *marine* quality I found in Rodia's work.

Down in the basement (he had to go there too) he was very much struck by my father's floor-set "Gate of Dreams" stone carving and studied it longer than any of the others. (I'd been feeling embarrassed about its bold motto and odd placement.) Finally he indicated the octopus eyes staring over the castle and observed, "Cutlu, perchance?"

It was the first reference of any sort to the research project that either of us had made since our meeting and it shook me strangely, but he appeared not to notice and continued with, "You know, Mr. Fischer, I'm tempted to get a reading with Atwood and Pabodie's infernal black box right here. Would you object?"

I told him certainly not and to go right ahead, but warned him there was only solid rock under the house (I had told him about my father's dowsing and even had mentioned Harley Warren, whom it turned out Wilmarth had heard of through a Randolph Carter).

He nodded, but said, "I'll take a shot at it nonetheless. We must start somewhere, you know," and he proceeded to set up the geo-scanner carefully so it was standing vertically on its three stubby legs right in the middle of the carving. He took off his shoes first so as not to risk damaging the rather fine stonework.

Then he opened the top of the geo-scanner. I glimpsed two dials and a large eyepiece. He knelt and applied his eye to it, drawing out a black hood and draping it over his head, very much like an old-fashioned photographer focusing for a picture. "Pardon me, but the indications I must look for are difficult to see," he said muffledly. "Hello, what's this?"

There was a longish pause during which nothing happened except his shoulders shifted a bit and there were a few faint clicks. Then he emerged from under the hood, tucked it back in the black box, closed the latter, and began to put on and relace his shoes.

"The scanner's gone crankish," he explained in answer to my inquiry, "and is seeing ghost vacuities. But not to worry—it only needs new warm-up cells, I fancy, which I have with me, and will be right as rain for tomorrow's expedition! That is, if—?" He rolled his eyes up at me in smiling inquiry.

"Of course I'll be able to show you my pet trails in the hills," I assured him. "In fact, I'm bursting to."

"Capital!" he said heartily.

But as we left the basement, its rock floor rang out a bit hollowly, it sounded to me, under his high-laced leather-soled and -heeled shoes (I was wearing sneakers).

It was getting dark, so I started dinner after giving him some iced tea, which he took with lots of lemon and sugar. I cooked eggs and small beefsteaks, figuring from his haggard looks he needed the most restorative sort of food. I also built a fire in the big fireplace against the almost invariable chill of evening.

As we ate by its dancing, crackling flames, he regaled me with brief impressions of his trip west—the cold, primeval pine woods of southern New Jersey with their somberly clad inhabitants speaking an almost Elizabethan English; the very narrow dark roads of West Virginia; the freezing waters of the Ohio flooding unruffled, silent, battleship gray, and ineffably menacing under lowering skies; the profound silence of Mammoth Cave; the southern Midwest with its Depression-spawned, but already legendary, bank robbers; the nervous Creole charms of New Orleans's restored French Quarter; the lonely, incredibly long stretches of road in Texas and Arizona that made one believe one was *seeing* infinity; the great, long, blue, mystery-freighted Pacific rollers ("so different from the Atlantic's choppier, shorter-spaced waves") which he'd watched with George Goodenough Akeley, who'd turned out to be a very solid chap and knowing more about his father's frightening Vermont researches than Wilmarth had expected.

When I mentioned finding *The Shadow Over Innsmouth* he nodded and murmured, "The original of its youthful hero has disappeared and his cousin from the Canton asylum. Down to Y'ha-nthlei? Who knows?" But when I remembered his accumulated mail he merely nodded his thanks, wincing a little, as though reluctant to face it. He really did look shockingly tired.

When we'd finished dinner, however, and he'd taken his black coffee (also with lots of sugar) and the fire was dancing flickeringly, both yellow and blue now, he turned to me with a little, venturesomely friendly smile and a big, wonderingly wide lifting of his eyebrows, and said quietly, "And now you'll quite rightly be expecting me to tell you, my dear Fischer, all the things about the project that I've been hesitant to write, the answers I've been reluctant to give to your cogent questions, the revelations I've been putting off making until we should meet in person. Really, you have been very patient, and I thank you."

Then he shook his head thoughtfully, his eyes growing distant, as he slowly and rather sinuously and somehow unwillingly shrugged his shoulders, which paradoxically were both frail and wide, and grimaced slightly, as if tasting something strangely bitter, and said even more quietly, "if only I had more to tell you that's been *definitely proved.* Somehow we always stop just short of that. Oh, the artifacts are real enough and certain—the Innsmouth jewelry, the Antarctic soapstones, Blake's Shining Trapezohedron, though that's lost in Narragansett Bay, the spiky baluster knob Walter Gilman brought back from his witchy dreamland (or the nontemporal fourth dimension, if you prefer), even the unknown elements, meteoric and otherwise, which defy all analysis, even the new magneto-optic probe which has given us virginium and alabamine. And it's almost equally certain that all, or almost all, those weird extraterrestrial and extra-cosmic creatures *have* existed—that's why I wanted you to read the Lovecraft stories, despite their lurid extravagances, so you'd have some picture of the entities that I'd be talking to you about. Except that they and the evidence for them do have a maddening way of vanishing upon extinction and from all records—Wilbur Whateley's mangled remains, his brother's vast invisible cadaver, the Plutonian old Akeley killed *and couldn't photograph*, the June 1882 meteor itself which struck Nahum Gardner's farm and which set old Armitage (young then) studying the *Necronomicon* (the start of everything at Miskatonic) and which Atwood's father saw with his own eyes and tried to analyze, or what Danforth saw down in Antarctica when he looked back at the horrible higher mountains beyond the Mountains of Madness—he's got amnesia for that now that he has regained his sanity…all, all gone!

"But whether any of those creatures exist *today*—there, there's the rub! The overwhelming question we can't answer, though always on the edge of doing so. The thing is," he went on with gathering urgency, "that *if they do exist*, they are so unimaginably powerful and resourceful, they might be" —and he looked around sharply—"anywhere at the moment!

"Take *Cthulhu*," he began.

I couldn't help starting as I heard that word pronounced for the first time in my life; the harsh, dark, abysmal *monosyllabic* growl it came to was so very like the sound that had originally come to me from my imagination, or my subconscious, or my otherwise unremembered dreams, or....

He continued, "If Cthulhu exists, then he (or she, or it) can go anywhere he wants through space, or air, or sea, or earth itself. We know from Johansen's account (it turned his hair white) that Cthulhu can exist as a gas, be torn to atoms, and then recombine. He wouldn't need tunnels to go through solid rock, he could *seep* through it—'not in the spaces we know, but between them.' And yet in his inscrutability he might choose tunnels—there's that to be reckoned with. Or—still another possibility—perhaps he neither exists nor does not exist but is in some half state—'waits dreaming,' as Angell's old chant has it. Perhaps his dreams, incarnated as your winged worms, Fischer, dig tunnels.

"It is those monstrous underground cavern-and-tunnel worlds, not all from Cthulhu by any means, that I have been assigned to investigate with the geo-scanner, partly because I was the first to hear of them from old Akeley and also—Merciful Creator! —from the Plutonian who masked as him—'great worlds of unknown life down there; blue-litten K'n-yan, red-litten Yoth, and black, lightless N'kai,' which was Tsathoggua's home, and even stranger inner spaces litten by colors from space and from Earth's nighted core. That's how I guessed the colors in your childhood dreams or nightmares (or personality exchanges), my dear Fischer. I've glimpsed them also in the geo-scanner, where they are, however, most fugitive and difficult to discern...."

His voice trailed off tiredly, just as my own concern became most feverishly intense with his mention of "personality exchanges."

He really did look shockingly fatigued. Nevertheless I felt impelled to nerve myself to say, "Perhaps those dreams can be repeated, if I take Dr. Morgan's drug. Why not tonight?"

"Out of the question," he replied, shaking his head slowly. "In the first place, I wrote too hopefully there. At the last minute Morgan was unable to supply me with the drug. He promised to send it along by mail, but hasn't yet. In the second place, I'm inclined to think now that it would be much too dangerous an experiment."

"But at least you'll be able to check those dream colors and the tunnels with your geo-scanner?" I pressed on, somewhat crestfallen. "If I can repair it..." he said, his head nodding and slumping to one side. The dying flames were all blue now as he whispered mumblingly, "...if I am *permitted* to repair it...."

I had to help him to bed and then retire to my own, shaken and unsatisfied, my mind a whirl. Wilmarth's alternating moods of breezy optimism and a seemingly *frightened* dejection were hard to adjust to. But now I realized that I was very tired myself—after all, I'd been up most of the previous night reading *Innsmouth*—and soon I slumbered.

(The voices stridently groan, "The pit of primal life, the Yellow Sign, Aza-thoth, the Magnum Innominandum, the shimmering violet and emerald wings, the cerulean and vermilion claws, Great Cthulhu's wasps..." Night has fallen. I have limpingly paced the house from the low attic with its circular portholes to the basement, where I touched my father's sledge and eyed "The Gate of Dreams." The moment draws nigh. I must write rapidly.)

I awoke to bright sunlight, feeling totally refreshed by my customary twelve hours of sleep. I found Wilmarth busily writing at the table that faced the north window of his bedroom. His smiling face looked positively youthful in the cool light, despite its neatly brushed thatch of white hair—I hardly recognized him. All his accumulated mail except for one item lay open and face downward on the far left-hand corner of the table, while on the far right-hand corner was an impressive pile of newly written and addressed postcards, each with its neatly affixed, fresh, one-cent stamp.

"Good morrow, Georg," he greeted me (properly pronouncing it GAY-org), "if I may so address you. And good news!—the scanner is recharged and be-having perfectly, ready for the day's downward surveying, while that letter George Goodenough forwarded is from Francis Morgan and contains a supply of the drug against tonight's inward researches! Two dosages exactly—Georg, I'll dream with you!" He waved a small paper packet.

"That's wonderful, Albert," I told him, meaning it utterly. "By the way, it's my birthday," I added.

"Congratulations!" he said joyfully. 'We'll celebrate it tonight with our drafts of Morgan's drug."

And our expedition did turn out to be a glorious one, at least until almost its very end. The Hollywood Hills put on their most youthfully winning face; even the underlying crumbling, wormeaten corruptions seemed fresh. The sun was hot, the sky bright blue, but there was a steady cool breeze from the west and occasional great high white clouds casting enormous shadows. Amazingly, Albert seemed to know the territory almost as well as I did—he'd studied his maps prodigiously and brought them along, including the penciled ones I'd sent him. And he instantly named correctly the manzanita, sumac, scrub oak, and other encroaching vegetation through which we wended our way.

Every so often and especially at my favorite pausing places, he would take readings with the geo-scanner, which he carried handily, while I had two can-teens and a small backpack. While his head was under the black hood, I would stand guard, my stick ready. Once I surprised a dark and pinkly pale, fat, large serpent, which went slithering into the underbrush. Before I could tell him, he said correctly, "A king snake, foe of the crotaloids—a good omen."

And...on every reading, Albert's black box showed vacuities of some sort—

tunnels or caves—immediately below us, at depths varying from a few to a few score meters. Somehow this did not trouble us by bright outdoor day. I think it was what we'd both been expecting. Coming out from under the hood, he'd merely nod and say, "Fifteen meters" (or the like) and note it down in his little book, and we'd tramp on. Once he let me try my luck under the hood, but all I could see through the eyepiece was what seemed like an intensification of the dancing points of colored light one sees in the dark with the eyes closed. He told me it took considerable training to learn to recognize the significant indications.

High in the Santa Monicas we lunched on beef sandwiches and the tea-flavored lemonade with which I'd filled both canteens. Sun and breeze bathed us. Hills were all around and beyond them to the west the blue Pacific. We talked of Sir Francis Drake and Magellan and of Captain Cook and his great circumpolar voyagings, and of the fabulous lands they'd all heard legends of—and of how the tunnels we were tracing were really no more strange. We spoke of Lovecraft's stories almost as if they were no more than that. Daytime viewpoints can be strangely unworrying and unconcerned.

Halfway back or so, Albert began looking very haggard once more—frighteningly so. I got him to let me carry the black box. To do that I had to abandon my flat backpack and empty canteens—he didn't seem to notice.

Almost home, we paused at my father's memorial. The sun had westered most of this way, and there were dark shadows and also shafts of ruddy light almost parallel to the ground. Albert, very weary now, was fumbling for phrases to praise Rodia's work, when there swiftly glided out of the undergrowth behind him what I first took to be a large rattlesnake. But as I lunged lurchingly toward it, lashing at it with my stick, and as it slid back into thick cover with preternatural rapidity, and as Albert whirled around, the sinuous, vanishing thing looked for an instant to me as if it were all shimmering violet-green above with beating wings and bluish-scarlet below with claws while its minatory rattle was more a skirling hum.

We raced home, not speaking of it at all, each of us concerned only that his comrade not fall behind. Somewhere mine found the strength.

His postcards had been collected from the box by the road and there were a half dozen new letters for him—and a notification of a registered package for me.

Nothing must do then but Albert must drive me down to Hollywood to pick up the package before the post office closed. His face was fearfully haggard, but he seemed suddenly flooded with a fantastic nervous energy and (when I protested that it could hardly be anything of great importance) a tremendous willpower that would brook no opposition.

He drove like a veritable demon and as though the fate of worlds depended on his speed—Hollywood must have thought it was Wallace Reid come back from the dead for another of his transcontinental racing pictures. The Tin Hind fled like a frightened one indeed, as he worked the gear lever smartly, shifting up and down. The wonders were that we weren't arrested and didn't crash. But I got to the proper window just before it closed and I signed for the package—a stoutly wrapped, tightly sealed, and heavily corded parcel from (it really startled me) Simon Rodia.

Then back again, just as fast despite my protests, the Tin Hind screeching on the corners and curves, my companion's face an implacable, watchful death's-mask, up into the crumbling and desiccated hills as the last streaks of the day faded to violet in the west and the first stars came out.

I forced Albert to rest then and drink hot black coffee freighted with sugar while I got dinner—when he'd stepped out of the car into the chilly night he'd almost fainted. I grilled steaks again—if he'd needed restorative food last night, he needed it doubly now after our exhausting hike and our Dance of Death along the dry, twisting roads, I told him roughly. ("Or Grim Reaper's Tarantella, eh, Georg?" he responded with a feeble but unvanquishable little grin.) Soon he was prowling around again—he wouldn't stay still—and peering out the windows and then lugging the geo-scanner down into the basement, "to round out our readings," he informed me. I had just finished building and lighting a big fire in the fireplace when he came hurrying back up. Its first white flare of flame as the kindling caught showed me his ashen face and white circled blue eyes. He was shaking all over, literally.

"I'm sorry, Georg, to be such a troublesome and seemingly ungrateful guest," he said, forcing himself with a great effort to speak coherently and calmly (though most imperatively), "but really you and I must get out of here at once. There's no place safe for us this side of Arkham—which is not safe either, but there at least we'll have the counsel and support of salted veterans of the Miskatonic project whose nerves are steadier than mine. Last night I got (and concealed from you—I was sure it had to be wrong) a reading of fifteen down there under the carving—*centimeters*, Georg, not meters. Tonight I have confirmed that reading beyond any question of a doubt, only it's shrunk to five under the carving. The floor there is the merest shell—it rings as hollow as a crypt in New Orleans's St. Louis One or Two—*they* have been eating at it from below and are feasting still. No, no arguments! You have time to pack one small bag—limit yourself to necessities, but bring that registered parcel from Rodia, I'm curious about it."

And with that he strode to his bedroom, whence he emerged in a short while with his packed valise and carried it and the black box out to the car.

Meanwhile I'd nerved myself to go down in the basement. The floor did ring much more hollowly than it had last night—it made me hesitate to tread upon it—but otherwise nothing appeared changed. Nevertheless it gave me a curious feeling of unreality, as if there were no real objects left in the world, only flimsy scenery, a few stage properties including a balsa sledgehammer, a registered parcel with nothing in it, and a cyclorama of nighted hills, and two actors.

I hurried back upstairs, took the steaks off the grill and set them on the table in front of the softly roaring fire (for they were done) and headed after Albert.

But he anticipated me, stepping back inside the door, looking at me sharply—his eyes were still wide and staring—and demanding, "Why aren't you packed?"

I said to him steadily, "Now look here, Albert, I thought last night the cellar floor sounded hollow, so that is not entirely a surprise. And any way you look at it, we can't drive to Arkharn on nervous energy. In fact, we can't get even decently started driving east without some food inside us. You say yourself it's dangerous everywhere, even at Miskatonic, and from what we (or at least I) saw at my father's grave there may be at least one of the things loose already. So let's eat dinner—I have a hunch terror hasn't taken away your appetite entirely—and have a look inside Rodia's package, and then leave if we must."

There was a rather long pause. Then his expression relaxed into a somewhat wan smile and he said, "Very well, Georg, that does make sense. I'm frightened all right, make no mistake of that, in fact I've walked in terror for the past ten years. But in this case, to speak as honestly as I'm able, I have been even more concerned for you—it suddenly seemed such a pity, such a disservice, that I should have dragged you into this dreadful business. But as you say, one must bow to necessity, bodily and otherwise…and try to show a little style about it," he added with a rather doleful chuckle.

So we sat down before the dancing, golden fire and ate our steaks and fixings (I had some burgundy, he stayed with his sweet black coffee) and talked of this and that—chiefly of Hollywood, as it turned out. He'd glimpsed a bookstore on our headlong drive, and now he asked about it and that led to other things.

Our dinner done, I refilled his cup and my glass, then cleared a space and opened Rodia's parcel, using the carving knife to cut its cords and slit its seals. It contained, carefully packed in excelsior, the casket of embossed copper and German silver which sits before me now. I recognized my father's handiwork at once, which reproduced quite closely in beaten metal his stone carving in the basement, though without the "Gate of Dreams" inscription. Albert's finger indicated the Cutlu eyes, though he did not speak the name. I opened the casket. It contained several sheets of heavy bond paper. This time it was my father's handwriting I recognized. Standing side by side, Albert and I read the document, which I append here:

15 Mar 1925

My dear Son:

Today you are 13 but I write to you and wish you well when you are 25. Why I do so you will learn as you read this. The box is yours—*Leb'wohl!* I leave it with a friend to send to you if I should go in the 12 years between—Nature has given me signs that that may be: jagged flashes of rare earth colors in my eyes from time to time. Now read with care, for I am telling secrets.

When I was a boy in Louisville I had dreams by day and could not remember them. They were black times in my mind that were minutes long, the longest half an hour. Sometimes I came to in another place and doing something different, but never harmful. I thought my black daydreams were a weakness or a judgment, but Nature was wise. I was not strong and did not know enough to bear them yet. Under my father's rule I learned my craft and made my body strong and always studied when and as I could.

When I was 25 I was deep in love—this was before your mother—with a beautiful girl who died of consumption. Pining upon her grave I had a daydream, but this time by the strength of my desire I kept my mind white. I swam down through the loam and I was joined with her in full bodily union. She said this coupling must be our last, but that I now would have the power to move at will under and through the earth from time to time. We kissed farewell forever, *Lorchen* and I, and I swam down and on, her knight of dreams, exulting in my strength like some old kobold breasting the rock. It is not black down there, my son, as one would think. There are glorious colors. Water is blue, metals bright red and yellow, rocks green and brown, *undsoweiter*. After a time I swam back and up into my body, standing on the new-made grave. I was no longer pining, but profoundly grateful.

So I learned how to divine, my son, to be a fish of earth when there is need and Nature wills, to dive into the Hall of the Mountain King dancing with light. Always the finest colors and the strangest hues lay west. Rare earths they are named by scientists, who are wise, though blind. That's why I brought us here. Under the greatest of oceans, earth is a rainbow web and Nature is a spider spinning and walking it.

And now you have shown you have my power, *mein Sohn*, but in a greater form. You have black nightdreams. I know, for I have sat by you as you slept and heard you talk and seen your terror, which would soon destroy you if you could recall it, as one night showed. But Nature in her wisdom blindfolds you until you have the needed strength and learning. As you know by now, I have provided for your education at a good Eastern school praised by Harley Warren, the finest employer that I ever had, who knew a lot about the nether realms.

And now you're strong enough, *mein Sohn*, to act—and wise, I hope, as Nature's acolyte. You've studied deep and made your body strong. You have the power and the hour has come. The triton blows his horn. Rise up, *mein Iieber Georg*, and follow me. Now is the time. Build upon what I've built, but build more greatly. Yours is the wider and the greater realm. Make your mind white. With or without some lovely woman's help, now burst the gate of dreams!

Your loving Father

At any other time that document would have moved and shaken me profoundly. Truth to tell, it did so move and shake me, but I had been already so moved and shaken by today's climactic events that my first thought was of how the letter applied to them.

I echoed from the letter, "Now burst the gate of dreams," and then added, suppressing another interpretation, "That means I should take Morgan's drug tonight. Let's do it, Albert, as you proposed this morning."

"Your father's last command," he said heavily, clearly much impressed by that aspect of the letter. Then, "Georg, this is a most fantastic, shattering missive! That sign he got—sounds like migraine. And his references to the rare-earth elements—that could be crucial. And colors in the earth perceived perhaps by extrasensory perception! The Miskatonic project should have started investigating dowsing years ago. We've been blind—" He broke off. "You're right, Georg, and I am strongly tempted. But the danger! How to choose? On the one hand a supreme parental injunction and our raging curiosities—for mine's a-boil. On the other hand Great Cthulhu and his minions. Oh, for an indication of how to decide!"

There was a sharp knocking at the door. We both started. After a moment's pause I moved rapidly, Albert following. With my hand on the latch I paused again. I had not heard a car stop outside. Through the stout oak came the cry, "Telegram!" I opened it.

There was revealed a skinny, somewhat jaunty-looking youth of pale complexion scattered with big freckles and with carrot red hair under his visored cap. His trousers were wrapped tightly around his legs by bicycle clips.

"Either of you Albert N. Wilmarth?" he inquired coolly. "I am he," Albert said, stepping forward.

"Then sign for this, please."

Albert did so and tipped him, substituting a dime for a nickel at the last instant.

The youth grinned widely, said, "G'night," and sauntered off. I closed the door and turned quickly back.

Albert had torn open the flimsy envelope and drawn out and spread the missive. He was pale already, but as his eyes flashed across it, he grew paler still. It was as if he were two-thirds of a ghost already and its message had made him a full one. He held the yellow sheet out to me wordlessly:

LOVECRAFT IS DEAD STOP THE WHIPPOORWILLS DID NOT SING STOP TAKE COURAGE STOP DANFORTH

I looked up. Albert's face was still as ghostly white, but its expression had changed from uncertainty and dread to decision and challenge.

"That tips the balance," he said. "What have I more to lose? By George, Georg, we'll have a look down into the abyss on whose edge we totter. Are you game?"

"I proposed it," I said. "Shall I fetch your valise from the car?"

"No need," he said, whipping from his inside breast pocket the small paper packet from Dr. Morgan he'd shown me that morning. "I had the hunch that we were going to use it, until that apparition at your father's tomb shattered my nerves."

I fetched small glasses. He split evenly between them the small supply of white powder, which dissolved readily in the water I added under his direction. Then he looked at me quizzically, holding his glass as if for a toast.

"No question of to whom we drink this," I said, indicating the telegram he was still holding in his other hand.

He winced slightly. "No, don't speak his name. Let's rather drink to *all* our brave comrades who have perished or suffered greatly in the Miskatonic project."

That "our" really warmed me. We touched glasses and drained them. The draft was faintly bitter.

"Morgan writes that the effects are quite rapid," he said. "First drowsiness, then sleep, and then hopefully dreams. He's tried it twice himself with Rice and doughty old Armitage, who laid the Dunwich Horror with him. The first time they visited in dream Gilman's Walpurgis hyperspace; the second, the inner city at the two magnetic poles—an area topologically unique."

Meanwhile I'd hurriedly poured a little more wine and lukewarm coffee and we'd settled ourselves comfortably in our easy chairs before the fire, the dancing flames of which became both a little blurred and a little dazzling as the drug began to take effect.

"Really, that was a most amazing missive from your father," he chatted on rapidly. "Spinning a rainbow web under the Pacific, the lines those weirdly litten tunnels—truly most vivid. Would Cthulhu be the spider? No, by Gad, I'd prefer your father's goddess Nature any day. She's kindlier at least."

"Albert," I said somewhat drowsily, thinking of personality exchanges, "could those creatures possibly be benign, or at least less malevolent than we infer? —as my father's subterranean visionings might indicate. My winged worms, even?"

"Most of our comrades did not find them so," he replied judiciously, "though of course there's our *Innsmouth* hero. What has he really found in Y'ha-nthlei? Wonder and glory? Who knows? Who can say he knows? Or old Akeley out in the stars—is his brain suffering the tortures of the damned in its shining metal cylinder? Or is it perpetually exalted by ever-changing true visions of infinity? And what did poor shoggoth-stampeded Danforth really think he saw beyond the two horrific mountain chains down there before he got amnesia? And is that last a blessing or a curse? Gad, he and I are suited to each other...the mind-smitten helping the nerve-shattered...fit nurses for felines...."

"That was surely heavy news he sent you," I observed with a little yawn, indicating the telegram about Lovecraft, which he still held tightly between finger and thumb. "You know, before that wire came, I had the craziest idea—that somehow you and he were the same person. I don't mean Danforth but—"

"Don't say it!" he said sharply. Then his voice went immediately drowsy as he continued, "But the roster of the perished is longer far...poor Lake and poor, poor Gedney and all those others under their Southern Cross and Magellanic shroud...the mathematical genius Walter Gilman who lost heart most terribly...the nonagenarian street-slain Angell and lightning-frozen Blake in Providence...Edward Pickman Derby, Arkham's plump Shelley deliquescing in his witch-wife's corpse...Gad, this is hardly the cheerfulest topic.... You know, Georg, down in San Diego young Akeley (G.G.) showed me a hidden sea-cave bluer than Capri and on its black beach of magnetite the webbed footprint of a merman...one of the Gnorri? ...and then...oh yes, of course... there's Wilbur Whateley, who was almost nine feet tall...though he hardly counts as a Miskatonic researcher...but the whippoorwills didn't get him either...or his big brother...."

I was still looking at the fire, and the dancing points of light in and around it had become the stars, thick as the Pleiades and Hyades, through which old Akeley journeyed eternally, when unconsciousness closed on me too, black as the wind-stirred, infinite gulf of darkness which Robert Blake saw in the Shining Trapezohedron, black as N'kai.

I awoke stiff and chilled. The fire at which I'd been staring was white ashes only. I felt a sharp pang of disappointment that I had not dreamed at all. Then I became aware of the low, irregular, inflected humming or buzzing that filled my ears.

I stood up with difficulty. My companion slumbered still, but his shut-eyed, death-pale face had a hideously tormented look and he writhed slowly and agonizedly from time to time as if in the grip of foulest nightmare. The yellow telegram had fallen from his fingers and lay on the floor. As I approached him I realized that the sound filling my ears was coming from between his lips, which were unceasingly a-twitch, and as I leaned my head close to them, the horridly articulate droning became recognizable words and phrases:

"The pulpy, tentacled head," I heard in horror, "*Cthulhu fhtagn*, the *wrong* geometry, the polarizing miasma, the prismatic distortion, *Cthulhu R'lyeh*, the positive blackness, the living nothingness..."

I could not bear to watch his dreadful agony or listen to those poisonous, *twangy* words an instant longer, so I seized him by the shoulders and shook him violently, though even as I did so there sprang into my mind my father's stern injunction never to do so.

His eyes came open wide in his white face and his mouth clamped shut as he came up with a powerful shove of his bent arms against the chair's arms which his hands had been clutching. It was as if it were happening in slow motion, though paradoxically it also seemed to be happening quite swiftly. He gave me a last mute look of utter horror and then he turned and ran, taking fantastically long strides, out through the door, which his outstretched hand threw wide ahead of him, and disappeared into the night.

I hobbled after him as swiftly as I could. I heard the motor catch at the starter's second prod. I screamed, "Wait, Albert, wait!" As I neared the Tin Hind, its lights flashed on and its motor roared and I was engulfed in acrid exhaust fumes as it screeched out the drive with a spattering of gravel and down the first curve.

I waited there then in the cold until all sight and sound of it had vanished in the night, which was already paling a little with the dawn.

And then I realized that I was still hearing those malignant, gloating, evilly resonant voices.

"*Cthulhu fhtagn,*" they were saying (and have been saying and are saying now and will forever), "the spider tunnels, the black infinities, the colors in pitch-darkness, the tiered towers of Yuggoth, the glittering centipedes, the winged worms...."

Somewhere not far off I heard a low, half-articulate whirring sound.

I went back into the house and wrote this manuscript.

And now I shall place the last with its interleafed communications and also the two books of poetry that led to all this in the copper and German silver casket, and I shall carry that with me down into the basement, where I shall take up my father's sledge (wondering in which body I shall survive, if at all) and literally carry out his last letter's last injunction.

Very early on the morning of Tuesday, March 16, 1937, the householders of Paradise Crest (then Vultures Roost) were disturbed by a clashing rumble and a sharp earth-shock which they attributed to an earthquake, and indeed very small tremors were registered at Griffith Observatory, UCLA, and USC, though on no other seismographs. Daylight revealed that the brick house locally known as Fischer's Folly had fallen in so completely that not one brick remained joined to another. Moreover, there appeared to be fewer bricks in view than the house would have accounted for, as if half of them had been trucked away during the night, or else fallen into some great space beneath the basement. In fact, the appearance of the ruin was of a gigantic ant lion's-pit lined by bricks instead of sand grains. The place was deemed, and actually was, dangerous, and was shortly filled in and in part cemented over, and apparently not long afterward rebuilt upon.

The body of the owner, a quietly spoken, crippled young man named Georg Reuter Fischer, was discovered flat on its face in the edge of the rubble with hands thrown out (the metal casket by one of them) as though he had been trying to flee outdoors when caught by the collapse. His death, however, was attributed to a slightly earlier accident or insane act of self-destruction involving acid, of which his eccentric father was once known to have kept a supply. It was well that easy identification was made possible by his conspicuously twisted right foot, for when the body was turned over it was discovered that something had eaten away the entire front of his face and also those portions of his skull and jaw and the entire forebrain.

Black Hill

Orrin Grey

That place was still called "Black Hill" when I come there, though it was as flat as a plate and nothing stood taller'n a man's shoulder far as the eye could see, 'cept the shacks and the derricks. Not a tree nor a lick of grass to be seen, everything stomped dead by the men and the horses and the trucks.

My first day there, I asked Burke why they called it "Black Hill" and he laughed and stamped his foot on the bare, brown dirt. "The hill's unner there," he said. "Not a lake nor a river, like they say it, but sure enough a hill, all piled up an' waitin', pressin' up on th' ground, clawin' ta get out. Nothin' but the dirt 'tween it an' us. We poke a hole in th' dirt an' up it jumps!"

Burke had been out there from the beginning. He was there when they drove the Stapleton #1, and he saw the black gold just well up from the ground and come pouring out. Enough, it seemed, to make any man rich.

He bought up a parcel of land out west of El Dorado with the money he made and started the Black Hill Oil Company. By the time he sent for me, the Black Hill field was already putting up more'n three hundred thousand barrels a day.

I didn't know why he needed me and I said as much, though I was thankful for the work. He just shook his head. "This here's only th' beginnin'," he said. "There's another world down there, Smith. Things the like-a-which Man ain't never dreamed, let alone seen. If all I wanted was ta be rich, I coulda quit by now, but there's somethin' more down there. Somethin' else. I cain't say what, exactly, but I aim ta find it."

Burke and I had worked together in Iowa for a spell, years back. I wasn't nothing but an amateur geologist. I'd delivered the mail, 'fore I ruint my leg, and I'd taught a bit of school. I had a wife and two girls back in Iowa, but there weren't no work for a man like me in those days anywhere but in the fields, so the fields was where I worked. And when Burke called for me, I came because the money was good and I knew him for a man I could put my back against.

I lived in the shacks, like most everyone else who worked the fields. As field geologist, I had one to myself, but it still weren't much more'n four walls and a bed. There was a desk against the wall, under the one window, and I sat there and wrote letters to Matilda and the girls when I could.

Burke worked the men hard but fair. He strode about the field, barking orders and working with 'em side-by-side. He was as tall and rudely constructed as a derrick hisself, and his hair and beard were as bristly and red as an oil fire. He was missing two-and-a-half fingers on his right hand, lost to one of the walking boards. His left ear was gone and half his face a mess of scars, owing to a mishap with some nitroglycerine.

He'd been married back when I knew him, but his wife had since passed and left him with a pretty little dark-eyed girl who, I gathered, lived with some spinster aunt at the hotel in town. Whenever I rode in with Burke on one errand or another, he'd always insist we stop by the hotel so he could buy her a root beer or an ice cream, and pick her up in his long arms and spin her above his head. It was a sweet sight, seeing how he doted on her. The only thing it made me regret was my own girls being so far away, and how I was missing watching them grow up.

ॐ

I'd been at the field three weeks when Burke rode up with a pair of horses, told me to mount up and follow him. We rode out past the edge of the field, past the last of the derricks, to a spot where a copse of trees once stood, 'fore they were all dragged down and sawed up for timber. The ground was swept as smooth and flat as if it was the floor of some fella's house.

"This here," Burke said, "is what I bought this land fer. There was somethin' here when I come out, a wheel a stones like them the Injuns set aside, though I could'n find nobody from 'round here could say which tribe mighta put 'em up. I come out 'fore the men, moved them stones myself, by hand. Didn' want nobody gettin' spooked off. They's a wild mix a folks works th' fields, as you well know, an' some of 'em are too superstitious fer their own good. But look here; I don' think this was no burial ground nor nothin' of th' sort. I think them Injuns, whichever ones they was, *knowed* they was somethin' unner this ground an' they marked th' spot."

"You mean oil?" I asked. I knew some folks believed oil was medicinal, that they'd set up shacks and stagecoach stops around tar springs and drunk the black stuff that bubbled up to cure everything from gout to infertility. And I knew the Indians were better geologists than anybody'd ever given 'em credit for, better able to find the flow of underground rivers and stratas of good rock than they'd any right to be. So, I didn't suppose it was unreasonable to think they mighta known there was oil down there, or marked the place to find it.

Burke just shrugged at me, didn't answer my question straight. Instead, he said, "Gonna build me a derrick here. Gonna dig deep, deeper'n any well we dug so far. I want you on it, 'cause I know I kin count by you."

And I didn't think nothing more of it, save that I was proud to be trusted, to be depended on. The next day, we started digging.

The digging didn't go easy. It seemed like every day, there was something new went wrong. A storm come up and dropped bucketfuls of hail on the whole field, blew a derrick over. Two of the men got into it over something, and one pulled a knife and killed the other. Three of the men took sick and couldn't work. Four more vanished over the course of a week and weren't never found. And, through it all, the pipe went down and down and down.

We passed over several promising-looking strikes, 'cause they weren't whatever Burke was looking for, and the men working the towers got restless. Still we went down and down, until finally we hit something else.

There was a sound come up from the hole, like a gasp. The men figured we'd hit a pocket of gas and everyone backed off in case it was like to burn. Then the derrick shook all the way up and the ground seemed to slide a little under our feet. There come a noise from the hole like I ain't never heard the ground make in all my years. When I was a boy, my pa'd known a man who worked a whaling ship and he said that whales *sang* to one another. He'd put his hands together over his mouth and blown a call that he said was as close as he could do to what they sounded like. This sounded like that call.

All the men went back another pace, not knowing if maybe we'd hit a sink-hole, or God knows what. There was another groan, then an old cave stink, and then the black stuff started coming up around the pipe like a tide. I'd seen gushers in my day, the pressurized wells that blew the tops off the derricks, but this weren't the same. This weren't no geyser; this were a flood, the oil *pouring* up from under the ground like a barrel that's been overturned. Everybody was silent for another minute and then the men gathered 'round all cheered, 'cause they knowed we'd finally hit whatever it was we'd been aiming at.

ॐ

I'd expected Burke to be blown over by our success, but when he come out to look at the well, his smile didn't touch his eyes none.

That night, he invited me to eat dinner with him in his shack, which weren't really much better'n mine, though it had a coupla rooms. I remembered his wife and little girl had lived in it with him when he started the field, back before his wife got carried off by whatever it was carried her off.

Burke served me a dinner of baked beans and set out a bottle of whiskey on the table between us. He seemed distracted, thoughtful. "Pensive," as they say. He told me I'd done a good job on the well, but didn't seem to want to talk much more about it.

"I got no need ta tell you what oil is," he finally said, after we'd drained most of the bottle. "Dead stuff. Rotted a thousand years, pressed down by th' dirt. You know who th' first wildcatters in this country consulted 'fore diggin'? Not geologists. Mediums. Spiritualists. They knowed, even then. Hell, mebbe they knowed better. Mebbe it's us has forgot."

He stopped and raised his glass, only to find it empty. He sat it back down and continued, without refilling it, "Somethin' dies an' you put it down in th' dirt; it' don' disappear. It stays, forever. They's not a place on this earth somethin' ain't died, where somethin' don' lay buried. All this world's a boneyard an' us just ghouls crouched on top, breakin' open tombs. I made my peace wi' it. A man does, ta live th' life we live. But here..." He reached over to a sideboard and took up an old, worn black Bible and opened it up. From the back, he took out a scrap of paper, brown and worn smooth by years of handling, and passed it to me. "Kin you read that?" he asked.

I could, but only just. The handwriting was careful but uneven, like it'd been copied down slow by a palsied hand. It was just one line: *THAT IS NOT DEAD WHICH CAN ETERNAL LIE.*

"Took that off a feller came ta shut down th' field," Burke said. "Fancied hisself some kinda preacher, though nota-th' Word a God. He said all sortsa things, crazy things, 'bout there bein' somethin' underneath us, somethin' that dreamed though it was dead. He had a gun. Managed to light a buncha th' place on fire. Took an ax ta one-a-th' derricks, 'fore I shot him wi' my rifle.

He had that in his pocket. Can't rightly say why I kept it, but I thought about it a lot since. An' damned if it ain't right, just a bit. Oil, right? It's dead, jus' dead stuff crammed down there in its tomb, but it can lay there forever, cain't it? An' when we dig it up, there it is, waitin' to come out, fulla heat an' fire an' life. What does that tell ya?"

I didn't get a chance to answer him and I don't rightly know what I'd've said if I had, because right then, he noticed the flicker of the shadows against the wall. "Fire," he breathed and my heart jumped up, 'cause fire's the worst curse there is when you're in the field.

Burke rushed out, already barking orders, and I followed him. If the doubtful and morbid thoughts of a few minutes before were still in him, as they must've been, then he kept 'em well hid. He shouted to the men and they jumped to, fighting to keep the fires away from the pipes and the nitroglycerine trucks.

I was a few paces behind Burke and when the ground shivered under my feet, I stopped and swung my eyes across the field. The fires seemed like they was burning everywhere, like they'd sprung up from every corner of the place at once. I could see the whole field, it seemed like, all licked with curling orange tongues, the derricks that wasn't yet burning standing like the silhouettes of ships' masts before the flames.

The ground gave another shake under me, like the flank of a horse shivering to throw off flies. Through the smoke, I saw my derrick sway. I ran toward it. The fire hadn't reached it yet and I was prob'ly needed someplace else, but I somehow had a feeling that the derrick was where I had to be.

As I got right up to it, I heard that same sound, the one I remembered from earlier in the day, and I saw the derrick start to topple. At the same time, a crack opened up below me like a mouth in the dirt. I felt my feet going out from under me and saw that big skeleton of wood and metal coming down toward my head. The next thing I remember, I was hanging from the derrick where it laid across an empty black chasm, a pit that seemed like it went down all the way to the center of the earth. Down in that darkness, I saw something move.

In the years that've intervened since that night, the doctors have tried their best to convince me that I misremember some of what come next, but I know they're wrong. I remember it clear as day. There was something down in the dark below me, something that heaved itself up toward the surface, toward the light, toward me. I remembered suddenly why that place was called "Black Hill." I saw that great bulk heave and slop toward me in the dark. I saw what looked like golden eyes opening and closing, and hungry mouths smacking. I smelt a smell like what sometimes comes up from caves and holes that've been closed away fer too long. I heard a hiss and a groan, and I believe I closed my eyes. Then I heard Burke's voice.

He was shouting, but there was something different about the sound. It was ragged and hoarse, but that wasn't it. It was like he was talking straight at a feller, not like he was yelling all around as he had been before.

I opened my eyes up again and I saw him, standing by the edge of the crack in the ground, looking like some heathen god with the fires burning behind him. He was shouting down into the pit.

"What more kin you take from me?" he demanded. "What more could you want? You took ma hand, ma face, ma wife! I done give you ever'thin' I got, damn you, ever'thin' I am. I ain't got nothin' left you kin take, nothin' but her, an' her y'll not have! I'll see you in hell myself, first."

And then he stepped into the hole. Other men in the field heard Burke shout and saw me hanging there on the tipped-over derrick. But if anyone else saw what happened to him, they pretended not to. They said they saw him standing there, and that they saw him fall, but that's it. I know, though, that he didn't fall. That he went down there to spite the Devil, or whatever it was he saw down there, and something came up to meet him, something black and old and putrid as a rotted log that's set for months at the bottom of a pond. I saw him go down into that blackness like a mammoth being pulled down into a tar pit. That's the last thing I saw 'fore I blacked out.

ಐ

By the time I come to, the fires had been put out. The men told me that, even though I'd been unconscious, it'd taken three of them to pry my arms off the derrick's supports.

Soon as I was able to walk again, I made a man take me out to survey the field. The damage was bad: nearly half the derricks lost, barrels of oil burned up, and one of the nitroglycerine trucks had exploded. My derrick still lay on its side, but there was little enough to show that the crack had ever been beneath it. I asked the man with me. He said that the ground had shaken again and the crack sealed up. There was just a scar to mark its passing, an uneven place where one lip of the ground was higher'n the other.

Burke had a business partner, a banker from Wichita, who took over his interest in the Black Hill Oil Company and sold it off to one of the other concerns. In his will, Burke had left a stipulation that his daughter never have a stake in it. By the time she was of an age to marry, she was provided fer nicely by the investment of Burke's money into other ventures.

I never worked the fields again. When my wife died, I come here to the sanitarium, where I've stayed ever since. My two girls are grown and married now, but they take turns coming to visit me. They've taken such good care of me since the incident.

There're days when I think I could leave this place, move in with one of them and have a life outside these walls, long as I stayed out of automobiles and away from oil fields. And maybe I would, were it not fer the dreams.

I dream, not of the world, but of the future. The future that Burke and I helped to bring about and that I'm powerless to prevent. I see a country criss-crossed with roads where thousands of automobiles drive every day. I see ships as big as whales, plying the sea with bellies full of black blood. I see a world of perpetual light and motion, powered by the unquiet dead.

The God of Dark Laughter

Michael Chabon

Thirteen days after the Entwhistle-Ealing Bros. Circus left Ashtown, beating a long retreat toward its winter headquarters in Peru, Indiana, two boys out hunting squirrels in the woods along Portwine Road stumbled on a body that was dressed in a mad suit of purple and orange velour. They found it at the end of a muddy strip of gravel that began, five miles to the west, as Yuggogheny County Road 22A. Another half mile farther to the east and it would have been left to my colleagues over in Fayette County to puzzle out the question of who had shot the man and skinned his head from chin to crown and clavicle to clavicle, taking ears, eyelids, lips, and scalp in a single grisly flap, like the cupped husk of a peeled orange. My name is Edward D. Satterlee, and for the last twelve years I have faithfully served Yuggogheny County as its district attorney, in cases that have all too often run to the outrageous and bizarre. I make the following report in no confidence that it, or I, will be believed, and beg the reader to consider this, at least in part, my letter of resignation.

The boys who found the body were themselves fresh from several hours' worth of bloody amusement with long knives and dead squirrels, and at first the investigating officers took them for the perpetrators of the crime. There was blood on the boys' cuffs, their shirttails, and the bills of their gray twill caps. But the country detectives and I quickly moved beyond Joey Matuszak

343

and Frankie Corro. For all their familiarity with gristle and sinew and the bright-purple discovered interior of a body, the boys had come into the station looking pale and bewildered, and we found ample evidence at the crime scene of their having lost the contents of their stomachs when confronted with the corpse.

Now, I have every intention of setting down the facts of this case as I understand and experienced them, without fear of the reader's doubting them (or my own sanity), but I see no point in mentioning any further *anatomical* details of the crime, except to say that our coroner, Dr. Sauer, though he labored at the problem with a sad fervor was hard-put to establish conclusively that the victim had been dead before his killer went to work on him with a very long, very sharp knife.

The dead man, as I have already mentioned, was attired in a curious suit—the trousers and jacket of threadbare purple velour, the waistcoat bright orange, the whole thing patched with outsized squares of fabric cut from a variety of loudly clashing plaids. It was on account of the patches, along with the victim's cracked and split-soled shoes and a certain undeniable shabbiness in the stuff of the suit, that the primary detective—a man not apt to see deeper than the outermost wrapper of the world (we do not attract, I must confess, the finest police talent in this doleful little corner of western Pennsylvania)—had already figured the victim for a vagrant, albeit one with extraordinarily big feet.

"Those cannot possibly be his real shoes, Ganz, you idiot," I gently suggested. The call, patched through to my boarding house from that gruesome clearing in the woods, had interrupted my supper, which by a grim coincidence had been a Brunswick stew (the specialty of my Virginia-born landlady) or pork and *squirrel.* "They're supposed to make you laugh."

"They *are* pretty funny," said Ganz. "Come to think of it." Detective John Ganz was a large-boned fellow, upholstered in a layer of ruddy flesh. He breathed through his mouth, and walked with a tall man's defeated stoop, and five times a day he took out his comb and ritually plastered his thinning blond hair to the top of his head with a dime-size dab of Tres Flores.

When I arrived at the clearing, having abandoned my solitary dinner, I found the corpse lying just as the young hunters had come upon it, supine, arms thrown up and to either side of the flayed face in a startled attitude that fuelled the hopes of poor Dr. Sauer that the victim's death by gunshot had preceded his mutilation. Ganz or one of the other investigators had kindly thrown a chamois cloth over the vandalized head. I took enough of a peek beneath it to provide me with everything that I or the reader could possibly need to know about the condition of the head—I will never forget the sight of that monstrous, fleshless grin—and to remark the dead man's unusual choice of cravat. It was a giant, floppy bow tie, white with orange and purple polka dots.

"Damn you, Ganz," I said, though I was not in truth addressing the poor fellow, who, I knew, would not be able to answer my question anytime soon. "What's a dead clown doing in my woods?"

We found no wallet on the corpse, nor any kind of identifying objects. My men, along with the better part of the Ashtown Police Department, went over and over the woods east of town, hourly widening the radius of their search. That day, when not attending to my other duties (I was then in the process of breaking up the Dushnyk cigarette-smuggling ring), I managed to work my way back along a chain of inferences to the Entwhistle-Ealing Bros. Circus, which, as I eventually recalled, had recently stayed on the eastern outskirts of Ashtown, at the fringe of the woods where the body was found.

The following day, I succeeded in reaching the circus's general manager, a man named Onheuser, at their winter headquarters in Peru. He informed me over the phone that the company had left Pennsylvania and was now en route to Peru, and I asked him if he had received any reports from the road manager of a clown's having suddenly gone missing.

"Missing?" he said. I wished that I could see his face, for I thought I heard the flatted note of something false in his tone. Perhaps he was merely nervous about talking to a county district attorney. The Entwhistle-Ealing Bros. Circus was a mangy affair, by all accounts, and probably no stranger to pursuit by officers of the court. "Why, I don't believe so, no."

I explained to him that a man who gave every indication of having once been a circus clown had turned up dead in a pinewood outside Ashtown, Pennsylvania.

"Oh, no," Onheuser said. "I truly hope he wasn't one of mine, Mr. Satterlee."

"It is possible you might have left one of your clowns behind, Mr. Onheuser?"

"Clowns are special people," Onheuser replied, sounding a touch on the defensive. "They love their work, but sometimes it can get to be a little, well, too much for them." It developed that Mr. Onheuser had, in his younger days, performed as a clown, under the name of Mr. Wingo, in the circus of which he was now the general manager. "It's not unusual for a clown to drop out for a little while, cool his heels, you know, in some town where he can get a few months of well-earned rest. It isn't *common*, I wouldn't say, but it's not unusual. I will wire my road manager—they're in Canton, Ohio—and see what I can find out."

I gathered, reading between the lines, that clowns were high-strung types, and not above going on the occasional bender. This poor fellow had probably jumped ship here two weeks ago, holing up somewhere with a case of rye, only to run afoul of a very nasty person, possibly one who harbored no great love of clowns. In fact, I had an odd feeling, nothing more than a hunch, really, that the ordinary citizens of Ashtown and its environs were safe, even though the killer was still at large. Once more, I picked up a slip of paper that I had tucked into my desk blotter that morning. It was something that Dr. Sauer had clipped from his files and passed along to me. *Coulrophobia: morbid, irrational fear of or aversion to clowns.*

"Er, listen, Mr. Satterlee," Onheuser went on. "I hope you won't mind my asking. That is, I hope it's not a, well, a confidential police matter, or something of the sort. But I know that when I do get through to them, out in Canton, they're going to want to know."

I guessed, somehow, what he was about to ask me. I could hear the prickling fear behind his curiosity, the note of dread in his voice. I waited him out.

"Did they—was there any—how did he die?"

"He was shot," I said, for the moment supplying the least interesting part of the answer, tugging on that loose thread of fear. "In the head."

"And there was... forgive me. No... no harm done? To the body? Other than the gunshot wound, I mean to say."

"Well, yes, his head *was* rather savagely mutilated," I said brightly. "Is that what you mean to say?"

"Ah! No, no, I don't—"

"The killer or killers removed all the skin from the cranium. It was very skillfully done. Now, suppose you tell me what you know about it."

There was another pause, and a stream of agitated electrons burbled along between us.

"I don't know anything, Mr. District Attorney. I'm really sorry. I really must go now. I'll wire you when I have some—"

The line went dead. He was so keen to hang up on me that he could not even wait to finish his sentence. I got up and went to the shelf where, in recent months, I had taken to keeping a bottle of whiskey tucked behind my bust of Daniel Webster. Carrying the bottle and a dusty glass back to my desk, I sat down and tried to reconcile myself to the thought that I was confronted—not, alas, for the first time in my tenure as chief law-enforcement officer of Yuggogheny County—with a crime whose explanation was going to involve not the usual amalgam of stupidity, meanness, and singularly poor judgment but the incalculable intentions of a being who is genuinely evil. What disheartened me was not that I viewed a crime committed out of the promptings of an evil nature as inherently less liable to solution than the misdeeds of the foolish, the unlucky, or the habitually cruel. On the contrary, evil often expresses itself through refreshingly discernible patterns, through schedules and syllogisms. But the presence of evil, once scented, tends to bring out all that is most irrational and uncontrollable in the public imagination. It is a catalyst for pea-brained theories, gimcrack scholarship, and the credulous cosmologies of hysteria.

At that moment, there was a knock on the door to my office, and Detective Ganz came in. At one time I would have tried to hide the glass of whiskey, behind the typewriter or the photo of my wife and son, but now it did not seem to be worth the effort. I was not fooling anyone. Ganz took note of the glass in my hand with a raised eyebrow and a school-marmish pursing of his lips.

"Well?" I said. There had been a brief period, following my son's death and the subsequent suicide of my dear wife, Mary, when I had indulged the pitying regard of my staff. I now found that I regretted having shown such weakness. "What is it, then? Has something turned up?"

"A cave," Ganz said. "The poor bastard was living in a cave."

The range of low hills and hollows separating lower Yuggogheny from Fayette County is rotten with caves. For many years, when I was a boy, a man named Colonel Earnshawe operated penny tours of the iridescent organ pipes and jagged stone teeth of Neighborsburg Caverns, before they collapsed in the mysterious earthquake of 1919, killing the Colonel and his sister Irene, and putting to rest many strange rumors about that eccentric old pair. My childhood friends and I, ranging in the woods, would from time to time come upon the root-choked mouth of a cave exhaling its cool plutonic breath, and dare one another to leave the sunshine and enter that world of shadow— that entrance, as it always seemed to me, to the legendary past itself, where the bones of Indians and Frenchmen might lie moldering. It was in one of these anterooms of buried history that the beam of a flashlight, wielded by a deputy sheriff from Plunkettsburg, had struck the silvery lip of a can of pork and beans. Calling to his companions, the deputy plunged through a curtain of spiderweb and found himself in the parlor, bedroom, and kitchen of the dead man. There were some cans of chili and hash, a Primus stove, a lantern, a bedroll, a mess kit, and an old Colt revolver, Army issue, loaded and apparently not fired for some time. And there were also books—a Scout guide to roughing it, a collected Blake, and a couple of odd texts, elderly and tattered: one in German called "Über das Finstere Lachen," by a man named Friedrich von Junzt, which appeared to be religious or philosophical in nature, and one a small volume bound in black leather and printed in no alphabet known to me, the letters sinuous and furred with wild diacritical marks.

"Pretty heavy reading for a clown," Ganz said.

"It's not all rubber chickens and hosing each other down with seltzer bottles, Jack."

"Oh, no?"

"No, sir. Clowns have unsuspected depths."

"I'm starting to get that impression, sir."

Propped against the straightest wall of the cave, just beside the lantern, there was a large mirror, still bearing the bent clasps and sheared bolts that had once, I inferred, held it to the wall of a filling-station men's room. At its foot was the item that had earlier confirmed to Detective Ganz—and now confirmed to me as I went to inspect it—the recent habitation of the cave by a painted circus clown: a large, padlocked wooden makeup kit, of heavy and rather elaborate construction. I directed Ganz to send for a Pittsburgh criminalist who had served us with discretion in the horrific Primm case, reminding him that nothing must be touched until this Mr. Espy and his black bag of dusts and luminous powders arrived.

The air in the cave had a sharp, briny tinge; beneath it there was a stale animal musk that reminded me, absurdly, of the smell inside a circus tent.

"Why was he living in a cave?" I said to Ganz. "We have a perfectly nice hotel in town."

"Maybe he was broke."

"Or maybe he thought that a hotel was the first place they would look for him."

Ganz looked confused, and a little bit annoyed, as if he thought I were being deliberately mysterious.

"*Who* was looking for him?"

"I don't know, Detective. Maybe no one. I'm just thinking out loud."

Impatience marred Ganz's fair, bland features. He could tell that I was in the grip of a hunch, and hunches were always among the first considerations ruled out by the procedural practices of Detective John Ganz. My hunches had, admittedly, an uneven record. In the Primm business, one had very nearly got both Ganz and me killed. As for the wayward hunch about my mother's old crony Thaddeus Craven and the strength of his will to quit drinking—I suppose I shall regret indulging that one for the rest of my life.

"If you'll excuse me, Jack..." I said. "I'm having a bit of a hard time with the stench in here."

"I was thinking he might have been keeping a pig." Ganz inclined his head to one side and gave an empirical sniff. "It smells like pig to me."

I covered my mouth and hurried outside in the cool, dank pinewood. I gathered in great lungfuls of air. The nausea passed, and I filled my pipe, walking up and down outside the mouth of the cave and trying to connect this new discovery to my talk with the circus man, Onheuser. Clearly, he had suspected that this clown might have met with a grisly end. Not only that, he had known that his fellow circus people would fear the very same thing—as if there were some coulrophobic madman with a knife who was as much a part of circus lore as the prohibition on whistling in the dressing room or on looking over your shoulder when you marched in a circus parade.

I got my pipe lit, and wandered down into the woods, toward the clearing where the boys had stumbled over the dead man, following a rough trail that the police had found. Really, it was not a trail so much as an impromptu alley of broken saplings and trampled ground that wound a convoluted course down the hill from the cave to the clearing. It appeared to have been blazed a few days before by the victim and his pursuer; near the bottom, where the trees gave way to open sky, there were grooves of plowed earth that corresponded neatly with encrustations on the heels of the clown's giant brogues. The killer must have caught the clown at the edge of the clearing, and then dragged him along by the hair, or by the collar of his shirt, for the last twenty-five yards, leaving this furrowed record of the panicked, slipping flight of the clown. The presumed killer's footprints were everywhere in evidence, and appeared to have been made by a pair of long and pointed boots. But the really puzzling thing was a third set of prints, which Ganz had noticed and mentioned to me, scattered here and there along the cold black mud of the path. They seemed to have been made by a barefoot child of eight or nine years. And damned, as Ganz had concluded his report to me, if that barefoot child did not appear to have been dancing!

I came into the clearing, a little short of breath, and stood listening to the wind in the pines and the distant rumble of the state highway, until my pipe went out. It was a cool afternoon, but the sky had been blue all day and the woods were peaceful and fragrant. Nevertheless, I was conscious of a mounting sense of disquiet as I stood over the bed of sodden leaves where the body had been found. I did not then, nor do I now, believe in ghosts, but as the sun dipped down behind the tops of the trees, lengthening the long shadows encompassing me, I became aware of an irresistible feeling that somebody was watching me. After a moment, the feeling intensified, and localized, as it were, so I was certain that to see who it was I need only turn around. Bravely—meaning not that I am a brave man but that I behaved as if I were—I took my matches from my jacket pocket and relit my pipe. Then I turned. I knew that when I glanced behind me I would not see Jack Ganz or one of the other policemen standing there; any of them would have said something to me by now. No, it was either going to be nothing at all or something that I could not even allow myself to imagine.

It was, in fact, a baboon, crouching on its hind legs in the middle of the trail, regarding me with close-set orange eyes, one hand cupped at its side. It had great puffed whiskers and a long canine snout. There was something in the barrel chest and the muttonchop sideburns that led me to conclude, correctly, as it turned out, that the specimen was male. For all his majestic bulk, the old fellow presented a rather sad spectacle. His fur was matted and caked with mud, and a sticky coating of pine needles clung to his feet. The expression in his eyes was unsettlingly forlorn, almost pleading, I would have said, and in his mute gaze I imagined I detected a hint of outraged dignity. This might, of course, have been due to the hat he was wearing. It was conical, parti-colored with orange and purple lozenges, and ornamented at the tip with a bright-orange pompom. Tied under his chin with a length of black ribbon, it hung from the side of his head at a humorous angle. I myself might have been tempted to kill the man who had tied it to my head.

"Was it you?" I said, thinking of Poe's story of the rampaging orang swinging a razor in a Parisian apartment. Had that story had any basis in fact? Could the dead clown have been killed by the pet or sidekick with whom, as the mystery of the animal smell in the cave now resolved itself, he had shared his fugitive existence?

The baboon declined to answer my question. After a moment, though, he raised his long crooked left arm and gestured vaguely toward his belly. The import of this message was unmistakable, and thus I had the answer to my question—if he could not open a can of franks and beans, he would not have been able to perform that awful surgery on his owner or partner.

"All right, old boy," I said. "Let's get you something to eat." I took a step toward him, watching for signs that he might bolt or, worse, throw himself at me. But he sat, looking miserable, clenching something in his right paw. I crossed the distance between us. His rancid-hair smell was unbearable. "You need a bath, don't you?" I spoke, by reflex, as if I were talking to somebody's tired old dog. "Were you and your friend in the habit of bathing together? Were you there when it happened, old boy? Any idea who did it?"

The animal gazed up at me, its eyes kindled with that luminous and sagacious sorrow that lends to the faces of apes and mandrills an air of cousinly reproach, as if we humans have betrayed the principles of our kind. Tentatively, I reached out to him with one hand. He grasped my fingers in his dry leather paw, and then the next instant he had leapt bodily into my arms, like a child seeking solace. The garbage-and-skunk stench of him burned my nose. I gagged and stumbled backward as the baboon scrambled to wrap his arms and legs around me. I must have cried out; a moment later a pair of iron lids seemed to slam against my skull, and the animal went slack, sliding, with a horrible, human sigh of disappointment, to the ground at my feet.

Ganz and two Ashtown policemen came running over and dragged the dead baboon away from me.

"He wasn't—he was just—" I was too outraged to form a coherent expression of my anger. "You could have hit *me*!"

Ganz closed the animal's eyes, and laid its arms out at its sides. The right paw was still clenched in a shaggy fist. Ganz, not without some difficulty, managed to pry it open. He uttered an unprintable oath.

In the baboon's palm lay a human finger. Ganz and I looked at each other, wordlessly confirming that the dead clown had been in possession of a full complement of digits.

"See that Espy gets that finger," I said. "Maybe we can find out whose it was."

"It's a woman's," Ganz said. "Look at that nail."

I took it from him, holding it by the chewed and bloody end so as not to dislodge any evidence that might be trapped under the long nail. Though rigid, it was strangely warm, perhaps from having spent a few days in the vengeful grip of the animal who had claimed it from his master's murderer. It appeared to be an index finger, with a manicured, pointed nail nearly three-quarters of an inch long. I shook my head.

"It isn't painted," I said. "Not even varnished. How many women wear their nails like that?"

"Maybe the paint rubbed off," one of the policemen suggested.

"Maybe," I said. I knelt on the ground beside the body of the baboon. There was, I noted, a wound on the back of his neck, long and deep and crusted over with dirt and dried blood. I now saw him in my mind's eye, dancing like a barefoot child around the murderer and the victim as they struggled down the path to the clearing. It would take a powerful man to fight such an animal off. "I can't believe you killed our only witness, Detective Ganz. The poor bastard was just giving me a hug."

This information seemed to amuse Ganz nearly as much as it puzzled him.

"He was a monkey, sir," Ganz said. "I doubt he—"

"He could make signs, you fool! He told me he was *hungry*."

Ganz blinked, trying, I supposed, to append to his personal operations manual this evidence of the potential usefulness of circus apes to police inquiries.

"If I had a dozen baboons like that one on my staff," I said, "I would never have to leave the office."

That evening, before going home, I stopped by the evidence room in the High Street annex and signed out the two books that had been found in the cave that morning. As I walked back into the corridor, I thought I detected an odd odor—odd, at any rate, for that dull expanse of linoleum and buzzing fluorescent tubes—of the sea: a sharp, salty, briny smell. I decided that it must be some new disinfectant being used by the custodian, but it reminded me of the smell of blood from the specimen bags and sealed containers in the evidence room. I turned the lock on the room's door and slipped the books, in their waxy protective envelope, into my briefcase, and walked down High Street to Dennistoun Road, where the public library was. It stayed open late on Wednesday nights, and I would need a German-English dictionary if my college German and I were going to get anywhere with Herr von Junzt.

The librarian, Lucy Brand, returned my greeting with the circumspect air of one who hopes to be rewarded for her forebearance with a wealth of juicy tidbits. Word of the murder, denuded of most of the relevant details, had made the Ashtown *Ambler* yesterday morning, and though I had cautioned the unlucky young squirrel hunters against talking about the case, already conjectures, misprisions, and outright lies had begun wildly to coalesce; I knew the temper of my home town well enough to realise that if I did not close this case soon things might get out of hand. Ashtown, as the events surrounding the appearance of the so-called Green Man, in 1932, amply demonstrated, has a lamentable tendency toward municipal panic.

Having secured a copy of Köhler's Dictionary of the English and German Languages, I went, on an impulse, to the card catalogue and looked up von Junzt, Friedrich. There was no card for any work by this author—hardly surprising, perhaps, in a small-town library like ours. I returned to the reference shelf, and consulted an encyclopedia of philosophical biography and comparable volumes of philologic reference, but found no entry for any von Junzt—a diplomate, by the testimony of his title page, of the University of Tübingen and of the Sorbonne. It seemed that von Junzt had been dismissed, or expunged, from the dusty memory of his discipline.

It was as I was closing the Encyclopedia of Archaeo-Anthropological Research that a name suddenly leapt out at me, catching my eye just before the pages slammed together. It was a word that I had noticed in von Junzt's book: "Urartu." I barely managed to slip the edge of my thumb into the encyclopedia to mark the place; half a second later and the reference might have been lost to me. As it turned out, the name of von Junzt was also contained—sealed up—in the sarcophagus of this entry, a long and tedious one devoted to the work of an Oxford man by the name of St. Dennis T.R. Gladfellow, "a noted scholar," as the entry had it, "in the field of inquiry into the beliefs of the ancient, largely unknown peoples referred to conjecturally today as proto-Urartians." The reference lay buried in a column dense with comparisons among various bits of obsidian and broken bronze:

G's analysis of the meaning of such ceremonial blades admittedly was aided by the earlier discoveries of Friedrich von Junzt, at the site of the former Temple of Yrrh, in north central Armenia, among them certain sacrificial artifacts pertaining to the worship of the proto-Urartian deity Yĕ-Heh, rather grandly (though regrettably without credible evidence) styled "the god of dark or mocking laughter" by the German, a notorious adventurer and fake whose work, nevertheless, in this instance, has managed to prove useful to science.

The prospect of spending the evening in the company of Herr von Junzt began to seem even less appealing. One of the most tedious human beings I have ever known was my own mother, who, early in my childhood, fell under the spell of Madame Blavatsky and her followers and proceeded to weary my youth and deplete my patrimony with her devotion to that indigestible caseation of balderdash and lies. Mother drew a number of local simpletons into her orbit, among them poor old drunken Thaddeus Craven, and burnt them up as thoroughly as the earth's atmosphere consumes asteroids. The most satisfying episodes of my career have been those which afforded me the opportunity to prosecute charlatans and frauds and those who preyed on the credulous; I did not now relish the thought of sitting at home with such a man all evening, in particular one who spoke only German.

Nevertheless, I could not ignore the undeniable novelty of a murdered circus clown who was familiar with scholarship—however spurious or misguided—concerning the religious beliefs of proto-Urartians. I carried the Köhler's over to the counter, where Lucy Brand waited eagerly for me to spill some small ration of beans. When I offered nothing for her delectation, she finally spoke.

"Was he a German?" she said, showing unaccustomed boldness, it seemed to me.

"Was *who* a German, my dear Miss Brand?"

"The victim." She lowered her voice to a textbook librarian's whisper, though there was no one in the building but old Bob Spherakis, asleep and snoring in the periodicals room over a copy of *Grit*.

"I—I don't know," I said, taken aback by the simplicity of her inference, or rather by its having escaped me. "I suppose he may have been, yes."

She slid the book across the counter toward me.

"There was another one of them in here this afternoon," she said. "At least, I think he was a German. A Jew, come to think of it. Somehow he managed to find the only book in Hebrew we have in our collection. It's one of the books old Mr. Vorzeichen donated when he died. A prayer book, I think it is. Tiny little thing. Black leather."

This information ought to have struck a chord in my memory, of course, but it did not. I settled my hat on my head, bid Miss Brand good night, and walked slowly home, with the dictionary under my arm and, in my briefcase, von Junzt's stout tome and the little black-leather volume filled with sinuous mysterious script.

I will not tax the reader with an account of my struggles with Köhler's dictionary and the thorny bramble of von Junzt's overheated German prose. Suffice to say that it took me the better part of the evening to make my way through the introduction. It was well past midnight by the time I arrived at the first chapter, and nearing two o'clock before I had amassed the information that I will now pass along to the reader, with no endorsement beyond the testimony of those pages, nor any hope of its being believed.

It was a blustery night; I sat in the study on the top floor of my old house's round tower, listening to the windows rattle in their casements, as if a gang of intruders were seeking a way in. In this high room, in 1885, it was said, Howard Ash, the last living descendant of our town's founder, General Hannaniah Ash, had sealed the blank note of his life and dispatched himself, with postage due, to his Creator. A fugitive draft blew from time to time across my desk and stirred the pages of the dictionary by my left hand. I felt, as I read, as if the whole world were asleep—benighted, ignorant, and dreaming—while I had been left to man the crow's nest, standing lonely vigil in the teeth of a storm that was blowing in from a tropic of dread.

According to the scholar or charlatan Friedrich von Junzt, the regions around what is now northern Armenia had spawned, along with an entire cosmology, two competing cults of incalculable antiquity, which survived to the present day: that of Yê-Heh, the God of Dark Laughter, and that of Ai, the God of Unbearable and Ubiquitous Sorrow. The Yê-Hehists viewed the universe as a cosmic hoax, perpetrated by the father-god Yrrh for unknowable purposes: a place of calamity and cruel irony so overwhelming that the only possible response was a malevolent laughter like that, presumably, of Yrrh himself. The laughing followers of baboon-headed Yê-Heh created a sacred burlesque, mentioned by Pausanias and by one of the travellers in Plutarch's dialogue "On the Passing of the Oracles," to express their mockery of life, death, and all human aspirations. The rite involved the flaying of a human head, severed from the shoulders of one who had died in battle or in the course of some other supposedly exalted endeavor. The clown-priest would don the bloodless mask and then dance, making a public travesty of the noble dead. Through generations of inbreeding, the worshippers of Yê-Heh had evolved into a virtual subspecies of humanity, characterized by distended grins and skin as white as chalk. Von Junzt even claimed that the tradition of painted circus clowns derived from the clumsy imitation, by noninitiates, of these ancient kooks.

The "immemorial foes" of the baboon boys, as the reader may have surmised, were the followers of Ai, the God Who Mourns. These gloomy fanatics saw the world as no less horrifying and cruel than did their archenemies, but their response to the whole mess was a more or less permanent wailing. Over the long millennia since the heyday of ancient Urartu, the Aiites had developed a complicated physical discipline, a sort of jujitsu or calisthenics of murder, which they chiefly employed in a ruthless hunt of followers of Yê-Heh. For they believed that Yrrh, the Absent One, the Silent Devisor who, an eternity ago, tossed the cosmos over his shoulder like a sheet of fish wrap and wandered away leaving not a clue as to his intentions, would not return to explain the meaning of his inexplicable and tragic creation until the progeny of Yê-Heh, along with all copies of the Yê-Hehist sacred book, "Khndzut Dzul," or "The Unfathomable Ruse," had been expunged from the face of the earth. Only then would Yrrh return from his primeval hiatus—"bringing what new horror or redemption," as the German intoned, "none can say."

All this struck me as a gamier variety of the same loony, Zoroastrian plonk that my mother had spent her life decanting, and I might have been inclined to set the whole business aside and leave the case to be swept under the administrative rug by Jack Ganz had it not been for the words with which Herr von Junzt concluded the second chapter of his tedious work:

While the Yê-Hehist gospel of cynicism and ridicule has, quite obviously, spread around the world, the cult itself has largely died out, in part through the predation of foes and in part through chronic health problems brought about by inbreeding. Today [von Junzt's book carried a date of 1849] it is reported that there may be fewer than 150 of the Yê-Hehists left in the world. They have survived, for the most part, by taking on work in travelling circuses. While their existence is known to ordinary members of the circus world, their secret has, by and large, been kept. And in the sideshows they have gone to ground, awaiting the tread outside the wagon, the shadow on the tent-flap, the cruel knife that will, in a mockery of their own long-abandoned ritual of mockery, deprive them of the lily-white flesh of their skulls.

Here I put down the book, my hands trembling from fatigue, and took up the other one, printed in an unknown tongue. "The Unfathomable Ruse"? I hardly thought so; I was inclined to give as little credit as I reasonably could to Herr von Junzt's account. More than likely the small black volume was some inspirational text in the mother tongue of the dead man, a translation of the Gospels perhaps. And yet I must confess there were a few tangential points in von Junzt's account that caused me some misgiving.

There was a scrape then just outside my window, as if a finger with a very long nail were being drawn almost lovingly along the glass. But the finger turned out to be one of the branches of a fine old horse-chestnut tree that stood outside the tower, scratching at the window in the wind. I was relieved and humiliated. Time to go to bed, I said to myself. Before I turned in, I went to the shelf and moved to one side the bust of Galen that I had inherited from my father, a country doctor. I took a quick snort of good Tennessee whiskey, a taste for which I had also inherited from my old man. Thus emboldened, I went over to the desk and picked up the books. To be frank, I would have preferred to leave them there—I would have preferred to burn them, to be really frank—but I felt that it was my duty to keep them about me while they were under my watch. So I slept with the books beneath my pillow, in their wax envelopes, and I had the worst dream of my life.

It was one of those dreams where you are a fly on the wall, a phantom bystander, disembodied and unable to speak or intervene. In it, I was treated to the spectacle of a man whose young son was going to die. The man lived in a corner of the world where, from time to time, evil seemed to bubble up from the rusty red earth like a black combustible compound of ancient things long dead. And yet, year after year, this man met each new outburst of horror, true to his code, with nothing but law books, statutes, and county ordinances, as if sheltering with only a sheet of newspaper those he had sworn to protect, insisting that the steaming black geyser pouring down on them was nothing but a light spring rain. That vision started me laughing, but the cream of the jest came when, seized by a spasm of forgiveness toward his late, mad mother, the man decided not to prosecute one of her old paramours, a rummy by the name of Craven, for driving under the influence. Shortly thereafter, Craven steered his old Hudson Terraplane the wrong way down a one-way street, where it encountered, with appropriate cartoon sound effects, an oncoming bicycle ridden by the man's heedless, darling, wildly pedalling son. That was the funniest thing of all, funnier than the amusing ironies of the man's profession, than his furtive drinking and his wordless, solitary suppers, funnier even than his having been widowed by suicide: the joke of a father's outliving his boy. It was so funny that, watching this ridiculous man in my dream, I could not catch my breath for laughing. I laughed so hard that my eyes popped from their sockets, and my smile stretched until it broke my aching jaw. I laughed until the husk of my head burst like a pod and fell away, and my skull and brains went floating off into the sky, white dandelion fluff, a cloud of fairy parasols.

Around four o'clock in the morning, I woke and was conscious of someone in the room with me. There was an unmistakable tang of sea in the air. My eyesight is poor and it took me a while to make him out in the darkness, though he was standing just beside my bed, with his long thin arm snaked under my pillow, creeping around. I lay perfectly still, aware of the tips of this slender shadow's fingernails and the scrape of his scaly knuckles, as he riled the contents of my head and absconded with them through the bedroom window, which was somehow also the mouth of the Neighborsburg Caverns, with tiny of Colonel Earnshaw taking tickets in the booth.

I awakened now in truth, and reached immediately under the pillow. The books were still there. I returned them to the evidence room at eight o'clock this morning. At nine, there was a call from Dolores and Victor Abbott, at their motor lodge out on the Plunkettsburg Pike. A guest had made an abrupt departure, leaving a mess. I got into a car with Ganz and we drove out to get a look. The Ashtown police were already there, going over the buildings and grounds of the Vista Dolores Lodge. The wastebasket of Room 201 was overflowing with blood-soaked bandages. There was evidence that the guest had been keeping some kind of live bird in the room; one of the neighboring guests reported that it had sounded like a crow. And over the whole room there hung a salt smell that I recognized immediately, a smell that some compared to the smell of the ocean, and others to that of blood. When the pillow, wringing wet, was sent up to Pittsburgh for analysis by Mr. Espy, it was found to have been saturated with human tears.

When I returned from court, late this afternoon, there was a message from Dr. Sauer. He had completed his postmortem and wondered if I would drop by. I took the bottle from behind Daniel Webster and headed on down to the county morgue.

"He was already dead, the poor son of a biscuit eater," Dr. Sauer said, looking less morose than he had the last time we spoke. Sauer was a gaunt old Methodist who avoided strong language but never, so long as I had known him, strong drink. I poured us each a tumbler, and then a second. "It took me a while to establish it because there was something about the fellow that I was missing."

"What was that?"

"Well, I'm reasonably sure that he was a hemophiliac. So my reckoning time of death by coagulation of the blood was all thrown off."

"Hemophilia," I said.

"Yes," Dr. Sauer said. "It is associated with inbreeding, as in the case of royal families in Europe."

Inbreeding. We stood there for a while, looking at the sad bulk of the dead man under the sheet.

"I also found a tattoo," Dr. Sauer added. "The head of a grinning baboon. On his left forearm. Oh, and one other thing. He suffered from some kind of vitiligo. There are white patches on his nape and throat."

Let the record show that the contents of the victim's makeup kit, when it was inventoried, included cold cream, rouge, red greasepaint, a powder puff, some brushes, cotton swabs, and five cans of foundation in a tint the label described as "Olive Male." There was no trace, however, of the white greasepaint with which clowns daub their grinning faces.

Here I conclude my report, and with it my tenure as district attorney for this blighted and unfortunate county. I have staked my career—my life itself—on the things I could see, on the stories I could credit, and on the eventual vindication, when the book was closed, of the reasonable and skeptical approach. In the face of twenty-five years of bloodshed, mayhem, criminality, and the universal human pastime of ruination, I have clung fiercely to Occam's razor, seeking always to keep my solutions unadorned and free of conjecture, and never to resort to conspiracy or any kind of prosecutorial woolgathering. My mother, whenever she was confronted by calamity or personal sorrow, invoked cosmic emanations, invisible empires, ancient prophecies, and intrigues; it has been the business of my life to reject such folderol and seek the simpler explanation. But we were fools, she and I, arrant blockheads, each of us blind to or heedless of the readiest explanation: that the world is an ungettable joke, and our human need to explain its wonders and horrors, our appalling genius for devising such explanations, is nothing more than the rim shot that accompanies the punch line.

I do not know if that nameless clown was the last, but in any case, with such pursuers, there can be few of his kind left. And if there is any truth in the grim doctrine of those hunters, then the return of our father Yrrh, with his inscrutable intentions, cannot be far off. But I fear that, in spite of their efforts over the last ten thousand years, the followers of Ai are going to be gravely disappointed when, at the end of all we know and everything we have ever lost or imagined, the rafters of the world are shaken by a single, terrible guffaw.

Sticks

Karl Edward Wagner

· i ·

The lashed-together framework of sticks jutted from a small cairn alongside the stream. Colin Leverett studied it in perplexity—half a dozen odd lengths of branch, wired together at cross angles for no fathomable purpose. It reminded him unpleasantly of some bizarre crucifix, and he wondered what might lie beneath the cairn.

It was spring of 1942—the kind of day to make the War seem distant and unreal, although the draft notice waited on his desk. In a few days Leverett would lock his rural studio, wonder if he would see it again—be able to use its pens and brushes and carving tools when he did return. It was good-bye to the woods and streams of upstate New York, too. No fly rods, no tramps through the countryside in Hitler's Europe. No point in putting off fishing that trout stream he had driven past once, exploring back roads of the Otselic Valley.

Mann Brook—so it was marked on the old geological survey map—ran southeast of DeRuyter. The unfrequented country road crossed over a stone bridge old before the first horseless carriage, but Leverett's Ford eased across and onto the shoulder. Taking fly rod and tackle, he included pocket flask and tied an iron skillet to his belt. He'd work his way downstream a few miles. By afternoon he'd lunch on fresh trout, maybe some fat bullfrog legs.

It was a fine clear stream, though difficult to fish, as dense bushes hung out from the bank, broken with stretches of open water hard to work without being seen. But the trout rose boldly to his fly, and Leverett was in fine spirits.

From the bridge the valley along Mann Brook began as fairly open pasture, but half a mile downstream the land had fallen into disuse and was thick with second-growth evergreens and scrub-apple trees. Another mile, and the scrub merged with dense forest, which continued unbroken. The land here, he had learned, had been taken over by the state many years back.

As Leverett followed the stream, he noted remains of an old railroad embankment. No vestige of tracks or ties—only the embankment itself, overgrown with large trees. The artist rejoiced in the beautiful dry-wall culverts spanning the stream as it wound through the valley. To his mind it seemed eerie, this forgotten railroad running straight and true through virtual wilderness.

He could imagine an old wood-burner with a conical stack, steaming along through the valley dragging two or three wooden coaches. It must be a branch of the old Oswego Midland Rail Road, he decided, abandoned rather suddenly in the 1870s. Leverett, who had a memory for detail, knew of it from a story his grandfather told of riding the line in 1871 from Otselic to DeRuyter on his honeymoon. The engine had so labored up the steep grade over Crumb Hill that he got off to walk alongside. Probably that sharp grade was the reason for the line's abandonment.

When he came across a scrap of board nailed to several sticks set into a stone wall, his darkest thought was that it might read "No Trespassing." Curiously, though the board was weathered featureless, the nails seemed quite new. Leverett scarcely gave it thought, until a short distance beyond he came upon another such contrivance. And another.

Now he scratched at the day's stubble on his long jaw. This didn't make sense. A prank? But on whom? A child's game? No, the arrangement was far too sophisticated. As an artist, Leverett appreciated the craftsmanship of the work—the calculated angles and lengths, the designed intricacy of the maddeningly inexplicable devices. There was something distinctly uncomfortable about their effect.

Leverett reminded himself that he had come here to fish, and continued downstream. But as he worked around a thicket he again stopped in puzzlement.

Here was a small open space with more of the stick lattices and an arrangement of flat stones laid out on the ground. The stones—likely taken from one of the many drywall culverts—made a pattern maybe twenty by fifteen feet that at first glance resembled a ground plan for a house. Intrigued, Leverett quickly saw this was not so. If the ground plan was for anything, it would have to be for a small maze.

The bizarre lattice structures were all around. Sticks from trees and bits of board nailed together in fantastic array. They defied description; no two seemed alike. Some were only one or two straight sticks lashed together in parallel or at angles. Others were worked into complicated lattices of dozens of sticks and boards. One could have been a child's tree house—it was built in three planes, but was so abstract and useless that it could be nothing more than an insane conglomeration of sticks and wire. Sometimes the contrivances were stuck in a pile of stones or a wall, maybe thrust into the railroad embankment or nailed to a tree.

It should have been ridiculous. It wasn't. Instead it seemed somehow sinister—these utterly inexplicable, meticulously constructed stick lattices spread through a wilderness where only a tree-grown embankment or a forgotten stone wall gave evidence that man had ever passed through. Leverett forgot about trout and frog legs, instead dug into his pockets for a notebook and stub of pencil. Busily he began to sketch the more intricate structures. Perhaps someone could explain them; perhaps there was something to their insane complexity that warranted closer study for his own work.

Leverett was roughly two miles from the bridge when he came upon the ruins of a house. It was an unlovely Colonial farmhouse, box-shaped and gambrel-roofed, fast falling into the ground. Windows were dark and empty; the chimneys on either end looked ready to topple. Rafters showed through open spaces in the roof, and the weathered boards of the walls had in places rotted away to reveal hewn timber beams. The foundation was stone and disproportionately massive. From the size of the unmortared stone blocks, its builder had intended the foundation to stand forever.

The house was nearly swallowed up by undergrowth and rampant lilac bushes, but Leverett could distinguish what had been a lawn with imposing shade trees. Farther back were gnarled and sickly apple trees and an overgrown garden where a few lost flowers still bloomed—wan and serpentine from years in the wild. The stick lattices were everywhere—the lawn, the trees, even the house were covered with the uncanny structures. They reminded Leverett of a hundred misshapen spider webs grouped so closely together as to almost ensnare the entire house and clearing. Wondering, he sketched page after page of them as he cautiously approached the abandoned house.

He wasn't certain just what he expected to find inside. The aspect of the farmhouse was frankly menacing, standing as it did in gloomy desolation where the forest had devoured the works of man—where the only sign that man had been here in this century were these insanely wrought latticeworks of sticks and board. Some might have turned back at this point. Leverett, whose fascination for the macabre was evident in his art, instead was intrigued. He drew a rough sketch of the farmhouse and grounds, overrun with the enigmatic devices, with thickets of hedges and distorted flowers. He regretted that it might be years before he could capture the eeriness of the place on sketchboard or canvas.

The door was off its hinges, and Leverett gingerly stepped within, hoping that the flooring remained sound enough to bear his sparse frame. The afternoon sun pierced the empty windows, mottling the decaying floorboards with great blotches of light. Dust drifted in the sunlight. The house was empty—stripped of furnishings other than indistinct tangles of rubble mounded over with decay and the drifted leaves of many seasons.

Someone had been here, and recently. Someone who had literally covered the mildewed walls with diagrams of the mysterious lattice structures. The drawings were applied directly to the walls, crisscrossing the rotting wallpaper and crumbling plaster in bold black lines. Some of vertiginous complexity covered an entire wall, like a mad mural. Others were small, only a few crossed lines, and reminded Leverett of cuneiform glyphics.

His pencil hurried over the pages of his notebook. Leverett noted with fascination that a number of the drawings were recognizable as schematics of lattices he had earlier sketched. Was this then the planning room for the madman or educated idiot who had built these structures? The gouges etched by the charcoal into the soft plaster appeared fresh—done days or months ago, perhaps.

A darkened doorway opened into the cellar. Were there drawings there as well? And what else? Leverett wondered if he should dare it. Except for streamers of light that crept through cracks in the flooring, the cellar was in darkness.

"Hello?" he called. "Anyone here?" It didn't seem silly just then. These stick lattices hardly seemed the work of a rational mind. Leverett wasn't enthusiastic with the prospect of encountering such a person in this dark cellar. It occurred to him that virtually anything might transpire here, and no one in the world of 1942 would ever know.

And that in itself was too great a fascination for one of Leverett's temperament. Carefully he started down the cellar stairs. They were stone and thus solid, but treacherous with moss and debris.

The cellar was enormous—even more so in the darkness. Leverett reached the foot of the steps, and paused for his eyes to adjust to the damp gloom. An earlier impression recurred to him. The cellar was too big for the house. Had another dwelling stood here originally—perhaps destroyed and rebuilt by one of lesser fortune? He examined the stonework. Here were great blocks of gneiss that might support a castle. On closer look they reminded him of a fortress—for the dry-wall technique was startlingly Mycenaean.

Like the house above, the cellar appeared to be empty, although without light Leverett could not be certain what the shadows hid. There seemed to be darker areas of shadow along sections of the foundation wall, suggesting openings to chambers beyond. Leverett began to feel uneasy in spite of himself.

There was something here—a large tablelike bulk in the center of the cellar. Where a few ghosts of sunlight drifted down to touch its edges, it seemed to be of stone. Cautiously he crossed the stone paving to where it loomed—waist high, maybe eight feet long, and less wide. A roughly shaped slab of gneiss, he judged, and supported by pillars of unmortared stone. In the darkness he could get only a vague conception of the object. He ran his hand along the slab. It seemed to have a groove along its edge.

His groping fingers encountered fabric, something cold and leathery and yielding. Mildewed harness, he guessed in distaste.

Something closed on his wrist, set icy nails into his flesh.

Leverett screamed and lunged away with frantic strength. He was held fast, but the object on the stone slab pulled upward.

A sickly beam of sunlight came down to touch one end of the slab. It was enough. As Leverett struggled backward and the thing that held him heaved up from the stone table, its face passed through the beam of light.

It was a lich's face—desiccated flesh tight over its skull. Filthy strands of hair were matted over its scalp; tattered lips were drawn away from broken yellowed teeth, and sunken in their sockets eyes that should be dead were bright with hideous life.

Leverett screamed again, desperate with fear. His free hand clawed the iron skillet tied to his belt. Ripping it loose, he smashed at the nightmarish face with all his strength.

For one frozen instant of horror the sunlight let him see the skillet crush through the mould-eaten forehead like an axe—cleaving the dry flesh and brittle bone. The grip on his wrist failed. The cadaverous face fell away, and the sight of its caved-in forehead and unblinking eyes from between which thick blood had begun to ooze would awaken Leverett from nightmare on countless nights.

But now Leverett tore free and fled. And when his aching legs faltered as he plunged headlong through the scrub-growth, he was spurred to desperate energy by the memory of the footsteps that had stumbled up the cellar stairs behind him.

· ii ·

When Colin Leverett returned from the War, his friends marked him a changed man. He had aged. There were streaks of grey in his hair; his springy step had slowed. The athletic leanness of his body had withered to an unhealthy gauntness. There were indelible lines to his face, and his eyes were haunted.

More disturbing was an alteration of temperament. A mordant cynicism had eroded his earlier air of whimsical asceticism. His fascination with the macabre had assumed a darker mood, a morbid obsession that his old acquaintances found disquieting. But it had been that kind of war, especially for those who had fought through the Apennines.

Leverett might have told them otherwise, had he cared to discuss his nightmarish experience on Mann Brook. But Leverett kept his own counsel, and when he grimly recalled that creature he had struggled with in the abandoned cellar, he usually convinced himself it had only been a derelict—a crazy hermit whose appearance had been distorted by the poor light and his own imagination. Nor had his blow more than glanced off the man's forehead, he reasoned, since the other had recovered quickly enough to give chase. It was best not to dwell upon such matters, and this rational explanation helped restore sanity when he awoke from nightmares of that face.

Thus Colin Leverett returned to his studio and once more plied his pens and brushes and carving knives. The pulp magazines, where fans had acclaimed his work before the War, welcomed him back with long lists of assignments. There were commissions from galleries and collectors, unfinished sculptures and wooden models. Leverett busied himself.

There were problems now. *Short Stories* returned a cover painting as "too grotesque." The publishers of a new anthology of horror stories sent back a pair of his interior drawings—"too gruesome, especially the rotted, bloated faces of those hanged men." A customer returned a silver figurine, complaining the martyred saint was too thoroughly martyred. Even *Weird Tales*, after heralding his return to its ghoul-haunted pages, began returning illustrations they considered "too strong, even for our readers."

Leverett tried halfheartedly to tone things down, found the results vapid and uninspired. Eventually the assignments stopped trickling in. Leverett, becoming more the recluse as years went by, dismissed the pulp days from his mind. Working quietly in his isolated studio, he found a living doing occasional commissioned pieces and gallery work, from time to time selling a painting or sculpture to the major museums. Critics had much praise for his bizarre abstract sculptures.

· iii ·

The War was twenty-five years history when Colin Leverett received a letter from a good friend of the pulp days—Prescott Brandon, now editor-publisher of Gothic House, a small press that specialized in books of the weird-fantasy genre. Despite a lapse in correspondence of many years, Brandon's letter began in his typically direct style:

The Eyrie/Salem, Mass./Aug. 2

To the Macabre Hermit of the Midlands:

Colin, I'm putting together a deluxe three-volume collection of H. Kenneth Allard's horror stories. I well recall that Kent's stories were personal favorites of yours. How about shambling forth from retirement and illustrating these for me? Will need two-color jackets and a dozen line interiors each. Would hope that you can startle fandom with some especially ghastly drawings for these—something different from the hackneyed skulls and bats and werewolves carting off half-dressed ladies.

Interested? I'll send you the material and details, and you can have a free hand. Let us hear—*Scotty*

Leverett was delighted. He felt some nostalgia for the pulp days, and he had always admired Allard's genius in transforming visions of cosmic horror into convincing prose. He wrote Brandon an enthusiastic reply.

He spent hours rereading the stories for inclusion, making notes and preliminary sketches. No squeamish subeditors to offend here; Scotty meant what he said. Leverett bent to his task with maniacal relish.

Something different, Scotty had asked. A free hand. Leverett studied his pencil sketches critically. The figures seemed headed the right direction, but the drawings needed something more—something that would inject the mood of sinister evil that pervaded Allard's work. Grinning skulls and leathery bats? Trite. Allard demanded more.

The idea had inexorably taken hold of him. Perhaps because Allard's tales evoked that same sense of horror, perhaps because Allard's visions of crumbling Yankee farmhouses and their depraved secrets so reminded him of that spring afternoon on Mann Brook...

Although he had refused to look at it since the day he had staggered in, half-dead from terror and exhaustion, Leverett perfectly recalled where he had flung his notebook. He retrieved it from the back of a seldom-used file, thumbed through the wrinkled pages thoughtfully. These hasty sketches reawakened the sense of foreboding evil, the charnel horror of that day. Studying the bizarre lattice patterns, it seemed impossible to Leverett that others would not share the feeling of horror the stick structures evoked in him.

He began to sketch bits of stick latticework into his pencil roughs. The sneering faces of Allard's degenerate creatures took on an added shadow of menace. Leverett nodded, pleased with the effect.

· iv ·

Some months afterward, a letter from Brandon informed Leverett he had received the last of the Allard drawings and was enormously pleased with the work. Brandon added a postscript:

> For God's sake, Colin—What is it with these insane sticks you've got poking up everywhere in the illos! The damn things get really creepy after awhile. How on earth did you get onto this?

Leverett supposed he owed Brandon some explanation. Dutifully he wrote a lengthy letter, setting down the circumstances of his experience on Mann Brook—omitting only the horror that had seized his wrist in the cellar. Let Brandon think him eccentric, but not a madman and murderer.

Brandon's reply was immediate:

> *Colin—*
> Your account of the Mann Brook episode is fascinating—and incredible! It reads like the start of one of Allard's stories! I have taken liberty of forwarding your letter to Alexander Stefroi in Pelham. Dr. Stefroi is an earnest scholar of this region's history—as you may already know. I'm certain your account will interest him, and he may have some light to shed on the uncanny affair.
> Expect 1st volume, *Voices from the Shadow,* to be ready from the binder next month. Pages looked great.
>
> *Best—Scotty*

The following week brought a letter postmarked Pelham, Mass.:

> A mutual friend, Prescott Brandon, forwarded your fascinating account of discovering curious sticks and stone artifacts on an abandoned farm in upstate New York. I found this most intriguing, and wonder if you can recall further details? Can you relocate the exact site after 30 years? If possible, I'd like to examine the foundations this spring, as they call to mind similar megalithic sites of this region. Several of us are interested in locating what we believe are remains of megalithic construction dating back to the Bronze Age, and to determine their possible use in rituals of black magic in Colonial days.
> Present archeological evidence indicates that ca. 1700–2000 B.C. there was an influx of Bronze Age peoples into the Northeast from Europe. We know that the Bronze Age saw the rise of an extremely

advanced culture, and that as seafarers they were to have no peers until the Vikings. Remains of a megalithic culture originating in the Mediterranean can be seen in the Lion Gate in Mycenae, in Stonehenge, and in dolmens, passage graves and barrow mounds throughout Europe. Moreover this seems to have represented far more than a style of architecture peculiar to the era. Rather, it appears to have been a religious cult whose adherents worshipped a sort of earth-mother, served her with fertility rituals and sacrifices, and believed that immortality of the soul could be secured through interment in megalithic tombs.

That this culture came to America cannot be doubted from the hundreds of megalithic remnants—found and now recognized—in our region. The most important site to date is Mystery Hill in N.H., comprising a great many walls and dolmens of megalithic construction—most notably the Y Cavern barrow mound and the Sacrificial Table (see postcard). Less spectacular megalithic sites include the group of cairns and carved stones at Mineral Mt., subterranean chambers with stone passageways such as at Petersham and Shutesbury, and uncounted shaped megaliths and buried "monk's cells" throughout this region.

Of further interest, these sites seem to have retained their mystic aura for the early Colonials, and numerous megalithic sites show evidence of having been used for sinister purposes by Colonial sorcerers and alchemists. This became particularly true after the witchcraft persecutions drove many practitioners into the western wilderness—explaining why upstate New York and western Mass. have seen the emergence of so many cultist groups in later years.

Of particular interest here is Shadrach Ireland's "Brethren of the New Light," who believed that the world was soon to be destroyed by sinister "Powers from Outside" and that they, the elect, would then attain physical immortality. The elect who died beforehand were to have their bodies preserved on tables of stone until the "Old Ones" came forth to return them to life. We have definitely linked the megalithic sites at Shutesbury to later unwholesome practices of the New Light cult. They were absorbed in 1781 by Mother Ann Lee's Shakers, and Ireland's putrescent corpse was hauled from the stone table in his cellar and buried.

Thus I think it probable that your farmhouse may have figured in similar hidden practices. At Mystery Hill a farmhouse was built in 1926 that incorporated one dolmen in its foundations. The house burned down ca. 1848–55, and there were some unsavory local stories as to what took place there. My guess is that your farmhouse had been built over or incorporated a similar megalithic site—and that your "sticks" indicate some unknown cult still survived there. I can recall certain vague references to lattice devices figuring in secret ceremonies, but can pinpoint nothing definite. Possibly they represent a development of occult symbols to be used in certain conjurations, but this is just a guess. I suggest you consult Waite's *Ceremonial Magic* or such to see if you can recognize similar magical symbols.

Hope this is of some use to you. Please let me hear back.

Sincerely,
Alexander Stefroi

There was a postcard enclosed—a photograph of a four-and-a-half-ton granite slab, ringed by a deep groove with a spout, identified as the Sacrificial Table at Mystery Hill. On the back Stefroi had written:

You must have found something similar to this. They are not rare—we have one in Pelham removed from a site now beneath Quabbin Reservoir. They were used for sacrifice—animal and human—and the groove is to channel blood into a bowl, presumably.

Leverett dropped the card and shuddered. Stefroi's letter reawakened the old horror, and he wished now he had let the matter lie forgotten in his files. Of course, it couldn't be forgotten—even after thirty years.

He wrote Stefroi a careful letter, thanking him for his information and adding a few minor details to his account. This spring, he promised, wondering if he would keep the promise, he would try to relocate the farmhouse on Mann Brook.

· v ·

Spring was late that year, and it was not until early June that Colin Leverett found time to return to Mann Brook. On the surface, very little had changed in three decades. The ancient stone bridge yet stood, nor had the country lane been paved. Leverett wondered whether anyone had driven past since his terror-sped flight.

He found the old railroad grade easily as he started downstream. Thirty years, he told himself—but the chill inside him only tightened. The going was far more difficult than before. The day was unbearably hot and humid. Wading through the rank underbrush raised clouds of black flies that savagely bit him.

Evidently the stream had seen severe flooding in past years, judging from piled logs and debris that blocked his path. Stretches were scooped out to barren rocks and gravel. Elsewhere, gigantic barriers of uprooted trees and debris looked like ancient and moldering fortifications. As he worked his way down the valley, he realized that his search would yield nothing. So intense had been the force of the long-ago flood that even the course of the stream had changed. Many of the dry-wall culverts no longer spanned the brook, but sat lost and alone far back from its present banks. Others had been knocked flat and swept away, or were buried beneath tons of rotting logs.

At one point Leverett found remnants of an apple orchard groping through weeds and bushes. He thought the house must be close by, but here the flooding had been particularly severe, and evidently even those ponderous stone foundations had been toppled over and buried beneath debris.

Leverett finally turned back to his car. His step was lighter.

A few weeks later he received a response from Stefroi to his reported failure:

> Forgive my tardy reply to your letter of 13 June. I have recently been pursuing inquiries which may, I hope, lead to discovery of a previously unreported megalithic site of major significance. Naturally I am disappointed that no traces remained of the Mann Brook site. While I tried not to get my hopes up, it did seem likely that the foundations would have survived. In searching through regional data, I note that there were particularly severe flash floods in the Otselic area in July 1942 and again in May 1946. Very probably your old farmhouse with its enigmatic devices was utterly destroyed not very long after your discovery of the site. This is weird and wild country, and doubtless there is much we shall never know.
>
> I write this with a profound sense of personal loss over the death two nights ago of Prescott Brandon. This was a severe blow to me—as I am sure it was to you and to all who knew him. I only hope the police will catch the vicious killers who did this senseless act—evidently thieves surprised while ransacking his office. Police believe the killers were high on drugs, from the mindless brutality of their crime.
>
> I had just received a copy of the third Allard volume, *Unhallowed Places.* A superbly designed book, and this tragedy becomes all the more insuperable with the realization that Scotty will give the world no more such treasures.
>
> *In sorrow,*
> *Alexander Stefroi*

Leverett stared at the letter in shock. He had not received news of Brandon's death—had only a few days before opened a parcel from the publisher containing a first copy of *Unhallowed Places*. A line of Brandon's last letter recurred to him—a line that had seemed amusing at the time:

> Your sticks have bewildered a good many fans, Colin, and I've worn out a ribbon answering inquiries. One fellow in particular—a Major George Leonard—has pressed me for details, and I'm afraid I told him too much. He has written several times for your address, but knowing how you value privacy I told him simply to permit me to forward any correspondence. He wants to see your original sketches, I gather, but these overbearing occult-types give me a pain. Frankly, I wouldn't care to meet the man myself.

· vi ·

"Mr. Colin Leverett?"

Leverett studied the tall, lean man who stood smiling at the doorway of his studio. The sports car he had driven up in was black, and looked expensive. The same held for the turtleneck and leather slacks he wore, and the sleek briefcase he carried. The blackness made his thin face deathly pale. Leverett guessed his age to be in the late forties by the thinning of his hair. Dark glasses hid his eyes, black driving gloves his hands.

"Scotty Brandon told me where to find you," the stranger said.

"Scotty?" Leverett's voice was wary.

"Yes, we lost a mutual friend, I regret to say. I'd been talking with him just before...But I see by your expression Scotty never had time to write." He fumbled awkwardly. "I'm Dana Allard."

"Allard?"

His visitor seemed embarrassed. "Yes—H. Kenneth Allard was my uncle."

"I hadn't realized Allard left a family," mused Leverett, shaking the extended hand. He had never met the writer personally, but there was a strong resemblance to the few photographs he had seen. And Scotty had been paying royalty checks to an estate of some sort, he recalled.

"My father was Kent's half-brother. He later took his father's name, but there was no marriage, if you follow."

"Of course." Leverett was abashed. "Please find a place to sit down. And what brings you here?"

Dana Allard tapped his briefcase. "Something I'd been discussing with Scotty. Just recently I turned up a stack of my uncle's unpublished manuscripts." He unlatched the briefcase and handed Leverett a sheaf of yellowed paper. "Father collected Kent's personal effects from the state hospital as next-of-kin. He never thought much of my uncle, or his writing. He stuffed this away in our attic and forgot about it. Scotty was quite excited when I told him of my discovery."

Leverett was glancing through the manuscript—page after page of cramped handwriting, with revisions pieced throughout like an indecipherable puzzle. He had seen photographs of Allard manuscripts. There was no mistaking this.

Or the prose. Leverett read a few passages with rapt absorption. It was authentic—and brilliant.

"Uncle's mind seems to have taken an especially morbid turn as his illness drew on," Dana hazarded. "I admire his work very greatly, but I find these last few pieces…well, a bit too horrible. Especially his translation of his mythical *Book of Elders.*"

It appealed to Leverett perfectly. He barely noticed his guest as he pored over the brittle pages. Allard was describing a megalithic structure his doomed narrator had encountered in the crypts beneath an ancient churchyard. There were references to "elder glyphics" that resembled his lattice devices.

"Look here." Dana pointed. "These incantations he records here from Al-orri-Zrokros's forbidden tome. 'Yogth-Yugth-Sut-Hyrath-Yogng'—hell, I can't pronounce them. And he has pages of them."

"This is incredible!" Leverett protested. He tried to mouth the alien syllables. It could be done. He even detected a rhythm.

"Well, I'm relieved you approve. I'd feared these last few stories and fragments might prove a little much for Kent's fans."

"Then you're going to have them published?"

Dana nodded. "Scotty was going to. I just hope those thieves weren't searching for this—a collector would pay a fortune. But Scotty said he was going to keep this secret until he was ready for announcement." His thin face was sad. "So now I'm going to publish it myself—in a deluxe edition. And I want you to illustrate it."

"I'd feel honored!" vowed Leverett, unable to believe it.

"I really liked those drawings you did for the trilogy. I'd like to see more like those—as many as you feel like doing. I mean to spare no expense in publishing this. And those stick things…"

"Yes?"

"Scotty told me the story of those. Fascinating! And you have a whole notebook of them? May I see it?"

Leverett hurriedly dug the notebook from his file, returned to the manuscript.

Dana paged through the book in awe. "These are totally bizarre—and there are references to such things in the manuscript, to make it even more fantastic. Can you reproduce them all for the book?"

"All I can remember," Leverett assured him. "And I have a good memory. But won't that be overdoing it?"

"Not at all! They fit into the book. And they're utterly unique. No, put everything you've got into this book. I'm going to entitle it *Dwellers in the Earth*, after the longest piece. I've already arranged for its printing, so we begin as soon as you can have the art ready. And I know you'll give it your all."

· vii ·

He was floating in space. Objects drifted past him. Stars, he first thought. The objects drifted closer.

Sticks. Stick lattices of all configurations. And then he was drifting among them, and he saw they were not sticks—not of wood. The lattice designs were of dead-pale substance, like streaks of frozen starlight. They reminded him of glyphics of some unearthly alphabet—complex, enigmatic symbols arranged to spell...what? And there was an arrangement—a three-dimensional pattern. A maze of utterly baffling intricacy...

Then somehow he was in a tunnel. A cramped, stone-lined tunnel through which he must crawl on his belly. The dank, moss-slimed stones pressed close about his wriggling form, evoking shrill whispers of claustrophobic dread.

And after an indefinite space of crawling through this and other stone-lined burrows, and sometimes through passages whose angles hurt his eyes, he would creep forth into a subterranean chamber. Great slabs of granite a dozen feet across formed the walls and ceiling of this buried chamber, and between the slabs other burrows pierced the earth. Altar-like, a gigantic slab of gneiss waited in the center of the chamber. A spring welled darkly between the stone pillars that supported the table. Its outer edge was encircled by a groove, sickeningly stained by the substance that clotted in the stone bowl beneath its collecting spout.

Others were emerging from the darkened burrows that ringed the chamber—slouched figures only dimly glimpsed and vaguely human. And a figure in a tattered cloak came toward him from the shadow—stretched out a claw-like hand to seize his wrist and draw him toward the sacrificial table. He followed unresistingly, knowing that something was expected of him.

They reached the altar, and in the glow from the cuneiform lattices chiselled into the gneiss slab he could see his guide's face. A moldering corpse-face, the rotted bone of its forehead smashed inward upon the foulness that oozed forth...

And Leverett would awaken to the echo of his own screams...

He'd been working too hard, he told himself, stumbling about in the darkness, getting dressed because he was too shaken to return to sleep. The nightmares had been coming every night. No wonder he was exhausted.

But in his studio his work awaited him. Almost fifty drawings completed now, and he planned another score. No wonder the nightmares.

It was a grueling pace, but Dana Allard was ecstatic with the work he had done. And *Dwellers in the Earth* was waiting. Despite problems with typesetting, with getting the special paper Dana wanted—the book only waited on him.

Though his bones ached with fatigue, Leverett determinedly trudged through the greying night. Certain features of the nightmare would be interesting to portray.

· viii ·

The last of the drawings had gone off to Dana Allard in Petersham, and Leverett, fifteen pounds lighter and gut-weary, converted part of the bonus check into a case of good whiskey. Dana had the offset presses rolling as soon as plates were shot from the drawings. Despite his precise planning, presses had broken down, one printer had quit for reasons not stated, there had been a bad accident at the new printer's—seemingly innumerable problems, and Dana had been furious at each delay. But production pushed along quickly for all that. Leverett wrote that the book was cursed, but Dana responded that a week would see it ready.

Leverett amused himself in his studio constructing stick lattices and trying to catch up on his sleep. He was expecting a copy of the book when he received a letter from Stefroi:

> Have tried to reach you by phone last few days, but no answer at your house. I'm pushed for time just now, so must be brief. I have indeed uncovered an unsuspected megalithic site of enormous importance. It's located on the estate of a long prominent Mass. family—and as I cannot receive authorization to visit it, I will not say where. Have investigated secretly (and quite illegally) for a short time one night and was nearly caught. Came across references to the place in collection of 17th-century letters and papers in a divinity school library. Writer denouncing the family as a brood of sorcerers and witches, reference to alchemical activities and other less savory rumors—and describes underground stone chambers, megalithic artifacts, etc. which are put to "foul usage and diabolic pracktise." Just got a quick glimpse, but his description was not exaggerated. And Colin—in creeping through the woods to get to the site, I came across dozens of your mysterious "sticks"! Brought a small one back and have it here to show you. Recently constructed and exactly like your drawings. With luck, I'll gain admittance and find out their significance—undoubtedly they have significance—though these cultists can be stubborn about sharing secrets. Will

explain my interest is scientific, no exposure to ridicule—and see what they say. Will get a closer took one way or another. And so— I'm off!

Sincerely,
Alexander Stefroi

Leverett's bushy brows rose. Allard had intimated certain dark rituals in which the stick lattices figured. But Allard had written over thirty years ago, and Leverett assumed the writer had stumbled onto something similar to the Mann Brook site. Stefroi was writing about something current.

He rather hoped Stefroi would discover nothing more than an inane hoax.

The nightmares haunted him still—familiar now, for all that their scenes and phantasms were visited by him only in dream. Familiar. The terror that they evoked was undiminished.

Now he was walking through forest—a section of hills that seemed to be those close by. A huge slab of granite had been dragged aside, and a pit yawned where it had lain. He entered the pit without hesitation, and the rounded steps that led downward were known to his tread. A buried stone chamber, and, leading from it, stone-lined burrows. He knew which one to crawl into.

And again the underground room with its sacrificial altar and its dark spring beneath, and the gathering circle of poorly glimpsed figures. A knot of them clustered about the stone table, and as he stepped toward them he saw they pinioned a frantically writhing man.

It was a stoutly built man, white hair disheveled, flesh gouged and filthy. Recognition seemed to burst over the contorted features, and he wondered if he should know the man. But now the lich with the caved-in skull was whispering in his ear, and he tried not to think of the unclean things that peered from that cloven brow, and instead took the bronze knife from the skeletal hand, and raised the knife high, and because he could not scream and awaken, did with the knife as the tattered priest had whispered.

And when after an interval of unholy madness, he at last did awaken, the stickiness that covered him was not cold sweat, nor was it nightmare the half-devoured heart he clutched in one fist.

· ix ·

Leverett somehow found sanity enough to dispose of the shredded lump of flesh. He stood under the shower all morning, scrubbing his skin raw. He wished he could vomit.

There was a news item on the radio. The crushed body of noted archeologist, Dr. Alexander Stefroi, had been discovered beneath a fallen granite slab near Whately. Police speculated the gigantic slab had shifted with the scientist's excavations at its base. Identification was made through personal effects.

When his hands stopped shaking enough to drive, Leverett fled to Petersham—reaching Dana Allard's old stone house about dark. Allard was slow to answer his frantic knock.

"Why, good evening, Colin! What a coincidence your coming here just now! The books are ready. The bindery just delivered them."

Leverett brushed past him. "We've got to destroy them!" he blurted. He'd thought a lot since morning.

"Destroy them?"

"There's something none of us figured on. Those stick lattices—there's a cult, some damnable cult. The lattices have some significance in their rituals. Stefroi hinted once they might be glyphics of some sort; I don't know. But the cult is still alive. They don't want their secrets revealed. They killed Scotty...they killed Stefroi. They're on to me—I don't know what they intend. They'll kill you to stop you from releasing this book!"

Dana's frown was worried, but Leverett knew he hadn't impressed him the right way. "Colin, this sounds insane. You really have been over-extending yourself, you know. Look, I'll show you the books. They're in the cellar."

Leverett let his host lead him downstairs. The cellar was quite large, flagstoned and dry. A mountain of brown-wrapped bundles awaited them.

"Put them down here where they wouldn't knock the floor out," Dana explained. "They start going out to distributors tomorrow. Here, I'll sign your copy."

Distractedly Leverett opened a copy of *Dwellers in the Earth*. He gazed at his lovingly rendered drawings of rotted creatures and buried stone chambers and stained altars—and everywhere the enigmatic latticework structures. He shuddered.

"Here." Dana Allard handed Leverett the book he had signed. "And to answer your question, they are elder glyphics."

But Leverett was staring at the inscription in its unmistakable handwriting: "For Colin Leverett, Without whom this work could not have seen completion—H. Kenneth Allard."

Allard was speaking. Leverett saw places where the hastily applied flesh-toned makeup didn't quite conceal what lay beneath. "Glyphics symbolic of alien dimensions—inexplicable to the human mind, but essential fragments of an evocation so unthinkably vast that the 'pentagram' (if you will) is miles across. Once before we tried—but your iron weapon destroyed part of Althol's brain. He erred at the last instant—almost annihilating us all. Althol had been formulating the evocation since he fled the advance of iron four millennia past.

"Then you reappeared, Colin Leverett—you with your artist's knowledge and diagrams of Althol's symbols. And now a thousand new minds will read the evocation you have returned to us, unite with our minds as we stand in the Hidden Places. And the Great Old Ones will come forth from the earth, and we, the dead who have steadfastly served them, shall be masters of the living."

Leverett turned to run, but now they were creeping forth from the shadows of the cellar, as massive flagstones slid back to reveal the tunnels beyond. He began to scream as Althol came to lead him away, but he could not awaken, could only follow.

Hand of Glory

Laird Barron

From the pages of a partially burned manuscript discovered in the charred ruins of a mansion in Ransom Hollow, Washington:

That buffalo charges across the eternal prairie, mad black eye rolling at the photographer. The photographer is Old Scratch's left hand man. Every few seconds the buffalo rumbles past the same tussock, the same tumbleweed, the same bleached skull of its brother or sister. That poor buffalo is Sisyphus without the stone, without the hill, without a larger sense of futility. The beast's hooves are worn to bone. Blood foams at its muzzle. The dumb brute doesn't understand where we are.

But I do.

CP, Nov. 1925

෨෪

This is the house my father built stone by stone in Anno Domini 1898. I was seven. Mother died of consumption that winter, and my baby brothers Earl and William followed her through the Pearly Gates directly. Hell of a housewarming.

Dad never remarried. He just dug in and redoubled his efforts on behalf

377

of his boss, Myron Arden. The Arden family own the politicos, the cops, the stevedores and the stevedores' dogs. They owned Dad too, but he didn't mind. Four bullets through the chest, a knife in the gut, two car wrecks, and a bottle a day booze habit weren't enough to rub him out. It required a broken heart from missing his wife. He collapsed, stone dead, on a job in Seattle in 1916 and I inherited his worldly possessions, such as they were. The debts, too.

The passing of Donald Cope was a mournful day commemorated with a crowded wake—mostly populated by Mr. Myron Arden's family and henchmen who constituted Dad's only real friends—and the requisite violins, excessive drinking of Jameson's, fistfights, and drunken profanities roared at passersby, although in truth, there hadn't been much left of the old man since Mother went.

My sister Lucy returned to Ireland and joined a convent. Big brother Acton lives here in Olympia. He's a surgeon. When his friends and associates ask about his kin at garden parties, I don't think my name comes up much. That's okay. Dad always liked me better.

I've a reputation in this town. I've let my share of blood, taken my share of scalps. You want an enemy bled, burnt, blasted into Kingdom Come, ask for Johnny Cope. My viciousness and cruelty are without peer. There are bad men in this business, and worse men, and then there's me. But I must admit, any lug who quakes in his boots at the mention of my name should've gotten a load of the old man. *There* was Mr. Death's blue-eyed boy himself, like mr. cummings said.

෦ଌ

A dark hallway parallels the bedroom. Dad was a short, wiry man from short wiry stock and he fitted the house accordingly. The walls are close, the windows narrow, and so the passage is dim even in daylight. When night falls it becomes a mineshaft and I lie awake, listening. Listening for a voice in the darkness, a dragging footstep, or something else, possibly something I've not heard in this life. Perversely, the light from the lamp down the street, or the moonlight, or the starlight, make that black gap of a bedroom door a deeper mystery.

I resemble Mother's people: lanky, with a horse's jaw and rawboned hands meant for spadework, or tying nooses on ropes, and I have to duck when passing through these low doorways; but at heart, I'm my father's son. I knock down the better portion of a bottle of Bushmill's every evening while I count my wins and losses from the track. My closet is stacked with crates of the stuff. I don't pay for liquor—it's a bequest from Mr. Arden, that first class bootlegger; a mark of sentimental appreciation for my father's steadfast service to the cause. When I sleep, I sleep fully dressed, suit and tie, left hand draped across the Thompson like a lover. Fear is a second heartbeat, my following shadow.

This has gone on a while.

৪৩

The first time I got shot was in the fall of 1914.

I was twenty-one and freshly escaped from the private academy Dad spent the last of his money shipping me off to. He loved me so much he'd hoped I wouldn't come back, that I'd join Acton in medicine, or get into engineering, or stow away on a tramp steamer and spend my life hunting ivory and drinking and whoring my way across the globe into Terra Incognita; anything but the family business. No such luck. My grades were pathetic, barely sufficient to graduate as I'd spent too many study nights gambling, and weekends fighting sailors at the docks. I wasn't as smart as Acton anyway, and I found it much easier and more satisfying to break things rather than build them. Mine was a talent for reading and leading people. I didn't mind manipulating them, I didn't mind destroying them if it came to that. It's not as if we dealt with real folks, anyway. In our world, everybody was part of the machine.

Dad had been teaching me the trade for a few months, taking me along on lightweight jobs. There was this Guinea named Alfonso who owed Mr. Arden big and skipped town on the debt. Dad and I tracked the fellow to Vancouver and caught him late one night, dead drunk in his shack. Alfonso didn't have the money, but we knew his relatives were good for it, so we only roughed him up: Knocked some teeth loose and broke his leg. Dad used a mattock handle with a bunch of bolts drilled into the fat end. It required more swings than I'd expected.

Unfortunately, Alfonso was entertaining a couple of whores from the dance hall. The girls thought we were murdering the poor bastard and that they'd be next. One jumped through a window, and the other, a half-naked, heavyset lass who was in no shape to run anywhere, pulled a derringer from her brassiere and popped me in the ribs. Probably aiming for my face. Dad didn't stop to think about the gun being a one-shot rig—he took three strides and whacked her in the back of the head with the mattock handle. Just as thick-skulled as Alfonso, she didn't die, although that was a pity, considering the results. One of her eyes fell out later and she never talked right again. Life is just one long train wreck.

They say you become a man when you lose your virginity. Not my baptism, alas, alack. Having a lima bean-sized hole blown through me and enduring the fevered hours afterward was the real crucible, the mettle-tester. I remember sprawling in the front seat of the car near the river and Dad pressing a doubled handkerchief against the wound. Blood dripped shiny on the floorboard. It didn't hurt much, more like the after-effects of a solid punch to the body. However, my vision was too acute, too close; black and white flashes scorched my brain.

Seagulls circled the car, their shadows so much larger than seemed possible, the shadows of angels ready to carry me into Kingdom Come. Dad gave me a dose of whiskey from his hip flask. He drove with the pedal on the floor and that rattletrap car shuddered on the verge of tearing itself apart, yet as I slumped against the door, the landscape lay frozen, immobile as the glacier that ended everything in the world the first time. Bands of light, God's pillars of blazing fire, bisected the scenery into a glaring triptych that shattered my mind. Dad gripped my shoulder and laughed and shook me now and again to keep me from falling unconscious.

Dr. Green, a sawbones on the Arden payroll, fished out the bullet and patched the wound and kept me on ice in the spare room at his house. That's when I discovered I had the recovery power of a brutish animal, a bear that retreats to the cave to lick its wounds before lumbering forth again in short order. To some, such a capacity suggests the lack of a higher degree of acumen, the lack of a fully developed imagination. I'm inured to pain and suffering, and whether it's breeding or nature I don't give a damn.

Two weeks later I was on the mend. To celebrate, I threw Gahan Kirk, a no account lackey for the Eastside crew, off the White Building roof for cheating at cards. Such is the making of a legend. The reality was, I pushed the man while he was distracted with begging Dad and Sonny Hopkins, Mr. Arden's number two enforcer, not to rub him out. Eight stories. He flipped like a ragdoll, smashing into a couple of fire escapes and crashing one down atop him in the alley. It was hideously spectacular.

The second time I got shot was during the Great War.

Mr. Arden was unhappy to see me sign on for the trip to Europe. He saw I was hell-bent to do my small part and thus gave his reluctant blessing, assuring me I'd have work when I came home from 'Killing the Huns.' Five minutes after I landed in France I was damned sorry for such a foolish impulse toward patriotism.

One night our platoon negotiated a mine field, smashed a machine gun bunker with a volley of pineapples, clambered through barbed wire, and assaulted an enemy trench. Toward the end of the action, me and a squad mate were in hand to hand combat with a German officer we'd cornered. I'd run dry on ammo five minutes before and gone charging like a rhino through the encampment, and thank Holy Mother Mary it was a ghost town from the shelling or else I'd have been ventilated inside of twenty paces. The German rattled off half a dozen rounds with his Luger before I stuck a bayonet through his neck. I didn't realize I was clipped until the sleeve of my uniform went sopping black. Two bullets, spaced tight as a quarter zipped through my left shoulder. Couldn't have asked for a cleaner wound and I hopped back into the fray come the dawn advance. I confiscated the German's pistol and the wicked bayonet he'd kept in his boot. They'd come in handy on many a bloody occasion since.

The third time...we'll get to that.

&bd;

11/11/25
Autumn of 1925 saw my existence in decline. Then I killed some guys and it was downhill in a wagon with no brakes from there.

Trouble followed after a string of anonymous calls to my home. Heavy breathing and hang-ups. The caller waited until the dead of night when I was drunk and too addled to do more than slur curses into the phone. I figured it was some dame I'd miffed, or a lug I'd thrashed, maybe even somebody with a real grudge—a widow or an orphan. My detractors are many. Whoever it was only spoke once upon the occasion of their final call. Amid crackling as of a bonfire, the male voice said, "I love you son. I love you son. I love you son."

I was drunk beyond drunk and I fell on the floor and wept. The calls stopped and I put it out of my mind.

Toward the end of September I hit a jackpot on a twenty to one pony and collected a cool grand at the window, which I used to pay off three markers in one fell swoop. I squandered the remainder on a trip to Seattle, embarking upon a bender that saw me tour every dance hall and speakeasy from the harbor inland. The ride lasted until I awakened flat broke one morning in a swanky penthouse suite of the Wilsonian Hotel in the embrace of an over the hill burlesque dancer named Pearl.

Pearl was statuesque, going to flab in the middle and the ass. Jesus, what an ass it was, though. We'd known one another for a while—I courted her younger sister Madison before she made for the bright lights of Chi-Town. Last I heard, she was a gangster's moll. Roy Night, a button man who rubbed out guys for Capone, could afford to keep Maddie in furs and diamonds and steak dinners. Good for her. Pearl wasn't any Maddie, but she wasn't half bad. Just slightly beaten down, a little tired, standing at the crossroads where Maddie herself would be in six or seven years. Me, I'd likely be dead by then so no time like the present.

I was hung-over and broke, and with two of my last ten bucks tipped the kid who pushed the breakfast cart. He handed me the fateful telegram, its envelope smudged and mussed. I must've paid the kid off pretty well during my stay, because he pocketed the money and said there were a couple of men downstairs asking what room I was in. They'd come around twice the day before, too. Bruisers, he said. Blood in their eyes, he said.

My first suspicion was of T-Men or Pinkertons. I asked him to describe the lugs. He did. I said thanks and told him to relay the gentlemen my room number on the sly and pick up some coin for his trouble. These were no lawmen, rather the opposite; a couple of Johnson brothers. Freelance guns, just like me.

Bobby Dirk and Curtis Bane, The Long and The Short, so-called, and that appellation had nothing to do with their stature, but rather stemmed from an embarrassing incident in a bathhouse.

I'd seen them around over the years, shared a drink or two in passing. Dirk was stoop-shouldered and sallow; Bane was stocky with watery eyes and a receding chin. Snowbirds and sad sack gamblers, both of them, which accounted for their uneven temperament and willingness to stoop to the foulest of deeds. Anybody could've put them on my trail. There were plenty of folks who'd be pleased to pony up the coin if it meant seeing me into a pine box.

While Pearl dressed I drank coffee and watched rain hit the window. Pearl knew the party was over—she'd fished through my wallet enough times. She was a good sport and rubbed my shoulders while I ate cold eggs. She had the grip of a stonemason. "You'd better get along," I said.

"Why's that?" she said.

"Because, in a few minutes a couple of men are probably going to break down the door and try to rub me out," I said, and lighted another cigarette.

She laughed and kissed my ear. "Day in the life of Johnny Cope. See ya around, doll. I'm hotfooting it outta here."

I unsnapped the violin case and leaned it against the closet. I assembled the Thompson on the breakfast table, locking pieces together while I watched the rain and thought about Pearl's ass. When I'd finished, I wiped away the excess cleaning oil with a monogrammed hotel napkin. I sipped the dregs of the coffee and opened a new deck of Lucky Strike and smoked a couple of them. After half an hour and still no visitors, I knotted my tie, slipped my automatic into its shoulder holster and shrugged on my suit jacket, then the greatcoat. Pacific Northwest gloom and rain has always agreed with me. Eight months out of the year I can comfortably wear bulky clothes to hide my weapons. Dad had always insisted on nice suits for work. He claimed Mr. Arden appreciated we dressed as gentlemen.

The hall was dim and I moved quickly to the stairwell exit. Elevators are deathtraps. You'd never catch me in one. I could tell you stories about fools who met their untimely ends like rats in a box. I descended briskly, paused at the door, then stepped into the alley. A cold drizzle misted everything, made the concrete slick and treacherous. I lighted a cigarette and stuck it in the corner of my mouth and began to move for the street.

For a couple of seconds I thought I had it made. Yeah. I always thought that.

Curtis Bane drifted from the inset threshold of a service door about ten feet to the street side. He raised his hand, palm out to forestall me. I wasn't buying. I hurled the empty violin case at his head and whipped around. And yes indeed, that rotten cur Bobby Dirk was sneaking up on my flank. I brought the trench broom from under my coat and squeezed off half the drum, rat-a-tat-tat. Oh, that sweet ratcheting burr; spurts of flame lighted the gloomy alley. Some of the bullets blasted brick from the wall, but enough ripped through a shocked and amazed Bobby Dirk to cut him nearly in half in a gout of black blood and smoke. What remained of him danced, baby, danced and flew backward and fell straight down, all ties to the here and now severed.

Curtis Bane screamed and though I came around fast and fired in the same motion, he'd already pulled a heater and begun pumping metal at me. We both missed and I was empty, that drum clicking uselessly. I went straight at him. Happily, he too was out of bullets and I closed the gap and slammed the butt of the rifle into his chest. Should've knocked him down, but no. The bastard was squat and powerful as a wild animal, thanks to being a coke fiend, no doubt. He ripped the rifle from my grasp and flung it aside. He locked his fists and swung them up into my chin, and it was like getting clobbered with a hammer, and I sprawled into a row of trash cans. Stars zipped through my vision. A leather cosh dropped from his sleeve into his hand and he knew what to do with it all right. He swung it in a short chopping blow at my face and I got my left hand up and the blow snapped my two smallest fingers, and he swung again and I turned my head just enough that it only squashed my ear and you better believe that hurt, but now I'd drawn the sawback bayonet I kept strapped to my hip, a fourteen-inch grooved steel blade with notched and pitted edges—Jesus-fuck who knew how many Yankee boys the Kraut who'd owned it gashed before I did for him—and stabbed it to the guard into Bane's groin. Took a couple of seconds for Bane to register it was curtains. His face whitened and his mouth slackened, breath steaming in the chill, his evil soul coming untethered. He had lots of gold fillings. He lurched away and I clutched his sleeve awkwardly with my broken hand and rose, twisting the handle of the blade side to side, turning it like a car crank into his guts and bladder, putting my shoulder and hip into it for leverage. He moaned in panic and dropped the cosh and pried at my wrist, but the strength was draining from him and I slammed him against the wall and worked the handle with murderous joy. The cords of his neck went taut and he looked away, as if embarrassed, eyes milky, a doomed petitioner gaping at Hell in all its fiery majesty. I freed the blade with a cork-like pop and blood spurted down his leg in a nice thick stream and he collapsed, folding into himself like a bug does when it dies.

Nobody had stuck their head into the alley to see what all the ruckus was about, nor did I hear sirens yet, so I took a moment to collect the dead men's wallets and light a fresh cigarette. Then I gathered my Thompson and its case and retreated into the hotel stairwell to pack the gun, scrape the blood from my shoes and comb my hair. Composed, I walked out through the lobby and the front door, winking at a rosy-cheeked lass and her wintery dame escort. A tear formed at the corner of my eye.

Two cops rolled up and climbed from their Model T. The taller of the pair barely fit into his uniform. He cradled a shotgun. The other pig carried a Billy club. I smiled at the big one as we passed, eyes level, our shoulders almost brushing, the heavy violin case bumping against my leg, the pistol hidden in the sleeve of my coat, already cocked. My hand burned like fire and I was close to vomiting, and surely the pig saw the gory lump of my ear, the snail-trail of blood streaking my cheek. His piggy little eyes were red and dulled, and I recognized him as a brother in inveterate drunkenness. We all kept walking, violent forces drifting along the razor's edge of an apocalyptic clash. They entered the hotel and I hopped a trolley to the train station. I steamed home to Olympia without incident, except by the time I staggered into the house and fell in a heap on the bed, I was out of my mind with agony and fever.

I didn't realize I'd been shot until waking to find myself lying in a pool of blood. There was a neat hole an inch above my hip. I plugged it with my pinky and went to sleep.

Number three. A banner day. Dad would be so proud.

‡

Dick found me a day and a half later, blood everywhere, like somebody had slaughtered a cow in my bed. Miraculously, the wound had clotted enough to keep me from bleeding out. He took a long look at me (I was partially naked and had somehow gotten hold of a couple of bottles of the Bushmill's, which were empty by this point, although I didn't recall drinking them) and then rang Leroy Bly to come over and help salvage the situation as I was in no condition to assist. I think he was also afraid I might be far enough gone to mistake him for a foe and start shooting or cutting. Later, he explained it was the unpleasant-looking man watching my house from a catbird's seat down the way that gave him pause. The guy screwed when Dick approached him, so there was no telling what his intentions were.

The two of them got me into the tub. Good old Dr. Green swung by with his little black bag of goodies and plucked the bullet from my innards, clucking and muttering as he worked. After stitching me inside and out, he put a cast on my hand, bandaged my ear, and shot enough dope into me to pacify a Clydesdale, then gave me another dose for the fever. The boys settled in to watch over me on account of my helpless condition. They fretted that somebody from Seattle was gunning for payback. News of my rubbing out The Long and Short had gotten around. Two or three of the Seattle bosses were partial to them, so it was reasonable to expect they might take the matter personally.

Dick's full name was Richard Stiff and he'd worked for the railroad since he was a boy, just as his father had before him. He was a thick, jowly lug with forearms as round as my calf. Unloading steel off boxcars all day will do that for a man. He was married and had eleven children—a devout Catholic, my comrade Dick. Mr. Arden used him on occasion when a bit of extra muscle was needed. Dick didn't have the stomach for killing, but was more than happy to give some sorry bugger an oak rubdown if that's what Mr. Arden wanted.

The honest money only went so far. The best story I can tell about him is that when the railroad boys gathered for their union hall meetings roll call was done surname first, thus the man reading off the muster would request "Stiff, Dick" to signal his attendance, this to the inevitable jeers and hoots from the rowdy crowd. As for Leroy Bly, he was a short, handsome middle-aged Irishman who kept an eye on a couple of local speakeasies for the Arden family and did a bit of enforcement for Arden's bookmakers as well. Not a button man by trade, nonetheless I'd heard he'd blipped off at least two men and left their remains in the high timber west of town. Rumor had it one of the poor saps was the boyfriend of a dame Bly had taken a shine to—so he was a jealous bastard as well. Nice to know as I'd never been above snaking a fella's chickadee if the mood was right.

A week passed in a confusion of *delirium tremens* and plain old delirium. Half dead from blood loss, sure, but it was the withdrawal from life-succoring whiskey and tobacco that threatened to do me in.

Eventually the fever broke I emerged into the light, growling for breakfast and hooch and a cigarette. Dick said someone from The Broadsword Hotel had called at least a dozen times—wouldn't leave a message, had to speak with me personal like. Meanwhile, Bly informed me that Mr. Arden was quite worried about the untimely deaths of The Long and Short. Dick's suspicions that the powers that be wanted my hide proved accurate. It had come down through the bush telegraph I'd do well to take to the air for a few weeks. Perhaps a holiday in a sunnier clime. Bly set a small butcher paper package on the table. The package contained three hundred dollars of "vacation" money. Bly watched as I stuck the cash into my pocket. He was ostensibly Dick's chum and to a lesser degree mine, however I suspected he'd cheerfully plant an ice pick between my shoulder blades should I defy Mr. Arden's wishes. In fact, I figured the old man had sent him to keep tabs on my activities.

I'd read the name of one Conrad Paxton scribbled on the back of a card in Curtis Bane's wallet, so it seemed possible this mystery man dispatched the pair to blip me. A few subtle inquiries led me to believe my antagonist resided somewhere in Western Washington beyond the principal cities. Since getting shy of Olympia was the order of the day, I'd decided to track Paxton down and pay him a visit. To this effect, would the boys be willing to accompany me for expenses and a few laughs?

Both Dick and Bly agreed, Bly with the proviso he could bring along his nephew Vernon. Yeah, I was in Dutch with Mr. Arden, no question—no way Bly would drop his gig here in town unless it was to spy on me, maybe awaiting the word to blip me off. And young master Vernon, he was a sad sack gambler and snowbird known for taking any low deed that presented itself, thus I assumed Bly wanted him to tag along as backup when the moment came to slip me the shiv. Mr. Arden was likely assessing my continued value to his family versus the ire of his colleagues in Seattle. There was nothing for it but to lie low for a while and see what was what after the dust settled.

I uncapped a bottle and poured myself the first shot of many to come. I stared into the bottom of the glass. The crystal ball hinted this Conrad Paxton fellow was in for a world of pain.

❧

Later that afternoon I received yet another call from management at the Broadsword Hotel passing along the message that an old friend of my father's, one Helios Augustus, desired my presence after his evening show. I hung up without committing, poured a drink and turned over the possibilities. In the end, I struggled into my best suit and had Dick drive me to the hotel.

The boys smuggled me out the back of the house and through a hole in the fence on the off chance sore friends of The Long and Short might be watching. I wondered who that weird bird lurking down the street repre-sented—a Seattle boss, or Paxton, or even somebody on Arden's payroll, a gun he'd called from out of town? I hated to worry like this; it gave me acid, had me jumping at shadows. Rattle a man enough he's going to make a mistake and get himself clipped.

I came into the performance late and took a seat on the edge of the smoky lounge where I could sag against the wall and ordered a steak sandwich and a glass of milk while the magician did his thing to mild applause.

Helios Augustus had grown a bit long in the tooth, a portly figure dressed in an elegant suit and a cape of darkest purple silk. However, his white hair and craggy features complemented the melodic and cultured timbre of his voice. He'd honed that voice in Shakespearean theatre and claimed descent from a distinguished lineage of Greek poets and prestidigitators. I'd met him at a nightclub in Seattle a couple of years before the Great War. He'd been slimmer and handsomer, and made doves appear and lovely female assistants disappear in puffs of smoke. Dad took me to watch the show because he'd known He-lios Augustus before the magician became famous and was dealing cards on a barge in Port Angeles. Dad told me the fellow wasn't Greek—his real name was Phillip Wary and he'd come from the Midwest, son of a meat packer.

I smoked and waited for the magician to wrap up his routine with a series of elaborate card tricks, all of which required the assistance of a mature lady in a low cut gown and jade necklace, a real duchess. The hand didn't need to be quicker than the eye with that much artfully-lighted bosom to serve as a distraction. As the audience headed for the exits, he saw me and came over and shook my hand. "Johnny Cope in the flesh," he said. "You look like you've been on the wrong end of a stick. I'm sorry about your father." He did not add, *he was a good man*. I appreciated a little honesty, so far as it went. Good-ness was not among Dad's virtues. He hadn't even liked to talk about it.

We adjourned to his dressing room where the old fellow produced a bot-tle of sherry and poured a couple of glasses. His quarters were plush, albeit cramped with his makeup desk and gold-framed mirror, steamer trunks plas-tered with stamps from exotic ports, a walnut armoire that scraped the ceiling, and shelves of arcane trinkets—bleached skulls and beakers, thick black books and cold braziers. A waxen, emaciated hand, gray as mud and severed at the wrist, jutted from an urn decorated with weird scrollwork like chains of teeny death's heads. The severed hand clutched a black candle. A brass kaleidoscope of particularly ornate make caught my attention. I squinted through the ap-erture and turned the dial. The metal felt damnably cold. Jigsaw pieces of painted crystal rattled around inside, revealing tantalizing glimpses of naked thighs and breasts, black corsets and red, pouty smiles. The image fell into place and it was no longer a burlesque dancer primping for my pleasure. Instead I beheld a horrid portrait of some rugose beast—all trunk and tentacle and squirming maw. I dropped the kaleidoscope like it was hot.

"Dear lad, you have to turn the opposite direction to focus the naked ladies." Helios Augustus smiled and shook his head at my provincial curiosity. He passed me a cigar, but I'd never acquired a taste for them and stuck with my Lucky Strike. He was in town on business, having relocated to San Francisco. His fortunes had waned in recent years; the proletariats preferred large stage productions with mirrors and cannon-smoke, acrobats and wild animals to his urbane and intimate style of magic. He lamented the recent deaths of the famed composer Moritz Moszkowski and the Polish novelist Wladislaw Reymont, both of whom he'd briefly entertained during his adventures abroad. Did I, by chance, enjoy classical arts? I confessed my tastes ran more toward Mark Twain and Fletch Henderson and Coleman Hawkins. "Well, big band is a worthy enough pleasure. A certain earthy complexity appropriate to an earthy man. I lived nearly eighteen years on the Continent. Played in the grandest and oldest theatres in Europe. Two shows on the Orient Express. Now I give myself away on a weeknight to faux royalty and well-dressed rabble. Woe is me!" He laughed without much bitterness and poured another drink.

Finally, I said, "What did you call me here to jaw about?"

"Rumor has it Conrad Paxton seeks the pleasure of your company."

"Yeah, that's the name. And let's get it straight—*I'm* looking for *him* with a passion. Who the hell is he?"

"Doubtless you've heard of Eadweard Muybridge, the rather infamous inventor. Muybridge created the first moving picture."

"Dad knew him from the Army. Didn't talk about him much. Muybridge went soft in the head and they parted ways." I had a sip of sherry.

"A brilliant, scandalous figure who was the pet of California high society for many years. He passed away around the turn of the century. Paxton was his estranged son and protégé. It's a long story—he put the boy up for adoption; they were later reconciled after a fashion. I met the lad when he debuted from the ether in Seattle as the inheritor of Muybridge's American estate. No one knew that he was actually Muybridge's son at the time. Initially he was widely celebrated as a disciple of Muybridge and a bibliophile specializing in the arcane and the occult, an acquirer of morbid photography and cinema as well. He owns a vault of Muybridge's photographic plates and short films I'm certain many historians would give an eye tooth to examine."

"According to my information, he lives north of here these days," I said.

"He didn't fare well in California and moved on after the war. Ransom

Hollow, a collection of villages near the Cascades. You shot two of his men in Seattle. Quite a rumpus, eh?"

"Maybe they were doing a job for this character, but they weren't his men. Dirk and Bane are traveling guns."

"Be that as it may, you would do well to fear Conrad's intentions."

"That's backwards, as I said."

"So, you *do* mean to track him to ground. Don't go alone. He's well-protected. Take some of your meaner hoodlum associates, is my suggestion."

"What's his beef? Does he have the curse on me?"

"It seems plausible. He killed your father."

I nodded and finished my latest round of booze. I set aside the glass and drew my pistol and chambered a round and rested the weapon across my knee, barrel fixed on the magician's navel. My head was woozy and I wasn't sure of hitting the side of a barn if push came to shove. "Our palaver has taken a peculiar and unwelcome turn. Please, explain how you've come into this bit of news. Quick and to the point is my best advice."

The magician puffed on his cigar, and regarded me with a half smile that the overly civilized reserve for scofflaws and bounders such as myself. I resisted the temptation to jam a cushion over his face and dust him then and there, because I knew slippery devils like him always came in first and they survived by stepping on the heads of drowning men. He removed the cigar from his mouth and said, "Conrad Paxton confessed it to some associates of mine several years ago."

"Horse shit."

"The source is…trustworthy."

"Dad kicked from a heart attack. Are you saying this lug got to him somehow? Poisoned him?" It was difficult to speak. My vision had narrowed as it did when blood was in my eye. I wanted to strangle, to stab, to empty the Luger. "Did my old man rub out somebody near and dear to Paxton? Thump him one? What?"

"Conrad didn't specify a method, didn't express a motive, only that he'd committed the deed."

"You've taken your sweet time reporting the news," I said.

"The pistol aimed at my John Thomas suggests my caution was well-founded. At the time I didn't believe the story, thinking Paxton a loud-mouthed eccentric. He *is* a loud-mouthed eccentric—I simply thought this more rubbish."

"I expect bragging of murder is a sure way to spoil a fellow's reputation in your refined circles." My collar tightened and my vision was streaky from my elevated pulse, which in turn caused everything on me that was broken, crushed, or punctured to throb. I kept my cool by fantasizing about what I was going to do to my enemy when I tracked him to ground. Better, much better.

"It also didn't help when the squalid details of Conrad's provenance and subsequent upbringing eventually came to light. The poor chap was in and out of institutions for most of his youth. He worked as a clerk at (*illegible*) University and there reunited with papa Muybridge and ultimately joined the photographer's staff. If not for Eadweard Muybridge's patronage, today Conrad would likely be in a gutter or dead."

"Oh, I see. Paxton didn't become a hermit by choice, your people shunned him like the good folks in Utah do it."

"In a nutshell, yes. Conrad's childhood history is sufficiently macabre to warrant such treatment. Not much is known about the Paxtons except they owned a fishery. Conrad's adoptive sister vanished when she was eight and he nine. All fingers pointed to his involvement. At age sixteen he drowned a rival at school and was sent to an asylum until he reached majority. The rich and beautiful are somewhat phobic regarding the criminally insane no matter how affluent the latter might be. Institutional taint isn't fashionable unless one derives from old money. Alas, Conrad is new money and what he's got isn't much by the standards of California high society."

"I don't know whether to thank you or shoot you," I said. "I'm inclined to accept your word for the moment. It would be an unfortunate thing were I to discover this information of yours is a hoax. Who are these associates that heard Paxton's confession?"

"The Corning Sisters. The sisters dwell in Luster, one of several rustic burghs in Ransom Hollow. If anyone can help you against Conrad, it'll be the crones. I admired Donald. Your father was a killer with the eye of an artist, the heart of a poet. A conflicted man, but a loyal friend. I'd like to know why Conrad wanted him dead."

"I'm more interested in discovering why he wants to bop me," I said. Actually, I was more preoccupied with deciding on a gun or a dull knife.

"He may not necessarily wish to kill you, my boy. It may be worse than that. Do you enjoy films? There's one that may be of particular importance to you."

ಒಲ

Dick gave me a look when I brought Helios Augustus to the curb. He drove us to the Redfield Museum of Natural History without comment, although Bly's nephew Vernon frowned and muttered and cast suspicious glances into the rearview. I'd met the lug once at a speakeasy on the south side; lanky kid with red-rimmed eyes and a leaky nose. Pale as milk and mean as a snake. No scholar, either. I smiled at him, though not friendly like.

Helios Augustus rang the doorbell until a pasty clerk who pulled duty as a night watchman and janitor admitted us. The magician held a brief, muttered conference and we were soon guided to the basement archives where the public was never ever allowed. The screening area for visiting big cheeses, donors and dignitaries was located in an isolated region near the boiler room and the heat was oppressive. At least the seats were comfortable old wingbacks and I rested in one while they fussed and bustled around and eventually got the boxy projector rolling. The room was already dim and then Helios Augustus killed the lone floor lamp and we were at the bottom of a mine shaft, except for a blotch of light from the camera aperture spattered against a cloth panel. The clerk cranked dutifully and Helios Augustus settled beside me. He smelled of brandy and dust and when he leaned in to whisper his narration of the film, tiny specks of fire glinted in his irises.

What he showed me was a silent film montage of various projects by Eadweard Muybridge. The first several appeared innocuous—simple renderings of the dead photographer's various plates and the famous *Horse in Motion* reel that settled once and for all the matter of whether all four feet of the animal leave the ground during full gallop. For some reason the jittering frames of the buffalo plunging across the prairie made me uneasy. The images repeated until they shivered and the beast's hide grew thick and lustrous, until I swore foam bubbled from its snout, that its eye was fixed upon me with a malign purpose, and I squirmed in my seat and felt blood from my belly wound soaking the bandages. Sensing my discomfort, Helios Augustus patted my arm and advised me to steel myself for what was to come.

After the horse and buffalo, there arrived a stream of increasingly disjointed images that the magician informed me originated with numerous photographic experiments Muybridge indulged during his years teaching at university. These often involved men and women, likely students or staff, performing mundane tasks such as arranging books, or folding clothes, or sifting flour, in mundane settings such as parlors and kitchens. The routine gradually segued into strange territory. The subjects continued their plebian labors, but did so partially unclothed, and soon modesty was abandoned as were all garments. Yet there was nothing overtly sexual or erotic about the succeeding imagery. No, the sensations that crept over me were of anxiety and revulsion as a naked woman of middle age silently trundled about the confines of a workshop, fetching pails of water from a cistern and dumping them into a barrel. Much like the buffalo charging in place, she retraced her route with manic stoicism, endlessly, endlessly. A three-legged dog tracked her circuit by swiveling its misshapen skull. The dog fretted and scratched behind its ear and finally froze, snout pointed at the camera. The dog shuddered and rolled onto its side and frothed at the mouth while the woman continued, heedless, damned.

Next came a sequence of weirdly static shots of a dark, watery expanse. The quality was blurred and seemed alternately too close and too far. Milk-white mist crept into the frame. Eventually something large disturbed the flat ocean—a whale breaching, an iceberg bobbing to the surface. Ropes, or cables lashed and writhed and whipped the water to a sudsy froth. Scores of ropes, scores of cables. The spectacle hurt my brain. Mist thickened to pea soup and swallowed the final frame.

I hoped for the lights to come up and the film to end. Instead, Helios Augustus squeezed my forearm in warning as upon the screen a boy, naked as a jay, scuttled on all fours from a stony archway in what might've been a cathedral. The boy's expression distorted in the manner of a wild animal caged, or of a man as the noose tightens around his neck. His eyes and tongue protruded. He raised his head so sharply it seemed impossible that his spine wasn't wrenched, and his alacrity at advancing and retreating was wholly un-natural…well, ye gods, that had to be a trick of the camera. A horrid trick. "The boy is quite real," Helios Augustus said. "All that you see is real. No il-lusion, no stagecraft."

I tugged a handkerchief from my pocket and dabbed my brow. My hand was clammy. "Why in hell did he take those pictures?"

"No one knows. Muybridge was a man of varied moods. There were sides to him seen only under certain conditions and by certain people. He conducted these more questionable film experiments with strict secrecy. I imagine the tone and content disturbed the prudish elements at university—"

"You mean the sane folks."

"As you wish, the sane folks. None dared stand in the way of his scientific pursuits. The administration understood how much glory his fame would bring them, and all the money."

"Yeah," I said. "Yeah. The money. Thanks for the show, old man. Could have done without it, all the same."

"I wanted you to meet young master Conrad," the magician said. "Before you met Conrad the elder."

The boy on the screen opened his mouth. His silent scream pierced my eye, then my brain. For the first time in I don't know, I made the sign of the cross.

ରଛ

We loaded my luggage then swung by Dick, Bly, and Vernon's joints to fetch their essentials—a change of clothes, guns, and any extra hooch that was lying around. Then we made for the station and the evening train. Ah, the silken rapture of riding the Starlight Express in a Pullman sleeper. Thank you, dear Mr. Arden, sir.

My companions shared the sleeper next to mine and they vowed to keep a watch over me as I rested. They'd already broken out a deck of cards and uncorked a bottle of whiskey as I limped from their quarters, so I wasn't expecting much in the way of protection. It was dark as the train steamed along between Olympia and Tacoma. I sat in the gloom and put the Thompson together and laid it beneath the coverlet. This was more from habit than expediency. Firing the gun would be a bastard with my busted fingers and I hoped it wouldn't come to that. I'd removed the bandages and let it be—a mass of purple and yellow bruises from the nails to my wrist. I could sort of make a fist and that was all that mattered, really.

I fell asleep, lulled by the rattle and sway of the car on the tracks, and dreamed of Bane's face, his bulging eyes, all that blood. Bane's death mask shimmered and sloughed into that of the boy in the film, an adolescent Conrad Paxton being put through his paces by an offstage tormentor. A celebrated ghoul who'd notched his place in the history books with some fancy imagination and a clever arrangement of lenses, bulbs, and springs.

Didn't last long, thank god as I snapped to when the train shuddered and slowed. Lamplight from some unknown station filtered through the blinds and sent shadows skittering across the ceiling and down the walls. I pointed the barrel at a figure hunched near the door, but the figure dissolved as the light shifted and revealed nothing more dangerous than my suitcase, the bulk of my jacket slung across a chair. I sat there a long while, breathing heavily as distant twinkly lights of passing towns floated in the great darkness.

The train rolled into Ransom Hollow and we disembarked at the Luster depot without incident. A cab relayed us to the Sycamore Hotel, the only game in the village. This was wild and wooly country, deep in the forested hills near the foot of the mountains. Ransom Hollow comprised a long, shallow river valley that eventually climbed into those mountains. An old roadmap marked the existence of three towns and a half dozen villages in the vicinity, each of them established during or prior to the westward expansion of the 1830s. Judging by the moss and shingle roofs of the squat and rude houses, most of them saltbox or shotgun shacks, the rutted boardwalks and goats wandering the unpaved lanes, not much had changed since the era of mountain men trappers and gold rush placer miners.

The next morning we ate breakfast at a shop a couple of blocks from the hotel, then Dick and Bly departed to reconnoiter Paxton's estate while Vernon stayed with me. My hand and ear were throbbing. I stepped into the alley and had a gulp from a flask I'd stashed in my coat, and smoked one of the reefers

Doc Green had slipped me the other day. Dope wasn't my preference, but it killed the pain far better than the booze did.

It was a scorcher of an autumn day and I hailed a cab and we rode in the back with the window rolled down. I smoked another cigarette and finished the whiskey; my mood was notably improved by the time the driver deposited us at our destination. The Corning sisters lived in a wooded neighborhood north of the town square. Theirs was a brick bungalow behind a steep walkup and gated entrance. Hedges blocked in the yard and its well-tended beds of roses and begonias. Several lawn gnomes crouched in the grass or peeked from the shrubbery; squat, wooden monstrosities of shin height, exaggerated features, pop-eyed and leering.

The bungalow itself had a European style peaked roof and was painted a cheery yellow. Wooden shutters bracketed the windows. Faces, similar to the sinister gnomes, were carved into the wood. The iron knocker on the main door was also shaped into a grinning, demonic visage. A naked man reclined against the hedge. He was average height, brawny as a Viking rower and sunburned. All over. His eyes were yellow. He spat in the grass and turned and slipped sideways through the hedge and vanished.

"What in hell?" Vernon said. He'd dressed in a bowler and an out of fashion jacket that didn't quite fit his lanky frame. He kept removing his tiny spectacles and smearing them around on his frayed sleeve. "See that lug? He was stark starin' nude!"

I doffed my Homburg and rapped the door, eschewing the knocker.

"Hello, Mr. Cope. And you must be Vernon. You're exactly how I imagined." A woman approached toward my left from around the corner of the house. She was tall, eye to eye with me, and softly middle-aged. Her hair was shoulder-length and black, her breasts full beneath a common-sense shirt and blouse. She wore pants and sandals. Her hands were dirty and she held a trowel loosely at hip level. I kept an eye on the trowel—her manner reminded me of a Mexican knife fighter I'd tangled with once. The scar from the Mexican's blade traversed a span between my collar bone and left nipple.

"I didn't realize you were expecting me," I said, calculating the implications of Helios Augustus wiring ahead to warn her of my impending arrival.

"Taller than your father," she said. Her voice was harsh. The way she carefully enunciated each syllable suggested her roots were far from Washington. Norway, perhaps. The garden gnomes were definitely Old World knick-knacks.

"You knew my father? I had no idea."

"I've met the majority of Augustus' American friends. He enjoys putting them on display."

"Mrs. Corning —"

"Not Mrs.," she said. "This is a house of spinsters. I'm Carling. You'll not encounter Groa and Vilborg, alas. Come inside from this hateful sunlight. I'll make you a pudding." She hesitated and looked Vernon north to south and then smiled an unpleasant little smile that made me happy for some reason. "Your friend can take his ease out here under the magnolia. We don't allow pets in the cottage."

"Shut up," I said to Vernon when he opened his mouth to argue.

Carling led me into the dim interior of the bungalow and barred the door. The air was sour and close. Meat hooks dangled from low rafter beams and forced me to stoop lest I whack my skull. An iron cauldron steamed and burbled upon the banked coals of a hearth. A wide plank table ran along the wall. The table was scarred. I noted an oversized meat cleaver stuck into a plank near a platter full of curdled blood. The floor was filthy. I immediately began to reassess the situation and kept my coat open in case I needed to draw my pistol in a hurry.

"Shakespearean digs you've got here, Ma'am," I said as I brushed dead leaves from a chair and sat. "No thanks on the pudding, if you don't mind."

"Your hand is broken. And you seem to be missing a portion of your ear. Your father didn't get into such trouble."

"He got himself dead, didn't he?"

In the next room, a baby cried briefly. Spinsters with a baby. I didn't like it. My belly hurt and my ear throbbed in time with my spindled fingers and I wondered, the thought drifting out of the blue, if she could smell the blood soaking my undershirt.

Carling's left eye drooped in either a twitch or a wink. She rummaged in a cabinet and then sprinkled a pinch of what appeared to be tea leaves into a cloudy glass. Down came a bottle of something that gurgled when she shook it. She poured three fingers into the glass and set it before me. Then she leaned against the counter and regarded me, idly drumming her fingers against her thigh. "We *weren't* expecting you. However, your appearance isn't particularly a surprise. Doubtless the magician expressed his good will by revealing Conrad Paxton's designs upon you. The magician was sincerely fond of your father. He fancies himself an urbane and sophisticated man. Such individuals always have room for one or two brutes in their menagerie of acquaintances."

"That was Dad, all right," I said and withdrew a cigarette, pausing before striking the match until she nodded. I smoked for a bit while we stared at one another.

"I'll read your fortune when you've finished," she said indicating the glass of alcohol and the noisome vapors drifting forth. In the bluish light her features seemed more haggard and vulpine than they had in the bright, clean sunshine. "Although, I think I can guess."

"Where's Groa and Vilborg?" I snapped open the Korn switchblade I carried in the breast pocket of my shirt and stirred the thick dark booze with the point. The knife was a small comfort, but I was taking it where I could find it.

"Wise, very wise to remember their names, Johnny, may I call you Johnny?—and to utter them. Names do have power. My sisters are in the cellar finishing the task we'd begun prior to this interruption. You have us at a disadvantage. Were it otherwise…But you lead a charmed life, don't you? There's not much chance of your return after this, more is the pity."

"What kind of task would that be?"

"The dark of the moon is upon us tonight. We conduct a ritual of longevity during the reaping season. It requires the most ancient and potent of sacrifices. Three days and three nights of intense labor, of which this morning counts as the first."

"Cutting apart a hapless virgin, are we?"

Carling ran her thumbnail between her front teeth. A black dog padded into the kitchen from the passage that let from the living room where the cries had emanated and I thought perhaps it had uttered the noise. The dog's eyes were yellow. It was the length and mass of a Saint Bernard, although its breed suggested that of a wolf. The dog smiled at me. Carling spoke a guttural phrase and unbarred the door and let it out. She shut the door and pressed her forehead against the frame.

"How do you know Paxton?" I said, idly considering her earlier comment about banning pets from the house.

"My sisters and I have ever been great fans of Eadweard's photography. Absolute genius, and quite the conversationalist. I have some postcards he sent us from his travels. Very thoughtful in his own, idiosyncratic way. Quite loyal to those who showed the same to him. Conrad is Eadweard Muybridge's dead wife's son, a few minutes the elder of his brother, Florado. The Paxtons took him to replace their own infant who'd died at birth the very night Muybridge's boys came into the world. Florado spent his youth in the institution. No talent to speak of. Worthless."

"But there must've been some question of paternity in Muybridge's mind. He left them to an institution in the first place. Kind of a rotten trick, you ask me."

"Eadweard tried to convince himself the children were the get of that retired colonel his wife had been humping."

"But they weren't."

"Oh, no—they belonged to Eadweard."

"Yet, one remained at the orphanage, and Conrad was adopted. Why did Muybridge come back into the kid's life? Guilt? Couldn't be guilt since he left the twin to rot."

"You couldn't understand. Conrad was special, possessed of a peculiar darkness that Eadweard recognized later, after traveling in Central America doing goddess knows what. The boy was key to something very large and very important. We all knew that. Don't ask and I'll tell you no lies. Take it up with Conrad when you see him."

"I don't believe Paxton murdered my father," I said. The baby in the other room moaned and I resisted the urge to look in that direction.

"Oh, then this is a social call? I would've fixed my hair, naughty boy."

"I'm here because he sent a pair of guns after me in Seattle. I didn't appreciate the gesture. Maybe I'm wrong, maybe he did blip my father. Two reasons to buzz him. Helios says you know the book on this guy. So, I come to you before I go to him."

"Reconnaissance is always wisest. Murder is not precisely what occurred. Conrad drained your father's life energy, siphoned it away via soul taking. You know of what I speak—photography, if done in a prescribed and ritualistic manner, can steal the subject's life force. This had a side consequence of effecting Mr. Cope's death. To be honest, Conrad didn't do it personally. He isn't talented in that area. He's a dilettante of the black arts. He had it done by proxy, much the way your employer Mr. Arden has *you* do the dirty work for him."

She was insane, obviously. Barking mad and probably very dangerous. God alone knew how many types of poison she had stashed up her sleeve. That cauldron of soup was likely fuming with nightshade, and my booze…I pushed it aside and brushed the blade against my pants leg. "Voodoo?" I said, just making conversation, wondering if I should rough her up a bit, if that was even wise, what with her dog and the naked guy roaming around. No confidence in Vernon whatsoever.

"There are many faiths at the crossroads here in the Hollow," Carling said, bending to stir the pot and good god her shoulders were broad as a logger's. "Voodoo is not one of them. I can't tell you who did in your father, only that it was done and that Conrad ordered it so. I recommend you make haste to the Paxton estate and do what you do best—rub the little shit out before he does for you. He tried once, he'll definitely take another crack at it."

"Awfully harsh words for your old chum," I said to her brawny backside. "Two of you must have had a lovers' quarrel."

"He's more of a godson. I don't have a problem with Conrad. He's vicious and vengeful and wants my head on a stick, but I don't hold that against him in the slightest."

"Then why are you so interested in seeing him get blipped?"

"You seem like a nice boy, Johnny." Carling turned slowly and there was something amiss with her face that I couldn't quite figure out. That nasty grin was back, though. "Speaking of treachery and violence, that other fellow you brought is no good. I wager he'll bite."

"Think so?" I said. "He's just along for the ride."

"Bah. Let us bargain. Leave your friend with us and I'll give you a present. I make knick-knacks, charms, trinkets and such. What you really need if you're going to visit the Paxton estate is a talisman to ward off the diabolic. It wouldn't do to go traipsing in there as you are."

"I agree. I'll be sure to pack a shotgun."

She cackled. Actually and truly cackled. "Yes, yes, for the best. Here's a secret few know—I wasn't always a spinster. In another life I traveled to India and China and laid with many, many men, handsomer than you even. They were younger and unspoiled. I nearly, very, very nearly married a rich Chinaman who owned a great deal of Hainan."

"Didn't work out, eh? Sorry to hear it, Ms. Corning."

"He raised monkeys. I hate monkeys worse than Christ." She went through the door into the next room and I put my hand on the pistol from reflex and perhaps a touch of fear, but she returned with nothing more sinister than a shriveled black leaf in her open palm. Not a leaf, I discovered upon receiving it, but a dry cocoon. She dropped it into my shirt pocket, just leaned over and did it without asking and up close she smelled of spice and dirt and unwashed flesh.

"Thanks," I said recoiling from the proximity of her many large, sharp teeth.

"Drink your whiskey and run along."

I stared at the glass. It smelled worse than turpentine.

"Drink your fucking whiskey," she said.

And I did, automatic as you please. It burned like acid.

She snatched the empty glass and regarded the constellation of dregs at the bottom. She grinned, sharp as a pickaxe. "He's throwing a party in a couple of nights. Does one every week. Costumes, pretty girls, rich trappers and furriers, our rustic nobility. It augers well for you to attend."

I finally got my breath back. "In that case, the furriers' ball it is."

She smiled and patted my cheek. "Good luck. Keep the charm on your person. Else..." She smiled sadly and straightened to her full height. "Might want to keep this visit between you and me."

ᗢ

Vernon was missing when I hit the street. The cab driver shrugged and said he hadn't seen anything. No reason not to believe him, but I dragged him by the hair from the car and belted him around some on the off chance he was lying. Guy wasn't lying, though. There wasn't any way I'd go back into that abattoir of a cottage to hunt for the lost snowbird, so I decided on a plausible story to tell the boys. Vernon was the type slated to end it face down in a ditch, anyway. Wouldn't be too hard to sell the tale and frankly, watching Bly stew and fret would be a treat.

Never did see Vernon again.

ଓଓ

Dick and Bly hadn't gotten very close to the Paxton mansion. The estate was guarded by a bramble-covered stone wall out of *Sleeping Beauty*, a half mile of wildwood and overgrown gardens, then croquet courses, polo fields, and a small barracks that housed a contingent of fifteen or so backwoods thugs armed with shotguns and dogs. God alone knew where Paxton had recruited such a gang. I figured they must be either locals pressed into service or real talent from out of state. No way to tell without tangling with them, though.

Dick had cased the joint with field glasses and concluded a daylight approach would be risky as hell. Retreat and regrouping seemed the preferable course, thus we decided to cool our heels and get skunk drunk.

The boys had caught wind of a nasty speakeasy in a cellar near Belson Creek in neighboring Olde Towne. A girl Bly had picked up in the parking lot of Luster's one and only hardware store claimed men with real hard bark on them hung around there. Abigail and Bly were real chummy, it seemed, and he told her we were looking to put the arm on a certain country gentleman. The girl suggested low at the heel scoundrels who tenanted the dive might be helpful.

The speakeasy was called Satan's Bung and the password at the door was Van Iblis, all of this Dick had discovered from his own temporary girls, Wanda and Clementine, which made me think they'd spent most of the day reconnoitering a watering hole rather than pursuing our mission with any zeal. In any event, we sashayed into that den of iniquity with sweet little chippies who still had most of their teeth, a deck of unmarked cards, and a bottle of sour mash. There were a few tough guys hanging around, as advertised; lumberjacks in wool coats and sawdust-sprinkled caps and cork boots; the meanest of the lot even hoisted his axe onto the bar. One gander at my crew and they looked the other way right smartly. Some good old boys came down from the hills or out of the swamp, hitched their overalls and commenced to picking banjos, banging drums, and harmonizing in an angelic chorus that belied their sodden, bloated, and warty features, their shaggy beards and knurled scalps. They clogged barefoot, stamping like bulls ready for battle.

Dick, seven sails to the wind, wondered aloud what could be done in the face of determined and violent opposition entrenched at the Paxton estate and I laughed and told him not to worry too much, this was a vacation. Relax and enjoy himself—I'd think of something. I always thought of something.

Truth of it was, I'd lost a bit of my stomach for the game after tea and cake at the Corning Sisters' house and the resultant disappearance of Vernon. If it hadn't been for the rifling of my home, the attack by the Long and the Short, the mystery of whether Paxton really bopped Dad would've remained a mystery. Thus, despite my reassurances to the contrary, I wasn't drinking and plotting a clever plan of assault or infiltration of the estate, but rather simply drinking and finagling a way to get my ashes hauled by one of the chippies.

One thing led to another, a second bottle of rotgut to a third, and Clementine climbed into my lap and nuzzled my neck and unbuttoned my pants and slipped her hand inside. Meanwhile a huge man in a red and black checkered coat and coonskin cap pranced, nimble as a Russian ballerina, and wheedled a strange tune on a flute of lacquered black ivory. This flautist was a hirsute, wiry fellow with a jagged visage hacked from a stone, truly more beast than man by his gesticulations and the manner he gyrated his crotch, thrusting to the beat, and likely the product of generations of inbreeding, yet he piped with an evil and sinuous grace that captured the admiration of me, my companions, the entire roomful of seedy and desperate characters. The lug seemed to fixate upon me, glaring and smirking as he clicked his heels and puffed his cheeks and capered among the tables like a faun.

I conjectured aloud as to his odd behavior, upon which Dick replied in a slur that if I wanted him to give the bird a thrashing, just make the sign. My girl, deep into her cups, mumbled that the flautist was named Dan Blackwood, last scion of a venerable Ransom Hollow family renowned as hunters and furriers without peer, but these days runners of moonshine. A rapist and murderer who'd skated out of prison by decree of the prince of Darkness Hissownself, or so the fireside talk went. A fearful and loathsome brute, his friends were few and of similar malignant ilk and were known as the Blackwood Boys. Her friend Abigail paused from licking Bly's earlobe to concur.

Dan Blackwood trilled his oddly sinister tune while a pair of hillbillies accompanied him with banjo and fiddle and a brawny lad with golden locks shouldered aside the piano player and pawed the ivories to create a kind of screeching cacophony not unlike a train wreck while the paper lanterns dripped down blood-red light and the cellar audience clenched into a tighter knot and swayed on their feet, their stools and stumps, stamping time against the muddy floor. From that cacophony a dark and primitive rhythm emerged as each instrument fell into line with its brother and soon that wattled and toad-like orchestra found unity with their piper and produced a song that put ice in my loins and welded me to my seat. Each staccato burst from the snare drum, each shrill from the flute, each discordant clink from the piano, each nails on slate shriek of violin and fiddle, pierced my brain, caused a sweet, agonizing lurch of my innards, and patient Clementine jerked my cock, out of joint, so to speak.

The song ended with a bang and a crash and the crowd swooned. More tunes followed and more people entered that cramped space and added to the sensation we were supplicants or convicts in a special circle of hell, such was the ripe taint of filthy work clothes and matted hair and belched booze like sulfurous counterpoint to the maniacal contortions of the performers, the rich foul effluvium of their concert.

During an intermission, I extricated myself from industrious Clementine and made my way up the stairs into the alley to piss against the side of the building. The darkness was profound, moonless as Carling had stated, and the stars were covered by a thin veil of cloud. Despite my best efforts, I wasn't particularly impaired and thus wary and ready for trouble when the door opened and a group of men, one bearing a lantern that oozed the hideous red glow, spilled forth and mounted the stairs. The trio stopped at the sight of me and raised the lantern high so that it scattered a nest of rats into the hinder of the lane. I turned to face them, hand on pistol, and I smiled and hoped Dick or Bly might come tripping up the steps at any moment.

But there was no menace evinced by this group, at least not aimed at me. The leader was the handsome blond lad who'd hammered the piano into submission. He saluted me with two fingers and said, "Hey, now city feller. My name's Candy. How'n ya like our burg?" The young man didn't wait for an answer, but grunted at his comrades, the toad-like fiddler and banjo picker who might've once been conjoined and later separated with an axe blow, then said to me in his thick, unfamiliar accent, "So, chum, the telegraph sez you in Ransom Holler on dirty business. My boss knows who yer gunnin' for and he'd be pleased as punch to make yer acquaintance."

"That's right civilized. I was thinking of closing this joint down, though…"

"Naw, naw, ol' son. Ya gotta pay the piper round this neck of the woods."

I asked who and where and the kid laughed and said to get my friends and follow him, and to ease my mind the men opened their coats to show they weren't packing heat. Big knives and braining clubs wrapped in leather and nail-studded, but no pea shooters and I thought again how Dick had managed to learn of this place and recalled something about one of the girls, perhaps

Abigail, whispering the name into his ear and a small chill crept along my spine. Certainly Paxton could be laying a trap, and he wasn't the only candidate for skullduggery. Only the good lord knew how strongly the Corning sisters interfered in the politics of the Hollow and if they'd set the Blackwood Gang upon us, and of course this caused my suspicious mind to circle back to Helios Augustus and his interest in the affair. Increasingly I kicked myself for not having shot him when I'd the chance and before he could take action against me, assuming my paranoid suppositions bore weight. So, I nodded and tipped my hat and told the Blackwood Boys to bide a moment.

Dick and Bly were barely coherent when I returned to gather them and the girls. Bly, collar undone, eyes crossed and blinking, professed incredulity that we would even consider traveling with these crazed locals to some as yet unknown location. Dick didn't say anything, although his mouth curved down at the corners with the distaste of a man who'd gulped castor oil. We both understood the score; no way on God's green earth we'd make it back to Luster and our heavy armament if the gang wanted our skins. Probably wouldn't matter even if we actually managed to get armed. This was the heart of midnight and the best and only card to turn was to go for a ride with the devil. He grabbed Bly's arm and dragged him along after me, the goodtime girls staggering in our wake. Ferocious lasses—they weren't keen on allowing their meal tickets to escape, and clutched our sleeves and wailed like the damned.

Young master Candy gave our ragged assembly a bemused once-over, then shrugged and told us to get a move on, starlight was wasting. He led us to a great creaking behemoth of a farm truck with raised sides to pen in livestock and bade us pile into the bed. His compatriot the fiddler was already a boulder slumped behind the steering wheel.

I don't recall the way because it was pitch black and the night wind stung my eyes. We drove along Belson Creek and crossed it on rickety narrow bridges and were soon among ancient groves of poplar and fir, well removed from Olde Towne or any other lighted habitation. The road was rutted and the jarring threatened to rip my belly open. I spent most of the thankfully brief ride doubled, hands pressed hard against the wound, hoping against hope to keep my guts on the inside.

The truck stopped briefly and Candy climbed down to scrape the ruined carcass of a raccoon or opossum from the dirt and chucked it into the bed near our feet. Bly groaned and puked onto his shoes and the girls screamed or laughed or both. Dick was a blurry white splotch in the shadows and from the manner he hunched, I suspected he had a finger on the trigger of the revolver in his pocket. Most likely, he figured I'd done in poor, stupid Vernon and was fixing to dust that weasel Bly next, hell maybe I'd go all in and make a play for

Mr. Arden. These ideas were far from my mind (well, dusting Bly was a possibility), naturally. Suicide wasn't my intent. Nonetheless, I couldn't fault Dick for worrying; could only wonder, between shocks to my kidneys and gut from the washboard track, how he would land if it ever came time to choose teams.

The fiddler swung the truck along a tongue of gravel that unrolled deep inside a bog and we came to a ramshackle hut, a trapper or fisherman's abode, raised on stilts that leaned every which way like a spindly, decrepit daddy longlegs with a house on its back. Dull, scaly light flickered through windows with tanned skins for curtains and vaguely illuminated the squelching morass of a yard with its weeds and moss and rusty barrels half sunk in the muck, and close by in the shadows came the slosh of Belson Creek churning fitfully as it dreamed. Another truck rolled in behind us and half a dozen more goons wordlessly unloaded and stood around, their faces obscured in the gloom. All of them bore clubs, mattock handles, and gaff hooks.

There was a kind of ladder descending from a trapdoor and on either side were strung moldering nets and the moth-eaten hides of beasts slaughtered decades ago and chains of animal bones and antlers that jangled when we bumped them in passing. I went first, hoping to not reinjure my hand while entertaining visions of a sledgehammer smashing my skull, or a machete lopping my melon at the neck as I passed through the opening. Ducks in Tin Pan Alley is what we were.

Nobody clobbered me with a hammer, nobody chopped me with an axe and I hoisted myself into the sooty confines of Dan Blackwood's shanty. Beaver hides were stretched into circles and tacked on the walls, probably to cover the knotholes and chinks in a vain effort to bar the gnats and mosquitoes that swarmed the bog. Bundles of fox and muskrat hide were twined at the muzzle and hung everywhere and black bear furs lay in heaps and crawled with sluggish flies. A rat crouched enthroned high atop one mound, sucking its paws. It regarded me with skepticism. Light came from scores of candles, coagulated slag of black and white, and rustic kerosene lamps I wagered had seen duty in Gold Rush mines. The overwhelming odors were that of animal musk, lye, and peat smoke. Already, already sweat poured from me and I wanted another dose of mash.

That sinister flautist Dan Blackwood tended a cast iron stove, fry pan in one fist, spatula in the other. He had already prepared several platters of flapjacks. He wore a pork pie hat cocked at a precipitous angle. A bear skin covered him after a burlesque fashion.

"Going to be one of those nights, isn't it?" I said as my friends and hangers on clambered through the hatch and stood blinking and gawping at their surroundings, this taxidermy post in Hades.

"Hello, cousin. Drag up a stump. Breakfast is at hand." Blackwood's voice was harsh and thin and came through his long nose. At proximity, his astounding grotesqueness altered into a perverse beauty, such were the chiseled planes and crags of his brow and cheek, the lustrous blackness of his matted hair that ran riot over his entire body. His teeth were perfectly white when he smiled, and he smiled often.

The cakes, fried in pure lard and smothered in butter and maple syrup, were pretty fucking divine. Blackwood ate with almost dainty precision and his small, dark eyes shone brightly in the candle flame and ye gods the heat from the stove was as the heat from a blast furnace and soon all of us were in shirt sleeves or less, the girls quickly divested themselves of blouse and skirt and lounged around in their dainties. I didn't care about the naked chickadees; my attention was divided between my recurrent pains of hand and ear, and gazing in wonder at our satyr host, lacking only his hooves to complete the image of the great god Pan taking a mortal turn as a simple gang boss. We had him alone—his men remained below in the dark—and yet, in my bones I felt it was me and Dick and Bly who were at a disadvantage if matters went south.

"Don't get a lot of fellows with your kind of bark around here," Blackwood said. He reclined in a heavy wooden chair padded with furs, not unlike the throne of a feudal lord who was contemplating the fate of some unwelcome itinerant vagabonds. "Oh, there's wild men and murderous types aplenty, but not professional gunslingers. I hear tell you've come to the Hollow with blood in your eye, and who put it there? Why dear little Connie Paxton, of course; the moneybags who rules from his castle a few miles yonder as the crow wings it."

"Friend of yours?" I said, returning his brilliant smile with one of my own as I gauged the speed I could draw the Luger and pump lead into that hairy torso. Clementine slithered over and caressed my shoulders and kissed my neck. Her husband had been a merchant marine during the Big One, had lain in Davey Jones's Locker since 1918. Her nipples were hard as she pressed against my back.

Blackwood kept right on smiling. "Friend is a powerful word, cousin. Almost as powerful as a true name. It's more proper to say Mr. Paxton and I have a pact. Keepin' the peace so we can all conduct our nefarious trades, well that's a sacred duty."

"I understand why you'd like things to stay peaceful," I said.

"No, cousin, you *don't* understand. The Hollow is far from peaceful. We do surely love our bloodlettin', make no mistake. Children go missin' from their beds and tender maidens are ravished by Black Bill of the Wood," he winked at slack-jawed and insensate Abigail who lay against Bly, "and just the other day the good constable Jarred Brown discovered the severed head of his best deputy floatin' in Belson Creek. Alas, poor Ned Smedley. I knew him, Johnny! Peaceful, this territory ain't. On the other hand, we've avoided full scale battle since that machine gun incident at the Luster court house in 1910. This fragile balance between big predators is oh so delicately strung. And along come you Gatlin-totin' hard-asses from the big town to upset everything. What shall I do with you, cousin, oh what?"

"Jesus, these are swell flapjacks, Mr. Blackwood," Bly said. His rummy eyes were glazed as a stuffed dog's.

"Why, thank you, sirrah. At the risk of soundin' trite, it's an old family recipe. Wheat flour, salt, sugar, eggs from a black speckled virgin hen, dust from the bones of a Pinkerton, a few drops of his heart blood. Awful decadent, I'll be so gauche as to agree."

None of us said anything until Clementine muttered into my good ear, "Relax, baby. You ain't a lawman, are you? You finer than frog's hair." She nipped me.

"Yes, it is true," Blackwood said. "Our faithful government employees have a tendency to get short shrift. The Hollow voted and decided we'd be best off if such folk weren't allowed to bear tales. This summer a couple government rats, Pinkerton men, came sniffin' round for moonshine stills and such. Leto, Brutus and Candy, you've met 'em, dragged those two agents into the bog and buried 'em chest deep in the mud. My lads took turns batterin' out their brains with those thumpers they carry on their belts. I imagine it took a while. Boys play rough. Candy worked in a stockyard. He brained the cattle when they came through the chute. Got a taste for it." He glanced at the trap door when he said this.

"Powerful glad I'm no Pinkerton," I said.

He opened his hand and reached across the space between us as if he meant to grasp my neck, and at the last moment he flinched and withdrew and his smile faded and the beast in him came near the surface. "You've been to see those bitches."

"The Corning ladies? Come to think of it, yes, I had a drink with the sisters. Now I'm having breakfast with you. Don't be jealous, Dan." I remained perfectly still and as poised as one can be with sweat in his eyes, a hard-on in progress, and consumed by rolling waves of blue-black pain. My own beast was growling and slamming its Stone Age muzzle against the bars. It wanted blood to quench its terror, wanted loose. "What do you have against old ladies. They didn't mention you."

"Our business interests lie at cross-purposes. I don't relish no competition. Wait. Wait a minute… Did you see the child?" Blackwood asked this in a hushed tone, and his face smoothed into a false calmness, probably a mirror of my own. Oh, we were trying very hard not to slaughter one another. He cocked his head and whispered, "John, did you see the child?"

That surely spooked me, and the teary light in his eyes spooked me too, but not half so much as the recollection of the cries in the dim room at the Corning bungalow. "No. I didn't."

He watched me for a while, watched me until even Dick and Bly began to rouse from their reveries to straighten and cast puzzled looks between us. Blackwood kept flexing his hand, clenching and tearing at an invisible throat, perhaps. "All right. That's hunkum-bunkum." His smile returned. "The crones don't have no children."

I wiped my palms to dry the sweat and lighted a cigarette and smoked it to cover my expression. After a few moments I said, "Does Paxton know I'm here?"

"Yes. Of course. The forest has eyes, the swamp ears. Why you've come to give him the buzz is the mystery."

"Hell with that. Some say he's at the root of trouble with my kin. Then there's the goons he sent my way. I didn't start this. Going to end it, though."

"Mighty enterprising, aren't you? A real dyed in the wool bad man."

"What is this pact? I wager it involves plenty of cabbage."

"An alliance, bad man. He and I versus the damnable crones and that rotgut they try to pass off as whiskey. Little Lord Paxton is moneyed up real good. He inherited well. In any event, he keeps palms greased at the Governor's mansion and in turn, I watch his back. Been that way for a while. It's not perfect; I don't cotton to bowing and scraping. Man does what man must."

"Who funds the sisters?"

"Some say they buried a fortune in mason jars. Gold ingots from the Old World. Maybe, after they're gone, me and the lads will go treasure hunting on their land."

So, I'd well and truly fallen from fry pan to fire. Paxton wanted me dead, or captured, thus far the jury remained out on that detail, and here I'd skipped into the grasp of his chief enforcer. "Hell, I made it easy for you lugs, eh? Walked right into the box." I nodded and decided that this was the end of the line and prepared to draw my pistol and go pay Saint Peter my respects with an empty clip. "Don't think I'll go quietly. We Copes die real hard."

"Hold on a second," Bly said, sobering in a hurry. I didn't think the Bly clan had a similar tradition.

Blackwood patted him on the head. "No need for heroics, gents. We've broken bread, haven't we? You can hop on Shank's Mare and head for the tall timber anytime you like. Nobody here's gonna try to stop you. On the other paw, I was kind of hoping you might stick around the Hollow, see this affair through."

I sat there and gaped, thunderstruck. "We can walk out of here." My senses strained, alert for the snare that must lurk within his affable offer. "What do you want, Dan?"

"Me and the boys recently were proposed a deal by…Well, that's none of your concern. A certain party has entered the picture, is enough to say. We been offered terms that trump our arrangement with Paxton. Trump it in spades. Problem is, I've sworn an oath to do him no harm, so that ties my hands."

"That's where I come in."

"You've said a mouthful, and no need to say more. We'll let it ride, see how far it takes us."

"And if I want to cash in and take my leave?"

He shrugged and left me to dangle in the wind. I started to ask another question, and thought better of it and sat quietly, my mind off to the races. Dan's smile got even wider. "Candy will squire you back to the Sycamore. There's a garden party and dinner. All the pretty folk will be there tying one on. Dress accordingly, eh?"

ೞ

Candy returned us to the hotel where my entourage collapsed, semi-clothed and pawing one another, into a couple of piles on the beds. Dawn leaked through the curtains and I was queerly energized despite heavy drinking and nagging wounds, so I visited the nearby café as the first customer. I drank bad coffee in a corner booth as locals staggered in and ordered plates of hash and eggs and muttered and glowered at one another; beasts awakened too soon from hibernation. I fished in my pocket and retrieved the cocoon Carling had given me and lay it on the edge of the saucer. It resembled a slug withered by salt and dried in the hot sun. I wondered if my father, a solid, yet philosophically ambiguous, Catholic, ever carried a good luck charm. What else was a crucifix or a rosary?

"You know you're playing the fool." I said this aloud, barely a mutter, just enough to clear the air between my passions and my higher faculties. Possibly I thought giving voice to the suspicion would formalize matters, break the spell and justify turning the boat around and sailing home, or making tracks for sunny Mexico and a few days encamping on a beach with a bottle of whiskey and a couple of *señoritas* who didn't habla inglés. At that moment a goose waddled over my grave and the light reflecting from the waitress's coffee pot bent strangely and the back of my neck went cold. I looked down the aisle through the doorway glass and spotted a couple of the Blackwood Boys loitering in the bushes of a vacant lot across the way. One was the big fiddler, the other wore overalls and a coonskin cap. The fiddler rested his weight on the handle of what at first I took for a shovel. When he raised the object and laid it across his shoulder I recognized it as a sword, one of those Scottish claymores.

A party and in my finest suit and tie it would be. Goddamn, if they were going to be this way about it I'd go see the barber after breakfast and have a haircut and a shave.

൱

It was as Blackwood promised. We drove over to the mansion in a Cadillac I rented from the night clerk at the hotel. Even if the guys hadn't scoped the joint out previously, we would've easily found our way by following a small parade of fancy vehicles bound for the estate. Bly rolled through the hoary, moss-encrusted gates and the mansion loomed like a castle on the horizon. He eased around the side and parked in the back. We came through the servants' entrance. Dick and Bly packing shotguns, me with the Thompson slung under my arm. Men in livery were frantically arranging matters for the weekly estate hoedown and the ugly mugs with the guns made themselves scarce.

Conrad Paxton was on the veranda. He didn't seem at all surprised when I barged in and introduced myself. He smiled a thin, deadly smile and waved to an empty seat. "*Et tu* Daniel?" he said to himself, and chuckled. "Please, have a drink. Reynolds," he snapped his fingers at a bland older man wearing a dated suit, "fetch, would you? And, John, please, tell your comrades to take a walk. Time for the men to chat."

Dick and Bly waited. I gave the sign and they put the iron away under their trench coats and scrammed. A minute or two later, they reappeared on the lawn amid the hubbub and stood where they could watch us. Everybody ignored them.

I leaned the Thompson against the railing and sat across from my host. We regarded each other for a while as more guests arrived and the party got underway.

Finally, he said, "This moment was inevitable. One can only contend with the likes of Blackwood and his ilk for a finite period before they turn on one like the wild animals they are. I'd considered moving overseas, somewhere with a more hospitable clime. No use, my enemies will never cease to pursue, and I'd rather die in my home. Well, Eadweard's, technically." Conrad Paxton's face was long and narrow. His fingers were slender. He smoked fancy

European cigarettes with a filter and an ivory cigarette holder. Too effete for cigars, I imagined. Well, me too, chum, me too.

"Maybe if you hadn't done me and mine dirt you'd be adding candles to your cake for a spell yet."

"Ah, *done you dirt.* I can only imagine what poppycock you've been told to set you upon me. My father knew your father. Now the sons meet. Too bad it's not a social call—I'm hell with social calls. You have the look of a soldier."

"Did my bit."

"What did you do in the war, John?"

"I shot people."

"Ha. So did my father, albeit with a camera. As for me, I do nothing of consequence except drink my inheritance, collect moldy tomes, and also the envy of those who'd love to appropriate what I safeguard in this place. You may think of me as a lonely, rich caretaker."

"Sounds miserable," I said.

Afternoon light was dimming to red through the trees that walled in the unkempt concourses of green lawn. Some twenty minutes after our arrival, and still more Model Ts, Packards and Studebakers formed a shiny black and white procession along the crushed gravel drive, assembling around the central fountain, a twelve-foot-tall marble faun gone slightly green around the gills from decades of mold. Oh, the feather boas and peacock feather hats, homburgs and stovepipes! Ponderously loaded tables of *hors d'oeuvres*, including a splendid tiered cake, and pails of frosty cold punch, liberally dosed with rum, were arrayed beneath fluttering silk pavilions. Servants darted among the gathering throng and unpacked orchestral instruments on a nearby dais. Several others worked the polo fields, hoisting buckets as they bent to reapply chalk lines, or smooth divots, or whatever.

Dick and Bly, resigned to their fate, loitered next to the punch, faces gray and pained even at this hour, following the legendary excesses of the previous evening. Both had cups in hand and were tipping them regularly. As for Paxton's goons, those gents continued to maintain a low profile, confined to the fancy bunkhouse at the edge of the property, although doubtless a few of them lurked in the shrubbery or behind the trees. My fingers were crossed that Blackwood meant to keep his bargain. Best plan I had.

A bluff man with a pretty young girl stuck on his arm waved to us. Paxton indolently returned the gesture. He inserted the filter between his lips and dragged exaggeratedly. "That would be the mayor. Best friend of whores and moonshiners in the entire county."

"I like that in a politician," I said. "Let's talk about you."

"My story is rather dreary. Father bundled me off to the orphanage then disappeared into Central America for several years. Another of his many expeditions. None of them made him famous. He became *famous* for murdering that colonel and driving Mother into an early grave. I also have his slide collection and his money." Paxton didn't sound too angry for someone with such a petulant mouth. I supposed the fortune he'd inherited when his father died sweetened life's bitter pills.

"My birth father, Eadweard Muybridge, died in his native England in 1904. I missed the funeral, and my brother Florado's as well. I'm a cad that way. Floddie got whacked by a car in San Francisco. Of all the bloody luck, eh? Father originally sent me and my brother to the orphanage where I was adopted by the Paxtons as an infant. My real mother named me Conrad after a distant cousin. Conrad Gallatry was a soldier and died in the Philippines fighting in the Spanish-American War.

"As a youth, I took scant interest in my genealogy, preferring to eschew the coarseness of these roots, and knew the barest facts regarding Eadweard Muybridge beyond his reputation as a master photographer and eccentric. Father was a peculiar individual. In 1875 Eadweard killed his wife's, and my dearest mum, presumed lover—he'd presented that worthy, a retired colonel, with an incriminating romantic letter addressed to Mrs. Muybridge in the Colonel's hand, uttered a pithy remark, and then shot him dead. Father's defense consisted of not insubstantial celebrity, his value to science, and a claim of insanity as the result of an old coach accident that crushed his skull, in addition to the understandable anguish at discovering Mum's betrayal. I can attest the attribution of insanity was correct, albeit nothing to do with the crash, as I seemed to have come by my moods and anxieties honestly. Blood will tell."

"You drowned a boy at your school," I said. "And before that, your stepsister vanished. Somewhat of a scoundrel as a lad, weren't you?"

"So they say. What they say is far kinder than the truth. Especially for my adopted Mum and Da. My stepsister left evidence behind, which, predictably, the Paxtons obscured for reasons of propriety. They suspected the truth and those suspicions were confirmed when I killed that nit Abelard Fries in our dormitory. A much bolder act, that murder. And again, the truth was obfuscated by the authorities, by my family. No, word of what I'd really done could not be allowed to escape our circle. You see, for me, it had already begun. I was already on the path of enlightenment, seeker and sometimes keeper of *Mysterium Tremendum et fascinans*. Even at that tender age."

"All of you kooky bastards in this county into black magic?" I'd let his insinuations regarding the fate of his sister slide from my mind, dismissing a host of ghastly speculative images as they manifested and hung between us like phantom smoke rings.

"Only the better class of people."

"You sold your soul at age nine, or thereabouts. Is that it, man? Then daddy came home from the jungle one day and took you in because...because why?"

"Sold my soul? Hardly. I traded up. You didn't come to me to speak of that. You're an interesting person, John. *Not* interesting enough for this path of mine. Your evils are definitely, tragically lowercase."

"Fine, let's not dance. Word is, you did for my father. Frankly, I was attached to him. That means we've got business."

"Farfetched, isn't it? Didn't he choke on a sandwich or something?"

"I'm beginning to wonder. More pressing: Why did you try to have me rubbed out? To keep me in the dark about you bopping my dad? That wasn't neighborly."

"I didn't harm your father. Never met the man, although Eadweard spoke of him, wrote of him. Your old man made a whale of an impression on people he didn't kill. Nor did I dispatch those hooligans who braced you in Seattle. Until you and your squad lumbered into Ransom Hollow, I had scant knowledge and exactly zero interest in your existence. Helios Augustus certainly engineered the whole charade. The old goat knew full well you'd respond unkindly to the ministrations of fellow Johnson Brothers, that you'd do for them, or they for you, and the winner, spurred by his wise counsel, would come seeking my scalp."

"Ridiculous. Hand them a roll of bills and they'll blip anyone you please, no skullduggery required."

"This is as much a game as anything. Your father was responsible for Eadweard's troubles with the law. Donald Cope is the one who put the idea of murder in his head, the one who mailed the gun that Eadweard eventually used on the retired officer who'd dallied with my mother. Eadweard wasn't violent, but your father was the devil on his shoulder telling him to be a man, to smite his enemy. After pulling the trigger, my father went off the rails, disappeared into the world and when he returned, he had no use for Helios Augustus, or anyone. He was his own man, in a demented fashion. Meanwhile, Helios Augustus, who had spent many painstaking years cultivating and mentoring Eadweard, was beside himself. The magician was no simple cardsharp on a barge whom your father just happened to meet. One of his myriad disguises. His posturing as a magician, famous or not, is yet another. Helios Augustus is a servant of evil and he manipulates everyone, your father included. Donald Cope was meant to be a tool, a protector of Eadweard. A loyal dog. He wasn't supposed to dispense wisdom, certainly not his own homespun brand of hooliganism. He ruined the magician's plan. Ruined everything, it seems."

I was accustomed to liars, bold-faced or wide-eyed, silver tongued or pleading, often with the barrel of my gun directed at them as they babbled their last prayers to an indifferent god, squirted their last tears into the indifferent earth. A man will utter any falsehood, commit any debasement, sell his own children down the river, to avoid that final sweet goodnight.

Paxton wasn't a liar, though. I studied him and his sallow, indolent affectation of plantation suzerainty, the dark power in his gaze, and beheld with clarity he was a being who had no need for deception, that all was delivered to him on a platter. He wasn't afraid, either. I couldn't decide whether that lack of fear depended upon his access to the Blackwood Boys, his supreme and overweening sense of superiority, an utter lack of self-preservation instincts, or something else as yet to make its presence felt. Something dread and terrible in the wings was my guess, based upon the pit that opened in my gut as we talked while the sun sank into the mountains and the shadows of the gibbering and jabbering gentry spread grotesquely across the grass.

"You said Augustus groomed Muybridge."

"Yes. Groomed him to spread darkness with his art. And Father did, though not to the degree or with the potency Helios Augustus desired. The sorcerer and his allies believed Eadweard was tantalizingly close to unlocking something vast and inimical to human existence."

The guests stirred and the band ascended the dais, each member lavishly dressed in a black suit, hair slicked with oil and banded in gold or silver, each cradling an oboe, a violin, a horn, a double bass, and of course, of fucking course, Dan Blackwood at the fore with his majestic flute, decked in a classical white suit and black tie, his buttered down hair shining like an angel's satin wing. They nodded to one another and began to play soft and sweet chamber music from some German symphony that was popular when lederhosen reigned at court. Music to calm a bellicose Holy Roman Emperor. Music beautiful enough to bring a tear to a killer's eye.

I realized Dick and Bly had disappeared. I stood, free hand pressed to my side to keep the bandage from coming unstuck. "Your hospitality is right kingly, Mr. Paxton, sir—"

"Indeed? You haven't touched your brandy. I'm guessing that's a difficult bit of self restraint for an Irishman. It's not poisoned. Heavens, man, I couldn't harm you if that were my fiercest desire."

"Mr. Paxton, I'd like to take you at your word. Problem is, Curtis Bane had a card with your name written on it in his pocket. That's how I got wind of you."

"Extraordinarily convenient. And world famous magician Phil Wary, oh dear, my mistake—Helios Augustus—showed you some films my father made and told you I'd set the dogs on your trail. Am I correct?"

"Yeah, that's right." The pit in my belly kept crumbling away. It would be an abyss pretty soon. It wasn't that the pale aristocrat had put the puzzle together that made me sick with nerves, it was his boredom and malicious glee at revealing the obvious to a baboon. My distress was honey to him.

"And let me ponder this… Unnecessary. Helios put you in contact with those women in Luster. The crones, as some rudely call them."

"I think the ladies prefer it, actually."

"The crones were coy, that's their game. As you were permitted to depart their presence with your hide, I'll wager they confirmed the magician's slander of my character. Wily monsters, the Corning women. Man-haters, man-eaters. Men are pawns or provender, often both. Word to the wise—never go back there."

Just like that the sun snuffed as a burning wick under a thumb and darkness was all around, held at bay by a few lanterns in the yard, a trickle of light from the open doors on the porch and a handful of windows. The guests milled and drank and laughed above the beautiful music, and several couples assayed a waltz before the dais. I squinted, becoming desperate to catch a glimpse of my comrades, and still couldn't pick them out of the moiling crowd. I swayed as the blood rushed from my head and there were two, no, three, Conrad Paxton's seated in the gathering gloom, faces obscured except for the glinting eyes narrowed in curiosity, the curve of a sardonic smile. "Why would they lie?" I said. "What's in it for them?"

Paxton rose and made as if to take my elbow to steady me, although if I crashed to earth, there wasn't much chance the bony bastard would be able to do more than slow my fall. Much as Blackwood had done, he hesitated and then edged away toward the threshold of the French doors that let into a study, abruptly loath to touch me. "You are unwell. Come inside away from the heat and the noise."

"Hands off. I asked a question."

"My destruction is their motivation and ultimate goal. Each for his or her personal reason. The sorcerer desires the secrets within my vault: the cases of photographic plates, the reels, a life's work. Father's store of esoteric theory. Helios Augustus can practically taste the wickedness that broods there, black as a tanner's chimney. Eadweard's macabre films caused quite a stir in certain circles. They suggest great depths of depravity, of a dehumanizing element inherent in photography. A property of anti-life."

"You're pulling my leg. That's—"

"Preposterous? Absurd? Any loonier than swearing your life upon a book that preaches of virgin births and wandering Jews risen from the grave to spare the world from blood and thunder and annihilation?"

"I've lapsed," I said.

"The magician once speculated to me that he had a plan to create moving images that would wipe minds clean and imprint upon them all manner of base, un-sublimated desires. The desire to bow and scrape, to lick the boots of an overlord. It was madness, yet appealing. How his face animated when he mused on the spectacle of thousands of common folk streaming from theatres, faces slack with lust and carnal hunger. For the magician, Eadweard's lost work is paramount. My enemies want the specimens as yet hidden from the academic community, the plates and reels whispered of in darkened council chambers."

"That what the crones want too? To see a black pope in the debauched Vatican, and Old Scratch on the throne?"

"No, no, those lovelies have simpler tastes. They wish to devour the souls my father supposedly trapped in his pictures. So delightfully primitive to entertain the notion that film can steal our animating force. Not much more sophisticated than the tribals who believe you mustn't point at another person, else they'll die. Eadweard was many, many things, and many of them repugnant. He was not, however, a soul taker. Soul taking is a myth with a single exception. There is but One and that worthy needs no aperture, no lens, no box.

"Look here, John: thaumaturgy, geomancy, black magic, all that is stuff and nonsense, hooey, claptrap, if you will. Certainly, I serve the master and attend Black Mass. Not a thing to do with the supernatural, I'm not barmy. It's a matter of philosophy, of acclimating oneself to the natural forces of the world and the universe. Right thinking, as it were. Ask me if Satan exists, I'll say yes and slice a virgin's throat in the Dark Lord's honor. Ask me if I believe He manipulates and rewards, again yes. Directly? Does He imbue his acolytes with the power of miracles as Helios Augustus surely believes, as the crones believe their old gods do? I will laugh in your face. Satan no more interferes in any meaningful way than God does. Which is to say, by no discernable measure."

"Color me relieved. Got to admit, the old magician almost had my goat. I thought there might be something to all this horseshit mumbo-jumbo."

"Of course, mysticism was invented for the peasantry. You are far out of your depth. You are being turned like a card between masters. The Ace of Clubs. In all of this you are but a blunt instrument. If anyone murdered your father, it was Helios Augustus. Likely by poison. Poison and lies are the sorcerer's best friends."

I took the blackened cocoon from my shirt pocket. So trivial a thing, so withered a husk, yet even as I brandished it between thumb and forefinger, my host shrank farther away until he'd stepped into the house proper and regarded me from the sweep of a velvet curtain, drawn across his face like a cowl or a cape, and for an instant the ice in my heart suggested that it was a trick, that he was indeed the creature of a forsaken angel, that he meant to lull me into complacency and would then laugh and devour me, skin, bones, and soul. Beneath the balcony the music changed; it sizzled and snapped and strange guttural cries and glottal croaks resounded here and there.

A quick glance, no more, but plenty for me to take it in—the guests were *all* pairing now, and many had already removed their clothes. The shorn and scorched patches of bare earth farther out hadn't suffered from the ravages of ponies or cleats. Servants were not reapplying chalk lines; it must've been pitch in their buckets, for one knelt and laid a torch down and flames shot waist high and quickly blossomed into a series of crisscross angles of an occult nature. The mighty pentagram spanned dozens of yards and it shed a most hellish radiance, which I figured was the point of the exercise. Thus, evidently, was the weekly spectacle at the Paxton estate.

"Don't look so horrified, it's not as if they're going to rut in the field," Paxton said from the safety of the door. "Granted, a few might observe the rituals. The majority will dance and make merry. Harmless as can be. I hadn't estimated you for a prude."

My hand came away from my side wet. I drew the Luger. "I don't care whether they fuck or not," I said, advancing until I'd backed him further into the study. It was dim and antiquated as could be expected. A marble desk and plush chairs, towering stacks of leathery tomes accessed by a ladder on a sliding rail. Obscured by a lush, ornamental tree was a dark statue of a devil missing its right arm. The horned head was intact, though, and its hollow eyes reminded me of the vacuous gaze of the boy in Muybridge's film. "No one is gonna hear it when I put a bullet in you. No one is gonna weep, either. You're not a likeable fella, Mr. Paxton."

"You aren't the first the sorcerer has sent to murder me. He's gathered so many fools over the years, sent them traipsing to their doom. Swine, apes, rodents. Whatever dregs take on such work, whatever scum stoop to such dirty deeds. I'm exhausted. Let this be the end of the tedious affair."

"I'm here for revenge," I said. "My heart is pure." I shot him in the gut.

"The road to Hell, etcetera, etcetera." Paxton slumped against the desk. He painstakingly lighted another cigarette. His silk shirt went black. "Father, the crones, other, much darker personages who shall remain nameless for both our sakes, had sky high ambitions for me when I was born. That's why I went to a surrogate family while Floddie got shuffled to a sty of an orphanage. It must be admitted that I'm a substantial disappointment. An individual of power, certainly. Still, they'd read the portents and dared hope I would herald a new age, that I would be the chosen one, that I would cast down the tyrants and

416 : Laird Barron

light the great fires of the end days. Alas, here I dwell, a philosopher hermit, a casual entertainer and dilettante of the left-hand path. I don't begrudge their bitterness and spite. I don't blame them for seeking my destruction. They want someone to shriek and bleed to repay their lost dreams. Who better than the architect of their disillusionment?"

To test my theory that no one would notice, or care, and to change the subject, I shot him again. In the thigh this time.

"See, I told you. I'm but a mortal, and now I die." He sagged to the floor, still clutching his cigarette. His eyes glittered and dripped. "Yes, yes, again." And after he took the third bullet, this one in the ribs an inch or two above the very first, he smiled and blood oozed from his mouth. "Frankly, I thought you'd extort me for money. Or use me to bargain for your friends whom you've so quaintly and clumsily searched for since they wandered away a few minutes ago."

"My friends are dead. Or dying. Probably chained in the cellar getting the Broderick with a hammer. It's what I'd do if I were in your shoes." I grudgingly admired his grit in the face of certain death. He'd a lot more pluck than his demeanor suggested.

"I hope your animal paranoia serves you well all the days of your life. Your friends aren't dead. Nor tortured; not on my account. Although, maybe Daniel wasn't satisfied with one double cross. I suppose it's possible he's already dug a hole for you in the woods. May you be so fortunate." He wheezed and his face drained of color, become gauzy in the dimness. After the fit subsided, he gestured at my chest. "Give me the charm, if you please."

I limped to his side and took the cigarette from him and had a drag. Then I placed the cocoon in his hand. He nodded and more blood dribbled forth as he popped the bits of leaf and silk and chrysalis into his mouth and chewed. He said, "A fake. What else could it be?" His voice was fading and his head lolled. "If I'd been born the Antichrist, none of this would've happened. Anyway...I'm innocent. You're bound for the fire, big fellow."

I knelt and grasped his tie to pull him close. "Innocent? The first one was for my dad. Don't really give a damn whether you done him or not, so I'll go with what feels good. And this does indeed feel good. The other two were for your sister and that poor sap in boarding school. Probably not enough fire in Hell for you. Should we meet down there? You'd best get shy of me."

"In a few minutes, then," Paxton said and his face relaxed. When I let loose of his tie, he toppled sideways and lay motionless. Jeeves, or Reynolds, or whatever the butler's name was, opened the door and froze in mid-stride. He calmly assessed the situation, turned sharply as a Kraut infantryman on parade, and shut it again.

Lights from the fires painted the window and flowed in the curtains and made the devil statue's grin widen until everything seemed to warp and I covered my eyes and listened to Dan Blackwood piping and the mad laughter of his thralls. I shook myself and fetched the Thompson and made myself comfortable behind the desk in the captain's chair, and waited. Smoked half a deck of ciggies while I did.

Betting man that I am, I laid odds that either some random goons, Blackwood, or one of my chums, would come through the door fairly soon, and in that order of likelihood. The universe continued to reveal its mysteries a bit later when Helios Augustus walked in, dressed to the nines in yellow and purple silk, with a stovepipe hat and a black cane with a lump of gold at the grip. He bowed, sweeping his hat, and damn me for an idiot, I should've cut him down right then, but I didn't. I had it in my mind to palaver since it had gone so swimmingly with Paxton.

Bad mistake, because, what with the magician and his expert prestidigitation and such, his hat vanished and he easily produced a weapon that settled my hash. For an instant my brain saw a gun and instinctively my finger tightened on the trigger of the Thompson. Or tried to. Odd, thing, I couldn't move a muscle, couldn't so much as bat a lash. My body sat, a big useless lump. I heard and felt everything. No difficulties there, and then I recognized what Helios had brandished was the mummified severed hand he'd kept in his dressing room at the Hotel Broadsword. I wondered when he'd gotten into town. Had Blackwood dialed him on the blower this morning? The way things were going, I half suspected the creepy bastard might've hidden in the shrubbery days ago and waited, patient as a spider, for this, his moment of sweet, sweet triumph.

That horrid, preserved hand, yet clutching a fat black candle captivated me…. I knew from a passage of a book on folklore, read to me by some chippie I humped in college, that what I was looking at must be a hand of glory. Hacked from a murderer and pickled for use in the blackest of magic rituals. I couldn't quite recall what it was supposed to do, exactly. Paralyzing jackasses such as myself, for one, obviously.

"Say, Johnny, did Conrad happen to tell you where he stowed the key to his vault?" The magician was in high spirits. He glided toward me, waltzing to the notes of Blackwood's flute.

I discovered my mouth was in working order. I coughed to clear my throat. "Nope," I said.

He nodded and poured himself a glass of sherry from a decanter and drank it with relish. "Indeed, I imagine this is the blood of my foes."

"Hey," I said. "How'd you turn the Blackwood Boys anyhow?"

"Them? The boys are true believers, and with good reason considering who roams the woods around here. I got my hands on a film of Eadweard's, one that might've seen him burned alive even in this modern age. In the film, young Conrad and some other nubile youths were having congress with the great ram of the black forest. Old Bill stepped from the grove of blood and took a bow. I must confess, it was a spectacular bit of photography. I informed the boys that instead of hoarding Muybridge's genius for myself, it would be share and share alike. Dan and his associates were convinced."

"I'm sorry I asked."

"Does everyone beg you for mercy at the end?"

"The ones who see it coming."

"Do you ever grant quarter?"

"Nope."

"Will *you* beg me for mercy?"

"Sure, why not?"

The magician laughed and snapped his fingers. "Alas! Alack! I would spare you, for sentimental reasons, and because I was such a cad to send the Long and the Short gunning for you, and to curse Donald purely from spite. Unfortunately, 'tis Danny of the Blackwood who means to skin you alive on a corroded altar to Old Bill. Sorry, lad. Entertaining as I'm sure that will prove, I'm on a mission. You sit tight, Uncle Phil needs to see to his prize. Thanks oodles, boy. As the heathens and savages are wont to say, you done good." He ignored the torrent of profanity that I unleashed upon his revelation that he'd killed my father, and casually swirled his elegant cape around his shoulders and used my own matches to strike a flame to the black candle. Woe and gloom, it was a macabre and chilling sight, that flame guttering and licking at dead fingers as he thrust it forth as a torch.

Helios Augustus proved familiar with the layout. He promptly made an adjustment to the devil statue and ten feet away one of the massive bookcases pivoted to reveal a steel door, blank save for a keyhole. The magician drew a deep breath and spent several minutes chanting in Latin or Greek, or bits of both and soon the door gave way with a mere push from his index finger. He threw back his head and laughed. I admit, that sound was so cold and diabolical if I'd been able to piss myself right then, I would've. Then he wiped his eyes and disappeared into a well of darkness and was gone for what felt like an age.

I spent the duration listening to the Blackwood Boys reciting an opera while straining with all of my might and main to lift my hand, turn my head, wiggle a toe, to no avail. This reminded me, most unpleasantly, of soldiers in France I'd seen lying trussed up in bandages at the hospital, the poor bastards unable to blink as they rotted in their ruined bodies. I sweated and tried to reconcile myself with an imminent fate worse than death, accompanied by death. 'Hacked to pieces by a band of hillbilly satanists' hadn't ever made my list of imagined ways of getting rubbed out—and as the Samurai warriors of yore meditated on a thousand demises, I too had imagined a whole lot of ways of kicking.

Helios Augustus's candle flame flickered in the black opening. He carried a satchel and it appeared heavily laden by its bulges; doubtless stuffed with Eadweard Muybridge's priceless lost films. He paused to set the grisly hand in its sconce before me on the desk. The candle had melted to a blob of shallow grease. It smelled of burnt human flesh, which I figured was about right. Probably baby fat, assuming my former chippie girlfriend was on the money in her description.

Helios said, "Tata, lad. By the by, since you've naught else to occupy you, it may be in order to inspect this talisman more closely. I'd rather thought you might twig to my ruse back in Olympia. You're a nice boy, but not much of a detective, sorry to say." He waved cheerily and departed.

I stared into the flame and thought murderous thoughts and a glint on the ring finger arrested my attention. The ring was slightly sunken into the flesh, and that's why I hadn't noted it straight away. My father's wedding band. Helios Augustus, that louse, that conniving, filthy sonofawhore, had not only murdered my father by his own admission, but later defiled his grave and chopped off his left hand to make a grotesque charm.

Rage had a sobering effect upon me. The agony from my wounds receded, along with the rising panic at being trapped like a rabbit in a snare and my brain ticked along its circuit, methodical and accountant-like. It occurred to me that despite his callous speech, the magician might've left me a chance, whether intentionally or as an oversight, the devil only knew. I huffed and puffed and blew out the candle, and the invisible force that had clamped me in its vise evaporated. Not one to sit around contemplating my navel, nor one to look askance at good fortune, I lurched to my feet and into action.

I took a few moments to set the curtains aflame, fueling the blaze with the crystal decanter of booze. I wrapped Dad's awful hand in a kerchief and jammed it into my pocket. Wasn't going to leave even this small, gruesome remnant of him in the house of Satan.

An excellent thing I made my escape when I did, because I met a couple of Blackwood's boys on the grand staircase. "Hello, fellas," I said, and sprayed them with hellfire of my own, sent them tumbling like Jack and Jill down the steps, notched the columns and the walls with bullet holes. I exulted at their destruction. My hand didn't bother me a whit.

Somebody, somewhere, cut the electricity and the mansion went dark as a tomb except for the fire licking along the upper reaches of the balcony and the sporadic muzzle flashes of my trench broom, the guns of my enemies, for indeed those rat bastards, slicked and powdered for the performance, yet animals by their inbred faces and bestial snarls, poured in from everywhere and I was chivvied through the foyer and an antechamber where I swung the Thompson like a fireman with a hose. When the drum clicked empty I dropped the rifle and jumped through the patio doors in a crash of glass and splintered wood, and loped, dragging curtains in my wake, across the lawn for the trees. I weaved between the mighty lines of the burning pentagrams that now merely smoldered, and the trailing edge of my train caught fire and flames consumed the curtains and began eating their way toward me, made me Kipling's rogue tiger zigzagging into the night, enemies in close pursuit. Back there in the yard echoed a chorus of screams as the top of the house bloomed red and orange and the hillbillies swarmed after me, small arms popping and cracking and it was just like the war all over again.

The fox hunt lasted half the night. I blundered through the woods while the enemy gave chase, and it was an eerie, eerie several hours as Dan Blackwood's pipe and his cousins' fiddle and banjo continued to play and they drove me through briar and marsh and barbwire fence until I stumbled across a lonely dirt road and stole a farm truck from behind a barn and roared out of the Hollow, skin intact. Didn't slow down until the sun crept over the horizon and I'd reached the Seattle city limits. The world tottered and fell on my head and I coasted through a guardrail and came to a grinding halt in a field, grass scraping against the metal of the cab like a thousand fingernails. It got hazy after that.

☙

Dick sat by my bedside for three days. He handed me a bottle of whiskey when I opened my eyes. I expressed surprise to find him among the living, convinced as I'd been that he and Bly got bopped and dumped in a shallow grave. Turned out Bly had snuck off with some patrician's wife and had a hump in the bushes while Dick accidentally nodded off under a tree. Everything was burning and Armageddon was in full swing when they came to, so they rendezvoused and did the smart thing—sneaked away with tails between legs.

Good news was, Mr. Arden wanted us back in Olympia soonest; he'd gotten into a dispute with a gangster in Portland. Seemed that all was forgiven in regard to my rubbing out the Long and the Short. The boss needed every gun in his army.

Neither Dick nor the docs ever mentioned the severed hand in my pocket. It was missing when I retrieved my clothes and I decided to let the matter drop. I returned to Olympia and had a warm chat with Mr. Arden and everything was peaches and cream. The boss didn't even ask about Vernon. Ha!

He sent me and a few of the boys to Portland with a message for his competition. I bought a brand spanking new Chicago-typewriter for the occasion. I also stopped by the Broadsword where the manager, after a little physical persuasion, told me that Helios Augustus had skipped town days prior on the Starlight Express, headed to California, if not points beyond. Yeah, well, revenge and cold dishes, and so forth. Meanwhile, I'd probably avoid motion pictures and stick to light reading.

During the ride to Portland, I sat in back and watched the farms and fields roll past and thought of returning to Ransom Hollow with troops and paying tribute to the crones and the Blackwood Boys; fantasized of torching the entire valley and its miserable settlements. Of course, Mr. Arden would never sanction such a drastic engagement. That's when I got to thinking that maybe, just maybe I wasn't my father's son, maybe I wanted more than a long leash and a pat on the head. Maybe the leash would feel better in my fist. I chuckled and stroked the Thompson lying across my knees.

"Johnny?" Dick said when he glimpsed my smile in the rearview.

I winked at him and pulled my Homburg down low over my eyes and had a sweet dream as we approached Portland in a black cloud like angels of death.

Acknowledgments

My sincere thanks to those who offered assistance, contacts, story sugges-
tions, and advice (both heeded and unheeded) as I assembled this anthology,
particularly John Joseph Adams, Matthew Carpenter, Scott Connors, Daniel
Corrick, Richard Curtis, Ellen Datlow, Mike Davis, Vanyel Harkema, Ron
Hilger, Dot Lumley, Kay McCauley, Silvia Moreno-Garcia, Merilee Heifetz,
Sarah Nagel, Cameron Pierce, Pete Rawlik, Martin Roberts, Jaynie Rodri-
guez, Jonathan Strahan, Allison Stumpf, Pam Valvera, Gordon van Gelder,
Jim Wagner, Jerad Walters, and everybody involved in the H. P. Lovecraft
Film Festival in Portland, OR. Apologies to anyone I might have forgotten.

Thanks to the entire Night Shade team: Jason Williams, for buying the
book; Jeremy Lassen, for agreeing that it was a good idea; Amy Popovich, for
mad layout skills and wrangling talents; Dave Palumbo, for art direction and
the myriad cover options; Tomra Palmer, for marketing expertise, and Liz Up-
son, for promoting the hell out of it. Thanks as well to Shannon Page for her
eagle-eyed copyediting, Mobius9 for the breathtaking cover art, and Claudia
Noble for her outstanding design.

Thanks to you, the reader, and aficionados of weird ficiton everywhere.
Thanks to all who helped #FeedCthulhu. Let's do it again this year.

Special thanks to my wife, Jennifer, for keeping me sane in a maddening,
carnivorous universe, and for continuing to put up with my proclivity for
keeping my nose in books.

Copyright Acknowledgments

"Hand of Glory" © 2012 Laird Barron. Original to this anthology.

"Boojum" © 2008 Elizabeth Bear and Sarah Monette. Originally published in *Fast Ships, Black Sails*. Reprinted by permission of the authors.

"The God of Dark Laughter" © 2001 Michael Chabon. Originally published in *The New Yorker*, April 9, 2001. Reprinted by arrangement with Mary Evans Inc.

"This is How the World Ends" © 2010 John R. Fultz. Originally published in *Cthulhu's Reign*. Reprinted by permission of the author.

"Shoggoth's Old Peculiar" © 1998 Neil Gaiman. Originally published in *The Mammoth Book of Comic Fantasy*. Reprinted by permission of the author.

"Once More, from the Top" © 2001 A. Scott Glancy. Originally published in *Delta Green: Dark Theatres*. Reprinted by permission of the author.

"Rapture of the Deep" © 2009 Cody Goodfellow. Originally published in *Dark Discoveries #15, Fall 2009*. Reprinted by permission of the author.

"Black Hill" © 2010 Orrin Grey. Originally published in *Historical Lovecraft: Tales of Horror Through Time*. Reprinted by permission of the author.

"Nor the Demons Down Under the Sea" © 2003 Caitlín R. Kiernan. Originally published in *The Children of Cthulhu: Chilling New Tales Inspired by H. P. Lovecraft*. Reprinted by permission of the author.

"The Terror from the Depths" © 1976 Fritz Leiber. Originally published in *The Disciples of Cthulhu*. Reprinted by permission of the author's literary estate.

"Take Your Daughters to Work" © 2007 Livia Llewellyn. Originally published in *Subterranean, Issue #6*. Reprinted by permission of the author.

About the Editor

Ross E. Lockhart is the managing editor of Night Shade Books. A lifelong fan of supernatural, fantastic, speculative, and weird fiction, he holds degrees in English from Sonoma State University (BA) and San Francisco State University (MA). In 2011, he edited the acclaimed anthology *The Book of Cthulhu*. His rock-and-roll novel, *Chick Bassist*, is forthcoming from Lazy Fascist Press. He lives in an old church in Petaluma, California, with his wife Jennifer, hundreds of books, and Elinor, who is fitting in nicely.

Find out more about *The Book of Cthulhu* at www.thebookofcthulhu.com

About the Editor